# QUEEN'S RANSOM
## A Mystery Guild Lost Classics Omnibus

# QUEEN'S RANSOM:

## THE ROMAN HAT MYSTERY

## CALAMITY TOWN

## CAT OF MANY TAILS

by
Ellery Queen

Mystery Guild
Garden City, New York

# Contents

# THE ROMAN HAT MYSTERY

Grateful acknowledgment

is made to

**PROFESSOR ALEXANDER GOETTLER**

*Chief Toxicologist of the City of New York*

for his friendly offices

in the preparation of this tale

# CONTENTS

# Lexicon of Persons
## Connected with the Investigation

*Note:* The complete list of individuals, male and female, brought into the story of Monte Field's murder and appended below is given solely for the convenience of the reader. It is intended to simplify rather than mystify. In the course of perusing mysterio-detective literature the reader is, like as not, apt to lose sight of a number of seemingly unimportant characters who eventually prove of primary significance in the solution of the crime. The writer therefore urges a frequent study of this chart during the reader's pilgrimage through the tale, if toward no other end than to ward off the inevitable cry of "Unfair!"—the consolation of those who read and do not reason.

ELLERY QUEEN

**Monte Field,** an important personage indeed—the victim.
**William Pusak,** clerk. Cranially a brachycephalic.
**Doyle,** a *gendarme* with brains.
**Louis Panzer,** a Broadway theatre manager.
**James Peale,** the Don Juan of "Gunplay."
**Eve Ellis.** The quality of friendship is not strained.
**Stephen Barry.** One can understand the perturbation of the juvenile lead.
**Lucille Horton,** the "lady of the streets"—in the play.
**Hilda Orange,** a celebrated English character actress.
**Thomas Velie,** Detective-Sergeant who knows a thing or two about crime.
**Hesse, Piggott, Flint, Johnson, Hagstrom, Ritter,** gentlemen of the Homicide Squad.
**Dr. Samuel Prouty,** Assistant to the Chief Medical Examiner.
**Madge O'Connell,** usherette on the fatal aisle.
**Dr. Stuttgard.** There is always a doctor in the audience.
**Jess Lynch,** the obliging orangeade boy.
**John Cazzanelli,** alias **"Parson Johnny,"** naturally takes a professional interest in "Gunplay."
**Benjamin Morgan.** What do you make of him?
**Frances Ives-Pope.** Enter the society interest.
**Stanford Ives-Pope,** man-about-town.
**Harry Neilson.** He revels in the sweet uses of publicity.

**Henry Sampson,** for once an intelligent District Attorney.
**Charles Michaels,** the fly—or the spider?
**Mrs. Angela Russo,** a lady of reputation.
**Timothy Cronin,** a legal ferret.
**Arthur Stoates,** another.
**Oscar Lewin,** the Charon of the dead man's office.
**Franklin Ives-Pope.** If wealth meant happiness.
**Mrs. Franklin Ives-Pope,** a maternal hypochondriac.
**Mrs. Phillips.** Middle-aged angels have their uses.
**Dr. Thaddeus Jones,** toxicologist of the City of New York.
**Edmund Crewe,** architectural expert attached to the Detective Bureau.
**Djuna,** an Admirable Crichton of a new species.

The Problem Is—

### Who Killed Monte Field?

Meet the astute gentlemen whose business
it is to discover such things—

**Mr. Richard Queen**                    **Mr. Ellery Queen**

*= a son of Erebus held in Greek myth to ferry
the souls of the dead over the Styx
THIS explanation
Written on July 28, 2011
I learned a "new" word!

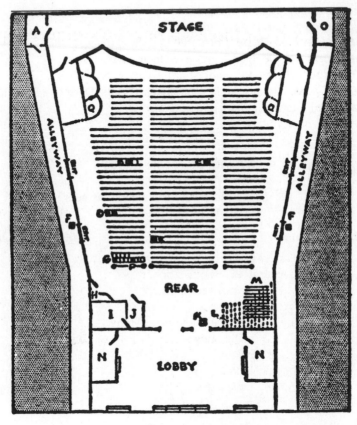

Map of the Roman Theatre
Drawn by Ellery Queen

# Explanation for the Map of the Roman Theatre

A:    Actors' dressing-rooms.

B:    Frances Ives-Pope's seat.

C:    Benjamin Morgan's seat.

D:    Aisle seats occupied by "Parson Johnny" Cazzanelli and Madge O'Connell.

E:    Dr. Stuttgard's seat.

F, F:    Orangeade boys' stands (only during intermissions).

G:    Area in vicinity of crime. Black square represents seat occupied by Monte Field. Three white squares to the right and four white squares directly in front represent vacant seats.

H:    Publicity office, occupied by Harry Neilson.

I:    Manager Louis Panzer's private office.

J:    Anteroom to manager's office.

K:    Ticket-taker's box.

L:    Only stairway leading to the balcony.

M:    Stairway leading downstairs to General Lounge.

N, N:    Cashiers' offices.

O:    Property Room.

P:    William Pusak's seat.

Q, Q:    Orchestra boxes.

# FOREWORD

I have been asked by both publisher and author to write a cursory preface to the story of Monte Field's murder. Let me say at once that I am neither a writer nor a criminologist. To make authoritative remarks, therefore, anent the techniques of crime and crime fiction is obviously beyond my capacity. Nevertheless, I have one legitimate claim to the privilege of introducing this remarkable story, based as it is upon perhaps the most mystifying crime of the past decade. . . . If it were not for me, *The Roman Hat Mystery* would never have reached the fiction-reading public. I am responsible for its having been brought to light; and there my pallid connection with it ends.

During the past winter I shook off the dust of New York and went a-traveling in Europe. In the course of a capricious roving about the corners of the Continent (a roving induced by that boredom which comes to every Conrad in quest of his youth)—I found myself one August day in a tiny Italian mountain village. How I got there, its location and its name do not matter; a promise is a promise, even when it is made by a stockbroker. Dimly I remembered that this toy hamlet perched on the lip of a sierra harbored two old friends whom I had not seen for two years. They had come from the seething sidewalks of New York to bask in the brilliant peace of an Italian countryside—well, perhaps it was as much curiosity about their regrets as anything else, that prompted me to intrude upon their solitude.

My reception at the hands of old Richard Queen, keener and grayer than ever, and of his son Ellery was cordial enough. We had been more than friends in the old days; perhaps, too, the vinous air of Italy was too heady a cure for their dust-choked Manhattan memories. In any case, they seemed profoundly glad to see me. Mrs. Ellery Queen—Ellery was now the husband of a glorious creature and the startled father of an infant who resembled his grandfather to an extraordinary degree—was as gracious as the name she bore. Even Djuna, no longer the scapegrace I had known, greeted me with every sign of nostalgia.

Despite Ellery's desperate efforts to make me forget New York and appreciate the lofty beauties of his local scenery, I had not been in their tiny villa for many days before a devilish notion took possession of me and I began to pester poor Ellery to death. I have something of a reputa-

tion for persistence, if no other virtue; so that before I left, Ellery in despair agreed to compromise. He took me into his library, locked the door
and attacked an old steel filing cabinet. After a slow search he managed
to bring out what I suspect was under his fingers all the time. It was a
faded manuscript bound Ellery-like in blue legal paper.

The argument raged. I wished to leave his beloved Italian shores with
the manuscript in my trunk, whereas he insisted that the sheaf of con-
tention remain hidden in the cabinet. Old Richard was wrenched away
from his desk, where he was writing a treatise for a German magazine on
"American Crime and Methods of Detection," to settle the affair. Mrs.
Queen held her husband's arm as he was about to close the incident with
a workmanlike fist; Djuna clucked gravely; and even Ellery, Jr., extracted
his pudgy hand from his mouth long enough to make a comment in his
gurgle-language.

The upshot of it all was that *The Roman Hat Mystery* went back to the
States in my luggage. Not unconditionally, however—Ellery is a peculiar
man. I was forced solemnly and by all I held dear to swear the identities
of my friends and of the important characters concerned in the story be
veiled by pseudonyms; and that, on pain of instant annihilation, their
names be permanently withheld from the reading public.

Consequently "Richard Queen" and "Ellery Queen" are not the true
names of those gentlemen. Ellery himself made the selections; and I
might add at once that his choices were contrived to baffle the reader
who might endeavor to ferret the truth from some apparent clue of ana-
gram.

*The Roman Hat Mystery* is based on actual records in the police
archives of New York City. Ellery and his father, as usual, worked hand-
in-hand on the case. During this period in his career Ellery was a
detective-story writer of no mean reputation. Adhering to the aphorism
that truth is often stranger than fiction, it was his custom to make notes of
interesting investigations for possible use in his murder tales. The affair
of the Hat so fascinated him that he kept unusually exhaustive notes, intending to publish it. Immediately after, however, he was plunged into
another investigation which left him scant opportunity for business; and
when this last case was successfully closed, Ellery's father, the Inspector,
consummated a lifelong ambition by retiring and moving to Italy, bag
and baggage. Ellery, who had in this affair found the lady of his heart,
was animated by a painful desire to do something "big" in letters, Italy
sounded idyllic to him; he married with his father's blessing and the
three of them, accompanied by Djuna, went off to their new European
home. The manuscript was utterly forgotten until I rescued it.

On one point, before I close this painfully unhandsome preface, I should like to make myself clear.

I have always found it extremely difficult to explain to strangers the peculiar affinity which bound Richard to Ellery Queen, as I must call them. For one thing, they are persons of by no means uncomplicated natures. Richard Queen, sprucely middle-aged after thirty-two years' service in the city police, earned his Inspector's chevrons not so much through diligence as by an extraordinary grasp of the technique of criminal investigation. It was said, for example, at the time of his brilliant detectival efforts during the now-ancient Barnaby Ross murder case, that "Richard Queen by this feat firmly establishes his fame beside such masters of crime detection as Tamaka Hiero, Brillon the Frenchman, Kris Oliver, Renaud, and James Redix the Younger."

Queen, with his habitual shyness toward newspaper eulogy, was the first to scoff at this extravagant statement; although Ellery maintains that for many years the old man secretly preserved a clipping of the story. However that may be—and I like to think of Richard Queen in terms of human personality, despite the efforts of imaginative journalists to make a legend of him—I cannot emphasize too strongly the fact that he was heavily dependent upon his son's wit for success in many of his professional achievements.

This is not a matter of public knowledge. Some mementoes of their careers are still reverently preserved by friends: the small bachelor establishment maintained during their American residence on West 87th Street, and now a semiprivate museum of curios collected during their productive years; the really excellent portrait of father and son, done by Thiraud and hanging in the art gallery of an anonymous millionaire; Richard's precious snuffbox, the Florentine antique which he had picked up at an auction and which he therefore held dearer than rubies, only to succumb to the blandishments of a charming old lady whose name he cleared of slander; Ellery's enormous collection of books on violence, perhaps as complete as any in the world, which he regretfully discarded when the Queens left for Italy; and, of course, the many as yet unpublished documents containing records of cases solved by the Queens and now stored away from prying eyes in the City's police archives.

But the things of the heart—the spiritual bonds between father and son—have until this time remained secret from all except a few favored intimates, among whom I was fortunate enough to be numbered. The old man, perhaps the most famous executive of the Detective Division in the last half-century, overshadowing in public renown, it is to be feared, even those gentlemen who sat briefly in the Police Commissioner's suite—the old man, let me repeat, owed a respectable portion of his reputation to his son's genius.

In matters of pure tenacity, when possibilities lay frankly open on every hand, Richard Queen was a peerless investigator. He had a crystal-clear mind for detail; a retentive memory for complexities of motive and plot; a cool viewpoint when the obstacle seemed insuperable. Give him a hundred facts, bungled and torn, out of proportion and sequence, and he had them assembled in short order. He was like a bloodhound who follows the true scent in the clutter of a hopelessly tangled trail.

But the intuitive sense, the gift of imagination, belonged to Ellery Queen, the fiction writer. The two might have been twins possessing abnormally developed faculties of mind, impotent by themselves but vigorous when applied one to the other. Richard Queen, far from resenting the bond which made his success so spectacularly possible—as a less generous nature might have done—took pains to make it plain to his friends. The slender, gray old man whose name was anathema to contemporary lawbreakers, used to utter his "confession," as he called it, with a naïveté explicable only on the score of his proud fatherhood.

One word more. Of all the affairs pursued by the two Queens this, which Ellery has titled *The Roman Hat Mystery* for reasons shortly to be made clear, was surely the crowning case of them all. The dilettante of criminology, the thoughtful reader of detective literature, will understand as the tale unfolds why Ellery considers the murder of Monte Field worthy of study. The average murderer's motives and habits are fairly accessible to the criminal specialist. Not so, however, in the case of the Field killer. Here the Queens dealt with a person of delicate perception and extraordinary finesse. In fact, as Richard pointed out shortly after the dénouement, the crime planned was as nearly perfect as human ingenuity could make it. As in so many "perfect crimes," however, a small mischance of fate coupled with Ellery's acute deductive analyses gave the hunting Queens the single clue which led ultimately to the destruction of the plotter.

J. J. McC.

*New York*
*March 1, 1929*

# PART ONE

*"The policeman must oft follow the precept of the 'bakadori'—those fool-birds who, though they know disaster awaits them at the hands and clubs of the beachcombers, brave ignominious death to bury their eggs in the sandy shore.... So the policeman. All Nippon should not deter him from hatching the egg of thoroughness."*

—*From* A THOUSAND LEAVES
by Tamaka Hiero

# 1

## In Which Are Introduced a Theatre Audience and a Corpse

The dramatic season of 192– began in a disconcerting manner. Eugene O'Neill had neglected to write a new play in time to secure the financial encouragement of the *intelligentsia*; and as for the "low-brows," having attended play after play without enthusiasm, they had deserted the legitimate theatre for the more ingenuous delights of the motion picture palaces.

On the evening of Monday, September 24th, therefore, when a misty rain softened the electric blaze of Broadway's theatrical district, it was viewed morosely by house managers and producers from 37th Street to Columbus Circle. Several plays were then and there given their walking papers by the men higher up, who called upon God and the weather bureau to witness their discomfiture. The penetrating rain kept the play-going public close to its radios and bridge tables. Broadway was a bleak sight indeed to those few who had the temerity to patrol its empty streets.

The sidewalk fronting the Roman Theatre, on 47th Street west of the "White Way," however, was jammed with a mid-season, fair-weather crowd. The title "Gunplay" flared from a gay marquee. Cashiers dextrously attended the chattering throng lined up at the "Tonight's Performance" window. The buff-and-blue doorman, impressive with the dignity of his uniform and the placidity of his years, bowed the evening's top-hatted and befurred customers into the orchestra with an air of satisfaction, as if inclemencies of weather held no terrors for those implicated in "Gunplay's" production.

Inside the theatre, one of Broadway's newest, people bustled to their seats visibly apprehensive, since the boisterous quality of the play was public knowledge. In due time the last member of the audience ceased rustling his program; the last latecomer stumbled over his neighbor's feet; the lights dimmed and the curtain rose. A pistol coughed in the silence, a man screamed . . . the play was on.

"Gunplay" was the first drama of the season to utilize the noises customarily associated with the underworld. Automatics, machine guns, raids on night-clubs, the lethal sounds of gang vendettas—the entire stock-in-trade of the romanticized crime society was jammed into three swift acts. It was an exaggerated reflection of the times—a bit raw, a bit nasty and altogether satisfying to the theatrical public. Consequently it played to packed houses in rain and shine. This evening's house was proof of its popularity.

The performance proceeded smoothly. The audience was thrilled at the thunderous climax to the first act. The rain having stopped, people strolled out into the side alley for a breath of air during the first ten-minute intermission. With the rising of the curtain on Act II, the detonations on the stage increased in volume. The second act hurtled to its big moment as explosive dialogue shot across the footlights. A slight commotion at the rear of the theatre went unnoticed, not unnaturally, in the noise and the darkness. No one seemed aware of anything amiss and the play crashed on. Gradually, however, the commotion increased in volume. At this point a few spectators at the rear of the left section squirmed about in their seats, to assert their rights in angry whispers. The protest was contagious. In an incredibly short time scores of eyes turned toward that section of the orchestra.

Suddenly a sharp scream tore through the theatre. The audience, excited and fascinated by the swift sequence of events on the stage, craned their necks expectantly in the direction of the cry, eager to witness what they thought was a new sensation of the play.

Without warning the lights of the theatre snapped on, revealing puzzled, fearful, already appreciative faces. At the extreme left, near a closed exit door, a large policeman stood holding a slight nervous man by the arm. He fended off a group of inquisitive people with a huge hand, shouting in stentorian tones, "Everybody stay right where he is! Don't get out of your seat, any of you!"

People laughed.

The smiles were soon wiped away. For the audience began to perceive a curious hesitancy on the part of the actors. Although they continued to recite their lines behind the footlights they were casting puzzled glances out into the orchestra. People, noting this, half-rose from their seats, panicky in the presence of a scented tragedy. The officer's Jovian voice continued to thunder, "Keep your seats, I say! Stay where you are!"

The audience suddenly realized that the incident was not play-acting but reality. Women shrieked and clutched their escorts. Bedlam broke loose in the balcony, whose occupants were in no position to see anything below.

The policeman turned savagely to a stocky, foreign-looking man in evening clothes who was standing by, rubbing his hands together.

"I'll have to ask you to close every exit this minute and see that they're kept closed, Mr. Panzer," he growled. "Station an usher at all the doors and tell 'em to hold everybody tryin' to get in or out. Send somebody outside to cover the alleys, too, until help comes from the station. Move fast, Mr. Panzer, before hell pops!"

The swarthy little man hurried away, brushing aside a number of excited people who had disregarded the officer's bellowed admonition and had jumped up to question him.

The bluecoat stood wide-legged at the entrance to the last row of the left section, concealing with his bulk the crumpled figure of a man in full evening dress, lying slumped in a queer attitude on the floor between rows. The policeman looked up, keeping a firm grip on the arm of the cowering man at his side, and shot a quick glance toward the rear of the orchestra.

"Hey, Neilson!" he shouted.

A tall tow-headed man hurried out of a small room near the main entrance and pushed his way through to the officer. He looked sharply down at the inert figure on the floor.

"What's happened here, Doyle?"

"Better ask this feller here," replied the policeman grimly. He shook the arm of the man he was holding. "There's a guy dead, and Mr."—he bent a ferocious glance upon the shrinking little man—"Pusak, W-William Pusak," he stammered—"this Mr. Pusak," continued Doyle, "says he heard him whisper he'd been croaked."

Neilson stared at the dead body, stunned.

The policeman chewed his lip. "I'm in one sweet mess, Harry," he said hoarsely. "The only cop in the place, and a pack of yellin' fools to take care of. . . . I want you to do somethin' for me."

"Say the word. . . . This is one hell of a note!"

Doyle wheeled in a rage to shout to a man who had just risen three rows ahead and was standing on his seat, peering at the proceedings. "Hey you!" he roared. "Get down offa there! Here—get back there, the whole bunch o' you. Back to your seats, now, or I'll pinch the whole nosey mob!"

He turned on Neilson. "Beat it to your desk, Harry, and give headquarters a buzz about the murder," he whispered. "Tell 'em to bring down a gang—make it a big one. Tell 'em it's a theatre—they'll know what to do. And here, Harry—take my whistle and toot your head off outside. I gotta get some help right away."

As Neilson fought his way back through the crowd, Doyle shouted after him: "Better ask 'em to send old man Queen down here, Harry!"

The tow-headed man disappeared into the office. A few moments later a shrill whistle was heard from the sidewalk in front of the theatre.

The swarthy theatre manager whom Doyle had commanded to place guards at the exits and alleys came scurrying back through the press. His dress shirt was slightly rumpled and he was mopping his forehead with an air of bewilderment. A woman stopped him as he wriggled his way forward. She squeaked,

"Why is this policeman keeping us here, Mr. Panzer? I've a right to leave, I should like you to know! I don't care if an accident *did* happen— I had nothing to do with it—that's your affair—please tell him to stop this silly disciplining of innocent people!"

The little man stammered, trying to escape. "Now, madam, please. I'm sure the officer knows what he is doing. A man has been killed here—it is a serious matter. Don't you see. . . . As manager of the theatre I must follow his orders. . . . Please be calm—have a little patience. . . ."

He wormed his way out of her grasp and was off before she could protest.

Doyle, his arms waving violently, stood on a seat and bellowed: "I told you to sit down and keep quiet, the pack o' you! I don't care if you're the Mayor himself, you—yeah, you there, in the monocle—stay down or I'll shove you down! Don't you people realize what's happened? Pipe down, I say!" He jumped to the floor, muttering as he wiped the perspiration from his capband.

In the turmoil and excitement, with the orchestra boiling like a huge kettle, and necks stretched over the railing of the balcony as the people there strove vainly to discover the cause of the confusion, the abrupt cessation of activity on the stage was forgotten by the audience. The actors had stammered their way through lines rendered meaningless by the drama before the footlights. Now the slow descent of the curtain put an end to the evening's entertainment. The actors, chattering, hurried toward the stagestairs. Like the audience they peered toward the nucleus of the trouble in bewilderment.

A buxom old lady, in garish clothes—the very fine imported actress billed in the character of Madame Murphy, "keeper of the public house"—her name was Hilda Orange; the slight, graceful figure of "the street waif, Nanette"—Eve Ellis, leading-lady of the piece; the tall robust hero of "Gunplay," James Peale, attired in a rough tweed suit and cap; the juvenile, smart in evening clothes, portraying the society lad who had fallen into the clutches of the "gang"—Stephen Barry; Lucille Horton, whose characterization of the "lady of the streets" had brought down a shower of adjectives from the dramatic critics, who had little enough to rant about that unfortunate season; a vandyked old man whose faultless evening clothes attested to the tailoring genius of M. Le Brun, costumer extraordinary to the entire cast of "Gunplay"; the heavy-set villain, whose stage scowl was dissolved in a foggy docility as he surveyed the frantic auditorium; in fact, the entire personnel of the play, bewigged and powdered, rouged and painted—some wielding towels as they hastily removed their make-up—scampered in a body under the lowering curtain and trooped down the stage steps into the orchestra, where they elbowed their way up the aisle toward the scene of the commotion.

Another flurry, at the main entrance, caused many people despite Doyle's vigorous orders to rise in their seats for a clearer view. A group of bluecoats were hustling their way inside, their night sticks ready. Doyle heaved a gargantuan sigh of relief as he saluted the tall man in plainclothes at their head.

"What's up, Doyle?" asked the newcomer, frowning at the pandemonium raging about them. The bluecoats who had entered with him were herding the crowd to the rear of the orchestra, behind the seat section. People who had been standing tried to slip back to their seats; they were apprehended and made to join the angry cluster jammed behind the last row.

"Looks like this man's been murdered, Sergeant," said Doyle.

"Uh-huh." The plainclothes man looked incuriously down at the one still figure in the theatre—lying at their feet, a black-sleeved arm flung over his face, his legs sprawled gawkily under the seats in the row before.

"What is it—gat?" asked the newcomer of Doyle, his eyes roving.

"No, sir—don't seem to be," said the policeman. "Had a doctor from the audience look him over the very first thing—thinks it's poison."

The Sergeant grunted. "Who's this?" he rapped, indicating the trembling figure of Pusak by Doyle's side.

"Chap who found the body," returned Doyle. "He hasn't moved from the spot since."

"Good enough." The detective turned toward a compact group huddled a few feet behind them and asked, generally: "Who's the manager here?"

Panzer stepped forward.

"I'm Velie, detective-sergeant from headquarters," said the plainclothes man abruptly. "Haven't you done anything to keep this yelling pack of idiots quiet?"

"I've done my best, Sergeant," mumbled the manager, wringing his hands. "But they all seem incensed at the way this officer"—he indicated Doyle apologetically—"has been storming at them. I don't know how I can reasonably expect them to keep sitting in their seats as if nothing had happened."

"Well, we'll take care of that," snapped Velie. He gave a rapid order to a uniformed man nearby. "Now"—he turned back to Doyle—"how about the doors, the exits? Done anything yet in that direction?"

"Sure thing, Sergeant," grinned the policeman. "I had Mr. Panzer here station ushers at every door. They've been there all night, anyway. But I just wanted to make sure."

"You were right. Nobody try to get out?"

"I think I can vouch for that, Sergeant," put in Panzer meekly. "The action of the play necessitates having ushers posted near every exit, for atmosphere. This is a crook play, with a good deal of shooting and screaming and that sort of thing going on, and the presence of guards around the doors heightens the general effect of mystery. I can very easily find out for you if . . ."

"We'll attend to that ourselves," said Velie. "Doyle, who'd you send for?"

"Inspector Queen," answered Doyle. "I had the publicity man, Neilson, phone him at headquarters."

Velie allowed a smile to crease his wintry face. "Thought of everything, didn't you? Now how about the body? Has it been touched at all since this fellow found it?"

The cowering man held in Doyle's hard grasp broke out, half-crying. "I—I only found him, officer—honest to God, I—"

"All right, all right," said Velie coldly. "You'll keep, won't you? What are you blubbering about? Well, Doyle?"

"Not a finger was laid on the body since I came over," replied Doyle, with a trace of pride in his voice. "Except, of course, for a Dr. Stuttgard. I got him out of the audience to make sure the man was dead. He was, and nobody else came near."

"You've been busy, haven't you, Doyle? I'll see you won't suffer by it," said Velie. He wheeled on Panzer, who shrank back. "Better trot up to the stage and make an announcement, Mr. Manager. The whole crew of 'em are to stay right where they are until Inspector Queen lets them go home—understand? Tell them it won't do any good to kick—and the more they kick the longer they'll be here. Make it plain, too, that they're to stick to their seats, and any suspicious move on anybody's part is going to make trouble."

"Yes. Yes. Good Lord, what a catastrophe!" groaned Panzer as he made his way down the aisle toward the stage.

At the same moment a little knot of people pushed open the big door at the rear of the theatre and stepped across the carpet in a body.

# 2

## In Which One Queen Works and Another Queen Watches

There was nothing remarkable in either the physique or the manner of Inspector Richard Queen. He was a small, withered, rather mild-appearing old gentleman. He walked with a little stoop and an air of deliberation that somehow accorded perfectly with his thick gray hair and mustaches, veiled gray eyes and slender hands.

As he crossed the carpet with short, quick steps Inspector Queen was far from impressive to the milling eyes that observed his approach from every side. And yet, so unusual was the gentle dignity of his appearance, so harmless and benevolent the smile that illumined his lined old face, that an audible rustle swept over the auditorium, preceding him in a strangely fitting manner.

In his own men the change was appreciable. Doyle retreated into a corner near the left exits. Detective-Sergeant Velie, poised over the body—sardonic, cold, untouched by the near-hysteria about him—relaxed a trifle, as if he were satisfied to relinquish his place in the sun. The bluecoats guarding the aisles saluted with alacrity. The nervous, muttering, angry audience sank back with an unreasoning relief.

Inspector Queen stepped forward and shook hands with Velie.

"Too bad, Thomas, my boy. I hear you were going home when this happened," he murmured. To Doyle he smiled in a fatherly fashion. Then, in a mild pity, he peered down at the man on the floor. "Thomas," he asked, "are all the exits covered?" Velie nodded.

The old man turned back and let his eyes travel interestedly about the scene. He asked a low-voiced question of Velie, who nodded his head in assent; then he crooked his finger at Doyle.

"Doyle, where are the people who were sitting in these seats?" He pointed to three chairs adjoining the dead man's and four directly to the front of them in the preceding row.

The policeman appeared puzzled. "Didn't see anybody there, Inspector. . . ."

Queen stood silent for a moment, then waved Doyle back with the low remark to Velie, "In a crowded house, too. . . . Remember that." Velie raised his eyebrows gravely. "I'm cold on this whole business," continued the Inspector genially. "All I can see right now are a dead man and a lot of perspiring people making noise. Have Hesse and Piggott direct traffic for a while, eh, son?"

Velie spoke sharply to two of the plainclothes men who had entered the theatre with the Inspector. They wriggled their way toward the rear and the people who had been crowding around found themselves pushed aside. Policemen joined the two detectives. The group of actors and actresses were ordered to move back. A section was roped off behind the central tier of seats and some fifty men and women packed into the small space. Quiet men circulated among them, instructing them to show their tickets and return to their seats one by one. Within five minutes not a member of the audience was left standing. The actors were cautioned to remain within the rope enclosure for the time being.

In the extreme left aisle Inspector Queen reached into his topcoat pocket, carefully extracted a brown carved snuffbox and took a pinch with every evidence of enjoyment.

"That's more like it, Thomas," he chuckled. "You know how fussy I am about noises. . . . Who is the poor chap on the floor—do you know?"

Velie shook his head. "I haven't even touched the body, Inspector," he said. "I got here just a few minutes before you did. A man on the 47th Street beat called me up from his box and reported Doyle's whistle. Doyle seems to have been doing things, sir. . . . His lieutenant reports favorably on his record."

"Ah," said the Inspector, "ah, yes. Doyle. Come here, Doyle."

The policeman stepped forward and saluted.

"Just what," went on the little gray man, leaning comfortably against a seat back, "just what happened here, Doyle?"

"All I know about it, Inspector," began Doyle, "is that a couple of minutes before the end of the second act this man"—he pointed to Pusak, who stood wretchedly in a corner—"came running up to me where I was standin' in the back, watchin' the show, and he says, 'A man's been murdered, officer! . . . A man's murdered!' He was blubberin' like a baby and I thought he was pie-eyed. But I stepped mighty quick and came over here—the place was dark and there was a lot of shootin' and screamin' on the stage—and I took a look at the feller on the floor. I didn't move him, but I felt his heart and there wasn't anything to feel. To make sure he was croakcd I asked for a doctor and a gent by the name of Stuttgard answered my call. . . ."

Inspector Queen stood pertly, his head cocked on a side like a parrot's. "That's excellent," he said. "Excellent, Doyle. I'll question Dr. Stuttgard later. Then what happened?" he went on.

"Then," continued the policeman, "then I got the usherette on this aisle to beat it back to the manager's office for Panzer. Louis Panzer — that's the manager right over there. . . ."

Queen regarded Panzer, who was standing a few feet to the rear talking to Neilson, and nodded. "That's Panzer, you say. All right, all right . . . Ellery! You got my message?"

He darted forward, brushing aside Panzer, who fell back apologetically, and clapped the shoulder of a tall young man who had slipped through the main door and was slowly looking about the scene. The old man passed his arm through the younger man's.

"Haven't inconvenienced you any, son? What bookstore did you haunt tonight? Ellery, I'm mighty glad you're here!"

He dipped into his pocket, again extracted the snuffbox, sniffed deeply — so deeply that he sneezed — and looked up into his son's face.

"As a matter of fact," said Ellery Queen, his eyes restlessly roving, "I can't return the compliment. You just lured me away from a perfect book-lover's paradise. I was at the point of getting the dealer to let me have a priceless Falconer first edition, intending to borrow the money from you at headquarters. I telephoned — and here I am. A Falconer — Oh, well. Tomorrow will do, I suppose."

The Inspector chuckled. "Now if you told me you were picking up an old snuffbox I might be interested. As it is — trot along. Looks as if we have some work tonight."

They walked toward the little knot of men on the left, the old man's hand grasping his son's coatsleeve. Ellery Queen towered six inches above his father's head. There was a square cut to his shoulders and an agreeable swing to his body as he walked. He was dressed in oxford gray and carried a light stick. On his nose perched what seemed an incongruous note in so athletic a man — a rimless pince-nez. But the brow above, the long delicate lines of the face, the bright eyes were those of a man of thought rather than action.

They joined the group at the body. Ellery was greeted respectfully by Velic. He bent over the seat, glanced earnestly at the dead man, and stepped back.

"Go on, Doyle," said the Inspector briskly. "You looked at the body, detained the man who found it, got the manager. . . . Then what?"

"Panzer at my orders closed all the doors at once and saw that no one either came in or went out," answered Doyle. "There was a lot of fuss here with the audience, but nothing else happened."

"Right, right!" said the Inspector, feeling for his snuffbox. "You did a mighty good job. Now—that gentleman there."

He gestured in the direction of the trembling little man in the corner, who stepped forward hesitantly, licked his lips, looked about him with a helpless expression, and then stood silent.

"What's your name?" asked the Inspector, in a kindly tone.

"Pusak—William Pusak," said the man. "I'm a bookkeeper, sir. I was just—"

"One at a time, Pusak. Where were you sitting?"

Pusak pointed eagerly to the sixth seat from the aisle, in the last row. A frightened young girl in the fifth seat sat staring in their direction.

"I see," said the Inspector. "Is that young lady with you?"

"Yes, sir—yes, sir. That's my fiancée, sir. Her name is Esther—Esther Jablow. . . ."

A little to the rear a detective was scribbling in a notebook. Ellery stood behind his father, glancing from one exit to another. He began to draw a diagram on the flyleaf of a small book he had taken from his top-coat pocket.

The Inspector scrutinized the girl, who immediately averted her eyes. "Now, Pusak, I want you to tell me just what happened."

"I—I didn't do a thing out of the way, sir."

Inspector Queen patted his arm. "Nobody is accusing you of anything, Pusak. All I want is your story of what happened. Take your time—tell it your own way. . . ."

Pusak gave him a curious glance. Then he moistened his lips and began. "Well, I was sitting there in that seat with my—with Miss Jablow—and we were enjoying the show pretty much. The second act was kind of exciting—there was a lot of shooting and yelling on the stage—and then I got up and started to go out the row to the aisle. This aisle—here." He pointed nervously to the spot of carpet on which he was standing. Queen nodded, his face benign.

"I had to push past my—Miss Jablow, and there wasn't anybody except one man between her and the aisle. That's why I went that way. I didn't sort of like to"—he hesitated apologetically—"to bother people going out that way in the middle of the most exciting part. . . ."

"That was very decent of you, Pusak," said the Inspector, smiling.

"Yes, sir. So I walked down the row, feeling my way, because it was pretty dark in the theatre, and then I came to—to this man." He shuddered, and continued more rapidly. "He was sitting in a funny way, I thought. His knees were touching the seat in front of him and I couldn't get past. I said, 'I'm sorry,' and tried again, but his knees hadn't moved an inch. I didn't know what to do, sir—I'm not nervy, like some fellows, and I was going to turn around and go back when all of a sudden I felt the man's body slip to the floor—I was still pressed up close to him. Of course, I got kind of scared—it was only natural. . . ."

"I should say," said the Inspector, with concern. "It must have given you quite a turn. Then what happened?"

"Well, sir. . . . Then, before I realized what was happening, he fell clean out of his seat and his head bumped against my legs. I didn't know what to do. I couldn't call for help—I don't know why, but I couldn't somehow—and I just naturally bent over him, thinking he was drunk or sick or something, and meant to lift him up. I hadn't figured on what I'd do after that. . . ."

"I know just how you felt, Pusak. Go on."

"Then it happened—the thing I told this policeman about. I'd just got hold of his head when I felt his hand come up and grab mine, just like he was trying awfully hard to get a grip on something, and he moaned. It was so low I could hardly hear it, but sort of horrible. I can't quite describe it exactly. . . ."

"Now, we're getting on," said the Inspector. "And?"

"And then he talked. It wasn't really talking—it was more like a gurgle, as if he was choking. He said a few words that I didn't catch at all, but I realized that this was something different from just being sick or drunk, so I bent even lower and listened hard. I heard him gasp, 'It's murder. . . . Been murdered . . .' or something like that. . . ."

"So he said, 'It's murder,' eh?" The Inspector regarded Pusak with severity. "Well, now. That must have given you a shock, Pusak." He snapped suddenly, "Are you certain this man said 'murder'?"

"That's what I heard, sir. I've got good hearing," said Pusak doggedly.

"Well!" Queen relaxed, smiling again. "Of course. I just wanted to make sure. Then what did you do?"

"Then I felt him squirm a little and all of a sudden go limp in my arms. I was afraid he'd died and I don't know how—but next thing I knew I was in the back telling it all to the policeman—this policeman here." He pointed to Doyle, who rocked on his heels impersonally.

"And that's all?"

"Yes, sir. Yes, sir. That's all I know about it," said Pusak, with a sigh of relief.

Queen grasped him by the coat front and barked, "That isn't all, Pusak. You forgot to tell us why you left your seat in the first place!" He glared into the little man's eyes.

Pusak coughed, teetered back and forth a moment, as if uncertain of his next words, then leaned forward and whispered into the Inspector's astonished ear.

"Oh!" Queen's lips twitched in the suspicion of a smile, but he said gravely, "I see, Pusak. Thank you very much for your help. Everything is all right now—you may go back to your seat and leave with the others later on." He waved his hand in a gesture of dismissal. Pusak, with a sickly glance at the dead man on the floor, crept around the rear wall of the last row and reappeared by the girl's side. She immediately engaged him in a whispered but animated conversation.

As the Inspector with a little smile turned to Velie, Ellery made a slight movement of impatience, opened his mouth to speak, appeared to reconsider, and finally moved quietly backwards, disappearing from view.

"Well, Thomas," sighed the Inspector, "let's have a look at this chap."

He bent nimbly over the dead man, on his knees in the space between the last row and the row directly before it. Despite the brilliant sparkle of light from the fixtures overhead, the cramped space near the floor was dark. Velie produced a flashlight and stooped over the Inspector, keeping its bright beam on the corpse, shifting it as the Inspector's hands roved about. Queen silently pointed to an ugly ragged brown stain on the otherwise immaculate shirtfront.

"Blood?" grunted Velie.

The Inspector sniffed the shirt cautiously. "Nothing more dangerous than whisky," he retorted.

He ran his hands swiftly over the body, feeling over the heart and at the neck, where the collar was loosened. He looked up at Velie.

"Looks like a poisoning case, all right, Thomas. Get hold of this Dr. Stuttgard for me, will you? I'd like to have his professional opinion before Prouty gets here."

Velie snapped an order and a moment later a medium-sized man in evening clothes, olive-skinned and wearing a thin black mustache, came up behind a detective.

"Here he is, Inspector," said Velie.

"Ah, yes." Queen looked up from his examination. "How do you do, Doctor? I am informed that you examined the body almost immediately after it was discovered. I see no obvious sign of death—what is your opinion?"

"My examination was necessarily a cursory one," said Dr. Stuttgard carefully, his fingers brushing a phantom speck from his satin lapel. "In the semidark and under these conditions I could not at first discern any abnormal sign of death. From the construction of the facial muscles I thought that it was a simple case of heart failure, but on closer examination I noticed that blueness of the face—it's quite clear in this light, isn't it? That combined with the alcoholic odor from the mouth seems to point to some form of alcoholic poisoning. Of one thing I can assure you—this man did not die of a gunshot wound or a stab. I naturally made sure of that at once. I even examined his neck—you see I loosened the collar— to make sure it was not strangulation."

"I see." The Inspector smiled, "Thank you very much, Doctor. Oh, by the way," he added, as Dr. Stuttgard with a muttered word turned aside, "do you think this man might have died from the effects of wood alcohol?"

Dr. Stuttgard answered promptly. "Impossible," he said. "It was some- thing much more powerful and quick-acting."

"Could you put a name to the exact poison which killed this man?"

The olive-skinned physician hesitated. Then he said stiffly, "I am very sorry, Inspector; you cannot reasonably expect me to be more precise. Under the circumstances . . ." His voice trailed off, and he backed away.

Queen chuckled as he bent again to his grim task.

The dead man sprawled on the floor was not a pleasant sight. The In- spector gently lifted the clenched hand and stared hard at the contorted face. Then he looked under the seat. There was nothing there. However, a black silk-lined cape hung carelessly over the back of the chair. He emp- tied all of the pockets of both dress suit and cape, his hands diving in and out of the clothing. He extracted a few letters and papers from the inside breast pocket, delved into the vest pockets and trouser pockets, heaping his discoveries in two piles—one containing papers and letters, the other coins, keys and miscellaneous material. A silver flask initialed "M. F." he found in one of the hip pockets. He handled the flask gingerly, holding it by the neck, and scanning the gleaming surface as if for fingerprints. Shaking his head, he wrapped the flask with infinite care in a clean hand- kerchief, and placed it aside.

A ticket stub colored blue and bearing the inscription "LL32 Left," he secreted in his own vest pocket.

Without pausing to examine any of the other objects individually, he ran his hands over the lining of the vest and coat, and made a rapid pass over the trouser legs. Then, as he fingered the coat-tail pocket, he exclaimed in a low tone, "Well, well, Thomas—here's a pretty find!" as he extracted a woman's evening bag, small, compact and glittering with rhinestones.

He turned it over in his hands reflectively, then snapped it open, glanced through it and took out a number of feminine accessories. In a small compartment, nestling beside a lipstick, he found a tiny cardcase. After a moment, he replaced all the contents and put the bag in his own pocket.

The Inspector picked up the papers from the floor and swiftly glanced through them. He frowned as he came to the last one—a letterhead.

"Ever hear of Monte Field, Thomas?" he asked, looking up.

Velie tightened his lips. "I'll say I have. One of the crookedest lawyers in town."

The Inspector looked grave. "Well, Thomas, this is Mr. Monte Field— what's left of him." Velie grunted.

"Where the average police system falls down," came Ellery's voice over his father's shoulder, "is in its ruthless tracking down of gentlemen who dispose of such fungus as Mr. Monte Field."

The Inspector straightened, dusted his knees carefully, took a pinch of snuff, and said, "Ellery, my boy, you'll never make a policeman. I didn't know you knew Field."

"I wasn't exactly on terms of intimacy with the gentleman," said Ellery. "But I remember having met him at the Pantheon Club, and from what I heard at the time I don't wonder somebody has removed him from our midst."

"Let's discuss the demerits of Mr. Field at a more propitious time," said the Inspector gravely. "I happen to know quite a bit about him, and none of it is pleasant."

He wheeled and was about to walk away when Ellery, gazing curiously at the dead body and the seat, drawled, "Has anything been removed, Dad—anything at all?"

Inspector Queen turned his head. "And why do you ask that bright question, young man?"

"Because," returned Ellery, with a grimace, "unless my eyesight fails me, the chap's tophat is not under the seat, on the floor beside him, or anywhere in the general vicinity."

"So you noticed that too, did you, Ellery?" said the Inspector grimly. "It's the first thing I saw when I bent down to examine him—or rather the first thing I didn't see." The Inspector seemed to lose his geniality as he spoke. His brow wrinkled and his gray mustache bristled fiercely. He shrugged his shoulders. "And no hat check in his clothes, either. . . . Flint!"

A husky young man in plain clothes hurried forward.

"Flint, suppose you exercise those young muscles of yours by getting down on your hands and knees and hunting for a tophat. It ought to be somewhere around here."

"Right, Inspector," said Flint cheerfully, and he began a methodical search of the indicated area.

"Velie," said Queen, in a businesslike tone, "suppose you find Ritter and Hesse and—no, those two will do—for me, will you?" Velie walked away.

"Hagstrom!" shouted the Inspector to another detective standing by.

"Yes, Chief."

"Get busy with this stuff"—he pointed to the two small piles of articles he had taken from Field's pockets and which lay on the floor—"and be sure to put them safely away in my own bags."

As Hagstrom knelt by the body, Ellery quietly bent over and opened the coat. He immediately jotted a memorandum on the flyleaf of the book in which he had drawn a diagram some time before. He muttered to himself, patting the volume, "And it's a Stendhause private edition, too!"

Velie returned with Ritter and Hesse at his heels. The Inspector said sharply, "Ritter, go to this man's apartment. His name is Monte Field, he was an attorney, and he lived at 113 West 75th Street. Stick around until you're relieved. If any one shows up, nab him."

Ritter, touching his hat, mumbled, "Yes, Inspector," and turned away.

"Now Hesse, my lad," continued the Inspector to the other detective, "hurry down to 51 Chambers Street, this man's office, and wait there until you hear from me. Get inside if you can, otherwise park outside the door all night."

"Right, Inspector." Hesse disappeared.

Queen turned about and chuckled as he saw Ellery, broad shoulders bent over, examining the dead man.

"Don't trust your father, eh, Ellery?" the Inspector chided. "What are you snooping for?"

Ellery smiled, straightening up. "I'm merely curious, that's all," he said. "There are certain things about this unsavory corpse that interest me hugely. For example, have you taken the man's head measurement?" He held up a piece of string, which he had slipped from a wrapped book in his coat pocket, and offered it for his father's inspection.

The Inspector took it, scowled and summoned a policeman from the rear of the theatre. He issued a low-voiced order, the string exchanged hands and the policeman departed.

"Inspector."

Queen looked up. Hagstrom stood by his elbow, eyes gleaming.

"I found this pushed way back under Field's seat when I picked up the papers. It was against the back wall."

He held up a dark-green bottle, of the kind used by ginger-ale manufacturers. A gaudy label read, "Paley's Extra Dry Ginger Ale." The bottle was half-empty.

"Well, Hagstrom, you've got something up your sleeve. Out with it!" the Inspector said curtly.

"Yes, sir! When I found this bottle under the dead man's seat, I knew that he had probably used it tonight. There was no matinee today and the cleaning women go over the place every twenty-four hours. It wouldn't have been there unless this man, or somebody connected with him, had used it and put it there tonight. I thought, 'Maybe this is a clue,' so I dug up the refreshment boy who had this section of the theatre and I asked him to sell me a bottle of ginger ale. He said"—Hagstrom smiled—"he said they don't sell ginger ale in this theatre!"

"You used your head that time, Hagstrom," said the Inspector approvingly. "Get hold of the boy and bring him here."

As Hagstrom left, a stout little man in slightly disarranged evening clothes bustled up, a policeman doggedly holding his arm. The Inspector sighed.

"Are you in charge of this affair, sir?" stormed the little man, drawing himself up to five feet two inches of perspiring flesh.

"I am," said Queen gravely.

"Then I want you to know," burst out the newcomer "—here, you, let go of my arm, do you hear?—I want you to know, sir . . ."

"Detach yourself from the gentleman's arm, officer," said the Inspector, with deepening gravity.

". . . that I consider this entire affair the most vicious outrage! I have been sitting here with my wife and daughter since the interruption to the play for almost an hour, and your officers refuse to allow us even to stand up. It's a damnable outrage, sir! Do you think you can keep this entire audience waiting at your leisure? I've been watching you—don't think I haven't. You've been dawdling around while we sat and suffered. I want you to know, sir—I want you to know!—that unless you permit my party to leave at once, I shall get in touch with my very good friend District Attorney Sampson and lodge a personal complaint against you!"

Inspector Queen gazed distastefully into the empurpled face of the stout little man. He sighed and said with a note of sternness, "My dear man, has it occurred to you that at this moment, while you stand beefing about a little thing like being detained an hour or so, a person who has committed murder may be in this very audience—perhaps sitting next to your wife and daughter? He is just as anxious as you to get away. If you wish to make a complaint to the District Attorney, your very good friend, you may do so after you leave this theatre. Meanwhile, I'll trouble you to return to your seat and be patient until you are permitted to go. . . . I hope I make myself clear."

A titter arose from some spectators nearby, who seemed to be enjoying the little man's discomfiture. He flounced away, with the policeman stolidly following. The Inspector, muttering "Jackass!" turned to Velie.

"Take Panzer with you to the box office and see if you can find complete tickets for these numbers." He bent over the last row and the row before it, scribbling the numbers LL30 Left, LL28 Left, LL26 Left, KK32 Left, KK30 Left, KK28 left, and KK26 Left on the back of an old envelope. He handed the memorandum to Velie, who went away.

Ellery, who had been leaning idly against the rear wall of the last row, watching his father, the audience, and occasionally restudying the geography of the theatre, murmured in the Inspector's ear: "I was just reflecting on the unusual fact that with such a popular bit of dramatic trash as 'Gunplay,' seven seats in the direct vicinity of the murdered man's seat should remain empty during the performance."

"When did you begin to wonder, my son?" said Queen, and while Ellery absently tapped the floor with his stick, barked, "Piggott!"

The detective stepped forward.

"Get the usherette who was on this aisle and the outside doorman— that middle-aged fellow on the sidewalk—and bring 'em here."

As Piggott walked off, a disheveled young man appeared by Queen's side, wiping his face with a handkerchief.

"Well, Flint?" asked Queen instantly.

"I've been over this floor like a scrubwoman, Inspector. If you're looking for a hat in this section of the theatre, it's mighty well hidden."

"All right, Flint, stand by."

The detective trudged off. Ellery said slowly, "Didn't really think your young Diogenes would find the tophat, did you, dad?"

The Inspector grunted. He walked down the aisle and proceeded to lean over person after person, questioning each in low tones. All heads turned in his direction as he went from row to row, interrogating the occupants of the two aisle seats successively. As he walked back in Ellery's direction, his face expressionless, the policeman whom he had sent out with the piece of string saluted him.

"What size, officer?" asked the Inspector.

"The clerk in the hat store said it was exactly 7⅛," answered the bluecoat. Inspector Queen nodded, dismissing him.

Velie strode up, with Panzer trailing worriedly behind. Ellery leaned forward with an air of keen absorption to catch Velie's words. Queen grew tense, the light of a great interest on his face.

"Well, Thomas," he said, "what did you find in the box office?"

"Just this, Inspector," reported Velie unemotionally. "The seven tickets for which you gave me the numbers are not in the ticket rack. They were sold from the box office window, what date Mr. Panzer has no way of knowing."

"The tickets might have been turned over to an agency, you know, Velie," remarked Ellery.

"I verified that, Mr. Queen," answered Velie. "Those tickets were not assigned to any agency. There are definite records to prove it."

Inspector Queen stood very still, his gray eyes gleaming. Then he said, "In other words, gentlemen, it would seem that at a drama which has been playing to capacity business ever since its opening, seven tickets in a group were bought—and then the purchasers conveniently forgot to attend the performance!"

# 3

## In Which a 'Parson' Came to Grief

There was a silence as the four men regarded each other with a dawning conviction. Panzer shuffled his feet and coughed nervously; Velie's face was a study in concentrated thought; Ellery stepped backward and fell into a rapt contemplation of his father's gray-and-blue necktie.

Inspector Queen stood biting his mustache. He shook his shoulders suddenly and turned on Velie.

"Thomas, I'm going to give you a dirty job," he said. "I want you to marshal a half-dozen or so of the uniformed men and set 'em to a personal examination of every soul in this place. All they have to do is get the name and address of each person in the audience. It's quite a job, and it will take time, but I'm afraid it's absolutely necessary. By the way, Thomas, in your scouting around, did you question any of the ushers who take care of the balcony?"

"I got hold of the very man to give me information," said Velie. "He's the lad who stands at the foot of the stairs in the orchestra, directing holders of balcony tickets to the upper floor. Chap by the name of Miller."

"A very conscientious boy," interposed Panzer, rubbing his hands.

"Miller is ready to swear that not a person in this theatre either went upstairs from the orchestra or came downstairs from the moment the curtain went up on the second act."

"That sort of cuts down your work, Thomas," remarked the Inspector, who had been listening intently. "Have your men go through the orchestra boxes and orchestra only. Remember I want the name and address of every person here—every single one. And Thomas—"

"Yes, Inspector?" said Velie, turning back.

"While they're at it, have 'em ask these people to show the ticket stubs belonging to the seats in which they are sitting. Every case of loss of stub should be noted beside the name of the loser; and in cases—it is a bare possibility—where a person holds a stub which does not agree with the seat number of the chair in which he's sitting, a notation is also to be made. Think you can get all that done, my boy?"

"Sure thing!" Velie grunted as he strode away.

The Inspector smoothed his gray mustache and took a pinch of snuff, inhaling deeply.

"Ellery," he said, "there's something worrying you. Out with it, son!"

"Eh?" Ellery started, blinking his eyes. He removed his pince-nez, and said slowly, "My very revered father, I am beginning to think that— Well, there's little peace in this world for a quiet book-loving man." He sat down on the arm of the dead man's seat, his eyes troubled. Suddenly he smiled. "Take care that you don't repeat the unfortunate error of that ancient butcher who, with his twoscore apprentices, sought high and low for his most treasured knife when all the time it reposed quietly in his mouth."

"You're very informative these days, my son," said the Inspector petulantly. "Flint!"

The detective came forward.

"Flint," said Queen, "you've had one pleasant job tonight and I've another for you. Think your back could stand a little more bending? Seems to me I remember you took a weight-lifting contest in the Police Games when you were pounding a beat."

"Yes, sir," said Flint, grinning broadly. "I guess I can stand the strain."

"Well, then," continued the Inspector, jamming his hands into his pockets, "here's your job. Get a squad of men together—good Lord, I should have brought the Reserves along with me!—and make an exhaustive search of every square foot of the theatre property, inside and out. You'll be looking for ticket stubs, do you understand? Anything resembling half a ticket has to be in my possession when you're through. Search the theatre floor particularly, but don't neglect the rear, the steps leading up to the balcony, the lobby outside, the sidewalk in front of the theatre, the alleyways at both sides, the lounge downstairs, the men's room, the ladies' room—Here, here! That'll never do. Call up the nearest precinct for a matron and have her do that. Thoroughly clear?"

Flint was off with a cheerful nod.

"Now, then." Queen stood rubbing his hands. "Mr. Panzer, would you step this way a minute? Very kind of you, sir. I'm afraid we're making unholy nuisances of ourselves tonight, but it can't be helped. I see the audience is on the verge of rebellion. I'd be obliged if you would trot up to the stage and announce that they will be held here just a little while longer, to have patience, and all that sort of thing. Thank you!"

As Panzer hurried down the center aisle, people clutching at his coat to detain him, Detective Hagstrom, standing a few feet away, caught the Inspector's eye. By his side was a small slim youth of nineteen, chewing gum with vehement motions of his jaw, and obviously quite nervous at the ordeal he was facing. He was clad in a black-and-gold uniform, very ornate and resplendent, and incongruously fitted out with a starched shirt front and a wing collar and bow tie. A cap resembling the headgear of a bellboy perched on his blond head. He coughed deprecatingly as the Inspector motioned him forward.

"Here is the boy who says they don't sell ginger ale in this theatre," said Hagstrom severely, grasping the lad's arm in a suggestive grip.

"You don't, eh, son?" asked Queen affably. "How is that?"

The boy was plainly in a funk. His eyes rolled alarmingly as they sought the broad face of Doyle. The policeman patted him encouragingly on the shoulder and said to the Inspector, "He's a little scared, sir—but he's a good boy. I've known him since he was a shaver. Grew up on my beat. Answer the Inspector, Jessie. . . ."

"Well, I—I don't know, sir," stammered the boy, shuffling his feet. "The only drinks we're allowed to sell during the intermissions is orangeade. We got a contract with the ——" —he mentioned the name of a well-known manufacturer of the concoction—"people and they give us a big discount if we sell their stuff and nobody else's. So—"

"I see," said the Inspector. "Are drinks sold only during intermissions?"

"Yes, sir," answered the boy, more naturally. "As soon as the curtain goes down the doors to the alleys on both sides are opened, and there we are—my partner and me, with our stands set up, and the cups filled ready to serve."

"Oh, so there are two of you, eh?"

"No, sir, three all together. I forgot to tell you—one feller is downstairs in the main lounge, too."

"Ummmm." The Inspector fixed him with a large and kindly eye. "Now, son, if the Roman Theatre sells nothing but orangeade, do you think you could explain how this ginger-ale bottle got here?"

His hand dove down and reappeared brandishing the dark-green bottle discovered by Hagstrom. The boy paled and began to bite his lips. His eyes roved from side to side as if they sought a quick avenue of escape. He inserted a large and dirty finger between his neck and collar and coughed.

"Why—why . . ." He had some difficulty in speaking.

Inspector Queen put down the bottle and rested his wiry length against the arm of a seat. He folded his arms sternly.

"What's your name?" he demanded.

The boy's color changed from blue-white to a pasty yellow. He furtively eyed Hagstrom, who had with a flourish taken a notebook and pencil from his pocket and was waiting forbiddingly.

The boy moistened his lips. "Lynch—Jess Lynch," he said hoarsely.

"And where is your station between acts, Lynch?" said the Inspector balefully.

"I'm—I'm right here, in the left-side alley, sir," stuttered the boy.

"Ah!" said the Inspector, knitting his brows ferociously. "And were you selling drinks in the left alley tonight, Lynch?"

"Why, why—yes, sir."

"Then you know something about this ginger-ale bottle?"

The boy peered about, saw the stout small form of Louis Panzer on the stage, about to make an announcement, and leaning forward, whispered, "Yes, sir—I do know about that bottle. I—I didn't want to tell before because Mr. Panzer's a strict guy when it comes to breaking rules, and he'd fire me in a minute if he knew what I did. You won't tell, sir?"

The Inspector started, then smiled. "Shoot, son. You've got something on your conscience—might as well get it off." He relaxed and at a flick of a finger Hagstrom unconcernedly walked away.

"This is how it happened, sir," began Jess Lynch eagerly. "I'd set my stand up in the alley here about five minutes before the end of the first act, like we're supposed to. When the girl on this aisle opened the doors after the first act, I began to give the people comin' out a nice refined selling chatter. We all do. A lot of people bought drinks and I was so busy I didn't have time to notice anything going on around me. In a little while I had a breathing spell, and then a man came up to me and said, 'Let me have a bottle of ginger ale, boy.' I looked up and saw he was a ritzy feller in evening dress, actin' kind of tipsy. He was laughing to himself and he looked pretty happy. I says to myself, 'I bet I know what *he* wants ginger ale for!' and sure enough he taps his back pocket and winks. Well—"

"Just a minute son," interrupted Queen. "Ever see a dead man before?"

"Why—why, no, sir, but I guess I could stand it once," said the boy nervously.

"Fine! Is this the man who asked you for the ginger ale?" The Inspector took the boy by the arm and made him bend over the dead body.

Jess Lynch regarded it with awed fascination. He bobbed his head vigorously.

"Yes, sir. That's the gentleman."

"You're sure of that now, Jess?" The boy nodded. "By the way, is that the outfit he was wearing when he accosted you?"

"Yes, sir."

"Anything missing, Jess?" Ellery, who had been nestling in a dark corner, leaned forward a little.

The boy regarded the Inspector with puzzlement on his face, looking from Queen to the body and back again. He was silent for a full minute, while the Queens hung on his words. Then his face lit up suddenly and he cried, "Why—yes, sir! He was wearin' a hat—a shiny topper—when he spoke to me!"

Inspector Queen looked pleased. "Go on, Jess—Doc Prouty! It's taken you a long time getting here. What held you up?"

A tall lanky man had come striding across the carpet, a black bag in his hand. He was smoking a vicious-looking cigar with no apparent concern for local fire rules, and appeared in something of a hurry.

"You said something there, Inspector," he said, setting down the bag and shaking hands with both Ellery and Queen. "You know we just moved and I haven't got my new phone yet. I had a hard day today and I was in bed anyway. They couldn't get hold of me—had to send a man around to my new place. I rushed down here as fast as I could. Where's the casualty?"

He dropped to his knees in the aisle as the Inspector indicated the body on the floor. A policeman was summoned to hold a flashlight as the Assistant Medical Examiner worked.

Queen took Jess Lynch by the arm and walked him off to one side. "What happened after he asked you for the ginger ale, Jess?"

The boy, who had been staring at the proceedings, gulped and continued. "Well, sir, of course I told him that we didn't sell ginger ale, only orangeade. He leaned a little closer, and then I could smell the booze on his breath. He says confidentially, 'There's a half dollar in it for you if you get me a bottle, kid! But I want it right away!' Well—you know how it is—they don't give tips nowadays. . . . Anyway, I said I couldn't get it that minute but that I'd duck out and buy a bottle for him right after the second act started. He walked away—after tellin' me where he was sitting—I saw him go back into the theatre. As soon as the intermission ended and the usherette closed the doors, I left my stand in the alleyway and hopped across the street to Libby's ice-cream parlor. I—"

"Do you usually leave your stand in the alley, Jess?"

"No, sir. I always hop inside the doors with the stand just before she locks the doors, and then take it downstairs to the lounge. But the man said he wanted the ginger ale right away, so I figured I'd save time by getting the bottle for him first. Then I thought I'd go back into the alley, get my stand, and bring it into the theatre through the front door. Nobody'd say anything. . . . Anyway, I left the stand in the alley and ran over to Libby's. I bought a bottle of Paley's ginger ale, sneaked it inside to this man, and he gave me a buck. Pretty nice of him, I thought, seeing as how he'd only promised me four bits."

"You told that very nicely, Jess," said the Inspector with approval. "Now, a few things more. Was he sitting in this seat—was this the seat he told you to come to?"

"Oh, yes, sir. He said LL32 Left, and sure enough that's where I found him."

"Quite right." The Inspector, after a pause, asked casually, "Did you notice if he was alone, Jess?"

"Sure thing, sir," returned the boy in a cheerful tone. "He was sittin' all alone on this end seat. The reason I noticed it was that the show's been packed ever since it opened, and I thought it was queer that there should be so many seats empty around here."

"That's fine, Jess. You'll make a detective yet. . . . You couldn't tell me how many seats were empty, I suppose?"

"Well, sir, it was kind of dark and I wasn't payin' much attention. I guess it was about half a dozen all told—some next to him in the same row and some right in the row in front."

"Just a moment, Jess." The boy turned, licking his lips in honest fright at the sound of Ellery's low cool voice. "Did you see anything more of that shiny topper when you handed him the bottle of ginger ale?" asked Ellery, tapping the point of his neat shoe with his stick.

"Why, yes—yes, sir!" stammered the boy. "When I gave him the bottle he was holding the hat in his lap, but before I left I saw him stick it underneath his seat."

"Another question, Jess." The boy sighed with relief at the sound of the Inspector's reassuring voice. "About how long, do you reckon, did it take you to deliver the bottle to this man after the second act started?"

Jess Lynch thought gravely for a moment, and then said with finality, "It was just about ten minutes, sir. We got to keep pretty close tabs on the time, and I know it was ten minutes because when I came into the theatre with the bottle it was just the part on the stage when the girl is caught in the gang's hangout and is being grilled by the villain."

"An observant young Hermes!" murmured Ellery, smiling suddenly. The orangeade boy caught the smile and lost the last vestige of his fear. He smiled back. Ellery crooked his finger and bent forward. "Tell me, Jess. Why did it take you ten minutes to cross the street, buy a bottle of ginger ale and return to the theatre? Ten minutes is a long time, isn't it?"

The boy turned scarlet as he looked appealingly from Ellery to the Inspector. "Well, sir—I guess I stopped to talk for a few minutes with my girl. . . ."

"Your girl?" The Inspector's voice was mildly curious.

"Yes, sir. Elinor Libby—her old man owns the ice-cream parlor. She—she wanted me to stay there in the store with her when I went for the ginger ale. I told her I had to deliver it in the theatre, so she said all right but wouldn't I come right back. And I did. We stayed there a couple of minutes and then I remembered the stand in the alley. . . ."

"The stand in the alley?" Ellery's tone was eager. "Quite so, Jess—the stand in the alley. Don't tell me that, by some remarkable whim of fortune, you went back to the alley!"

"Sure I did!" rejoined the boy, in surprise. "I mean—we both did, Elinor and me."

"Elinor and you, eh, Jess?" said Ellery softly. "And how long were you there?"

The Inspector's eyes flashed at Ellery's question. He muttered approvingly to himself and listened intently as the boy answered.

"Well, I wanted to take the stand right away, sir, but Elinor and me—we got to talking there—and Elinor said why not stay in the alley till the next intermission. . . . I figured that was a good idea. I'd wait till a few minutes before 10:05, when the act ends, and I'd duck down for some more orangeade, and then when the doors opened for the second intermission, I'd be all ready. So we stayed there, sir. . . . It wasn't wrong, sir. I didn't mean anything wrong."

Ellery straightened and fixed the boy with his eyes. "Jess, I want you to be very careful now. At exactly what time did you and Elinor get to the alley?"

"Well. . . ." Jess scratched his head. "It was about 9:25 when I gave that man the ginger ale. I went across for Elinor, stayed a few minutes and then came over to the alley. Musta been just about 9:35—just about—when I went back for my orangeade stand."

"Very good. And what time exactly did you leave the alley?"

"It was just ten o'clock, sir. Elinor looked at her wrist watch when I asked her if it was time to go in for my orangeade refills."

"You didn't hear anything going on in the theatre?"

"No, sir. We were too busy talking, I guess. . . . I didn't know anything had happened inside until we walked out of the alley and I met Johnny Chase, one of the ushers, standing there, like he was on guard. He told me there was an accident inside and Mr. Panzer had sent him to stand outside the left alley."

"I see. . . ." Ellery removed his pince-nez in some agitation and flourished it before the boy's nose. "Carefully now, Jess. Did anyone go in or out of the alley all the time you were there with Elinor?"

The boy's answer was immediate and emphatic. "No, sir. Not a soul."

"Right, my lad." The Inspector gave the boy a spanking slap on the back and sent him off grinning. Queen looked around sharply, spied Panzer, who had made his announcement on the stage with ineffectual results, and beckoned with an imperative finger.

"Mr. Panzer," he said abruptly, "I want some information about the time schedule of the play. . . . At what times does the curtain go up on the second act?"

"The second act begins at 9:15 sharp and ends at 10:05 sharp," said Panzer instantly.

"Was tonight's performance run according to this schedule?"

"Certainly. We must be on the dot because of cues, lights, and so on," responded the manager.

The Inspector muttered some calculations to himself. "That makes it 9:25 the boy saw Field alive," he mused. "He was found dead at . . ."

He swung about and called for Officer Doyle. The man came running.

"Doyle," asked the Inspector, "Doyle, do you remember exactly at what time this fellow Pusak approached you with his story of the murder?"

The policeman scratched his head. "Why, I don't remember exactly, Inspector," he said. "All I do know is that the second act was almost over when it happened."

"Not definite enough, Doyle," said Queen irritably. "Where are the actors now?"

"Got 'em herded right over there back of the center section, sir," said Doyle. "We didn't know what to do with 'em except that."

"Get one of them for me!" snapped the Inspector.

Doyle ran off. Queen beckoned to Detective Piggott, who was standing a few feet to the rear between a man and a woman.

"Got the doorman there, Piggott?" asked Queen. Piggott nodded and a tall, corpulent old man, cap trembling in his hand, uniform shrunken on his flabby body, stumbled forward.

"Are you the man who stands outside the theatre—the regular doorman?" asked the Inspector.

"Yes, sir," the doorman answered, twisting the cap in his hands.

"Very well. Now think hard. Did anyone—anyone, mind you—leave the theatre by the front entrance during the second act?" The Inspector was leaning forward, like a small greyhound.

The man took a moment before replying. Then he said slowly, but with conviction, "No, sir. Nobody went out of the theatre. Nobody, I mean, but the orangeade boy."

"Were you there all the time?" barked the Inspector.

"Yes, sir."

"Now then. Do you remember anybody *coming in* during the second act?"

"We-e-ll . . . Jessie Lynch, the orangeade boy, came in right after the act started."

"Anybody else?"

There was silence as the old man made a frenzied effort at concentration. After a moment he looked helplessly from one face to another, eyes despairing. Then he mumbled, "I don't remember, sir."

The Inspector regarded him irritably. The old man seemed sincere in his nervous way. He was perspiring and frequently looked sidewise at Panzer, as if he sensed that his defection of memory would cost him his position.

"I'm awfully sorry, sir," the doorman repeated. "Awfully sorry. There might've been someone, but my memory ain't as good as it used to be when I was younger. I—I just can't seem to recall."

Ellery's cool voice cut in on the old man's thick accents.

"How long have you been a doorman?"

The old man's bewildered eyes shifted to this new inquisitor. "Nigh onto ten years, sir. I wasn't always a doorman. Only when I got old and couldn't do nothin' else—"

"I understand," said Ellery kindly. He hesitated a moment, then added inflexibly, "A man who has been a doorman for as many years as you have might forget something about the first act. But people do not often come into a theatre during the second act. Surely if you think hard enough you can answer positively, one way or the other?"

The response came painfully. "I—I don't remember, sir. I could say no one did, but that mightn't be the truth. I just can't answer."

"All right." The Inspector put his hand on the old man's shoulder. "Forget it. Perhaps we're asking too much. That's all for the time being." The doorman shuffled away with the pitiful alacrity of old age.

Doyle clumped toward the group, a tall handsome man dressed in rough tweeds in his wake, traces of stage make-up streaking his face.

"This is Mr. Peale, Inspector. He's the leading man of the show," reported Doyle.

Queen smiled at the actor, offering his hand. "Pleased to make your acquaintance, Mr. Peale. Perhaps you can help us out with a little information."

"Glad to be of service, Inspector," replied Peale, in a rich baritone. He glanced at the back of the Medical Examiner, who was busy over the dead man; then looked away with repugnance.

"I suppose you were on the stage at the time the hue-and-cry went up in this unfortunate affair?" pursued the Inspector.

"Oh, yes. In fact, the entire cast was. What is it you would like to know?"

"Could you definitely place the time that you noticed something wrong in the audience?"

"Yes, I can. We had just about ten minutes before the end of the act. It was at the climax of the play, and my role demands the discharge of a pistol. I remember we had some discussion during rehearsals of this point in the play, and that is how I can be so sure of the time."

The Inspector nodded. "Thank you very much, Mr. Peale. That's exactly what I wanted to know. . . . Incidentally, let me apologize for having kept you people crowded back here in this fashion. We were quite busy and had no time to make other arrangements. You and the rest of the cast are at liberty to go backstage now. Of course, make no effort to leave the theatre until you are notified."

"I understand completely, Inspector. Happy to have been able to help." Peale bowed and retreated to the rear of the theatre.

The Inspector leaned against the nearest seat, absorbed in thought, Ellery, at his side, was absently polishing the lenses of his pince-nez. Father motioned significantly to son.

"Well, Ellery?" Queen asked in a low voice.

"Elementary, my dear Watson," murmured Ellery. "Our respected victim was last seen alive at 9:25, and he was found dead at approximately 9:55. Problem: What happened between times? Sounds ludicrously simple."

"You don't say?" muttered Queen. "Piggott!"

"Yes, sir."

"Is that the usherette? Let's get some action."

Piggott released the arm of the young woman standing at his side. She was a pert and painted lady with even white teeth and a ghastly smile. She minced forward and regarded the Inspector brazenly.

"Are you the regular usherette on this aisle, Miss—?" asked the Inspector briskly.

"O'Connell, Madge O'Connell. Yes, I am!"

The Inspector took her arm gently. "I'm afraid I'll have to ask you to be as grave as you are impertinent, my dear," he said. "Step over here for a moment." The girl's face was deathly white as they paused at the LL row. "Pardon me a moment, Doc. Mind if we interrupt your work?"

Dr. Prouty looked up with an abstracted scowl. "No, go right ahead, Inspector. I'm nearly through." He stood up and moved aside, biting the cigar between his teeth.

Queen watched the girl's face as she stooped over the dead man's body. She drew her breath in sharply.

"Do you remember ushering this man to his seat tonight, Miss O'Connell?"

The girl hesitated. "Seems like I do. But I was very busy tonight, as usual, and I must have ushered two hundred people all told. So I couldn't say positively."

"Do you recall whether these seats which are empty now"—he indicated the seven vacant chairs—"were unoccupied all during the first and second acts?"

"Well . . . I do seem to remember noticing them that way as I walked up and down the aisle. . . . No, sir. I don't think anybody sat in those seats all night."

"Did anyone walk up or down this aisle during the second act, Miss O'Connell? Think hard, now; it's important that you answer correctly."

The girl hesitated once more, flashing bold eyes at the impassive face of the Inspector. "No—I didn't see anybody walk up or down the aisle." She quickly added, "I couldn't tell you much. I don't know a thing about this business. I'm a hard-working girl, and I—"

"Yes, yes, my dear, we understand that. Now where do you generally stand when you're not ushering people to their seats?"

The girl pointed to the head of the aisle.

"Were you there all during the second act, Miss O'Connell?" asked the Inspector softly.

The girl moistened her lips before she spoke. "Well—yes, I was. But, honest, I didn't see anything out of the way all night."

"Very well." Queen's voice was mild. "That's all." She turned away with quick, light steps.

There was a stir behind the group. Queen wheeled to confront Dr. Prouty, who had risen to his feet and was closing his bag. He was whistling dolefully.

"Well, Doc—I see you're through. What's the verdict?" asked Queen.

"It's short and snappy, Inspector. Man died about two hours ago. Cause of death puzzled me for a while but it's pretty well settled in my mind as poison. The signs all point to some form of alcoholic poisoning—you've probably noticed the sallow blue color of the skin. Did you smell his breath? Sweetest odor of bum booze I ever had the pleasure of inhaling. He must have been drunk as a lord. At the same time, it couldn't have been ordinary alcoholic poisoning—he wouldn't have dropped off so fast. That's all I can tell you right now." He paused, buttoning his coat.

Queen took Field's kerchief-wrapped flask from his pocket and handed it to Dr. Prouty. "This is the dead man's flask, Doc. Suppose you analyze the contents for me. Before you handle it, though, let Jimmy down at the laboratory look it over for fingerprints. And—but wait a minute." The Inspector peered about and picked up the half-empty ginger-ale bottle where it stood in a corner on the carpet. "You can analyze this ginger ale for me, too, Doc," he added.

The Assistant Medical Examiner, after stowing the flask and bottle
into his bag, tenderly adjusted the hat on his head.

"Well, I'll be going, Inspector," he drawled. "I'll have a fuller report
for you when I've performed the autopsy. Ought to give you something
to work on. Incidentally, the morgue-wagon must be outside—I phoned
for one on my way down. So long." He yawned and slouched away.

As Dr. Prouty disappeared, two white-garbed orderlies hurried across
the carpet, bearing a stretcher between them. At a sign from Queen they
lifted the inert body, deposited it on the stretcher, covered it with a blanket and hustled out. The detectives and policemen around the door
watched with relief as the grisly burden was borne away—the main work
of the evening for them was almost over. The audience—rustling, shifting, coughing, murmuring—twisted about with a renewal of interest as
the body was unceremoniously carted off.

Queen had just turned to Ellery with a weary sigh when from the extreme right-hand side of the theatre came an ominous commotion. People
everywhere popped out of their seats staring while policemen shouted for
quiet. Queen spoke rapidly to a uniformed officer nearby. Ellery slipped
to one side, eyes gleaming. The disturbance came nearer by jerky degrees. Two policemen appeared hauling a struggling figure between
them. They dragged their capture to the head of the left aisle and hustled
the man to his feet, holding him up by main force.

The man was short and ratlike. He wore cheap storeclothes of a sombre cut. On his head was a black hat of the kind sometimes worn by
country dominies. His mouth writhed in an ugly manner; imprecations
issued from it venomously. As he caught the eye of the Inspector fixed
upon him, however, he ceased struggling and went limp at once.

"Found this man tryin' to sneak out the alley door on the other side of
the buildin', Inspector," panted one of the bluecoats, shaking the captive
roughly.

The Inspector chuckled, took his brown snuffbox from his pocket, inhaled, sneezed his habitual joyful sneeze, and beamed upon the silent
cowering man between the two officers.

"Well, well, Parson," he said genially. "Mighty nice of you to turn up
so conveniently!"

# 4

## In Which Many Are Called and Two Are Chosen

Some natures, through peculiar weakness, cannot endure the sight of a whining man. Of all the silent, threatening group ringed about the abject figure called "Parson," Ellery alone experienced a sick feeling of disgust at the spectacle the prisoner was making of himself.

At the hidden lash in Queen's words, the Parson drew himself up stiffly, glared into the Inspector's eyes for a split second, then with a resumption of his former tactics began to fight against the sturdy arms which encircled him. He writhed and spat and cursed, finally becoming silent again. He was conserving his breath. The fury of his threshing body communicated itself to his captors; another policeman joined the melee and helped pin the prisoner to the floor. And suddenly he wilted and shrank like a pricked balloon. A policeman hauled him roughly to his feet, where he stood, eyes downcast, body still, hat clutched in his hand.

Ellery turned his head.

"Come now, Parson," went on the Inspector, just as if the man had been a balky child at rest after a fit of temper, "you know that sort of business doesn't go with me. What happened when you tried it last time at the Old Slip on the riverfront?"

"Answer when you're spoken to!" growled a bluecoat, prodding him in the ribs.

"I don't know nothin' and besides I got nothin' to say," muttered the Parson, shifting from one foot to the other.

"I'm surprised at you, Parson," said Queen gently. "I haven't asked you what you know."

"You got no right to hold an innocent man!" shouted the Parson indignantly. "Ain't I as good as anybody else here? I bought a ticket and I paid for it with real dough, too! Where do you get that stuff—tryin' to keep me from goin' home!"

"So you bought a ticket, did you?" asked the Inspector, rocking on his heels. "Well, well! Suppose you snap out the old stub and let Papa Queen look it over."

The Parson's hand mechanically went to his lower vest pocket, his fingers dipping into it with a quite surprising deftness. His face went blank as he slowly withdrew his hand, empty. He began a search of his other pockets with an appearance of fierce annoyance that made the Inspector smile.

"Hell!" grunted the Parson. "If that ain't the toughest luck. I always hangs onto my ticket stubs, an' just tonight I have to go and throw it away. Sorry, Inspector!"

"Oh, that's quite all right," said Queen. His face went bleak and hard. "Quit stalling, Cazzanelli! What were you doing in this theatre tonight? What made you decide to duck out so suddenly? Answer me!"

The Parson looked about him. His arms were held very securely by two bluecoats. A number of hard-looking men surrounded him. The prospect of escape did not seem particularly bright. His face underwent another change. It assumed a priestly, outraged innocence. A mist filmed his little eyes, as if he were truly the Christian martyr and these tyrants his pagan inquisitors. The Parson had often employed this trick of personality to good purpose.

"Inspector," he said, "you know you ain't got no right to grill me this way, don't you, Inspector? A man's got a right to his lawyer, ain't he? Sure he's got a right!" And he stopped as if there were nothing more to be said.

The Inspector eyed him curiously. "When did you see Field last?" he asked.

"Field? You don't mean to say—Monte Field? Never heard of him, Inspector," muttered the Parson, rather shakily. "What are you tryin' to put over on me?"

"Not a thing, Parson, not a thing. But as long as you don't care to answer now, suppose we let you cool your heels for a while. Perhaps you'll have something to say later. . . . Don't forget, Parson, there's still that little matter of the Bonomo Silk robbery to go into." He turned to one of the policemen. "Escort our friend to that anteroom off the manager's office, and keep him company for a while, officer."

Ellery, reflectively watching the Parson being dragged toward the rear of the theatre, was startled to hear his father say, "The Parson isn't too bright, is he? To make a slip like that—!"

"Be thankful for small favors," smiled Ellery. "One error breeds twenty more."

The Inspector turned with a grin to confront Velie, who had just arrived with a sheaf of papers in his hand.

"Ah, Thomas is back," chuckled the Inspector, who seemed in good spirits. "And what have you found, Thomas?"

"Well, Inspector," replied the detective, ruffling the edges of his papers, "it's hard to say. This is half of the list—the other half isn't ready yet. But I think you'll find something interesting here."

He handed Queen a batch of hastily written names and addresses. They were the names which the Inspector had ordered Velie to secure by interrogation of the audience.

Queen, with Ellery at his shoulder, examined the list, studying each name carefully. He was halfway through the sheaf when he stiffened. He squinted at the name which had halted him and looked up at Velie with a puzzled air.

"Morgan," he said thoughtfully. "Benjamin Morgan. Sounds mighty familiar, Thomas. What does it suggest to you?"

Velie smiled frostily. "I thought you'd ask me that, Inspector. Benjamin Morgan was Monte Field's law partner until two years ago."

Queen nodded. The three men stared into each other's eyes. Then the old man shrugged his shoulders and said briefly, "Have to see some more of Mr. Morgan, I'm afraid."

He turned back to the list with a sigh. Again he studied each name, looking up at intervals reflectively, shaking his head, and going on. Velie, who knew Queen's reputation for memory even more thoroughly than Ellery, watched his superior with respectful eyes.

Finally the Inspector handed the papers back to the detective. "Nothing else, there, Thomas," he said. "Unless you caught something that escaped me. Did you?" His tone was grave.

Velie stared at the old man wordlessly, shook his head and started to walk away.

"Just a minute, Thomas," called Queen. "Before you get that second list completed, ask Mr. Morgan to step into Panzer's office will you? Don't scare him. And by the way, see that he has his ticket stub before he goes to the office." Velie departed.

The Inspector motioned to Panzer, who was watching a group of policemen being marshaled by detectives for Queen's work. The stout little manager hurried up.

"Mr. Panzer," inquired the Inspector, "at what time do your scrubwomen generally start cleaning up?"

"Why, they've been here for quite a while now, Inspector, waiting to get to work. Most theatres are tidied early in the morning, but I've always had my employees come immediately after the evening performance. Just what is on your mind?"

Ellery, who had frowned slightly when the Inspector spoke, brightened at the manager's reply. He began to polish his pince-nez with satisfaction.

"Here's what I want you to do, Mr. Panzer," continued Queen evenly. "Arrange to have your cleaning women make a particularly thorough search tonight, after everybody is gone. They must pick up and save everything—everything, no matter how seemingly trivial—and they're to watch especially for ticket stubs. Can you trust these people?"

"Oh, absolutely, Inspector. They've been with the theatre ever since it was built. You may be sure that nothing will be overlooked. What shall I do with the sweepings?"

"Wrap them carefully, address them to me and send them by a trustworthy messenger to headquarters tomorrow morning." The Inspector paused. "I want to impress upon you, Mr. Panzer, the importance of this task. It's much more important than it seems. Do you understand?"

"Certainly, certainly!" Panzer hastened away.

A detective with grizzled hair walked briskly across the carpet, turned down the left aisle and touched his hat to Queen. In his hand was a sheaf of papers resembling the one which Velie had presented.

"Sergeant Velie had asked me to give you this list of names. He says that it's the rest of the names and addresses of the people in the audience, Inspector."

Queen took the papers from the detective's hand with a sudden show of eagerness. Ellery leaned forward. The old man's eyes traveled slowly from name to name as his thin finger moved down each sheet. Near the bottom of the last one he smiled, looked at Ellery triumphantly, and finished the page. He turned and whispered into his son's ear. A light came over Ellery's face as he nodded.

The Inspector turned back to the waiting detective. "Come here, Johnson," he said. Queen spread out the page he had been studying for the man's scrutiny. "I want you to find Velie and have him report to me at once. After you've done that, get hold of this woman"—his finger pointed to a name and a row and seat number next to it—"ask her to step into the manager's office with you. You'll find a man by the name of Morgan there. Stay with both of them until you hear from me. Incidentally, if there's any conversation between them keep your ears open—I want to know what is said. Treat the woman courteously."

"Yes, sir. Velie also asked me to tell you," continued Johnson, "that he has a group of people separated from the rest of the audience—they're the ones who have no ticket stubs. He'd like to know what you want done with them."

"Do their names appear on both lists, Johnson?" asked Queen, handing him the second sheaf for return to Velie.

"Yes, sir."

"Then tell Velie to let them leave with the others, but not before he makes a special list of their names. It won't be necessary for me to see or speak to them."

Johnson saluted and disappeared.

Queen turned to converse in low tones with Ellery, who seemed to have something on his mind. They were interrupted by the reappearance of Panzer.

"Inspector?" The manager coughed politely.

"Oh, yes, Panzer!" said the Inspector, whirling about. "Everything straight with regard to the cleaning women?"

"Yes, sir. Is there anything else you would like me to do . . . ? And, Inspector, I hope you will pardon me for asking, but how much longer will the audience have to wait? I have been receiving most disturbing inquiries from many people. I am hoping no trouble comes of this affair." His dark face was glistening with perspiration.

"Oh, don't worry about that, Panzer," said the Inspector casually. "Their wait is almost over. In fact I am ordering my men to get them out of here in a few minutes. Before they leave, however, they'll have one thing more to complain about," he added with a grim smile.

"Yes, Inspector?"

"Oh, yes," said Queen. "They're going to submit to a search. No doubt they'll protest, and you'll hear threats of lawsuits and personal violence, but don't worry about it. I'm responsible for everything done here tonight, and I'll see that you're kept out of trouble. . . . Now, we'll need a woman searcher to help our men. We have a police matron here, but she's busy downstairs. Do you think you could get me a dependable woman— middle-aged preferably—who won't object to a thankless job and will know how to keep her mouth shut?"

The manager pondered for a moment. "I think I can get you the woman you want. She's a Mrs. Phillips, our wardrobe mistress. She's well on in years and as pleasant as anyone you could get for such a task."

"Just the person," said Queen briskly. "Get her at once and station her at the main exit. Detective-Sergeant Velie will give her the necessary instructions."

Velie had come up in time to hear the last remark. Panzer bustled down the aisle toward the boxes.

"Morgan set?" asked Queen.

"Yes, Inspector."

"Well, then, you have one more job and you'll be through for the night, Thomas. I want you to superintend the departure of the people seated in the orchestra and boxes. Have them leave one by one, and overhaul them as they go out. No one is to leave by any exit except the main door, and just to make sure tell the men at the side exits to keep 'em moving toward the rear." Velie nodded. "Now, about the search. Piggott!" The detective came on the run. "Piggott, you accompany Mr. Queen and Sergeant Velie and help search every man who goes out the main door. There'll be a matron there to search the women. Examine every parcel. Go over their pockets for anything suspicious; collect all the ticket stubs; and watch especially for *an extra hat*. The hat I want is a silk topper. But if you find any other kind of extra hat, nab the owner and be sure he's nabbed properly. Now, boys, get to work!"

Ellery, who had been lounging against a pillar, straightened up and followed Piggott. As Velie stalked behind, Queen called, "Don't release the people in the balcony until the orchestra is empty. Send somebody up there to keep them quiet."

With his last important instruction given the Inspector turned to Doyle, who was standing guard nearby, and said quietly, "Shoot downstairs to the cloakroom, Doyle, my lad, and keep your eyes open while the people are getting their wraps. When they're all gone, search the place with a fine comb. If there is anything left in the racks, bring it to me."

Queen leaned back against the pillar which loomed, a marble sentinel, over the seat in which murder had been done. As he stood there, eyes blank, hands clutching his lapels, the broad-shouldered Flint hurried up with a gleam of excitement in his eyes. Inspector Queen regarded him critically.

"Found something, Flint?" he asked, fumbling for his snuffbox.

The detective silently offered him a half-ticket, colored blue, and marked "LL30 Left."

"Well, well!" exclaimed Queen. "Where did you find that?"

"Right inside the main door," said Flint. "Looked as if it was dropped just as the owner came into the theatre."

Queen did not answer. With a swooping dip of his fingers he extracted from his vest pocket the blue-colored stub he had found on the dead man's person. He regarded them in silence—two identically colored and marked stubs, one with the inscription LL32 Left, the other LL30 Left.

His eyes narrowed as he studied the innocent-appearing pasteboards. He bent closer, slowly turning the stubs back to back. Then, with a puzzled light in his gray eyes, he turned them front to front. Still unsatisfied, he turned them back to front.

In none of the three positions did the torn edges of the tickets coincide!

# 5

## In Which Inspector Queen Conducts
## Some Legal Conversations

Queen made his way across the broad red carpet covering the rear of the orchestra, his hat pulled down over his eyes. He was searching the recesses of his pocket for the inevitable snuffbox. The Inspector was evidently engaged in a weighty mental process, for his hand closed tightly upon the two blue ticket stubs and he grimaced, as if he were not at all satisfied with his thoughts.

Before opening the green-speckled door marked "Manager's Office," he turned to survey the scene behind him. The stir in the audience was businesslike. A great chattering filled the air; policemen and detectives circulated among the rows, giving orders, answering questions, hustling people out of their seats, lining them up in the main aisles to be searched at the huge outer door. The Inspector noticed absently that there was little protest from the audience at the ordeal they were facing. They seemed too tired to resent the indignity of a search. A long queue of half-angry, half-amused women was lined up at one side being examined rapidly, one by one, by a motherly woman dressed in black. Queen glanced briefly at the detectives blocking the door. Piggott with the experience of long practice was making rapid passes over the clothing of the men. Velie, at his side, was studying the reaction of the various people undergoing examination. Occasionally he searched a man himself. Ellery stood a little apart, hands in his capacious topcoat pockets smoking a cigarette and seeming to be thinking of nothing more important than the first edition he had missed buying.

Queen sighed, and went in.

The anteroom to the main office was a tiny place, fitted out in bronze and oak. On one of the chairs against the wall, burrowed into the deep leather cushions, sat Parson Johnny, puffing at a cigarette with a show of unconcern. A policeman stood by the chair, one massive hand on the Parson's shoulder.

"Trail along, Parson," said Queen casually, without stopping. The little gangster lounged to his feet, spun his cigarette butt deftly into a shining brass cuspidor, and slouched after the Inspector, the policeman treading on his heels.

Queen opened the door to the main office, glancing quickly about him as he stood on the threshold. Then he stepped aside, allowing the gangster and the bluecoat to precede him. The door banged shut behind them.

Louis Panzer had an unusual taste in office appointments. A clear green lightshade shone brilliantly above a carved desk. Chairs and smoking stands; a skillfully wrought clothes-tree; silk-covered divan—these and other articles were strewn tastefully about the room. Unlike most managers' offices, Panzer's did not exploit photographs of stars, managers, producers and "angels." Several delicate prints, a huge tapestry, and a Constable oil painting hung on the wall.

But Inspector Queen's scrutiny at the moment was not for the artistic quality of Mr. Panzer's private chamber. It was rather for the six people who faced him. Beside Detective Johnson sat a middle-aged man inclining to corpulence, with shrewd eyes and a puzzled frown. He wore faultless evening clothes. In the next chair sat a young girl of considerable beauty, attired in a simple evening gown and wrap. She was looking up at a handsome young man in evening clothes, hat in hand, who was bending over her chair and talking earnestly in an undertone. Beside them were two other women, both leaning forward and listening intently.

The stout man held aloof from the others. At Inspector Queen's entrance he immediately got to his feet with an inquiring look. The little group became silent and turned solemn faces on Queen.

With a deprecating cough Parson Johnny, accompanied by his escort, sidled across the rug into a corner. He seemed overwhelmed by the splendor of the company in which he found himself. He shuffled his feet and cast a despairing look in the direction of the Inspector.

Queen moved over to the desk and faced the group. At a motion of his hand Johnson came quickly to his side.

"Who are the three extra people, Johnson?" he asked in a tone inaudible to the others.

"The old fellow there is Morgan," whispered Johnson, "and the good-looker sitting near him is the woman you told me to get. When I went for her in the orchestra I found the young chap and the other two women with her. The four of 'em were pretty chummy. I gave her your message, and she seemed nervous. But she stood up and came along like a major—

only the other three came, too. I didn't know but what you'd like to see 'em, Inspector. . . ."

Queen nodded. "Hear anything?" he asked in the same low tone.

"Not a peep, Inspector. The old chap doesn't seem to know any of these people. The others have just been wondering why you could possibly want *her*."

The Inspector waved Johnson to a corner and addressed the waiting group.

"I've summoned two of you," he said pleasantly, "for a little chat. And since the others are here, too, it will be all right for them to wait. But for the moment I must ask you all to step into the anteroom while I conduct a little business with this gentleman." He inclined his head toward the gangster, who stiffened indignantly.

With a flutter of excited conversation the two men and three women departed, Johnson closing the door behind them.

Queen whirled on Parson Johnny.

"Bring that rat here!" he snapped to the policeman. He sat down in Panzer's chair and drew the tips of his fingers together. The gangster was jerked to his feet and marched across the carpet, to be pushed directly in front of the desk.

"Now, Parson," said Queen menacingly. "I've got you where I want you. We're going to have a nice little talk with nobody to interrupt. Get me?"

The Parson was silent, his eyes liquid with distrust.

"So you won't say anything, eh, Johnny? How long do you think I'll let you get away with that?"

"I told you before—I don't know nothin' and besides I won't say nothin' till I see my lawyer," the gangster said sullenly.

"Your lawyer? Well, Parson, who *is* your lawyer?" asked the Inspector in an innocent tone.

The Parson bit his lip, remaining silent. Queen turned to Johnson.

"Johnson, my boy, you worked on the Babylon stickup, didn't you?" he asked.

"Sure did, Chief," said the detective.

"That," explained Queen gently, to the gangster, "was when you were sent up for a year. Remember, Parson?"

Still silence.

"And Johnson," continued the Inspector, leaning back in his chair, "refresh my memory. Who was the lawyer defending our friend here?"

"Field. By—" Johnson exclaimed, staring at the Parson.

"Exactly. The gentleman now lying on one of our unfeeling slabs at the morgue. Well, what about it? Cut the comedy! Where do you come off saying you don't know Monte Field? You knew his first name, all right, when I mentioned only his last. Come clean, now!"

The gangster had sagged against the policeman, a furtive despair in his eyes. He moistened his lips and said, "You got me there, Inspector. I—I don't know nothin' about this, though, honest. I ain't seen Field in a month. I didn't—my Gawd, you're not tryin' to tie this croakin' around my neck, are you?"

He stared at Queen in anguish. The policeman jerked him straight.

"Parson, Parson," said Queen, "how you do jump at conclusions. I'm merely looking for a little information. Of course, if you want to confess to the murder I'll call my men in and we can get your story all straight and go home to bed. How about it?"

"No!" shouted the gangster, thrashing out suddenly with his arm. The officer caught it deftly and twisted it behind the squirming back. "Where do you get that stuff? I ain't confessin' nothin'. I don't know nothin'. I didn't see Field tonight an' I didn't even know he was here! Confess. . . . I got some mighty influential friends, Inspector—you can't pull that stuff on me, I'll tell you!"

"That's too bad, Johnny," sighed the Inspector. He took a pinch of snuff. "All right, then. You didn't kill Monte Field. What time did you get here tonight, and where's your ticket?"

The Parson twisted his hat in his hands. "I wasn't goin' to say nothin' before, Inspector, because I figured you was tryin' to railroad me. I can explain when and how I got here all right. It was about half past eight, and I got in on a pass, that's how. Here's the stub to prove it." He searched carefully in his coat pocket and produced a perforated blue stub. He handed it to Queen, who glanced at it carefully and put it in his pocket.

"And where," he asked, "and where did you get the pass, Johnny?"

"I—my girl give it to me, Inspector," replied the gangster nervously.

"Ah—the woman enters the case," said Queen jovially. "And what might this young Circe's name be, Johnny?"

"Who?—why, she's—hey, Inspector, don't get her in no trouble, will you?" burst out Parson Johnny. "She's a reg'lar kid, an' she don't know nothin' either. Honest, I—"

"Her name?" snapped Queen.

"Madge O'Connell," whined Johnny. "She's an usher here."

Queen's eyes lit up. A quick glance passed between him and Johnson. The detective left the room.

"So," continued the Inspector, leaning back again comfortably, "so my old friend Parson Johnny doesn't know a thing about Monte Field. Well, well, well! We'll see how your lady-friend's story backs you up." As he talked he looked steadily at the hat in the gangster's hand. It was a cheap black fedora, matching the sombre suit which the man was wearing. "Here, Parson," he said suddenly. "Hand over that hat of yours."

He took the head piece from the gangster's reluctant hand and examined it. He pulled down the leather band inside, eyed it critically and finally handed it back.

"We forgot something, Parson," he said. "Officer, suppose you frisk Mr. Cazzanelli's person, eh?"

The Parson submitted to the search with an ill grace, but he was quiescent enough. "No gat," said the policeman briefly, and continued. He put his hand into the man's hip pocket, extracting a fat wallet. "Want this, Inspector?"

Queen took it, counted the money briskly, and handed it back to the policeman, who returned it to the pocket.

"One hundred and twenty-two smackers, Johnny," the old man murmured. "Seems to me I can smell Bonomo silk in these bills. However!" He laughed and said to the bluecoat, "No flask?" The policeman shook his head. "Anything under his vest or shirt?" Again a negative. Queen was silent until the search was completed. Parson Johnny relaxed with a sigh.

"Well, Johnny, mighty lucky night this is for you— Come in!" Queen said at a knock on the door. It opened to disclose the slender girl in usherette's uniform whom he had questioned earlier in the evening. Johnson came in after her and closed the door.

Madge O'Connell stood on the rug and stared with tragic eyes at her lover, who was thoughtfully studying the floor. She flashed a glance at Queen. Then her mouth hardened and she snapped at the gangster. "Well? So they got you after all, you sap! I told you not to try to make a break for it!" She turned her back contemptuously on the Parson and began to ply a powderpuff with vigor.

"Why didn't you tell me before, my girl," said Queen softly, "that you got a pass for your friend John Cazzanelli?"

"I ain't telling everything, Mr. Cop," she answered pertly. "Why should I? Johnny didn't have anything to do with this business."

"We won't discuss that," said the Inspector, toying with his snuffbox. "What I want you to tell me now, Madge, is whether your memory has improved any since I spoke to you."

"What d'ya mean?" she demanded.

"I mean this. You told me that you were at your regular station just before the show started—that you conducted a lot of people to their seats— that you didn't remember whether you ushered Monte Field, the dead man, to his row or not—and that you were standing up at the head of the

lcft aisle all during the performance. *All* during the performance, Madge.
Is that correct?"

"Sure it is, Inspector. Who says I wasn't?" The girl was growing excited, but Queen glanced at her fluttering fingers and they became still.

"Aw, cut it out, Madge," snapped the Parson unexpectedly. "Don't
make it no worse than it is. Sooner or later he'll find out we were together anyways, and then he'd have something on you. You don't know
this bird. Come clean, Madge!"

"So!" said the Inspector, looking pleasantly from the gangster to the
girl. "Parson, you're getting sensible in your old age. Did I hear you say
you two were together? When, and why, and for how long?"

Madge O'Connell's face had gone red and white by turns. She favored
her lover with a venomous glance, then turned back to Queen.

"I guess I might as well spill it," she said disgustedly, "after this
halfwit shows a yellow streak. Here's all I know, Inspector—and Gawd
help you if you tell that little mutt of a manager about it!" Queen's eyebrows went up, but he did not interrupt her. "I got the pass for Johnny all
right," she continued defiantly, "because—well, Johnny kind of likes
blood-and-thunder stuff, and it was his offnight. So I got him the pass. It
was for two—all the passes are—so that the seat next to Johnny was
empty all the time. It was an aisle seat on the left—best I could get for
that loud-mouthed shrimp! During the first act I was pretty busy and
couldn't sit with him. But after the first intermission, when the curtain
went up on Act II, things got slack and it was a good chance to sit next to
him. Sure, I admit it—I was sittin' next to him nearly the whole act! Why
not—don't I deserve a rest once in a while?"

"I see." Queen bent his brows. "You would have saved me a lot of
time and trouble, young lady, if you'd told me this before. Didn't you get
up at all during the second act?"

"Well, I did a couple of times, I guess," she said guardedly. "But
everything was okay, and the manager wasn't around, so I went back."

"Did you notice this man Field as you passed?"

"No—no, sir."

"Did you notice if anybody was sitting next to him?"

"No, sir. I didn't know he was there. Wasn't—wasn't looking that
way, I guess."

"I suppose, then," continued Queen coldly, "you don't remember ushering somebody into the last row, next to the last seat, during the second
act?"

"No, sir. . . . Aw, I know I shouldn't have done it, maybe, but I didn't
see a thing wrong all night." She was growing more nervous at each

question. She furtively glanced at the Parson, but he was staring at the floor.

"You're a great help, young lady," said Queen, rising suddenly. "Beat it."

As she turned to go, the gangster with an innocent leer slid across the rug to follow her. Queen made a sign to the policeman. The Parson found himself yanked back to his former position.

"Not so fast, Johnny," said Queen icily. "O'Connell!" The girl turned, trying to appear unconcerned. "For the time being I shan't say anything about this to Mr. Panzer. But I'd advise you to watch your step and learn to keep your mouth clean when you talk to your superiors. Get on now, and if I ever hear of another break on your part God help *you!*"

She started to laugh, wavered and fled from the room.

Queen whirled on the policeman. "Put the nippers on him, officer," he snapped, jerking his finger toward the gangster, "and run him down to the station!"

The policeman saluted. There was a flash of steel, a dull click, and the Parson stared stupidly at the handcuffs on his wrists. Before he could open his mouth he was hustled out of the room.

Queen made a disgusted motion of his hand, threw himself into the leather-covered chair, took a pinch of snuff, and said to Johnson in an entirely different tone, "I'll trouble you, Johnson my boy, to ask Mr. Morgan to step in here."

Benjamin Morgan entered Queen's temporary sanctum with a firm step that did not succeed entirely in concealing a certain bewildered agitation. He said in a cheerful, hearty baritone, "Well, sir, here I am," and sank into a chair with much the same air of satisfaction that a man exhales when he seats himself in his clubroom after a hard day. Queen was not taken in. He favored Morgan with a long, earnest stare, which made the paunchy grizzled man squirm.

"My name is Queen, Mr. Morgan," he said in a friendly voice, "Inspector Richard Queen."

"I suspected as much," said Morgan, rising to shake hands. "I think you know who I am, Inspector. I was under your eye more than once in the Criminal Court years ago. There was a case—do you remember it?—I was defending Mary Doolittle when she was being tried for murder. . . ."

"Indeed, yes!" exclaimed the Inspector heartily. "I wondered where I'd seen you before. You got her off, too, if I'm not mistaken. That was a mighty nice piece of work, Morgan—very, very nice. So *you're* the fellow! Well, well!"

Morgan laughed. "Was pretty nice, at that," he admitted. "But those days are over, I'm afraid, Inspector. You know—I'm not in the criminal end of it any more."

"No?" Queen took a pinch of snuff. "I didn't know that. Anything"—
he sneezed—"anything go wrong?" he asked sympathetically.

Morgan was silent. After a moment he crossed his legs and said,
"Quite a bit went wrong. May I smoke?" he asked abruptly. On Queen's
assent he lit a fat cigar and became absorbed in its curling haze.

Neither man spoke for a long time. Morgan seemed to sense that he
was under a rigid inspection, for he crossed and uncrossed his legs re-
peatedly, avoiding Queen's eyes. The old man appeared to be ruminating,
his head sunk on his breast.

The silence became electric, embarrassing. There was not a sound in
the room, except the ticking of a floor-clock in a corner. From somewhere
in the theatre came a sudden burst of conversation. Voices were raised to
a high pitch of indignation or protest. Then even this was cut off.

"Come now, Inspector. . . ." Morgan coughed. He was enveloped in a
thick rolling smoke from his cigar, and his voice was harsh and strained.
"What is this—a refined third degree?"

Queen looked up, startled. "Eh? I beg your pardon, Mr. Morgan. My
thoughts went wool-gathering, I guess. Been rubbing it in, have I? Dear
me! I must be getting old." He rose and took a short turn about the room,
his hands clasped loosely behind his back. Morgan's eyes followed him.

"Mr. Morgan"—the Inspector pounced on him with one of his habitual
conversational leaps—"do you know why I've asked you to stay and talk
to me?"

"Why—I can't say I do, Inspector. I suppose, naturally, that it has to
do with the accident here tonight. But what connection it can possibly
have with me, I'll confess I don't know." Morgan puffed violently at his
weed.

"Perhaps, Mr. Morgan, you will know in a moment," said Queen,
leaning back against the desk. "The man murdered here tonight—it
wasn't any accident, I can assure you of that—was a certain Monte
Field."

The announcement was placid enough but the effect upon Morgan was
astounding. He fairly leaped from his chair, eyes popping, hands trembling, breath hoarse and heavy. His cigar dropped to the floor. Queen regarded him with morose eyes.

"Monte—Field!" Morgan's cry was terrible in its intensity. He stared
at the Inspector's face. Then he collapsed in the chair, his whole body
sagging.

"Pick up your cigar, Mr. Morgan," said Queen. "I shouldn't like to
abuse Mr. Panzer's hospitality." The lawyer stooped mechanically and
retrieved the cigar.

"My friend," thought Queen to himself, "either you are one of the world's greatest actors or you just got the shock of your life!" He straightened up. "Come now, Mr. Morgan—pull yourself together. Why should the death of Field affect you in this way?"

"But—but, man! Monte Field . . . Oh, my God!" And he threw back his head and laughed—a wild humor that made Queen sit up alertly. The spasm continued, Morgan's body rocking to and fro in hysteria. The Inspector knew the symptoms. He slapped the lawyer in the face, pulling him to his feet by his coat collar.

"Don't forget yourself, Morgan!" commanded Queen. The rough tone had its effect. Morgan stopped laughing, regarded Queen with a blank expression, and dropped heavily into the chair—still shaken, but himself.

"I'm—I'm sorry, Inspector," he muttered, dabbing his face with a handkerchief. "It was—quite a surprise."

"Evidently," said Queen dryly. "You couldn't have acted more surprised if the earth had opened under your feet. Now, Morgan, what's this all about?"

The lawyer continued to wipe the perspiration from his face. He was shaking like a leaf, his jowls red. He gnawed at his lip in indecision.

"All right, Inspector," he said at last. "What do you want to know?"

"That's better," said Queen approvingly. "Suppose you tell me when you last saw Monte Field?"

The lawyer cleared his throat nervously. "Why—why, I haven't seen him for ages," he said in a low voice. "I suppose you know that we were partners once—we had a successful legal practice. Then something happened and we broke up. I—I haven't seen him since."

"And that was how long ago?"

"A little over two years."

"Very good." Queen leaned forward. "I'm anxious to know, too, just why the two of you broke up your partnership."

The lawyer looked down at the rug, fingering his cigar. "I—well, I guess you know Field's reputation as well as I. We didn't agree on ethics, had a little argument and decided to dissolve."

"You parted amicably?"

"Well—under the circumstances, yes."

Queen drummed on the desk. Morgan shifted uneasily. He was evidently still laboring under the effects of his astonishment.

"What time did you get to the theatre tonight, Morgan?" asked the Inspector.

Morgan seemed surprised at the question. "Why—about a quarter after eight," he replied.

"Let me see your ticket stub, please," said Queen.

The lawyer handed it over after fumbling for it in several pockets.

Queen took it, extracted from his own pocket the three stubs he had secreted there, and lowered his hands below the level of the desk. He
looked up in a moment, his eyes expressionless as he returned the four
bits of pasteboard to his own pocket.

"So you were sitting in M2 Center, were you? Pretty good seat, Morgan," he remarked. "Just what made you come to see 'Gunplay' tonight,
anyway?"

"Why, it *is* a rum sort of show, isn't it, Inspector?" Morgan appeared
embarrassed. "I don't know that I would ever have thought of coming—
I'm not a theatre-going man, you know—except that the Roman management was kind enough to send me a complimentary ticket for this
evening's performance."

"Is that a fact?" exclaimed Queen ingenuously. "Quite nice of them,
I'd say. When did you receive the ticket?"

"Why, I got the ticket and the letter Saturday morning, Inspector, at
my office."

"Oh, you got a letter too, eh? You don't happen to have it around you,
do you?"

"I'm—pretty—sure I—have," grunted Morgan as he began to search
his pockets. "Yes! Here it is."

He offered the Inspector a small, rectangular sheet of paper, deckle-
edged and of crushed bond stock. Queen handled it gingerly as he held it
up to the light. Through the few typewritten lines on it a watermark was
distinctly visible. His lips puckered, and he laid the sheet cautiously on
the desk blotter. As Morgan watched, he opened the top drawer of
Panzer's desk and rummaged about until he found a piece of notepaper. It
was large, square, and heavily glazed with an ornate theatre insignia engraved on an upper quarter. Queen put the two pieces of paper side by
side, thought a moment, then sighed and picked up the sheet which Morgan had handed him. He read it through slowly.

The Management of the Roman Theatre cordially invites the
attendance of Mr. Benjamin Morgan at the Monday evening, September twenty-fourth performance of GUNPLAY. As a leading figure
of the New York bar, Mr. Morgan's opinion of the play as a social
and legal document is earnestly solicited. This, however, is by no
means obligatory; and the Management wishes further to assure
Mr. Morgan that the acceptance of its invitation entails no obliga-
tion whatsoever.

(Signed) THE ROMAN THEATRE
Per: S.

The "S" was a barely decipherable ink scrawl.

Queen looked up, smiling. "Mighty nice of the Theatre, Mr. Morgan. I just wonder now—" Still smiling, he signalled to Johnson, who had been sitting in a corner chair, silent spectator to the interview.

"Get Mr. Panzer, the manager, for me, Johnson," said Queen. "And if the publicity man—chap by the name of Bealson, or Pealson, or something—is around, have him step in here, too."

He turned to the lawyer after Johnson left.

"Let me trouble you for your gloves a moment, Mr. Morgan," he said lightly.

With a puzzled stare, Morgan dropped them on the desk in front of Queen, who picked them up curiously. They were of white silk—the conventional gloves for eveningwear. The Inspector pretended to be very busy examining them. He turned them inside out, minutely scrutinized a speck on the tip of one finger, and even went so far as to try them on his own hands, with a jesting remark to Morgan. His examination concluded, he gravely handed the gloves back to the lawyer.

"And—oh, yes, Mr. Morgan—that's a mighty spruce-looking tophat you've got there. May I see it a moment?"

Still silently, the lawyer placed his hat on the desk. Queen picked it up with a carefree air, whistling in a slightly flat key, "The Sidewalks of New York." He turned the hat over in his hand. It was a glistening affair of extremely fine quality. The lining was of shimmering white silk, with the name of the maker, "James Chauncey Co.," stamped in gold. Two initials, "B.M.," were similarly inlaid on the band.

Queen grinned as he placed the hat on his own head. It was a close fit. He doffed it almost immediately and returned it to Morgan.

"Very kind of you to allow me these liberties, Mr. Morgan," he said as he hastily scribbled a note on a pad which he took from his pocket.

The door opened to admit Johnson, Panzer and Harry Neilson. Panzer stepped forward hesitantly and Neilson dropped into an armchair.

"What can we do for you, Inspector?" quavered Panzer, making a valiant attempt to disregard the presence of the grizzled aristocrat slumped in his chair.

"Mr. Panzer," said Queen slowly, "how many kinds of stationery are used in the Roman Theatre?"

The manager's eyes opened wide. "Just one, Inspector. There's a sheet of it on the desk in front of you."

"Ummmm." Queen handed Panzer the slip of paper which he had received from Morgan. "I want you to examine that sheet very carefully, Mr. Panzer. To your knowledge, are there any samples of it in the Roman?"

The manager looked it over with an unfamiliar stare. "No, I don't think so. In fact, I'm sure of it. What's this?" he exclaimed as his eye caught the first few typewritten lines. "Neilson!" he cried, whirling on the publicity man. "What's this—your latest publicity stunt?" He waved the sheet in Neilson's face.

Neilson snatched it from his employer's hand and read it quickly. "Well, I'll be switched!" he said softly. "If that doesn't beat the nonstop exploitation record!" He reread it, an admiring look on his face. Then, with four pairs of eyes trained accusingly on him, he handed it back to Panzer. "I'm sorry I have to deny any share in this brilliant idea," he drawled. "Why the deuce didn't *I* think of it?" And he retreated to his corner, arms folded on his chest.

The manager turned to Queen in bewilderment. "This is very peculiar, Inspector. To my knowledge the Roman Theatre has never used this stationery, and I can state positively that I never authorized any such publicity stunt. And if Neilson denies a part in it—" He shrugged his shoulders.

Queen placed the paper carefully in his pocket. "That will be all, gentlemen. Thank you." He dismissed the two men with a nod.

He looked appraisingly at the lawyer, whose face was suffused with a fiery color that reached from his neck to the roots of his hair. The Inspector raised his hand and let it drop with a little bang on the desk.

"What do you think of *that*, Mr. Morgan?" he asked simply.

Morgan leaped to his feet. "It's a damned frame-up!" he shouted, shaking his fist in Queen's face. "I don't know any more about it than— than *you* do, if you'll pardon a little impertinence! What's more, if you think you can scare me by this hocus-pocus searching of gloves and hats and—and, by God, you haven't examined my underwear yet, Inspector!" He stopped for lack of breath, his face purple.

"But, my dear Morgan," said the Inspector mildly, "why do you upset yourself so? One would think I've been accusing you of Monte Field's murder. Sit down and cool off, man; I asked you a simple question."

Morgan collapsed in his chair. He passed a quivering hand over his forehead and muttered, "Sorry, Inspector. Lost my temper. But of all the rotten deals—" He subsided, mumbling to himself.

Queen sat staring quizzically at him. Morgan was making a great to-do with his handkerchief and cigar. Johnson coughed deprecatingly, looking up at the ceiling. Again a burst of sound penetrated the walls, only to be throttled in mid-air.

Queen's voice cut sharply into the silence. "That's all, Morgan. You may go."

The lawyer lumbered to his feet, opened his mouth as if to speak, clamped his legs together and, clapping his hat on his head, walked out of the room. Johnson innocently lounged forward to help him with the door, on a signal from the Inspector. Both men disappeared.

Queen, left alone in the room, immediately fell into a fierce preoccupation. He took from his pockets the four stubs, the letter Morgan had given him and the woman's rhinestone evening bag which he had found in the dead man's pocket. This last article he opened for the second time that evening and spread its contents on the desk before him. A few calling cards, with the name "Frances Ives-Pope" neatly engraved; two dainty lace handkerchiefs; a vanity case filled with powder, rouge and lipstick; a small change purse containing twenty dollars in bills and a few coins; and a house-key. Queen fingered these articles thoughtfully for a moment, returned them to the handbag and putting bag, stubs and letter back into his pocket once more, rose and looked slowly about. He crossed the room to the clothestree, picked up the single hat, a derby, hanging there and examined its interior. The initials "L.P." and the head-size "6⅞," seemed to interest him.

He replaced the hat and opened the door.

The four people sitting in the anteroom jumped to their feet with expressions of relief. Queen stood smiling on the threshold, his hands jammed into his pockets.

"Here we are at last," he said. "Won't you all please step into the office?"

He politely stood aside to let them pass—the three women and the young man. They trooped in with a flurry of excitement, the women sitting down as the young man busied himself setting chairs for them. Four pairs of eyes gazed earnestly at the old man by the door. He smiled paternally, took one quick glance into the anteroom, closed the door and marched in a stately way to the desk, where he sat down, feeling for his snuffbox.

"Well!" he said genially. "I must apologize for having kept you people waiting so long—official business, you know. . . . Now, let's see. Hmmm. Yes. . . . Yes, yes. I must— All right! Now, in the first place, ladies and gentleman, how do we stand?" He turned his mild gaze on the most beautiful of the three women. "I believe, miss, that your name is Frances Ives-Pope, although I haven't had the pleasure of being introduced. Am I correct?"

The girl's eyebrows went up. "That's quite correct, sir," she said in a vibrant musical voice. "Although I don't quite understand how you know my name."

She smiled. It was a magnetic smile, full of charm and a certain strong womanliness that was extremely attractive. A full-bodied creature in the bloom of youth, with great brown eyes and a creamy complexion, she radiated a wholesomeness that the Inspector found refreshing.

He beamed down at her. "Well, Miss Ives-Pope," he chuckled, "I suppose it is mysterious to a layman. And the fact that I am a policeman no doubt heightens the general effect. But it's quite simple. You are by no means an unphotographed young lady—I saw your picture in the paper today, as a matter of fact, on the society page."

The girl laughed, a trifle nervously. "So that's how it was!" she said. "I was beginning to be frightened. Just what is it, sir, that you want of me?"

"Business—always business," said the Inspector ruefully. "Just when I'm getting interested in someone I'm brought bang-up against my profession. . . . Before we conduct our inquisition, may I ask who your friends are?"

An embarrassed coughing arose from the three people on whom Queen bent his eyes. Frances said charmingly, "I'm sorry—Inspector, is it? Allow me to introduce Miss Hilda Orange and Miss Eve Ellis, my very dear friends. And this is Mr. Stephen Barry, my fiancé."

Queen glanced at them in some surprise. "If I'm not mistaken—aren't you members of the cast of 'Gunplay'?"

There was a unanimous nodding of heads.

Queen turned to Frances. "I don't want to seem too officious, Miss Ives-Pope, but I want you to explain something. . . . Why are you accompanied by your friends?" he asked with a disarming smile. "I know it sounds impertinent, but I distinctly recall ordering my man to summon you—alone. . . ."

The three thespians rose stiffly. Frances turned from her companions to the Inspector with a pleading look.

"I—please forgive me, Inspector," she said swiftly. "I—I've never been questioned by the police before. I was nervous and—and I asked my fiancé and these two ladies, who are my most intimate friends, to be present during the interview. I didn't realize that I was going against your wishes. . . ."

"I understand," returned Queen, smiling. "I understand completely. But you see—" He made a gesture of finality.

Stephen Barry leaned over the girl's chair. "I'll stay with you, dear, if you give the word." He glared at the Inspector belligerently.

"But, Stephen, dear—" Frances cried helplessly. Queen's face was adamant. "You—you'd better all go. But please wait for me outside. It won't take long, will it, Inspector?" she asked, her eyes unhappy.

Queen shook his head. "Not so very long." His entire attitude had changed. He seemed to be growing truculent. His audience sensed the metamorphosis in him and in an intangible manner grew antagonistic.

Hilda Orange, a large buxom woman of forty, with traces of a hand-some youth in her face, now brutally shorn of its make-up in the cold light of the room, leaned over Frances and glared at the Inspector.

"We'll be waiting outside for you, my dear," she said grimly. "And if you feel faint, or something, just screech a little and you'll see what action means." She flounced out of the room. Eve Ellis patted Frances' hand. "Don't worry, Frances," she said in her soft, clear voice. "We're with you." And taking Barry's arm, she followed Hilda Orange. Barry looked back with a mixture of anger and solicitude, shooting a vitriolic glance at Queen as he slammed the door.

Queen was instantly on his feet, his manner brisk and impersonal. He gazed fully into Frances' eyes, his palms pressed against the top surface of the desk. "Now, Miss Frances Ives-Pope," he said curtly, "this is all the business I have to transact with you. . . ." He dipped into his pocket and produced with something of the stage-magician's celerity the rhine-stone bag. "I want to return your bag."

Frances half-rose to her feet, staring from him to the shimmering purse, the color drained from her face. "Why, that's—that's my evening bag!" she stammered.

"Precisely, Miss Ives-Pope," said Queen. "It was found in the the-atre—tonight."

"Of course!" The girl dropped back into her seat with a little nervous laugh. "How stupid of me! And I didn't miss it until now. . . ."

"But, Miss Ives-Pope," the little Inspector continued deliberately, "the finding of your purse is not nearly so important as the place in which it was found." He paused. "You know that there was a man murdered here this evening?"

She stared at him open-mouthed, a wild fear gathering in her eyes. "Yes, I heard so," she breathed.

"Well, your bag, Miss Ives-Pope," continued Queen inexorably, "was found in the murdered man's pocket!"

Terror gleamed in the girl's eyes. Then, with a choked scream, she toppled forward in the chair, her face white and strained.

Queen sprang forward, concern and sympathy instantly apparent on his face. As he reached the limp form, the door burst open and Stephen Barry, coat tails flying, catapulted into the room. Hilda Orange, Eve Ellis and Johnson, the detective, hurried in behind him.

"What in hell have you done to her, you damned snooper!" the actor cried, shouldering Queen out of the way. He gathered Frances' body ten-derly in his arms, pushing aside the wisps of black hair tumbled over her eyes, crooning desperately in her ear. She sighed and looked up in bewil-

derment as she saw the flushed young face close to hers. "Steve, I—
fainted," she murmured, and dropped back in his arms.

"Get some water, somebody," the young man growled, chafing her
hands. A tumbler was promptly pushed over his shoulder by Johnson.
Barry forced a few drops down Frances' throat and she choked, coming
back to consciousness. The two actresses pushed Barry aside and
brusquely ordered the men to leave. Queen meekly followed the protesting actor and the detective.

"You're a fine cop, you are!" said Barry scathingly, to the Inspector.
"What did you do to her—hit her over the head with the policeman's
usual finesse?"

"Now, now, young man," said Queen mildly, "no harsh words, please.
The young lady simply received a shock."

They stood in a strained silence until the door opened and the actresses appeared supporting Frances between them. Barry flew to her
side. "Are you all right now, dear?" he whispered, pressing her hand.

"Please—Steve—take me—home," she gasped, leaning heavily on
his arm.

Inspector Queen stood aside to let them pass. There was a mournful
look in his eyes as he watched them walk slowly to the main door and
join the short line going out.

# 6

## In Which the District Attorney
## Turns Biographer

Inspector Richard Queen was a peculiar man. Small and wiry, thatched with gray and wrinkled in fine lines of experience, he might have been a business executive, a night watchman, or what he chose. Certainly, in the proper raiment, his quiet figure would mold itself to any disguise.

This ready adaptability was carried out in his manner as well. Few people knew him as he was. To his associates, to his enemies, to the forlorn scraps of humanity whom he turned over to the due processes of the law, he remained ever a source of wonder. He could be theatrical when he chose, or mild, or pompous, or fatherly, or bulldogging.

But underneath, as someone had said with an overemphatic sentimentality, the Inspector had "a heart of gold." Inside he was harmless, and keen, and not a little hurt by the cruelties of the world. It was true that to the people who officially came under his eye he was never twice the same. He was constantly whirling into some new facet of personality. He found this to be good business; people never understood him, never knew what he was going to do or say, and consequently they were always a little afraid of him.

Now that he was alone, back in Panzer's office, the door shut tight, his investigations temporarily halted, the true character of the man shone from his face. At this moment it was an old face—old physically, old and wise spiritually. The incident of the girl he had startled into unconsciousness was uppermost in his mind. The memory of her drawn, horrified face made him wince. Frances Ives-Pope seemed to personify everything a man of years could hope for in his own daughter. To see her shrink under the lash pained him. To see her fiancé turn fiercely in her defense made him blush.

Abstemious except for his one mild dissipation, the Inspector reached for his snuffbox with a sigh and sniffed freely. . . .

When there came a peremptory knock on the door, he was the chameleon again—a detective-inspector sitting at a desk and no doubt thinking clever and ponderous thoughts. In truth, he was wishing that Ellery would come back.

At his hearty "Come in!" the door swung open to admit a thin, bright-eyed man dressed in heavy overclothes, a woolen muffler wound about his neck.

"Henry!" exclaimed the Inspector, starting to his feet. "What the dickens are you doing here? I thought the doctor had ordered you to stay in bed!"

District Attorney Henry Sampson winked as he slumped into an arm-chair.

"Doctors," he said didactically, "doctors give me a pain in the neck. How are tricks?"

He groaned and felt his throat gingerly. The Inspector sat down again.

"For a grown man, Henry," he said decisively, "you're the most unruly patient I've ever seen. Man alive, you'll catch pneumonia if you don't watch out!"

"Well," grinned the District Attorney, "I carry a lot of insurance, so I should worry. . . . You haven't answered my question."

"Oh, yes," grunted Queen. "Your question. How's tricks, I think you asked? Tricks, my dear Henry, are at present in a state of complete nullity. Does that satisfy you?"

"Kindly be more explicit," said Sampson. "Remember, I'm a sick man and my head is buzzing."

"Henry," said Queen, leaning forward earnestly, "I warn you that we're in the midst of one of the toughest cases this department has ever handled. . . . Is *your* head buzzing? I'd hate to tell you what's happening in mine!"

Sampson regarded him with a frown. "If it's as you say—and I suppose it is—this comes at a rotten time. Election's not so far off—an unsolved murder handled by the improper parties. . . ."

"Well, that's one way of looking at it," remarked Queen, in a low voice. "I wasn't exactly thinking of this affair in terms of votes, Henry. A man's been killed—and at the moment I'll be frank enough to admit that I haven't the slightest idea who did the job or how."

"I accept your well-meant rebuke, Inspector," said Sampson, in a lighter tone. "But if you'd heard what I did a few moments ago—over the telephone . . ."

"One moment, my dear Watson, as Ellery would say," chuckled Queen, with that startling change of temperament so characteristic of him. "I'll bet I know what happened. You were at home, probably in bed.

Your telephone rang. A voice began to crab, protest, gurgle, and do all the other things a voice does when its owner is excited. The voice said, 'I won't stand for being cooped up by the police, like a common criminal! I want that man Queen severely reprimanded! He's a menace to personal liberty!' And so on, in words of that general tenor. . . ."

"My dear fellow!" said Sampson, laughing.

"This gentleman, the owner of the protesting voice," continued the Inspector, "is short, rather stout, wears gold-rimmed eyeglasses, has an exceedingly disagreeable feminine voice, displays a really touching concern for his 'very good friend, District Attorney Sampson.' Correct?"

Sampson sat staring at him. Then his keen face creased into a smile.

"Perfectly astounding, my dear Holmes!" he murmured. "Since you know so much about my friend, perhaps it would be child's play for you to give me his name?"

"Er—but that was the fellow, wasn't it?" said Queen, his face scarlet. "I—Ellery, my boy! I'm glad to see you!"

Ellery had entered the room. He shook hands cordially with Sampson, who greeted him with a pleasure born of long association, and made a remark about the dangers of a District Attorney's life, briskly setting down on the desk a huge container of coffee and a paper bag pleasantly suggestive of French pastry.

"Well, gentlemen, the great search is finished, over, *kaput*, and the perspiring detectives will now partake of midnight tiffin." He laughed and slapped his father affectionately on the shoulder.

"But, Ellery!" cried Queen delightedly. "This is a welcome surprise! Henry, will you join us in a little celebration?" He filled three paper cups with the steaming coffee.

"I don't know what you're celebrating, but count me in," said Sampson and the three men fell to with enthusiasm.

"What's happened, Ellery?" asked the old man, sipping his coffee contentedly.

"Gods do not eat, neither do they drink," murmured Ellery from behind a cream puff. "I am not omnipotent, and suppose you tell me what happened in your impromptu torture chamber. . . . I can tell you one thing you don't know, however. Mr. Libby, of Libby's ice-cream parlor, whence came these elegant cakes, confirms Jess Lynch's story about the ginger ale. And Miss Elinor Libby nicely corroborated the alley story."

Queen wiped his lips daintily with a huge handkerchief. "Well, let Prouty make sure about the ginger ale, anyway. As for me, I interviewed several people and now I have nothing to do."

"Thank you," remarked Ellery dryly. "That was a perfect recitation.

Have you acquainted the D. A. with the events of this tumultuous evening?"

"Gentlemen," said Sampson, setting down his cup, "here's what I know. About a half-hour ago I was telephoned by 'one of my very good friends'—who happens to wield a little power behind the scenes—and he told me in no uncertain terms that during tonight's performance a man was murdered. Inspector Richard Queen, he said, had descended upon the theatorium like a whirlwind, accompanied by his minor whirlwinds, and had proceeded to make everybody wait over an hour—an inexcusable, totally unwarranted procedure, my friend charged. He further deposed that said Inspector even went so far as to accuse him personally of the crime, and had domineering policemen search him and his wife and daughter before they were allowed to leave the theatre.

"So much for my informant's story—the rest of his conversation, being rather profane, is irrelevant. The only other thing I know is that Velie told me outside who the murdered man was. And *that*, gentlemen, was the most interesting part of the whole story."

"You know almost as much about this case as I do," grunted Queen. "Probably more, because I have an idea you are thoroughly familiar with Field's operation. . . . Ellery, what happened outside during the search?"

Ellery crossed his legs comfortably. "As you might have guessed, the search of the audience was entirely without result. Nothing out of the way was found. Not one solitary thing. Nobody looked guilty, and nobody took it upon himself to confess. In other words, it was a complete fiasco."

"Of course, of course," said Queen. "There's somebody almighty clever behind this business. I suppose you didn't even come across the suspicion of an extra hat?"

"That, Dad," remarked Ellery, "was what I was decorating the lobby for. No—no hat."

"Are they all through out there?"

"Just finished when I strolled across the street for the refreshments," said Ellery. "There was nothing else to do but allow the angry mob in the gallery to file downstairs and out into the street. Everybody's out now—the galleryites, the employees, the cast. . . . Queer species, actors. All night they play God and then suddenly they find themselves reduced to ordinary street clothes and the ills that flesh is heir to. By the way, Velie also searched the five people who came out of this office. Quite a motor that young lady possesses. Miss Ives-Pope and her party, I gathered. . . . Didn't know but that you might have forgotten them," he chuckled.

"So we're up a tree, eh?" muttered the Inspector. "Here's the story,

Henry." And he gave a concise résumé of the evening's events to Sampson, who sat silently throughout, frowning.

"And that," concluded Queen, after describing briefly the scenes enacted in the little office, "is that. Now, Henry, you must have something to tell us about Monte Field. We know that he was a slick article—but that's all we do know."

"That would be putting it mildly," said Sampson savagely. "I can give you almost by rote the story of his life. It looks to me as if you're going to have a difficult time and some incident in his past might give you a clue.

"Field first came under the scrutiny of my office during my predecessor's regime. He was suspected of negotiating a swindle connected with the bucket-shop scandals. Cronin, an assistant D. A. at the time, couldn't get a thing on him. Field had covered his operations well. All we had was the telltale story, which might or might not have been true, of a 'stool pigeon' who had been kicked out of the mob. Of course, Cronin never let on to Field directly or indirectly that he was under suspicion. The affair blew over and although Cronin was a bulldog, every time he thought he had something he found that he had nothing after all. Oh, no question about it—Field was slick.

"When I came into office, on Cronin's fervent suggestion we began an exhaustive investigation of Field's background. On the q. t., of course. And this is what we discovered: Monte Field came of a blue-blood New England family—the kind that doesn't brag about its Mayflower descendants. He had private tutoring as a kid, went to a swanky prep school, got through by the skin of his teeth and then was sent to Harvard by his father as a sort of last despairing gesture. He seems to have been a pretty bad egg even as a boy. Nothing criminal, but just wild. On the other hand, he must have had a grain of pride because when the blow-up came he actually shortened his name. The family name was Fielding—and he became Monte Field."

Queen and Ellery nodded, Ellery's eyes introspective, Queen staring steadily at Sampson.

"Field," resumed Sampson, "wasn't a total loss, understand. He had brains. He studied law brilliantly at Harvard. He seemed to have a flair for oratory that was considerably aided by his profound knowledge of legal technology. But just after graduation, before his family could get even the bit of pleasure out of his scholastic career that should have been theirs, he was mixed up in a dirty deal with a girl. His father cut him off in jigtime. He was through—out—he'd disgraced the family name—you know the sort of thing. . . .

"Well, this friend of ours didn't let grief overwhelm him, evidently.

He made the best of being done out of a nice little legacy, and decided to go out and make some money on his own. How he managed to get along during this period we couldn't find out, but the next thing we hear of him is that he has formed a partnership with a fellow by the name of Cohen. One of the smoothest shysters in the business. What a partnership that was! They cleaned up a fortune between them establishing a select clientele chosen from among the biggest crooks in crookdom. Now, you know as well as I just how hard it is to 'get' anything on a bird who knows more about the loopholes of the law than the Supreme Court judges. They got away with everything—it was a golden era for crime. Crooks considered themselves top-notch when Cohen & Field were kind enough to defend them.

"And then Mr. Cohen, who was the experienced man of the combination, knowing the ropes, making the 'contacts' with the firm's clients, fixing the fees—and he could do that beautifully in spite of his inability to speak untainted English—Mr. Cohen, I say, met a very sad end one winter night on the North River waterfront. He was found shot through the head, and although it's twelve years since the happy event, the murderer is still unknown. That is—unknown in the legal sense. We had grave suspicions as to his identity. I shouldn't be at all surprised if Mr. Field's demise this evening removed the Cohen case from the register."

"So that's the kind of playboy he was," murmured Ellery. "Even in death his face is most disagreeable. Too bad I had to lose my first edition on his account."

"Forget it, you bookworm," growled his father. "Go on, Henry."

"Now," said Sampson, taking the last piece of cake from the desk and munching it heartily, "now we come to a bright spot in Mr. Field's life. For after the unfortunate decease of his partner, he seemed to turn over a new leaf. He actually went to work—real legal work—and of course he had the brains to pull it through. For a number of years he worked alone, gradually effacing the bad reputation he had built up in the profession and even gaining a little respect now and then from some of our hoity-toity legal lights.

"This period of apparent good behavior lasted for six years. Then he met Ben Morgan—a solid man with a spotless record and a good reputation, although perhaps lacking the vital spark which makes the great lawyer. Somehow Field persuaded Morgan to join him in partnership. Then things began to hum.

"You'll remember that in that period some highly shady things were happening in New York. We got faint inklings of a gigantic criminal ring, composed of 'fences,' crooks, lawyers, and in some cases politicians. Some smashing big robberies were pulled off; bootlegging got to be a distinct art in the city environs; and a number of daring hold-ups resulting in murder put the department on its toes. But you know that as well as I do. You fellows 'got' some of them; but you never broke the ring, and you never reached the men higher up. And I have every reason to believe that our late friend Mr. Monte Field was the brains behind the whole business.

"See how easy it was for a man of his talents. Under the tutelage of Cohen, his first partner, he had become thoroughly familiar with the underworld moguls. When Cohen outlived his usefulness, he was conveniently bumped off. Then Field—remember, I am working now on speculation chiefly, because the evidence is practically nil—then Field, under the cloak of a respectable legal business, absolutely aboveboard, quietly built up a far-flung criminal organization. How he accomplished this we have no way of knowing, of course. When he was quite ready to shoot the works, he tied up with a well-known respectable partner, Morgan, and now secure in his legal position, began to engineer most of the big crooked deals pulled off in the last five years or so. . . ."

"Where does Morgan come in?" asked Ellery idly.

"I was coming to that. Morgan, we have every reason to believe, was absolutely innocent of any connection with Field's undercover operations. He was as straight as a die and in fact had often refused cases in which the defendant was a shady character. Their relations must have become strained when Morgan got a hint of what was going on. Whether this is so or not I don't know—you could easily find out from Morgan himself. Anyway, they broke up. Since the dissolution, Field has operated a little more in the open, but still not a shred of tangible evidence which would count in a court of law."

"Pardon me for interrupting, Henry," said Queen reflectively, "but can't you give me a little more information on their break-up? I'd like to use it as a check on Morgan when I talk to him again."

"Oh, yes!" replied Sampson grimly. "I'm glad you reminded me. Before the last word was written in the dissolving of the partnership, the two men had a terrific blow-up which almost resulted in tragedy. At the Webster Club, where they were lunching, they were heard quarreling violently. The argument increased until it was necessary for the bystanders to interfere. Morgan was beside himself with rage and actually threatened Field's life right then and there. Field, I understand, was quite calm."

"Did any of the witnesses get an inkling of the cause of the quarrel?" asked Queen.

"Unfortunately, no. The thing blew over soon enough; they dissolved quietly and that was the last anybody ever heard of it. Until, of course, tonight."

There was a pregnant silence when the District Attorney stopped talking. Ellery whistled a few bars of a Schubert air, while Queen frankly took a pinch of snuff with a ferocious vigor.

"I'd say, offhand," murmured Ellery, looking off into space, "that Mr. Morgan is in deucedly hot water."

His father grunted. Sampson said seriously, "Well, that's your affair, gentlemen. I know what my job is. Now that Field is out of the way, I'm going to have his files and records gone over with a fine comb. If nothing else, his murder will accomplish eventually, I hope, the complete annihilation of his gang. I'll have a man at his office in the morning."

"One of my men is camping there already," remarked Queen absently. "So you think it's Morgan, do you?" he asked Ellery, with a flash of his eyes.

"I seem to recall making a remark a minute ago," said Ellery calmly, "to the effect that Mr. Morgan is in hot water. I did not commit myself further. I admit that Morgan seems to be the logical man—except, gentlemen, for one thing," he added.

"The hat," said Inspector Queen instantly.

*"No,"* said Ellery, *"the other hat."*

# 7

## The Queens Take Stock

"Let's see where we stand," continued Ellery without pausing. "Let's consider this thing in its most elementary light.

"These, roughly, are the facts: A man of shady character, Monte Field, probable head of a vast criminal organization, with undoubtedly a host of enemies, is found murdered in the Roman Theatre ten minutes before the end of the second act, at precisely 9:55 o'clock. He is discovered by a man named William Pusak, a clerk of an inferior type of intelligence, who is sitting five seats away in the same row. This man, attempting to leave, pushes his way past the victim who before he dies mutters, 'Murder! Been murdered!' or words to that effect.

"A policeman is called and to make sure the man is dead, secures the services of a doctor in the audience, who definitely pronounces the victim killed by some form of alcoholic poisoning. Subsequently Dr. Prouty, the Assistant Medical Examiner, confirms this statement, adding that there is only one disturbing factor—that a man would not die so soon from lethal alcohol. The question of the cause of death, therefore, we must leave for the moment, since only an autopsy can definitely determine it.

"With a large audience to attend to, the policeman calls for help, officers of the vicinity come in to take charge and subsequently the headquarters men arrive to conduct the immediate investigation. The first important issue that arises is the question of whether the murderer had the opportunity to leave the scene of the crime between the time it was committed and the time it was discovered. Doyle, the policeman who was first on the scene, immediately ordered the manager to station guards at all exits and both alleys.

"When I arrived, I thought of this point the very first thing and conducted a little investigation of my own. I went around to all the exits and questioned the guards. I discovered that there was a guard at every door of the auditorium during the entire second act, with two exceptions which I shall mention shortly. Now, it had been determined from the testimony of the orangeade boy, Jess Lynch, that the victim was alive not only during the intermission between Act I and Act II—when he saw and talked to Field in the alleyway—but that Field was also in apparently good health ten minutes after the raising of the curtain for Act II. This was when the boy delivered a bottle of ginger ale to Field at the seat in which he was later found dead. Inside the theatre, an usher stationed at the foot of the stairs leading to the balcony swore that no one had either gone up or come down during the second act. This eliminates the possibility that the murderer had access to the balcony.

"The two exceptions I noted a moment ago are the two doors on the extreme left aisle, which should have been guarded but were not because the usherette, Madge O'Connell, was sitting in the audience next to her lover. This presented to my mind the possibility that the murderer might have left by one of these two doors, which were conveniently placed for an escape should the murderer have been so inclined. However, even this possibility was eliminated by the statement of the O'Connell girl, whom I hunted up after she was questioned by Dad."

"You talked to her on the sly, did you, you scalawag?" roared Queen, glaring at Ellery.

"I certainly did," chuckled Ellery, "and I discovered the one important fact that seems pertinent to this phase of the investigation. O'Connell swore that before she left the doors to sit down next to Parson Johnny she stepped on the inside floorlock that latches them top and bottom. When the commotion began the girl sprang from the Parson's side and finding the doors locked as she had left them, unlatched them while Doyle was attempting to quiet the audience. Unless she was lying—and I don't think she was—this proves that the murderer did not leave by these doors, since at the time the body was found they were still locked from the inside."

"Well, I'll be switched!" growled Queen. "She didn't tell me a thing about that part of it, drat her! Wait till I get my hands on her, the little snip!"

"Please be logical, *M. le Gardien de la Paix*," laughed Ellery. "The reason she didn't tell you about bolting the doors was that you didn't ask her. She felt that she was in enough of an uncomfortable position already.

"At any rate, that statement of hers would seem to dispose of the two side doors near the murdered man's seat. I will admit that all sorts of possibilities enter into the problem—for example, Madge O'Connell might have been an accomplice. I mention this only as a possibility, and not even as a theory. At any rate, it seems to me that the murderer would not have run the risk of being seen leaving from side doors. Besides, a departure in so unusual a manner and at so unusual a time would have been all the more noticeable especially since few people leave during a second act. And again—the murderer could have no foreknowledge of the O'Connell girl's dereliction in duty—if she were not an accomplice. As the crime was carefully planned—and we must admit that from all indications it was—the murderer would have discarded the side doors as a means of escape.

"This probe left, I felt, only one other channel of investigation. That was the main entrance. And here again we received definite testimony from the ticket-taker and the doorman outside to the effect that no one *left* the building during the second act by that route. Except, of course, the harmless orangeade boy.

"All the exits having been guarded or locked, and the alley having been under constant surveillance from 9:35 on by Lynch, Elinor, Johnny Chase—the usher—and after him the police—these being the facts, all my questioning and checking, gentlemen," continued Ellery in a grave tone, "lead to the inevitable conclusion that, from the time the murder was discovered and all the time thereafter while the investigation was going on, *the murderer was in the theatre!*"

A silence followed Ellery's pronouncement. "Incidentally," he added calmly, "it occurred to me when I talked to the ushers to ask if they had seen anyone leave his seat after the second act started, and they can't recall anyone changing seats!"

Queen idly took another pinch of snuff. "Nice work—and a very pretty piece of reasoning, my son—but nothing, after all, of a startling or conclusive nature. Granted that the murderer was in the theatre all that time—how could we possibly have laid our hands on him?"

"He didn't say you could," put in Sampson, smiling. "Don't be so sensitive, old boy; nobody's going to report you for negligence in the performance of your duty. From all I've heard tonight you handled the affair well."

Queen grunted. "I'll admit I'm a little peeved at myself for not following up that matter of the doors more thoroughly. But even if it were possible for the murderer to have left directly after the crime, I nevertheless would have had to pursue the inquiry as I did, on the chance that he was still in the theatre."

"But Dad—of course!" said Ellery seriously. "You had so many things to attend to, while all I had to do was stand around and look Socratic."

"How about the people who have come under the eye of the investigation so far?" asked Sampson curiously.

"Well, what about them?" challenged Ellery. "We certainly can draw
no definite conclusions from either their conversation or their actions.
We have Parson Johnny, a thug, who was there apparently for no other
reason than to enjoy a play giving some interesting sidelights on his own
profession. Then there is Madge O'Connell, a very doubtful character
about whom we can make no decision at this stage of the game. She
might be an accomplice—she might be innocent—she might be merely
negligent—she might be almost anything. Then there is William Pusak,
who found Field. Did you notice the moronic cast of his head? And Benjamin Morgan—here we strike fallow ground in the realm of probability.
But what do we know of his actions tonight? True, his story of the letter
and the complimentary ticket sounds queer, since anyone could have
written the letter, even Morgan himself. And we must always remember
the public threat against Field; and also the enmity, reason unknown,
which has existed between them for two years. And, lastly, we have Miss
Frances Ives-Pope. I'm exceedingly sorry I was absent during that interview. The fact remains—and isn't it an interesting one?—that her
evening bag was found in the dead man's pocket. Explain that if you can.

"So you see where we are," Ellery continued ruefully. "All we have
managed to derive from this evening's entertainment is a plethora of suspicions and a poverty of facts."

"So far, son," said Queen casually, "you have kept on mighty safe
ground. But you've forgotten the important matter of the suspiciously vacant seats. Also the rather startling fact that Field's ticket stub and the
only other stub that could be attributed to the murderer—I refer to the
LL30 Left stub found by Flint—that these two stubs do not coincide.
That is to say, that the torn edges indicate they were gathered by the
ticket-taker at different times!"

"Check," said Ellery. "But let's leave that for the moment and get on
to the problem of Field's tophat."

"The hat—well, what do you think of it?" asked Queen curiously.

"Just this. In the first place, we have fairly established the fact that the
hat is not missing through accident. The murdered man was seen by Jess
Lynch with the hat in his lap ten minutes after Act II began. Now—for
the moment, let's forget the problem of where the hat is now. The immediate conclusion to draw is that the hat was taken away for one of two
reasons: first, that it was in some way incriminating in itself, so that if it
were left behind it would point to the murderer's identity. What the nature of this incriminating indication is we cannot even guess at the moment. Second, the hat may have contained something which the murderer
wanted. You will say: Why couldn't he take this mysterious object and
leave the hat? Probably, if this supposition is true, because he either had

not sufficient time to extract it, or else did not know *how* to extract it and therefore took the hat away with him to examine it at his leisure. Do you agree with me so far?"

The District Attorney nodded slowly. Queen sat still, his eyes vaguely troubled.

"Let us for a moment consider what the hat could possibly have contained," resumed Ellery, as he vigorously polished his glasses. "Due to its size, shape and cubic content our field of speculation is not a broad one. What could be hidden in a tophat? The only things that present themselves to my mind are: papers of some sort, jewelry, banknotes, or any other small object of value which could not easily be detected in such a place. Obviously, this problematical object would not be carried merely in the crown of the hat since it would fall out whenever the wearer uncovered his head. We are led to believe therefore that, whatever the object was, it was concealed in the lining of the hat. This immediately narrows our list of possibilities. Solid objects of bulk must be eliminated. A jewel might have been concealed; banknotes or papers might have been concealed. We can, I think, discard the jewel, from what we know of Monte Field. If he was carrying anything of value, it would probably be connected in some way with his profession.

"One point remains to be considered in this preliminary analysis of the missing tophat. And, gentlemen, it may very well become a pivotal consideration before we are through. It is of paramount importance for us to know whether the murderer knew in advance of his crime that it would be necessary for him to take away Monte Field's tophat. In other words, did the murderer have *foreknowledge* of the hat's significance, whatever it may prove to be? I maintain that the facts prove deductively, as logically as facts *can* prove deductively, that the murderer had no foreknowledge.

"Follow me closely. . . . Since Monte Field's tophat is missing, and since no other tophat has been found in its place, it is an undeniable indication that it was essential that it be taken away. You must agree that, as I pointed out before, the murderer is most plausibly the remover of the hat. Now! Regardless of *why* it had to be taken away, we are faced with two alternatives: one, that the murderer knew in advance that it had to be taken away; or two, that he did *not* know in advance. Let us exhaust the possibilities in the former case. If he knew in advance, it may be surely and logically assumed that he would have brought with him to the theatre a hat to replace Field's, rather than leave an obvious clue by the provocative absence of the murdered man's hat. To bring a replacement hat would have been the safe thing to do. The murderer would have had no difficulty in securing a replacement hat, since knowing its importance in advance, he could certainly have armed himself with a further knowledge of Field's head-size, style of tophat, and other minor details. *But there is no replacement hat.* We have every right to expect a replacement hat in a crime so carefully concocted as this one. There being none, our only conclusion can be that the murderer did not know beforehand the importance of Field's hat; otherwise he would assuredly have taken the intelligent precaution of leaving another hat behind. In this way the police would never know that Field's hat had any significance at all.

"Another point in corroboration. Even if the murderer didn't desire, for some dark reason of his own, to leave a replacement hat, he certainly would have arranged to secure what was in the hat by cutting it out. All he had to do was to provide himself in advance with a sharp instrument—a pocket knife, for example. The *empty* hat, though cut, would not have presented the problem of disposal that the *missing* hat would. Surely the murderer would have preferred this procedure, had he foreknowledge of the hat's contents. But he did not do even this. This, it seems to me, is strong corroborative evidence that he did not know before he came to the Roman Theatre that he would have to take away a hat or its contents. *Quod erat demonstrandum.*"

The District Attorney gazed at Ellery with puckered lips. Inspector Queen seemed sunk in a lethargy. His hand hovered midway between his snuffbox and his nose.

"Just what's the point, Ellery?" inquired Sampson. "Why is it important for you to know that the murderer had no foreknowledge of the hat's significance?"

Ellery smiled. "Merely this. The crime was committed after the beginning of the second act. I want to be sure in my own mind that the murderer, by not knowing in advance of the hat's significance, could not have used the first intermission in any manner whatsoever as an essential element of his plan. . . . Of course, Field's hat may turn up somewhere on the premises, and its discovery would invalidate all these speculations. But—I don't think it will. . . ."

"That analysis of yours might be elementary, boy, but it sounds quite logical to me," said Sampson approvingly. "You should have been a lawyer."

"You can't beat the Queen brains," chuckled the old man suddenly, his face wreathed in a wide smile. "But I'm going to get busy on another tack that ought to jibe somewhere with this puzzle of the hat. You noticed, Ellery, the name of the clothier sewed into Field's coat?"

"No sooner said than done," grinned Ellery. Producing one of the small volumes which he carried in his topcoat pocket, he opened it and pointed to a notation on the flyleaf. "Browne Bros., gentlemen—no less."

"That's right; and I'll have Velie down there in the morning to check up," said the Inspector. "You must have realized that Field's clothing is of exceptional quality. That evening-suit cost three hundred dollars, if it cost a penny. And Browne Bros. are the artists to charge such fashionable prices. But there's another point in this connection: every stitch of clothing on the dead man's body had the same manufacturer's mark. That's not uncommon with wealthy men; and Browne's made a specialty of outfitting their customers from head to foot. What more probable to assume—"

"Than that Field bought his hats there, too!" exclaimed Sampson, with an air of discovery.

"Exactly, Tacitus," said Queen, grinning. "Velie's job is to check up on this clothing business and if possible secure an exact duplicate of the hat Field wore tonight. I'm mighty anxious to look it over."

Sampson rose with a cough. "I suppose I really ought to get back to bed," he said. "The only reason I came down here was to see that you didn't arrest the Mayor. Boy, that friend of mine was sore! I'll never hear the end of it!"

Queen looked up at him with a quizzical smile. "Before you go, Henry, suppose you tell me just where I stand on this thing. I know that I used a pretty high hand tonight, but you must realize how necessary it was. Are you going to put one of your own men on the case?"

Sampson glared at him. "When did you get the idea I wasn't satisfied with your conduct of the investigation, you old canary bird!" he growled. "I've never checked you up yet, and I'm not going to start now. If you can't bring this thing to a successful conclusion, I certainly don't think any of my men can. My dear Q, go ahead and detain half of New York if you think it's necessary. I'll back you up."

"Thanks, Henry," said Queen. "I just wanted to be sure. Add now, since you're so nice about it, watch my smoke!"

He ambled across the room into the anteroom, stuck his head past the doorway into the theatre, and shouted, "Mr. Panzer, will you come here a moment?"

He came back smiling grimly to himself, the swarthy theatre manager close on his heels.

"Mr. Panzer, meet District Attorney Sampson," said Queen. The two men shook hands. "Now, Mr. Panzer, you've got one more job and you can go home and go to sleep. I want this theatre shut down so tight a mouse couldn't get into it!"

Panzer grew pale. Sampson shrugged his shoulders, as if to indicate that he washed his hands of the entire affair. Ellery nodded sagely in approval.

"But—but Inspector, just when we're playing to capacity!" groaned the little manager. "Is it absolutely necessary?"

"So necessary, my dear man," answered the Inspector coolly, "that I'm going to have two men here patrolling the premises all the time."

Panzer wrung his hands, looking furtively at Sampson. But the District Attorney was standing with his back to them, examining a print on the wall.

"This is terrible, Inspector!" wailed Panzer. "I'll never hear the end of it from Gordon Davis, the producer. . . . But of course—if you say so, it will be done."

"Heck, man, don't look so blue," said Queen, more kindly. "You'll be getting so much publicity out of this that when the show reopens you'll have to enlarge the theatre. I don't expect to have the theatre shut down more than a few days, anyway. I'll give the necessary orders to my men outside. After you've transacted your routine business here tonight, just tip off the men I've left and go home. I'll let you know in a few days when you can reopen."

Panzer waggled his head sadly, shook hands all around and left. Sampson immediately whirled on Queen and said, "By the Lord Harry, Q, that's going some! Why do you want the theatre closed? You've milked it dry, haven't you?"

"Well, Henry," said Queen slowly, "the hat hasn't been found. All those people filed out of the theatre and were searched—and each one had just one hat. Doesn't that indicate that the hat we're looking for is still here somewhere? And if it's still here, I'm not giving anybody a chance to come in and take it away. If there's any taking to be done, I'll do it."

Sampson nodded. Ellery was still wearing a worried frown as the three men walked out of the office into the almost deserted orchestra. Here and there a busy figure was stooping over a seat, examining the floor. A few men could be seen darting in and out of the boxes up front. Sergeant Velie stood by the main door, talking in low tones to Piggott and Hagstrom. Detective Flint, superintending a squad of men, was working far to the front of the orchestra. A small group of cleaning women operated vacuum cleaners tiredly here and there. In one corner, to the rear, a buxom police matron was talking with an elderly woman—the woman Panzer had called Mrs. Phillips.

The three men walked to the main door. While Ellery and Sampson were silently surveying the always depressing scene of an untenanted auditorium, Queen spoke rapidly to Velie, giving orders in an undertone. Finally he turned and said, "Well, gentlemen, that's all for tonight. Let's be going."

On the sidewalk a number of policemen had roped off a large space, behind which a straggling crowd of curiosity-seekers was gaping.

"Even at two o'clock in the morning these nightbirds patrol Broadway," grunted Sampson. With a wave of the hand he entered his automobile after the Queens politely refused his offer of a "lift." A crowd of businesslike reporters pushed through the lines and surrounded the two Queens.

"Here, here! What's this, gentlemen?" asked the old man, frowning.

"How about the lowdown on tonight's job, Inspector?" asked one of them urgently.

"You'll get all the information you want, boys, from Detective-Sergeant Velie—inside." He smiled as they charged in a body through the glass doors.

Ellery and Richard Queen stood silently on the curb, watching the policemen herd back the crowd. Then the old man said with a sudden wave of weariness, "Come on, son, let's walk part of the way home."

# PART TWO

*"... To illustrate: Once young Jean C.—— came to me after a month of diligent investigation on a difficult assignment. He wore a forlorn expression. Without a word he handed me a slip of official paper. I read it in surprise. It was his resignation.*

*" 'Here, Jean!' I cried. 'What is the meaning of this?'*

*" 'I have failed, M. Brillon,' he muttered. 'A month's work gone to the devil. I have been on the wrong track. It is a disgrace.'*

*" 'Jean, my friend,' said I solemnly, 'this for your resignation.' Wherewith I tore it to bits before his astonished eyes. 'Go now,' I admonished him, 'and begin from the beginning. For remember always the maxim: He who would know right must first know wrong!' "*

—*From* Reminiscences of a Prefect
by Auguste Brillon

PART TWO

# 8

## In Which the Queens Meet Mr. Field's Very Best Friend

The Queens' apartment on West 87th Street was a man's domicile from the pipcrack over the hearth to the shining sabers on the wall. They lived on the top floor of a three-family brownstone house, a relic of late Victorian times. You walked up the heavily carpeted stairs through seemingly endless halls of dismal rectitude. When you were quite convinced that only mummified souls could inhabit such a dreary place, you came upon the huge oaken door marked, "The Queens"—a motto lettered neatly and framed. Then Djuna grinned at you from behind a crack and you entered a new world.

More than one individual, exalted in his own little niche, had willingly climbed the uninviting staircases to find sanctuary in this haven. More than one card bearing a famous name had been blithely carried by Djuna through the foyer into the living room.

The foyer was Ellery's inspiration, if the truth were told. It was so small and so narrow that its walls appeared unnaturally towering. With a humorous severity one wall had been completely covered by a tapestry depicting the chase—a most appropriate appurtenance to this medieval chamber. Both Queens detested it heartily, preserving it only because it had been presented to them with regal gratitude by the Duke of—, the impulsive gentleman whose son Richard Queen had saved from a noisome scandal, the details of which have never been made public. Beneath the tapestry stood a heavy mission table, displaying a parchment lamp and a pair of bronze bookends bounding a three-volume set of the Arabian Nights' Entertainment.

Two mission chairs and a small rug completed the foyer.

When you walked through this oppressive place, always gloomy and almost always hideous, you were ready for anything except the perfect cheeriness of the large room beyond. This study in contrast was Ellery's private jest, for if it wcre not for him the old man would long since have thrown the foyer and its furnishings into some dark limbo.

The living room was lined on three sides with a bristling and leathern-reeking series of bookcases, rising tier upon tier to the high ceiling. On the fourth wall was a huge natural fireplace, with a solid oak beam as a mantel and gleaming ironwork spacing the grate. Above the fireplace were the famous crossed sabers, a gift from the old fencing master of Nuremberg with whom Richard had lived in his younger days during his studies in Germany. Lamps winked and gleamed all over the great sprawling room; easychairs, armchairs, low divans, footstools, bright-colored leather cushions were everywhere. In a word, it was the most comfortable room two intellectual gentlemen of luxurious tastes could devise for their living quarters. And where such a place might after a time have become stale through sheer variety, the bustling person of Djuna, man-of-work, general factotum, errand boy, valet and mascot prevented such a dénouement.

Djuna had been picked up by Richard Queen during the period of Ellery's studies at college, when the old man was very much alone. This cheerful young man, nineteen years old, an orphan for as long as he could remember, ecstatically unaware of the necessity for a surname—slim and small, nervous and joyous, bubbling over with spirit and yet as quiet as a mouse when the occasion demanded—this Djuna, then, worshipped old Richard in much the same fashion as the ancient Alaskans bowed down to their totempoles. Between him and Ellery, too, there was a shy kinship which rarely found expression except in the boy's passionate service. He slept in a small room beyond the bedroom used by father and son and, according to Richard's own chuckling expression, "could hear a flea singing to its mate in the middle of the night."

On the morning after the eventful night of Monte Field's murder, Djuna was laying the cloth for breakfast when the telephone rang. The boy, accustomed to early morning calls, lifted the receiver:

"This is Inspector Queen's man Djuna talking. Who is calling, please?"

"Oh, it is, is it?" growled a bass voice over the wire. "Well, you son of a gypsy policeman, wake the Inspector for me and be quick about it!"

"Inspector Queen may not be disturbed, sir, unless his man Djuna knows who's calling." Djuna, who knew Sergeant Velie's voice especially well, grinned and stuck his tongue in his cheek.

A slim hand firmly grasped Djuna's neck and propelled him halfway across the room. The Inspector, fully dressed, his nostrils quivering appreciatively with his morning's first ration of snuff, said into the mouthpiece, "Don't mind Djuna, Thomas. What's up? This is Queen talking."

"Oh, that you, Inspector? I wouldn't have buzzed you so early in the morning except that Ritter just phoned from Monte Field's apartment. Got an interesting report," rumbled Velie.

"Well, well!" chuckled the Inspector. "So our friend Ritter's bagged someone, eh? Who is it, Thomas?"

"You guessed it, sir," came Velie's unmoved voice. "He said he's got a lady down there in an embarrassing state of deshabille and if he stays alone with her much longer his wife will divorce him. Orders, sir?"

Queen laughed heartily. "Sure enough, Thomas. Send a couple of men down there right away to chaperon him. I'll be there myself in two shakes of a lamb's tail—which is to say, as soon as I can drag Ellery out of bed."

He hung up, grinning. "Djuna!" he shouted. The boy's head popped out from behind the kitchenette door immediately. "Hurry up with the eggs and coffee, son!" The Inspector turned toward the bedroom to find Ellery, collarless but unmistakably on the road to dress, confronting him with an air of absorption.

"So you're really up?" grumbled the Inspector, easing himself into an armchair. "I thought I'd have to drag you out of bed, you sluggard!"

"You may rest easy," said Ellery absently. "I most certainly am up, and I am going to stay up. And as soon as Djuna replenishes the inner man I'll be off and out of your way." He lounged into the bedroom, reappearing a moment later brandishing his collar and tie.

"Here! Where d'ye think you're going, young man?" roared Queen, starting up.

"Down to my bookshop, Inspector darling," replied Ellery judicially. "You don't think I'm going to allow that Falconer first edition to get away from me? Really—it may still be there, you know."

"Falconer fiddlesticks," said his father grimly. "You started something and you're going to help finish it. Here—Djuna—where in time is that kid?"

Djuna stepped briskly into the room balancing a tray in one hand and a pitcher of milk in the other. In a twinkling he had the table ready, the coffee bubbling, the toast browned; and father and son hurried through their breakfast without a word.

"Now," remarked Ellery, setting down his empty cup, "now that I've finished this Arcadian repast, tell me where the fire is."

"Get your hat and coat on and stop asking pointless questions, son of my grief," growled Queen. In three minutes they were on the sidewalk hailing a taxicab.

The cab drew up before a monumental apartment building. Lounging on the sidewalk, a cigarette drooping from his lips, was Detective Piggott. The Inspector winked and trotted into the lobby. He and Ellery were whisked up to the fourth floor where Detective Hagstrom greeted them, pointing to an apartment door numbered 4-D. Ellery, leaning forward to catch the inscription on the nameplate, was about to turn on his father with an amused expostulation when the door swung open at Queen's imperious ring and the broad flushed face of Ritter peered out at them.

"Morning, Inspector," the detective mumbled, holding the door open. "I'm glad you've come, sir."

Queen and Ellery marched inside. They stood in a small foyer, profusely furnished. Directly in their line of vision was a living room, and beyond that a closed door. A frilled feminine slipper and a slim ankle were visible at the edge of the door.

The Inspector stepped forward, changed his mind and quickly opening the hall door called to Hagstrom, who was sauntering about outside. The detective ran up.

"Come inside here," said Queen sharply. "Got a job for you."

With Ellery and the two plainclothesmen following at his heels, he strode into the living room.

A woman of mature beauty, a trifle worn, the pastiness of a ruined complexion apparent beneath heavily applied rouge, sprang to her feet. She was dressed in a flowing flimsy negligee and her hair was tousled. She nervously crushed a cigarette underfoot.

"Are you the big cheese around here?" she yelled in a strident fury to Queen. He stood stock still and examined her impersonally. "Then what the hell do you mean by sending one o' your flatfoots to keep me locked up all night, hey?"

She jumped forward as if to come to grips with the old man. Ritter lumbered swiftly toward her and squeezed her arm. "Here you," he growled, "shut up until you're spoken to."

She glared at him. Then with a tigerish twist she was out of his grasp and in a chair, panting, wild-eyed.

Arms akimbo, the Inspector stood looking her up and down with unconcealed distaste. Ellery glanced at the woman briefly and began to putter about the room, peering at the wall hangings and Japanese prints, picking up a book from an end table, poking his head into dark corners.

Queen motioned to Hagstrom. "Take this lady into the next room and keep her company for a while," he said. The detective unceremoniously hustled the woman to her feet. She tossed her head defiantly and marched into the next room, Hagstrom following.

"Now, Ritter, my boy," sighed the old man, sinking into an easychair, "tell me what happened."

Ritter answered stiffly. His eyes were strained, bloodshot. "I followed out your orders last night to the dot. I beat it down here in a police car, left it on the corner because I didn't know but what somebody might be keeping a lookout, and strolled up to this apartment. Everything was quiet—and I hadn't noticed any lights either, because before I went in I beat it down to the court and looked up at the back windows of the apartment. So I gave 'em a nice short ring on the bell and waited.

"No answer," continued Ritter, with a tightening of his big jaw. "I buzzed again—this time longer and louder. This time I got results. I heard the latch on the inside rattle and this woman yodels, 'That you, honey? Where's your key?' Aha—thinks I—Mr. Field's lady friend! So I shoved my foot in the door and grabbed her before she knew what was what. Well, sir, I got a surprise. Sort of expected," he grinned sheepishly, "sort of expected to find the woman dressed, but all I grabbed was a thin piece o' silk nightgown. I guess I must have blushed. . . ."

"Ah, the opportunities of our good minions of the law!" murmured Ellery, head bent over a small lacquered vase.

"Anyway," continued the detective, "I got my hands on her and she yelped—plenty. Hustled her into the living room here where she'd put on the light, and took a good look at her. She was scared blue but she was kind of plucky, too, because she began to cuss me and she wanted to know who in hell I was, what I was tryin' to do in a woman's apartment at night, and all that sort of stuff. I flashed my badge. And Inspector, that hefty Sheba—the minute she sees the badge, she shuts up tight like a bluepoint and won't answer a question I ask her!"

"Why was that?" The old man's eyes roved from floor to ceiling as he looked over the appointments of the room.

"Hard to tell, Inspector," said Ritter. "First she seemed scared, but when she saw my badge she bucked up wonderful. And the longer I was here the more brazen she became."

"You didn't tell her about Field, did you?" queried the Inspector, in a sharp, low tone.

Ritter gave his superior a reproachful glance. "Not a peep out o' me, sir," he said. "Well, when I saw it was no go tryin' to get anything out of her—all she'd yell was, 'Wait till Monte gets home, you bozo!'—I took a look at the bedroom. Nobody there, so I shoved her inside, kept the door open and the light on and stayed all night. She climbed into bed after a while and I guess she went to sleep. At about seven this morning she popped out and started to yell all over again. Seemed to think that Field had been grabbed by headquarters. Insisted on having a newspaper. I told her nothin' doin' and then phoned the office. Not another thing happened since."

"I say, Dad!" exclaimed Ellery suddenly, from a corner of the room.

"What do you think our legal friend reads—you'll never guess. 'How to Tell Character from Handwriting'!"

The Inspector grunted as he rose. "Stop fiddling with those eternal books," he said, "and come along."

He flung open the bedroom door. The woman was sitting cross-legged on the bed, an ornate affair of a bastard French period style, canopied and draped from ceiling to floor with heavy damask curtains. Hagstrom leaned stolidly against the window.

Queen looked quickly about. He turned to Ritter. "Was that bed mussed up when you came in here last night—did it look as if it had been slept in?" he whispered aside.

Ritter nodded. "All right, then, Ritter," said Queen in a genial tone. "Go home and get some rest. You deserve it. And send up Piggott on your way out." The detective touched his hat and departed.

Queen turned on the woman. He walked to the bed and sat down beside her, studying her half-averted face. She lit a cigarette defiantly.

"I am Inspector Queen of the police, my dear," announced the old man mildly. "I warn you that any attempt to keep a stubborn silence or lie to me will only get you into a heap of trouble. But there! Of course you understand."

She jerked away. "I'm not answering any questions, Mr. Inspector, until I know what right you have to ask 'em. I haven't done anything wrong and my slate's clean. You can put that in your pipe and smoke it!"

The Inspector took a pinch of snuff, as if the woman's reference to the vile weed had reminded him of his favorite vice. He said: "That's fair enough," in dulcet tones. "Here you are, a lonely woman suddenly tumbled out of bed in the middle of the night—you *were* in bed, weren't you—?"

"Sure I was," she flashed instantly, then bit her lip.

"—and confronted by a policeman. . . . I don't wonder you were frightened, my dear."

"I was not!" she said shrilly.

"We'll not argue about it," rejoined the old man benevolently. "But certainly you have no objection to telling me your name?"

"I don't know why I should but I can't see any harm in it," retorted the woman. "My name is Angela Russo—Mrs. Angela Russo—and I'm, well, I'm engaged to Mr. Field."

"I see," said Queen gravely. "Mrs. Angela Russo and you are engaged to Mr. Field. Very good! And what were you doing in these rooms last night, Mrs. Angela Russo?"

"None of your business!" she said coolly. "You'd better let me go now—I haven't done a thing out of the way. You've got no right to jabber at me, old boy!"

Ellery, in a corner peering out of the window, smiled. The Inspector leaned over and took the woman's hand gently.

"My dear Mrs. Russo," he said, "believe me—there is every reason in the world why we should be anxious to know what you were doing here last night. Come now—tell me."

"I won't open my mouth till I know what you've done with Monte!" she cried, shaking off his hand. "If you've got him, why are you pestering me! I don't know anything."

"Mr. Field is in a very safe place at the moment," snapped the Inspector, rising, "I've given you plenty of rope, madam. Monte Field is dead."

"Monte—Field—is—" The woman's lips moved mechanically. She leaped to her feet, clutching the negligee to her plump figure, staring at Queen's impassive face.

She laughed shortly and threw herself back on the bed. "Go on—you're taking me for a ride," she jeered.

"I'm not accustomed to joking about death," returned the old man with a little smile. "I assure you that you may take my word for it—Monte Field is dead." She was staring up at him, her lips moving soundlessly. "And what is more, Mrs. Russo, he has been murdered. Perhaps now you'll deign to answer my questions. Where were you at a quarter to ten last night?" he whispered in her ear, his face close to hers.

Mrs. Russo relaxed limply on the bed, a dawning fright in her large eyes. She gaped at the Inspector, found little comfort in his face and with a cry whirled to sob into the rumpled pillow. Queen stepped back and spoke in a low tone to Piggott, who had come into the room a moment before. The woman's heaving sobs subsided suddenly. She sat up, dabbing her face with a lace handkerchief. Her eyes were strangely bright.

"I get you now," she said in a quiet voice. "I was right here in this apartment at a quarter to ten last night."

"Can you prove that, Mrs. Russo?" asked Queen fingering his snuffbox.

"I can't prove anything and I don't have to," she returned dully. "But if you're looking for an alibi, the doorman downstairs must have seen me come into the building at about nine-thirty."

"We can easily check that up," admitted Queen. "Tell me—why did you come here last night at all?"

"I had an appointment with Monte," she explained lifelessly. "He called me up at my own place yesterday afternoon and we made a date for last night. He told me he'd be out on business until about ten o'clock, and I was to wait here for him. I come up"—she paused and continued brazenly—"I come up quite often like that. We generally have a little 'time' and spend the evening together. Being engaged—you know."

"Ummm. I see, I see." The Inspector cleared his throat in some embarrassment. "And then, when he didn't come on time—?"

"I thought he might've been detained longer than he'd figured. So I—well, I felt tired and took a little nap."

"Very good," said Queen quickly. "Did he tell you where he was going, or the nature of his business?"

"No."

"I should be greatly obliged to you, Mrs. Russo," said the Inspector carefully, "if you would tell me what Mr. Field's attitude was toward theatre-going."

The woman looked at him curiously. She seemed to be recovering her spirits. "Didn't go very often," she snapped. "Why?"

The Inspector beamed. "Now, that's a question, isn't it?" he asked. He motioned to Hagstrom, who pulled a notebook out of his pocket.

"Could you give me a list of Mr. Field's personal friends?" resumed Queen. "And any business acquaintances you might know of?"

Mrs. Russo put her hands behind her head, coquettishly. "To tell the truth," she said sweetly, "I don't know any. I met Monte about six months ago at a masque ball in the Village. We've kept our engagement sort of quiet, you see. In fact, I've never met his friends at all. . . . I don't think," she confided, "I don't think Monte had many friends. And of course I don't know a thing about his business associates."

"What was Field's financial condition, Mrs. Russo?"

"Trust a woman to know those things!" she retorted, completely restored to her flippant manner. "Monte was always a good spender. Never seemed to run out of cash. He's spent five hundred a night on me many a time. That was Monte—a damned good sport. Tough luck for him!—poor darling." She wiped a tear from her eye, sniffling hastily.

"But—his bank account?" pursued the Inspector firmly.

Mrs. Russo smiled. She seemed to possess an inexhaustible fund of shifting emotions. "Never got nosey," she said. "As long as Monte was treating me square it wasn't any of my business. At least," she added, "he wouldn't tell me, so what did I care?"

"Where were you, Mrs. Russo," came Ellery's indifferent tones, "*before* nine-thirty last night?"

She turned in surprise at the new voice. They measured each other carefully, and something like warmth crept into her eyes. "I don't know who you are, mister, but if you want to find out ask the lovers in Central Park. I was taking a little stroll in the Park—all by my lonesome—from about half-past seven until the time I reached here."

"How fortunate!" murmured Ellery. The Inspector hastily went to the door, crooking his finger at the other three men. "We'll leave you now to dress, Mrs. Russo. That will be all for the present." She watched quizzically as they filed out. Queen, last, shut the door after a fatherly glance at her face.

In the living room the four men proceeded to make a hurried but thorough search. At the Inspector's command Hagstrom and Piggott went through the drawers of a carved desk in one corner of the room. Ellery was interestedly rifling the pages of the book on character through handwriting. Queen prowled restlessly about, poking his head into a clothes closet just inside the room, off the foyer. This was a commodious storage compartment for clothes—assorted topcoats, capes and the like hung from a rack. The Inspector rifled the pockets. A few miscellaneous articles—handkerchiefs, keys, old personal letters, wallets—came to light. These he put to one side. A top shelf held several hats.

"Ellery—hats," he grunted.

Ellery quickly crossed the room, stuffing into his pocket the book he had been reading. His father pointed out the hats meaningly; together they reached up to examine them. There were four—a discolored Panama, two fedors, one gray and one brown, and a derby. All bore the imprint of Browne Bros.

The two men turned the hats over in their hands. Both noticed immediately that three of them had no linings—the Panama and the two fedoras. The fourth hat, an excellent derby, Queen examined critically. He felt the lining, turned down the leather sweatband, then shook his head.

"To tell the truth, Ellery," he said slowly, "I'll be switched if I know why I should expect to find clues in these hats. We know that Field wore a tophat last night and obviously it would be impossible for that hat to be in these rooms. According to our findings the murderer was still in the theatre when we arrived. Ritter was down here by eleven o'clock. The hat therefore *couldn't* have been brought to this place. For that matter, what earthly reason would the murderer have for such an action, even if it were physically possible for him to do it? He must have realized that we would search Field's apartment at once. No, I guess I'm feeling a little offcolor, Ellery. There's nothing to be squeezed out of these hats." He threw the derby back onto the shelf disgustedly.

Ellery stood thoughtful and unsmiling. "You're right enough, Dad; these hats mean nothing. But I have the strangest feeling. . . . By the way!" He straightened up and took off his pince-nez. "Did it occur to you last night that something else belonging to Field might have been missing besides the hat?"

"I wish they were all as easy to answer as that," said Queen grimly.

"Certainly—a walking stick. But what could I do about that? Working on the premise that Field brought one with him—it would have been simple enough for someone who had entered the theatre without a walking stick to leave the theatre with Field's. And how could we stop him or identify the stick? So I didn't even bother thinking about it. And if it's still on the Roman premises, Ellery, it will keep—no fear about that."

Ellery chuckled. "I should be able to quote Shelley or Wordsworth at this point," he said, "in proof of my admiration for your prowess. But I can't think of a more poetical phrase than 'You've got one over on me.' Because I didn't think of it until just now. But here's the point: there is no cane of any kind in the closet. A man like Field, had he possessed a swanky halberd to go with evening dress, would most certainly have owned other sticks to match other costumes. That fact—unless we find sticks in the bedroom closet, which I doubt, since all the overclothes seem to be here—that fact, therefore, eliminates the possibility that Field had a stick with him last night. *Ergo*—we may forget all about it."

"Good enough, El," returned the Inspector absently. "I hadn't thought of that. Well—let's see how the boys are getting on."

They walked across the room to where Hagstrom and Piggott were rifling the desk. A small pile of papers and notes had accumulated on the lid.

"Find anything interesting?" asked Queen.

"Not a thing of value that I can see, Inspector," answered Piggott. "Just the usual stuff—some letters, chiefly from this Russo woman, and pretty hot too!—a lot of bills and receipts and things like that. Don't think you'll find anything here."

Queen went through the papers. "No, nothing much," he admitted. "Well, let's get on." They restored the papers to the desk. Piggott and Hagstrom rapidly searched the room. They tapped furniture, poked beneath cushions, picked up the rug—a thorough, workmanlike job. As Queen and Ellery stood silently watching, the bedroom door opened. Mrs. Russo appeared, saucily appareled in a brown walking suit and toque. She paused at the door, surveying the scene with wide, innocent eyes. The two detectives proceeded with their search without looking up.

"What are they doing, Inspector?" she inquired in a languid tone. "Looking for pretty-pretties?" But her eyes were keen and interested.

"That was remarkably rapid dressing for a female, Mrs. Russo," said the Inspector admiringly. "Going home?"

Her glance darted at him. "Sure thing," she answered, looking away.

"And you live at—?"

She gave an address on MacDougal Street in Greenwich Village.

"Thank you," said Queen courteously, making a note. She began to walk across the room. "Oh, Mrs. Russo!" she turned. "Before you go—perhaps you could tell us something about Mr. Field's convivial habits. Was he, now, what you would call a heavy drinker?"

She laughed merrily. "Is that all?" she said. "Yes and no. I've seen Monte drink half a night and be sober as a—as a parson. And then I've seen him at other times when he was pickled silly on a couple of tots. It all depended—don't you know?" She laughed again.

"Well, many of us are that way," murmured the Inspector. "I don't want you to abuse any confidences, Mrs. Russo—but perhaps you know the source of his liquor supply?"

She stopped laughing instantly, her face reflecting an innocent indignation. "What do you think I am, anyway?" she demanded. "I don't know, but even if I did I wouldn't tell. There's many a hard-working bootlegger who's head and shoulders above the guys who try to run 'em in, believe me!"

"The way of all flesh, Mrs. Russo," said Queen soothingly. "Nevertheless, my dear," he continued softly, "I'm sure that if I need that information eventually, you will enlighten me. Eh?" There was a silence. "I think that will be all, then, Mrs. Russo. Just stay in town, won't you? We may require your testimony soon."

"Well—so long," she said, tossing her head. She marched out of the room to the foyer.

"Mrs. Russo!" called Queen suddenly, in a sharp tone. She turned with her gloved hand on the front-door knob, the smile dying from her lips. "What's Ben Morgan been doing since he and Field dissolved partnership—do you know?"

Her reply came after a split second of hesitation. "Who's he?" she asked, her forehead wrinkled into a frown.

Queen stood squarely on the rug. He said sadly, "Never mind. Good day," and turned his back on her. The door slammed. A moment later Hagstrom strolled out, leaving Piggott, Queen and Ellery in the apartment.

The three men, as if inspired by a single thought, ran into the bedroom. It was apparently as they had left it. The bed was disordered and Mrs. Russo's nightgown and negligee were lying on the floor. Queen opened the door of the bedroom clothes closet. "Whew!" said Ellery. "This chap had a quiet taste in clothes, didn't he? Sort of Mulberry Street Beau Brummell." They ransacked the closet with no results. Ellery craned his neck at the shelf above. "No hats—no canes; that settles *that!*" he murmured with an air of satisfaction. Piggott, who had disappeared into a small kitchen, returned staggering under the burden of a half-empty case of liquor bottles.

Ellery and his father bent over the case. The Inspector removed a cork gingerly, sniffed the contents, then handed the bottle to Piggott, who followed his superior's example critically.

"Looks and smells okay," said the detective. "But I'd hate to take a chance tasting this stuff—after last night."

"You're perfectly justified in your caution," chuckled Ellery. "But if you should change your mind and decide to invoke the spirit of Bacchus, Piggott, let me suggest this prayer: O wine, if thou hast no name to be known by, let us call thee Death."*

"I'll have the firewater analyzed," growled Queen. "Scotch and rye mixed, and the labels look like the real thing. But then you never can tell. . . ." Ellery suddenly grasped his father's arm, leaning forward tensely. The three men stiffened.

A barely audible scratching came to their ears, proceeding from the foyer.

"Sounds as if somebody is using a key on the door," whispered Queen. "Duck out, Piggott—jump whoever it is as soon as he gets inside!"

Piggott darted through the living room into the foyer. Queen and Ellery waited in the bedroom, concealed from view.

There was utter silence now except for the scraping on the outer door. The newcomer seemed to be having difficulty with the key. Suddenly the rasp of the lock tumblers falling back was heard and an instant later the door swung open. It slammed shut almost immediately.

A muffled cry, a hoarse bull-like voice, Piggott's half-strangled oath, the frenzied shuffling of feet—and Ellery and his father were speeding across the living room to the foyer.

Piggott was struggling in the arms of a burly, powerful man dressed in black. A suitcase lay on the floor to one side, as if it had been thrown there during the tussle. A newspaper was fluttering through the air, settling on the parquet just as Ellery reached the cursing men.

It took the combined efforts of the three to subdue their visitor. Finally, panting heavily, he lay on the floor, Piggott's arm jammed tightly across his chest.

The Inspector bent down, gazed curiously into the man's red, angry features and said softly, "And who are you, mister?"

---

* Ellery Queen was here probably paraphrasing the Shakespearian quotation: "O thou invisible spirit of wine, if thou hast no name to be known by, let us call thee devil."

# 9

## In Which the Mysterious Mr. Michaels Appears

The intruder rose awkwardly to his feet. He was a tall, ponderous man with solemn features and blank eyes. There was nothing distingishing in either his appearance or his manner. If anything unusual could be said of him at all, it was that both his appearance and manner were so unremarkable. It seemed as if, whoever he was or whatever his occupation, he had made a deliberate effort to efface all marks of personality.

"Just what's the idea of the strong-arm stuff?" he said in a bass voice. But even his tones were flat and colorless.

Queen turned to Piggott. "What happened?" he demanded, with a pretense of severity.

"I stood behind the door, Inspector," gasped Piggott, still winded, "and when this wildcat stepped in I touched him on the arm. He jumped me like a trainload o' tigers, he did. Pushed me in the face—he's got a wallop, Inspector. . . . Tried to get out the door again."

Queen nodded judicially. The newcomer said mildly, "That's a lie, sir. He jumped me and I fought back."

"Here, here!" murmured Queen. "This will never do. . . ."

The door swung open suddenly and Detective Johnson stood on the threshold. He took the Inspector to one side. "Velie sent me down the last minute on the chance you might need me, Inspector. . . . And as I was coming up I saw that chap there. Didn't know but what he might be snooping around, so I followed him up." Queen nodded vigorously. "Glad you came—I can use you," he muttered and motioning to the others, he led the way into the living room.

"Now, my man," he said curtly to the big intruder, "the show is over. Who are you and what are you doing here?"

"My name is Charles Michaels—sir. I am Mr. Monte Field's valet." The Inspector's eyes narrowed. The man's entire demeanor had in some intangible manner changed. His face was blank, as before, and his attitude seemed in no way different. Yet the old man sensed a metamorphosis; he glanced quickly at Ellery and saw a confirmation of his own thought in his son's eyes.

"Is that so?" inquired the Inspector steadily. "Valet, eh? And where are you going at this hour of the morning with that traveling bag?" He jerked his hand toward the suitcase, a cheap black affair, which Piggott had picked up in the foyer and carried into the living room. Ellery suddenly strolled away in the direction of the foyer. He bent over to pick up something.

"Sir?" Michaels seemed upset by the question. "That's mine, sir," he confided. "I was just going away this morning on my vacation and I'd arranged with Mr. Field to come here for my salary check before I left."

The old man's eyes sparkled. He had it! Michaels' expression and general bearing had remained unchanged, but his voice and enunciation were markedly different.

"So you arranged to get your check from Mr. Field this morning?" murmured the Inspector. "That's mighty funny now, come to think of it."

Michaels permitted a fleeting amazement to scud across his features. "Why—why, where is Mr. Field?" he asked.

" 'Massa's in de cold, cold ground,' " chuckled Ellery, from the foyer. He stepped back into the living room, flourishing the newspaper which Michaels had dropped during the fracas with Piggott. "Really, now, old chap, that's a bit thick, you know. Here is the morning paper you brought in with you. And the first thing I see as I pick it up is the nice black headline describing Mr. Field's little accident. Smeared over the entire front page. And—er, you failed to see the story?"

Michaels stared stonily at Ellery and the paper. But his eyes fell as he mumbled, "I didn't get the opportunity of reading the paper this morning, sir. What has happened to Mr. Field?"

The Inspector snorted. "Field's been killed, Michaels, and you knew it all the time."

"But I didn't, I tell you, sir," objected the valet respectfully.

"Stop lying!" rasped Queen. "Tell us why you're here or you'll get plenty of opportunity to talk behind bars!"

Michaels regarded the old man patiently. "I've told you the truth, sir," he said. "Mr. Field told me yesterday that I was to come here this morning for my check. That's all I know."

"You were to meet him here?"

"Yes, sir."

"Then why did you forget to ring the bell? Used a key as if you didn't expect to find anyone here, my man," said Queen.

"The bell?" The valet opened his eyes wide. "I always use my key, sir. Never disturb Mr. Field if I can help it."

"Why didn't Field give you a check yesterday?" barked the Inspector.

"He didn't have his checkbook handy, I think, sir."

Queen's lip curled. "You haven't even a fertile imagination, Michaels. At what time did you last see him yesterday?"

"At about seven o'clock, sir," said Michaels promptly. "I don't live here at the apartment. It's too small and Mr. Field likes—liked privacy. I generally come early in the morning to make breakfast for him and prepare his bath and lay out his clothes. Then when he's gone to the office I clean up a bit and the rest of the day is my own until dinnertime. I return about five, prepare dinner unless I've heard from Mr. Field during the day that he is dining out, and get his dinner or evening clothes ready. Then I am through for the night. . . . Yesterday after I laid out his things he told me about the check."

"Not an especially fatiguing itinerary," murmured Ellery. "And what things did you lay out last evening, Michaels?"

The man faced Ellery respectfully. "There was his underwear, sir, and his socks, his evening shoes, stiff shirt, studs, collar, white tie, full evening dress, cape, hat—"

"Ah, yes—his hat," interrupted Queen. "And what kind of hat was it, Michaels?"

"His regular tophat, sir," answered Michaels. "He had only one, and a very expensive one it was, too," he added warmly. "Browne Bros., I think."

Queen drummed lazily on the arm of his chair. "Tell me, Michaels," he said, "what did you do last night after you left here—that is, after seven o'clock?"

"I went home, sir. I had my bag to pack and I was rather fatigued. I went right to sleep after I'd had a bite to eat—it must have been near nine-thirty when I climbed into bed, sir," he added innocently.

"Where do you live?" Michaels gave a number of East 146th Street, in the Bronx section. "I see. . . . Did Field have any regular visitors here?" went on the Inspector.

Michaels frowned politely. "That's hard for me to say, sir. Mr. Field wasn't what you would call a friendly person. But then I wasn't here evenings, so I can't say who came after I left. But—"

"Yes?"

"There was a lady, sir. . . ." Michaels hesitated primly. "I dislike mentioning names under the circumstances—"

"Her name?" said Queen wearily.

"Well, sir—it isn't sort of right—Russo. Mrs. Angela Russo, her name is," answered Michaels.

"How long did Mr. Field know this Mrs. Russo?"

"Several months, sir. I think he met her at a party in Greenwich Village somewhere."

"I see. And they were engaged, perhaps?"

Michaels seemed embarrassed. "You might call it that, sir, although it was a little less formal. . . ."

Silence. "How long have you been in Monte Field's employ, Michaels?" pursued the Inspector.

"Three years next month."

Queen switched to a new line of questioning. He asked Michaels about Field's addiction to theatre-going, his financial condition and his drinking habits. In these particulars Michaels corroborated Mrs. Russo's statements. Nothing of a fresh nature was disclosed.

"A few moments ago you said you have been working for Field a matter of three years," continued Queen, settling back in his chair. "How did you get the job?"

Michaels did not answer immediately. "I followed up an ad in the papers, sir."

"Quite so. . . . If you have been in Field's service for three years, Michaels, you should know Benjamin Morgan."

Michaels permitted a proper smile to cross his lips. "Certainly I know Mr. Benjamin Morgan," he said heartily. "And a very fine gentleman he is, too, sir. He was Mr. Field's partner, you know, in their law business. But then they separated about two years ago and I haven't seen much of Mr. Morgan since."

"Did you see him often before the split?"

"No, sir," returned the burly valet, in a tone which implied regret. "Mr. Field was not Mr. Mogan's—ah—type, and they didn't mix socially. Oh, I remember seeing Mr. Morgan in this apartment three or four times, but only when it was a matter of most urgent business. Even then I couldn't say much about it since I didn't stay all evening. . . . Of course, he hasn't been here, so far as I know, since they broke up the firm."

Queen smiled for the first time during the conversation. "Thank you for your frankness, Michaels. . . . I'm going to be an old gossip—do you recall any unpleasantness about the time they dissolved?"

"Oh, no, sir!" protested Michaels. "I never heard of a quarrel or anything like that. In fact, Mr. Field told me immediately after the dissolution that he and Mr. Morgan would remain friends—very good friends, he said."

Michaels turned with his politely blank expression at a touch of his arm. He found himself face to face with Ellery. "Yes, sir?" he asked respectfully.

"Michaels, dear man," said Ellery with severity, "I detest raking up old coals, but why haven't you told the Inspector about the time you were in jail?"

As if he had stepped on an exposed live-wire Michaels' body stiffened and grew still. The ruddy color drained out of his face. He stared openmouthed, aplomb swept away, into Ellery's smiling eyes.

"Why—why—how did you find that out?" gasped the valet, his speech less soft and polished. Queen appraised his son with approval. Piggott and Johnson moved closer to the trembling man.

Ellery lit a cigarette. "I didn't know it at all," he said cheerfully. "That is, not until you told me. It would pay you to cultivate the Delphic oracles, Michaels."

Michaels' face was the color of dead ashes. He turned, shaking, toward Queen. "You—you didn't ask me about that, sir," he said weakly. Nevertheless his tone had again become taut and blank. "Besides, a man doesn't like to tell things like that to the police. . . ."

"Where did you do time, Michaels?" asked the Inspector in a kindly voice.

"Elmira Reformatory, sir," muttered Michaels. "It was my first offense—I was up against it, starving, stole some money. . . . I got a short stretch, sir."

Queen rose. "Well, Michaels, of course you understand that you are not exactly a free agent at present. You may go home and look for another job if you want to, but stay at your present lodgings and be ready for a call at any time. . . . Just a moment, before you go." He strode over to the black suitcase and snapped it open. A jumbled mass of clothing—a dark suit, shirts, ties, socks—some clean, some dirty—was revealed. Queen rummaged swiftly through the bag, closed it and handed it to Michaels, who was standing to one side with an expression of sorrowful patience.

"Seems to me you were taking mighty few duds with you, Michaels," remarked Queen, smiling. "It's too bad that you've been done out of your vacation. Well! That's the way life is!" Michaels murmured a low good-by, picked up the bag and departed. A moment later Piggott strolled out of the apartment.

Ellery threw back his head and laughed delightedly. "What a mannerly beggar! Lying in his teeth, Pater. . . . And what did he want here, do you think?"

"He came to get something, of course," mused the Inspector. "And that means there's something here of importance that we have apparently overlooked. . . ."

He grew thoughtful. The telephone bell rang.

"Inspector?" Sergeant Velie's voice boomed over the wire. "I called headquarters but you weren't there, so I guessed you were still at Field's place. . . . I've some interesting news for you from Browne Bros. Do you want me to come up to Field's?"

"No," returned Queen. "We're through here. I'll be at my office just as soon as I've paid a visit to Field's on Chambers Street. I'll be there if anything important comes up in the interim. Where are you now?"

"Fifth Avenue—I've just come out of Browne's."

"Then go back to headquarters and wait for me. And, Thomas—send a uniformed man up here right away."

Queen hung up and turned to Johnson.

"Stay here until a cop shows up—it won't be long," he grunted. "Have him keep a watch in the apartment and arrange for a relief. Then report back to the main office. . . . Come along, Ellery. This is going to be a busy day!"

Ellery's protests were in vain. His father fussily hustled him out of the building and into the street, where the roar of a taxicab's exhaust effectually drowned out his voice.

# 10

## In Which Mr. Field's Tophats Begin to Assume Proportions

It was exactly ten o'clock in the morning when Inspector Queen and his son opened the frosted glass door marked:

MONTE FIELD

ATTORNEY-AT-LAW

The large waiting room they entered was decorated in just such a fashion as might have been expected from a man of Field's taste in clothes. It was deserted, and with a puzzled glance Inspector Queen pushed through the door, Ellery strolling behind, and went into the General Office. This was a long room filled with desks. It resembled a newspaper "city room" except for its rows of bookcases filled with ponderous legal tomes.

The office was in a state of violent upheaval. Stenographers chattered excitedly in small groups. A number of male clerks whispered in a corner; and in the center of the room stood Detective Hesse, talking earnestly to a lean saturnine man with grayed temples. It was evident that the demise of the lawyer had created something of a stir in his place of business.

At the entrance of the Queens the employees looked at each other in a startled way and began to slip back to their desks. An embarrassed silence fell. Hesse hurried forward. His eyes were red and strained.

"Good morning, Hesse," said the Inspector abruptly. "Where's Field's private office?"

The detective led them across the room to still another door, a large PRIVATE lettered on its panels. The three men went into a small office which was overwhelmingly luxurious.

"This chap went for atmosphere, didn't he?" Ellery chuckled, sinking into a red-leather armchair.

"Let's have it, Hesse," said the Inspector, following Ellery's suit.

Hesse began to talk rapidly. "Got here last night and found the door locked. No sign of a light inside. I listened pretty closely but couldn't hear a sound, so I took it for granted that there was no one inside and camped in the corridor all night. At about a quarter to nine this morning the office manager breezed in and I collared him. He was that tall bird I was talking to when you came in. Name's Lewin—Oscar Lewin."

"Office manager, eh?" remarked the old man, inhaling snuff.

"Yes, Chief. He's either dumb or else he knows how to keep his mouth shut," continued Hesse. "Of course, he'd already seen the morning papers and was upset by the news of Field's murder. I could see he didn't like my questions any too well, either. . . . I didn't get a thing out of him. Not a thing. He said he'd gone straight home last night—it seems Field had left about four o'clock and didn't come back—and he didn't know anything about the murder until he read the papers. We've been sort of sliding along here all morning, waiting for you to come."

"Get Lewin for me."

Hesse returned with the lanky office manager in his wake. Oscar Lewin was physically unprepossessing. He had shifty black eyes and was abnormally thin. There was something predatory in his beaked nose and bony figure. The Inspector looked him over coldly.

"So you're the office manager," he remarked. "Well, what do you think of this affair, Lewin?"

"It's terrible—simply terrible," groaned Lewin. "I can't imagine how it happened or why. Good Lord, I was talking to him only four o'clock yesterday afternoon!" He seemed genuinely distressed.

"Did Mr. Field appear strange or worried when you spoke to him?"

"Not at all, sir," replied Lewin nervously. "In fact, he was in unusually good spirits. Cracked a joke about the Giants and said he was going to see a darned good show last night—'Gunplay.' And now I see by the papers that he was killed there!"

"Oh, he told you about the play, did he?" asked the Inspector. "He didn't happen to remark by any chance that he was going with anybody?"

"No, sir." Lewin shuffled his feet.

"I see." Queen paused. "Lewin, as manager you must have been closer to Field than any other of his employees. Just what do you know about him personally?"

"Not a thing, sir, not a thing," said Lewin hastily. "Mr. Field was not a man with whom an employee could become familiar. Occasionally he said something about himself, but it was always of a general nature and more jesting than serious. To us outside he was always a considerate and generous employer—that's all."

"What exactly was the caliber of the business he conducted, Lewin? You must certainly know something about that."

"Business?" Lewin seemed startled. "Why, it was as fine a practice as any I've encountered in the law profession. I've worked for Field only two years or so, but he had some high-and-mighty clients, Inspector. I can give you a list of them. . . ."

"Do that and mail it to me," said Queen. "So he had a flourishing and respectable practice, eh? Any personal visitors to your knowledge—especially recently?"

"No. I can't remember ever seeing any one up here except his clients. Of course, he may have known some of them socially. . . . Oh, yes! Of course his valet came here at times—tall, brawny fellow by the name of Michaels."

"Michaels? I'll have to remember that name," said the Inspector thoughtfully. He looked up at Lewin. "All right, Lewin. That will be all now. You might dismiss the force for the day. And—just stay around for a while. I expect one of Mr. Sampson's men soon, and undoubtedly he will need your help." Lewin nodded gravely and retired.

The moment the door closed Queen was on his feet. "Where's Field's private washroom, Hesse?" he demanded. The detective pointed to a door in a far corner of the room.

Queen opened it, Ellery crowding close behind. They were peering into a tiny cubicle spaced off in an angle of the wall. It contained a washbowl, a medicine chest and a small clothes closet. Queen looked into the medicine chest first. It held a bottle of iodine, a bottle of peroxide, a tube of shaving cream, and other shaving articles. "Nothing there," said Ellery. "How about the closet?" The old man pulled the door open curiously. A suit of street clothes hung there, a half-dozen neckties and a fedora hat. The Inspector carried the hat back into the office and examined it. He handed it to Ellery, who disdainfully returned it at once to its peg in the closet.

"Dang those hats!" exploded the Inspector. There was a knock on the door and Hesse admitted a bland young man.

"Inspector Queen?" inquired the newcomer politely.

"Right," snapped the Inspector, "and if you're a reporter you can say the police will apprehend the murderer of Monte Field within twenty-four hours. Because that's all I'm going to give you right now."

The young man smiled. "Sorry, Inspector, but I'm not a reporter. I'm Arthur Stoates, new man at District Attorney Sampson's office. The Chief couldn't reach me until this morning and I was busy on something else—that's why I'm a little late. Too bad about Field, isn't it?" He grinned as he threw his coat and hat on a chair.

"It's all in the point of view," grumbled Queen. "He's certainly causing a heap of trouble. Just what were Sampson's instructions?"

"Well, I'm not as familiar with Field's career as I might be, naturally, but I'm pinch-hitting for Tim Cronin, who's tied up this morning on something else. I'm to make a start until Tim gets untangled, which will be some time this afternoon. Cronin, you know, was the man after Field a couple of years ago. He's aching to get busy with these files."

"Fair enough. From what Sampson told me about Cronin—if there's anything incriminating in these records and files, he'll ferret it out. Hesse, take Mr. Stoates outside and introduce him to Lewin—that's the office manager, Stoates. Keep your eye on him—he looks like a wily bird. And, Stoates—remember you're looking not for legitimate business and clientele in these records, but for something crooked. . . . See you later."

Stoates gave him a cheery smile and followed Hesse out. Ellery and his father faced each other across the room.

"What's that you've got in your hand?" asked the old man sharply.

"A copy of 'What Handwriting Tells,' which I picked up in this bookcase," replied Ellery lazily. "Why?"

"Come to think of it now, El," declared the Inspector slowly, "there's something fishy about this handwriting business." He shook his head in despair and rose. "Come along, son, there isn't a blamed thing here."

On their way through the main office, now empty except for Hesse, Lewin and Stoates, Queen beckoned to the detective. "Go home, Hesse," he said kindly. "Can't have you coming down with the grippe." Hesse grinned and sped through the door.

In a few minutes Inspector Queen was sitting in his private office at Center Street. Ellery termed it "the star chamber." It was small and cozy and homelike. Ellery draped himself over a chair and began to con the books on handwriting which he had filched from Field's apartment and office. The Inspector pressed a buzzer and the solid figure of Thomas Velie loomed in the doorway.

"Morning, Thomas," said Queen. "What is this remarkable news you have for me from Browne Bros.?"

"I don't know how remarkable it is, Inspector," said Velie coolly, seating himself in one of the straight-backed chairs which lined the wall, "but it sounded like the real thing to me. You told me last night to find out about Field's tophat. Well, I've an exact duplicate of it on my desk. Like to see it?"

"Don't be silly, Thomas," said Queen. "On the run!" Velie departed and was back in a moment carrying a hatbox. He tore the string and un-

covered a shining tophat, of such fine quality that Queen blinked. The Inspector picked it up curiously. On the inside was marked the size: 7 1/8.

"I spoke to the clerk, an old-timer, down at Browne's. Been waiting on
Field for years," resumed Velie. "It seems that Field bought every stitch
of his clothing there—for a long time. And it happens that he preferred
one clerk. Naturally the old buzzard knows quite a bit about Field's tastes
and purchases.

"He says, for one thing, that Field was a fussy dresser. His clothes
were always made to order by Browne's special tailoring department. He
went in for fancy suits and cuts and the latest in underclothes and neck-
wear. . . ."

"What about his taste in hats?" interposed Ellery, without looking up
from the book he was reading.

"I was coming to that, sir," continued Velie. "This clerk made a particular point of the hat business. For instance, when I questioned him about
the tophat, he said: 'Mr. Field was almost a fanatic on the subject. Why,
in the last six months he has bought no less than *three* of them!' I caught
that up, of course—made him check back with the sales records. Sure
enough, Field bought three silk toppers in the last half-year!"

Ellery and his father found themselves staring at each other, the same
question on their lips.

"Three—" began the old man.

"Now . . . isn't that an extraordinary circumstance?" asked Ellery
slowly, reaching for his pince-nez.

"Where in heaven's name are the other two?" continued Queen, in a
bewildered manner.

Ellery was silent.

Queen turned impatiently toward Velie. "What else did you find out,
Thomas?"

"Nothing much of value, except for this point"—answered Velie—
"that Field was an absolute fiend when it came to clothes. So much so
that last year he bought fifteen suits and no less than a dozen hats, including the toppers!"

"Hats, hats, hats!" groaned the Inspector. "The man must have been a
lunatic. Look here—did you find out whether Field ever bought walking
sticks at Browne's?"

A look of consternation spread over Velie's face. "Why—why, Inspector," he said ruefully, "I guess I slipped up there. I never even thought of
asking, and you hadn't told me last night—"

"Heck! We're none of us perfect," growled Queen. "Get that clerk on
the wire for me, Thomas."

Velie picked up one of the telephones on the desk and a few moments later handed the instrument to his superior.

"This is Inspector Queen speaking," said the old man rapidly. "I understand that you served Monte Field for a good many years? . . . Well, I want to check up on a little detail. Did Field ever purchase canes or walking sticks from you people? . . . What? Oh, I see. . . . Yes. Now, another thing. Did he ever give special orders about the manufacture of his clothes—extra pockets, or things like that? . . . You don't think so. All right. . . . What? Oh, I see. Thank you very much."

He hung up the receiver and turned about.

"Our lamented friend," he said disgustedly, "seems to have had as great an aversion to sticks as he had a love for hats. This clerk said he tried many times to interest Field in canes, and Field invariably refused to buy. Didn't like 'em, he said. And the clerk just confirmed his own impression about the special pockets—nothing doing. So that leaves us up a blank alley."

"On the contrary," said Ellery coolly, "it does nothing of the kind. It proves fairly conclusively that *the only article of apparel* taken away by the murderer last night was the hat. It seems to me that simplifies matters."

"I must have a moron's intelligence," grunted his father. "It doesn't mean a thing to me."

"By the way, Inspector," put in Velie, scowling, "Jimmy reported about the fingerprints on Field's flask. There are a few, but there's no question, he says, that they're all Field's. Jimmy got a print from the Morgue, of course, to check up."

"Well," said the Inspector, "maybe the flask has nothing to do with the crime at all. We'll have to wait, anyway, for Prouty's report on its contents."

"There's something else, Inspector," added Velie. "That junk—the sweepings of the theatre—that you told Panzer to send over to you this morning came a couple of minutes ago. Want to see it?"

"Sure thing, Thomas," said Queen. "And while you're out bring me the list you made last night containing the names of the people who had no stubs. The seat numbers are attached to each name, aren't they?"

Velie nodded and disappeared. Queen was looking morosely at the top of his son's head when the Sergeant returned with an unwieldy package and a typewritten list.

They spread the contents of the package carefully on the desk. For the most part the collected material consisted of crumpled programs, stray scraps of paper, chiefly from candy boxes, and many ticket stubs—those which had not been found by Flint and his searchers. Two women's gloves of different design; a small brown button, probably from a man's coat; the cap of a fountain pen; a woman's handkerchief and a few other scattered articles of the kind usually lost or thrown away in theatres came to light.

"Doesn't look as if there's much here, does it?" commented the Inspector. "Well, at least we'll be able to check up on the ticket-stub business."

Velie heaped the lost stubs in a small pile and began to read off their numbers and letters to Queen, who checked them off on the list Velie had brought him. There were not many of these and the checking-off process was completed in a few moments.

"That's all, Thomas?" inquired the Inspector, looking up.

"That's all, Chief."

"Well, there are about fifty people still unaccounted for according to this list. Where's Flint?"

"He's in the building somewhere, Inspector."

Queen picked up his telephone and gave a rapid order. Flint appeared almost at once.

"What did you find last night?" asked Queen abruptly.

"Well, Inspector," answered Flint sheepishly, "we practically dry-cleaned that place. We found quite a bit of stuff, but most of it was programs and things like that, and we left those for the cleaning women, who were working along with us. But we did pick up a raft of ticket stubs, especially out in the alleys." He brought forth from his pocket a package of pasteboards neatly bound with a rubber band. Velie took them and continued the process of reading off numbers and letters. When he was finished Queen slapped the typewritten list down on the desk before him.

"No fruit in the loom?" murmured Ellery, looking up from the book.

"Ding it, every one of those people who had no stubs is accounted for!" growled the Inspector. "There isn't a stub or a name left unchecked. . . . Well, there's one thing I can do." He searched through the pile of stubs, referring to the lists, until he found the stub which had belonged to Frances Ives-Pope. He fished from his pocket the four stubs he had collected Monday night and carefully tested the girl's stub with the one for Field's seat. The torn edges did not coincide.

"There's one consolation," the Inspector continued, stuffing the five tickets into his vest pocket, "we haven't found a trace of the six tickets for the seats next to and in front of Field's seat!"

"I didn't think you would," remarked Ellery. He put the book down and regarded his father with unwonted seriousness. "Have you ever stopped to consider, Dad, that we don't know definitely *why* Field was in the theatre last night?"

Queen knit his gray brows. "That particular problem has been puzzling me, of course. We know from Mrs. Russo and Michaels that Field did not care for the theatre—"

"You can never tell what vagary will seize a man," said Ellery decisively. "Many things might make a nontheatre-going man decide suddenly to go in for that sort of entertainment. The fact remains—he was there. But what I want to know is *why* he was there."

The old man shook his head gravely. "Was it a business appointment? Remember what Mrs. Russo said—that Field had promised to be back at 10 o'clock."

"I fancy the business appointment idea," applauded Ellery. "But consider how many probabilities there are—the Russo woman might be lying and Field said nothing of the sort; or if he did, he might have had no intention of keeping the appointment with her at 10 o'clock."

"I've quite made up my mind, Ellery," said the Inspector, "whatever the probabilities, that he didn't go the Roman Theatre last night to see the show. He went there with his eyes open—for business."

"I think that's correct, myself," returned Ellery, smiling. "But you can never be too careful in weighing possibilities. Now, if he went on business, he went to meet somebody. Was that somebody the murderer?"

"You ask too many questions, Ellery," said the Inspector.

"Thomas, let's have a look at the other stuff in that package."

Velie carefully handed the Inspector the miscellaneous articles one by one. The gloves, fountain-pen cap, button and handkerchief Queen threw to one side after a quick scrutiny. Nothing remained except the small bits of candy paper and the crumpled programs. The former yielding no clues, Queen took up the programs. And suddenly, in the midst of his examination, he cried delightedly: "See what I've found, boys!"

The three men leaned over his shoulder. Queen held a program in his hand, its wrinkles smoothed out. It showed evidences of having been crushed and thrown away. On one of the inside pages, bordering the usual article on men's wear, was a number of varied marks, some forming letters, some forming numbers, still others forming cabalistic designs such as a person scribbles in moments of idle thought.

"Inspector, it looks as if you've found Field's own program!" exclaimed Flint.

"Yes, sir, it certainly does," said Queen sharply. "Flint, look through the papers we found in the dead man's clothing last night and bring me a letter showing his signature." Flint hurried out.

Ellery was studying the scrawls intently. On the top margin of the paper appeared:

Flint returned with a letter. The Inspector compared the signatures — they were plainly by the same hand.

"We'll have them checked by Jimmie down in the laboratory," muttered the old man. "But I guess this is pretty authentic. It's Field's program, there can't be any doubt-of that. . . . What do you make of it, Thomas?"

Velie grated: "I don't know what those other numbers refer to, but that '50,000' couldn't mean anything but dollars, Chief."

"The old boy must have been figuring his bank account," said Queen. "He loved the sight of his own name, didn't he?"

"That's not quite fair to Field," protested Ellery. "When a man is sitting idle, waiting for something to happen — as he will when he is in a theatre before the performance begins — one of his most natural actions is to scribble his initials or his name on the handiest object. In a theatre the handiest object would be the program. . . . The writing of one's own name is fundamental in psychology. So perhaps Field wasn't as egotistical as this seems to make him."

"It's a small point," said the Inspector, studying the scrawls with a frown.

"Perhaps," returned Ellery. "But to get back to a more pressing matter — I don't agree with you when you say the '50,000' probably refers to Field's bank account. When a man jots down his bank balance he will not do it in such round numbers."

"We can prove or disprove that easily enough," retorted the Inspector, picking up a telephone. He asked the police operator to get him the number of Field's office. When he had spoken to Oscar Lewin for some time, he turned back to Ellery with a crestfallen air.

"You were right, El," he said. "Field had an amazingly small personal account. All his accounts balance to less than six thousand dollars. And this despite the fact that he frequently made deposits of ten and fifteen thousand dollars. Lewin himself was surprised. He hadn't known, he said, how Field's personal finances stood until I asked him to look the matter up. . . . I'll bet dollars to doughnuts Field played the stock market or the horses!"

"I'm not particularly overwhelmed by the news," remarked Ellery. "It points to the probable reason for the '50,000' on the program. That number not only represents dollars, but more than that—it indicates a business deal in which the stakes were fifty thousand! Not a bad night's work, if he had come out of it alive."

"How about the other two numbers?" asked Queen.

"I'm going to mull over them a bit," replied Ellery, subsiding in his chair. "I *would* like to know what the business deal was that involved such a large financial consideration," he added, absently polishing his pince-nez.

"Whatever the business deal was," said the Inspector sententiously, "you may be sure, my son, it was an evil one."

"An evil one?" inquired Ellery in a serious tone.

"Money's the root of all evil," retorted the Inspector with a grin.

Ellery's tone did not change. "Not only the root, Dad—but the fruit, too."

"Another quotation?" mocked the old man.

"Fielding," said Ellery imperturbably.

# 11

## In Which the Past Casts a Shadow

The telephone bell tinkled.

"Q? Sampson speaking," came the District Attorney's voice over the wire.

"Good morning, Henry," said Queen. "Where are you and how do you feel this morning?"

"I'm at the office and I feel rotten," returned Sampson, chuckling. "The doctor insists I'll be a corpse if I keep this up and the office insists the City will go under unless I attend to business. So what's a feller to do? . . . I say, Q."

The Inspector winked at Ellery across the table, as if to say, "I know what's coming!"

"Yes, Henry?"

"There's a gentleman in my private office whom I think it would be greatly to your advantage to meet," continued Sampson in a subdued tone. "He wants to see you and I'm afraid you'll have to chuck whatever you're doing and hotfoot it up here. He"—Sampson's voice became a whisper—"he's a man I can't afford to antagonize unnecessarily, Q, old boy."

The Inspector frowned. "I suppose you're referring to Ives-Pope," he said. "Riled, is he, because we questioned the apple of his eye last night?"

"Not exactly," said Sampson. "He's really a decent old chap. Just—er—just be nice to him, Q, won't you?"

"I'll handle him with silk gloves," chuckled the old man. "If it will ease your mind any I'll drag my son along. He generally attends to our social obligations."

"That will be fine," said Sampson gratefully.

The Inspector turned to Ellery as he hung up. "Poor Henry's in something of a mess," he said quizzically, "and I can't say I blame him for trying to please. Sick as a dog and the politicians hopping on him, this Crœsus howling in his front office. . . . Come along, son, we're going to meet the celebrated Franklin Ives-Pope!"

Ellery groaned, stretching his arms. "You'll have another sick man on your hands if this continues." Nevertheless he jumped up and clamped his hat on his head. "Let's look over this captain of industry."

Queen grinned at Velie. "Before I forget, Thomas. . . . I want you to do a bit of sleuthing today. Your job is to find out why Monte Field, who did a rushing legal business and lived in princely style, had only six thousand dollars in his personal account. It's probably Wall Street and the racetrack but I want you to make sure. You might learn something from the cancelled vouchers—Lewin down at Field's office could help you there. . . . And while you're at it—this might be extremely important, Thomas—get a complete line-up on Field's movements all day yesterday."

The two Queens departed for Sampson's headquarters.

The office of the District Attorney was a busy place and even an Inspector of Detectives was treated with scant ceremony in the sacred chambers. Ellery was wroth, and his father smiled, and finally the District Attorney himself came rushing out of his sanctum with a word of displeasure to the clerk who had allowed his friends to cool their heels on a hard bench.

"Watch your throat, young man," warned Queen, as Sampson led the way to his office, muttering maledictions on the head of the offender. "Are you sure I look all right to meet the money-mogul?"

Sampson held the door open. The two Queens on the threshold saw a man, hands clasped behind his back, looking through the window on the uninteresting vista outside. As the District Attorney closed the door the occupant of the room wheeled about with astonishing agility for a man of his weight.

Franklin Ives-Pope was a relic of more virile financial days. He resembled the strong self-assertive type of magnate who like old Cornelius Vanderbilt had dominated Wall Street as much by force of personality as by extent of wealth. Ives-Pope had clear gray eyes, iron-gray hair, a grizzled mustache, a husky body still springy with youth and an air of authority unmistakably masterful. Standing against the light of the dingy window, he was a most impressive figure of a man and Ellery and Queen, stepping forward, realized at once that here was an individual whose intelligence required no patronage.

The financier spoke in a deep pleasant voice even before Sampson, slightly embarrassed, could make the introduction. "I suppose you're Queen, the manhunter," he said. "I've been anxious to meet you for a long time, Inspector." He offered a large square hand, which Queen took with dignity.

"It would be unnecessary for me to echo that statement, Mr. Ives-Pope," he said, smiling a little. "Once I took a flyer in Wall Street and I think you've got some of my money. This, sir, is my son Ellery, who is the brains and beauty of the Queen family."

The big man's eyes measured Ellery's bulk appreciatively. He shook hands, saying, "You've got a smart father there, son!"

"Well!" sighed the District Attorney, setting three chairs. "I'm glad that's over. You haven't the slightest idea, Mr. Ives-Pope, how nervous I've been about this meeting. Queen is the devil himself when it comes to the social amenities and I shouldn't have been surprised if he had clapped his handcuffs on you as you shook hands!"

The tension snapped with the big man's hearty chuckle.

The District Attorney came abruptly to the point. "Mr. Ives-Pope is here, Q, to find out for himself just what can be done in the matter of his daughter." Queen nodded. Sampson turned to the financier. "As I told you before, sir, we have every confidence in Inspector Queen—always have had. He generally works without any check or supervision from the District Attorney's office. In view of the circumstances, I thought I should make that clear."

"That's a sane method, Sampson," said Ives-Pope, with approval. "I've always worked on that principle in my own business. Besides, from what I've heard about Inspector Queen, your confidence is well placed."

"Sometimes," said Queen gravely, "I have to do things that go against the grain. I will be frank to say that some things I did last night in the line of duty were extremely disagreeable to me. I suppose, Mr. Ives-Pope, your daughter is upset because of our little talk last night?"

Ives-Pope was silent for a moment. Then he raised his head and met the Inspector's gaze squarely. "Look here, Inspector," he said. "We're both men of the world and men of business. We've had dealings with all sorts of queer people, both of us; and we have, too, solved problems that presented enormous difficulties to others. So I think we can converse frankly. . . . Yes, my daughter Frances is more than a little upset. Incidentally, so is her mother, who is an ill woman at the best of times; and her brother Stanford, my son—but we needn't go into that. . . . Frances told me last night when she got home with—her friends—everything that happened. I know my daughter, Inspector, and I'd stake my fortune that there isn't the slightest connection between her and Field."

"My dear sir," returned the Inspector quietly, "I didn't accuse her of anything. Nobody knows better than I what peculiar things can happen in the course of a criminal investigation; therefore I never let the slightest blind spot escape my notice. All I did was to ask her to identify the bag. When she did so, I told her where it was found. I was waiting, of course, for an explanation. It did not come. . . . You must understand, Mr. Ives-Pope, that when a man is murdered and a woman's bag is found in his pocket it is the duty of the police to discover the owner of the bag and his or her connection with the crime. But of course—I do not have to convince you of that."

The magnate drummed on the arm of his chair. "I see your point of view, Inspector," he said. "It was obviously your duty, and it is still your duty to go to the bottom of the thing. In fact, I want you to make every effort to. My own personal opinion is that she is the victim of circumstances. But I don't want to plead her case. I trust you sufficiently to rely on your judgment after you've thoroughly probed the problem." He paused. "Inspector Queen, how would you like to have me arrange a little interview at my home tomorrow morning? I would not ask you to go to this trouble," he added apologetically, "except that Frances is quite ill, and her mother insists she stay at home. May we expect you?"

"Very good of you, Mr. Ives-Pope," remarked Queen calmly. "We'll be there."

The financier seemed indisposed to end the interview. He shifted heavily in his chair. "I've always been a fair man, Inspector," he said. "I feel somehow that I may be accused of using my position as a means of securing special privileges. That is not so. The shock of your tactics last night made it impossible for Frances to tell her story. At home, among the members of her family, I am sure she will be able to clear up her connection with the affair to your satisfaction." He hesitated for a moment, then continued in a colder tone. "Her fiancé will be there and perhaps his presence will help to calm her." His voice expressed the thought that he personally did not think so. "May we expect you, let us say, at ten-thirty?"

"That will be fine," said Queen, nodding. "I should like to know more definitely, sir, just who will be present."

"I can arrange it as you wish, Inspector," replied Ives-Pope, "but I imagine Mrs. Ives-Pope will want to be there and I know that Mr. Barry will—my future son-in-law," he explained dryly. "Perhaps a few of Frances' friends—theatrical friends. My son Stanford may also grace us with his presence—a very busy young man, you know," he added with a suspicion of bitterness.

The three men shifted embarrassedly. Ives-Pope rose with a sigh and Ellery, Queen and Sampson followed suit. "That's all, I think, Inspector," said the financier in a lighter tone. "Is there anything else I can do?"

"Not a thing."

"Then I'll be getting along." Ives-Pope turned to Ellery and Sampson.

"Of course, Sampson, if you can get away, I'd like you to be there. Do you think you can make it?" The District Attorney nodded. "And Mr. Queen"—the big man turned to Ellery—"will you come also? I understand that you have been following the investigation very closely at your father's side. We shall be happy to have you."

"I'll be there," said Ellery softly, and Ives-Pope left the office.

"Well, what do you think, Q?" asked Sampson, fidgeting in his swivel chair.

"A most interesting man," returned the Inspector. "How fairminded he is!"

"Oh, yes—yes," said Sampson. "Er—Q, he asked me before you came if you wouldn't go easy on the publicity. Sort of special favor, you know."

"He didn't have the nerve to come out with it to me, eh?" chuckled the Inspector. "He's quite human. . . . Well, Henry, I'll do my best, but if that young woman is implicated seriously, I won't vouch for hands off with the press."

"All right, all right, Q—it's up to you," said Sampson irritably. "Damn this throat of mine!" He took an atomizer from a desk drawer and sprinkled his throat wryly.

"Didn't Ives-Pope recently donate a hundred thousand dollars to the Chemical Research Foundation?" asked Ellery suddenly, turning to Sampson.

"I seem to remember something of that sort," said Sampson, gargling. "Why?"

Ellery mumbled an inaudible explanation that was lost in Sampson's violent gyrations with the sprayer. Queen, who was regarding his son speculatively, shook his head, consulted his watch and said, "Well, son, it's time we knocked off for lunch. What do you say—Henry, think you'd like to join us in a bite?"

Sampson grinned with an effort. "I'm full up to my neck with work, but even a District Attorney has to eat," he said. "I'll go on only one condition—that I pay the check. I owe you something, anyway."

As they donned their coats Queen picked up Sampson's telephone.

"Mr. Morgan? . . . Oh, hello, Morgan. I say, do you think you can find a little time this afternoon for a chat? . . . Right. Two-thirty will be fine. Good-by."

"That settles that," said the Inspector comfortably. "Always pays to be polite, Ellery—remember that."

At two-thirty promptly the two Queens were ushered into the quiet law office of Benjamin Morgan. It was noticeably different from Field's lavish suite—richly furnished but with a more businesslike simplicity. A smiling young woman closed the door after them. Morgan greeted them with some reserve. He held out a box of cigars as they sat down.

"No thanks—my snuff will do," said the Inspector genially, while Ellery after being introduced lit a cigarette and blew smoke rings. Morgan lit a cigar with shaking fingers.

"I suppose you're here to continue that talk of ours last night, Inspector?" said Morgan.

Queen sneezed, replaced his snuffbox, and leaned back in the chair. "Look here, Morgan old man," he said evenly. "You haven't been quite on the up-and-up with me."

"What do you mean?" asked Morgan, coloring.

"You told me last night," said the Inspector reflectively, "you told me last night that you parted amicably with Field two years ago, when you dissolved the firm of Field & Morgan. Did you say that?"

"I did," said Morgan.

"How, then, my dear fellow," asked Queen, "do you explain the little incident of the quarrel at the Webster Club? I certainly would not call a threat against another man's life an 'amicable' way of dissolving a partnership!"

Morgan sat quietly for several minutes while Queen stared patiently at him and Ellery sighed. Then he looked up and began to speak in a passionate undertone.

"I'm sorry, Inspector," he muttered, glancing away. "I might have known that a threat like that would be remembered by somebody. . . . Yes, it's true enough. We had lunch one day in the Webster Club at Field's suggestion. As far as I was concerned, the less I had to do with him socially the better I liked it. But the purpose of the luncheon was to go over some last details of the dissolution, and of course I had no choice. . . . I'm afraid I lost my temper. I did make a threat against his life, but it was—well, it was said in the heat of an angry moment. I forgot the whole thing before the week was over."

The Inspector nodded sagely. "Yes, things do happen like that sometimes. But"—and Morgan licked his lips in despairing anticipation—"a man doesn't threaten another man's life, even if he doesn't mean it, merely over a matter of business detail." He leveled his finger at Morgan's shrinking body. "Come on now, man—out with it. What are you holding back?"

Morgan's entire body had gone flaccid. His lips were ashy as he turned from one Queen to the other, mute appeal in his eyes. But their glances were inexorable and Ellery, who was regarding him much as a vivisectionist regards a guinea pig, interrupted.

"My dear Morgan," he said coldly, "Field had something on you, and he thought that that was a good time to tell you about it. It's as obvious as the red in your eye."

"You've guessed it in part, Mr. Queen. I've been one of the most unfortunate men God ever created. That devil Field—whoever killed him deserves to be decorated for his service to humanity. He was an octopus—a soulless beast in human form. I can't tell you how happy—yes, happy!— I am that he is dead!"

"Softly there, Morgan," said Queen. "Although I gather our mutual friend was a good deal of a skunk, your remarks might be overheard by a less sympathetic audience. And—?"

"Here's the whole story," mumbled Morgan, his eyes fixed on the desk blotter. "It's a hard one to tell. . . . When I was a kid at college I got into some trouble with a girl—a waitress in the college restaurant. She was not bad—just weak, and I suppose I was wild in those days. At any rate she had a child—my child. . . . I suppose you know that I come from a straitlaced family. If you don't, you would find out soon enough on investigation. They had great plans for me, they were socially ambitious— to cut it short, I couldn't very well marry the girl and bring her to father's house as my wife. It was a caddish thing to do. . . ."

He paused.

"But it was done, and that's all that matters. I've—I've always loved her. She was sensible enough about the arrangements. . . . I managed to provide for her out of my generous allowance. No one—I'll swear not a soul in this world with the exception of her widowed mother, a fine old lady—knew about the affair. I'll swear to that, I say. And yet—" His fist clenched, but he resumed with a sigh. "Eventually, I married the girl whom my family had selected for me." There was a painful silence as he stopped to clear his throat. "It was a *mariage de convenance*—just that and nothing else. She came from an old aristocratic family, and I had the money. We have lived fairly happily together. . . . And then I met Field. I curse the day I ever consented to go into partnership with him—but my own business was not exactly all it might have been and Field, if nothing else, was an aggressive and clever lawyer."

The Inspector took a pinch of snuff.

"Everything went smoothly at first," continued Morgan in the same low tone. "But by degrees I began to suspect that my partner was not everything he should have been. Queer clients—queer clients indeed— would enter his private office after hours; he would evade my questions about them; things began to look peculiar. Finally I decided my own reputation would suffer if I continued to be linked with the man, and I broached the subject of dissolution. Field objected strenuously, but I was stubborn and after all he could not dominate my desires. We dissolved." *Please see page 25*

Ellery's fingers tapped an absent tattoo on the handle of his stick.

"Then the affair at the Webster. He insisted we have lunch together for the settlement of the last few details. That wasn't his purpose at all, of course. You can guess, I suppose, his intentions. . . . He came out quite suavely with the overwhelming statement that he knew I was supporting a woman and my illegitimate child. He said that he had some of my letters to prove it, and a number of cancelled vouchers of checks I had sent her. . . . He admitted he had stolen them from me. I hadn't looked at them for years, of course. . . . Then he blandly announced that he meant to make capital out of this evidence!"

"Blackmail!" muttered Ellery, a light creeping into his eyes.

"Yes, blackmail," retorted Morgan bitterly. "Nothing less. He described in very graphic terms what would happen if the story should come out. Oh, Field was a clever crook! I saw the entire structure of social position I had built up—a process which took years—destroyed in an instant. My wife, her family, my own family—and more than that, the circle in which we moved—I shouldn't have been able to lift my head out of the muck. And as for business—well, it doesn't take much to make important clients go elsewhere for their legal work. I was trapped—I knew it and he knew it."

"Just how much did he want, Morgan?" asked Queen.

"Enough! He wanted twenty-five thousand dollars—just to keep quiet. I didn't even have any assurances that the affair would end there. I was caught and caught properly. Because, remember, this was not an affair which had died years before. I was still supporting that poor woman and my son. I am supporting them now. I will—continue to support them." He stared at his fingernails.

"I paid the money," he resumed morosely. "It meant stretching a bit but I paid it. But the harm was done. I saw red there at the Club, and— but you know what happened."

"And this blackmail has continued all the while, Morgan?" asked the Inspector.

"Yes, sir—for two solid years. The man was insatiable, I tell you! Even today I can't completely understand it. He must have been earning tremendous fees in his own practice, and yet he always seemed to be needing money. No small change, either—I have never paid him less than ten thousand dollars at one time!"

Queen and Ellery looked at each other fleetingly. Queen said, "Well, Morgan, it's a pretty kettle of fish. The more I hear about Field the more I dislike putting the irons on the fellow who did away with him. However! In the light of what you've told me, your statement last night that you hadn't seen Field for two years is patently untrue. When *did* you see him last?"

Morgan appeared to be racking his memory. "Oh, it was about two months ago, Inspector," he said at last.

The Inspector shifted in his chair. "I see. . . . I'm sorry you didn't tell me all this last night. You understand, of course, that your story is perfectly safe with the police. And it's mighty vital information. Now then—do you happen to know a woman by the name of Angela Russo?"

Morgan stared. "Why, no, Inspector. I've never heard of her."

Queen was silent for a moment. "Do you know a gentleman called 'Parson Johnny'?"

"I think I can give you some information there, Inspector. I'm certain that during our partnership Field was using the little thug for some shady business of his own. I caught him sneaking up into the office a number of times after hours, and when I asked Field about him, he would sneer and say, 'Oh, that's only Parson Johnny, a friend of mine!' But it was sufficient to establish the man's identity. What their connection was I can't tell you, because I don't know."

"Thanks, Morgan," said the Inspector. "I'm glad you told me that. And now—one last question. Have you ever heard the name Charles Michaels?"

"To be sure I have," responded Morgan grimly. "Michaels was Field's so-called valet—he acted in the capacity of bodyguard and was really a blackguard, or I'm greatly mistaken in my judgment of men. He came to the office once in a while. I can't think of anything else about him, Inspector."

"He knows you, of course?" asked Queen.

"Why—I suppose so," returned Morgan doubtfully. "I never spoke to him, but undoubtedly he saw me during his visits to the office."

"Well, now, that's fine, Morgan," grunted Queen, rising. "This has been a most interesting and informative chat. And—no, I don't think there's anything else. That is, at the moment. Just ride along, Morgan, and keep in town—available if we need you for anything. Remember that, won't you?"

"I'm not likely to forget it," said Morgan dully. "And—of course the story I told you—about my son—it won't come out?"

"You needn't have the slightest fear—about that, Morgan," said Queen, and a few moments later he and Ellery were on the sidewalk.

"So it was blackmail, Dad," murmured Ellery. "That gives me an idea, do you know?"

"Well, son, I've a few ideas of my own!" chuckled Queen, and in a telepathic silence they walked briskly down the street in the direction of headquarters.

# 12

## In Which the Queens Invade Society

Wednesday morning found Djuna pouring the coffee before a bemused Inspector and a chattering Ellery. The telephone bell rang. Both Ellery and his father jumped for the instrument.

"Here! What are you doing?" exclaimed Queen. "I'm expecting a call and that's it!"

"Now, now, sir, allow a bibliophile the privilege of using his own telephone," retorted Ellery. "I have a feeling that that's my friend the bookdealer calling me about the elusive Falconer."

"Look here, Ellery, don't start—" While they were chaffing each other good-naturedly across the table, Djuna picked up the telephone.

"The Inspector—the Inspector, did you say? Inspector," said Djuna, grinning as he held the mouthpiece to his thin chest, "it's for you."

Ellery subsided in his chair while Queen, with an air of triumph, snatched the instrument.

"Yes?"

"Stoates calling from Field's office, Inspector," came a fresh cheery young voice. "I want to put Mr. Cronin on the wire."

The Inspector's brow wrinkled in anticipation. Ellery was listening intently, and even Djuna, with the monkeylike eagerness of his sharp features, had become rooted to his corner, as if he, too, awaited important news. Djuna in this respect resembled his brother anthropoid—there was an alertness, a bright inquisitiveness in his attitude and mien which delighted the Queens eternally.

Finally a high-pitched voice came over the wire. "This is Tim Cronin speaking, Inspector," came Cronin's excited tones. "As you know, I've been watching this bird Field for years. He's been my pet nightmare for as long as I can remember. The D. A. tells me that he gave you the story night before last, so I needn't go into it. But in all these years of watching and waiting and digging I've never been able to find a solitary piece of evidence against that crook that I could bring into a courtroom. And he was a crook, Inspector—I'd stake my life on that. . . . Anyway, it's the old story here. I really shouldn't have hoped for anything better, knowing Field as I did. And yet—well, I couldn't help praying that somewhere, somehow, he would slip up, and that I'd nail it when I could get my hands on his private records. Inspector—there's nothing doing."

Queen's face reflected a fleeting disappointment, which Ellery interpreted with a sigh, rising as he did so to walk restlessly up and down the room.

"I guess we can't help it, Tim," returned Queen, with an effort at heartiness. "Don't worry—we've other irons in the fire."

"Inspector," said Cronin abruptly, "you've got your hands full. Field was a really slick article. And from the way it looks to me, the genius who could get past his guard and put him away is a really slick article, too. He couldn't be anything else. Incidentally, we're not halfway through with the files and maybe what we've looked over isn't as unpromising as I made it sound. There's plenty here to suggest shady work on Field's part—it's just that there's no direct incriminating evidence. We're hoping that we find something as we go on."

"All right, Tim—keep up the good work," muttered the Inspector. "And let me know how you make out. . . . Is Lewin there?"

"You mean the office manager?" Cronin's voice lowered. "He's around somewhere. Why?"

"You want to keep your eye peeled," said Queen. "I have a sneaking suspicion he's not as stupid as he sounds. Just don't let him get too familiar with any records lying around. For all we know, he may have been in on Field's little sideline."

"Right, Inspector. Call you sometime later," and the receiver clicked as Cronin hung up.

At ten-thirty Queen and Ellery pushed open the high gate at the entrance to the Ives-Pope residence on Riverside Drive. Ellery was moved to remark that the atmosphere was a perfect invitation to formal morning dress and that he was going to feel extremely uncomfortable when they were admitted through the stone portals.

In truth, the house which concealed the destinies of the Ives-Popes was in many respects awe-inspiring to men of the modest tastes of the Queens. It was a huge rambling old stone house, set far back from the Drive, hunched on the greensward of a respectable acreage. "Must have cost a pretty penny," grunted the Inspector as his eyes swept the rolling lawns surrounding the building. Gardens and summer-houses; walks and bowered nooks—one would have thought himself miles away from the city which roared by a scant few rods away, behind the high iron palings which circled the mansion. The Ives-Popes were immensely wealthy and brought to this not uncommon possession a lineage stretching back into the dim recesses of American colonization.

The front door was opened by a whiskered patrician whose back seemed composed of steel and whose nose was elevated at a perilous angle toward the ceiling. Ellery lounged in the doorway, surveying this uniformed nobleman with admiration, while Inspector Queen fumbled in his pockets for a card. He was a long time producing one; the stiff-backed flunkey stood graven into stone. Red-faced, the Inspector finally discovered a battered card. He placed it on the extended salver and watched the butler retreat to some cavern of his own.

Ellery chuckled as his father drew himself up at the sight of Franklin Ives-Pope's burly figure emerging from a wide carved doorway.

The financier hurried toward them.

"Inspector! Mr. Queen!" he exclaimed in a cordial tone. "Come right in. Have you been waiting long?"

The Inspector mumbled a greeting. They walked through a high-ceilinged shining-floored hall, decorated with austere old furniture.

"You're on the dot, gentlemen," said Ives-Pope, standing aside to allow them to pass into a large room. "Here are some additional members of our little board meeting. I think you know all of us present."

The Inspector and Ellery looked about. "I know everybody, sir, except that gentleman—I presume he is Mr. Stanford Ives-Pope," said Queen. "I'm afraid my son has still to make the acquaintance of—Mr. Peale, is it?—Mr. Barry—and, of course, Mr. Ives-Pope."

The introductions were made in a strained fashion. "Ah, Q!" murmured District Attorney Sampson, hurrying across the room. "I wouldn't have missed this for the world," he said in a low tone. "First time I've met most of the people who'll be present at the inquisition."

"What is that fellow Peale doing here?" muttered Queen to the District Attorney, while Ellery crossed the room to engage the three young men on the other side in conversation. Ives-Pope had excused himself and disappeared.

"He's a friend of young Ives-Pope, and, of course, he's chummy with Barry there, too," returned the District Attorney. "I gathered from the chitchat before you came that Stanford, Ives-Pope's son, originally introduced these professional people to his sister Frances. That's how she met Barry and fell in love with him. Peale seems on good terms with the young lady, too."

"I wonder how much Ives-Pope and his aristocratic spouse like the bourgeois company their children keep," said the Inspector, eyeing the small group on the other side of the room with interest.

"You'll find out soon enough," chuckled Sampson. "Just watch the icicles dripping from Mrs. Ives-Pope's eyebrows every time she sees one of these actors. I imagine they're about as welcome as a bunch of Bolsheviks."

Queen put his hands behind his back and stared curiously about the room. It was a library, well stocked with rich and rare books, catalogued carefully and immaculate behind shining glass. A desk dominated the center of the room. It was unpretentious for a millionaire's study, the Inspector noted with approval.

"Incidentally," resumed Sampson, "Eve Ellis, the girl who you said was with Miss Ives-Pope and her fiancé at the Roman Theatre Monday night is here, too. She's upstairs keeping the little heiress company, I imagine. Don't think the old lady likes it much. But they're both charming girls."

"What a pleasant place this must be when the Ives-Popes and the actors get together in private!" grunted Queen.

The four young men strolled towards them. Stanford Ives-Pope was a slender, well-manicured young man, fashionably dressed. There were deep pouches under his eyes. He wore a restless air of boredom that Queen was quick to note. Both Peale and Barry, the actors, were attired faultlessly.

"Mr. Queen tells me that you've got a pretty problem on your hands, Inspector," drawled Stanford Ives-Pope. "We're all uncommonly sorry to see poor Sis dragged into it. How in the world did her purse ever get into that chap's pocket? Barry hasn't slept for days over Frances' predicament, I give you my word!"

"My dear young man," said the Inspector, with a twinkle in his eye, "if I knew how Miss Ives-Pope's purse found its way into Monte Field's pocket, I wouldn't be here this morning. That's just one of the things that make this case so infernally interesting."

"The pleasure's all yours, Inspector. But you certainly can't think Frances had the slightest connection with all this?"

Queen smiled. "I can't think anything yet, young man," he protested. "I haven't heard what your sister has to say about it."

"She'll explain all right, Inspector," said Stephen Barry, his handsome face drawn into lines of fatigue. "You needn't worry about that. It's the damnable suspicion that she's open to that makes me angry—the whole thing is ridiculous!"

"I know just how you feel, Mr. Barry," said the Inspector kindly. "And

I want to take this opportunity of apologizing for my conduct the other night. I was perhaps a little—harsh."

"I suppose I ought to apologize, too," returned Barry, with a wan smile. "I guess I said a few things I didn't mean in that office. In the heat of the moment—seeing Frances—Miss Ives-Pope go off in a faint—" He paused awkwardly.

Peale, a massive giant, ruddy and wholesome in his morning clothes, put his arm affectionately about Barry's shoulders. "I'm sure the Inspector understood, Steve old boy," he said cheerfully. "Don't take it so much to heart—everything's bound to come out all right."

"You can leave it to Inspector Queen," said Sampson, nudging the Inspector jovially in the ribs. "He's the only bloodhound I've ever met who has a heart under his badge—and if Miss Ives-Pope can clear this thing up to his satisfaction, even to a reasonable extent, that will be the end of it."

"Oh, I don't know," murmured Ellery thoughtfully. "Dad's a great one for surprises. As for Miss Ives-Pope"—he smiled ruefully and bowed to the actor—"Mr. Barry, you're a deucedly lucky fellow."

"You wouldn't think so if you saw the mater," drawled Stanford Ives-Pope. "If I'm not mistaken, here she barges in now."

The men turned toward the door. An enormously stout woman was waddling in. A uniformed nurse supported her carefully under one huge arm, holding a large green bottle in her other hand. The financier followed briskly, by the side of a white-haired youngish looking man, wearing a dark coat and holding a black bag in his hand.

"Catharine, my dear," said Ives-Pope in a low voice to the stout woman as she sank into a greatchair, "these are the gentlemen whom I told you about—Inspector Richard Queen and Mr. Ellery Queen."

The two Queens bowed, receiving a stony glance from the myopic eyes of Mrs. Ives-Pope. "Charmed, I'm sure," she shrilled. "Where's Nurse? Nurse! I feel faint, please."

The uniformed girl hurried to her side, the green bottle ready. Mrs. Ives-Pope closed her eyes and inhaled, sighing with relief. The financier hurriedly introduced the white-haired man, Dr. Vincent Cornish, the family physician. The physician made swift apologies and disappeared behind the butler. "Great chap, this Cornish," whispered Sampson to Queen. "Not only the most fashionable doctor on the Drive, but a genuine scientist as well." The Inspector elevated his brows, but said nothing.

"The mater's one reason why I never cared for the medical profession," Stanford Ives-Pope was saying in a loud whisper to Ellery.

"Ah! Frances, my dear!" Ives-Pope hurried forward, followed by Barry, who dashed for the door. Mrs. Ives-Pope's fishy stare enveloped his back with cold disapproval. James Peale coughed embarrassedly and made a mumbled remark to Sampson.

Frances, attired in a filmy morning gown, her face pale and drawn, entered the room leaning heavily on the arm of Eve Ellis, the actress. Her smile was somewhat forced as she murmured a greeting to the Inspector. Eve Ellis was introduced by Peale and the two girls seated themselves near Mrs. Ives-Pope. The old lady was sitting squarely in her chair, glaring about her like a lioness whose cub has been threatened. Two servants appeared silently and set chairs for the men. At Ives-Pope's urgent request Queen sat down at the big desk. Ellery refused a chair, preferring to lean against a bookcase behind and to the side of the company.

When the conversation had died away the Inspector cleared his throat and turned toward Frances, who after a startled flutter of the eyelids returned his glance steadily.

"First of all Miss Frances—I hope I may call you that," began Queen in a fatherly tone, "allow me to explain my tactics of Monday night and to apologize for what must have seemed to you a totally unwarranted severity. From what Mr. Ives-Pope has told me, you can explain your actions on the night of the murder of Monte Field. I take it, therefore, that as far as you are concerned our little chat this morning will effectually remove you from the investigation. Before we have that chat, please believe me when I say that Monday night you were to me merely one of a number of suspicious characters. I acted in accordance with my habits in such cases. I see now how, to a woman of your breeding and social position, a grilling by a policeman under such tense circumstances would cause sufficient shock to bring on your present condition."

Frances smiled wearily. "You're forgiven, Inspector," she said in a clear, low voice. "It was my fault for being so foolish. I'm ready to answer any questions you may care to ask me."

"In just a moment, my dear." The Inspector shifted a bit to include the entire silent company in his next remark. "I should like to make one point, ladies and gentlemen," he said gravely. "We are assembled here for a definite purpose, which is to discover a possible connection, and there must be one, between the fact that Miss Ives-Pope's bag was found in the dead man's pocket, and the fact that Miss Ives-Pope apparently was unable to explain this circumstance. Now, whether this morning's work bears fruit or not, I must ask you all to keep whatever is said a profound secret. As District Attorney Sampson knows very well, I do not generally conduct an investigation with such a large audience. But I am making this exception because I believe you are all deeply concerned in the unfortunate young lady who has been drawn into this crime. You can-

not, however, expect any consideration at my hands if one word of today's conversation reaches outside ears. Do we understand each other?"

"I say, Inspector," protested young Ives-Pope, "that's putting it a bit
strong, don't you think? We all of us know the story, anyway."

"Perhaps, Mr. Ives-Pope," retorted the Inspector with a grim smile,
"that is the reason I have consented to have all of you here."

There was a little rustle and Mrs. Ives-Pope opened her mouth as if to
burst into wrathful speech. A sharp look from her husband made her lips
droop together, with the protest unuttered. She transferred her glare to the
actress sitting by Frances' side. Eve Ellis blushed. The nurse stood by
Mrs. Ives-Pope with the smelling salts, like a setter dog about to point.

"Now, Miss Frances," resumed Queen kindly, "this is where we stand.
I examine the body of a dead man named Monte Field, prominent lawyer,
who was apparently enjoying an interesting play before he was so unceremoniously done away with, and find, in the rear coattail pocket of his
full-dress suit, an evening bag. I identify this as yours by a few calling
cards and some personal papers inside. I say to myself, 'Aha! A lady enters the problem!'—naturally enough. And I send one of my men to summon you, with the idea of allowing you to explain a most suspicious circumstance. You come—and you faint on being confronted with your
property and the news of its place of discovery. At the time, I say to myself, 'This young lady knows something!'—a not unnatural conclusion.
Now, in what way can you convince me that you know nothing—and that
your fainting was caused only by the shock of the thing? Remember,
Miss Frances—I am putting the problem not as Richard Queen but as a
policeman looking for the truth."

"My story is not as illuminating, perhaps, as you might like it to be,
Inspector," answered Frances quietly, in the deep hush that followed
Queen's peroration. "I don't see how it is going to help you at all. But
some facts which I think unimportant may be significant to your trained
mind. . . . Roughly, this is what happened.

"I came to be in the Roman Theatre Monday night in a natural way.
Since my engagement to Mr. Barry, although it has been a very quiet affair"—Mrs. Ives-Pope sniffed; her husband looked steadfastly at a point
beyond his daughter's dark hair—"I have often dropped into the theatre,
following a habit of meeting my fiancé after the performance. At such
times he would either escort me home or take me to some place in the
neighborhood for supper. Generally we make arrangements beforehand
for these theatre meetings; but sometimes I drop in unexpectedly if the
opportunity presents itself. Monday night was one of those times. . . .

"I got to the Roman a few minutes before the end of the first act, since
I have of course seen 'Gunplay' any number of times. I had my regular

seat—arranged for me many weeks ago by Mr. Barry through Mr. Panzer—and had no more than settled myself to watch the performance when the curtain came down for the first intermission. I was feeling a little warm; the air was none too good. . . . I went first to the ladies' restroom downstairs off the general lounge. Then I came up again and went out into the alley through the open door. There was quite a crowd of people there, enjoying the air."

She paused for a moment and Ellery, leaning against the bookcase, sharply surveyed the faces of the little audience. Mrs. Ives-Pope was looking about in her leviathan manner: Ives-Pope was still staring at the wall above Frances' head; Stanford was biting his fingernails; Peale and Barry were both watching Frances with nervous sympathy, looking furtively at Queen as if to gauge the effect of her words upon him; Eve Ellis' hand had stolen forward to clasp Frances' firmly.

The Inspector cleared his throat once more.

"Which alley was it, Miss Frances—the one on the left or the one on the right?" he asked.

"The one on the left, Inspector," she answered promptly. "You know I was sitting in M8 Left, and I suppose it was natural for me to go to the alley on that side."

"Quite so," said Queen smiling. "Go on, please."

"I stepped out into the alley," she resumed, less nervously, "and, not seeing any one I knew, stood close to the brick wall of the theatre, a little behind the open iron door. The freshness of the night air after the rain was delightful. I hadn't been standing there more than two minutes when I felt somebody brush up against me. I naturally moved a little to one side, thinking the person had stumbled. But when he—it was a man— when he did it again, I became a little frightened and started to walk away. He—he grasped my wrist and pulled me back. We were halfway behind the iron door, which was not pushed back completely and I doubt if anyone noticed his action."

"I see—I see," murmured the Inspector sympathetically. "It seems an unusual thing for a total stranger to do in a public place."

"It seemed as if he wanted to kiss me, Inspector. He leaned over and whispered, 'Good evening, honey!' and—well, of course, I jumped to that conclusion. I drew back a little and said as coldly as I could, 'Please let me go, or I will call for help.' He just laughed at that and bent closer. The reek of whisky on his breath was overpowering. It made me ill."

She stopped. Eve Ellis patted her hand reassuringly. Peale nudged Barry forcibly as the young man half-rose to his feet in muttered protest. "Miss Frances, I'm going to ask you a peculiar question—it's almost ridiculous when you come to think of it," said the Inspector, leaning back

in his chair. "Did the reek on his breath suggest good liquor or bad
liquor? . . . There! I knew you'd smile." And the entire company tittered
at the whimsical expression on Queen's face.

"Well, Inspector—it's hard to answer that," returned the girl freely.
"I'm afraid I'm not on intimate terms with spirits. But from what I can
remember, it had the odor of rather fine liquor. Fine liquor—but plenty of
it!" she concluded with a grim little toss of her head.

"I would've spotted the vintage in a minute if I'd been there!" muttered Stanford Ives-Pope.

His father's lips tightened, but after a moment they relaxed into the
suspicion of a grin. He shook his head warningly at his son.

"Go ahead, Miss Frances," said the Inspector.

"I was terribly frightened," the girl confessed, with a tremor of her red
lips. "And feeling nauseated and all—I wrenched away from his out-
stretched hand and stumbled blindly into the theatre. The next thing I remember is sitting in my seat listening to the warning ring of the backstage bell, announcing the beginning of the second act. I really don't
remember how I got there. My heart was in my throat and now I distinctly recall thinking that I would not tell Stephen—Mr. Barry—anything about the incident for fear he would want to look up this man and
punish him. Mr. Barry is terribly jealous, you know." She smiled tenderly
at her fiancé, who suddenly smiled back at her.

"And that, Inspector, is all I know about what happened Monday
night," she resumed. "I know you're going to ask me where my purse
comes into it. Well—it doesn't at all, Inspector. Because on my word of
honor I can't remember a thing about it!"

Queen shifted in his chair. "And how is that, Miss Frances?"

"Actually, I didn't even know I had lost it until you showed it to me in
the manager's office," she answered bravely. "I recall taking it with me
when I rose at the end of the first act to go to the restroom; and also opening it there to use my powderpuff. But whether I left it there or dropped it
later, somewhere else, I don't know to this minute."

"Don't you think, Miss Frances," interposed Queen, reaching for his
snuffbox and then guiltily dropping it back into his pocket as he met the
icy gaze of Mrs. Ives-Pope, "that you might have dropped it in the alley
after this man accosted you?"

A look of relief spread over the girl's face, and it became almost animated. "Why, Inspector!" she cried. "That was just what I have thought
about it all the time, but it seemed such a lame explanation—and I was so
horribly afraid that I might be caught in a sort of—of spider's web. . . . I
just couldn't bring myself to tell you that! While I don't actually remem-

ber, it seems logical, doesn't it?—that I dropped it when he grasped my wrist and entirely forgot about it afterward."

The Inspector smiled. "On the contrary, my dear," he said, "it is the only explanation which seems to cover the facts. In all probability this man found it there—picked it up—and in a moment of half-drunken amorousness put it into his pocket, probably intending to return it to you later. In this way he would have had another opportunity to meet you. He seems to have been quite smitten by your charms, my dear—and no wonder." And the Inspector bowed a little stiffly while the girl, the color in her face now completely restored, favored him with a dazzling smile.

"Now—a few things more, Miss Frances, and this little inquisition will be over," continued Queen. "Can you describe his physical appearance?"

"Oh, yes!" Frances returned quickly. "He made a rather forcible impression on me, as you can imagine. He was a trifle taller than I—that would make him about five feet eight—and inclined to corpulence. His face was bloated and he had deep leaden-colored pouches under his eyes. I've never seen a more dissipated-looking man. He was clean-shaven. There was nothing remarkable about his features except perhaps a prominent nose."

"That would be our friend Mr. Field, all right," remarked the Inspector grimly. "Now—think carefully, Miss Frances. Did you ever meet this man anywhere before—did you recognize him at all?"

The girl responded instantly. "I don't have to think much about that, Inspector. I can answer positively that I never saw the man before in my life!"

The pause which ensued was broken by the cool, even tones of Ellery. All heads turned toward him in a startled manner as he spoke.

"I beg your pardon, Miss Ives-Pope, for interrupting," he said affably. "But I am curious to know whether you noticed how the man who accosted you was dressed."

Frances turned her smile upon Ellery, who blinked quite humanly. "I didn't take particular notice of his clothes, Mr. Queen," she said, displaying white, brilliant teeth. "But I seem to remember his wearing a full-dress suit—his shirt bosom was a little stained—they were like liquor stains—and a tophat. From what I recall of his attire, it was rather fastidious and in good taste, except, of course, for the stains on his shirt."

Ellery murmured a fascinated thanks and subsided against the bookcase. With a sharp look at his son, Queen rose to his feet.

"Then that will be all, ladies and gentlemen. I think we may safely consider the incident closed."

There was an instantaneous little burst of approval and everybody rose to press in on Frances, who was radiant with happiness. Barry, Peale and Eve Ellis bore Frances off in triumphal march, while Stanford, with a lugubrious smile, offered his mother a carefully elbowed arm.

"Thus endeth the first lesson," he announced gravely. "Mater, my arm before you faint!" A protesting Mrs. Ives-Pope departed, leaning ponderously on her son.

Ives-Pope shook Queen's hand vigorously. "Then you think it's all over as far as my girl is concerned?" he asked.

"I think so, Mr. Ives-Pope," answered the Inspector. "Well, sir, thank you for your courtesy. And now we must be going—lots of work to do. Coming, Henry?"

Five minutes later Queen, Ellery and District Attorney Sampson were striding side by side down Riverside Drive toward 72nd Street, earnestly discussing the events of the morning.

"I'm glad that line of investigation is cleared up with no result," said Sampson dreamily. "By the Lord Harry, I admire that girl's pluck, Q!"

"Good child," said the Inspector. "What do you think, Ellery?" he asked suddenly, turning on his son, who was walking along staring at the River.

"Oh, she's charming," Ellery said at once, his abstracted eyes brightening.

"I didn't mean the girl, my son," said his father irritably. "I meant the general aspect of the morning's work."

"Oh, that!" Ellery smiled a little. "Do you mind if I become Æsopian?"

"Yes," groaned his father.

"A lion," said Ellery, "may be beholden to a mouse."

# 13

## Queen to Queen

Djuna had just cleared the table of the dinner dishes and was serving coffee to the two Queens at six-thirty that evening when the outer doorbell rang. The little man-of-all-work straightened his tie, pulled down his jacket (while the Inspector and Ellery eyed him in twinkling amusement), and marched gravely into the foyer. He was back in a moment bearing a silver tray upon which lay two calling cards. The Inspector picked them up with beetling brows. *The author certainly "captured" the world in the 1920s. A time Capsule was read these words on July 29, 1982.*

"Such ceremony, Djuna!" he murmured. "Well, well! So 'Doc' Prouty's bringing a visitor. Show 'em in, you imp!"

Djuna marched back and returned with the Chief Assistant Medical Examiner and a tall, thin, emaciated man, entirely bald and wearing a closely clipped beard. Queen and Ellery rose.

"I've been expecting to hear from you, Doc!" Queen grinned, shaking hands with Prouty. "And if I'm not mistaken, here's Professor Jones himself! Welcome to our castle, Doctor." The thin man bowed.

"This is my son and keeper of my conscience, Doctor," Queen added, presenting Ellery. "Ellery—Dr. Thaddeus Jones."

Dr. Jones offered a large limp hand. "So you're the chap Queen and Sampson keep prattling about!" he boomed. "Certainly happy to meet you, sir."

"I've been fairly itching to be introduced to New York City's Paracelsus and eminent Toxicologist," smiled Ellery. "The honor of rattling the city's skeletons is all yours." He shuddered elaborately and indicated some chairs. The four men sat down.

"Join us in some coffee, gentlemen," urged Queen, and shouted to Djuna, whose bright eyes were visible from behind the kitchenette door. "Djuna! You rascal! Coffee for four!" Djuna grinned and disappeared, to pop out a moment later like a jack-in-the-box, bearing four cups of steaming coffee. yum  *I AM a coffee fan!  July 23, 2011*

Prouty, who resembled the popular conception of Mephistopheles, whipped from his pocket one of his black, dangerous-looking cigars and began to puff away furiously.

"This chitter-chatter may be all right for you men of leisure," he said briskly, between puffs, "but I've been working like a beaver all day analyzing the contents of a lady's stomach, and I want to get home for some sleep."

"Hear, hear!" murmured Ellery, "I gather from your soliciting the aid of Professor Jones that you met with some obstruction in your analysis of Mr. Field's corporeal remains. Lay on, Æsculapius!"

"I'll lay on," returned Prouty grimly. "You're right—I met with a violent obstruction. I've had some little experience, if you'll pardon the professional modesty, in examining the innards of deceased ladies and gentlemen, but I'll confess I never saw 'em in such a mess as this chap Field's. Seriously, Jones will attest to the truth of *that*. His æsophagus, for example, and the entire tracheal tract looked as if some one had taken a blowtorch and played it gently over his insides."

"What was it—couldn't have been bichloride of mercury, could it, Doc?" asked Ellery, who prided himself on a complete ignorance of the exact sciences.

"Hardly," growled Prouty. "But let me tell you what happened. I analyzed for every poison on the calendar, and although this one had familiar petroleum components I couldn't place it exactly. Yes, sir—I was stumped good and proper. And to let you in on a secret—the Medical Examiner himself, who thought I was pie-eyed from overwork, made a stab at it with his own fine Italian hand. The net result in his case, my boys, was zero. And the M. E.'s not exactly a novice either when it comes to chemical analysis. So we surrendered the problem to our fountainhead of learning. Let him spout his own story."

Dr. Thaddeus Jones cleared his throat forbiddingly. "Thank you, my friend, for a most dramatic introduction," he said in his deep lumbering voice. "Yes, Inspector, the remains were turned over to me, and in all seriousness, I want to say here and now that my discovery was the most startling the Toxicologist's office has made in fifteen years!"

"My, my!" murmured Queen, taking a pinch of snuff. "I'm beginning to respect the mentality of our friend the murderer. So many things point to the unusual lately! And what did you find, Doctor?"

"I took it for granted that Prouty and the Medical Examiner had done the preliminaries very well," began Dr. Jones, crossing his bony knees. "They generally do. And so, before anything else, I analyzed for the obscure poisons. Obscure, that is to say, from the standpoint of the criminal user. To show you how minutely I searched—I even thought of that favorite standby of our friends the fiction writers: *curare*, the South American toxin which makes the grade in four out of five detective stories. But even that sadly abused member of the toxic family disappointed me. . . ."

Ellery leaned back and laughed. "If you're referring in a mildly satirical way to my profession, Dr. Jones, let me inform you that I have never used *curare* in any of my novels."

The toxicologist's eyes twinkled. "So you're one of them, too, eh? Queen, old man," he added dolorously, turning to the Inspector, who was thoughtfully chewing on a piece of French pastry, "allow me to offer you my condolences. . . . At any rate, gentlemen, let me explain that in the case of rare poisons we can generally come to a definite conclusion without much trouble—that is, rare poisons that are in the pharmacopœia. Of course, there are any number of rare poisons of which we have no knowledge whatever—Eastern drugs particularly.

"Well, to make a long story short, I found myself faced with the unpleasant conclusion that I was up a tree." Dr. Jones chuckled in reminiscence. "It wasn't a pleasant conclusion. The poison I analyzed had certain properties which were vaguely familiar, as Prouty has said, and others which didn't jibe at all. I spent most of yesterday evening mulling over my retorts and testtubes, and late last night I suddenly got the answer."

Ellery and Queen sat up straight and Dr. Prouty relaxed in his chair with a sigh, reaching for a second cup of coffee. The toxicologist uncrossed his legs, his voice booming more terrifyingly than ever.

"The poison that killed your victim, Inspector, is known as tetra ethyl lead!"

To a scientist this announcement, in Dr. Jones's profoundest tones, might have carried a dramatic quality. To the Inspector it meant less than nothing. As for Ellery, he murmured, "Sounds like a mythological monster to me!"

Dr. Jones went on, smiling. "So it hasn't impressed you much, eh? But let me tell you a little about tetra ethyl lead. It is almost odorless—to be more exact, it resembles chloroform in physical appearance. Point number one. Point number two—it has an odor—faint, to be sure—but distinctly like that of ether. Point number three—it is fearfully potent. So potent—but let me illustrate just what this devilishly powerful chemical substance will do to living tissue."

By this time the toxicologist had gained the entire attention of his audience.

"I took a healthy rabbit, of the sort we use for experiment, and

painted—just painted, mind you—the tender area behind the creature's
ear with an undiluted dose of the stuff. Remember, this was not an internal injection. It was merely a painting of the skin. It would have to be absorbed through the dermis before it reached the bloodstream. I watched
the rabbit for an hour—and after that I didn't have to watch him any
more. He was as dead as any dead rabbit I ever saw."

"That doesn't seem so powerful to me, Doctor," protested the Inspector.

"It doesn't, eh? Well, take my word for it that it's extraordinary. For a
mere daubing of whole, healthy skin—I tell you, I was astounded. If the
skin had an incision of some sort, or if the poison were administered internally, that would be a different story. You can imagine, therefore, what
happened to Field's insides when he *swallowed* the stuff—and he swallowed plenty!"

Ellery's brow was wrinkled in thought. He began to polish the lenses
of his pince-nez.

"And that isn't all," resumed Dr. Jones. "As far as I know—and I have
been in the service of the city for God knows how many years, and I've
not kept uninformed about the progress of my science in other parts of
the world, either—as far as I know, tetra ethyl lead has never before been
used for criminal purposes!"

The Inspector drew up, startled. "That's saying something, Doctor!"
he muttered. "Are you sure?"

"Positive. That's why I'm so keenly interested."

"Just how long would it take for this poison to kill a man, Doctor?"
asked Ellery slowly.

Dr. Jones grimaced. "That's something I can't answer definitely, for
the very good reason that to my knowledge no human being has ever
died of its effects before. But I can make a fairly good guess. I can't con-
ceive of Field having lived more than fifteen to twenty minutes at the utmost after having taken the poison internally."

The silence that followed was broken by a cough from Queen. "On the
other hand, Doctor, this very strangeness of the poison should make it
fairly easy to trace. What, would you say, is its commonest source?
Where does it come from? How would I go about getting it if I wanted
some for a criminal purpose and didn't want to leave a trail?"

A gaunt smile lit up the features of the toxicologist. "The job of tracing this stuff, Inspector," he said fervently, "I'll leave to you. You can
have it. Tetra ethyl lead, as far as I've been able to determine—remember, it is almost entirely new to us—occurs most commonly in certain petroleum products. I tinkered around quite a bit before I found the easiest

way of making it in quantity. You'll never guess how it's done. It can be extracted from common, ordinary, everyday gasoline!"

The two Queens exclaimed under their breaths. "Gasoline!" cried the Inspector. "Why—how on earth could a man trace that?"

"That's the point," answered the toxicologist. "I could go to the corner gas station, fill up the tank of my car, run it home, extract some of the gasoline from the tank, go into my laboratory and distill the tetra ethyl lead in remarkably little time with remarkably little effort!"

"Doesn't that imply, Doctor," put in Ellery hopefully, "that the murderer of Field had some laboratory experience—knew something about chemical analysis, and all that sort of rot?"

"No, it doesn't. Any man with a home-brew 'still' in his house could distill that poison without leaving a trace. The beauty of the process is that the tetra ethyl lead in the gasoline has a higher boiling point than any other of the fluid's constituents. All you have to do is distill everything out up to a certain temperature, and what's left is this poison."

The Inspector took a pinch of snuff with trembling fingers. "All I can say is—I take my hat off to the murderer," he muttered. "Tell me—Doctor—wouldn't a man have to know quite a bit about toxicology to possess such knowledge? How could he ever know this without some special interest—and therefore training—in the subject?"

Dr. Jones snorted. "Inspector, I'm surprised at you. Your question is already answered."

"How? What do you mean?"

"Haven't I just told you how to do it? And if you heard about the poison from a toxicologist, couldn't you make some provided you had the 'still'? You would require no knowledge except the boiling point of tetra ethyl lead. Get along with you, Queen! You haven't a chance in the world of tracing the murderer through the poison. In all probability he overheard a conversation between two toxicologists, or even between two medical men who had heard about the stuff. The rest was easy. I'm not saying this is so. The man might be a chemist, at that. But I'm concerned only in giving you the possibilities."

"I suppose it was administered in whisky, eh, Doctor?" asked Queen abstractedly.

"No doubt about it," returned the toxicologist. "The stomach showed a large whisky content. Certainly, it would be an easy way for the murderer to slip it over on his victim. With the whisky you get nowadays, most of it smells etherized, anyway. And besides, Field probably had it down before he realized anything was wrong—if he did at all."

"Wouldn't he taste the stuff?" asked Ellery wearily.

"I've never tasted it, young man, so I can't say definitely," answered

Dr. Jones, a trifle tartly. "But I doubt whether he would—sufficiently to alarm him, at any rate. Once he had it down it wouldn't make any difference."

Queen turned to Prouty, whose cigar had gone out. He had fallen into a hearty doze. "Say, Doc!"

Prouty opened his eyes sleepily. "Where are my slippers—I can't even seem to find my slippers, damn it!"

Despite the tension of the moment, there was a spontaneous roar of amusement at the expense of the Assistant Medical Examiner. When he had come to with sufficient thoroughness to understand what he had said, he joined the chuckling group and said, "Just goes to prove that I'd better be going home, Queen. What did you want to know?"

"Tell me," said Queen, still shaking, "what did you get from your analysis of the whisky?"

"Oh!" Prouty sobered instantly. "The whisky in the flask was as fine as any I've ever tested—and I've been doing nothing but testing booze for years now. It was the poison in the liquor on his breath that made me think at first that Field had drunk rotten booze. The Scotch and rye that you sent me in bottles from Field's apartment were also of the very highest quality. Probably the flask's contents came from the same place as the bottled stuff. In fact, I should say that both samples were imported goods. I haven't come across domestic liquor of that caliber ever since the war—that is, except for the pre-war stuff that was stored away. . . . And I suppose Velie communicated my report to you that the ginger ale is okay."

Queen nodded. "Well, that seems to settle it," he said heavily. "It looks as if we're up against a blank wall on this tetra ethyl lead business. But just to make sure, Doc—work along with the professor here and try to locate a possible leak somewhere in the distribution of the poison. You fellows know more about that than anybody I could put on the case. It's just a stab in the dark and probably nothing will come of it."

"There's no question about it," murmured Ellery. "A novelist should stick to his last."

--------

"I think," remarked Ellery eagerly, after the two doctors had gone, "that I'll amble down to my bookseller for that Falconer." He rose and began a hasty search for his coat.

"Here!" bellowed the Inspector, pulling him down into a chair. "Nothing doing. That blasted book of yours won't run away. I want you to sit here and keep my headache company."

Ellery nestled into the leather cushions with a sigh. "Just when I get to feeling that all investigations into the foibles of the human mind are use-less and a waste of time, my worthy sire puts the onus of thought upon me again. Heigh-ho! What's on the menu?"

"I'm not putting any onus on you at all," growled Queen. "And stop using such big words. I'm dizzy enough. What I want you to do is help me go over this confounded mess of a case and see—well, what we can see."

"I might have suspected it," said Ellery. "Where do I start?"

"You don't," grunted his father. "I'm doing the talking tonight and you're going to listen. And you might make a few notes, too.

"Let's begin with Field. I think, in the first place, that we can take it for granted our friend went to the Roman Theatre Monday night not for pleasure but for business. Right?"

"No doubt about it in my mind," said Ellery. "What did Velie report about Field's movements Monday?"

"Field got to his office at 9:30—his usual morning arrival hour. He worked until noon. He had no personal visitors all day. At twelve o'clock he lunched at the Webster Club alone, and at 1:30 returned to his office. He worked steadily until 4:00—and seems to have gone straight home, as the doorman and elevatorman both testify he arrived at the apartment about 4:30. Velie could get no further data except that Michaels arrived at 5:00 and left at 6:00. Field left at 7:30, dressed as we found him. I have a list of the clients whom he saw during the day, but it doesn't tell much."

"How about the reason for his small bank account?" asked Ellery.

"Just what I figured," returned Queen. "Field has been losing steadily on the stock market—and not chicken feed, either. Velie's just run a little tip to earth which makes Field out as a frequent visitor to the racetrack, where he's also dropped plenty. For a shrewd man, he certainly was an easy mark for the wiseacres. Anyway, that explains his having so little cash in his personal account. And more than that—it probably also explains more conclusively the item of '50,000' on the program we found. That meant money, and the money it referred to was in some way connected, I'm sure, with the person he was to meet at the theatre.

"Now, I think that we can pretty well conclude that Field knew his murderer rather intimately. For one thing, he accepted a drink obviously without suspicion, or at least question; for another, the meeting seems to have been definitely arranged for purposes of concealment—why, else, if that is not so, was the theatre chosen for the meeting at all?"

"All right. Let me ask you the same question," interposed Ellery, puckering his lips. "Why *should* a theatre be chosen as a meeting place to transact a secret and undoubtedly nefarious business? Wouldn't a park be more secret? Wouldn't a hotel lobby have its advantages? Answer that."

"Unfortunately, my son," said the Inspector mildly, "Mr. Field could have had no definite knowledge that he was going to be murdered. As far as he was concerned, all he was going to do was to take care of his part of the transaction. As a matter of fact, Field *himself* might have chosen the theatre as the place of meeting. Perhaps he wanted to establish an alibi for something. There's no way of telling yet just what he wanted to do. As for the hotel lobby—certainly he would run a grave risk of being seen. He might have been unwilling, further, to risk himself in such a lonely place as a park. And, lastly, he may have had some particular reason for not wanting to be seen in the company of the second party. Remember—the ticket stubs we found showed that the other person did not come into the theatre at the same time as Field. But this is all fruitless conjecture—"

Ellery smiled in a thoughtful manner, but said nothing. He was thinking to himself that the old man had not completely satisfied the objection, and that this was a strange thing in a man of Inspector Queen's direct habits of thought. . . .

But Queen was continuing. "Very well. We must always bear in mind the further possibility that the person with whom Field transacted his business was *not* his murderer. Of course, this is merely a possibility. The crime seems to have been too well planned for that. But if this *is* so, then we must look for *two* people in the audience Monday night who were directly connected with Field's death."

"Morgan?" asked Ellery idly.

The Inspector shrugged his shoulders. "Perhaps. Why didn't he tell us about it when we spoke to him yesterday afternoon? He confessed everything else. Well, maybe because he felt that a confession of having paid blackmail to the murdered man, together with the fact that he was found in the theatre, would be too damning a bit of circumstantial evidence."

"Look at it this way," said Ellery. "Here we find a man dead who has written on his program the number '50,000,' obviously referring to dollars. We know from what both Sampson and Cronin have told us about Field that he was a man of unscrupulous and probably criminal character. Further, we know from Morgan that he was also a blackmailer. I think, therefore, we can deduce safely that he went to the Roman Theatre on Monday night to collect or arrange for the payment of $50,000 in blackmail from some person unknown. Right so far?"

"Go ahead," grunted the Inspector noncommittally.

"Very well," continued Ellery. "If we conclude that the person blackmailed that night and the murderer were one and the same, we need look no further for a motive. There's the motive ready made—to choke off the blackmailing Field. *If*, however, we proceed on the assumption that the murderer and the person blackmailed were not the same, but two entirely different individuals, *then* we must still scrabble about looking for a motive for the crime. My personal opinion is that this is unnecessary—that the murderer and the black-mailed person are one. What do you think?"

"I'm inclined to agree with you, Ellery," said the Inspector. "I merely mentioned the other possibility—did not state my own conviction. Let us proceed, for the time being, then, on the assumption that Field's blackmail victim and his murderer were the same. . . .

"Now—I want to clear up the matter of the missing tickets."

"Ah—the missing tickets," murmured Ellery. "I was wondering what you made of that."

"Don't be funny, now, you rascal," growled Queen. "Here's what I make of it. All in all, we are dealing with eight seats—one in which Field sat, for which we have the stub found on Field's person; one in which the murderer sat, for which we have the stub found by Flint; and finally the six empty seats for which tickets were bought, as established by the box-office report, and for which stubs were not found, torn or whole, anywhere in the theatre or box office. First of all, it is barely possible that all of those six whole tickets were in the theatre Monday night, and went out of the theatre on somebody's person. Remember, the search of individuals was necessarily not so exhaustive as to include an examination for small things like tickets. This, however, is highly improbable. The best explanation is that either Field or his murderer bought all eight tickets at one time, intending to use two and reserving the other six to insure absolute privacy during the short time that the business was to be transacted. In this case, the most sensible thing to have done was to destroy the tickets as soon as they were bought; which was probably done by either Field or the murderer, according to who made the arrangements. We must, therefore, forget those six tickets—they're gone and we'll never get our hands on them.

"To proceed," continued the Inspector. "We know that Field and his victim entered the theatre separately. This may positively be deduced from the fact that when I put the two stubs back to front, the torn edges did not match. When two people enter together, the tickets are presented together and are invariably torn together. Now—this does not say that they did not come in at practically the same time, because for purposes of safety they may have come in one after the other, as if they did not know each other. However, Madge O'Connell claims no one sat in LL30 during Act I, and the orangeade boy, Jess Lynch, testified that ten minutes after Act II had started, there was still no one in LL30. This means that the murderer either had not yet entered the theatre, *or* he had come in before

but was sitting in some other part of the orchestra, having a ticket necessarily for another seat."

Ellery shook his head. "I realize that as well as you, son," said the old
man testily. "I'm just following the thought through. I was going to say
that it doesn't seem likely the murderer had come into the theatre at the
regular time. It's probable that he entered at least ten minutes after the
second act started."

"I can give you proof of that," said Ellery lazily.

The Inspector took a pinch of snuff. "I know—those cabalistic figures
on the program. How did they read?

930
815
50,000

"We know what the fifty thousand represented. The other two figures
must have referred not to dollars, but to time. Look at the '815.' The play
started at 8:25. In all likelihood Field arrived about 8:15, or if he arrived
sooner, he had some cause to refer to his watch at that time. Now, if he
had an appointment with some one who, we assume, arrived much later,
what more likely than that Field should have idly jotted down on his program—first, the '50,000,' which indicates that he was thinking about the
impending transaction, which involved $50,000 in blackmail; then 8:15,
the time he was thinking about it; and finally 9:30—the time the blackmail victim was due to arrive! It's the most natural thing in the world for
Field to have done this, as it would be for anyone who is in the habit
of scribbling in idle moments. It's very fortunate for us, because it points
to two things: first, to the exact time of the appointment with the murderer—9:30; and, second, it corroborates our conjecture as regards the
actual time the murder was committed. At 9:25 Lynch saw Field alive
and alone; at 9:30, by Field's written evidence, the murderer was due to
arrive, and we take it for granted he did; according to Dr. Jones' statement it would take the poison from fifteen to twenty minutes to kill
Field—and in view of Pusak's discovery at 9:55 of the dead body, we
may say that the poison was administered about 9:35. If the tetra ethyl
lead took at the most twenty minutes—that gives us 9:55. Much before
then, of course, the murderer left the scene of the crime. Remember—he
could not have known that our friend Mr. Pusak would suddenly desire to
rise and leave his seat. The murderer was probably figuring that Field's
body would not be discovered until the intermission, at 10:05, which
would have been ample time for Field to have died without being able to
murmur any message at all. Luckily for our mysterious murderer Field

was discovered too late to gasp more than the information that he'd been murdered. If Pusak had walked out five minutes earlier we'd have our elusive friend behind the bars right now."

"Bravo!" murmured Ellery, smiling affectionately. "A perfect recitation. My congratulations."

"Oh, go jump in the bathtub," growled his father. "At this point I just want to repeat what you brought out Monday night in Panzer's office—the fact that although the murderer quitted the scene of the crime between 9:30 and 9:55, he was present in the theatre all the rest of the evening until we allowed everybody to go home. Your examination of the guards and the O'Connell girl, together with the doorman's evidence, Jess Lynch's presence in the alley, the usher's corroboration of this fact and all the rest of it, takes care of that. . . . He was there, all right.

"This leaves us momentarily up a tree. All we can do now is consider some of the personalities we've bumped into in the course of the investigation," went on the Inspector with a sigh. "First—did Madge O'Connell tell the truth when she said she had seen no one pass up or down the aisle during the second act? And that she had not seen, at anytime during the evening at all, the person who we know sat in LL30 from half-past nine until ten or fifteen minutes before the body was discovered?"

"It's a tricky question, Dad," remarked Ellery seriously, "because if she was lying about these things, we are losing a mine of information. If she *was* lying—good Lord!—she might be in a position at this moment either to describe, or identify, or possibly name the murderer! However, her nervousness and peculiar attitude might be ascribed to her knowledge that Parson Johnny was in the theatre, with a pack of policemen just aching to get their fingers on him."

"Sounds reasonable to me," grumbled Queen. "Well, what about Parson Johnny? How does he fit into this—or does he fit into it at all? We must always remember that, according to Morgan's statement, Cazzanelli was actively associated with Field. Field had been his lawyer, and perhaps had even bought the Parson's services for this shady business Cronin is nosing around about. If the Parson was not there by accident, was he there through Field or through Madge O'Connell, as she and he both say? I think, my son," he added with a fierce tug at his mustache, "that I'm going to give Parson Johnny a taste of the lash—it won't hurt his thick hide! And that snippy little O'Connell chit—won't do any harm to scare the wits out of her either. . . ."

He took an enormous pinch of snuff, sneezing to the tune of Ellery's sympathetic chuckles.

"And dear old Benjamin Morgan," continued the Inspector, "was he telling the truth about the anonymous letter which so conveniently gave him a mysterious source for his theatre ticket?

"And that most interesting lady, Mrs. Angela Russo. . . . Ah, the ladies, bless 'em! They always muddle a man's logic so. What did she say—that she came to Field's apartment at 9:30? Is her alibi perfectly sound? Of course, the doorman at the apartment house confirmed her statement. But it's easy to 'fix' doormen. . . . Does she know more than she had indicated about Field's business—particularly his private business? Was she lying when she said that Field told her he would be back at ten o'clock? Remember, we know that Field had an appointment in the Roman Theatre beginning at 9:30—did he really expect to keep it and be back at his rooms by ten o'clock? By cab it would be a fifteen or twenty-minute drive, through traffic, which would leave only ten minutes for the transaction—possible, of course. Couldn't do it much sooner by subway, either. We mustn't forget, too, that this woman was not in the theatre at any time during the evening."

"You'll have your hands full with that fair flower of Eve," remarked Ellery. "It's so beautifully evident that she's keeping back a story of some sort. Did you notice that brazen defiance? Wasn't mere bravado. She knows something, Dad. I would certainly keep my eye on her—sooner or later she'll give herself away."

"Hagstrom will take care of her," said Queen abstractedly. "Now, how about Michaels? He has no supported alibi for Monday evening. But then it might not make any difference. He wasn't in the theatre. . . . There's something fishy about that fellow. Was he really looking for something when he came to Field's apartment Tuesday morning? We've made a thorough search of the premises—is it possible we've overlooked something? It's quite evident that he was lying when he spilled that story about the check, and not knowing that Field was dead. And consider this—he *must* have realized that he was running into danger in coming to Field's rooms. He'd read about the murder and couldn't have hoped that the police would delay going to the place. So he was taking a desperate chance—for what reason? Answer that one!"

"It might have had something to do with his imprisonment—by George, he looked surprised when I accused him, didn't he?" chuckled Ellery.

"Might at that," returned the Inspector. "By the way, I've heard from Velie about Michaels' term up in Elmira. Thomas reports that it was a hushed-up case—much more serious than the light sentence in the Reformatory indicates. Michaels was suspected of forgery—and it looked mighty black for him. Then Lawyer Field nicely got Mr. Michaels off on an entirely different count—something to do with petty larceny—and nothing was ever heard about the forgery business again. This boy Michaels looks like the real thing—have to step on his heels a bit."

"I have a little idea of my own about Michaels," said Ellery thoughtfully. "But let it go for the present."

Queen seemed not to hear. He stared into the fire roaring in the stone fireplace. "There's Lewin, too," he said. "Seems incredible that a man of Lewin's stamp should have been so confidentially associated with his employer without knowing a good deal more than he professes. Is he keeping something back? If he is, heaven help him—because Cronin will just about pulverize him!"

"I rather like that chap Cronin," sighed Ellery. "How on earth can a fellow be so set on one idea? . . . Has this occurred to you? I wonder if Morgan knows Angela Russo? Despite the fact that both of them deny a mutual acquaintance. Would be deucedly interesting if they did, wouldn't it?"

"My son," groaned Queen, "don't go looking for trouble. We've a peck of it now without going out of our way for more. . . . By jingo!"

There was a comfortable silence as the Inspector sprawled in the light of the leaping flames. Ellery munched contentedly on a succulent piece of pastry. Djuna's bright eyes gleamed from the far corner of the room, where he had stolen noiselessly and squatted on his thin haunches on the floor, listening to the conversation.

Suddenly the old man's eyes met Ellery's in a spasmodic transference of thought.

"The hat . . ." muttered Queen. "We always come back to the hat."

Ellery's glance was troubled. "And not a bad thing to come back to, Dad. Hat—hat—hat! Where does it fit in? Just what do we know about it?"

The Inspector shifted in his chair. He crossed his legs, took another pinch of snuff and proceeded with a fresh vigor. "All right. We can't afford to be lazy in the matter of that blamed silk topper," he said briskly. "What do we know so far? First, that the hat did not leave the theatre. It seems funny, doesn't it? Doesn't seem possible that we would find no trace at all after such a thorough search. . . . Nothing was left in the cloakroom after everybody was gone; nothing was found in the sweepings that might indicate a hat torn to small pieces or burned; in fact, not a trace, not a thing for us to go on. Therefore, Ellery, the only sensible conclusion we can make at this point is *that we haven't looked for the hat in the right place!* And further, wherever it is, it's still there, due to our precaution of closing the theatre down since Monday night. Ellery, we've got to go back tomorrow morning and turn that place upside down. I won't sleep until we see light somewhere in this matter."

Ellery was silent. "I'm not at all satisfied with things as you've stated them, Dad," he muttered at last. "Hat—hat—there's something wrong somewhere!" He fell silent once more. "No! The hat is the focal point of this investigation—I cannot see any other way out of it. Solve the mystery of Field's hat and you will find the one essential clue that will point to the murderer. I'm so convinced of this that I'll be satisfied we're on the right track only when we're making progress in the explanation of the hat."

The old man nodded his head vigorously. "Ever since yesterday morning, when I had time to think over the hat business, I've felt that we had gone astray somewhere. And here it is Wednesday night—still no light. We've done necessary things—they've led nowhere. . . ." He stared into the fire. "Everything is so badly muddled. I've got all the loose ends at my fingertips, but for some blasted reason I can't seem to make them cohere—fit together—*explain* anything. . . . Undoubtedly, son, what is missing is the story of the top piece."

The telephone bell rang. The Inspector sprang for the instrument. He listened attentively to a man's unhurried tones, made a brisk comment and finally hung up.

"Who's the latest midnight babbler, O recipient of many confidences?" asked Ellery, grinning.

"That was Edmund Crewe," said Queen. "You may remember I asked him yesterday morning to go over the Roman. He spent all of yesterday and today at it. And he reports positively that there is no secret hiding place anywhere on the premises of the theatre. If Eddie Crewe, who is about the last word in architectural matters of this kind, says there's no hiding place there, you may rest assured it's so."

He jumped to his feet and espied Djuna squatting on his hams in the corner. "Djuna! Get the old bed ready," he roared. Djuna slipped through the room and disappeared with a silent grin. Queen wheeled on Ellery, who had already taken off his coat and was fumbling with his tie.

"The first thing we do tomorrow morning is go down to the Roman Theatre and start all over again!" the old man said decisively. "And let me tell you, son—I'm through fooling around! Somebody'd better watch out!"

Ellery affectionately encircled his father's shoulders with one great arm. "Come on to bed, you old fraud!" he laughed.

# PART THREE

*"A good detective is born, not made. Like all genius, he springs not from a carefully nurtured* polizei *but from all mankind. The most amazing detective I ever knew was a dirty old witch doctor who had never been out of the bush. . . . It is the peculiar gift of the truly great detective that he can apply to the inexorable rules of logic three catalyzers: an abnormal observation of events, a knowledge of the human mind and an insight into the human heart."*

—*From* THE MANHUNTER'S MANUAL
by James Redix (the Younger)

# 14

## In Which the Hat Grows

On Thursday, September 27th, the third morning after the events of the crime in the Roman Theatre, Inspector Queen and Ellery rose at an early hour and dressed hastily. They repaired to a makeshift breakfast under the protesting eye of Djuna, who had been pulled bodily from his bed and thrust into the sober habiliments which he affected as major-domo of the Queen ménage.

While they were munching at anæmic pancakes, the old man asked Djuna to get Louis Panzer on the telephone. In a few moments the Inspector was speaking genially into the mouthpiece. "Good morning, Panzer. Please forgive me for hauling you out of bed at this ungodly time of the morning. . . . There's something important in the wind and we need your help."

Panzer murmured a sleepy reassurance.

"Can you come down to the Roman Theatre right away and open it for us?" went on the old man. "I told you that you wouldn't be shut down very long and now it looks as if you'll be able to cash in on the publicity the affair has been getting. I'm not sure when we can reopen, you understand, but it's barely possible that you'll be able to put your show on tonight. Can I count on you?"

"This is excellent!" Panzer's voice came over the wire in a tremulous eagerness. "Do you want me to come down to the theatre at once? I'll be there in a half-hour—I'm not dressed."

"That will be fine," returned Queen. "Of course, Panzer—no one is to be allowed inside yet. Wait for us on the sidewalk before you use your keys and don't notify anyone, either. We'll talk it all over at the theatre. . . . Just a moment."

He clamped the mouthpiece against his chest and looked up inquiringly at Ellery, who was gesturing frantically. Ellery formed his lips around the syllables of a name and the old man nodded approvingly. He spoke into the telephone again.

"There's one other thing you can do for me at present, Panzer," he continued. "Can you get hold of that nice old lady, Mrs. Phillips? I'd like to have her meet us at the theatre as soon as she can."

"Certainly, Inspector. If it's at all possible," said Panzer. Queen replaced the receiver on its hook.

"Well, that's that," he remarked, rubbing his hands together and delving into his pocket for the snuffbox. "Ah-h-h! Bless Sir Walter and all those hardy pioneers who championed the cause of the filthy weed!" He sneezed joyously. "One minute, Ellery, than we'll go."

He picked up the telephone once more and called detective headquarters. He gave a few cheery orders, banged the instrument back on the table and hustled Ellery into his coat. Djuna watched them leave with a mournful expression: he had often pleaded with the Inspector to be allowed to accompany the Queens on their sporadic excursions into the byways of New York. The Inspector, who had his own ideas on the subject of rearing adolescents, invariably refused. And Djuna, who regarded his patron much as the Stone Age man regarded his amulets, accepted the inevitable and hoped for a more auspicious future.

It was a raw, wet day. Ellery and his father turned up their coat collars as they walked towards Broadway and the subway. Both were extraordinarily taciturn, but the keen anticipatory looks on their faces — so curiously alike and yet so different — portended an exciting and revealing day.

Broadway and its threaded canyons were deserted in the chill wind of the morning as the two men walked briskly down 47th Street towards the Roman Theatre. A drab-coated man lounged on the sidewalk before the closed glass doors of the lobby; another leaned comfortably against the high iron fence which cut off the left alley from the street. The dumpy form of Louis Panzer was visible standing before the central door of the theatre, in conversation with Flint.

Panzer shook hands excitedly. "Well, well!" he cried. "So the ban is to be lifted at last! . . . Exceedingly happy to hear that, Inspector."

"Oh, it isn't exactly lifted, Panzer," smiled the old man. "Have you the keys? Morning, Flint. Rest up any since Monday night?"

Panzer produced a heavy bunch of keys and unlocked the central door of the lobby. The four men filed in. The swarthy manager fumbled with the lock of the inside door and finally managed to swing it open. The dark interior of the orchestra yawned in their faces.

Ellery shivered. "With the possible exceptions of the Metropolitan

Opera House and Titus' Tomb, this is the most dismal theatorium I've ever entered. It's a fitting mausoleum for the dear departed. . . ."

The more prosaic Inspector grunted as he pushed his son into the maw of the dark orchestra. "Get along with you! You'll be giving us all the 'willies.' "

Panzer, who had hurried ahead, turned on the main electric switch. The auditorium leaped into more familiar outlines by the light of the big arcs and chandeliers. Ellery's fanciful comparison was not so fantastic as his father had made it appear. The long rows of seats were draped with dirty tarpaulin; murky shadows streaked across the carpets, already dusty; the bare whitewashed wall at the rear of the empty stage made an ugly splotch in the sea of red plush.

"Sorry to see that tarpaulin there," grumbled the Inspector to Panzer. "Because it will have to be rolled up. We're going to conduct a little personal search of the orchestra. Flint, get those two men outside, please. They may as well do something to earn the city's money."

Flint sped away and returned shortly with the two detectives who had been on guard outside the theatre. Under the Inspector's direction they began to haul the huge sheets of rubberized seat covers to the sides, disclosing rows of cushioned chairs. Ellery, standing to one side near the extreme left aisle, withdrew from his pocket the little book in which he had scribbled notes and drawn a rough map of the theatre on Monday night. He was studying this and biting his under-lip. Occasionally he looked up as if to verify the layout of the theatre.

Queen bustled back to where Panzer was nervously pacing the rear. "Panzer, we're going to be mighty busy here for a couple of hours and I was too shortsighted to bring extra men with me. I wonder if I may impose upon you. . . . I have something in mind that requires immediate attention—it would take only a small part of your time and it would help me considerably."

"Of course, Inspector!" returned the little manager. "I'm only too glad to be of assistance."

The Inspector coughed. "Please don't feel that I'm using you as an errand boy or anything like that, old man," he explained apologetically. "But I need these fellows, who are trained in searches of this kind—and at the same time I must have some vital data from a couple of the District Attorney's men who are working downtown on another aspect of the case. Would you mind taking a note for me to one of them—name of Cronin—and bring back the parcel he gives you? I hate to ask you to do this, Panzer," he muttered. "But it's too important to trust to an ordinary messenger, and—ding it all! I'm in a hole."

Panzer smiled in his quick birdlike fashion. "Not another word, Inspector. I'm entirely at your service. I've the materials in my office if you care to write the note now."

The two men retired to Panzer's office. Five minutes later they re-entered the auditorium. Panzer held a sealed envelope in his hand and hurried out into the street. Queen watched him go, then turned with a sigh to Ellery, who had perched himself on the arm of the seat in which Field had been murdered and was still consulting the penciled map.

The Inspector whispered a few words to his son. Ellery smiled and clapped the old man vigorously on the back.

"What do you say we get a move on, son?" said Queen. "I forgot to ask Panzer if he had succeeded in reaching this Mrs. Phillips. I guess he did, though, or he would have said something about it. Where in thunder is she?"

He beckoned to Flint, who was helping the other two detectives in the back-breaking task of removing the tarpaulin.

"I've one of those popular bending exercises for you this morning, Flint. Go up to the balcony and get busy."

"What am I supposed to be looking for today, Inspector?" grinned the broad-shouldered detective. "Because I hope I have better luck than I did Monday night."

"You're looking for a hat—a nice, shiny top piece such as the swells wear, my boy," announced the Inspector. "But if you should come across anything else, use your lungs!" Flint trotted up the wide marble staircase towards the balcony. Queen looked after him, shaking his head. "I'm afraid the poor lad is doomed to another disappointment," he remarked to Ellery. "But I must make absolutely certain that there's nothing up there—and that the usher Miller who was guarding the balcony staircase Monday night was telling the truth. Come along, lazybones."

Ellery shed his topcoat reluctantly and tucked the little book away in his pocket. The Inspector wriggled out of his ulster and preceded his son down the aisle. Working side by side they began to search the orchestra pit at the extreme end of the auditorium. Finding nothing there, they clambered out into the orchestra again and, Ellery taking the right side and his father the left, began a slow, methodical combing of the theatre premises. They lifted the seats; probed experimentally into the plush cushions with long needles which the Inspector had produced mysteri-ously from his breast pocket; and kneeled to examine every inch of the carpet by the light of electric torches.

The two detectives who had by now completed the task of rolling up the tarpaulin began, on the Inspector's brief command, to work through the boxes, a man to each side of the theatre.

For a long time the four men proceeded in silence, unbroken except for the somewhat labored breathing of Inspector Queen. Ellery was working swiftly and efficiently, the old man more slowly. As they met near the center after completing the search of a row, they would regard each other significantly, shake their heads and continue afresh.

About twenty minutes after Panzer's departure the Inspector and Ellery, absorbed in their examination, were startled by the ringing of a telephone bell. In the silence of the theatre the clear trill of the bell rang out with astonishing sharpness. Father and son looked at each other blankly for an instant, then the old man laughed and plodded up the aisle in the direction of Panzer's office.

He returned shortly, smiling. "It was Panzer," he announced. "Got down to Field's office and found the place closed. No wonder—it's only a quarter of nine. But I told him to wait there until Cronin comes. It can't be long now."

Ellery laughed and they set to work again.

Fifteen minutes later, when the two men were almost finished, the front door opened and a small elderly woman dressed in black stood blinking in the brilliant arc lights. The Inspector sprang forward to meet her.

"You're Mrs. Phillips, aren't you?" he cried warmly. "It's mighty nice of you to come so soon, madam. I think you know Mr. Queen here?"

Ellery came forward, smiling one of his rare smiles and bowing with genuine gallantry. Mrs. Phillips was representative of a lovable old womanhood. She was short and of motherly proportions. Her gleaming white hair and air of kindliness endeared her immediately to Inspector Queen, who had a sentimental weakness for middle-aged ladies of presence.

"I certainly do know Mr. Queen," she said, extending her hand. "He was very nice to an old woman Monday night. . . . And I was so afraid you'd have to wait for me, sir!" she said softly, turning to the Inspector. "Mr. Panzer sent a messenger for me this morning—I haven't a telephone, you see. There was a time, when I was on the stage. . . . I came just as soon as I could."

The Inspector beamed. "For a lady it was remarkably prompt, re*mark*ably prompt, Mrs. Phillips!"

"My father kissed the Blarney Stone several centuries ago, Mrs. Phillips," said Ellery gravely. "Don't believe a word av 'im. . . . I suppose it will be *au fait* if I leave you to tackle the rest of the orchestra, Dad? I'd like to have a little chat with Mrs. Phillips. Do you think you're physically able to complete the job alone?"

"Physically able—!" snorted the Inspector. "You plump right down that aisle and go about your business, son. . . . I should appreciate your giving Mr. Queen all the help you can, Mrs. Phillips."

The white-haired lady smiled and Ellery, taking her arm, led her off in the direction of the stage. Inspector Queen, looking after them wistfully, shrugged his shoulders after a moment and turned back to resume the search. A short time later, when he chanced to straighten up, he espied Ellery and Mrs. Phillips seated on the stage conversing earnestly, like two players rehearsing their roles. Queen proceeded slowly up and down the rows, weaving in and out among the empty seats, shaking his head dolefully as he approached the last few rows still empty-handed. When he looked up again the two chairs on the stage held no occupants. Ellery and the old lady had disappeared.

Queen came at last to LL32 Left—the seat in which Monte Field had died. He made a painstaking examination of the cushions, a light of resignation in his eyes. Muttering to himself he walked slowly across the carpet at the rear of the theatre and entered Panzer's office. A few moments later he reappeared, only to make his way to the cubicle which was used as an office by the publicity man, Harry Neilson. He was in this compartment for some time. He came out and visited the cashiers' offices. Shutting the door behind him when he had finished, he wended his way down the steps on the right of the theatre leading to the general lounge, on the floor below the orchestra. Here he took his time, delving into every corner, every niche in the wall, every waste container—all of which he found to be empty. He speculatively eyed the large bin standing directly under the water fountain. He peered into this receptacle and pottered away, finding nothing. Thereupon with a sigh he opened the door on which was gilt-lettered, LADIES' REST ROOM, and went inside. A few moments later he reappeared to push his way through the swinging doors marked GENTLEMEN.

When his meticulous search of the lower floor was completed he trudged up the steps again. In the orchestra he found Louis Panzer waiting, slightly flushed from his exertions but displaying a triumphant smile. The little manager was carrying a small parcel wrapped in brown paper.

"So you saw Cronin after all, Panzer?" said the Inspector, scurrying forward. "This is mighty nice of you, my boy—I appreciate it more than I can say. Is this the package Cronin gave you?"

"It is. A very nice chap, Cronin. I didn't have to wait long after I telephoned you. He came in with two other men named Stoates and Lewin. He didn't keep me more than ten minutes altogether. I hope it was important, Inspector?" Panzer continued, smiling. "I should like to feel that I've been instrumental in clearing up part of the puzzle."

"Important?" echoed the Inspector, taking the parcel from the manager's hand. "You have no idea how important it is. Some day I'll tell you more about it. . . . Will you excuse me a moment, Panzer?"

The little man nodded in a fleeting disappointment as the Inspector grinned, backing off into a dark corner. Panzer shrugged and disappeared into his office.

When he came out, hat and coat left behind, the Inspector was stuffing the parcel into his pocket.

"Did you get what you wanted, sir?" inquired Panzer.

"Oh, yes, yes, indeed!" Queen said, rubbing his hands. "And now—I see Ellery is still gone—suppose we go into your office for a few minutes and while away the time until he returns."

They went into Panzer's sanctum and sat down. The manager lit a long Turkish cigarette while the Inspector dipped into his snuffbox.

"If I'm not presuming, Inspector," said Panzer casually, crossing his short fat legs and emitting a cloud of smoke, "how are things going?"

Queen shook his head sadly. "Not so well—not so well. We don't seem to be getting anywhere with the main angles of the case. In fact, I don't mind telling you that unless we get on the track of a certain object we face failure. . . . It's pretty hard on me—I've never encountered a more puzzling investigation." He wore a worried frown as he snapped the lid of his snuffbox shut.

"That's too bad, Inspector," Panzer clucked in sympathy. "And I was hoping—Ah, well! We can't put our personal concerns above the demands of justice, I suppose! Just what is it you are seeking, Inspector, if you don't mind telling an outsider?"

Queen brightened. "Not at all. You've done me a good turn this morning and— By jingo, how stupid of me not to think of this before!" Panzer leaned forward eagerly. "How long have you been manager of the Roman Theatre, Panzer?"

The manager raised his eyebrows. "Ever since it was built," he said. "Before that I managed the old Electra on 43rd Street—it is also owned by Gordon Davis," he explained.

"Oh!" The Inspector seemed to reflect deeply. "Then you would know this theatre from top to bottom—you would be as familiar with its construction as the architect, perhaps?"

"I have a rather thorough knowledge of it, yes," confessed Panzer, leaning back.

"That's excellent! Let me give you a little problem, then, Panzer. . . . Suppose you wished to conceal a—let us say, a tophat—somewhere in the building, in such a way that not even an exhaustive search of the premises would bring it to light. What would you do? Where would you hide it?"

Panzer scowled thoughtfully at his cigarette. "A rather unusual question, Inspector," he said at last, "and one which is not easy to answer. I know the plans of the theatre very well; I was consulted about them in a

conference with the architect before the theatre was built. And I can positively state that the original blueprints did not provide for such medieval
devices as concealed passageways, secret closets or anything of that sort.
I could enumerate any number of places where a man might hide a com-
paratively small object like a tophat, but none of them would be proof
against a really thorough search."

"I see." The Inspector squinted at his fingernails in an appearance of
disappointment. "So that doesn't help. We've been over the place from
top to bottom, as you know, and we can't find a trace of it. . . ."

The door opened and Ellery, a trifle begrimed but wearing a cheerful
smile, entered. The Inspector glanced at him in eager curiosity. Panzer
rose hesitantly with the evident intention of leaving father and son alone.
A flash of intelligence shot between the Queens.

"It's all right, Panzer—don't go," said the Inspector peremptorily.
"We've no secrets from you. Sit down, man!"

Panzer sat down.

"Don't you think, Dad," remarked Ellery, perching on the edge of the
desk and reaching for his pince-nez, "that this would be an opportune
moment to inform Mr. Panzer of tonight's opening? You remember we
decided while he was gone that the theatre might be thrown open to the
public this evening and a regular performance given. . . ."

"How could I have forgotten—!" said the Inspector without blinking,
although this was the first time he had heard about the mythical decision.
"I think we're about ready, Panzer, to lift the ban on the Roman. We find
that we can do nothing further here, so there is no reason for depriving
you of your patronage any longer. You may run a performance tonight—
in fact, we are most anxious to see a show put on, aren't we Ellery?"

" 'Anxious' is hardly the word," said Ellery, lighting a cigarette. "I
should say we insist upon it."

"Exactly," murmured the Inspector severely. "We insist upon it,
Panzer."

The manager had bobbed out of his chair, his face shining. "That's
simply splendid, gentlemen!" he cried. "I'll telephone Mr. Davis immediately to let him know the good news. Of course"—his face fell—"it's
terribly late to expect any sort of response from the public for tonight's
performance. Such short notice . . ."

"You needn't worry about that, Panzer," retorted the Inspector. "I've
caused your shutdown and I'll see that the theatre is compensated for it
tonight. I'll get the newspaper boys on the wire and ask them to ballyhoo
the opening in the next edition. It will mean a lot of unexpected publicity
for you and undoubtedly the free advertising, combined with the normal
curiosity of the public, will give you a sellout."

"That's sporting of you, Inspector," said Panzer, rubbing his hands. "Is there anything else I can do for you at the moment?"

"There's one item you've forgotten, Dad," interposed Ellery. He turned to the swart little manager. "Will you see that LL32 and LL30 Left are not sold tonight? The Inspector and I would enjoy seeing this evening's performance. We've not really had that pleasure yet, you know. And naturally we wish to preserve a stately incognito, Panzer—dislike the adulation of the crowd and that sort of thing. You'll keep it under cover, of course."

"Anything you say, Mr. Queen. I'll instruct the cashier to put aside those tickets," returned Panzer pleasantly. "And now, Inspector—you said you would telephone the press, I believe—?"

"Certainly." Queen took up the telephone and held pithy conversations with the city editors of a number of metropolitan newspapers. When he had finished Panzer bade them a hurried good-by to get busy with the telephone.

Inspector Queen and his son strolled out into the orchestra, where they found Flint and the two detectives who had been examining the boxes awaiting them.

"You men hang around the theatre on general principles," ordered the Inspector. "Be particularly careful this afternoon. . . . Any of you find anything?"

Flint scowled. "I ought to be digging clams in Canarsie," he said with a disgruntled air. "I fell down on the job Monday night, Inspector, and I'm blamed if I could find a thing for you today. That place upstairs is swept as clean as a hound's tooth. Guess I ought to go back to pounding a beat."

Queen slapped the big detective on the shoulder. "What's the matter with you? Don't be acting like a baby, lad. How on earth could you find anything when there wasn't anything to find? You fellows get something?" he demanded, swinging on the other two men.

They shook their heads in a gloomy negation.

A moment later the Inspector and Ellery climbed into a passing taxi-cab and settled back for the short drive to headquarters. The old man carefully closed the glass sliding window separating the driver's seat from the interior of the car.

"Now, my son," he said grimly, turning on Ellery, who was puffing dreamily at a cigarette, "please explain to your old daddy that hocus-pocus in Panzer's office!"

Ellery's lips tightened. He stared out of the window before replying. "Let me start this way," he said. "You have found nothing in your search today. Nor have your men. And although I scouted about myself, I was

just as unsuccessful. Dad, make up your mind to this one primary point:
The hat which Monte Field wore to the performance of 'Gunplay' on
Monday night, in which he was seen at the beginning of the second act,
and which presumably the murderer took away after the crime was committed, *is not in the Roman Theatre now and has not been there since
Monday night*. To proceed." Queen stared at him with grizzled brows.
"In all likelihood Field's tophat no longer exists. I would stake my Falconer against your snuffbox that it has fled this life and now enjoys a
reincarnation as ashes in the City dumps. That's point number one."

"Go on," commanded the Inspector.

"Point number two is so elementary as to be infantile. Nevertheless,
allow me the privilege of insulting the Queen intelligence. . . . If Field's
hat is not in the Roman Theatre now and has not been in the Roman Theatre since Monday night, it must of necessity have been taken *out* of the
Roman Theatre sometime during the course of that evening!"

He paused to gaze thoughtfully through the window. A traffic officer
was waving his arms at the juncture of 42nd Street and Broadway.

"We have established therefore," he continued lightly, "the factual basis of a point which has been running us ragged for three days: to wit, did
the hat for which we are looking leave the Roman Theatre. . . . To be di-
alectic—yes, it did. It left the Roman Theatre the night of the murder.
Now we approach a greater problem—*how* did it leave and *when*." He
puffed at his cigarette and regarded the glowing tip. "We know that no
person left the Roman Monday night with two hats or no hat at all. In no
case was there anything incongruous in the attire of any person leaving
the theatre. That is, a man wearing a full-dress costume did not go out
with a fedora. In a similar way, no one wearing a silk topper was dressed
in ordinary street clothes. Remember, we noticed nothing wrong from
this angle in *anyone*. . . . This leads us inevitably, to my staggering mind,
to the third fundamental conclusion: that Monte Field's hat left the theatre in the most natural manner in the world: *id est*, by way of some
man's head, its owner being garbed in appropriate evening clothes!"

The Inspector was keenly interested. He thought over Ellery's statement for a moment. Then he said seriously, "That's getting us somewhere, son. But you say a man left the theatre wearing Monte Field's
hat—an important and enlightening statement. But please answer this
question: What did he do with his own hat, since no one left with two?"

Ellery smiled. "You now have your hand on the heart of our little mystery, Dad. But let it hold for the moment. We have a number of other
points to mull over. For example, the man who departed wearing Monte
Field's hat could have been only one of two things: either he was the actual murderer, or he was an accomplice of the murderer."

"I see what you're driving at," muttered the Inspector. "Go on."

"If he was the murderer, we have definitely established the sex and also the fact that our man was wearing evening clothes that night—perhaps not a very illuminating point, since there were scores of such men in the theatre. If he was only an accomplice, we must conclude that the murderer was one of two possibilities: either a man dressed in ordinary clothes, whose possession of a tophat as he lcft would be patently suspicious; or else a woman, who of course could not sport a tophat at all!"

The Inspector sank back into the leather cushions. "Talk about your logic!" he chortled. "My son, I'm almost proud of you—that is, I would be if you weren't so disgustingly conceitcd. . . . Things standing where they do, therefore, the reason you pulled your little drama in Panzer's office. . . ."

His voice lowered as Ellery leaned forward. They continued to converse in inaudible tones until the taxicab drew up beforc the headquarters building.

No sooner had Inspector Queen, who had proceeded blithely through the somber corridors with Ellery striding at his side, entered his tiny office than Sergeant Velie lumbered to his feet.

"Thought you were lost, Inspector!" he exclaimed. "That Stoates kid was in here not long ago with a suffering look on his face. Said that Cronin was tearing his hair at Field's office—that they still hadn't found a thing in the files of an incriminating nature."

"Go away, go away, Thomas my lad," gurgled the Inspector softly. "I can't bother myself with petty problems like putting a dead man behind bars. Ellery and I—"

The telephone bell rang. Queen sprang forward and snatched the instrument from the desk. As he listened the glow left his thin cheeks and a frown settled once more on his forehead. Ellery watched him with a strange absorption.

"Inspector?" came the hurried voice of a man. "This is Hagstrom reporting. Just got a minute—can't say much. Been tailing Angela Russo all morning and had a tough time. . . . Seems to be wise that I'm following her. . . . A half hour ago she thought she'd given me the slip—she hopped into a cab and beat it downtown. . . . And say, Inspector—just three minutes ago I saw her enter Benjamin Morgan's office!"

Queen barked, "Nail her the instant she comes out!" and slammed the receiver down. He turned slowly to Ellery and Velie and repeated Hagstrom's report. Ellery's face became a study in frowning astonishment. Velie appeared unmistakably pleased.

But the old man's voice was strained as he sat down weakly in his swivel chair. Finally he groaned, "What do you know about that!"

# 15

## In Which an Accusation Is Made

Detective Hagstrom was a phlegmatic man. He traced his ancestry to the mountains of Norway, where stolidity was a virtue and stoicism the ultimate cult. Nevertheless, as he leaned against a gleaming marble wall on the twentieth floor of the Maddern Building, thirty feet to the side of the bronze-and-glass door marked:

BENJAMIN MORGAN
ATTORNEY AT LAW

his heart beat a trifle faster than usual. He shuffled his feet nervously as his jaw masticated a wad of chewing tobacco. If the truth were told Detective Hagstrom, a man of varied experience on the service of the police department, had never clamped his hand on the shoulder of a female with intent to arrest. He faced his coming assignment therefore in some trepidation, remembering with appalling clarity the fiery temperament of the lady for whom he was waiting.

His apprehension was well founded. When he had been lounging in the corridor some twenty minutes, and wondering whether his quarry had not slipped away through another exit, Benjamin Morgan's office door suddenly swung open and the large, curved figure of Mrs. Angela Russo garbed in a modish tweed ensemble, appeared. An unbecoming snarl distorted her carefully made-up features; she swung her purse menacingly as she strode toward the line of elevators. Hagstrom glanced quickly at his wrist watch. It was ten minutes to twelve. In a short time the offices would be disgorging their occupants for the lunch hour, and he was most desirous of making his arrest in the quiet of the deserted hall.

Accordingly he straightened up, adjusted his orange-and-blue necktie and stepped with a fair assumption of coolness into full view of the approaching woman. As she caught sight of him she slackened her stride perceptibly. Hagstrom hurried toward her, anticipating flight. But Mrs. Angela Russo was made of sterner stuff. She tossed her head and came on brazenly.

Hagstrom fixed his large red hand on her arm. "I guess you know what I want you for," he said fiercely. "Come along now, and don't make a fuss or I'll put the nippers on you!"

Mrs. Russo shook off his hand. "My, my—aren't you the big rough cop?" she murmured. "Just what do you think you're doing, anyway?"

Hagstrom glared. "None o' your lip, now!" His finger pressed savagely on the "Down" signal for the elevators. "You just shut up and come along!"

She faced him sweetly. "Are you trying to arrest me, by any chance?" she cooed. "Because you know, my big he-man, you've got to have a warrant to do that!"

"Aw, stow it!" he growled. "I'm not arresting you—I'm just inviting you to step down to headquarters for a little gab with Inspector Queen. You coming, or do I have to call the wagon?"

An elevator flashed to a stop. The elevatorman snapped, "Going down!" The woman glanced with momentary uncertainty at the car, peered slyly at Hagstrom and finally stepped into the elevator, the detective's hand firmly clasped on her elbow. They descended in silence under the curious scrutiny of several passengers.

Hagstrom, uneasy but determined, sensing somehow a storm brewing in the breast of the woman who strode so calmly by his side, was taking no chances. He did not relax his grasp until they sat side by side in a taxicab, bound for headquarters. Mrs. Russo's face had gone pasty under her rouge, despite the bold smile curving her lips. She turned suddenly to face her captor, leaning close to his rigidly official body.

"Mr. Cop, darling," she whispered, "do you think you could use a hundred-dollar bill?"

Her hand fumbled suggestively in her purse. Hagstrom lost his temper.

"Bribery, huh?" he sneered. "We'll have to chalk that one up for the Inspector!"

The woman's smile faded. For the rest of the journey she sat looking fixedly at the back of the driver's neck.

It was only when she was being marched, like a soldier on parade, down the dark corridors of the big police structure that her poise returned. And when Hagstrom held open the door of Inspector Queen's office, she passed inside with an airy tilt to her head and a pleasant smile that would have deceived a police matron.

Inspector Queen's office was a cheery affair of sunlight and color. At the moment it resembled a clubroom. Ellery's long legs were stretched comfortably across the thick carpet, his eyes pleasantly absorbed in the contents of a small cheaply bound book entitled "The Complete Guide to Handwriting Analysis." The smoke of a cigarette curled from his slack fingers. Sergeant Velie was sitting stolidly in a chair against the far wall, engrossed in a contemplation of Inspector Queen's snuffbox, which was held lovingly between the thumb and forefinger of the old police official himself. Queen was seated in his comfortable armchair, smiling in hazy introspection at some secret thought.

"Ah! Mrs. Russo! Come in, come in!" exclaimed the Inspector, bouncing to his feet. "Thomas—a chair for Mrs. Russo, if you please." The Sergeant silently placed one of the bare wooden chairs by the side of the Inspector's desk and as silently retreated to his corner. Ellery had not even glanced in the woman's direction. He read on, the same pleasantly abstracted smile on his lips. The old man was bowing with hospitable courtesy to Mrs. Russo.

She looked about at the peaceful scene with bewilderment. She had been prepared for severity, harshness, brutality—the domestic atmosphere of the little office took her completely by surprise. Nevertheless she seated herself and, the instant of hesitation gone, she exhibited the same agreeable smile, the same ladylike demeanor that she had practiced so successfully in the corridors.

Hagstrom was standing inside the doorway, glaring with offended dignity at the profile of the seated woman.

"She tried to slip me a century note," he said indignantly. "Tried to bribe me, Chief!"

Queen's eyebrows instantly rose in shocked surprise. "My dear Mrs. Russo!" he exclaimed in a sorrowful voice. "You really didn't intend to make this excellent officer forget his duty to the city, did you? But of course not! How stupid of me! Hagstrom, certainly you must be mistaken, my dear fellow. A hundred dollars—" He shook his head dolefully sinking back into the leather swivel chair.

Mrs. Russo smiled. "Isn't it queer how these cops get the wrong impression?" she asked in a lovely voice. "I assure you, Inspector—I was just having a little fun with him. . . ."

"Exactly," said the Inspector, smiling again, as if this statement restored his faith in human nature. "Hagstrom, that'll be all."

The detective, who was staring open-mouthed from his superior to the smiling woman, recovered in time to intercept a wink which passed from Velie to Queen across the woman's head. He went out quickly, muttering to himself.

"Now, Mrs. Russo," began the Inspector, in a businesslike tone, "what can we do for you today?"

She stared at him. "Why—why, I thought you wanted to see me. . . ." Her lips tightened. "Cut the comedy, Inspector!" she said shortly. "I'm not paying any social calls on my own hook to this place and you know it. What did you pinch me for?"

The Inspector spread his sensitive fingers deprecatingly, his mouth pursed in protest. "But, my dear lady!" he said. "Certainly you have something to tell me. Because, if you are here—and we cannot evade that evident fact—you are here for a reason. Granted that you did not come exactly of your own free will—still you were brought here because you have something to say to me. Don't you see?"

Mrs. Russo stared fixedly into his eyes. "What the— Hey, look here, Inspector Queen, what are you driving at? What do you think I've got to tell you? I answered everything you asked me Tuesday morning."

"Well!" The old man frowned. "Let us say that you did *not* answer every question Tuesday morning with absolute veracity. For example— do you know Benjamin Morgan?"

She did not flinch. "All right. You take the cake on that one. Your bloodhound caught me coming out of Morgan's office—what of it?" She deliberately opened her purse and began to dab powder on her nose. As she did so she glanced slyly at Ellery from the corner of her eyes. He was still engrossed in his book, oblivious to her presence. She turned back to the Inspector with a toss of the head.

Queen was looking at her sadly. "My dear Mrs. Russo, you're not being fair to a poor old man. I wanted merely to point out that you had— shall I say—lied to me the last time I spoke to you. Now that's a very dangerous procedure with police Inspectors, my dear—very dangerous."

"Listen here!" the woman said suddenly. "You're not going to get anywhere with this soft soap, Inspector. I *did* lie to you Tuesday morning. Because, you see, I didn't think you had anyone here who could follow me very long. Well, I took a gambler's chance and I lost. So you found out I was lying, and you want to know what it's all about. I'll tell you— and then maybe again I won't!"

"Oho!" exclaimed Queen softly. "So you feel you're in a safe enough position to dictate terms, eh? But Mrs. Russo—believe me you're putting your very charming neck into a noose!"

"Yeh?" The mask was fairly off now; the woman's face was stripped to its essential character of intrigue. "You got nothing on me and you know it damn well. All right—I did lie to you—what are you going to do about it? I'm admitting it now. And I'll even tell you what I was doing in that guy Morgan's office, if that'll help you any! That's the kind of a squareshooter *I* am, Mr. Inspector!"

"My dear Mrs. Russo," returned the Inspector in a pained voice, a little puffed smile in his cheeks, "we know already what you were doing in Mr. Morgan's office this morning, so you won't be conferring such a great favor on us after all. . . . I'm really surprised that you should be willing to incriminate yourself to that extent, Mrs. Russo. Blackmail is a mighty serious offense!"

The woman grew deathly white. She half rose in the chair, gripping its arms.

"So Morgan squealed after all, the dirty dog!" she snarled. "And I thought he was a wise guy. I'll get him something to squeal about, take it from me!"

"Ah, now you're beginning to talk my language," murmured the Inspector, leaning forward. "And just what is it you know about our friend Morgan?"

"I know this about him—but look here, Inspector, I can give you a redhot tip. You wouldn't frame a poor lonely woman on a blackmail charge, would you?"

The Inspector's face lengthened. "Now, now, Mrs. Russo!" he said. "Is that a nice thing to say? Certainly I can't make any promises. . . ." He rose, his slender body deadly in its immobility. She shrank back a little. "You will tell me what you have on your mind, Mrs. Russo," he said deliberately, "on the bare chance that I may show my gratitude in the generally accepted fashion. You will please talk—truthfully, do you understand?"

"Oh, I know well enough you're a tough nut, Inspector!" she muttered. "But I guess you're fair, too. . . . What do you want to know?"

"Everything."

"Well, it isn't my funeral," she said, in a more composed voice. There was a pause while Queen examined her curiously. In accusing her of blackmailing Morgan he had made a successful stab in the dark; now a flash of doubt assailed him. She seemed much too sure of herself if all she knew were the details of Morgan's past, as the Inspector had taken for granted from the beginning of the interview. He glanced at Ellery and was apprehensively quick to note that his son's eyes were no longer on the book but riveted on the profile of Mrs. Russo.

"Inspector," said Mrs. Russo, a shrill triumph creeping into her voice, "I know who killed Monte Field!"

"What's that?" Queen jumped out of his seat, a flush suffusing his white features. Ellery had straightened convulsively in his chair, his sharp eyes boring into the woman's face. The book he had been reading slipped out of his fingers and dropped to the floor with a thud.

"I said I know who killed Monte Field," repeated Mrs. Russo, evidently enjoying the sensation she had caused. "It's Benjamin Morgan, and I heard him threaten Monte *the night before he was murdered!*"

"Oh!" said the Inspector, sitting down. Ellery picked up his book and resumed his interrupted study of "The Complete Guide to Handwriting Analysis." Quiet descended once more. Velie, who had been staring at father and son in struggling amazement, seemed at a loss to understand their suddenly changed manner.

Mrs. Russo grew angry. "I suppose you think I'm lying again, but I'm not!" she screamed. "I tell you I heard with my own ears Ben Morgan tell Monte Sunday night that he'd put him away!"

The Inspector was grave, but undisturbed. "I don't doubt your word in the least, Mrs. Russo. Are you sure it was Sunday night?"

"Sure?" she shrilled. "I'll say I'm sure!"

"And where did this happen?"

"Right in Monte Field's own apartment, that's where!" she said bitingly. "I was with Monte all evening Sunday, and as far as I know he wasn't expecting company, because we didn't usually have company when we spent the evening together. . . . Monte himself jumped when the doorbell rang about eleven o'clock and said, 'Who in hell could that be?' We were in the living room at the time. But he got up and went to the door, and right after that I heard a man's voice outside. I figured Monte wouldn't want me to be seen by anybody, so I went into the bedroom and closed the door, just leaving a crack open. I could hear Monte trying to stall the man off. Anyway, they finally came into the living room. Through the crack in the door I saw it was this fellow Morgan—I didn't know who he was at the time, but later on I got it during the talk they had. And afterward Monte told me."

She stopped. The Inspector listened imperturbably and Ellery was paying not the slightest attention to her words. She went on desperately.

"For about a half hour they talked till I could have howled. Morgan was sort of cold and set; he didn't get excited till the last. From what I gathered, Monte had asked Morgan not long before for a big wad of dough in return for some papers; and Morgan said he didn't have the money, couldn't raise it. Said he'd decided to drop into Monte's place for one last reckoning. Monte was kind of sarcastic and mean—he could be awfully mean when he wanted to. Morgan kept getting madder and madder, and I could see he was holding his temper in. . . ."

The Inspector interrupted. "Just what was the reason for Field's demand for money?"

"I wish I knew, Inspector," she returned savagely. "But both of 'em were mighty careful not to mention the reason. . . . Anyway, it was something about those papers that Monte wanted Morgan to buy. It wouldn't take much brains to guess that Monte had something on Morgan and was pushing it to the limit."

At the mention of the word "papers" Ellery's interest in Mrs. Russo's story had revived. He had put the book down and begun to listen intently. The Inspector gave him a fleeting glance as he addressed the woman.

"Just how much money was Field demanding, Mrs. Russo?"

"You wouldn't believe me if I told you," she said, laughing disdainfully. "Monte was no piker. All he wanted was—fifty thousand dollars!"

The Inspector seemed unmoved. "Go on."

"So there they were," she continued, "jabbering back and forth, with Monte getting colder and Morgan getting madder. Finally Morgan picked up his hat and yelled, 'I'll be damned, you crook, if I'm going to be milked any more! You can do what you please—I'm through, do you understand? I'm through for good!' He was blue in the face. Monte didn't get up from his chair. He just said, 'You can do as you please, Benjamin my friend, but I give you exactly three days to hand that money over. And no bargaining, remember! Fifty thousand, or—but surely I don't have to remind you of the unpleasant consequences of refusal.' Monte sure was slick," she added admiringly. "Could sling the lingo like a professional.

"Morgan kept fiddling with his hat," she went on, "just as if he didn't know what to do with his hands. Then he exploded with, 'I told you where you get off, Field, and I mean every word of it. Publish those papers, and if it means ruin to me—I'll see to it that it's the last time you'll ever blackmail *anybody!*' He shook his fist under Monte's nose, and looked for a minute as if he was going to do him in then and there. Then all of a sudden he quieted down and without saying another word walked himself out of the apartment."

"And that's the story, Mrs. Russo?"

"Isn't it enough?" she flared. "What are you trying to do—protect that murdering coward? . . . But it isn't all. After Morgan left, Monte said to me, 'Did you hear what my friend said?' I made believe I didn't, but Monte was wise. He took me on his lap and said playfully, 'He'll regret it, Angel. . . .' He always called me Angel," she added coyly.

"I see. . . ." The Inspector mused. "And just what did Mr. Morgan say—that you took for a threat against Field's life?"

She stared at him incredulously. "Good gravy, are you dumb, or what?" she cried. "He said, 'I'll see to it it's the last time you'll ever blackmail *anybody!*' And then when my darling Monte was killed the very next night . . ."

"A very natural conclusion," smiled Queen. "Do I understand that you are preferring charges against Benjamin Morgan?"

"I'm not preferring anything except a little peace, Inspector," she retorted. "I've told you the story—now do what you want with it." She shrugged her shoulders and made as if to rise.

"One moment, Mrs. Russo." The Inspector held up a small and delicate finger. "You referred in your story to some 'papers' that Field was holding over Morgan's head. Did Field at any time during the quarrel between them actually bring out these papers?"

Mrs. Russo looked the old man coolly in the eye. "No, sir, he didn't. And make believe I'm not sorry he didn't, too!"

"A charming attitude of yours, Mrs. Russo. One of these days . . . I hope you understand that your skirts are not entirely—ah—clean in this matter, in a manner of speaking," said the Inspector. "So please consider very carefully before you answer my next question. Where did Monte Field keep his private documents?"

"I don't have to consider, Inspector," she snapped. "I just don't know. If there was any chance of my knowing I would, don't worry."

"Perhaps you made a few personal forays of your own when Field was absent from his apartment?" pursued Queen, smiling.

"Perhaps I did," she answered with a dimpling cheek. "But it didn't do any good. I'd swear they're not in those rooms. . . . Well, Inspector, anything else?"

The clear voice of Ellery seemed to startle her. But she coquettishly patted her hair as she turned towards him.

"As far as you know, Mrs. Russo," said Ellery icily, "from long and no doubt intimate association with your gallant Leander—how many different silk tophats did he possess?"

"You're the original crossword puzzle, aren't you?" she gurgled. "As far as I know, Mr. Man, he had only one. How many does a guy need?"

"You're certain of that, I suppose," said Ellery.

"Sure's you're born, Mr.—Queen." She contrived to slip a caress into her voice. Ellery stared at her as one stares at a strange zoological specimen. She made a little *moue* and turned about gayly.

"I'm not so popular around here so I'll beat it. . . . You're not going to put me in a nasty cell, are you, Inspector? I can go now, can't I?"

The Inspector bowed. "Oh yes—you may go, Mrs. Russo, under a certain amount of surveillance. . . . But please understand that we may still require your delightful company at some not distant date. Will you remain in town?"

"Charmed, I'm sure!" she laughed and swept out of the room.

Velie snapped to his feet like a soldier and said, "Well, Inspector, I guess that settles it!"

The Inspector sank wearily into his chair. "Are you insinuating, Thomas, like some of Ellery's stupid fiction sergeants—which you are not—that Mr. Morgan be arrested for the murder of Monte Field?"

"Why—what else?" Velie seemed at a loss.

"We'll wait a while, Thomas," returned the old man heavily.

# 16

## In Which the Queens Go to the Theatre

Ellery and his father regarded each other across the length of the little office. Velie had resumed his seat with a puzzled frown. He sat quietly for a time in the growing silence, seemed suddenly to make a decision and asking permission left the room.

The Inspector grinned as he fumbled with the lid of his snuffbox.

"Did you get a scare, too, Ellery?"

Ellery, however, was serious. "That woman gives me a case of Wodehouse 'willies,' " he said, shuddering. "Scare is much too mild a word."

"I couldn't for the moment grasp the significance of her attitude," said Inspector Queen. "To think that she *knew*, while we have been fumbling around. . . . It scattered my wits."

"I should say the interview was highly successful," commented Ellery. "Principally because I've been gathering a few interesting facts from this ponderous tome on chirography. But Mrs. Angela Russo does not measure up to my conception of perfect womanhood. . . ."

"If you ask me," chuckled the Inspector, "our beauteous friend has a crush on you. Consider the opportunities, my son—!"

Ellery made a grimace of profound distaste.

"Well!" Queen reached for one of the telephones on the desk. "Do you think we ought to give Benjamin Morgan another chance, Ellery?"

"Hanged if he deserves it," grumbled Ellery. "But I suppose it's the routine thing to do."

"You forget the papers, son—the papers," retorted the Inspector, a twinkle in his eye.

He spoke to the police operator in pleasant accents and a few moments later the buzzer sounded.

"Good afternoon, Mr. Morgan!" Queen said cheerfully. "And how are you today?"

"Inspector Queen?" asked Morgan after a slight hesitation. "Good afternoon to you, sir. How is the case progressing?"

"That's a fair question, Mr. Morgan," laughed the Inspector. "One, however, which I daren't answer for fear of being accused of incompetency. . . . Mr. Morgan, are you free this evening by any chance?"

Pause. "Why—not free exactly." The lawyer's voice was barely audible. "I am due at home, of course, for dinner, and I believe my wife has arranged a little bridge. Why, Inspector?"

"I was thinking of asking you to dine with my son and me this evening," said the Inspector regretfully. "Could you possibly get away for the dinner hour?"

A longer pause. "If it's absolutely necessary, Inspector—?"

"I wouldn't put it that way exactly, Mr. Morgan. . . . But I would appreciate your accepting the invitation."

"Oh." Morgan's voice came more resolutely now. "In that case I'm at your command, Inspector. Where shall I meet you?"

"That's fine, that's fine!" said Queen. "How about Carlos', at six?"

"Very well, Inspector," returned the lawyer quietly and hung up the receiver.

"I can't help feeling sorry for the poor chap," murmured the old man.

Ellery grunted. He was not feeling inclined to sympathize. The taste of Mrs. Angela Russo was still strong in his mouth, and it was not a pleasant taste at all.

Promptly at six o'clock Inspector Queen and Ellery joined Benjamin Morgan in the convivial atmosphere of Carlos' restaurant foyer. He was sitting dejectedly in a red-leather chair, staring at the backs of his hands. His lips drooped sadly, his knees were widely separated in an instinctive attitude of depression.

He made a laudable attempt to smile as the two Queens approached. He rose with a firmness that indicated to his keen hosts a mind determined upon a fixed course of action. The Inspector was at his bubbling best, partly because he felt a genuine liking for the corpulent attorney and partly because it was his business. Ellery, as usual, was noncommittal.

The three men shook hands like old friends.

"Glad to see you're on time, Morgan," said the Inspector, as a stiff headwaiter conducted them to a corner table. "I really must apologize for taking you away from your dinner at home. There was a time once—" He sighed and they sat down.

"No apology necessary," said Morgan with a wan smile. "I suppose you know that every married man relishes a bachelor dinner at times. . . . Just what is it, Inspector, you wanted to talk to me about?"

The old man raised a warning finger. "No business now, Morgan," he said. "I have an idea Louis has something up his sleeve in the way of solid refreshment—right, Louis?"

The dinner was a culinary delight. The Inspector who was quite indifferent to the nuances of the art, had left the details of the menu to his son. Ellery was fanatically interested in the delicate subject of foods and their preparation. Consequently the three men dined well. Morgan was at first inclined to taste his food abstractedly, but he became more and more alive to the delightful concoctions placed before him, until finally he forgot his troubles altogether and chatted and laughed with his hosts.

With *café au lait* and excellent cigars, which Ellery smoked cautiously, the Inspector diffidently, and Morgan with enjoyment, Queen came to the point.

"Morgan, I'm not going to beat around the bush. I have an idea you know why I asked you here tonight. I'm going to be perfectly honest. I want the true explanation for your silence regarding the events of Sunday night, September the twenty-third—four nights ago."

Morgan had become grave immediately after the Inspector began to speak. He put the cigar on the ashtray and regarded the old man with an expression of ineffable weariness.

"It was bound to come," he said. "I might have known that you would find out sooner or later. I suppose Mrs. Russo told you out of spite."

"She did," confessed Queen frankly. "As a gentleman I refuse to listen to tales; as a policeman it is my duty. Why have you kept this from me, Morgan?"

Morgan traced a meaningless figure on the cloth with a spoon. "Because—well, because a man is always a fool until he is made to realize the extent of his folly," he said quietly, looking up. "I hoped and prayed—it is a human failing, I suppose—that the incident would remain a secret between a dead man and myself. And to find that that prostitute was hiding in the bedroom—listening to every word I said—it rather took the wind out of my sails."

He gulped down a glass of water, rushing ahead. "The God's honest truth, Inspector, is that I thought I was being drawn into a trap and I couldn't bring myself to furnish contributory evidence. There I found myself in the theatre, not so far away from my worst enemy found murdered. I could not explain my presence except by an apparently silly and unsubstantiated story; and I remembered in a bitter flash that I had actually quarreled with the dead man the night before. It was a tight position, Inspector—take my word for it."

Inspector Queen said nothing. Ellery was leaning far back in his chair, watching Morgan with gloomy eyes. Morgan swallowed hard and went on.

"That's why I didn't say anything. Can you blame a man for keeping quiet when his legal training warns him so decisively of the net of circumstantial evidence he is helping to manufacture?"

Queen was silent for a moment. Then—"We'll let that pass for the moment, Morgan. Why did you go to see Field Sunday night?"

"For a very good reason," answered the lawyer bitterly. "On Thursday, a week ago, Field called me up at my office and told me that he was making a last business venture that entailed his procuring fifty thousand dollars at once. Fifty thousand dollars!" Morgan laughed dryly. "After he had milked me until I was as flabby financially as an old cow. . . . And his 'business venture'—can you imagine what it was? If you knew Field as well as I did, you would find the answer on the race tracks and the stockmarket. . . . Perhaps I'm wrong. Perhaps he was hard pressed for money and was cleaning up his old 'accounts.' At any rate, he wanted the fifty thousand on a brand-new proposition—that he would actually return the original documents to me for that sum! It was the first time he had even suggested such a thing. Every time—before—he had insolently asked blackmail for silence. This time it was a buy-and-sell proposition."

"That's an interesting point, Mr. Morgan," put in Ellery, with a flicker of his eyes. "Did anything in his conversation definitely lead you to suspect that he was 'clearing up old accounts,' as you phrase it?"

"Yes. That is why I said what I did. He gave me the impression that he was hard up, meant to take a little vacation—vacation to him would be a three-year jaunt on the continent, nothing less—and was soliciting all his 'friends.' I never knew that he was in the blackmailing business on a large scale; but this time—!"

Ellery and the Inspector exchanged glances. Morgan forged ahead.

"I told him the truth. That I was in a bad way financially, chiefly through him, and that it would be absolutely impossible for me to raise the preposterous amount he demanded. He merely laughed—insisted on getting the money. I was most anxious to get the papers back, of course. . . ."

"Had you verified from your cancelled vouchers the fact that some were missing?" asked the Inspector.

"It wasn't necessary, Inspector," grated Morgan. "He actually exhibited the vouchers and letters for my benefit in the Webster Club two years ago—when we had the quarrel. Oh, there is no question about it. He was top man."

"Go on."

"He hung up on me with a thinly veiled threat last Thursday. I had tried desperately during the conversation to make him believe that I would in some way meet his demands, because I knew that he would have no scruples at all about publishing the papers once he realized he had sucked me dry. . . ."

"Did you ask him if you could see the documents?" asked Ellery.

"I believe I did—but he laughed at me and said I would see the color of my checks and letters when he saw the color of my money. He was nobody's fool, that crook—he was taking no chances on my doing him in while he brought out the damning evidence. . . . You see how frank I am. I will even admit that at times the thought of violence entered my head. What man could keep from thinking such thoughts under those circumstances? But I never entertained homicidal fancies seriously, gentlemen—for a very good reason." He paused.

"It wouldn't have done you any good," said Ellery softly. "You didn't know where the documents were!"

"Exactly," returned Morgan with a tremulous smile. "I didn't know. And with those papers liable to come to light at any time—to fall into anybody's hands—what good would Field's death have done me? I would probably have exchanged a bad taskmaster for a worse. . . . On Sunday night, after trying for three terrible days to get together the money he asked for—with no result—I decided to come to a final settlement with him. I went to his apartment and found him in a dressing gown, much surprised and not at all apprehensive at seeing me. The living room was upset—I did not know at the time that Mrs. Russo was hiding in the next room."

He relit the cigar with shaking fingers.

"We quarreled—or rather I quarreled and he sneered. He would listen to no argument, to no plea. He wanted the fifty thousand or he would send the story around—and the proofs. It sort of got on my nerves after a while. . . . I left before I lost control of myself utterly. And that's all, Inspector, on my word of honor as a gentleman and as an unfortunate victim of circumstances."

He turned his head away. Inspector Queen coughed and threw his cigar into the ashtray. He fumbled in his pocket for the brown snuffbox, took a pinch, inhaled deeply and leaned back in his chair. Ellery suddenly poured a glass of water for Morgan, who took it and drained it.

"Thank you, Morgan," said Queen. "And since you have been so frank in your story, please be honest and tell me whether you threatened Field's life Sunday night during your quarrel. It is only fair to let you know that Mrs. Russo flatly accused you of Field's murder because of something you said in the heat of the moment."

Morgan grew pale. His brows twitched and his eyes, glazed and worried, stared pitifully at the Inspector.

"She was lying!" he cried hoarsely. Several diners nearby looked around curiously, and Inspector Queen tapped Morgan's arm. He bit his lip and lowered his voice. "I did nothing of the sort, Inspector. I was honest with you a moment ago when I said that I had thought savagely from time to time of killing Field. It was a crippled, silly, pointless thought. I—I wouldn't have the courage to kill a man. Even at the Webster Club when I lost my temper completely and shouted that threat I didn't mean it. Certainly Sunday night—please believe me rather than that unscrupulous, money-grubbing harlot, Inspector—you must!"

"I merely want you to explain what you said. Because," said the Inspector quietly, "strange as it may seem, I do believe that you made the statement she attributes to you."

"What statement?" Morgan was in a sweat of fear; his eyes started from his head.

" 'Publish those papers, and if it means ruin to me—I'll see to it that it's the last time you'll ever blackmail *anybody!*' " replied the Inspector. "Did you say that, Mr. Morgan?"

The lawyer stared incredulously at the Queens, then threw back his head and laughed. "Good heavens!" he gasped, at last. "Is that the 'threat' I made? Why, Inspector, what I meant was that if he published those documents, in the event that I couldn't meet his blackguard demands, that I'd make a clean breast of it to the police and drag him down with me. That's what I meant! And she thought I was threatening his life—" He wiped his eyes hysterically.

Ellery smiled, his finger summoning the waiter. He paid the check and lit a cigarette, looking sidewise at his father, who was regarding Morgan with a mixture of abstraction and sympathy.

"Very well, Mr. Morgan." The Inspector rose, pushed back his chair. "That's all we wanted to know." He stood aside courteously to allow the dazed, still trembling lawyer to precede them toward the cloakroom.

The sidewalk fronting the Roman Theatre was jammed when the two Queens strolled up 47th Street from Broadway. The crowd was so huge that police lines had been established. Traffic was at a complete standstill along the entire length of the narrow thoroughfare. The electric lights of the marquee blared forth the title "Gunplay" in vigorous dashes of light and in smaller lights the legend, "Starring—James Peale and Eve Ellis, Supported by an All-Star Cast." Women and men wielded frenzied elbows to push through the milling mob; policemen shouted hoarsely, demanding tickets for the evening's performance before they would allow anyone to pass through the lines.

The Inspector showed his badge and he and Ellery were hurled with the jostling crowd into the small lobby of the theatre. Beside the box office, his Latin face wreathed in smiles, stood Manager Panzer, courteous, firm and authoritative, helping to speed the long line of cash customers from the box office window to the ticket taker. The venerable doorman, perspiring mightily, was standing to one side, a bewildered expression on his face. The cashiers worked madly. Harry Neilson was huddled in a corner of the lobby, talking earnestly to three young men who were obviously reporters.

Panzer caught sight of the two Queens and hurried forward to greet them. At an imperious gesture from the Inspector he hesitated, then with an understanding nod turned back to the cashier's window. Ellery stood meekly in line and procured two reserved tickets from the box office. They entered the orchestra in the midst of a pushing throng.

A startled Madge O'Connell fell back as Ellery presented two tickets plainly marked LL32 Left and LL30 Left. The Inspector smiled as she fumbled with the pasteboards and threw him a half-fearful glance. She led them across the thick carpet to the extreme left aisle, silently indicated the last two seats of the last row and fled. The two men sat down, placed their hats in the wire holders below the seats and leaned back comfortably, for all the world like two pleasure-seekers contemplating an evening's gory entertainment.

The auditorium was packed. Droves of people being ushered down the aisles were rapidly consuming the empty seats. Heads twisted expectantly in the direction of the Queens, who became unwittingly the center of a most unwelcome scrutiny.

"Heck!" grumbled the old man. "We should have come in after the curtain went up."

"You're much too sensitive to public acclaim, *mon père*," laughed Ellery. "I don't mind the limelight." He consulted his wrist watch and their glances met significantly. It was exactly 8:25. They wriggled in their seats and settled down.

The lights were blotted out, one by one. The chatter of the audience died in a responsive sympathy. In total darkness the curtain rose on a weirdly dim stage. A shot exploded the silence; a man's gurgling shout raised gasps in the theatre. "Gunplay" was off in its widely publicized and theatrical manner.

Despite the preoccupation of his father, Ellery, relaxed in the chair which three nights before had held the dead body of Monte Field, was able to sit still and enjoy the exceedingly mellow melodrama. The fine rich voice of James Peale, ushered onto the stage by a series of climactic incidents, rang out and thrilled him with its commanding art. Eve Ellis's utter absorption in her role was apparent—at the moment she was conversing in low throbbing tones with Stephen Barry, whose handsome face and pleasant voice were evoking admiring comment from a young girl seated directly to the Inspector's right. Hilda Orange was huddled in a corner, dressed flamboyantly as befitted her stage character. The old "character-man" pottered aimlessly about the stage. Ellery leaned toward his father.

"It's a well-cast production," he whispered. "Watch that Orange woman!"

The play stuttered and crackled on. With a crashing symphony of words and noise the first act came to an end. The Inspector consulted his watch as the lights snapped on. It was 9:05.

He rose and Ellery followed him lazily. Madge O'Connell, pretending not to notice them, pushed open the heavy iron doors across the aisle and the audience began to file out into the dimly lit alleyway. The two Queens sauntered out among the others.

A uniformed boy standing behind a neat stand covered with paper cups was crying his wares in a subdued, "refined" voice. It was Jess Lynch, the boy who had testified in the matter of Monte Field's request for ginger ale.

Ellery strolled behind the iron door—there was a cramped space between the door and the brick wall. He noticed that the wall of the building flanking the other side of the alley was easily six stories high and unbroken. The Inspector bought an orangedrink from the boy. Jess Lynch recognized him with a start and Inspector Queen greeted the boy pleasantly.

People were standing in small groups, their attitudes betokening a strange interest in their surroundings. The Inspector heard a woman remark, in a fearful, fascinated voice, "They say he was standing right out here Monday night, buying an orangedrink!"

The warning bell soon clanged inside the theatre, and those who had come outside for a breath of air hurried back into the orchestra. Before he sat down, the Inspector glanced over across the rear of the auditorium to the foot of the staircase leading to the balcony. A stalwart, uniformed young man stood alertly on the first step.

The second act exploded into being. The audience swayed and gasped in the approved fashion while the dramatic fireworks were shot off on the stage. The Queens seemed suddenly to have become absorbed in the action. Father and son leaned forward, bodies taut, eyes intent. Ellery consulted his watch at 9:30—and the two Queens settled back again while the play rumbled on.

At 9:50 exactly they rose, took their hats and coats and slipped out of the LL row into the clear space behind the orchestra. A number of people were standing—at which the Inspector smiled and blessed the power of the press beneath his breath. The white-faced usherette, Madge O'Connell, was leaning stiffly against a pillar, staring unseeingly ahead.

The Queens, espying Manager Panzer in the doorway of his office beaming delightedly at the crowded auditorium, made their way towards him. The Inspector motioned him inside and rapidly stepped into the little anteroom, Ellery close behind. The smile faded from Panzer's face.

"I hope you've had a profitable evening?" he asked nervously.

"Profitable evening? Well—it depends upon what you mean by the word." The old man gestured briefly and led the way through the second door into Panzer's private office.

"Look here, Panzer," he said, pacing up and down in some excitement, "have you a plan of the orchestra handy which shows each seat, numbered, and all the exits?"

Panzer stared. "I think so. Just a moment." He fumbled in a filing cabinet, rummaged among some folders and finally brought out a large map of the theatre separated into two sections—one for the orchestra and the other for the balcony.

The Inspector brushed the second away impatiently as he and Ellery bent over the orchestra plan.* They studied it for a moment. Queen looked up at Panzer, who was shifting from one foot to another on the rug, evidently at a loss to know what would be required of him next.

"May I have this map, Panzer?" asked the Inspector shortly. "I'll return it unharmed in a few days."

"Certainly, certainly!" said Panzer. "Is there anything else I can do for you now, Inspector? . . . I want to thank you for your consideration in the matter of publicity, sir—Gordon Davis is extremely pleased at the 'house' tonight. He asked me to relay his thanks."

"Not at all—not at all," grumbled the Inspector, folding the map and putting it in his breast pocket. "It was coming to you—what's right is right. . . . And now, Ellery—if you'll come along. . . . Good night, Panzer. Not a word about this, remember!"

The two Queens slipped out of Panzer's office while he was babbling his reassurances of silence.

They crossed the rear of the orchestra once more, in the direction of the extreme left aisle. The Inspector beckoned curtly to Madge O'Connell.

"Yes," she breathed, her face chalky.

"Just open those doors wide enough to let us through, O'Connell, and forget all about it afterward. Understand?" said the Inspector grimly.

She mumbled under her breath as she pushed open one of the big iron

---

* The plan illustrated on page 8 and drawn by Ellery Queen was designed from Manager Panzer's map.—THE EDITOR

doors opposite the LL row. With a last warning shake of the head the Inspector slipped through, Ellery following—and the door came softly back into place again.

At 11 o'clock, as the wide exits were disgorging their first flocks of theatre-goers after the final curtain, Richard and Ellery Queen re-entered the Roman Theatre through the main door.

# 17

## In Which More Hats Grow

"Sit down, Tim—have a cup of coffee?"

Timothy Cronin, a keen-eyed man of medium height thatched plentifully with fire-red hair, seated himself in one of the Queens' comfortable chairs and accepted the Inspector's invitation in some embarrassment.

It was Friday morning and the Inspector and Ellery, garbed romantically in colorful dressing gowns, were in high spirits. They had retired the night before at an uncommonly early hour—for them; they had slept the sleep of the just; now Djuna had a pot of steaming coffee, of a variety which he blended himself, ready on the table; and indubitably all seemed right with the world.

Cronin had stalked into the cheery Queen quarters at an ungodly hour—disheveled, morose and unashamedly cursing. Not even the mild protests of the Inspector were able to stem the tide of profanity which streamed from his lips; and as for Ellery, he listened to the lawyer's language with an air of grave enjoyment, as an amateur harkens to a professional.

Then Cronin awoke to his environment, and blushed, and was invited to sit down, and stared at the unbending back of Djuna as that nimble man-of-affairs busied himself with the light appurtenances of the morning meal.

"I don't suppose you're in a mood to apologize for your shocking language, Tim Cronin, me lad," chided the Inspector, folding his hands Buddhalike over his stomach. "Do I have to inquire the reason for the bad temper?"

"Not much, you don't," growled Cronin, shifting his feet savagely on the rug. "You ought to be able to guess. I'm up against a blank wall in the matter of Field's papers. Blast his black soul!"

"It's blasted, Tim—it's blasted, never fear," said Queen sorrowfully.

"Poor Field is probably roasting his toes over a sizzling little coalfire in Hell just now—and chortling to himself over your profanity. Exactly what is the situation—how do things stand?"

Cronin grasped the cup Djuna had set before him and drained its scalding contents in a gulp. "Stand?" he cried, banging down the cup. "They don't stand—they're nil, nit, not! By Christopher, if I don't get my hands on some documentary evidence soon I'll go batty! Why, Inspector—Stoates and I ransacked that swell office of Field's until I don't think there's a rat in the walls who dares show his head outside a ten-foot hole—and there's nothing. Nothing! Man—it's inconceivable. I'd stake my reputation that somewhere—the Lord alone knows where—Field's papers are hidden, just begging somebody to come along and carry them away."

"You seem possessed of a phobia on the subject of hidden papers, Cronin," remarked Ellery mildly. "One would think we are living in the days of Charles the First. There's no such thing as hidden papers. You merely have to know where to look."

Cronin grinned impertinently. "That's very good of you, Mr. Queen. Suppose you suggest the place Mr. Monte Field selected to hide *his* papers."

Ellery lit a cigarette. "All right. I accept the challenge to combat. . . . You say—and I don't doubt your word in the least—that the documents you suppose to be in existence are not in Field's office. . . . By the way, what makes you so sure that Field kept papers which would incriminate him in this vast clique of gangsters you told us about?"

"He must have," retorted Cronin. "Queer logic, but it works. . . . My information absolutely establishes the fact that Field had correspondence and written plans connecting him with men higher up in gangdom whom we're constantly trying to 'get' and whom we haven't been able to touch so far. You'll have to take my word for it; it's too complicated a story to go into here. But you mark my words, Mr. Queen—Field had papers that he couldn't afford to destroy. Those are the papers I'm looking for."

"Granted," said Ellery in a rhetorical tone. "I merely wished to make certain of the facts. Let me repeat, then, these papers are not in his office. We must therefore look for them farther afield. For example, they might be secreted in a safety-deposit vault."

"But, El," objected the Inspector, who had listened to the interplay between Cronin and Ellery in amusement, "didn't I tell you this morning that Thomas had run that lead to earth? Field did not have a box in a safety-deposit vault. That is established. He had no general delivery or private post-office box either—under his real name or any other name.

"Thomas has also investigated Field's club affiliations and discovered that the lawyer had no residence, permanent or temporary, besides the flat on 75th Street. Furthermore, in all Thomas' scouting around, he found not the slightest indication of a possible hiding place. He thought that Field might have left the papers in a parcel or bag in the keeping of a shop-keeper, or something of the sort. But there wasn't a trace. . . . Velie's a good man in these matters, Ellery. You can bet your bottom dollar that hypothesis of yours is false."

"I was making a point for Cronin's benefit," retorted Ellery. He spread his fingers on the table elaborately and winked. "You see, we must narrow the field of search to the point where we can definitely say: 'It must be here.' The office, the safety-deposit vault, the post-office boxes have been ruled out. Yet we know that Field could not afford to keep these documents in a place difficult of access. I cannot vouch for the papers *you're* seeking, Cronin; but it's different with the papers *we're* seeking. No, Field had them somewhere near at hand. . . . And, to go a step further, it's reasonable to assume that he would have kept all his important secret papers in the same hiding place."

Cronin scratched his head and nodded.

"We shall now apply the elementary precepts, gentlemen." Ellery paused as if to emphasize his next statement. "Since we have narrowed our area of inquiry to the exclusion of all possible hiding places save one—the papers must be in that one hiding place. . . . Nothing to that."

"Now that I pause to consider," interpolated the Inspector, his good humor suddenly dissipated into gloom, "perhaps we weren't as careful in that place as we might have been."

"I'm as certain we're on the right track," said Ellery firmly, "as that today is Friday and there will be fish suppers in thirty million homes tonight."

Cronin was looking puzzled. "I don't quite get it, Mr. Queen. What do you mean when you say there's only one possible hiding place left?"

"Field's apartment, Cronin," replied Ellery imperturbably. "The papers are there."

"But I was discussing the case with the D. A. only yesterday," objected Cronin, "and he said you'd already ransacked Field's apartment and found nothing."

"True—true enough," said Ellery. "We searched Field's apartment and found nothing. The trouble was, Cronin, that we didn't look in the right place."

"Well, by ginger, if you know now, let's get a move on!" cried Cronin, springing from his chair.

The Inspector tapped the red-haired man's knee gently and pointed to the seat. "Sit down, Tim," he advised. "Ellery is merely indulging in his favorite game of ratiocination. He doesn't know where the papers are any

more than you do. He's guessing. . . . In detective literature," he added
with a sad smile, "they call it the 'art of deduction.' "

"I should say," murmured Ellery, emitting a cloud of smoke, "that I am
being challenged once more. Nevertheless, although I haven't been back
to Field's rooms I intend, with Inspector Queen's kind permission, to return there and find the slippery documents."

"In the matter of these papers—" began the old man, when he was interrupted by the doorbell ringing. Djuna admitted Sergeant Velie, who
was accompanied by a small, furtive young man so ill at ease as to be
trembling. The Inspector sprang to his feet and intercepted them before
they could enter the living room. Cronin stared as Queen said, "This the
fellow, Thomas?" and the big detective answered with grim levity, "Large
as life, Inspector."

"Think you could burgle an apartment without being caught, do you?"
inquired the Inspector genially, taking the newcomer by the arm. "You're
just the man I want."

The furtive young man seemed overcome by a species of terrified
palsy. "Say, Inspector, yer not takin' me fer a ride, are ya?" he stammered.

The Inspector smiled reassuringly and led him out into the foyer. They
held a whispered and one-sided conversation, with the stranger grunting
assents at every second word uttered by the old man. Cronin and Ellery in
the living room caught the flash of a small sheet of paper as it passed from
the Inspector's hand into the clutching paw of the young man.

Queen returned, stepping spryly. "All right, Thomas. You take care of
the other arrangements and see that our friend here gets into no trouble. . . . Now, gentlemen—"

Velie made his adieu monosyllabically and led the frightened stranger
from the apartment.

The Inspector sat down. "Before we go over to Field's rooms, boys," he
said thoughtfully, "I want to make certain things plain. In the first place,
from what Benjamin Morgan has told us, Field's business was law but his
great source of income—blackmail. Did you know that, Tim? Monte Field
sucked dozens of prominent men dry, in all likelihood to the tune of hundreds of thousands of dollars. In fact, Tim, we're convinced that the motive behind Field's murder was connected with this phase of his undercover activites. There is no doubt but that he was killed by somebody who
was being taken in for huge sums of hush-money and could stand the gaff
no longer.

"You know as well as I, Tim, that blackmail depends largely for its ugly
life on the possession of incriminating documents by the blackmailer.
That's why we're so sure that there are hidden papers about somewhere—
and Ellery here maintains that they're in Field's rooms. Well, we'll see. If

eventually we find those papers, the documents you've been hunting so long will probably come to light also, as Ellery pointed out a moment ago."

He paused reflectively. "I can't tell you, Tim, how badly I want to get my hands on those confounded documents of Field's. They mean a good deal to me. They'd clear up a lot of questions about which we're still in the dark. . . ."

"Well, then, let's get going!" cried Cronin, leaping from his chair. "Do you realize, Inspector, that I've worked for years on Field's tail for this one purpose? It will be the happiest day of my life. . . . Inspector—come on!"

Neither Ellery nor his father, however, seemed to be in haste. They retired to the bedroom to dress while Cronin fretted in the living room. If Cronin had not been so preoccupied with his own thoughts he would have noticed that the light spirits which had suffused the Queens when he arrived were now scattered into black gloom. The Inspector particularly seemed out of sorts, irritable and for once slow to push the investigation into an inevitable channel.

Eventually the Queens appeared fully dressed. The three men descended to the street. As they climbed into a taxicab Ellery sighed.

"Afraid you're going to be shown up, son?" muttered the old man, his nose buried in the folds of his topcoat.

"I'm not thinking of that," returned Ellery. "It's something else. . . . The papers will be found, never fear."

"I hope to Christmas you're right!" breathed Cronin fervently, and it was the last word spoken until the taxicab ground to a stop before the lofty apartment house on 75th Street.

The three men took the elevator to the fourth floor and stepped out into the quiet corridor. The Inspector peered about quickly, then punched the doorbell of the Field apartment. There was no answer, although they could hear the vague rustling of someone behind the door. Suddenly it swished open to reveal a red-faced policeman whose hand hovered uneasily in the region of his hip pocket.

"Don't be scared, man—we won't bite you!" growled the Inspector, who was completely out of temper for no reason that Cronin, nervous and springy as a racing colt, could fathom.

The uniformed man saluted. "Didn't know but it might be someone snoopin' around, Inspector," he said feebly.

The three men walked into the foyer, the slim, white hand of the old man pushing the door violently shut.

"Anything been happening around here?" snapped Queen, striding to the entrance to the living room and looking inside.

"Not a thing, sir," said the policeman. "I'm on four-hour shifts with Cassidy as relief and once in a while Detective Ritter drops in to see if everything is all right."

"Oh, he does, does he?" The old man turned back. "Anybody try to get into the place?"

"Not while I was here, Inspector—nor Cassidy neither," responded the policeman nervously. "And we've been alternating ever since Tuesday morning. There hasn't been a soul near these rooms except Ritter."

"Park out here in the foyer for the next couple of hours, officer," commanded the Inspector. "Get yourself a chair and take a snooze if you want to—but if anybody should start monkeying with the door tip us off pronto."

The policeman dragged a chair from the living room into the foyer, sat down with his back against the front door, folded his arms and unashamedly closed his eyes.

The three men took in the scene with gloomy eyes. The foyer was small but crowded with oddments of furniture and decoration. A bookcase filled with unused-appearing volumes; a small table on which perched a "modernistic" lamp and some carved ivory ashtrays; two Empire chairs; a peculiar piece of furniture which seemed half sideboard and half secretary; and a number of cushions and rugs were scattered about. The Inspector stood regarding this melange wryly.

"Here, son—I guess the best way for us to tackle the search is for the three of us to go through everything piece by piece, one checking up on the other. I'm not very hopeful about it. I'll tell you that."

"The gentleman of the Wailing Wall," groaned Ellery. "Grief is writ fine and large on his noble visage. You and I, Cronin—we're not such pessimists, are we?"

Cronin growled, "I'd say—less talk and more action, with all the respects in the world for these little family ructions."

Ellery stared at him with admiration. "You're almost insectivorous in your determination, man. More like an army ant than a human being. And poor Field's lying in the morgue, too. . . . *Allons, enfants!*"

They set to work under the nodding head of the policeman. They worked silently for the most part. Ellery's face reflected a calm expectancy; the Inspector's a doleful irritation; Cronin's a savage indomitability. Book after book was extracted from the case and carefully inspected—leaves shaken out—covers examined minutely—backboards pinched and pierced. There were over two hundred books and the thorough search took a long time. Ellery, after a period of activity, seemed inclined to allow his father and Cronin to do the heavier work of inspection while he devoted his attention more and more to the titles of the volumes.

At one point he uttered a delighted exclamation and held up to the light a thin, cheaply bound book. Cronin leaped forward immediately, his eyes blazing. The Inspector looked up with a flicker of interest. But Ellery had merely discovered another volume on handwriting analysis.

The old man stared at his son in silent curiosity, his lips puckered thoughtfully. Cronin turned back to the bookcase with a groan. Ellery, however, riffling the pages rapidly cried out again. The two men craned over his shoulder. On the margins of several pages were some penciled notations. The words spelled names: "Henry Jones," "John Smith," "George Brown." They were repeated many times on the margins of the page, as if the writer were practicing different styles of penmanship.

"Didn't Field have the most adolescent yen for scribbling?" asked Ellery, staring fascinatedly at the penciled names.

"As usual you have something up your sleeve, my son," remarked the Inspector wearily. "I see what you mean, but I don't see that it helps us any. Except for— By jinks, that's an idea!"

He bent forward and attacked the search once more, his body vibrant with fresh interest. Ellery, smiling, joined him. Cronin stared uncomprehendingly at both.

"Suppose you let me in on this thing, folks," he said in an aggrieved voice.

The Inspector straightened up. "Ellery's hit on something that, if it's true, is a bit of luck for us and reveals still another sidelight on Field's character. The blackhearted rascal! See here, Tim—if a man's an inveterate blackmailer and you find continual evidence that he has been practicing handwriting from textbooks on the subject, what conclusion would you draw?"

"You mean that he's a forger, too?" frowned Cronin. "I never suspected that in spite of all these years of hounding him."

"Not merely a forger, Cronin," laughed Ellery. "I don't think you will find Monte Field has penned somebody else's name to a check, or anything of that sort. He was too wily a bird to make such a grievous error. What he probably did do was secure original and incriminating documents referring to a certain individual, make copies of them and sell the *copies* back to the owner, retaining the originals for further use!"

"And in that case, Tim," added the Inspector portentously, "if we find this gold mine of papers somewhere about—which I greatly doubt—we'll also find, as like as not, the original or originals of the papers for which Monte Field was murdered!"

The red-haired Assistant District Attorney pulled a long face at his two companions. "Seems like a lot of 'if's' " he said finally, shaking his head.

They resumed the search in growing silence.

Nothing was concealed in the foyer. After an hour of steady, back-breaking work they were forced reluctantly to that conclusion. Not a square inch was left unexamined. The interior of the lamp and of the bookcase; the slender, thin-topped table; the secretary, inside and outside; the cushions; even the walls tapped carefully by the Inspector, who by now was aroused to a high pitch of excitement, suppressed but remarkable in his tight lips and color-touched cheeks.

They attacked the living room. Their first port-of-call was the wall, searching for signs of tampered woodwork. And still the big clothes closet inside the room directly off the foyer. Again the Inspector and Ellery went through the topcoats, overcoats and capes hanging on the rack. Nothing. On the shelf above were the four hats they had examined on Tuesday morning: the old Panama, the derby and the two fedoras. Still nothing. Cronin bumped down on his knees to peer savagely into the darker recesses of the closet, tapping the wall, searching for signs of tampered woodwork. And still nothing. With the aid of a chair the Inspector poked into the corners of the area above the shelf. He climbed down, shaking his head.

"Forget the closet, boys," he muttered. They descended upon the room proper.

The large carved desk which Hagstrom and Piggott had rifled three days before invited their scrutiny. Inside was the pile of papers, canceled bills and letters they had offered for the old man's inspection. Old Queen actually peered through these torn and ragged sheets as if they might conceal messages in invisible ink. He shrugged his shoulders and threw them down.

"Darned if I'm not growing romantic in my old age," he growled. "The influence of a fiction-writing rascal of a son."

He picked up the miscellaneous articles he himself had found on Tuesday in the pockets of the closet coats. Ellery was scowling now; Cronin was beginning to wear a forlorn, philosophical expression; the old man shuffled abstractedly among the keys, old letters, wallets, and then turned away.

"Nothing in the desk," he announced wearily. "I doubt if that clever limb of Satan would have selected anything as obvious as a desk for a hiding place."

"He would if he'd read Edgar Allen Poe," murmured Ellery. "Let's get on. Sure there is no secret drawer here?" he asked Cronin. The red head was shaken sadly but emphatically.

They probed and poked about in the furniture, under the carpets and lamps, in bookends, curtain rods. With each successive failure the apparent hopelessness of the search was reflected in their faces. When they had finished with the living room it looked as if it had innocently fallen in the path of a hurricane—a bare and comfortless satisfaction.

"Nothing left but the bedroom, kitchenette and lavatory," said the Inspector to Cronin; and the three men went into the room which Mrs. Angela Russo had occupied Monday night.

Field's bedroom was distinctly feminine in its accoutrements—a characteristic which Ellery ascribed to the influence of the charming Greenwich Villager. Again they scoured the premises, not an inch of space eluding their vigilant eyes and questing hands; and again there seemed nothing to do but admit failure. They took apart the bedding and examined the spring of the bed; they put it together again and attacked the clothes closet. Every suit was mauled and crushed by their insistent fingers—bathrobes, dressing gowns, shoes, cravats. Cronin halfheartedly repeated his examination of the walls and moldings. They lifted rugs and picked up chairs; shook out the pages of the telephone book in the bedside telephone table. The Inspector even lifted the metal disk which fitted around the steampipe at the floor, because it was loose and seemed to present possibilities.

From the bedroom they went into the kitchenette. It was so crowded with kitchen furnishings that they could barely move about. A large cabinet was rifled; Cronin's exasperated fingers dipped angrily into the flour and sugar bins. The stove, the dish closet, the pan closet—even the single marble washtub in a corner—was methodically gone over. On the floor to one side stood the half empty case of liquor bottles. Cronin cast longing glances in this direction, only to look guiltily away as the Inspector glared at him.

"And now—the bathroom," murmured Ellery. In an ominous silence they trooped into the tiled lavatory. Three minutes later they came out, still silently, and went into the living room where they disposed themselves in chairs. The Inspector drew out his snuffbox and took a vicious pinch; Cronin and Ellery lit cigarettes.

"I should say, my son," said the Inspector in sepulchral tones after a painful interval broken only by the snores of the policeman in the foyer, "I should say that the deductive method which has brought fame and fortune to Mr. Sherlock Holmes and his legions has gone awry. Mind you, I'm not scolding. . . ." But he slouched into the fastnesses of the chair.

Ellery stroked his smooth jaw with nervous fingers. "I seem to have made something of an ass of myself," he confessed. "And yet those papers are here somewhere. Isn't that a silly notion to have? But logic bears me out. When ten is the whole and two plus three plus four are discarded, only one is left. . . . Pardon me for being old-fashioned. I insist the papers are here."

Cronin grunted and expelled a huge mouthful of smoke.

"Your objection sustained," murmured Ellery, leaning back. "Let's go over the ground again. No, no!" he explained hastily, as Cronin's face lengthened in dismay—"I mean orally. . . . Mr. Field's apartment consists of a foyer, a living room, a kitchenette, a bedroom and a lavatory. We have fruitlessly examined a foyer, a living room, a kitchenette, a bedroom and a lavatory. Euclid would regretfully force a conclusion here. . . ." He mused, "How have we examined these rooms?" he asked suddenly. "We have gone over the obvious things, pulled the obvious things to pieces. Furniture, lamps, carpets—I repeat, the obvious things. And we have tapped floors, walls and moldings. It would seem that nothing has escaped the search. . . ."

He stopped, his eyes brightening. The Inspector threw off his look of fatigue at once. From experience he was aware that Ellery rarely grew excited over inconsequential things.

"And yet," said Ellery slowly, gazing in fascination at his father's face, "by the Golden Roofs of Seneca, we've overlooked something—actually overlooked something!"

"What!" growled Cronin. "You're kidding."

"Oh, but I'm not," chuckled Ellery, lounging to his feet. "We have examined floors and we have examined walls, but have we examined—ceilings?"

He shot the word forth theatrically while the two men stared at him in amazement.

"Here, what are you driving at, Ellery?" asked his father, frowning.

A—Ceiling
B—Door to Living Room
C—Mirror
D—Dressing Table

E—Damask curtains around bed, from ceiling to floor, concealing shaded portino which represents panel containing hats.

Ellery briskly crushed his cigarette in an ashtray. "Just this," he said. "Pure reasoning has it that when you have exhausted every possibility but one in a given equation that one, no matter how impossible, no matter how ridiculous it may seem in the postulation—*must be the correct one*. . . . A theorem analogous to the one by which I concluded that the papers were in this apartment."

"But, Mr. Queen, for the love of Pete—ceilings!" exploded Cronin, while the Inspector looked guiltily at the living room ceiling. Ellery caught the look and laughed, shaking his head.

"I'm not suggesting that we call in a plasterer to maul these lovely middle-class ceilings," he said. "Because I have the answer already. What is it in these rooms somewhere that is on the ceiling?"

"The chandeliers," muttered Cronin doubtfully, gazing upward at the heavily bronzed fixture above their heads.

"By jinks—the canopy over the bed!" shouted the Inspector. He jumped to his feet and ran into the bedroom. Cronin pounded hard after him, Ellery sauntering interestedly behind.

They stopped at the foot of the bed and stared up at the canopy. Unlike the conventional canopies of American style, this florid ornament was not merely a large square of cloth erected on four posts, an integral part of the bed only. The bed was so constructed that the four posts, beginning at the four corners, stretched from floor to ceiling. The heavy maroon-colored damask of the canopy also reached from floor to ceiling, connected at the top by a ringed rod from which the folds of the damask hung gracefully.

"Well, if it's anywhere," grunted the Inspector, dragging one of the damask-covered bedroom chairs to the bed, "it's up here. Here, boys, lend a hand."

He stood on the chair with a fine disregard for the havoc his shoes were wreaking on the silken material. Finding upon stretching his arms above his head that he was still many feet short of touching the ceiling, he stepped down.

"Doesn't look as if you could make it either, Ellery," he muttered. "And Field was no taller than you. There must be a ladder handy somewhere by which Field himself got up here!"

Cronin dashed into the kitchenette at Ellery's nod in that direction. He was back in a moment with a six-foot stepladder. The Inspector, mounting to the highest rung, found that his fingers were still short of touching the rod. Ellery solved the difficulty by ordering his father down and climbing to the top himself. Standing on the ladder he was in a position to explore the top of the canopy.

He grasped the damask firmly and pulled. The entire fabric gave way and fell to the sides, revealing a wooden panel about twelve inches deep—a framework which the hangings had concealed. Ellery's fingers swept swiftly over the wooden reliefwork of this panel. Cronin and the Inspector were staring with varying expressions up at him. Finding nothing that at the moment presented a possibility of entrance, Ellery leaned forward and explored the damask directly beneath the floor of the panel.

"Rip it down!" growled the Inspector.

Ellery jerked violently at the material and the entire canopy of damask fell to the bed. The bare unornamented floor of the panel was revealed.

"It's hollow," announced Ellery, rapping his knuckles on the underside paneling.

"That doesn't help much," said Cronin. "It wouldn't be a solid chunk, anyway. Why don't you try the other side of the bed, Mr. Queen?"

But Ellery, who had drawn back and was again examining the side of the panel, exclaimed triumphantly. He had been seeking a complicated, Machiavellian "secret door"—he found now that the secret door was nothing more subtle than a sliding panel. It was cleverly concealed—the juncture of sliding and stationary panels was covered by a row of wooden rosettes and clumsy decorations—but it was nothing that a student of mystery lore would have hailed as a triumph of concealment.

"It begins to appear as if I were being vindicated," Ellery chuckled as he peered into the black recesses of the hole he had uncovered. He thrust a long arm into the aperture. The Inspector and Cronin were staring at him with bated breath.

"By all the pagan gods," shouted Ellery suddenly, his lean body quivering with excitement. "Do you remember what I told you, Dad? Where would those papers be except in—hats!"

His sleeve coated with dust, he withdrew his arm and the two men below saw in his hand a musty silk tophat!

Cronin executed an intricate jig as Ellery dropped the hat on the bed and dipped his arm once more into the yawning hole. In a moment he had brought out another hat—and another—and still another! There they lay on the bed—two silk hats and two derbies.

"Take this flashlight, son," commanded the Inspector. "See if there's anything else up there."

Ellery took the proffered electric torch and flashed its beam into the aperture. After a moment he clambered down, shaking his head.

"That's all," he announced, dusting his sleeve, "but I should think it would be enough."

The Inspector picked up the four hats and carried them into the living room, where he deposited them on a sofa. The three men sat down gravely and regarded each other.

"I'm sort of itching to see what's what," said Cronin finally, in a hushed voice.

"I'm rather afraid to look," retorted the Inspector.

"*Mene mene tekel upharsin*," laughed Ellery. "In this case it might be interpreted as 'the handwriting on the panel.' Examine on, Macduff!"

The Inspector picked up one of the silk hats. It bore on the rich satiny lining the chaste trademark of Browne Bros. Ripping out the lining and finding nothing beneath, he tried to tear out the leather sweat-band. It resisted his mightiest efforts. He borrowed Cronin's pocket knife and with difficulty slashed away the band. Then he looked up.

"This hat, Romans and countrymen," he said pleasantly, "contains nothing but the familiar ingredients of hat-wear. Would you care to examine it?"

Cronin uttered a savage cry and snatched it from the Inspector's hand. He literally tore the hat to pieces in his rage.

"Heck!" he said disgustedly, throwing the remnants on the floor. "Explain that to my undeveloped brain, will you, Inspector?"

Queen smiled, taking up the second silk hat and regarding it curiously.

"You're at a disadvantage, Tim," he said. "We know why one of these hats is a blank. Don't we, Ellery?"

"Michaels," murmured Ellery.

"Exactly—Michaels," returned the Inspector.

"Charley Michaels!" exclaimed Cronin. "Field's strong-arm guy, by all that's holy! Where does he come into this?"

"Can't tell yet. Know anything about him?"

"Nothing except that he hung onto Field's coattails pretty closely. He's an ex-jailbird, did you know that?"

"Yes," replied the Inspector dreamily. "We'll have a talk about that phase of Mr. Michaels some other time. . . . But let me explain that hat: Michaels on the evening of the murder laid out, according to his statement, Field's evening clothes, including a silk hat. Michaels swore that as far as he knew Field possessed only *one* topper. Now if we suppose that Field used hats for concealing papers, and was going to the Roman Theatre that night wearing a 'loaded' one he must necessarily have substituted the loaded hat for the empty one which Michaels prepared. Since he was so careful to keep only one silk hat in the closet, he realized that Michaels, should he find a topper, would be suspicious. So, in switching hats, he had to conceal the empty one. What more natural than that he should put it in the place from which he had taken the loaded hat—the panel above the bed?"

"Well, I'll be switched!" exclaimed Cronin.

"Finally," resumed the Inspector, "We can take it as gospel that Field, who was devilishly careful in the matter of his headgear, intended to re-store the theatre hat to its hideaway when he got home from the Roman. Then he would have taken out this one which you've just torn up and put it back in the clothes closet. . . . But let's get on."

He pulled down the leather innerband of the second silk hat, which also bore the imprint of Browne Bros. "Look at this, will you!" he ex-claimed. The two men bent over and saw on the inner surface of the band, lettered with painful clarity in a purplish ink, the words BENJAMIN MORGAN.

"I've got to pledge you to secrecy, Tim," said the Inspector immedi-ately, turning to the red-haired man. "Never let on that you were a wit-ness to the finding of papers in any way implicating Benjamin Morgan in this affair."

"What do you think I am, Inspector?" growled Cronin. "I'm as dumb as an oyster, believe me!"

"All right, then." Queen felt the lining of the hat. There was a distinct crackle.

"Now," remarked Ellery calmly, "we know for the first time definitely why the murderer *had* to take away the hat Field wore Monday night. In all likelihood the murderer's name was lettered in the same way—that's indelible ink, you know—and the murderer couldn't leave a hat with his own name in it at the scene of the crime."

"By gosh, if you only had that hat, now," cried Cronin, "you'd know who the murderer is!"

"I'm afraid, Tim," replied the Inspector dryly, "that hat is gone for-ever."

He indicated a row of careful stitches at the base of the inner band, where the lining was attached to the fabric. He ripped these stitches swiftly and inserted his fingers between the lining and the crown. Silently he drew out a sheaf of papers held together by a thin rubber band.

"If I were as nasty as some people think I am," mused Ellery, leaning back, "I might with perfect justice say, 'I told you so.' "

"We know when we're licked, my son—don't rub it in," chortled the Inspector. He snapped off the rubber band, glanced hastily through the papers and with a satisfied grin deposited them in his breast pocket.

"Morgan's, all right," he said briefly, and attacked one of the derbies.

The inner side of the band was marked cryptically with an X. The In-spector found a row of stitches exactly as in the silk hat. The papers he drew out—a thicker bundle than Morgan's—he examined cursorily. Then he handed them to Cronin, whose fingers were trembling.

"A stroke of luck, Tim," he said slowly. "The man you were angling for is dead, but there are a lot of big names in this. I think you'll find yourself a hero one of these days."

Cronin grasped the bundle and feverishly unfolded the papers, one by one. "They're here—they're here!" he shouted. He jumped to his feet, stuffing the sheaf into his pocket.

"I've got to beat it, Inspector," he said rapidly. "There's a lot of work to do at last—and besides, what you find in that fourth hat is none of my business. I can't thank you and Mr. Queen enough! So long!"

He dashed from the room, and a moment later the snores of the policeman in the foyer came to an abrupt end. The outer door banged shut.

Ellery and the Inspector looked at each other.

"I don't know what good this stuff is going to do us," grumbled the old man, fumbling with the inner band of the last hat, a derby. "We've found things and deduced things and run rings around our imaginations—well . . ." He sighed as he held the band up to the light.

It was marked: MISC.

# 18

## Stalemate

At Friday noon, while Inspector Queen, Ellery and Timothy Cronin were deep in their search of Monte Field's rooms, Sergeant Velie, sombre and unmoved as usual, walked slowly up 87th Street from Broadway, mounted the brownstone steps of the house in which the Queens lived and rang the bell. Djuna's cheery voice bade him ascend, which the good Sergeant did with gravity.

"Inspector's not home!" announced Djuna pertly, his slim body completely hidden behind an enormous housewife's apron. Odorous traces of an onion-covered steak pervaded the air.

"Get on with you, you imp!" growled Velie. He took from his inner breast pocket a bulky envelope sealed, and handed it to Djuna. "Give this to the Inspector when he comes home. Forget, and I'll dip you into the East River."

"You and who else?" breathed Djuna, with a remarkable twitching of his lips. Then he added decorously, "Yes, sir."

"All right, then." Velie deliberatley turned about and descended to the street, where his broad back was visible in formidable proportions to the grinning Djuna from the fourth-story window.

When, at a little before six, the two Queens trudged wearily into their rooms, the alert eyes of the Inspector pounced upon the official envelope where it lay on his plate.

He tore off a corner of the envelope and pulled out a number of type-written sheets on the stationery of the Detective Bureau.

"Well, well!" he muttered to Ellery, who was lazily pulling off his top-coat. "The clans are gathering. . . ."

Sinking into an armchair, his hat forgotten on his head, his coat still buttoned, he set about reading the reports aloud.

The first slip read:

## REPORT OF RELEASE

28 September 192–

John Cazzanelli, alias Parson Johnny, alias John the Wop, alias Peter Dominick, released from custody today on parole.

Undercover investigation of J. C.'s complicity in the robbery of the Bonomo Silk Mills (June 2, 192–) not successful. We are searching for "Dinky" Morehouse, police informer, who has disappeared from usual haunts, for further information.

Release effected under advice of District Attorney Sampson. J. C. under surveillance and is available at any time.

T. V.

The second report which the Inspector picked up, laying aside the advices concerning Parson Johnny with a frown, read as follows:

## REPORT ON WILLIAM PUSAK

September 28, 192–

Investigation of the history of William Pusak reveals the following:

32 years old; born in Brooklyn, N.Y., of naturalized parents; unmarried; regular habits; socially inclined; has "dates" three or four nights a week; religious. Is bookkeeper at Stein & Rauch, clothing merchants, 1076 Broadway. Does not gamble or drink. No evil companions. Only vice seems fondness for girls.

Activities since Monday night normal. No letters sent, no money withdrawn from bank, hours fairly regular. No suspicious movements of any kind.

Girl, Esther Jablow, seems Pusak's "steadiest." Has seen E. J. twice since Monday—Tuesday at lunch, Wednesday evening. Went to movies and Chinese restaurant Wednesday evening.

Operative No. 4

OK'd: T. V.

The Inspector grunted as he threw the sheet aside. The third report was headed:

## REPORT ON MADGE O'CONNELL

To Friday, Sept. 28, '2–

O'Connell, lives at 1436 10th Avenue. Tenement, 4th floor. No father. Idle since Monday night, due to shutting down of Roman Theatre. Left theatre Monday night at general release of public.

Went home, but stopped in drugstore corner 8th Avenue and 48th Street to telephone. Unable to trace call. Overheard reference to Parson Johnny in phone conversation. Seemed excited.

Tuesday did not leave house until 1 o'clock. No attempt to get in touch with Parson Johnny at Tombs. Went around theatre employment agencies looking for usherette position after finding out Roman Theatre was closed indefinitely.

Nothing new Wednesday all day or Thursday. Returned to work at Roman Thursday night after call from manager. No attempt see or communicate with Parson Johnny. No incoming calls, no visitors, no mail. Seemed suspicious—think she is "wise" to tailing.

Operative No. 11<br>OK'd: T. V.

"Hmph!" muttered the Inspector as he picked up the next sheet of paper. "Let's see what this one says. . . ."

## REPORT ON FRANCES IVES-POPE

September 28, 192–

F. I.-P. left Roman Theatre Monday night directly after release from Manager's Office by Inspector Queen. Examined with other departing members of audience at main door. Left in company of Eve Ellis, Stephen Barry, Hilda Orange, of the cast. Took taxi to Ives-Pope house on Riverside Drive. Taken out in half-unconscious condition. Three actors left house soon after.

Tuesday she did not leave house. Learned from a gardener she was laid up in bed all day. Learned she received many calls during day.

Did not appear formally until Wednesday morning at interview in house with Inspector Queen. After interview, left house in company of Stephen Barry, Eve Ellis, James Peale, her brother Stanford. Ives-Pope limousine drove party out into Westchester. Outing revived F. Evening stayed at home with Stephen Barry. Bridge party on.

Thursday went shopping on Fifth Avenue. Met Stephen Barry for luncheon. He took her to Central Park; spent afternoon in open. S. B. escorted her home before five. S. B. stayed to dinner, leaving after dinner for work at Roman Theatre on call from stage manager. F. I.-P. spent evening at home with family.

No report Friday morning. No suspicious actions all week. At no time accosted by strange persons. No communication from or to Benjamin Morgan.

Operative No. 39<br>OK'd: T. V.

"And that's that," murmured the Inspector. The next report he selected was extremely short.

## REPORT ON OSCAR LEWIN

September 28, 192–

Lewin spent all day Tuesday, Wednesday, Thursday and Friday morning at office of Monte Field working with Messrs. Stoates and Cronin. Three men lunched together on each day.

Lewin married, lives in Bronx, 211 E. 156th Street. Spent every evening at home. No suspicious mail, no suspicious calls. No evil habits. Leads sober, modest life. Has good reputation.

Operative No. 16

NOTE: Full details of Oscar Lewin's history, habits, etc., available on request through Timothy Cronin, Assistant District Attorney.

T. V.

The Inspector sighed as he deposited the five sheets of paper on his plate, rose, doffed his hat and coat, flung them into Djuna's waiting arms and sat down again. Then he picked up the last report from the contents of the envelope—a larger sheet to which was pinned a small slip marked: MEMORANDUM TO R. Q.

This slip read:

Dr. Prouty left the attached report with me this morning for transmission to you. He is sorry he could not report in person, but the Burbridge poison case is taking all his time.

It was signed with Velie's familiar scrawling initials.

The attached sheet was a hastily typewritten message on the letterhead of the Chief Medical Examiner's office.

Dear Q [the message ran]: Here's the dope on the tetra ethyl lead. Jones and I have been superintending an exhaustive probe of all possible sources of dissemination. No success, and I think you can resign yourself to your fate in this respect. You'll never trace the poison that killed Monte Field. This is the opinion not merely of your humble servant but of the Chief and of Jones. We all agree that the most logical explanation is the gasoline theory. Try to trace *that*, Sherlocko!

A postscript in Dr. Prouty's handwriting ran:

Of course, if anything turns up, I'll let you know immediately. Keep sober.

"Fat lot of good *that* is!" mumbled the Inspector, as Ellery without a word attacked the aromatic and tempting meal that the priceless Djuna had prepared. The Inspector dug viciously into the fruit salad. He looked far from happy. He grumbled beneath his breath, cast baleful glances at the sheaf of reports by his plate, peered up at Ellery's tired face and heartily munching jaws and finally threw down his spoon altogether.

"Of all the useless, exasperating, empty bunch of reports I ever saw—!" he growled.

Ellery smiled. "You remember Periander, of course. . . . Eh? You might be polite, sir. . . . Periander of Corinth, who said in a moment of sobriety, 'To industry nothing is impossible!' "

With the fire roaring, Djuna curled up on the floor in a corner, his favorite attitude. Ellery smoked a cigarette and stared comfortably into the flames while old Queen crammed his nose vengefully with the contents of his snuffbox. The two Queens settled down to a serious discussion. To be more exact—Inspector Queen settled down and lent the tone of seriousness to the conversation, since Ellery seemed in a sublimely dreamy mood far removed from the sordid details of crime and punishment.

The old man brought his hand down on the arm of his chair with a sharp slap. "Ellery, did you ever in your born days see a case so positively nerve-racking?"

"On the contrary," commented Ellery, staring with half-closed eyes into the fire. "You are developing a natural case of nerves. You allow little things like apprehending a murderer to upset you unduly. Pardon the hedonistic philosophy. . . . If you will recall, in my story entitled 'The Affair of the Black Widow,' my good sleuths had no difficulty at all in laying their hands on the criminal. And why? Because they kept their heads. Conclusion: Always keep your head. . . . I'm thinking of tomorrow. Glorious vacation!"

"For an educated man, my son," growled the Inspector petulantly, "you show a surprising lack of coherence. You say things that mean nothing and mean things when you say nothing. No—I'm all mixed up—"

Ellery burst into laughter. "The Maine woods—the russet—the good Chauvin's cabin by the lake—a rod—air—Oh, Lord, won't tomorrow ever come?"

Inspector Queen regarded his son with a pitiful eagerness. "I—I sort of wish . . . Well, never mind." He sighed. "All I do say, El, is that if my little burglar fails—it's all up with us."

"To the blessed Gehenna with burglars!" cried Ellery. "What has Pan to do with human tribulation? My next book is as good as written, Dad."

"Stealing another idea from real life, you rascal," muttered the old man. "If you're borrowing the Field case for your plot, I'd be extremely interested to read your last few chapters!"

"Poor Dad!" chuckled Ellery. "Don't take life so seriously. If you fail, you fail. Monte Field wasn't worth a hill of legumes, anyway."

"That's not the point," said the old man. "I hate to admit defeat. . . . What a queer mess of motives and schemes this case is, Ellery. This is the first time in my entire experience that I have had such a hard nut to crack. It's enough to give a man apoplexy! I know WHO committed the murder—I know WHY the murder was committed—I even know HOW the murder was committed! And where am I? . . ." He paused and savagely took a pinch of snuff. "A million miles from nowhere, that's where!" he growled, and subsided.

"Certainly a most unusual situation," murmured Ellery. "Yet—more difficult things have been accomplished. . . . Heigh-ho! I can't wait to bathe myself in that Arcadian stream!"

"And get pneumonia, probably," said the Inspector anxiously. "You promise me now, young man, that you don't do any back-to-Nature stunts out there. I don't want a funeral on my hands—I . . ."

Ellery grew silent suddenly. He looked over at his father. The Inspector seemed strangely old in the flickering light of the fire. An expression of pain humanized the deeply sculptured lines of his face. His hand, brushing back his thick gray hair, looked alarmingly fragile.

Ellery rose, hesitated, colored, then bent swiftly forward and patted his father on the shoulder.

"Brace up, Dad," he said in a low voice. "If it weren't for my arrangements with Chauvin . . . Everything will be all right—take my word for it. If there were the slightest way in which I could help you by remaining. . . . But there isn't. It's your job now, Dad—and there's no man in the world who can handle it better than you. . . ." The old man stared up at him with a strange affection. Ellery turned abruptly away. "Well," he said lightly, "I'll have to pack now if I expect to make the 7:45 out of Grand Central tomorrow morning."

He disappeared into the bedroom. Djuna, who had been sitting Turkishwise in his corner, got quickly to his feet and crossed the room to the Inspector's chair. He slipped to the floor, his head resting against the old man's knees. The silence was punctuated by the snapping of wood in the fireplace and the muffled sounds of Ellery moving about in the next room.

Inspector Queen was very tired. His face, worn, thin, white, lined, was like a cameo in the dull red light. His hand caressed Djuna's curly head.

"Djuna, lad," he muttered, "never be a policeman when you grow up."

Djuna twisted his neck and stared gravely at the old man. "I'm going to be just what you are," he announced. . . .

The old man leaped to his feet as the telephone bell rang. He snatched the instrument from its table, his face livid, and said in a choked voice: "Queen speaking. Well?"

After a time he put down the phone and trudged across the room toward the bedroom. He leaned against the lintel heavily. Ellery straightened up from his suitcase—and jumped forward.

"Dad!" he cried. "What's the matter?"

The Inspector essayed a feeble smile. "Just—a—little tired, son, I guess," he grunted. "I just heard from our housebreaker. . . ."

"And—?"

"He found absolutely nothing."

Ellery gripped his father's arm and led him to the chair by the bed. The old man slumped into it, his eyes ineffably weary. "Ellery, old son," he said, "the last shred of evidence is gone. It's maddening! Not a morsel of physical, tangible evidence that would convict the murderer in court. What have we? A series of perfectly sound deductions—and that's all. A good lawyer would make Swiss cheese out of our case. . . . Well! The last word hasn't been spoken yet," he added with a sudden grimness as he rose from the chair. He pounded Ellery's broad back in returning vigor.

"Get to bed, son," he said. "You've got to get up early tomorrow morning. I'm going to sit up and think."

# *INTERLUDE*

### IN WHICH THE READER'S ATTENTION
### IS RESPECTFULLY REQUESTED

The current vogue in detective literature is all for the practice of placing the reader in the position of chief sleuth. I have prevailed upon Mr. Ellery Queen to permit at this point in THE ROMAN HAT MYSTERY the interpolation of a challenge to the reader. . . . "Who killed Monte Field?" "How was the murder accomplished?" . . . Mr. Queen agrees with me that the alert student of mystery tales, now being in possession of all the pertinent facts, should at this stage of the story have reached definite conclusions on the questions propounded. The solution—or enough of it to point unerringly to the guilty character—may be reached by a series of logical deductions and psychological observations. . . . In closing my last personal appearance in the tale let me admonish the reader with a variation of the phrase *Caveat Emptor:* "Let the reader beware!"

J. J. McC.

July 30, 2011! I cannot figure out this incredible mystery! I have read other Ellery Queen mysteries where he also is "a challenge to the reader." On THIS challenge I'm Stumped!

I have read CALAMITY TOWN many years ago – in fact, MANY, MANY, MANY!! *

A Stunner of A MYSTERY. I sure had a fascinating time reading Calamity Town, way back when! (In the 1970s)

# PART FOUR

*"The perfect criminal is a superman. He must be meticulous in his techniques: unseen, unseeable, a Lone Wolf. He must have neither friends nor dependents. He must be careful to a fault, quick of brain, hand and foot. . . . But these are nothing. There have been such men. . . . On the other hand, he must be a favored child of Fate—for circumstances over which he cannot have the remotest control must never contrive his downfall. This, I think, is more difficult to achieve. . . . But the last is most difficult of all.* He must never repeat his crime, his weapon or his motive! *. . . In all my two-score years as an official of the American police I have not once encountered the perfect criminal nor investigated the perfect crime."*

—*From* AMERICAN CRIME AND METHODS OF DETECTION
by Richard Queen

# 19

## In Which Inspector Queen Conducts
## More Legal Conversations

It was notable, particularly to District Attorney Sampson, that on Saturday evening Inspector Richard Queen was far from being himself. The old man was irritable, snappish and utterly uncongenial. He paced fretfully across the carpet of Manager Louis Panzer's office, biting his lips and muttering beneath his breath. He seemed oblivious to the presence of Sampson, Panzer and a third person who had never been in that theatrical sanctum before and was seated, mouselike, in one of Panzer's big chairs, his eyes like saucers. This was bright-eyed Djuna, granted the unprecedented privilege of accompanying his gray patron on this last incursion into the Roman Theatre.

In truth, Queen was singularly depressed. He had many times in his official life been confronted by apparently insoluble problems; he had as many times brought triumph out of failure. The Inspector's strange manner therefore was doubly inexplicable to Sampson, who had been associated with the old man for years and had never seen him so completely unstrung.

The old man's moodiness was not due to the progress of the Field investigation, as Sampson worriedly thought. Wiry little Djuna, sitting open-mouthed in his corner, was the only spectator to the Inspector's mad pacing who could have put his finger on the truth. Djuna, wise by virtue of *gamin* perspicacity, observant by nature, familiar with Queen's temperament through a loving association, knew that his patron's manner was due solely to Ellery's absence from the scene. Ellery had left New York on the 7:45 express that morning, having been gloomily accompanied to the station by his father. At the last moment the younger man had changed his mind, announcing his decision to forego the trip to Maine and abide in New York by his father's side until the case was concluded. The old man would have none of it. With his shrewd insight into Ellery's nature, he realized how keenly his highly strung son had been looking forward to this first vacation in over a year. It was not in his heart, impatient as he was for the constant presence of his son, to deprive him of this long contemplated pleasure trip.

Accordingly, he had swept aside Ellery's proposal and pushed him up the steps of the train, with a parting clap and a wan smile. Ellery's last words, shouted from the platform as the train glided out of the station, were: "I'm not forgetting you, Dad. You'll hear from me sooner than you expect!"

Now, torturing the nap of Manager Panzer's rug, the Inspector was feeling the full impact of their separation. His brain was addled, his constitution flabby, his stomach weak, his eyes dim. He felt completely out of tune with the world and its denizens, and he made no attempt to conceal his irritation.

"Should be about time now, Panzer," he growled to the stout little manager. "How long does this infernal audience take to clear out, anyway?"

"In a moment, Inspector, in a moment," replied Panzer. The District Attorney sniffed away the remnants of his cold. Djuna stared in fascination at his god.

A rap on the door twisted their heads about. Tow-headed Harry Neilson, the publicity man, poked his rugged face into the room. "Mind if I join the little party, Inspector?" he inquired cheerfully. "I was in at the birth, and if there's going to be a death—why, I'm aiming to stick around, with your permission!"

The Inspector shot him a dour glance from beneath his shaggy eyebrows. He stood in a Napoleonic attitude, his every hair and muscle bristling with ill-nature. Sampson regarded him in surprise. Inspector Queen was showing an unexpected side to his temper.

"Might's well," he barked. "One more won't hurt. There's an army here as it is."

Neilson reddened slightly and made a move as if to withdraw. The Inspector's eye twinkled with a partial return to good spirits.

"Here—sit down, Neilson," he said, not unkindly. "Mustn't mind an old fogey like me. I'm just frazzled a bit. Might need you tonight at that."

"Glad to be let in on it, Inspector," grinned Neilson. "What's the idea—sort of Spanish Inquisition?"

"Just about." The old man bent his brows. "But—we'll see."

At this moment the door opened and the tall, broad figure of Sergeant Velie stepped quickly into the room. He was carrying a sheet of paper which he handed to the Inspector.

"All present, sir," he said.

"Everybody out?" snapped Queen.

"Yes, sir. I've told the cleaning women to go down into the lounge and hang around until we're through. Cashiers have gone home, so have the ushers and usherettes. Cast is backstage, I guess, getting dressed."

"Right. Let's go, gentlemen." The Inspector stalked out of the room followed closely by Djuna, who had not opened his mouth all evening except to emit noiseless gasps of admiration, for no reason that the amused District Attorney could see. Panzer, Sampson and Neilson also followed, Velie bringing up the rear.

The auditorium was again a vast and deserted place, the empty rows of seats stark and cold. The lights of the theatre had been switched on in full and their cold radiance lit up every corner of the orchestra.

As the five men and Djuna swung toward the extreme left aisle, there was a concerted bobbing of heads from the left section of seats. It was apparent now that a small group of people were awaiting the arrival of the Inspector, who walked heavily down the aisle and took up a position in front of the left boxes, so that all the seated people faced him. Panzer, Neilson and Sampson stood at the head of the aisle with Djuna at one side, a feverish spectator.

The assembled party was placed peculiarly. From the row nearest the Inspector, who stood about halfway down the orchestra, and proceeding towards the rear the only seats occupied were those directly on the left aisle. The end two seats of the dozen rows were filled by a motley aggregation—men and women, old and young. They were the same people who had occupied these chairs on the night of the fatal performance and whom Inspector Queen had personally examined after the discovery of the body. In the section of eight seats—Monte Field's and the empty ones which had surrounded it—were grouped William Pusak, Esther Jablow, Madge O'Connell, Jess Lynch and Parson Johnny—the Parson furtive-eyed, uneasy and whispering to the usherette behind nicotined fingers.

At the Inspector's sudden gesture all became silent as the grave. Sampson, looking about him at the bright chandeliers and lights, the deserted theatre, the lowered curtain, could not help feeling that the stage was being set for dramatic revelations. He leaned forward interestedly. Panzer and Neilson were quiet and watchful. Djuna kept his eyes fixed on the old man.

"Ladies and gentlemen," Queen announced curtly, staring at the assembled company, "I've brought you here for a definite purpose. I will not keep you any longer than is absolutely necessary, but what is necessary and what is not necessary is entirely up to me. If I find that I do not receive what I consider truthful answers to my questions, everybody will stay here until I am satisfied. I want that thoroughly understood before we proceed."

He paused and glared about. There was a ripple of apprehension, a sudden crackle of conversation which died as quickly as it was born.

"On Monday night," continued the Inspector frostily, "you people attended the performance at this theatre and, with the exception of certain employees and others now seated at the rear, occupied the seats in which you now find yourselves." Sampson grinned as he noticed the stiffening of backs at these words, as if each individual felt his seat grow suddenly warm and uncomfortable beneath him.

"I want you to imagine that this is Monday night. I want you to think back to that night and try to remember everything that happened. By everything I mean any occurrence, no matter how trivial or apparently unimportant, that might have left an impression on your memory. . . ."

As the Inspector warmed to his words, a number of people drifted into the orchestra at the rear. Sampson greeted them in whispers. The little party was composed of Eve Ellis, Hilda Orange, Stephen Barry, James Peale and three or four other members of the cast of "Gunplay." They were dressed in their street clothes. Peale whispered to Sampson that they had just come from their dressing rooms and had dropped into the auditorium on hearing voices.

"Queen's holding a little powwow," whispered Sampson in return.

"Do you think the Inspector has any objections to our staying a while and listening?" asked Barry in a low tone, with an apprehensive glance toward the Inspector, who had stopped and was staring icily in their direction.

"Don't see why—" began Sampson worriedly, when Eve Ellis murmured, "Shhh!" and they all became silent.

"*Now*—" said the Inspector venomously, when the flurry had subsided, "this is the situation. Remember, you are now back in Monday evening. The curtain has gone up on the second act and the theatre is dark. There is a lot of noise from the stage and you are intent on the exciting sequences of the play. . . . Did any of you, especially those sitting in the aisle seats, notice anything peculiar, unusual or disturbing around or near you at that time?"

He paused expectantly. There were puzzled, fearful shakings of the head. No one answered.

"Think hard," growled the Inspector. "You remember on Monday night I went down this aisle and questioned all of you in the same vein. Naturally I don't want lies, and I can't reasonably expect that you will tell me something startling now when you could remember nothing Monday night. But this is a desperate situation. A man was murdered here and we are frankly up against it. One of the most difficult cases we have ever encountered! In the light of such a condition, when we find ourselves against a blank wall with not the slightest idea where to turn—I am being honest with you as I expect you to be with me—I *must* turn to you as the only members of the audience five nights ago who were in a position to see something important, if anything important occurred. . . . It has been my experience that often, under stress of nervousness and excitement, a man or woman will forget a little detail that returns to memory after a few hours, days, weeks of normalcy. It is my hope that something of the sort has taken place with you. . . ."

As Inspector Queen spoke, the words dropping acidly from his lips, the company lost its nervousness in its fascinated interest. When he paused, people put their heads together and whispered excitedly, shaking their heads at times, arguing in fierce, low tones at others. The Inspector waited in a resigned patience.

"Raise your hands if you have something to tell me . . ." he said.

A woman's timid white hand fluttered aloft.

"Yes, madam?" commanded Queen, pointing his finger. "Do you recall anything unusual?"

A withered old lady rose embarrassedly to her feet and began to stammer in a squeaking voice. "I don't know whether it's important or not, sir," she said tremulously. "But I do remember some time during the second act a woman, I think it was, walking down the aisle and a few seconds later walking up again."

"Yes? That's interesting, madam," commented the Inspector. "About what time was this—can you recall?"

"I don't remember the time, sir," shrilled the old lady, "but it was about ten minutes or so after the beginning of the act."

"I see. . . . And do you recall anything of her appearance? Was she young or old? What did she wear?"

The old lady looked troubled. "I don't exactly remember, sir," she quavered. "I wasn't paying—"

A high, clear voice interrupted from the rear. Heads twisted about. Madge O'Connell had jumped to her feet.

"You don't have to mess around with that any more, Inspector," she announced coldly. "That lady saw *me* walking down the aisle and back again. That was before I—you know." She winked pertly in the Inspector's direction.

People gasped. The old lady stared with pitiful bewilderment at the usherette, then at the Inspector and finally sat down.

"I'm not surprised," said the Inspector quietly. "Well, anybody else?"

There was no answer. Realizing that the company might feel shy of announcing their thoughts in public Queen started up the aisle, working from row to row, questioning each person separately in tones inaudible to the rest. When he had finished he returned slowly to his original position.

"I see that I must allow you ladies and gentlemen to return to your peaceful firesides. Thank you very much for your help. . . . Dismissed!"

He flung the word at them. They stared at him dazedly, then rose in muttering groups, took up their coats and hats and under Velie's stern eye began to file out of the theatre. Hilda Orange, standing in the group behind the last row, sighed.

"It's almost embarrassing to see that poor old gentleman's disappointment," she whispered to the others. "Come on, folks, let's be going, too."

The actors and actresses left the theatre among the departing company.

When the last man and woman had disappeared, the Inspector marched back up the aisle and stood gloomily staring at the little group who were left. They seemed to sense the seething fire in the old man and they cowered. But the Inspector, with a characteristic lightning change of front, became human again.

He sat down in one of the seats and folded his arms over the back, surveying Madge O'Connell, Parson Johnny and the others.

"All right, folks," he said in a genial tone. "How about you, Parson? You're a free man, you don't have to worry about silks any more and you can speak up now like any self-respecting citizen. Can you give us any help in this affair?"

"Naw," grunted the little gangster. "I told you all I knew. Ain't got a thing to say."

"I see. . . . You know, Parson, that we're interested in your dealings with Field." The gangster looked up in shocked surprise. "Oh, yes," continued the Inspector. "We want you to tell us sometime about your business with Mr. Field in the past. You'll keep that in mind, won't you? . . . Parson," he said sharply, "who killed Monte Field? Who had it in for him? If you know—out with it!"

"Aw, Inspector," the Parson whined, "you ain't pullin' that stuff on me again, are you? How should I know? Field was one slick guy—he didn't go around welching on his enemies. No, sir! *I* wouldn't know. . . . He was pretty good to me—got me off on a couple of charges," he admitted unblushingly. "But I didn't have no more idea he was here Monday night than—hell, than anything."

The Inspector turned to Madge O'Connell.

"How about you, O'Connell?" he asked softly. "My son, Mr. Queen, tells me that on Monday night you confided in him about closing the exit doors. You didn't say anything to me about that. What do *you* know?"

The girl returned his stare coolly. "I told you once, Inspector. I haven't a thing to say."

"And you, William Pusak—" Queen turned to the wizened little book-keeper. "Do you remember anything now that you forgot Monday night?"

Pusak wiggled uncomfortably. "Meant to tell you, Inspector," he mumbled. "And when I read about it in the papers it came back to me. . . . As I bent over Mr. Field Monday night I smelled a terrible smell of whisky. I don't remember if I told you that before."

"Thank you," remarked the Inspector dryly, rising. "A very important contribution to our little investigation. You may go, the whole lot of you. . . ."

The orangeade boy, Jess Lynch, looked disappointed. "Don't you want to talk to me, too, sir?" he asked anxiously.

The Inspector smiled despite his abstraction. "Ah, yes. The helpful purveyor of orangeade. . . . And what have you to say, Jess?"

"Well, sir, before this fellow Field came over to my stand to ask for the ginger ale, I happened to notice that he picked up something in the alleyway," said the boy eagerly. "It was shiny, sort of, but I couldn't see it clear enough. He put it in his hip pocket right away."

He concluded triumphantly, glancing about him as if to invite applause. The Inspector seemed interested enough.

"What was this shiny object like, Jess?" he inquired. "Might it have been a revolver?"

"Revolver? Gosh, I don't think so," said the orangeade boy doubtfully. "It was square, like. . . ."

"Might it have been a woman's purse?" interrupted the Inspector.

The boy's face brightened. "That's it!" he cried. "I'll bet that's what it was. Shined all over, like colored stones."

Queen sighed. "Very good, Lynch," he said. "You go home now like a good boy."

Silently the gangster, the usherette, Pusak and his feminine charge, and the orangeade boy rose and departed. Velie accompanied them to the outer door.

Sampson waited until they had gone before he took the Inspector to one side.

"What's the matter, Q?" he demanded. "Aren't things going right?"

"Henry, my boy," smiled the Inspector, "we've done as much as mortal brains could. Just a little more time. . . . I wish—" He did not say what he wished. He grasped Djuna firmly by the arm and bidding Panzer, Neilson, Velie and the District Attorney a placid good night, left the theatre.

At the apartment, as the Inspector wielded his key and the door swung open, Djuna pounced on a yellow envelope lying on the floor. It had evidently been stuck through the crack at the bottom of the door. Djuna flourished it in the old man's face.

"It's from Mr. Ellery, I'll bet!" he cried. "I knew he wouldn't forget!" He seemed more extraordinarily like a monkey than ever as he stood grinning, the telegram in his hand.

The Inspector snatched the envelope from Djuna's hand and, not pausing to take off his hat or coat, switched on the lights in the living room and eagerly extracted the yellow slip of paper.

Djuna had been correct.

ARRIVED SAFELY [it ran] CHAUVIN WILD WITH DELIGHT FISHING PROSPECT EXCEPTIONAL stop THINK I HAVE SOLVED YOUR LITTLE PROBLEM stop JOIN DISTINGUISHED COMPANY OF RABELAIS CHAUCER SHAKESPEARE DRYDEN WHO SAID MAKE A VIRTUE OF NECESSITY stop WHY NOT GO INTO BLACKMAILING BUSINESS YOURSELF stop DON'T GROWL DJUNA TO DEATH AFFECTIONATELY ELLERY

The Inspector stared down at the harmless yellow slip, a startled comprehension transmuting the harsh lines of his face.

He whirled on Djuna, clapped that young gentleman's cap on his tousled head and pulled his arm purposefully.

"Djuna, old son," he said gleefully, "let's go around the corner and celebrate with a couple of ice-cream sodas!"

# 20

## In Which Mr. Michaels Writes a Lecture

For the first time in a week Inspector Queen was genuinely himself as he strode cheerfully into his tiny office at the headquarters building and shied his coat at a chair.

It was Monday morning. He rubbed his hands, hummed "The Sidewalks of New York," as he plumped down at his desk and briskly ran through his voluminous mail and reports. He spent a half-hour issuing instructions by word of mouth and telephone to subordinates in various offices of the Detective Bureau, studied briefly a number of reports which a stenographer placed before him and finally pressed one of a row of buttons on his desk.

Velie appeared at once.

"Howdy, Thomas," said the Inspector heartily. "How are you this fine Fall morning?"

Velie permitted himself a smile. "Well enough, Inspector," he said. "And you? You seemed a little under the weather Saturday night."

The Inspector chuckled. "Let bygones be bygones, Thomas, my lad. Djuna and I visited the Bronx Zoo yesterday and spent a delightful four hours among our brethren, the animals."

"That imp of yours was in his element, I'll bet," growled Velie, "among the monkeys especially."

"Now, now, Thomas," chided the Inspector. "Don't be mistaken about Djuna. He's a smart little whippersnapper. Going to be a great man some day, mark my words!"

"Djuna?" Velie nodded gravely. "Guess you're right, Inspector. I'd give my right paw for that kid. . . . What's the program today, sir?"

"There's a lot on the program today, Thomas," Queen said mysteriously. "Did you get hold of Michaels after I telephoned you yesterday morning?"

"Sure thing, Inspector. He's been waiting outside for an hour. Came in early, with Piggott hanging on his heels. Piggott's been tailing him all over creation and he's pretty disgusted."

"Well, I always said a man's a fool to become a policeman," chuckled Queen. "Bring in the lamb."

Velie went out, to reappear a moment later with the tall, portly Michaels. Field's valet was dressed sombrely. He seemed nervous and ill at ease.

"Now, Thomas, my lad," said the Inspector after he had motioned Michaels to the chair beside his desk, "you go out and lock that door and don't let the Commissioner himself disturb me. Get that?"

Velie repressed a curious glance, grunted and departed. A few moments later a bulky figure was dimly discernible in silhouette through the frosted glass of the door.

At the expiration of a half-hour Velie was summoned by telephone to his superior's office. He unlocked the door. On the desk before the Inspector reposed a cheap square envelope unsealed, a sheet of notepaper partly visible as it lay inside. Michaels was on his feet, pale and trembling, his hat crushed in two beefy hands. Velie's sharp eyes noticed a generous ink stain on the fingers of the man's left hand.

"You are going to take *very* good care of Mr. Michaels, Thomas," said the Inspector genially. "Today, for instance, I want you to entertain him. I have no doubt you'll find something to do—go to a movie—there's an idea! In any event be friendly with the gentleman until you hear from me. . . . No communication with anybody, Michaels, do you hear?" he added brusquely, turning to the big man. "Just you tag along with Sergeant Velie and play nicely."

"You know I'm on the square, Inspector," mumbled Michaels sullenly. "You don't have to—"

"Just a precaution, Michaels—just an elementary precaution," interrupted the Inspector, smiling. "Have a nice time, boys!"

The two men left. Seated at his desk, Queen tilted his swivel chair, picked up the envelope before him reflectively, took out the slip of cheap white paper and read it over with a little smile.

The note bore neither date nor salutation. The message began abruptly.

"The writer is Chas. Michaels, I think you know me. I have been Monte Field's right-hand man for over two years.

I won't beat around the bush. Last Monday night you killed Field in the Roman Theatre. Monte Field told me Sunday he had an appointment with you at the Theatre. And I am the only one who does know this.

Another thing. I also know *why* you killed him. You put him away to get hold of the papers in Field's hat. But you do not know that the papers you stole from him *are not the originals*. To prove this to you, I am enclosing one sheet from the testimony of Nellie Johnson which was in Field's possession. If the papers you took from Field's hat are still in existence, compare what you have with this one. You will soon see that I am giving you the straight goods. And I have the rest of the originals safely put away where you will never lay hands on them. I might say that the police are looking for them with their tongues hanging out. Wouldn't it be nice if I stepped into Inspector Queen's office with the papers and my little story?

I will give you a chance to buy these papers. You can bring $25,000 in cold cash to the place I describe, and I will hand them over to you. I need money and you need the papers and my silence.

Meet me tomorrow, Tuesday night, at twelve o'clock, at the seventh bench on the right-hand side of the paved path in Central Park which starts at the northwest corner of 59th Street and 5th Avenue. I will be dressed in a gray overcoat and a gray slouch hat. Just say the word Papers to me.

This is the only way you can get the papers. Don't look for me before the appointment. If you are not there, I know what I have to do."

The scrawl, closely and painfully written, was signed: "Charles Michaels."

Inspector Queen sighed, licked the flap of the envelope and sealed it. He stared steadily at the name and address written in the same handwriting on the envelope. Unhurriedly he affixed a stamp on one corner.

He pressed another button. The door opened to admit Detective Ritter. "Good morning, Inspector."

"Morning, Ritter." The Inspector weighed the envelope reflectively in his hand. "What are you working on now?"

The detective shuffled his feet. "Nothing special, Inspector. I was helping Sergeant Velie up to Saturday, but I haven't had any work yet on the Field case this morning."

"Well, then, I'll give you a nice little job." The Inspector suddenly grinned, holding out the envelope. Ritter took it with a bewildered air. "Here, son, go to the corner of 149th Street and Third Avenue and post this letter in the nearest mailbox!"

Ritter stared, scratched his head, looked at Queen and finally went out, depositing the letter in his pocket.

The Inspector tilted his chair and took a pinch of snuff with every evidence of satisfaction.

# 21

## In Which Inspector Queen Makes a Capture

On Tuesday evening, October second, promptly at 11:30 P.M., a tall man wearing a soft black hat and a black overcoat, the collar pulled up around his face to keep out the raw night air, sauntered out of the lobby of a small hotel on 53rd Street near Seventh Avenue and proceeded at a sharp pace up Seventh Avenue toward Central Park.

Arrived at 59th Street he turned to the east and made his way along the deserted thoroughfare in the direction of Fifth Avenue. When he reached the Fifth Avenue entrance to Central Park, off the Plaza circle, he stopped in the shadow of one of the big concrete corner posts and leaned back idly. As he lit a cigarette the flare from a match illumined his face. It was that of an elderly man, a trifle lined. A grizzled mustache drooped in a straggling line from his upper lip. Under his hat a gray patch of hair was visible. Then the light from the match flickered out.

He stood quietly against the concrete post, hands jammed into his overcoat pockets, puffing away at his cigarette. An observer would have noticed, had he been keen, that the man's fingers trembled slightly and that his black-shod feet tapped the sidewalk in an unsteady tattoo.

When his cigarette burned down, he threw it away and glanced at a watch on his wrist. The hands stood at 11:50. He swore impatiently and stepped past the portals of the Park entrance.

The light from the overhead arcs bordering the Plaza dimmed as he walked up the stone lane. Hesitating, as if he were undecided as to his course of action, he looked about him, considered for a moment, then crossed over to the first bench and sat down heavily—like a man tired from his day's work and contemplating a restful quarter of an hour in the silence and darkness of the Park.

Slowly his head dropped; slowly his figure grew slack. He seemed to have fallen into a doze.

The minutes ticked away. No one passed the quiet figure of the black-clad man as he sat on his bench. On Fifth Avenue the motors roared past. The shrill whistle of the traffic officer in the Plaza pierced the chill air periodically. A cold wind soughed through the trees. From somewhere in the Stygian recesses of the Park came a girl's clear laugh—soft and far-off, but startlingly distinct. The minutes drowsed on; the man was falling into a deeper sleep.

And yet, just as the bells of the neighborhood churches began to toll the hour of twelve, the figure tensed, waited an instant and then rose determinedly.

Instead of heading toward the entrance he turned and plodded farther up the walk, his eyes bright and inquisitive in the gloomy depths created by his hat brim and coat collar. He seemed to be counting the benches as he proceeded in a steady, unhurried gait. Two—three—four—five— He stopped. In the semidarkness ahead he could barely make out a still gray figure seated on a bench.

The man walked slowly on. Six—seven— He did not pause, but went straight ahead. Eight—nine—ten. . . . Only then did he wheel and retrace his steps. This time his gait was brisker, more definite. He approached the seventh bench rapidly, then stopped short. Suddenly, as if he had made up his mind, he crossed over to the spot where the indistinctly looming figure rested quietly and sat down. The figure grunted and moved over a trifle to give the newcomer more room.

The two men sat in silence. After a time the black-garbed man dipped into the folds of his coat and produced a packet of cigarettes. He lit one and held the match for a moment after the tip of the cigarette glowed red. In the ray of the match light he covertly examined the quiet man at his side. The brief moment told him little—the occupant of the bench was as well muffled and concealed as himself. Then the light puffed out and they were in darkness once more.

The black-coated man seemed to come to a decision. He leaned forward, tapped the other man sharply on the knee and said in a low, husky voice the one word:

"Papers!"

The second man came to life immediately. He half-shifted his position, scrutinized his companion and grunted as if in satisfaction. He carefully leaned away from the other man on the bench and with his right gloved hand dug into his right overcoat pocket. The first man bent eagerly forward, his eyes bright. The gloved hand of his companion came out of the pocket, holding something tightly.

Then the owner of the hand did a surprising thing. With a fierce bunching of muscles he sprang from the bench and leaped backward, away from the first man. At the same time he leveled his right hand straight at the crouched frozen figure. And a fragmentary gleam of light from an arc lamp far off revealed the thing he held in his hand—a revolver.

Crying out hoarsely, the first man sprang to his feet with the agility of a cat. His hand plunged with a lightninglike movement into his overcoat pocket. He darted, reckless of the weapon pointed at his heart, straight forward at the tense figure before him.

But things were happening. The peaceful tableau, so suggestive a bare instant before of open spaces and dark country silence, was transformed magically into a scene of intense activity—a writhing, yelling pandemonium. From a cluster of bushes a few feet behind the bench a swiftly moving group of men with drawn guns materialized. At the same time, from the farther side of the walk, a similar group appeared, running toward the pair. And from both ends of the walk—from the entrance about a hundred feet away and from the opposite direction, in the blackness of the Park—came several uniformed policemen, brandishing revolvers. The groups converged almost as one.

The man who had drawn his gun and leaped from the bench did not await the arrival of reinforcements. As his companion of a moment before plunged his hand into his coat pocket the gun-wielder took careful aim and fired. The weapon roared, awakening echoes in the Park. An orange flame streaked into the body of the black-coated man. He lurched forward, clutching his shoulder spasmodically. His knees buckled and he fell to the stone walk. His hand still fumbled in his coat.

But an avalanche of men's bodies kept him from whatever furious purpose was in his mind. Ungentle fingers gripped his arms and pinned them down, so that he could not withdraw his hand from his pocket. They held him in this way, silently, until a crisp voice behind them said, "Careful, boys—watch his hands!"

Inspector Richard Queen wriggled into the hard-breathing group and stood contemplatively above the writhing figure on the pavement.

"Take his hand out, Velie—easy, now! Hold it stiff, and—stiff, man stiff! He'd jab you in a flash!"

Sergeant Thomas Velie, who was straining at the arm, gingerly pulled it from the pocket despite the violent flounderings of the man's body. The hand appeared—empty, muscles loosened at the last moment. Two men promptly fastened it in a vise.

Velie made a movement as if to explore the pocket. The Inspector stopped him with a sharp word and himself bent over the threshing man on the walk.

Carefully, delicately, as if his life depended upon caution, the old man lowered his hand into the pocket and felt about its exterior. He gripped something and just as cautiously withdrew it, holding it up to the light.

It was a hypodermic needle. The light of the arc lamp made its pale limpid contents sparkle.

Inspector Queen grinned as he knelt by the wounded man's side. He jerked off the black felt hat.

"Disguised and everything," he murmured.

He snatched at the gray mustache, passed his hand rapidly over the man's lined face. A smudge immediately appeared on the skin.

"Well, well!" said the Inspector softly, as the man's feverish eyes glared up at him. "Happy to meet you again, Mr. Stephen Barry, and your good friend, Mr. Tetra Ethyl Lead!"

# 22

## —and Explains

Inspector Queen sat at the writing desk in his living room scribbling industriously on a long narrow sheet of notepaper headed THE QUEENS.

It was Wednesday morning—a fair Wednesday morning, with the sun streaming into the room through the dormer windows and the cheerful noises of 87th Street faintly audible from the pavements below. The Inspector wore his dressing gown and slippers. Djuna was busy at the table clearing away the breakfast dishes.

The old man had written:

> DEAR SON: As I wired you late last night, the case is finished. We got Stephen Barry very nicely by using Michaels' name and handwriting as bait. I really ought to congratulate myself on the psychological soundness of the plan. Barry was desperate and like so many other criminals thought he could duplicate his crime without being caught.
>
> I hate to tell you how tired I am and how unsatisfying spiritually the job of manhunter is sometimes. When I think of that poor lovely little girl Frances, having to face the world as the sweetheart of a murderer. . . . Well, El, there's little justice and certainly no mercy in this world. And, of course, I'm more or less responsible for her shame. . . . Yet Ives-Pope himself was quite decent a while ago when he telephoned me on hearing the news. I suppose in one way I did him and Frances a service. We—

The doorbell rang and Djuna, drying his hands hastily on a kitchen towel, ran to the door. District Attorney Sampson and Timothy Cronin walked in—excited, happy, both talking at once. Queen rose, covering the sheet of paper with a blotter.

"Q, old man!" cried Sampson, extending both hands. "My congratulations! Have you seen the papers this morning?"

"Glory to Columbus!" grinned Cronin, holding up a newspaper on which in screaming headlines New York was apprised of the capture of Stephen Barry. The Inspector's photograph was displayed prominently and a rhapsodic story captioned "Queen Adds Another Laurel!" ran two full columns of type down the sheet.

The Inspector, however, seemed singularly unimpressed. He waved his visitors to chairs, and called for coffee, and began to talk about a projected change in the personnel of one of the city departments as if the Field case interested him not at all.

"Here, here!" growled Sampson. "What's the matter with you? You ought to be throwing out your chest, Q. You act as if you'd pulled a dud rather than succeeded."

"It's not that, Henry," said the Inspector with a sigh. "I just can't seem to be enthusiastic about anything when Ellery isn't by my side. By jingo, I wish he were here instead of in those blamed Maine woods!"

The two men laughed. Djuna served the coffee and for a time the Inspector was too occupied with his pastry to brood. Over his cigarette Cronin remarked: "I for one merely dropped in to pay my respects, Inspector, but I'm curious about some aspects of this case. . . . I don't know much about the investigation as a whole, except what Sampson told me on the way up."

"I'm rather at sea myself, Q," put in the District Attorney. "I imagine you have a story to tell us. Let's have it!"

Inspector Queen smiled sadly. "To save my own face I'll have to relate it as if I did most of the work. As a matter of fact, the only really intelligent work in the whole sordid business was Ellery's. He's a sharp lad, that son of mine."

Sampson and Cronin relaxed as the Inspector took some snuff and settled back in his armchair. Djuna folded himself quietly in a corner, ears cocked.

"In going over the Field case," began the Inspector, "I will have to refer at times to Benjamin Morgan, who is really the most innocent victim of all.* I want you to bear in mind, Henry, that whatever I say about Morgan is to go no further, either professionally or socially. I already have Tim's assurance of silence. . . ."

Both men nodded wordlessly. The Inspector continued:

---

'Inspector Queen's statement here is not altogether true. Benjamin Morgan was far from "innocent." But the Inspector's sense of justice compelled him to shield the lawyer and keep his word regarding silence. —E. Q.

"I needn't explain that most investigations of crime begin with a search for the motive. Many times you can discard suspect after suspect when you know the reason behind the crime. In this case the motive was obscure for a long time. There were certain indications, like Benjamin Morgan's story, but these were inconclusive. Morgan had been blackmailed by Field for years—a part of Field's activities of which you gentlemen were ignorant, despite your knowledge of his other social habits. This seemed to point to blackmail as a possible motive—or rather the choking off of blackmail. But then any number of things could have been the motive—revenge, by some criminal whom Field had been instrumental in 'sending up.' Or by a member of his criminal organization. Field had a host of enemies, and undoubtedly a host of friends who were friends only because Field held the whiphand. Any one of scores of people—men and women both—might have had a *motive* for killing the lawyer. So that, since we had so many other pressing and immediate things to think about and do that night at the Roman Theatre, we did not bother much with motive. It was always in the background, waiting to be called into service.

"But mark this point. If it was blackmail—as Ellery and I eventually decided, since it seemed the most likely possibility—there were most certainly some papers floating about in Field's possession which would be enlightening, to say the least. We knew that Morgan's papers existed. Cronin insisted that the papers for which *he* was looking were about somewhere. So we had to keep our eyes constantly on the alert for papers—tangible evidence which might or might not make clear the essential circumstances behind the crime.

"At the same time, in the matter of documents, Ellery was piqued by the great number of books on handwriting analysis he found among Field's effects. We concluded that a man like Field, who had blackmailed once to our knowledge (in the case of Morgan) and many times to our suspicions; and who was keenly interested in the science of handwriting, might have been a forger to boot. If this were true, and it seemed a plausible explanation, then it probably meant that Field made a habit of forging the original blackmail papers. The only reason he could have for doing this, of course, would be to sell the forgeries and keep the originals for further extortion. His association with the underworld undoubtedly helped him master the tricks of the trade. Later, we discovered that this hypothesis was true. And by that time we had definitely established blackmail as the motive of the crime. Remember, though, that this led us nowhere, since any one of our suspects might have been the blackmail victim and we had no way of telling who it was."

The Inspector frowned, settled back into his seat more comfortably.

"But I'm tackling this explanation the wrong way. It just goes to show you how habit will take hold of a man. I'm so accustomed to beginning with motive. . . . However! There is only one important and central circumstance which stands out in the investigation. It was a confounding clue—rather, the lack of a clue. I refer to the missing hat. . . .

"Now the unfortunate thing about the missing hat was that we were so busy pressing the immediate inquiry at the Roman Theatre on Monday night we couldn't grasp the full significance of its absence. Not that we weren't bothered by it from the beginning—far from it. It was one of the first things I noticed when I examined the body. As for Ellery, he caught it as soon as he entered the theatre and bent over the dead man. But what could we do? There were a hundred details to take care of—questions to ask, orders to give, discrepancies and suspicious discoveries to clean up—so that, as I say, we inadvertently missed our great opportunity. If we had analyzed the meaning of the hat's disappearance then and there—we might have clinched the case that very night."

"Well, it hasn't taken so long after all, you growler," laughed Sampson. "This is Wednesday and the murder was committed a week ago Monday. Only nine days—what are you kicking about?"

The Inspector shrugged. "But it would have made a considerable difference," he said. "If only we had reasoned it out— Well! When finally we did get around to dissecting the problem of the hat, we asked ourselves first of all: Why was the hat taken? Only two answers seemed to make sense: one, that the hat was incriminating in itself; two, that it contained something which the murderer wanted and for which the crime was committed. As it turned out, both were true. The hat was incriminating in itself because on the underside of the leather sweatband was Stephen Barry's name, printed in indelible ink; and the hat contained something which the murderer very emphatically wanted—the blackmail papers. He thought at the time, of course, that they were the originals.

"This did not get us very far, but it was a starting point. By the time we left Monday night with the command to shut down the theatre, we had not yet found the missing hat despite a sweeping search. However, we had no way of knowing whether the hat had managed in some mysterious manner to leave the theatre, or whether it was still there though unrevealed by our search. When we returned to the theatre on Thursday morning we settled once and for all the question of the location of Monte Field's pesky topper—that is, negatively. It was *not* in the theatre—that much was certain. And since the theatre had been sealed since Monday night, it follows that the hat must have left that same evening.

"Now everybody who left Monday night left with only one hat. In the light of our second search, therefore, we were compelled to conclude that somebody had walked out that night with Monte Field's hat in his hand or on his head, necessarily leaving his own in the theatre.

"He could not have disposed of the hat outside the theatre except when he left at the time the audience was allowed to leave; for up to that time all exits were guarded or locked, and the left-hand alley was blocked first by Jess Lynch and Elinor Libby, next by John Chase, the usher, and after that by one of my policemen. The right-hand alley, having no exit other than the orchestra doors, which were guarded all night, offered no avenue of disposal.

"To go on with the thought—since Field's hat was a tophat, and since nobody left the theatre dressed in a tophat who was not wearing evening clothes—this we watched for very closely—therefore the man who took away the missing hat *must* have been garbed in full dress. You might say that a man planning such a crime in advance would have come to the theatre without a hat, and therefore would have none to dispose of. But if you will stop to think, you must see that this is highly improbable. He would have been quite conspicuous, especially while entering the theatre, if he went in minus a tophat. It was a possibility, of course, and we kept it in mind; but we reasoned that a man working out such a consummate crime as this would have shied from taking any unnecessary chance of being identified. Also, Ellery had satisfied his own mind that the murderer had no foreknowledge of the Field hat's importance. This made still more improbable the possibility that the murderer arrived without a hat of his own. Having a hat of his own, he might have disposed of it, we thought, during the first intermission—which is to say, before the crime was committed. But Ellery's deductions proving the murderer's lack of foreknowledge made this impossible, since he would not have known at the first intermission of the *necessity* of doing away with his own hat. At any rate, I think we were justified in assuming that our man had to leave his own hat in the theatre and that it must have been a tophat. Does it follow so far?"

"It seems logical enough," admitted Sampson, "though very complicated."

"You have no idea how complicated it was," said the Inspector grimly, "since at the same time we had to bear in mind the other possibilities— such as the man walking out with Field's hat being not the murderer but an accomplice. But let's get on.

"The next question we asked ourselves was this: what *happened* to the tophat which the murderer left behind in the theatre? What did he do with it? Where did he leave it? . . . I can tell you that was a puzzler. We had ransacked the place from top to bottom. True, we found several hats backstage which Mrs. Phillips, the wardrobe mistress, identified as the personal property of various actors. But none of these was a personally owned tophat. Where then was the tophat which the murderer had left behind in the theatre? Ellery with his usual acumen struck right at the heart of the truth. He said to himself, 'The murderer's tophat must be here. We have not found any tophat whose presence is remarkable or out of the ordinary. Therefore the tophat we are seeking must be one whose presence is *not* out of the ordinary.' Fundamental? Almost ridiculously so. And yet I myself did not think of it.

"What tophats were there whose *presence* was not out of the ordinary—so natural and in so natural a place that they were not even questioned? In the Roman Theatre, where all the costumes were hired from Le Brun, the answer is simple: the rented tophats being used for purposes of the play. Where would such tophats be? Either in the actors' dressing rooms or in the general wardrobe room backstage. When Ellery had reached this point in his reasoning he took Mrs. Phillips backstage and checked up on every tophat in the actors' rooms and the wardrobe room. Every tophat there—and all were accounted for, none being missing— was a property tophat bearing on its lining the Le Brun insignia. Field's hat, which we had proved to be a Browne Bros. topper, was not among the property tophats or anywhere backstage.

"Since no one left the theatre Monday night with more than one tophat, and since Monte Field's hat was unquestionably taken out of the theatre that same night, it was positively established that the murderer's own tophat must have been in the Roman all the time the house was sealed, and was still there at the time of our second search. Now, the only tophats remaining in the theatre were property tophats. It therefore follows that the murderer's own tophat (which he was forced to leave behind because he walked out with Field's) *must* have been one of the property hats backstage, since let me repeat, these were the only tophats of which it could physically have been one.

"In other words—one of these property tophats backstage belonged to the man who left the theatre Monday night in full dress wearing Field's silk topper.

"If this man were the murderer—and he could scarcely be anyone else—then our field of inquiry was narrowed to a considerable degree. He could only have been either a male member of the cast who left the theatre in evening clothes, or somebody closely connected with the theatre and similarly dressed. In the latter case, such a person would have had to have, first, a property tophat to leave behind; second, undisputed access to the wardrobe and dressing rooms; and, third, the opportunity to leave his property tophat in either place.

"Now let us examine the possibilities in the latter case—that the murderer was closely connected with the theatre, yet not an actor." The Inspector paused to sniff deeply of the snuff in his treasured box. "The workmen backstage could be discarded because none of them wore the evening clothes which were necessary in order to take away Field's tophat. The cashiers, ushers, doormen and other minor employees were eliminated for the same reason. Harry Neilson, the publicity man, was also dressed in ordinary street clothes. Panzer, the manager, was attired in full dress, it is true, but I took the trouble to check up his head size and found it to be 6¾—an unusually small size. It would be virtually impossible for him to have *worn* Field's hat, which was 7⅛. It is true that we left the theatre before he did. On my way out, however, I definitely instructed Thomas Velie to make no exception in Panzer's case, but to search him as the others had been searched. I had examined Panzer's hat merely from a sense of duty while in his office earlier in the evening, and found it to be a derby. Velie subsequently reported that Panzer walked out with this derby on his head and no other hat in his possession. Now—if Panzer had been the man we were looking for, he might have walked out with Field's hat despite its larger size by merely holding it in his hand. But when he left with a derby, that was conclusive that he could not have taken away Field's hat, since the theatre was shut down immediately after his departure and no one—my men on duty saw to that—no one entered the premises until Thursday morning under my own eye. Theoretically it was possible for Panzer, or anyone else in the Roman personnel, to have been the murderer had he been able to secrete Field's tophat in the theatre. But this last hypothesis was dissipated by the report of Edmund Crewe, our official architectural expert, who definitely stated that there was no secret hiding place anywhere in the Roman Theatre.

"The elimination of Panzer, Neilson and the employees left only the cast as possibilities. How we finally narrowed down the field of inquiry until we got to Barry, let's leave for the moment. The interesting part of this case is really the startling and complex series of deductions which gave us the truth purely through logical reasoning. I say 'us'—I should say Ellery. . . ." *July 31, 2011*

"For a police Inspector you are certainly a shrinking violet," chuckled Cronin. "By gee, this is better than a detective story. I ought to be working now, but since my boss seems to be as interested as I am—keep going, Inspector!"

Queen smiled, forging ahead.

"The fact that the murderer was traced to the cast," he continued, "answers a question which has probably occurred to you and which certainly troubled us in the beginning. We could not at first understand why the theatre should have been chosen as a meeting place for the transaction of secret business. When you stop to think about it, a theatre presents enormous disadvantages under ordinary circumstances. Extra tickets, to mention only one thing, have to be bought to insure privacy through empty seats in the vicinity. What a silly tangle to get into when other meeting places are so much more convenient! A theatre is dark most of the time and disturbingly quiet. Any untoward noise or conversation is remarked. The crowds present a constant danger— one of recognition. However, all this is automatically explained when you realize that Barry was a member of the cast. From his standpoint the theatre was ideal—for who would dream of suspecting an actor of murder when the victim is found dead in the orchestra? Of course Field acquiesced, never suspecting what was in Barry's mind and that he was conniving his own death. Even if he were a little suspicious, you must remember that he was accustomed to dealing with dangerous people and probably felt capable of taking care of himself. This may have made him a little overconfident—we have no way, of course, of knowing.

"Let me get back to Ellery again—my favorite subject," continued the Inspector, with one of his recurrent dry chuckles. "Aside from these deductions about the hat—as a matter of fact, before the deductions were completely worked out—Ellery got his first indication of which way the wind blew during the meeting at the Ives-Pope house. It was clear that Field had not accosted Frances Ives-Pope in the alleyway between acts with merely flirtatious intentions. It seemed to Ellery that some connection existed between the two widely separated individuals. Now, this does not mean that Frances had to be aware of the connection. She was positive that she had never heard of or seen Field before. We had no reason to doubt her and every reason to believe her. That possible connection might have been Stephen Barry, provided Stephen Barry and Field knew each other without Frances' knowledge. If, for example, Field had an appointment at the theatre Monday night with the actor and suddenly saw Frances, it was possible that in his half-drunken mood he would venture to approach her, especially since the subject he and Barry had in common concerned her so deeply. As for recognizing her—thousands of people who read the daily papers know every line of her features—she is a much-photographed young society lady. Field certainly would have acquainted himself with her description and appearance out of sheer thoroughness of business method. . . . But to return to the triangle connection—Field, Frances, Barry—which I will go into detail later. You realize that no one else in the cast except Barry, who was engaged to Frances and had been publicly announced as her fiancé, with pictures and all the rest of the journalistic business, could have satisfied so well the question: Why did Field accost Frances?

"The other disturbing factor concerning Frances—the discovery of her bag in Field's clothes—was plausibly explained by her dropping it in the natural excitement of the moment when the drunken lawyer approached her. This was later confirmed by Jess Lynch's testimony to the effect that he saw Field pick up Frances' bag. Poor girl—I feel sorry for her." The Inspector sighed.

"To get back to the hat—you'll notice we always return to that blasted top piece," resumed Queen, after a pause. "I never knew of a case in which a single factor so dominated every aspect of the investigation. . . . Now mark this: Of the entire cast Barry was *the only one* who left the Roman Theatre Monday night dressed in evening clothes and tophat. As Ellery watched at the main door Monday night while the people were fil-ing out, his mind characteristically registered the fact that the entire cast, except Barry, left the theatre wearing street clothes; in fact, he even mentioned this to Sampson and me in Panzer's office later, although at the time neither of us realized its full significance. . . . Barry was therefore the only member of the cast who could have taken away Field's tophat. Think this over a moment and you will see that, in view of Ellery's hat deductions, we could now pin the guilt to Barry's shoulders beyond the shadow of a doubt.

"Our next step was to witness the play, which we did the evening of the day on which Ellery made the vital deductions—Thursday. You can see why. We wanted to confirm our conclusion by seeing whether Barry had the *time* during the second act to commit the murder. And, amazingly enough, of all the members of the cast, Barry was the only one who did have the time. He was absent from the stage from 9:20—he opened the business of the act and left almost at once—until 9:50, when he returned to the stage to remain there until the act ended. This was incontrovert-ible—part of a fixed and unchanging time schedule. Every other player was either on the stage all the time or else went on and off at extremely short intervals. This means that last Thursday night, more than five days ago—and the whole case took only nine days to consummate—we had solved our mystery. But solving the mystery of the murderer's identity was a far cry from bringing him to justice. You'll see why in a moment.

"The fact that the murderer could not enter until 9:30 or thereabouts explains why the torn edges of LL32 Left and LL30 Left did not coin-cide. It was necessary for Field and Barry, you see, to come in at different times. Field could not very well enter with Barry or even at a noticeably later hour—the matter of secrecy was too important to Barry, and Field understood, or thought he did, how necessary it was for him to play the secret game.

"When we pinned the guilt on Barry Thursday night, we resolved to question subtly the other members of the cast as well as workmen backstage. We wanted to find out, of course, whether any one had actually seen Barry leave or return. As it happened, no one had. Everybody was busy either acting, redressing, or working backstage. We conducted this little investigation after the performance that night, when Barry had already left the theatre. And it was checkmate, right enough.

"We had already borrowed a seating plan from Panzer. This map, together with the examination of the alleyway on the left and the dressing-room arrangement backstage—an examination made directly after the second act Thursday night—showed us how the murder was committed."

Sampson stirred. "I've been puzzling my wits about that," he confessed. "After all, Field was no babe-in-the-woods. This Barry must be a wizard, Q. How did he do it?"

"Every riddle is simple when you know the answer," retorted the Inspector. "Barry, whose freedom began at 9:20, immediately returned to his dressing room, slapped on a quick but thorough facial disguise, donned an evening cloak and the tophat which was part of his costume—you'll remember he was already dressed in evening clothes—and slipped out of his room into the alley.

"Of course you can't be expected to know the topography of the theatre. There is a series of tiers in a wing of the building backstage, facing the left alley, which is made up of dressing rooms. Barry's room is on the lowest tier, the door opening into the alleyway. There is a flight of iron steps leading down to the pavement.

"It was through this door that he quitted the dressing room, walking through the dark alley while the side doors of the theatre were shut during Act II. He sneaked out into the street, since there was no guard at the head of the alley at that time—and he knew it—nor had Jess Lynch and his 'girl' arrived, luckily for him; and entered the theatre brazenly through the regular front entrance, as if he were a latecomer. He presented his ticket—LL30 Left—at the door, muffled in his cloak and of course well disguised. As he passed into the theatre he deliberately threw away his ticket stub. This appeared to him to be a wise move, since he figured that if the ticket stub were found there, it would point to a member of the audience and directly away from the stage. Also, if his plans fell through and he were later searched carefully, the finding of the stub on his person would be damning evidence. All in all, he thought his move not only misleading but protective."

"But how did he plan to get to the seat without being ushered to it—and therefore seen?" objected Cronin.

"He hadn't planned to evade the usher," returned the Inspector. "Naturally, he had hoped, since the play was well on and the theatre dark, to gain the last row, the nearest to the door, before the usher could approach. However, even if the usher forestalled him and escorted him to the seat he was well disguised and the blackness of the theatre was proof enough against recognition. So that, if things turned out as badly as possible for him, the most that would be remembered was that some man, unknown, barely describable in general contour, arrived during the second act. As it happened he was not accosted, since Madge O'Connell was luckily seated with her lover. He managed to slip into the seat next to Field without being noticed.

"Remember, what I've just told you," went on the Inspector, clearing his dry throat, "is not the result of deduction or investigation. We could have no means of discovering such facts. Barry made his confession last night and cleared up all these points. . . . Knowing the culprit was Barry, of course, we might have reasoned out the entire procedure—it follows simply and is the natural situation if you know the criminal. It wasn't necessary, however. Does that sound like an alibi for Ellery or myself? Hmph!" The old man barely smiled.

"When he sat down next to Field he had a carefully planned idea of his course of action. Don't forget that he was on a strict time schedule and could not afford to waste a minute. On the other hand, Field, too, knew that Barry had to get back so he made no unnecessary delays. The truth of the matter, as Barry has told us, is that he expected to have a more difficult time with Field than he actually did have. But Field was sociably amenable to Barry's suggestions and conversation, probably because he was quite drunk and expected to receive a huge sum of money within a short time.

"Barry first requested the papers. When Field cannily asked for the money before he produced the documents, Barry showed him a wallet bulging with apparently genuine bills. It was quite dark in the theatre and Barry did not take the bills apart. Actually they were stage money. He patted them suggestively and did what Field must have expected: refused to hand over the money until he had checked the documents. Bear in mind that Barry was an accomplished actor and could handle the difficult situation with the confidence imparted to him by his stage training. . . . Field reached under his seat and to Barry's utter astonishment and consternation produced his tophat. Barry says that Field remarked: 'Never thought I'd keep the papers in this, did you? As a matter of fact, I've dedicated this hat to your history quite exclusively. See—it has your name in it.' And with this astounding statement he turned back the band! Barry used his pocket pencil flashlight and saw his name inked in on the underside of the leather sweatband.

"Just imagine what went through his mind at this moment. Here he saw what seemed at the moment a ruinous accident to his careful plans. Should Field's hat be examined—and of course it would be—at the time of the discovery of the body, then the name Stephen Barry on the band would be overwhelming evidence. . . . Barry had no time to rip out the band. In the first place he had no knife—unfortunately for him; and in the second place the hatband was closely and securely stitched to the tough fabric. Working on split-time, he saw at once that the only course open to him was to take the hat away after he killed Field. Since he and Field were of the same general physique, with Field wearing an average sized hat, 7 1/8, he immediately decided to leave the theatre wearing or carrying Field's hat. He would deposit his own in the dressing room, where its presence was not out of the way, take Field's hat from the theatre with him and destroy it as soon as he reached his rooms. It also occurred to him that if the hat were by some chance examined as he was leaving the theatre, his name printed inside would certainly ward off suspicion. In all probability it was this fact that made Barry feel he was running into no particular danger, even though he had not foreseen the unexpected circumstance."

"Clever rogue," murmured Sampson.

"The quick brain, Henry, the quick brain," said Queen gravely. "It has run many a man's neck into the noose. . . . As he made the lightning decision to take the hat, he realized that he could not leave his own in its place. For one thing, his hat was a snapdown—an opera hat—but more important, it had the name of Le Brun, the theatrical costumer, stamped in it. You can see that this would immediately point to someone in the cast—just the thing he wished to avoid. He told me also that at the moment, and for quite some time thereafter, he felt that the most the police could deduce from the hat's being missing was that it was taken because it contained something valuable. He could not see how this investigatory guess would point the finger of suspicion anywhere near him. When I explained to him the series of deductions Ellery made from the mere fact that the tophat was missing, he was utterly astounded. . . . You can see, now, that the only really fundamental weakness of his crime was due not to an oversight or a mistake on his part, but to an occurrence which he could not possibly have foreseen. It forced his hand and the entire chain was started. Had Barry's name not been lettered in Field's hat, there is no question in my mind but that he would be a free and unsuspected man today. The police records would carry another unsolved murder on its pages.

"I need not state that this entire train of thought flashed through his brain in less time than it takes to describe. He saw what he had to do and his plans adjusted themselves instantly to the new development. . . . When Field extracted the papers from the hat, Barry examined them cursorily under the lawyer's watchful eye. He did this by the same pencil flashlight—a tiny streak of illumination quite obscured by their shielding bodies. The papers seemed in good order and complete. But Barry did not spend much time over the papers at the moment. He looked up with a rueful smile and said: 'Seem to be all here, damn you'—very naturally, as if they were enemies under a truce and he was being a good sport. Field interpreted the remark for what it was intended to convey. Barry dipped into his pocket—the light was out now—and, as if he was nervous, took a swig at a pocket-flask of good whisky. Then as if recollecting his manners, he asked Field pleasantly enough if he would not take a drink to bind the bargain. Field, having seen Barry drink from the flask, could have no suspicion of foul play. In fact, he probably never dreamed that Barry would try to do him in. Barry handed him a flask. . . .

"But it wasn't the same flask. Under cover of the darkness he had taken out two flasks—the one he himself used coming from his left hip pocket. In handing it over to Field, he merely switched flasks. It was very simple—and made simpler because of the darkness and the fuddled condition of the lawyer. . . . The ruse of the flask worked. But Barry had taken no chances. He had in his pocket a hypodermic filled with the poison. If Field had refused to drink Barry was prepared to plunge the needle into the lawyer's arm or leg. He possessed a hypodermic needle which a physician had procured for him many years before. Barry had suffered from nervous attacks and could not remain under a doctor's care since he was traveling from place to place with a stock company. The hypodermic was untraceable, therefore, on a cold trail years old; and he was ready if Field refused to drink. So you see—his plan, even in this particular, was fool-proof. . . .

"The flask from which Field drank contained good whisky, all right, but mixed with tetra ethyl lead in a copious dose. The poison's slight ether smell was lost in the reek of the liquor; and Field, drinking, gulped down a huge mouthful before he realized that anything was wrong, if he did at all.

"Mechanically he returned the flask to Barry, who pocketed it and said: 'I guess I'll look over these papers more carefully—there's no reason why I should trust you, Field. . . .' Field, who was feeling extremely disinterested by this time, nodded in a puzzled sort of way and slumped

down in his seat. Barry really did examine the papers but he watched
Field like a hawk out of the corner of his eye all the time. In about five
minutes he saw that Field was out—out for good. He was not entirely unconscious but well under way; his face was contorted and he was gasping
for breath. He seemed unable to make any violent muscular movement or
outcry. Of course, he'd utterly forgotten Barry—in his agony—perhaps
didn't remain conscious very long. When he groaned those few words to
Pusak it was the superhuman effort of a practically dead man. . . .

"Barry now consulted his watch. It was 9:40. He had been with Field
only ten minutes. He had to be back on the stage at 9:50. He decided to
wait three minutes more—it had taken less time than he had figured—to
make sure that Field would not raise a rumpus. At 9:43 exactly, with
Field terribly inanimate in his internal agonies, Barry took Field's hat,
snapped down his own and slipped it under his cloak, and rose. The way
was clear. Hugging the wall, walking down the aisle as carefully and un-
obtrusively as possible, he gained the rear of the leftside boxes without
anyone noticing him. The play was at its highest point of tension. All
eyes were riveted on the stage.

"In the rear of the boxes he ripped off the false hair, rapidly adjusted
his make-up and passed through the stage door. The door leads into a narrow passageway which in turn leads into a corridor, branching out to various parts of the backstage area. His dressing room is a few feet from the
entrance to the corridor. He slipped inside, threw his stage hat among his
regular effects, dashed the remaining contents of the death flask into the
wash bowl and cleaned out the flask. He emptied the contents of the hypodermic into the toilet drain and put away the needle, cleaned. If it was
found—what of it? He had a perfectly sound excuse for owning it and
besides the murder had not been committed by such an instrument at
all. . . . He was now ready for his cue, calm, debonair, a little bored. The
call came at exactly 9:50, he went on the stage and was there until the
hue-and-cry was raised at 9:55 in the orchestra. . . ."

"Talk about your complicated plots!" ejaculated Sampson.

"It is not so complicated as it seems at first hearing," returned the Inspector. "Remember that Barry is an exceptionally clever young man and
above all an excellent actor. No one *but* an accomplished actor could have
carried off such a plan. The procedure was simple, after all; his hardest job
was to keep to his time schedule. If he was seen by any one he was disguised. The only dangerous part of his scheme was the getaway—when he
walked down the aisle and went backstage through the box stagedoor. The
aisle he took care of by keeping an eye out for the usher while he sat next
to Field. He had known beforehand, of course, that the ushers, due to the
nature of the play, kept their stations more or less faithfully, but he

counted on his disguise and hypodermic to help him through any emergency that might arise. However, Madge O'Connell was lax in her duty and so even this was in his favor. He told me last night, not without a certain pride, that he had prepared for every contingency. . . . As for the stagedoor, he knew from experience that at that period in the play's progress practically every one was on the stage. The technical men were busy at their stations, too. . . . Remember that he planned the crime knowing in advance the exact conditions under which he would have to operate. And if there was an element of danger, of uncertainty—well, it was all a risky business, wasn't it?—he asked me last night, smiling; and I had to admire him for his philosophy if for nothing else."

The Inspector shifted restlessly. "This makes clear, I hope, just how Barry did the job. As for our investigation. . . . With the hat deductions made and our knowledge of the murderer's identity, we still had no inkling of the exact circumstances behind the crime. If you've been keeping in mind the material evidence which we had collected on Thursday night, you will see that we had nothing at all with which to work. The best thing we could hope for was that somewhere among the papers for which all of us were looking was a clue which would tie up to Barry. Even that would not be enough, but. . . . So the next step," said the Inspector, after a sigh, "was the discovery of the papers in Field's neat hiding place at the top of the bed canopy in his apartment. This was Ellery's work from start to finish. We had found out that Field had no safety-deposit box, no post-office box, no outside residence, no friendly neighbor or tradesman, and that the documents were not in his office. By a process of elimination Ellery insisted that they must be somewhere in Field's rooms. You know how this search ended—an ingenious bit of pure reasoning on Ellery's part. We found Morgan's papers; we found Cronin's stuff relating to the gang activities—and by the way, Tim, I'm going to be keenly alive to what happens when we start on the big clean-up—and we found finally a wad of miscellaneous papers. Among these were Michaels' and Barry's. . . . You'll remember, Tim, that Ellery, from the handwriting analysis business, deducted that possibly we would find the originals of Barry's papers—and so we did.

"Michaels' case was interesting. That time he went to Elmira on the 'petty larceny' charge, it was through Field's clever manipulations with the law. But Field had the goods on Michaels and filed the documentary evidence of the man's real guilt away in his favorite hiding place, in the event that he might wish to use it at some future date. A very saving person, this Field. . . . When Michaels was released from prison Field used him unscrupulously for his dirty work, holding the threat of those papers over the man's head.

"Now Michaels had been on the lookout for a long time. He wanted the papers badly, as you may imagine. At every opportunity he searched the apartment for them. And when he didn't find them time after time, he became desperate. I don't doubt that Field, in his devilishly sardonic way, enjoyed the knowledge that Michaels was ransacking the place day after day. . . . On Monday night Michaels did what he said he did—went home and to bed. But early Tuesday morning, when he read the papers and learned that Field had been killed, he realized that the jig was up. He had to make one last search for the papers—if he didn't find them, the police might and he would be in hot water. So he risked running into the police net when he returned to Field's rooms Tuesday morning. The story about the check was nonsense, of course.

"But let's get on to Barry. The original papers we found in the hat marked 'Miscellaneous' told a sordid story. Stephen Barry, to make it short and ugly, has a strain of negroid blood in his veins. He was born in the South of a poor family and there was definite documentary evidence—letters, birth records and the like—to prove that his blood had the black taint. Now Field, as you know, made it his business to run things like this to earth. In some way he got hold of the papers, how long ago we can't say, but certainly quite a while back. He looked up Barry's status at the time and found him to be a struggling actor, on his uppers more often than he was in funds. He decided to let the fellow alone for the time. If ever Barry came into money or in the limelight, there would be time enough to blackmail him. . . . Field's wildest dreams could not have foreseen Barry's engagement to Frances Ives-Pope, daughter of a multi-millionaire and blue-blood society girl. I needn't explain what it would have meant to Barry to have the story of his mixed blood become known to the Ives-Popes. Besides—and this is quite important—Barry was in a constant state of impoverishment due to his gambling. What money he earned went into the pockets of the bookmakers at the race-track and in addition he had contracted enormous debts which he could never have wiped out unless his marriage to Frances went through. So pressing was his need, in fact, that it was he who subtly urged an early marriage. I have been wondering just how he regarded Frances sentimentally. I don't think, in all fairness to him, that he was marrying wholly because of the money involved. He really loves her, I suppose—but then, who wouldn't?"

The old man smiled reminiscently and went on. "Field approached Barry some time ago with the papers—secretly, of course. Barry paid what he could, but it was woefully little and naturally did not satisfy the insatiable blackmailer. He kept putting Field off desperately. But Field himself was getting into hot water because of his own gambling and was 'calling in' his little business deals one by one. Barry, pushed to the wall, realized that unless Field were silenced everything would be lost. He planned the murder. He saw that even if he did manage to raise the $50,000 Field demanded—a palpable impossibility—and even if he did get the original papers, yet Field might still wreck his hopes by merely circulating the story. There was only one thing to do—kill Field. He did it."

"Black blood, eh?" murmured Cronin. "Poor devil."

"You would scarcely guess it from his appearance," remarked Sampson. "He looks as white as you or I."

"Barry isn't anywhere near a full-blooded Negro," protested the Inspector. "He has just a drop in his veins—just a drop, but it would have been more than enough for the Ives-Popes. . . . To get on. When the papers had been discovered and read—we knew everything. Who—how—why the crime was committed. So we took stock of our evidence to bring about a conviction. You can't hale a man into court on a murder charge without evidence. . . . Well, what do you think we had? Nothing!

"Let me discuss the clues which might have been useful as evidence. The lady's purse—that was out. Valueless, as you know. . . . The source of the poison—a total failure. Incidentally, Barry did procure it exactly as Dr. Jones suggested—Jones, the toxicologist. Barry bought ordinary gasoline and distilled the tetra ethyl lead from it. There was no trace left. . . . Another possible clue—Monte Field's hat. It was gone. . . . The extra tickets for the six vacant seats—we had never seen them and there seemed little chance that we ever would. . . . The only other material evidence—the papers—indicated motive but proved nothing. By this token Morgan might have committed the crime, or any member of Field's criminal organization.

"Our only hope for bringing about a conviction depended upon our scheme to have Barry's apartment burglarized in the hope that either the hat, or the tickets, or some other clue like the poison or the poison apparatus, would be found. Velie got me a professional housebreaker and Barry's apartment was rifled Friday night while he was acting his role in the theatre. Not a trace of any of these clues came to light. The hat, the tickets, the poison—everything had been destroyed. Obviously, Barry would have done that; we could only make sure.

"In desperation, I called a meeting of a number of the Monday night audience, hoping that I would find someone who remembered seeing Barry that night. Sometimes, you know, people recall events later which they forgot completely in the excitement of a previous quizzing. But this

too, as it happened, was a failure. The only thing of value that turned up
was the orangeade boy's testimony about seeing Field pick up an evening
bag in the alley. This got us nowhere as far as Barry was concerned, however. And remember that when we questioned the cast Thursday night we
got no direct evidence from them.

"So there we were with a beautifully hypothetical statement of facts
for a jury, but not a shred of genuine evidence. The case we had to present would have offered no difficulties to a shrewd defending attorney. It
was all circumstantial evidence, based chiefly on reasoning. You know as
well as I do what a chance such a case would have in court. . . . Then my
troubles really began, for Ellery had to leave town.

"I racked my brains—the few I have." Queen scowled at his empty
coffee cup. "Things looked black enough. How could I convict a man
without evidence? It was maddening. And then Ellery did me the final
service of wiring me a suggestion."

"A suggestion?" asked Cronin.

"A suggestion that I do a little blackmailing myself. . . ."

"Blackmailing yourself?" Sampson stared. "I don't see the point."

"Trust Ellery to make a point that on the surface is obscure," retorted
the Inspector. "I saw at once that the only course left open to me was to
*manufacture* evidence!"

Both men frowned in puzzlement.

"It's simple enough," said Queen. "Field was killed by an unusual poison. And Field was killed because he was blackmailing Barry. Wasn't it
fair for me to assume that if Barry were suddenly blackmailed on the
identical score, he would again use poison—and in all likelihood the
*same* poison? I don't have to tell you that 'Once a poisoner always a poisoner.' In the case of Barry, if I could only get him to try to use that tetra
ethyl lead on somebody else, I'd have him! The poison is almost unknown—but I needn't explain further. You can see that if I caught him
with tetra ethyl lead, that would be all the evidence I needed.

"How to accomplish the feat was another matter. . . . The blackmail
opportunity fitted the circumstances perfectly. I actually had the original
papers pertaining to Barry's parentage and tainted blood. Barry thought
these destroyed—he had no reason to suspect that the papers he took
from Field were clever forgeries. If I blackmailed him he was in the same
boat as before. Consequently he would have to take the same action.

"And so I used our friend Charley Michaels. The only reason I utilized
him was that to Barry it would seem logical that Michaels, Field's crony
and bully and constant companion, should be in possession of the original papers. I got Michaels to write a letter, dictated by me. The reason I
wanted Michaels to write it was that possibly Barry, through association

with Field, was familiar with the man's handwriting. This may seem a small point but I couldn't take any chances. If I slipped up on my ruse, Barry would see through it at once and I'd never get him again.

"I enclosed a sheet of the original papers in the letter, to show that the new blackmailing threat had teeth. I stated that Field had brought Barry copies—the sheet enclosed proved my statement. Barry had no reason in the world to doubt that Michaels was milking him as his master had done before. The letter was so worded as to be an ultimatum. I set the time and the place and, to make a long story short, the plan worked. . . .

"I guess that's all, gentlemen. Barry came, he had his trusty little hypodermic filled with tetra ethyl lead, also a flask—an exact replica, you see, of the Field crime except for locale. My man—it was Ritter—was instructed to take no chances. As soon as he recognized Barry he covered him and raised the alarm. Luckily we were almost at their elbows behind the bushes. Barry was desperate and would have killed himself and Ritter, too, if he'd had half a chance."

There was a significant silence as the Inspector finished, sighed, leaned forward and took some snuff.

Sampson shifted in his chair. "Listens like a thriller, Q," he said admiringly. "But I'm not clear on a few points. For example, if this tetra ethyl lead is so little known, how on earth did Barry ever find out about it—to the degree of actually making some himself?"

"Oh." The Inspector smiled. "That worried me from the moment Jones described the poison. I was in the dark even after the capture. And yet—it just goes to show how stupid I am—the answer was under my nose all the time. You will remember that at the Ives-Pope place a certain Dr. Cornish was introduced. Now Cornish is a personal friend of the old financier and both of them are interested in medical science. In fact, I recall Ellery's asking at one time: "Didn't Ives-Pope recently donate $100,000 to the Chemical Research Foundation?" That was true. It was on the occasion of a meeting in the Ives-Pope house one evening several months ago that Barry accidentally found out about tetra ethyl lead. A delegation of scientists had called upon the magnate, introduced by Cornish, to request his financial aid in the Foundation. In the course of the evening, the talk naturally turned to medical gossip and the latest scientific discoveries. Barry admitted that he overheard one of the directors of the Foundation, a famous toxicologist, relate to the group the story of the poison. At this time Barry had no idea that he would put the knowledge to use; when he decided to kill Field, he saw the advantages of the poison and its untraceable source immediately."

"What the deuce was the significance of that message you sent to me by Louis Panzer Thursday morning, Inspector?" inquired Cronin curiously. "Remember? Your note requested that I watch Lewin and Panzer when they met to see if they knew each other. As I reported to you, I asked Lewin later and he denied any acquaintance with Panzer. What was the idea?"

"Panzer," repeated the Inspector softly. "Panzer has always intrigued me, Tim. At the time I sent him to you, remember the hat deductions which absolved him had not yet been made. . . . I sent him to you merely out of a sense of curiosity. I thought that if Lewin recognized him, it might point to a connection between Panzer and Field. My thought was not borne out; it wasn't too hopeful to begin with. Panzer might have been acquainted with Field on the outside without Lewin's knowledge. On the other hand, I didn't particularly want Panzer hanging around the theatre that morning; so the errand did both of us a lot of good."

"Well, I hope you were satisfied with that package of newspapers I sent you in return, as you instructed," grinned Cronin.

"How about the anonymous letter Morgan received? Was that a blind, or what?" demanded Sampson.

"It was a sweet little frame-up," returned Queen grimly. "Barry explained that to me last night. He had heard of Morgan's threat against Field's life. He didn't know, of course, that Field was blackmailing Morgan. But he thought it might plant a strong false trail if he got Morgan to the theatre on a thin story Monday night. If Morgan didn't come, there was nothing lost. If he did— He worked it this way. He chose ordinary cheap notepaper, went down to one of the typewriter agencies and, wearing gloves, typed the letter, signed it with that useless scrawled initial, and mailed the thing from the general post-office. He was careful about fingerprints and certainly the note could never be traced to him. As luck would have it, Morgan swallowed the bait and came. The very ridiculousness of Morgan's story and the obvious falsity of the note, as Barry figured, made Morgan a strong suspect. On the other hand, Providence seems to provide compensations. For the information we got from Morgan about Field's blackmailing activities did Mr. Barry a heap of harm. He couldn't have foreseen that, though."

Sampson nodded. "I can think of only one other thing. How did Barry arrange for the purchase of the tickets—or did he arrange for it at all?"

"He certainly did. Barry convinced Field that as a matter of fairness to himself, the meeting and the transfer of papers should take place in the theatre under a cloak of absolute secrecy. Field was agreeable and was easily persuaded to purchase the eight tickets at the box office. He himself realized that the six extra tickets were needed to insure privacy. He sent Barry seven and Barry promptly destroyed them all except LL30 Left."

The Inspector rose, smiling tiredly. "Djuna!" he said in a low voice. "Some more coffee."

Sampson stopped the boy with a protesting hand. "Thanks, Q, but I've got to be going. Cronin and I have loads of work on this gang affair. I couldn't rest, though, until I got the whole story from your own lips. . . . Q, old man," he added awkwardly, "I'm really sincere when I say that I think you've done a remarkable piece of work."

"I never heard of anything like it," put in Cronin heartily. "What a riddle, and what a beautiful piece of clear reasoning, from beginning to end!"

"Do you really think so?" asked the Inspector quietly. "I'm so glad, gentlemen. Because all the credit rightfully belongs to Ellery. I'm rather proud of that boy of mine. . . ." *July 30, 2011 (I made a mistake on the date.)*

When Sampson and Cronin had departed and Djuna had retired to his tiny kitchen to wash the breakfast dishes, the Inspector turned to his writing desk and took up his fountain pen. He rapidly read over what he had written to his son. Sighing, he put pen to paper once more.

Let's forget what I just wrote. More than an hour has passed since then. Sampson and Tim Cronin came up and I had to crystallize our work on the case for their benefit. I never saw such a pair! Kids, both of 'em. Gobbled the story as if it were a fairy tale. . . . As I talked, I saw with appalling clarity how little I actually did and how much you did. I'm pining for the day when you will pick out some nice girl and be married, and then the whole darned Queen family can pack off to Italy and settle down to a life of peace. . . . Well, El, I've got to dress and go down to headquarters. A lot of routine work has collected since last Monday and my job is just about cut out for me. . . .

When are you coming home? Don't think I want to rush you, but it's so gosh-awful lonesome, son. I—No, I guess I'm selfish as well as tired. Just a doddering old fogey who needs coddling. But you *will* come home soon, won't you? Djuna sends his regards. The rascal is taking my ears off with the dishes in the kitchen.

Your loving
FATHER

*I re-read first part of the FOREWORD on July 30, 2011. My goodness this mystery definitely is a keeper and I cherished reading The Roman Hat mystery.*

# CALAMITY TOWN

# CONTENTS

# PART ONE

# 1

## Mr. Queen Discovers America

Ellery Queen stood knee-deep in luggage on the Wrightsville station platform and thought: This makes me an admiral. Admiral Columbus.

The station was a squatty affair of black-red brick. On a rusty hand truck under the eaves, two small boys in torn blue overalls swung their dirty legs and chewed gum in unison, staring at him without expression.

The gravel about the station was peppered with horse droppings. Cramped two-story frame houses and little stoop-shouldered shops with a cracker-barrel look huddled to one side of the tracks — the city side, for up a steep street paved with square cobbles, Mr. Queen could see taller structures beyond and the fat behind of a retreating bus.

To the other side of the station, there were merely a garage, an ex-trolley labeled PHIL'S DINER, and a smithy with a neon sign. The rest was verdure and delight.

Country looks good, by jake, murmurs Mr. Queen enthusiastically. Green and yellow. Straw colors. And sky of blue and clouds of white — bluer blue and whiter white than he recalled ever having seen before.

City — country; and here they meet, where Wrightsville station flings the twentieth century into the astonished face of the land.

Yes, sir, my boy. You've found it.

*Porter!*

The Hollis Hotel, Upham House, and the Kelton among them could not offer the stranger at their desks one pitiful room. It seemed boom times had hit Wrightsville two jumps ahead of Mr. Queen. The last room at the Hollis was filched from under his nose by a portly man with "defense industry" written all over him.

Undiscouraged, Mr. Queen checked his bags at the Hollis, ate a leisurely lunch in the Coffee Shoppe, and read a copy of the *Wrightsville Record*—Frank Lloyd, Publisher and Editor.

He memorized as many of the names mentioned in the *Record* as seemed to have local prominence, bought two packs of Pall Malls and a Wrightsville street map from Mark Doodle's son Grover at the lobby cigar stand, then struck out across the red-cobbled Square under the hot sun.

At the horse trough in the center of the Square, Mr. Queen paused to admire Founder Wright. Founder Wright had once been a bronze, but he now looked mossy, and the stone trough on which he stood had obviously been unused for years. There were crusty bird droppings on the Founder's Yankee nose. Words on a plaque said that Jezreel Wright had founded Wrightsville when it was an abandoned Indian site, in the Year of Our Lord 1701, had tilled the land, started a farm, and prospered. The chaste windows of the Wrightsville National Bank, *John F. Wright, Pres.*, smiled at Mr. Queen from across the Square, and Mr. Queen smiled back: O Pioneers!

Then he circumnavigated the Square (which was round); peered into Sol Gowdy's Men's Shop, the Bon Ton Department Store, Dunc MacLean—Fine Liquors, and William Ketcham—Insurance; examined the three gilded balls above the shop of J. P. Simpson, the jardinieres of green and red liquid in the window of the High Village Pharmacy, *Myron Garback, Prop.;* and turned to survey the thoroughfares which radiated like spokes from the hub of the Square.

One spoke was a broad avenue: the red-brick Town Hall, the Carnegie Library, a glimpse of park, tall praying trees, and beyond, a cluster of white new WPA-looking buildings. Another spoke was a street lined with stores and full of women in house-dresses and men in work clothes. Consulting his street map, Mr. Queen ascertained that this avenue of commerce was Lower Main; so he made for it.

Here he found the *Record* office; he peered in and saw the big press being shined up by old Phinny Baker after the morning's run. He sauntered up Lower Main, poking his nose into the crowded five-and-dime, past the new Post Office building, past the Bijou Theater, past J. C. Pettigrew's real-estate office; and he went into Al Brown's Ice Cream Parlor and had a New York College Ice and listened to the chatter of tanned boys and red-cheeked girls of high-school age. He heard Saturday night "dates" being arranged right and left—for Danceland, in the Grove, which he gathered was at Wrightsville Junction three miles down the line, admission one dollar per person, and for Pete's sake Marge keep your mother away from the parking lot, will you? I don't wanna get caught like two weeks ago and have you start bawling!

Mr. Queen strolled about the town, approving and breathing deeply of wet leaves and honeysuckle. He liked the stuffed eagle in the Carnegie Library vestibule; he even liked Miss Aikin, the elderly Chief Librarian, who gave him a very sharp look, as if to say: "Don't you try to sneak a book out of *here!*" He liked the twisting narrow streets of Low Village, and he went into Sidney Gotch's General Store and purchased a package of Old Mariner Chewing Tobacco just as an excuse to smell the coffee and rubber boots and vinegar, the cheeses and kerosene.

He liked the Wrightsville Machine Shop, which had just reopened, and the old cotton-mill factory, diagonally across from the Low Village World War Memorial. Sidney Gotch told him about the cotton mill. It had been a cotton mill, then an empty building, then a shoe shop, then an empty building again; he could see for himself the splintery holes in the windows where the Low Village boys threw rocks in summer and snowballs in winter on their way to that vine-covered building up Lower Dade Street there—St. John's Parochial School. But now "specials" prowled around the mill with long fat holsters strapped to their thighs and eyes in their heads that would not smile; the boys, said Sidney Gotch, just yelled "Yahhhh!" and took it out on Mueller's Feed Store three doors up the block, near the corner of Whistling Avenue.

And the woolen mill had taken on extra help—army orders.

"Boom times, brother! No wonder you couldn't get a room. I've got an uncle from St. Paul and a cousin from Pittsburgh doublin' up with me and Betsy right now!"

In fact, Mr. Queen liked everything.

He glanced up at the big clock on the Town Hall steeple. Two-thirty. No room, eh?

Walking rapidly, he made his way back to Lower Main and neither paused nor pried until he reached the shop marked J.C. PETTIGREW, REAL ESTATE.

# 2

## Calamity House

His number twelves up on his desk, J.C. was napping when Mr. Queen came in. He had just come from the weekly Chamber of Commerce lunch at Upham House, and he was full of Ma Upham's fried chicken.

Mr. Queen woke him up. "My name," said Mr. Queen, "is Smith, I've just landed in Wrightsville, and I'm looking for a small furnished house to rent on a month-to-month basis."

"Glad to know you, Mr. Smith," said J.C., struggling into his gabardine "office" jacket. "My, it's warm! Furnished house, hey? I can see you're a stranger. No furnished houses in Wrightsville, Mr. Smith."

"Then perhaps a furnished apartment—"

"Same thing." J.C. yawned. "Excuse *me!* Certainly is hotting up, isn't it?"

"It certainly is," said Ellery.

Mr. Pettigrew leaned back in his swivel chair and picked a strand of chicken out of his teeth with an ivory pick, after which he examined it intently. "Housing's a problem. Yes, sir. People pouring into town like grain in a hopper. To work in the Machine Shop especially. Wait a minute!"

Mr. Queen waited.

"Course!" J.C. flicked the shred of chicken off his pick delicately. "Mr. Smith, you superstitious?"

Mr. Queen looked alarmed. "I can't say I am."

"In that case," said J.C., brightening; then he stopped. "What business you in? Not that it makes any difference, but—"

Ellery hesitated. "I'm a writer."

The real-estate man gaped. "You write *stories?*"

"That's it, Mr. Pettigrew. Books and such."

"Well, well," beamed J.C. "I'm real honored to meet you, Mr. Smith.

Smith . . . Now that's funny," said J.C. "I'm a reading man myself, but I just don't seem to recollect an author named—What did you say your first name was, Mr. Smith?"

"I didn't say, but it's Ellery. Ellery Smith."

"Ellery Smith," said J.C., concentrating.

Mr. Queen smiled. "I write under a pen name."

"Ah! Name of . . . ?" But when Mr. Pettigrew saw that Mr. "Smith" simply kept smiling, he rubbed his jaw and said: "Course you'd give references?"

"Would three months' rent in advance give me a good character in Wrightsville, Mr. Pettigrew?"

"Well, I should smile!" grinned J.C. "You come with me, Mr. Smith. I've got exactly the house you're looking for."

"What did you mean by asking me if I'm superstitious?" asked Ellery as they climbed into J.C.'s pea-green coupe and drove off. "Is the house haunted?"

"Uh . . . no," said J.C. "Though there *is* a sort of a queer yarn connected with that house—might give you an idea for one of your, now, books, hey?" Mr. "Smith" agreed; it might. "This house, it's next door to John F.'s own place on the Hill. John F. Wright, that is. He's President of the Wrightsville National. Oldest family in town.

"Well, sir, three years ago one of John F.'s three daughters—the middle one, Nora—Nora got herself engaged to this Jim Haight. Jim was head cashier at John F.'s bank. Wasn't a local boy—he'd come to Wrightsville from New York a couple of years before that with fine recommendations. Started out as an assistant teller, and he was making good. Steady boy, Jim; stayed away from the bad element, went to the library a lot, didn't have much fun, I s'pose—a movie at Louie Cahan's Bijou, or standing around Band Concert Nights with the rest of the boys, watching the girls parade up and down eating popcorn, and joshing 'em. Worked hard—plenty of up-and-go, Jim had, and independent? Say, I never saw a lad stand on his two feet like Jim did. We all liked him a heap."

Mr. Pettigrew sighed, and Ellery wondered why such a glowing subject should depress him.

"I take it Miss Nora Wright liked him more than anyone," said Ellery to grease the wheels of the story.

"That's a fact," muttered J.C. "Wild about the boy. Nora'd been the quiet kind before Jim came along—has to wear specs, and I guess it made her think she wasn't attractive to boys, 'cause she used to sit in the house while Lola and Patty went out with fellows—reading or sewing or helping her ma with organization work.

"Well, sir, Jim changed all that. Jim wasn't the kind to be stopped by a pair of eyeglasses. Nora's a pretty girl, and Jim started to rush her, and she changed . . . My, she changed!"

J.C. frowned. "S'pose I'm blabbing too much. Anyway, you get the idea. When Jim and Nora got engaged, the town said it was a fine match, especially after what had happened to John's oldest daughter, Lola."

Ellery said quickly: "And what was that, Mr. Pettigrew?"

J.C. swung the coupe into a broad country road. They were well away from town now, and Ellery feasted his eyes on the succulent greens of the countryside.

"Did I say something about Lola?" asked the real-estate man feebly. "Why . . . Lola, she'd run away from home. Eloped with an actor from a visiting stock company. After a while she came back home to Wrightsville. Divorced." J.C. set his lips stubbornly, and Mr. Queen realized he wasn't going to hear any more about Miss Lola Wright.

"Well, anyway," continued J.C., "John and Hermione Wright decided to give Jim and their Nora a furnished house for a wedding present. John cut off part of his property near his own house and built. Right next door, 'cause Hermy wanted Nora as close by as possible, seeing she'd . . . lost one of her girls already."

"Lola," nodded Mr. Queen. "Divorced, you said? Came back home afterwards. Then Lola Wright doesn't live with her father and mother anymore?"

"No," said J.C. shortly. "So John built Jim and Nora a sweet little six-roomer next door. Hermione was putting in rugs and furniture and drapes and linen and silver—the works—when all of a sudden it happened."

"What happened?" asked Mr. Queen.

"To tell the truth, Mr. Smith, nobody knows," said the real-estate man sheepishly. "Nobody 'cepting Nora Wright and Jim Haight. It was the day before the wedding and everything looked fine as corn silk, when Jim Haight ups and leaves town! Fact. Ran away. That was three years ago, and he's not been back since."

They were on a winding, rising road. Ellery saw wide old houses on voluptuous lawns, and elms and maples and cypress and weeping willows taller than the houses.

Mr. Pettigrew scowled at the Hill road. "The next morning John F. found a note of resignation on his desk at the bank, but not a word as to why Jim'd skipped town. And Nora wouldn't say a blessed word. Just shut herself up in her bedroom and wouldn't come out for her father or mother or sister Patricia or even old Ludie, the hired girl who's practically brought the three Wright girls up. Nora just kept bawling in her room. My daughter Carmel and Patty Wright are thick as molasses, and Pat told Carmel the whole thing. Pat did a heap of crying herself that day. I guess they all did."

"And the house?" murmured Mr. Queen.

J.C. drove his car to the side of the road and shut off the motor. "Wedding was called off. We all thought Jim'd turn up, thinking it was just a lovers' spat; but he didn't. Whatever broke those two up must have been awful important!" The real-estate man shook his head. "Well, there was the new house, all ready to be lived in, and no one to live in it. Terrible blow to Hermione. Hermy let out that Nora'd jilted Jim. But people did keep jawing about it, and after a while . . ." Mr. Pettigrew paused.

"Yes?" prompted Ellery.

"After a while people began saying Nora'd gone . . . crazy and that that little six-roomer was jinxed."

"Jinxed!"

J.C. smiled a sickly smile. "Funny how some folks are, isn't it? Thinking the house had anything to do with Jim and Nora's breaking up! And of course ain't nothing wrong with Nora. I mean, she's not crazy. Crazy!"

J.C. snorted. "That wasn't the whole of it. When it looked like Jim wasn't coming back, John F. decided to sell that house he'd built for his daughter. Pretty soon along came a buyer—relative of Judge Martin's wife, Clarice, man named Hunter of the Boston branch of the family. I was handling the deal."

J.C. lowered his voice. "Mr. Smith, I give you my word I'd taken this Mr. Hunter over to the house for a last inspection before signing the papers, and we were looking around the living room and Mr. Hunter was saying, 'I don't like the sofa just there,' when he gets kind of a scared look all of a sudden and grabs his heart and falls down right in front of me! Died on the spot! I didn't sleep for a week."

He swabbed his forehead.

"Doc Willoughby said it was heart failure. But that's not what the town said. The town said it was the house. First Jim ran away, then a buyer dropped dead. And to make it worse, some smart-aleck of a cub reporter on Frank Lloyd's *Record* wrote up Hunter's death and he called the house 'Calamity House' in his yarn. Frank fired him. Frank's friendly with the Wrights."

"Of all the nonsense!" chuckled Mr. Queen.

"Just the same, nobody'd buy," muttered J.C. "John offered to rent. Nobody's rent. Too unlucky, people said. Still want to rent, Mr. Smith?"

"Yes, indeed," said Mr. Queen cheerfully.

So J.C. started his car again.

"Family seems ill-fated," observed Ellery. "One daughter running off and another's life blasted by a love affair. Is the youngest daughter normal?"

"Patricia?" J.C. beamed. "Prettiest, smartest filly in town next to my Carmel! Pat's going steady with Carter Bradford. Cart's our new County Prosecutor . . . Here we are!"

The real-estate man steered his coupe into the driveway of a Colonial-style house sunk into the hillside far off the road. It was the largest house, and the trees on its lawns were the tallest trees that Ellery had seen on the Hill. There was a small white frame house close by the large one, its windows shuttered.

Mr. Queen kept looking at the blind and empty little house he intended to rent all the way up to the wide Wright porch.

Then J.C. rang the bell, and old Ludie in one of her famous starched aprons opened the front door and asked them what in tarnation.

# 3

## "Famed Author to Live in Wrightsville"

"I'll tell Mr. John you're callin'," sniffed Ludie, and she stalked out, her apron standing to each side of her like a Dutch cap.

"Guess Ludie knows we're here to rent Calamity House," grinned Mr. Pettigrew.

"Why should that make her look at me as if I were a Nazi *Gauleiter?*" asked Mr. Queen.

"I expect Ludie doesn't think it proper for folks like the John F. Wrights to be renting out houses. Sometimes I don't know who's got more pride in the family name, Ludie or Hermy!"

Mr. Queen took inventory. Lived in. There were a few aged mahogany pieces of distinction and a beautiful fireplace of Italian marble. And at least two of the oil paintings had merit.

J.C. noticed his interest. "Hermione picked out all the pictures herself. Knows a lot about art, Hermy does. Here she is now. And John."

Ellery rose. He had expected to meet a robust, severe-faced female; instead, he saw Hermy. Hermy always fooled strangers that way; she's so tiny and motherly and sweet-looking.

John Fowler Wright was a delicate little man with a brown country-club face. Ellery liked him at sight. He was carrying a stamp album with practiced care.

"John, this is Mr. Ellery Smith. He's looking to rent a furnished house," said J.C. nervously. "Mr. Wright, Mrs. Wright, Mr. Smith. A-hrmm!"

John F. said in his reedy voice that he was mighty proud to meet Mr. Smith, and Hermy held out her hand at arm's length with a sweet "How do you do, Mr. Smith," but Mr. "Smith" saw the iced gleam in Hermy's pretty blue eyes and decided that in this instance, too, the female was deadlier than the male. So he was most gallant with her. Hermy unbent a little at that and poked her slender lady's fingers in her sleek gray hair, the way she always did when she was pleased, or fussed, or both.

"Of course," said J.C. respectfully, "I thought right off of that beautiful little six-roomer you built next door, John—"

"I don't at all like the idea," said Hermione in her coolest voice, "of renting, John. I can't imagine, Mr. Pettigrew—"

"Maybe if you knew who Mr. Smith *is*," said J.C. quickly.

Hermy looked startled. John F. hitched forward in his wing chair near the fireplace.

"Well?" demanded Hermy. "Who is he?"

"Mr. Smith," said J.C., throwing it away, "is Ellery Smith, the famous author."

"Famous *author!*" gasped Hermy. "But I'm so bowled *over!* Here on the coffee table, Ludie!" Ludie clanked down a tray bearing a musical pitcher filled with ice and grape-juice-and-lemonade punch, and four handsome crystal goblets. "I'm *sure* you'll like our house, Mr. Smith," Hermy went on swiftly. "It's a little dream house. I decorated it with my own hands. Do you ever lecture? Our Women's Club—"

"Good golfing hereabouts, too," said John F. "How long would you want to rent for, Mr. Smith?"

"I'm sure Mr. Smith is going to like Wrightsville so well he'll stay on and *on*," interrupted Hermy. "Do have some of Ludie's punch, Mr. Smith—"

"Thing is," said John F., frowning, "the way Wrightsville's shooting up, I'll probably be able to sell pretty soon—"

"That's easy, John!" said J.C. "We can write in the lease that in case a buyer comes along, Mr. Smith is to vacate pending reasonable notice—"

"Business, business!" said Hermy gaily. "What Mr. Smith wants is to *see* the house. Mr. Pettigrew, you stay here and keep John and his poky old stamps company. Mr. Smith?"

Hermy held on to Ellery's arm all the way from the big house to the little house, as if she were afraid he'd fly away if she let go.

"Of course, the furniture's protected by dustcovers now, but it's really lovely. Early American bird's-eye maple and brand-new. Just look, Mr. Smith. Isn't it *darling?*"

Hermy dragged Ellery upstairs and downstairs, from cellar to peaked attic, exhibited the chintzy master bedroom, extolled the beauties of the living room with its maple pieces and art-filled niches and hooked rug and half-empty bookshelves . . .

"Yes, yes," said Ellery feebly. "Very nice, Mrs. Wright."

"Of course, I'll see you get a housekeeper," said Hermy happily. "Oh, dear! Where will you do your Work? We could fix over the second bedroom upstairs into a study. You *must* have a study for your Work, Mr. Smith."

Mr. "Smith" said he was sure he'd manage handsomely.

"Then you do like our little house? I'm so glad!" Hermione lowered her voice. "You're in Wrightsville incognito, of course?"

"Such an impressive word, Mrs. Wright . . ."

"Then except for a few of our *closest* friends, I'll make sure nobody knows who you are," beamed Hermy. "What kind of Work are you planning, Mr. Smith?"

"A novel," said Ellery faintly. "A novel of a particular sort, laid in a typical small city, Mrs. Wright."

"Then you're here to get Color! How *apt!* You chose our own dear Wrightsville! You must meet my daughter Patricia immediately, Mr. Smith. She's the cleverest child. I'm sure Pat would be a great help to you in getting to know Wrightsville . . ."

Two hours later Mr. Ellery Queen was signing the name "Ellery Smith" to a lease whereunder he agreed to rent Number 460 Hill Drive, furnished, for a period of six months beginning August 6, 1940, three months' rental paid in advance, one month's vacating notice to be given by lessor in event of a sale, at the rental of $75 per month.

"The truth is, Mr. Smith," confided J.C. as they left the Wright house, "I kind of held my breath in there for a minute."

"When was that?"

"When you took that pen of John F.'s and signed the lease."

"You held your breath?" Ellery frowned. "Why?"

J.C. guffawed. "I remembered the case of poor old Hunter and how he dropped dead in that very house. Calamity House! That's a hot one! Here you are, still fit as a fiddle!"

And he got into his coupe still overcome by mirth, bound for town to pick up Ellery's luggage at the Hollis Hotel . . . and leaving Ellery in the Wright driveway feeling irritated.

When Ellery returned to his new residence, there was a tingle in his spine.

There *was* something about the house, now that he was out of Mrs. Wright's clutches, something—well, *blank*, unfinished, like Outer Space. Ellery almost said to himself the word "inhuman," but when he got to that point, he took himself in hand sternly. Calamity House! As sensible as calling Wrightsville Calamity Town! He removed his coat, rolled up his shirtsleeves, and sailed into things.

"Mr. Smith," cried a horrified voice, "what are you *doing?*"

Ellery guiltily dropped a dustcover as Hermione Wright rushed in, her cheeks flushed and her gray hair no longer sleek. "Don't you dare touch a thing! Alberta, come in. Mr. Smith won't bite you." A bashful Amazon shuffled in. "Mr. Smith, this is Alberta Manaskas. I'm sure you'll find her most satisfactory. Alberta, don't stand there. Start the upstairs!" Alberta fled.

Ellery murmured his gratitude and sank into a chintz-cloaked chair as Mrs. Wright attacked the room about him with terrifying energy.

"We'll have this in apple-pie order in a jiffy! By the way, I trust you don't mind. On my trip into town to fetch Alberta, I *happened* to drop into the *Record* office—whoo! this dust!—and had a confidential chat with Frank Lloyd. The editor and publisher, you know."

Ellery's heart scuttled itself.

"By the way, I also took the liberty of giving Logan's a grocery and meat order for you. Although, of course, you'll dine with *us* tonight. Oh, dear, did I forget . . . ? Electricity . . . gas . . . water . . . No, I attended to everything. Oh, the telephone! I'll do that first thing tomorrow. Well, as I was saying, I knew that no matter *how* hard we tried, sooner or later everyone would know you're in Wrightsville, Mr. Smith, and of course as a newspaperman, Frank would *have* to do a story on you, so I thought I'd better ask Frank as a personal favor not to mention in his write-up that you're the famous author—Patty baby! Carter! Oh, my darlings, I have *such* a surprise for you!"

Mr. Queen rose, fumbling for his jacket.

His only coherent thought was that she had eyes the color of brook water bubbling in the sun.

"So you're the famous author," said Patricia Wright, looking at him with her head cocked. "When Pop told Carter and me just now what Mother had snagged, I thought I'd meet a baggy-pantsed poet with a hangdog look, melancholy eyes, and a pot. I'm *pleased*."

Mr. Queen tried to look suave and mumbled something.

"Isn't it wonderful, dearest?" cried Hermy. "You must forgive me, Mr. Smith. I know you think I'm terribly provincial. But I really *am* over-whelmed. Pat dear, introduce Carter."

"Carter! Darling, I'm so sorry. Mr. Smith, Mr. Bradford." Shaking hands with a tall young man, intelligent-looking but worried, Ellery wondered if he were worried about how to hold on to Miss Patricia Wright. He felt an instant sympathy.

"I suppose," said Carter Bradford politely, "we must all seem provincial to you, Mr. Smith. Fiction or nonfiction?"

"Fiction," said Ellery. So it was war.

"I'm *pleased*," said Pat again, looking Ellery over. Carter frowned; Mr. Queen beamed. "I'll do this room, Muth . . . You won't be hurting *my* feelings, Mr. Smith, if after we've stopped interfering in your life, you change things around again. But for now—"

As he watched Pat Wright setting his house in order under Carter Bradford's suspicious eye, Ellery thought: May the saints grant me calamities like this each blessed day. Carter, my boy, I'm sorry, but I'm cultivating your Patty!

His good humor was not dispelled even when J. C. Pettigrew hurried back from town with his luggage and flourished the last edition of the *Wrightsville Record.*

Frank Lloyd, Publisher and Editor, had kept his word to Hermione Wright only technically.

He had said nothing about Mr. Smith in the body of the news item except that he was "Mr. Ellery Smith of New York."

But the headline on the story ran:

FAMED AUTHOR TO
LIVE IN WRIGHTSVILLE!

# 4

## The Three Sisters

Mr. Ellery "Smith" was a sensation with the *haut monde* on the Hill and the local intelligentsia: Miss Aikin, the Librarian, who had studied Greek; Mrs. Holmes, who taught Comparative Lit at Wrightsville High; and, of course, Emmeline DuPré, known to the irreverent as the "Town Crier," who was nevertheless envied by young and old for having the miraculous good fortune to be *his neighbor*. Emmy DuPré's house was on Ellery's other side.

Automobile traffic suddenly increased on the Hill. Interest became so hydra-headed that Ellery would have been unmoved if the Wrightsville Omnibus Company had started running a sightseeing bus to his door.

Then there were Invitations. To tea, to dinner, to luncheon; and one—from Emmeline DuPré—asking him to breakfast, "so that we may discuss the Arts in the coolth of a Soft Morning, before the Dew vanishes from the Sward."

Ben Danzig, High Village Rental Library and Sundries, said he had never had such a rush on Fine Stationery.

So Mr. Queen began to look forward to escaping with Pat in the mornings, when she would call for him dressed in slacks and a pullover sweater and take him exploring through the County in her little convertible. She knew everybody in Wrightsville and Slocum Township, and introduced him to people named variously O'Halleran, Zimbruski, Johnson, Dowling, Goldberger, Venuti, Jacquard, Wladislaus, and Broadbeck—journeymen machinists, toolers, assembly-line men, farmers, retailers, hired hands, white and black and brown, with children of unduplicated sizes and degrees of cleanliness. In a short time, through the curiously wide acquaintanceship of Miss Wright, Mr. Queen's notebook was rich with funny lingos, dinner-pair details, Saturday-night brawls down on Route 16, square dances and hep-cat contests, noon whistles whistling, lots of smoke and laughing and pushing, and the color of America, Wrightsville edition.

"I don't know what I'd do without you," Ellery said one morning as they returned from Low Village. "You seem so much more the country-club, church-social, Younger-Set type of female. How come, Pat?"

"I'm that, too," grinned Pat. "But I'm a Sociology Major, or I was— got my degree in June; and I guess I just can't help practicing on the helpless population. If this war keeps up—"

"Milk Fund?" asked Ellery vaguely. "That sort of thing?"

"Barbarian! Milk Funds are Muth's department. My dear man, sociology is concerned with more than calcium for growing bones. It's the science of civilization. Now take the Zimbruskis—"

"Spare me," moaned Mr. Queen, having met the Zimbruskis. "By the way, what does Mr. Bradford, your local Prosecutor, think of all this, Patty?"

"Of me and sociology?"

"Of me and you."

"Oh." Pat tossed her hair to the wind, looking pleased. "Cart's jealous."

"Hmm. Look here, my little one—"

"Now don't start being noble," said Pat. "Trouble with Cart, he's taken me for granted too long. We've practically grown up together. Do him good to be jealous."

"I don't know," smiled Ellery, "that I entirely relish the role of love-irritant."

"Oh, please!" Pat was shocked. "I *like* you. And this is more fun." Suddenly, with one of her quick sidelong glances: "You know what people are saying, incidentally—or don't you?"

"What now?"

"You told Mr. Pettigrew that you're a famous writer—"

"Mr. Pettigrew supplied the adjective 'famous' all by himself."

"You've also said you don't write under the name Ellery Smith, that you use a pseudonym . . . but you didn't tell anyone *which* pseudonym."

"Lord, no!"

"So people are saying that maybe you aren't a famous author after all," murmured Pat. "Nice town, huh?"

"Which people?"

"People."

"Do *you* think I'm a fraud?"

"Never mind what I think," retorted Pat. "But you should know there's been a run on the Author's Photograph File at the Carnegie Library, and Miss Aikin reports you're simply not there."

"Pish," said Ellery. "And a couple of tushes. I'm just not famous enough."

"That's what I told her. Mother was furious at the very thought, but I said: 'Muth, how do we *know?*' and do you know, poor Mother didn't sleep a wink all night?"

They laughed together. Then Ellery said: "Which reminds me. Why haven't I met your sister Nora? Isn't she well?"

He was appalled by the way Pat stopped laughing at mention of her sister's name.

"Nora?" repeated Pat in a perfectly flat voice, a voice that told nothing at all. "Why, Nora's all right. Let's call it a morning, Mr. Smith."

That night Hermione officially unveiled her new treasure.

The list was *intime*. Just Judge and Clarice Martin, Doc Willoughby, Carter Bradford, Tabitha Wright, John F.'s only living sister—Tabitha was the "stiff-necked" Wright who had never quite "accepted" Hermione Bluefield—and Editor-Publisher Frank Lloyd of the *Record*.

Lloyd was talking politics with Carter Bradford, but both men merely pretended to be interested in each other. Carter was hurling poisonous looks at Pat and Ellery in the "love seat" by the Italian fireplace; while Lloyd, a brown bear of a man, kept glancing restlessly at the staircase in the foyer.

"Frank had a crush on Nora before Jim . . . He's still crazy about her," explained Pat. "When Jim Haight came along and Nora fell for him, Frank took the whole thing pretty badly."

Ellery inspected the mountainous newspaper editor from across the room and inwardly agreed that Frank Lloyd would make a dangerous adversary. There was iron in those deep-sunk green eyes.

"And when Jim walked out on Nora, Frank said that—"

"Yes?"

"Never mind what Frank said." Pat jumped up. "I'm talking too much." And she rustled toward Mr. Bradford to break another little piece off his heart. Pat was wearing a blue taffeta dinner gown that swished faintly as she moved.

"Milo, this is *the* Ellery Smith," said Hermy proudly, coming over with big, lumbering Doc Willoughby in tow.

"Don't know whether you're a good influence or not, Mr. Smith," chuckled Doc. "I just came from another confinement at the Jacquards'. Those Canucks! Triplets this time. Only difference between me and Dr. Dafoe is that no lady in Wright County's been considerate enough to bear more than four at one time. Like our town?"

"I've fallen in love with it, Dr. Willoughby."

"It's a good town. Hermy, where's my drink?"

"If you're broad-minded," snorted Judge Martin, strolling up with Clarice hanging—heavily—on his arm. Judge Martin was a gaunt little man with sleepy eyes and a dry manner. He reminded Ellery of Arthur Train's Mr. Tutt.

"Eli Martin!" cried Clarice. "Mr. Smith, you just ignore this husband of mine. He's miserable about having to wear his dinner jacket, and he'll take it out on you because you're the cause. Hermy, everything's just *perfect*."

"It's nothing at all," murmured Hermione, pleased. "Just a little intimate dinner, Clarice."

"I don't like these doodads," growled the Judge, fingering his bow tie. "Well, Tabitha, and what are *you* sniffing about?"

"Comedian!" said John F.'s sister, glaring at the old jurist. "I can't imagine what Mr. Smith must be thinking of us, Eli!"

Judge Martin observed dryly that if Mr. Smith thought less of him for being uncomfortable in doodads, then *he* thought less of Mr. Smith.

A crisis was averted by the appearance of Henry Clay Jackson announcing dinner. Henry Clay was the only trained butler in Wrightsville, and the ladies of the upper crust, by an enforced Communism, shared him and his rusty "buttlin' suit." It was an unwritten law among them that Henry Clay was to be employed on ultra-special occasions only.

"Dinnuh," announced Henry Clay Jackson, "is heaby suhved!"

Nora Wright appeared suddenly between the roast lamb-wreathed-in-mint-jelly-flowers and the pineapple mousse.

For an instant the room was singing-still.

Then Hermione quavered: "Why, *Nora* darling," and John F. said gladly: "Nora baby," through a mouthful of salted nuts, and Clarice Martin gasped: "Nora, how *nice!*" and the spell was broken.

Ellery was the first man on his feet. Frank Lloyd was the last; the thick neck under his shaggy hair was the color of brick.

Pat saved the day. "I must say this is a fine time to come down to dinner, Nora!" she said briskly. "Why, we've finished Ludie's best lamb. Mr. Smith, Nora."

Nora offered him her hand. It felt as fragile and cold as a piece of porcelain.

"Mother's told me all about you," said Nora in a voice that sounded unused.

"And you're disappointed. Naturally," smiled Ellery. He held out a chair.

"Oh, no! Hello, Judge, Mrs. Martin. Aunt Tabitha . . . Doctor . . . Carter . . ."

Frank Lloyd said: "Hullo, Nora," in gruff tones; he took the chair from Ellery's hands neither rudely nor politely; he simply took it and held it back for Nora. She turned pink and sat down. Just then Henry Clay marched in with the magnificent mousse, molded in the shape of a book, and everybody began to talk.

Nora Wright sat with her hands folded, palms up, as if exhausted; her colorless lips were twisted into a smile. Apparently she had dressed with great care, for her candy-striped dinner gown was fresh and perfectly draped, her nails impeccable, and her coiffure without a single stray wine-brown hair. Ellery glimpsed a sudden, rather appalling, vision of this slight bespectacled girl in her bedroom upstairs, fussing with her nails, fussing with her hair, fussing with her attractive gown . . . fussing, fussing, so that everything might be just so . . . fussing so long and so needlessly that she had been an hour late to dinner.

And now that she had achieved perfection, now that she had made the supreme effort of coming downstairs, she seemed emptied, as if the effort had been too much and not entirely worthwhile. She listened to Ellery's casual talk with a fixed smile, white face slightly lowered, not touching her mousse or demitasse, murmuring a monosyllable occasionally . . . but not as if she were bored, only as if she were weary beyond sensation.

And then, as suddenly as she had come in, she said: "Excuse me, please," and rose. All conversation stopped again.

Frank Lloyd jumped up and drew her chair back. He devoured her with a huge and clumsy hunger; she smiled at him, and at the others, and floated out . . . her step quickening as she approached the archway from the dining room to the foyer.

Then she disappeared, and everyone began to talk at once and ask for more coffee.

Mr. Queen was mentally sifting the evening's grist as he strolled back to his house in the warm darkness. The leaves of the big elms were talking, there was an oversize cameo moon, and his nose was filled with the scents of Hermione Wright's flowers.

But when he saw the small roadster parked by the curb before his house, dark and empty, the sweetness fled. It was simply night, and something was about to happen.

A gun-metal cloud slipped across the moon, and Mr. Queen made his way along the edge of his lawn on the muffling grass toward the little house. A point of fire took shape on his porch. It was swaying back and forth about waist-high to a standing man.

"Mr. Smith, I presume?"

A woman's contralto. Slightly fuzzed with husk. It had a mocking quality.

"Hullo!" he called, mounting the porch steps. "Mind if I turn on the porch light? It's so beastly dark—"

"Please do. I'm as curious to see you as you are to see me."

Ellery touched the light switch.

She was curled up in a corner of the slide-swing blinking at him from behind the streaming veil of her cigarette. The dove suede of her slacks was tight over her thighs; a cashmere sweater molded her breasts boldly. Ellery gathered a full-armed impression of earthiness, overripe, and growing bitter. *WOW, what an incredible description. MP July 31 2011*

She laughed, a little nervously he thought, and flipped her cigarette over the porch rail into the darkness.

"You may turn off the light now, Mr. Smith. I'm a fright; and besides, I shouldn't want to embarrass my family by making them aware I'm in their immediate neighborhood."

Ellery obediently switched off the porch light. "Then you're Lola Wright." The one who had eloped and come back divorced. The daughter the Wrights never mentioned.

"As if you didn't know!" Lola Wright laughed again, and it turned into a hiccup. "Excuse *me*. Seventh hiccup of a seventh Scotch. I'm famous, too, you know. The *drinking* Wright girl."

Ellery chuckled. "I've heard the vile slanders."

"I was all prepared to hate your guts, from the kowtowing that's been going on, but you're all right. Shake!" The swing creaked, and steps shuffled to the tune of an unsteady laugh, and then the moist heat of her hand warmed his neck as she groped. He gripped her arms to save her from falling.

"Here," he said. "You should have stopped at number six."

She placed her palms against his starched shirt and pushed strongly. "Whoa, Geronimo! The man'll think li'l Lola's stinko." He heard her totter back to the swing, and its creak. "Well, Mr. Famous Author Smith, and what do you think of us all? Pygmies and giants, sweet and sour, snaggle-toothed and slick-magazine ads—good material for a book, eh?"

"Elegant."

"You've come to the right place." Lola Wright lit another cigarette; the flame trembled. "Wrightsville! Gossipy, malicious, intolerant . . . the great American slob. More dirty linen to the square inch of backyard than New York or Marseilles."

"Oh, I don't know," argued Mr. Queen. "I've spent a lot of loose time prowling, and it seems a pretty nice place to me."

"Nicc!" She laughed. "Don't get me started. I was born here. It's wormy and damp—a breeding place of nastiness."

"Then why," murmured Mr. Queen, "did you come back to it?"

The red tip of her cigarette waxed three times in rapid succession. "None of your business. Like my family?"

"Immensely. You resemble your sister Patricia. Same physical glow, too."

"Only Patty's young, and my light's going out." Lola Wright mused for a moment. "I suppose you'd have to be polite to an old bag named Wright. Look, Brother Smith. I don't know why you came to Wrightsville, but if you're going to be palsy with my kin, you'll hear a lot about little Lola eventually, and . . . well . . . I don't give a damn what Wrightsville thinks of me, but an alien . . . that's different. Good grief! I still have vanity!"

"I haven't heard anything about you from your family."

"No?" He heard her laugh again. "I feel like baring my bosom tonight. You'll hear I drink. True. I learned it from— I learned it. You'll hear I'm seen in all the awful places in town, and what's worse, *alone*. Imagine! I'm supposed to be 'fast.' The truth is I do what I damned please, and all these vultures of women on the Hill, they've been tearing at me with their claws!"

She stopped.

"How about a drink?" asked Ellery.

"Not now. I don't blame my mother. She's narrow, like the rest of them; her social position is her whole life. But if I'd play according to her rules, she'd still take me back. She's got spunk, I'll give her that. Well, I won't play. It's my life, and to hell with rules! Understand?" She laughed once more. "Say you understand. Go on. Say it."

"I understand," Ellery said.

She was quiet. Then she said: "I'm boring you. Good night."

"I want to see you again."

"No. Good-bye."

Her shoes scraped the invisible porch floor. Ellery turned on the light again. She put up her arm to hide her eyes.

"Well, then, I'll see you home, Miss Wright."

"Thanks, no. I'm—"

She stopped.

Patricia Wright's gay voice called from the darkness below: "Ellery? May I come up and have a good-night cigarette with you? Carter's gone home and I saw your porch light—" Pat stopped, too.

The two sisters stared at each other.

"Hel*lo*, Lola!" cried Pat. She vaulted up the steps and kissed Lola vigorously. "Why didn't you tell me you were coming?"

Mr. Queen put the light out again very quickly. But he had time to see how Lola clung—briefly—to her taller, younger sister.

"Lay off, Snuffles," he heard Lola say in a muffled voice. "You're mussing my hairdo."

"And that's a fact," said Pat cheerfully. "You know, Ellery, this sister of mine is the most attractive girl ever to come out of Wrightsville. And she insists on hiding her light under frumpy old slacks!"

"You're a darling, Pats," said Lola, "but don't try so hard. It's no dice, and you know it."

Pat said miserably: "Lo dear . . . why don't you come back?"

"I think," remarked Mr. Queen, "I'll walk down to that hydrangea bush and see how it's making out."

"Don't," said Lola. "I'm going now. I really am."

"Lola!" Pat's voice was damp.

"You see, Mr. Smith? Snuffles. She was always snuffling as a brat. Pat, now stop it. This is old hat for us two."

"I'm all right." Pat blew her nose in the darkness. "I'll drive home with you."

"No, Patsy. Night, Mr. Smith."

"Good night."

"And I've changed my mind. Come over and have a drink with me any time you like. Night, Snuffy!"

And Lola was gone.

When the last rattle of Lola's 1932 coupe died, Pat said in a murmur: "Lo lives in a two-room hole down in Low Village, near the Machine Shop. She wouldn't take alimony from her husband, who was a rat till the day he died, and she won't accept money from Pop. Those clothes she wears—six years old. Part of her trousseau. She supports herself by giving piano lessons to Low Village hopefuls at fifty cents a throw."

"Pat, why does she stay in Wrightsville? What brought her back after her divorce?"

"Don't salmon or elephants or something come back to their birthplace . . . to die? Sometimes I think it's almost as if Lola's . . . hiding." Pat's silk taffeta rustled suddenly. "You make me talk and talk. Good night, Ellery."

"Night, Pat."

Mr. Queen stared into the dark night for a long time.

Yes, it was taking shape. He'd been lucky. The makings were here, rich and bloody. But the crime—the crime. Where was it?

*Or had it already occurred?*

Ellery went to bed in Calamity House with a sense of events past, present, and future.

On the afternoon of Sunday, August twenty-fifth, nearly three weeks from the day of Ellery's arrival in Wrightsville, he was smoking a post-prandial cigarette on his porch and enjoying the improbable sunset when Ed Hotchkiss's taxicab charged up the Hill and squealed to a stop before the Wright house next door.

A hatless young man jumped out of the cab.

Mr. Queen felt a sudden agitation and rose for a better view.

The young man shouted something to Ed Hotchkiss, bounded up the steps, and jabbed at the Wright doorbell.

Old Ludie opened the door. Ellery saw her fat arm rise as if to ward off a blow. Then Ludie scuttled back out of sight, and the young man dashed after her. The door banged.

Five minutes later it was yanked open; the young man rushed out, stumbled into the waiting cab, and yelled to be driven away.

Ellery sat down slowly. It might be. He would soon know. Pat would come flying across the lawn . . . There she was.

"Ellery! You'll never guess!"

"*Jim Haight's come back*," said Ellery.

Pat stared. "You're wonderful. Imagine—after three years! After the way Jim ran out on Nora! I can't believe it yet. He looks so much *older* . . . He had to see Nora, he yelled. Where was she? Why didn't she come down? Yes, he knew what Muth and Pop thought of him, but that could wait. Where was Nora? And all the time he kept shaking his fist in poor Pop's face and hopping up and down on one foot like a maniac!"

"What happened then?"

"I ran upstairs to tell Nora. She went deathly pale and plopped down on her bed. She said: '*Jim?*' and started to bawl. Said she'd rather be dead, and why hadn't he stayed away, and she wouldn't see him if he came crawling to her on his hands and knees—the usual feminine tripe. Poor Nora!"

Pat was near tears herself.

"I knew it was no good arguing with her—Nora's awfully stubborn when she wants to be. So I told Jim, and he got even more excited and wanted to run upstairs, and Pop got mad and waved his best mashie at the foot of the stairs, like Horatius at the bridge, and ordered Jim out of the house, and—well, Jim would have had to knock Pop down to get by him, so he ran out of the house screaming that he'd see Nora if he had to throw bombs to get in. And all this time I was trying to revive Muth, who'd conveniently fainted as a sort of strategic diversion . . . I've got to get back!" Pat ran off. Then she stopped and turned around. "Why in heaven's name," she asked slowly, "do I come running to you with the most intimate details of my family's affairs, Mr. Ellery Smith?"

"Maybe," smiled Ellery, "because I have a kind face."

"Don't be foul. Do you suppose I'm f—" Pat bit her lip, a faint blush staining her tan. Then she loped away.

Mr. Queen lit another cigarette with fingers not quite steady.

Despite the heat, he felt chilled suddenly.

He threw the unsmoked butt into the grass and went into the house to haul out his typewriter.

# 5

## Lover Come Back

Gabby Warrum, the one-toothed agent at the railroad station, saw Jim Haight get off the train.

Gabby told Emmeline DuPré.

By the time Ed Hotchkiss dropped Jim off at Upham House, where Ma for old times' sake managed to wangle a bed for him, Emmy DuPré had phoned nearly everyone in town who wasn't picnicking in Pine Grove or swimming in Slocum Lake.

Opinion, as Mr. Queen ascertained by prowling around town Monday and keeping his steel-trap ears open, was divided. J. C. Pettigrew, Donald Mackenzie, and the rest of the Rotary bunch, who were half-Country Club and half-tradespeople, generally opined that Jim Haight ought to be run out on a rail. The ladies were stoutly against this: Jim was a nice young man; whatever'd happened between him and Nora Wright three years ago wasn't *his* fault, you can bet your last year's bonnet!

Frank Lloyd disappeared. Phinny Baker said his boss had gone off on a hunting trip up in the Mahoganies. Emmeline DuPré sniffed. "It's funny Frank Lloyd should go hunting *the very next morning* after James Haight gets back to Wrightsville. Ran away, of course. That big windbag!" Emmy was disappointed that Frank hadn't taken one of his deer rifles and gone stalking through the streets of Wrightsville for Jim, like Owen Wister's Virginian (starring, however, Gary Cooper).

Old Soak Anderson, the town problem, discovered by Mr. Queen Monday noon lying on the stone pedestal of the Low Village World War Memorial, rubbed his salt-and-pepper stubble and declaimed: " 'O most lame and impotent conclusion!' "

"Are you feeling well this morning, Mr. Anderson?" asked Ellery, concerned.

"Never better, sir. But my point is one with the Proverb, the twenty-sixth, I believe, which states: 'Whoso diggeth a pit shall fall therein.' I refer, of course, to the reappearance in this accursed community of Jim Haight. Sow the wind, sir; sow the wind!"

The yeast in all this ferment acted strangely. Having returned to Wrightsville, Jim Haight shut himself up in his room at Upham House; he even had his meals served there, according to Ma Upham. Whereas Nora Wright, the prisoner, began to show herself!

Not in public, of course. But on Monday afternoon she watched Pat and Ellery play three sets of tennis on the grass court behind the Wright house, lying in a deck chair in the sun, her eyes protected by dark glasses hooked over her spectacles; and she kept smiling faintly. On Monday evening she strolled over with Pat and a hostile Carter Bradford "to see how you're coming along with your book, Mr. Smith." Ellery had Alberta Manaskas serve tea and oatmeal cookies; he treated Nora quite as if she were in the habit of dropping in. And then on Tuesday night . . .

Tuesday night was bridge night at the Wrights'. Carter Bradford usually came to dinner, and Carter and Pat paired against Hermione and John F.

Hermy thought it might be "nice" to have Mr. Smith in on Tuesday, August twenty-seventh, to make a fifth; and Ellery accepted with alacrity.

"I'd much rather watch tonight," said Pat. "Carter dear, you and Pop against Ellery and Mother. I'll heckle."

"Come on, come on, we're losing time," said John F. "Stakes, Smith? It's your option."

"Makes no difference to me," said Ellery. "Suppose I toss the honor over to Bradford."

"In that case," said Hermy quickly, "let's play for a tenth. Carter, *why* don't they pay Prosecutors more?" Then she brightened. "When you're Governor . . ."

"Penny a point," said Carter; his lean face was crimson.

"But Cart, I didn't mean—" wailed Hermione.

"If Cart wants to play for a cent, by all means *play* for a cent," said Pat firmly. "I'm sure he'll win!"

"Hello," said Nora.

She had not come down to dinner—Hermy had said something about a "headache." Now Nora was smiling at them from the foyer. She came in with a basket of knitting and sat down in the big chair under a piano lamp.

"I'm really winning the war for Britain," she smiled, "all by myself. This is my tenth sweater!"

Mr. and Mrs. Wright exchanged startled glances, and Pat absently began to ruffle Ellery's hair.

"Play cards," said Carter in a smothered voice.

The game began under what seemed to Ellery promising circumstances, considering the warm vital hand in his hair and Carter's outthrust lower lip. And, in fact, after two rubbers Cart slammed his cards down on the table.

"Why, Cart!" gasped Pat.

"Carter Bradford," said Hermy, "I never *heard*—"

"What on earth?" said John F., staring at him.

"If you'd stop *jumping around*, Pat," cried Carter, "I'd be able to concentrate on this ding-busted game!"

"Jumping *around?*" said Pat indignantly. "Cart Bradford, I've been sitting here on the arm of Ellery's chair all evening not saying a word!"

"If you want to play with his beautiful hair," roared Cart, "why don't you take him outside under the moon?"

Pat turned the machine-gun of her eyes on him. Then she said contritely to Ellery: "I'm sure you'll forgive Cart's bad manners. He's really had a decent bringing-up, but associating with hardened criminals so much—"

Nora yelped.

Jim Haight stood in the archway. His Palm Beach suit hung tired and defeated; his shirt was dark with perspiration. He looked like a man who has been running at top speed in a blazing heat without purpose or plan—just running.

And Nora's face was a cloud-torn sky.

"Nora."

The pink in Nora's cheeks spread and deepened until her face seemed a mirror to flames.

Nobody moved. Nobody said a word.

Nora sprang toward him. For an instant Ellery thought she meant to attack him in a spasm of fury. But then Ellery saw that Nora was not angry; she was in a panic. It was the fright of a woman who had long since surrendered hope of life to live in a suspension of life, a kind of breathing death; it was the fear of joyous rebirth. Powerful writing. MP July 31, 2011

Nora darted by Jim and skimmed up the stairs.

Jim Haight looked exultant. Then he ran after her.

And silence.

Living Statues, thought Ellery. He ran his finger between his neck and his collar; it came away dripping.

John F. and Hermy Wright were saying secretive things to each other with their eyes, as a man and woman learn to do who have lived together for thirty years.

Pat kept glaring at the empty foyer, her chest rising and falling visibly; and Carter kept glaring at Pat, as if the thing that was happening between Jim and Nora had somehow become confused in his mind with what was happening between him and Pat.

Later . . . later there were overhead sounds: the opening of a bedroom door, a slither of feet, steps on stairs.

Nora and Jim appeared in the foyer.

"We're going to be married," said Nora. It was as if she were a cold lamp and Jim had touched the button. She glowed from within and gave off a sort of heat.

"Right off," said Jim. He had a deep defiant voice; it was harsher than he meant, rasped by emery strain. "Right off!" Jim said. "Understand?" He was scarlet from the roots of his sandy hair to the chicken skin below his formidable Adam's apple. But he kept blinking at John F. and Hermy with a dogged, nervous bellicosity.

"Oh, Nora!" cried Pat, and she pounced and kissed Nora's mouth and began to cry and laugh. Hermy was smiling the stiff smile of a corpse. John F. mumbled, "I'll be dinged," and heaved out of his chair and went to his daughter and took her hand, and he took Jim's hand, just standing there helplessly. Carter said: "It's high time, you two lunatics!" and slipped his arm about Pat's waist.

Nora did not cry. She kept looking at her mother.

And then Hermy's petrifaction broke into little pieces and she ran to Nora, pushing Pat and John F. and Carter aside. She kissed Nora and kissed Jim and said something in a hysterical tone that made no sense but seemed the right thing to say just the same.

Mr. Queen slipped out, feeling a little lonely.

# 6

## "Wright-Haight Nuptials Today"

Hermy planned the wedding like a general in his field tent surrounded by maps of the terrain and figures representing the accurate strength of the enemy's forces.

While Nora and Pat were in New York shopping for Nora's trousseau, Hermione held technical discussions with old Mr. Thomas, sexton of the First Methodist Church; horticultural conferences with Andy Birobatyan, the one-eyed Armenian florist in High Village; histrionic conversations with the Reverend Dr. Doolittle *in re* rehearsals and choirboy arrangements; talks with Mrs. Jones the caterer, with Mr. Graycee of the travel agency, and with John F. at the bank on intrafamiliar banking business.

But these were Quartermaster's chores. The General Staff conversations were with the ladies of Wrightsville.

"It's just like a movie, dear!" Hermy gushed over the telephone. "It was nothing more than a lovers' quarrel to begin with—Oh, yes, darling, *I* know what people are saying!" said Hermy coldly. "But my Nora doesn't have to grab anybody. I don't suppose you recall last year how that handsome young Social Registrite from Bar Harbor . . . Of *course* not! Why should we have a *quiet* wedding? My dear, they'll be married in church and . . . *Naturally* as a bride . . . Yes, to South America for six weeks . . . Oh, John is taking Jim back into the bank . . . Oh, no, dear, an *officer's* position . . . Of course, darling! Do you think I'd marry my Nora off and not have *you* at the wedding?"

On Saturday, August thirty-first, one week after Jim's return to Wrightsville, Jim and Nora were married by Dr. Doolittle in the First Methodist Church. John F. gave the bride away, and Carter Bradford was Jim's best man.

After the ceremony, there was a lawn reception on the Wright grounds. Twenty Negro waiters in mess jackets served; the rum punch was prepared from the recipe John F. had brought back with him from Bermuda in 1928. Emmeline DuPré, full-blown in an organdy creation and crowned with a real rosebud tiara, skittered from group to group remarking how "well" Hermione Wright had carried off a "delicate" situation, and didn't Jim look interesting with those purple welts under his eyes? Do you suppose he's been drinking these three years? How romantic! Clarice Martin said rather loudly that *some* people were born troublemakers.

During the lawn reception Jim and Nora escaped by the service door. Ed Hotchkiss drove the bride and groom over to Slocum Township in time to catch the express. Jim and Nora were to stay overnight in New York and sail on Tuesday for Rio.

Mr. Queen, who was prowling, spied the fleeing couple as they hurried into Ed's cab. Wet diamonds in her eyes, Nora clung to her husband's hand. Jim looked solemn and proud; he handed his wife into the cab gingerly, as if she might bruise under less careful manipulation.

Mr. Queen also saw Frank Lloyd. Lloyd, returning from his "hunting trip" the day before the wedding, had sent a note to Hermy "regretting" that he couldn't attend the ceremony or reception as he had to go upstate that very evening to attend a newspaper publishers' convention in the Capital. Gladys Hemmingworth, his Society reporter, would cover the wedding for the *Record*. "Please extend to Nora my very best wishes for her happiness. Yours, F. Lloyd."

But F. Lloyd, who should have been two hundred miles away, was skulking behind a weeping willow near the grass court behind the Wright house. Mr. Queen experienced trepidation. What had Patty once said? "Frank took the whole thing pretty badly." And Frank Lloyd was a dangerous man . . . Ellery, behind a maple, actually picked up a rock as Jim and Nora ran out of the kitchen to get into the cab.

But the weeping willow wept quietly, and as soon as the taxi disappeared, F. Lloyd left his hiding place and stamped off into the woods behind the house.

Pat Wright trudged up onto Ellery's porch the Tuesday night after the wedding and said with an artificial cheeriness: "Well, Jim and Nora are somewhere on the Atlantic."

"Holding hands under the moon."

Pat sighed. Ellery sat down beside her on the swing. They rocked together, shoulders touching.

"What happened to your bridge game tonight?" Ellery finally asked.

"Oh, Mother called it off. She's exhausted—been in bed practically since Sunday. And poor old Pop's pottering around with his stamp albums, looking lost. I didn't realize—quite—what it means to lose a daughter."

"I noticed your sister Lola—"

"Lola wouldn't come. Mother drove down to Low Village to ask her. Let's not talk about . . . Lola."

"Then whom shall we talk about?"

Patty mumbled: "You."

"Me?" Ellery was astonished. Then he chuckled. "The answer is yes."

"*What?*" cried Pat. "Ellery, you're ribbing me!"

"Not at all. Your dad has a problem. Nora's just married. This house, under lease to me, was originally designed for her. He's thinking—"

"Oh, El, you're such a darling! Pop hasn't known *what* to do, the coward! So he asked me to talk to you. Jim and Nora do want to live in their . . . Well, I mean—who'd have thought it would turn out this way? As soon as they get back from their honeymoon. But it's not fair to you—"

"All's fair," said Ellery. "I'll vacate at once."

"Oh, no!" said Pat. "You've a six-month lease, you're writing your novel, we've really no right, Pop feels just awful—"

"Nonsense," smiled Ellery. "That hair of yours drives me quite mad. It isn't human. I mean it's like raw silk with lightning bugs in it."

Pat grew very still. And then she wiggled into the corner of the swing and pulled her skirt down over her knees.

"Yes?" said Pat in a queer voice.

Mr. Queen fumbled for a match. "That's all. It's just—extraordinary."

"I see. My hair isn't human, it's just—extraordinary," Pat mocked him. "Well, in that case I must dash. Cart's waiting."

Mr. Queen abruptly rose.

"Mustn't offend Carter! Will Saturday be time enough? I imagine your mother will want to renovate the house, and I'll be leaving Wrightsville, considering the housing shortage—"

"How stupid of me," said Pat. "I almost forgot the most important thing." She got off the swing and stretched lazily. "Pop and Mother are inviting you to be our houseguest for as long as you like. Good niiiiiight!"

And she was gone, leaving Mr. Queen on the porch of Calamity House in a remarkably better humor.

# 7

## Hallowe'en: The Mask

Jim and Nora returned from their honeymoon cruise in the middle of October, just when the slopes of Bald Mountain looked as if they had been set on fire and everywhere you went in town you breathed the cider smoke of leaves burning. The State Fair was roaring full blast in Slocum: Jess Watkins's black-and-white milker, *Fanny IX*, took first prize in the Fancy Milch class, making Wrightsville proud. Kids were sporting red-rubber hands from going without gloves, the stars were frostbitten, and the nights had a twang to them. Out in the country you could see the pumpkins squatting in mysterious rows, like little orange men from Mars. Town Clerk Amos Bluefield, a distant cousin of Hermione's, obligingly died of thrombosis on October eleventh, so there was even the usual "important" fall funeral.

Nora and Jim stepped off the train the color of Hawaiians. Jim grinned at his father-in-law. "What! Such a small reception committee?"

"Town's thinking about other things these days, Jim," said John F. "Draft registration tomorrow."

"Holy smoke!" said Jim. "Nora, I clean forgot!"

"Oh, Lordy," breathed Nora. "Now I've got something else to worry about!" And she clung to Jim's arm all the way up the Hill.

"The town's just agog," declared Hermy. "Nora baby, you look *wonderful!*"

Nora did. "I've put on ten pounds," she laughed.

"How's married life?" demanded Carter Bradford.

"Why not get married and find out for yourself, Cart?" asked Nora. "Pat dear, you're ravishing!"

"What chance has a man got," growled Carter, "with that smooth-talking hack writer in the house—"

"Unfair competition," grinned Jim.

"In the *house*," exclaimed Nora. "Mother, you never wrote me!"

"It was the least we could do, Nora," said Hermy, "seeing how sweet he was about giving up his lease."

"Nice fella," said John F. "Bring back any stamps?"

But Pat said impatiently: "Nora, shake off these men and let's you and I go somewhere and . . . talk."

"Wait till you see what Jim and I brought—" Nora's eyes grew big as the family limousine stopped in the Wright driveway. "Jim, *look!*"

"Surprise!"

The little house by the big one glistened in the October sunshine. It had been repainted: the fresh white of the clapboard walls, the turkey-red of the shutters and "trim," the Christmas green of the newly relandscaped grounds made it look like a delectable gift package.

"It certainly looks fine," said Jim. Nora smiled at him and squeezed his hand.

"And just wait, children," beamed Hermy, "till you see the *inside*."

"Absolutely spick and utterly span," said Pat. "Ready to receive the lovebirds. Nora, you're blubbing!"

"It's so beautiful," wept Nora, hugging her father and mother. And she dragged her husband off to explore the interior of the house that had lain empty, except for Mr. Queen's short tenure, for three frightened years.

Mr. Queen had packed an overnight bag the day before the newly-weds' return and had taken the noon train. It was a delicate disappearance, under the circumstances, and Pat said it showed he had "a fine character." Whatever his reason, Mr. Queen returned on October seventeenth, the day after national registration, to find bustle and laughter in the little house next door, and no sign whatever that it had recently been known as Calamity House.

"We do want to thank you for giving up the house, Mr. Smith," said Nora. There was a housewifely smudge on her pert nose.

"That hundred-watt look is my reward."

"Flatterer!" retorted Nora, and tugged at her starchy little apron. "I look a sight—"

"For ailing eyes. Where's the happy bridegroom?"

"Jim's down at the railroad station picking his things up. Before he came back from his apartment in New York, he'd packed his books and clothes and things and shipped them to Wrightsville care of General Delivery, and they've been held in the baggage room ever since. Here he is! Jim, did you get everything?"

Jim waved from Ed Hotchkiss's cab, which was heaped with suitcases and nailed boxes and a wardrobe trunk. Ed and Jim carried them into the house.

Ellery remarked how fit Jim looked, and Jim with a friendly handclasp thanked him for "being so decent about moving out," and Nora wanted Mr. "Smith" to stay for lunch. But Mr. "Smith" laughed and said he'd take advantage of that invitation when Nora and Jim weren't so busy getting settled, and he left as Nora said: "Such a mess of boxes, Jimmy!" and Jim grunted: "You never know how many books you've got till you start packing 'em. Ed, lug these boxes down the cellar meanwhile, huh?"

The last thing Ellery saw was Jim and Nora in each other's arms.

Mr. Queen grinned. If the bride's house hid a calamity within its walls, the calamity was hidden superlatively well.

Ellery attacked his novel with energy. Except for mealtimes he remained within the sanctuary of his quarters on the top floor, the whole of which Hermy had placed at his disposal. Hermy and Pat and Ludie could hear his portable clacking away until immoral hours. He saw little of Jim and Nora, although at dinner he kept his ears alert for dissonances in the family talk.

But Jim and Nora seemed happy. At the bank Jim had found waiting for him a private office with a new oak desk and a bronze plaque saying MR. HAIGHT V.-PRES. Old customers dropped in to wish him luck and ask about Nora, not without a certain vulturous hope.

The little house was popular, too. The ladies of the Hill called and called, and Nora gave them tea and smiles. Sharp eyes probed corners, looking for dust and despair; but they were disappointed, and Nora giggled over their frustrated curiosity. Hermy was very proud of her married daughter.

So Mr. Queen decided he had been an imaginative fool and that Calamity House was buried beyond resurrection. He began to make plans to invent a crime in his novel, since life was so uncooperative. And, because he liked all the characters, he was very glad.

The twenty-ninth of October came and went, and with it the published figures of the Federal draft lottery in Washington. Jim and Carter Bradford drew high order-numbers; Mr. Queen was observed to drop in at the Hollis Hotel early on the morning of the thirtieth for a New York newspaper, upon reading which he was seen by Mark Doodle's son Grover to shrug and toss the paper away.

The thirty-first was mad. People on the Hill answered mysterious doorbells all day. Menacing signs in colored chalk appeared on pavements. As evening came on, costumed gnomes began to flit about town,

their faces painted and their arms flapping. Big sisters complained bitterly about the disappearance of various compacts and lipsticks, and
many a gnome went to bed with a tingling bottom.

It was all gay and nostalgic, and Mr. Queen strolled about the neighborhood before dinner wishing he were young again so that he, too,
might enjoy the wicked pleasures of Hallowe'en. On his way back to the
Wright house, he noticed that the Haight place next door was lit up; and
on impulse he went up the walk and rang his ex-doorbell.

But it was Pat, not Nora, who answered the door.

"Thought you'd run out on me," said Pat. "We *never* see you anymore." Ellery fed his eyes for a moment. "Now what?" demanded Pat,
blushing. "If you aren't the wackiest man! No*ra?* It's the famous author."

"Come in!" called Nora from the living room. He found her struggling
with an armful of books, trying to pick up more from disorderly stacks
on the floor.

"Here, let me help you," said Ellery.

"Oh, dear, no," said Nora. "You just watch us." And Nora plodded up
the stairs.

"Nora's turning the second bedroom upstairs into a study for Jim," explained Pat.

Pat was stacking books from the floor in her arms and Ellery was idly
examining titles on the half-filled bookshelves when Nora came downstairs for more books.

"Where's Jim, Nora?" asked Ellery.

"At the bank," said Nora, stooping. "An awfully important directors'
meeting—" And just then a book slid off the top of the fresh pile in her
arms, and another, and another, while Nora crouched there, horrified at
the cascade. Half the books were on the floor again.

Pat said: "Oh, look, Nor! Letters!"

"Letters? Where? Of all— They are!"

One of the volumes which had fallen from Nora's arms was oversized
and fat, bound in tan cloth. From among the leaves some envelopes had
tumbled.

Nora picked them up curiously. They were not sealed.

"Oh, three poky old envelopes," said Pat. "Let's get going with these
books, or we'll never be through, Nora."

But Nora frowned. "There's something inside each one, Pat. These are
Jim's books. I wonder if . . ." She removed a single sheet of folded
notepaper from one of the envelopes and spread it smooth, reading
slowly to herself.

"Nora," said Mr. Queen, "what's the matter?"

Nora said faintly: "I don't understand—" and returned the sheet to its envelope. She took a similar sheet from the second envelope, read it, returned it to its envelope, the third, read it . . . And as she thrust it back into the third envelope, her cheeks were the color of wet sand. Pat and Ellery glanced at each other, puzzled.

"*Boo!*"

Nora whirled, shrieking. In the doorway crouched a man wearing a papier-mâché mask; his fingers were curled before his fantastic face, opening and closing hungrily.

Nora's eyes turned up until they were all whites. And then she crumpled, still clutching the three envelopes.

"Nora!" Jim ripped off the ludicrous Hallowe'en mask. "Nora, I didn't mean—"

"Jim, you fool," panted Pat, flinging herself to her knees by Nora's still body. "That's a smart joke! Nora dear—Nora!"

"Look out, Pat," said Jim hoarsely; he seized Nora's limp figure, scooped her up, half-ran up the stairs with her.

"It's only a faint," said Ellery as Pat dashed into the kitchen. "She'll be all right, Patty!"

Pat came stumbling back with a glass of water, which slopped over with each step.

"Here, wench." Ellery took it from her and sped up the stairs with the glass, Pat treading on his heels.

They found Nora on her bed, in hysterics, while Jim chafed her hands and groaned self-abasements.

"Excuse me," said Ellery. He shouldered Jim aside and put the glass to Nora's blue lips. She tried to push his hand away. He slapped her, and she cried out; but she drank the water, choking. Then she sank back on the pillow, covering her face with her palms. "Go away," she sobbed.

"Nora, you all right now?" asked Pat anxiously.

"Yes. Please. Leave me alone. Please!"

"Go on, now," said Jim. "Leave us alone."

Nora let her hands fall. Her face was swollen and puffed.

"You, too, Jim."

Jim gaped at her. Pat steered him out. Ellery shut the bedroom door, frowning, and they went downstairs.

Jim made for the liquor cabinet, poured himself a stiff Scotch, and tossed it down with one desperate motion.

"You know how nervous Nora is," said Pat disapprovingly. "If you hadn't had too much to drink tonight—"

Jim was angry, sullen. "Who's tight? Don't you go telling Nora I've been drinking! Understand?"

"Yes, Jim," said Pat quietly. They waited. Pat kept going to the foot of the stairs and looking up. Jim shuffled around. Ellery whistled a noiseless tune.

Suddenly Nora appeared.

"Nora! Feeling better?" cried Pat.

"Worlds." Nora came downstairs smiling. "Please forgive me, Mr. Smith. It was just being scared all of a sudden."

Jim seized her in his arms. "Oh, Nora—"

"Forget it, dear," laughed Nora.

There was no sign of the three envelopes.

# 8

## Hallowe'en: The Scarlet Letters

When Jim and Nora came up on the porch after dinner, Nora was quite gay.

"Pat told me about that silly mask, Jim Haight," said Hermy. "Nora dearest, you're sure you're all right?"

"Of course, Mother. All this fuss over a scare!"

John F. was studying his son-in-law in a puzzled, secretive way. Jim seemed a little sheepish; he grinned vaguely.

"Where's Carter, Pat?" demanded Hermy. "Wasn't he supposed to go with us to Town Hall tonight?"

"I've a headache, Muth. I phoned Cart to say I was going to bed. Night!" Pat went quickly into the house.

"Come along, Smith," said John F. "There's a good speaker—one of those war correspondents."

"Thanks, Mr. Wright, but I've some work on my novel. Have a nice time!"

When Jim's new car rolled off down the Hill, Mr. Ellery Queen stepped off the Wright porch and, by the light of the pumpkin moon, noiselessly crossed the lawn.

He circled Nora's house once, inspecting the windows. All dark. Then Alberta had already left—Thursday night was her night off.

Ellery opened the kitchen door with a skeleton key, locked it behind him and, using his flashlight sparingly, made his way through the hall to the living room. He climbed the stairs making no sound.

At the landing, he paused, frowning. There was a luminous line under Nora's bedroom door!

He listened intently. Inside, drawers were being pulled open and pushed shut. A thief? Another Hallowe'en prank?

Gripping the flashlight like a club, Ellery kicked the door open.

Miss Patricia Wright screamed as she sprang from her stooped position over the lowest drawer of Nora's vanity.

"Hello," said Mr. Queen affably.

"Worm!" gasped Pat. "I thought I'd *die*." Then she blushed under his amused glance. "At least *I* have an excuse! I'm her sister. But you . . . you're just a plain snoop, *Mr. Ellery Queen!*"

Ellery's jaw waggled. "You little demon," he said admiringly. "You've known me all along."

"Of course," retorted Pat. "I heard you lecture once on *The Place of the Detective Story in Contemporary Civilization*. Very pompous it was, too."

"Wellesley?"

"Sarah Lawrence. I thought at the time you were very handsome. *Sic transit gloria*. Don't look so concerned. I shan't give your precious incognito away."

Mr. Queen kissed her.

"Mmm," said Pat. "Not bad. But inopportune . . . No, please, Ellery. Some other time. Ellery, those letters—you're the only one I can confide in. Muth and Pop would worry themselves sick—"

"And Carter Bradford?" suggested Mr. Queen dryly.

"Cart," said Miss Wright, flushing, "is . . . Well, I just wouldn't want Cart to know anything's wrong. If it is," she added quickly. "I'm not sure anything is."

Ellery said: "Yes, you are. Delicious lipstick."

"Wipe it off. Yes," said Pat damply, "I am . . . Why didn't Nora say what was in those letters?" she burst out. "Why did she come back to the living room tonight without them? *Why did she chase us all out of her bedroom?* Ellery, I'm . . . scared."

Ellery squeezed her cold hands. "Let's look for them."

He found them in one of Nora's hatboxes. The hatbox lay on the shelf of Nora's closet, and the three envelopes had been tucked between the tissue paper and the floor of the box, beneath a little flowered hat with a saucy mauve veil.

"Very clumsy technique," mourned Mr. Queen.

"Poor Nor," said Pat. Her lips were pale. "Let me see!" Ellery handed her the three letters.

In the upper right-hand corner of each envelope, where a stamp should have been, appeared a date written in red crayon.

Pat frowned. Ellery took the envelopes from her and arranged them in chronological order, according to the crayoned dates. The dates were: 11/28, 12/25, and 1/1.

"And all three," mused Pat, "are addressed to 'Miss Rosemary Haight.' She's Jim's only sister. We've never met her. But it's queer there's no street or city address . . ."

"Not necessarily," said Ellery, his brows together. "The queerness lies in the use of the crayon."

"Oh, Jim's always used a thin red crayon instead of a pencil—it's a habit of his."

"Then his sister's name on these envelopes is in Jim's handwriting?"

"Yes. I'd recognize this scrawl of Jim's anywhere. For Pete's sake, Ellery, what's *in* them?"

Ellery removed the contents of the first envelope, crumpled a bit from Nora's clutch when she had fainted.

The note was in Jim's handwriting, too, Pat said, and written in the same red crayon:

Nov. 28

DEAR SIS: I know it's been a long time, but you can imagine I've been rushed. Haven't time to drop you more than a line, because my wife got sick today. Doesn't seem like much, but I don't know. If you ask me, the doctor doesn't know what it is, either. Let's hope it's nothing. Of course, I'll keep you posted. Write me soon.

Love,
Jim

"I can't understand it," said Pat slowly. "Nora's never felt better. Muth and I were just remarking about it the other day. Ellery—"

"Has Nora seen Dr. Willoughby recently?"

"No. Unless . . . But I'm sure she hasn't."

"I see," said Ellery in a voice that told nothing.

"Besides, that date—November twenty-eighth. That's a month away, Ellery! How could Jim know . . . ?" Pat stopped. Then she said hoarsely: "Open the second one!"

The second note was shorter than the first, but it was written in the same red crayon in the same scrawl.

December 25th

SIS: I don't want to worry you. But I've got to tell you. It's much worse.

My wife is terribly ill. We're doing everything we can.

In haste,
Jim

"In haste, Jim," repeated Pat. "In haste—and dated December twenty-fifth!"

Ellery's eyes were clouded over now, hiding.

"But how could Jim know Nora's illness is worse when Nora isn't even sick?" cried Pat. "And two months in advance!"

"I think," said Mr. Queen, "we'd best read the third note." And he took the sheet of paper from the last envelope.

"Ellery, what . . . ?"

He handed it to her and began to walk up and down Nora's bedroom, smoking a cigarette with short, nervous puffs.

Pat read the note wide-eyed. Like the others, it was in Jim's hand, a red-crayon scrawl. It said:

Jan. 1

DEAREST SIS: She's dead. She passed away today.

My wife, gone. As if she'd never been. Her last moments were—
I can't write anymore.

Come to me if you can.

Jim

Ellery said: "Not now, honey child," and threw his arm about Pat's waist.

"What does it mean?" she sobbed.

"Stop blubbering."

Pat turned away, hiding her face.

Ellery replaced the messages in their envelopes and returned the envelopes to their hiding place exactly as he had found them. He set the hatbox back on the shelf of the closet, closed the vanity drawer in which Pat had been rummaging, straightened Nora's hand mirror. Another look around, and he led Pat from the room, switching off the ceiling light by the door.

"Find the door open?" he asked Pat.

"Closed," she replied in a strangled voice.

He closed it.

"Wait. Where's that fat tan book—the one the envelopes fell out of this evening?"

"In Jim's study." Pat seemed to have difficulty pronouncing her brother-in-law's name.

They found the book on one of the newly installed shelves in the bedroom Nora had converted into a study for her husband. Ellery had switched on the mica-shaded desk lamp, and it threw long shadows on the walls.

Pat clung to his arm, throwing glances over her shoulder.

"Pretty fresh condition," said Ellery in a mutter, plucking the book from the shelf. "Cloth hasn't even begun to fade, and the edges of the pages are clean."

"What is it?" whispered Pat.

"Edgcomb's *Toxicology*."

"Toxicology!" Pat stared at it in horror.

Ellery sharply scrutinized the binding. Then he let the book fall open in his hands.

It broke obediently to a dog-eared page—the only dog-eared page he could find. The book's spine showed a deep crack which ran parallel with the place in the book where it had broken open to reveal the dog-eared page.

The three envelopes, then, had been lying between these two pages, thought Ellery. He began to read—to himself.

"What," said Pat feverishly, "what would Jim Haight be doing with a book on toxicology?"

Ellery looked at her. "These two facing pages deal with various arsenious compounds—formulae, morbific effects, detection in organs and tissues, antidotes, fatal dosages, treatment of diseases arising from arsenious poisoning—"

*"Poisoning!"*

Ellery laid the book down within the brightest focus of the lamp. His finger pointed to the words in bold type: *Arsenious Oxid* ($As_2O_3$).

His finger moved down to a paragraph which described arsenious oxid as "white, tasteless, poisonous," and gave the fatal dosage.

This paragraph had been underlined in light red crayon.

In a quite clear voice that emerged from between wry, unwilling lips, Pat said: *"Jim is planning to murder Nora."*

# PART TWO

# 9

## Burnt Offering

"Jim is planning to murder Nora."

Ellery set the book upon the shelf. With his back to Pat, he said: "Nonsense."

"You saw the letters yourself! You read them!"

Mr. Queen sighed. They went downstairs in the dark, his arm about her waist.

Outside, there was the old moon and a stencil of cold stars. Pat shivered against him, and his clasp tightened. They drifted across the silver lawn and came to rest beneath the tallest elm.

"Look at the sky," said Ellery, "and tell me that again."

"Don't feed me philosophy! Or poetry. This is the good old U.S.A. in the Year of Our Madness nineteen-forty. Jim is insane. He must be!" She began to cry.

"The human mind—" began Mr. Queen, and he stopped. He had been about to say that the human mind was a curious and wonderful instrument. But it occurred to him in time that this was a two-way phrase, a Delphic hedge. The fact was . . . it looked bad. Very bad.

"Nora's in danger," sobbed Pat. "Ellery, what am I going to do?"

"Time may spade up some bones of truth, Patty."

"But I can't take this alone! Nora—you saw how Nora took it. Ellery, she was scared green. And then . . . just as if nothing had happened. She's decided already, don't you see? *She's decided not to believe it*. If you waved those letters under her nose, Nora wouldn't admit anything now! Her mind opened for just a second; now it's shut down tight, and she'd lie to God."

"Yes," said Ellery, and his arms comforted her.

"He was so much in love with her! You saw it all happen. You saw the look on his face that night when they came downstairs to say they were

going to be married. Jim was *happy*. When they got back from their honeymoon, he seemed even happier." Pat whispered: "Maybe he *has* gone
mad. Maybe that's been the whole thing all along. A dangerous maniac!"

Ellery said nothing.

"How can I tell Mother? Or my father? It would kill them, and it
wouldn't do any good. And yet—I've got to!"

A car throbbed up the Hill in the darkness.

"You're letting your emotions get in the way of your thinking, Pat,"
said Ellery. "A situation like this calls for observation and caution. And a
disciplined tongue."

"I don't understand . . ."

"One false accusation, and you might wreck the lives not only of Jim
and Nora, but of your father and mother, too."

"Yes . . . And Nora waited so long—"

"I said there's time. There is. We'll watch, and we'll see, and meanwhile it will be a secret between us . . . Did I say 'we'?" Ellery sounded
rueful. "It seems I've declared myself in."

Pat gasped. "You wouldn't back out *now?* I took it for granted. I
mean, I've counted on you from that first awful moment. Ellery, you've
*got* to help Nora! You're trained to this sort of thing. Please don't go
away!" Pat shook him.

"I just said 'we,' didn't I?" said Ellery, almost irritably. There was
something wrong. A sound had gone wrong somewhere. A sound that had
stopped. A car? Had that been a car before? It hadn't passed . . . "Cry it
out now; but when it's over, it's over. Do you understand?" And now he
shook her.

"Yes," wept Pat. "I'm a snuffling fool. I'm sorry."

"You're not a fool, but you must be a heroine. No word, no look, no
*attitude*. As far as the rest of Wrightsville is concerned, those letters don't
exist. Jim is your brother-in-law, and you like him, and you're happy
about him and Nora." She nodded against his shoulder. "We mustn't tell
your father or mother or Frank Lloyd or—"

Pat raised her head. "Or whom?"

"No," said Ellery with a frown. "I can't make *that* decision for you,
too."

"You mean Cart," said Pat steadily.

"I mean the Prosecutor of Wright County."

Pat was silent. Ellery was silent. The moon was lower now, its bosom
ruffled with slate flounces of cloud.

"I couldn't tell Carter," murmured Pat. "It never even occurred to me.
I can't tell you why. Maybe it's because he's connected with the police.
Maybe it's because he's not in the family—"

"I'm not in the family, either," said Mr. Queen.

"You're different!"

Despite himself, Mr. Queen experienced a chill of pleasure. But his voice was impersonal. "At any rate, you've got to be my eyes and ears, Pat. Stay with Nora as much as possible without arousing her suspicions. Watch Jim without seeming to. Report everything that happens. And whenever possible, you must work me into your family gatherings. Is all that clear?"

Pat actually smiled up at him. "I *was* being silly. Now it doesn't seem half so bad, with you under this tree, and the moonlight touching that flat plane of your right cheek . . . You're very handsome, you know, Ellery—"

"Then why in hell," growled a male voice from the darkness, "don't you kiss him?"

"Cart!" Pat snuggled against the black chest of the elm.

They could hear Bradford breathing somewhere near—breathing short deep ones.

Too absurd, thought Mr. Queen. A man of logic should evade such encirclements by chance. But at least it cleared up the minor irritation of the sound-that-had-stopped. It had been Carter Bradford's car.

"Well, he *is* handsome," said Pat's voice from the tree trunk. Ellery grinned to himself.

"You lied to me," cried Carter. He materialized: no hat and his chestnut hair angry. "Don't hide in a bush, Pat!"

"I'm not hiding," said Pat peevishly, "and it isn't a bush, it's a tree." She came out of the darkness, too; and they faced each other with punctilio.

Mr. Queen watched with silent enjoyment.

"You told me over the phone that you had a headache!"

"Yes."

"You said you were going to bed!"

"I am."

"Don't quibble!"

"Why not? You raise such unimportant points, Mr. Bradford."

Carter's arms flapped under the unfriendly stars. "You lied to get rid of me. You didn't want me around. You had a date with this scribbler! Don't deny it!"

"I do deny it." Pat's voice softened. "I did lie to you, Cart, but I didn't have a date with Ellery."

"That," remarked Mr. Queen from his observation post, "happens to be the truth."

"Stick your two cents out, Smith!" shouted Carter. "I'm trying to keep my temper, or I'd drape you over the lawn!"

Mr. "Smith" grinned and held his peace.

"All right, so I'm jealous," muttered Cart. "But you don't have to be a sneak, Pat! If you don't want me, say so."

"This has nothing to do with my wanting you or not wanting you," said Pat in a timid-turtle voice.

"Well, do you or don't you?"

Pat's eyes fell. "You've no right to ask me that—here—now." Her eyes flashed up. "You wouldn't want a sneak, anyway, would you?"

"All right! Have it your way!"

"Cart . . . !"

His voice came back in a bellow of defiance. "I'm through!"

Pat ran off toward the big white house.

Thought Mr. Queen as he watched her slim figure race across the lawn: In a way it's better . . . much better. You don't know what you're in for. And Mr. Carter Bradford, when you meet him next, may very well be an enemy.


When Ellery returned from his pre-breakfast walk the next morning, he found Nora and her mother whispering on the Wright porch.

"Good morning!" he said cheerfully. "Enjoy the lecture last night?"

"It was very interesting." Nora looked distressed, and Hermione pre-occupied, so Ellery began to go into the house.

"Mr. Smith," said Hermy. "Oh, dear, I don't know how to say it! Nora dear—"

"Ellery, what happened here last night?" asked Nora.

"Happened?" Ellery looked blank.

"I mean with Pat and Carter. You were home—"

"Is anything wrong with Pat?" asked Ellery quickly.

"Of course there is. She won't come down to breakfast. She won't answer any questions. And when Pat sulks—"

"It's Carter's fault," Hermy burst out. "I *thought* there was something queer about her 'headache' last night! Please, Mr. Smith, if you know anything about it—if something happened after we went to Town Hall last night which her mother ought to know—"

"Has Pat broken off with Cart?" asked Nora anxiously. "No, you don't have to answer, Ellery. I can see it in your face. Mother, you'll simply have to give Patty a talking-to. She can't keep doing this sort of thing to Cart."

Ellery walked Nora back to the little house. As soon as they were out of earshot of Mrs. Wright, Nora said: "Of course you had something to do with it."

"I?" asked Mr. Queen.

"Well . . . don't you agree Pat's in love with Carter? I'm sure you could help by not making Carter jealous—"

"Mr. Bradford," said Mr. Queen, "would be jealous of a postage stamp Patty licked."

"I know. He's so hotheaded, too! Oh, dear." Nora sighed. "I'm making a mess of it. Will you forgive me? And come in to breakfast?"

"Yes to both questions." And as he helped Nora up the porch steps, he wondered just how guilty he really was.

Jim was full of political talk, and Nora . . . Nora was wonderful. No other word for it, thought Ellery. Watching and listening, he could detect no least tinkle of falsity. They seemed so much like two young people luxuriating in the blessedness of early marriage that it was a temptation to dismiss the incidents of the previous evening as fantasy.

Pat arrived, with Alberta and eggs, in a rush.

"Nora! How nice," she said, as if nothing at all had happened. "Can you spare a starving gal an egg or two? Morning, Jim! Ellery! Not that Ludie didn't have breakfast for me. She *did*. But I just felt that nosy impulse to look in on the lovebirds . . ."

"Alberta, another setting," said Nora, and she smiled at Pat. "You *do* talk in the morning! Ellery, sit down. The honeymoon being over, *my* husband doesn't rise for my family anymore."

Jim stared. "Who—Patso?" He grinned. "Say, you *are* grown-up! Let me look. Yep. A real glamour girl. Smith, I envy you. If I were a bachelor—"

Ellery saw the swift cloud darken Nora's face. She pressed more coffee on her husband.

Pat kept chattering. She wasn't a very good actress—couldn't look Jim in the eye. Heroic, though. Remembering instructions in the midst of her own troubles . . .

But Nora was superb. Yes, Pat had been right. Nora had decided not to *think* about the letters or their horrible implication. And she was using the minor crisis of Pat and Cart to help her not to think.

"I'll fix your eggs myself, darling," said Nora to Pat. "Alberta's a jewel, but how could she know you like four-minute coddling, to the second? Excuse me." Nora left the dining room to join Alberta in the kitchen.

"That Nora," chuckled Jim. "She's a real hen. Say! What time is it?

I'll be late at the bank. Patty, you been crying? You're talking sort of funny, too. Nora!" he shouted. "Didn't the mail come yet?"

"Not yet!" Nora called from the kitchen.

"Who, me?" said Pat feebly. "Don't—don't be a goop, Jim."

"*All* right, *all* right," said Jim, laughing. "So it's none of my damn business. Ah! There's Bailey now. 'Scuse!"

Jim hurried out to the foyer to answer the postman's ring. They heard him open the front door; they heard old Mr. Bailey's cracked "Mornin', Mr. Haight," Jim's joshing response, the little slam of the door, and Jim's slow returning footsteps, as if he were shuffling through the mail as he came back.

Then he walked into the field of their vision and stopped, and they saw him staring at one of the several envelopes the postman had just delivered. His face was liverish.

And then he vaulted upstairs. They heard his feet pound on the carpeting and a moment later a door bang.

Pat was gaping at the spot Jim had just vacated.

"Eat your cereal," said Ellery.

Pat flushed and bent quickly over her plate.

Ellery got up and walked without noise to the foot of the staircase. After a moment he returned to the breakfast table.

"He's in his study, I think. Heard him *lock the door* . . . No! Not now. Here's Nora."

Pat choked over her Crackle-Crunch.

"Where's Jim?" asked Nora as she set the eggs before her sister.

"Upstairs," said Ellery, reaching for the toast.

"Jim?"

"Yes, Nora." Jim reappeared on the stairs; he was still pale, but rigidly controlled. He had his coat on and carried several unopened letters of assorted sizes.

"Jim! Is anything wrong?"

"Wrong?" Jim laughed. "I never saw such a suspicious woman! What the devil should be wrong?"

"I don't know. But you look so pale—"

Jim kissed her. "You ought to've been a nurse! Well, got to be going. Oh, by the way. Here's the mail. The usual junk. Bye, Patty! Smith! See you soon." Jim raced out.

After breakfast Ellery said something about "strolling in the woods" behind the house and excused himself.

A half hour later Pat joined him. She came hurrying through the underbrush with a Javanese scarf tied around her head, looking back over her shoulder as if someone were chasing her.

"I thought I'd never get away from Nora," Pat panted. She dropped to a stump. "Whoo!"

Ellery blew smoke thoughtfully. "Pat, we've got to read that letter Jim just received."

"Ellery . . . where's this all going to end?"

"It stirred Jim up tremendously. Can't be coincidence. Somehow this morning's letter ties in with the rest of this puzzle. Can you lure Nora out of the house?"

"She's going to High Village this morning with Alberta to do some shopping. There's the station wagon! I'd recognize that putt-putt in Detroit."

Mr. Queen ground out his cigarette carefully. "All right, then," he said.

Pat kicked a twig. Her hands were trembling. Then she sprang off the stump. "I feel like a skunk," she moaned. "But what else can we do?"

"I doubt if we'll find anything," said Ellery as Pat let him into Nora's house with her duplicate key. "Jim locked the door when he ran upstairs. He didn't want to be caught doing . . . whatever it was he did."

"You think he destroyed the letter?"

"Afraid so. But we'll have a look, anyway."

In Jim's study, Pat set her back against the door. She looked ill.

Ellery sniffed. And went directly to the fireplace. It was clean except for a small mound of ash.

"He burned it!" said Pat.

"But not thoroughly enough."

"Ellery, you've found something!"

"A scrap that wasn't consumed by the fire."

Pat flew across the room. Ellery was examining a scrap of charred paper very carefully.

"Part of the envelope?"

"The flap. Return address. But the address has been burned off. Only thing left is the sender's name."

Pat read: " 'Rosemary Haight.' Jim's sister." Her eyes widened. "Jim's sister, Rosemary! Ellery, the one he wrote those three letters to about Nora!"

"It's possible that—" Ellery did not finish.

"You were going to say it's possible there was a first letter we didn't find, because he'd already sent it! And that this is the remains of his sister's answer."

"Yes." Ellery tucked the burnt scrap away in his wallet. "But on second thought I'm not so sure. Why should his sister's reply bother him so much, if that's what it is? No, Patty, this is something different, something new."

"But what?"

"That," said Mr. Queen, "is what we've got to find out." He took her arm, looking about. "Let's get out of here."

That night they were all sitting on the Wright porch watching the wind blow the leaves across the lawn. John F. and Jim were debating the presidential campaign with some heat, while Hermy anxiously appeased and Nora and Pat listened like mice. Ellery sat by himself in a corner, smoking.

"John, you know I don't like these political arguments!" said Hermy. "Goodness, you men get so hot under the collar—"

John F. grunted. "Jim, there's dictatorship coming in this country, you mark my words—"

Jim grinned. "And you'll eat 'em . . . *All* right, Mother!" Then he said casually: "Oh, by the way, darling, I got a letter from my sister, Rosemary, this morning. Forgot to tell you."

"Yes?" Nora's tone was bright. "How nice. What does she write, dear?"

Pat drifted toward Ellery and in the darkness sat down at his feet. He put his hand on her neck; it was clammy.

"The usual stuff. She does say she'd like to meet you—all of you."

"Well, I should think so!" said Hermy. "I'm very anxious to meet your sister, Jim. Is she coming out for a visit?"

"Well . . . I *was* thinking of asking her, but—"

"Now, Jim," said Nora. "You know I've asked you dozens of times to invite Rosemary to Wrightsville."

"Then it's all right with you, Nor?" asked Jim quickly.

"All right!" Nora laughed. "What's the matter with you? Give me her address, and I'll drop her a note tonight."

"Don't bother, darling. I'll write her myself."

When they were alone, a half hour later, Pat said to Ellery: "Nora was scared."

"Yes. It's a poser." Ellery circled his knees with his arms. "Of course, the letter that stirred Jim up this morning was the same letter he just said he got from his sister."

"Ellery, Jim's holding something back."

"No question about it."

"If his sister, Rosemary, just wrote about wanting to come out for a visit, or anything as trivial as that . . . *why did Jim burn her letter?*"

Mr. Queen kept the silence for a long time. Finally he mumbled: "Go to bed, Patty. I want to think."

On November the eighth, four days after Franklin Delano Roosevelt had been elected to the Presidency of the United States for a third term, Jim Haight's sister came to Wrightsville.

# 10

## Jim and the Fleshpot

"Miss Rosemary Haight," wrote Gladys Hemmingworth in the Society column of the *Wrightsville Record*, "was strikingly accoutered in a *naturel* French suede traveling suit with sleeveless jerkin to match, a dashing jacket of platinum-fox fur topped with the jauntiest fox-trimmed archery hat of forest green, and green suede wedgies and bag . . ."

Mr. Ellery Queen happened to be taking a walk that morning . . . to the Wrightsville station. So he saw Rosemary Haight get off the train at the head of a *safari* bearing luggage and pose for a moment, in the sun, like a movie actress. He saw her trip over to Jim and kiss him, and turn to Nora with animation and embrace her, presenting a spruce cheek; and Mr. Queen also saw the two women laugh and chatter as Jim and the *safari* picked up the visitor's impedimenta and made for Jim's car.

And Mr. Queen's weather eye clouded over.

That night, at Nora's, he had an opportunity to test his first barometric impression.

And he decided that Rosemary Haight was no bucolic maiden on an exciting journey; that she was pure metropolis, insolent and bored and trying to conceal both. Also, she was menacingly attractive. Hermy, Pat, and Nora disliked her instantly; Ellery could tell that from the extreme politeness with which they treated her. As for John F., he was charmed, spryly gallant. Hermy reproached him in the silent language of the eye.

And Ellery spent a troubled night trying to put Miss Rosemary Haight together in the larger puzzle and not succeeding.

Jim was busy at the bank these days and, rather with relief, Ellery thought, left the problem of entertaining his sister to Nora. Dutifully Nora drove Rosemary about the countryside, showing her the "sights." It was a little difficult for Nora to sustain the charming-hostess illusion, Pat confided in Ellery, since Rosemary had a supercilious attitude toward everything and wondered "how in heaven's name you can be *happy* in such a dull place, Mrs. H!"

Then there was the gauntlet of the town's ladies to run . . . teas for the guest, very correct with hats on in the house and white gloves, an ambitious mah-jongg party, a wiener roast on the lawn one moonlit night, a church social . . .

The ladies were cold. Emmeline DuPré said Rosemary Haight had a streak of "commerce," whatever that was, Clarice Martin thought her clothes too "you-know," and Mrs. Mackenzie at the Country Club said she was a born bitch and look at those silly men drooling at her!

The Wright women found themselves constrained to defend her, which was hard, considering that secretly they agreed to the truth of all the charges.

"I wish she'd leave," said Pat to Ellery a few days after Rosemary's arrival. "Isn't that a horrid thing to say? But I do. And now she's sent for her trunks!"

"But I thought she didn't like it here."

"That's what I can't understand, either. Nora says it was supposed to be a 'flying' visit, but Rosemary acts as if she means to dig in for the winter. And Nora can't very well discourage her."

"What's Jim say?"

"Nothing to Nora, but"—Pat lowered her voice and looked around—"apparently he's said something to Rosemary, because I happened in just this morning and there was Nora trapped in the serving pantry while Jim and Rosemary, who evidently thought Nora was upstairs, were having an argument in the dining room. That woman has a temper!"

"What was the argument about?" asked Ellery eagerly.

"I came in at the tail end and didn't hear anything important, but Nora says it was . . . well, frightening. Nora wouldn't tell me what she'd heard, but she was terribly upset—she looked the same way as when she read those three letters that tumbled out of the toxicology book."

Ellery muttered: "I wish I'd heard that argument. Why can't I put my finger on *something?* Pat, you're a rotten assistant detective!"

"Yes, sir," said Pat miserably.

Rosemary Haight's trunk arrived on the fourteenth. Steve Polaris, who ran the local express agency, delivered the trunk himself—an overgrown affair that looked as if it might be packed with imported evening gowns. Steve lugged it up Nora's walk on his broad back; and Mr. Queen, who was watching from the Wright porch, saw him carry it into Nora's house and come out a few minutes later accompanied by Rosemary, who was wearing a candid red, white, and blue negligee. She looked like an enlistment poster.

Ellery saw Rosemary sign Steve Polaris's receipt book and go back into the house. Steve slouched down the walk grinning—Steve had the most wolfish eye, Pat said, in all of Low Village.

"Pat," said Ellery urgently, "do you know this truckman well?"

"Steve? That's the only way you *can* know Steve."

Steve tossed his receipt book on the driver's seat of his truck and began to climb in.

"Then distract him. Kiss him, vamp him, do a striptease—anything, but get him out of sight of that truck for two minutes!"

Pat instantly called: "Oh, Ste-e-e-eve!" and tripped down the porch steps. Ellery followed in a saunter. No one was in sight anywhere on the Hill.

Pat was slipping her arm through Steve's and giving him one of her quick little-girl smiles, saying something about her piano, and there wasn't a man she knew strong enough to move it from where it was to where she wanted it, and, of course, when she saw Steve . . .

Steve went with Pat into the Wright house, visibly swollen.

Ellery was at the truck in two bounds. He snatched the receipt book from the front seat. Then he took a piece of charred paper from his wallet and began riffling the pages of the book . . .

When Pat reappeared with Steve, Mr. Queen was at Hermione's zinnia bed surveying the dead and dying blossoms with the sadness of a poet. Steve gave him a scornful look and passed on.

"Now you'll have to move the piano back," said Pat. "I *am* sorry—I could have thought of something not quite so bulky . . . Bye, Stevie!" The truck rolled off with a flirt of its exhaust.

"I was wrong," mumbled Ellery.

"About what?"

"About Rosemary."

"Stop being cryptic! And why did you send me to lure Steve away from his truck? The two are connected, Mr. Queen!"

"I had a flash from on high. It said to me: 'This woman Rosemary doesn't seem cut from the same cloth as Jim Haight. They don't seem like brother and sister at all—' "

"Ellery!"

"Oh, it was possible. But my flash was wrong. She *is* his sister."

"And you proved that through Steve Polaris's truck? Wonderful man!"

"Through his receipt book, in which this woman had just signed her name. I *have* the real Rosemary Haight's signature, you'll recall, my dear Watson."

"On that charred flap of envelope we found in Jim's study—the remains of his sister's letter that he'd burned!"

"Precisely, my dear Watson. And the signature 'Rosemary Haight' on the flap of the letter and the signature 'Rosemary Haight' in Steve's receipt book are the work of the same hand."

"Leaving us," remarked Pat dryly, "exactly where we were."

"No," said Mr. Queen with a faint smile. "Before we only *believed* this woman was Jim's sister. Now we *know* it. Even your primitive mind can detect the distinction, my dear Watson?"

The longer Rosemary Haight stayed at Nora's, the more inexplicable the woman became. Jim was busier and busier at the bank; sometimes he did not even come home to dinner. Yet Rosemary did not seem to mind her brother's neglect half so much as her sister-in-law's attentions. The female Haight tongue was forked; more than once its venom reduced Nora to tears . . . shed, it was reported to Mr. Queen by his favorite spy, in her own room, alone. Toward Pat and Hermione, Rosemary was less obvious. She rattled on about her "travels"—Panama, Rio, Honolulu, Bali, Banff, surf riding and skiing and mountain climbing and "exciting" men—much talk about exciting men—until the ladies of the Wright family began to look harried and grim, and retaliated.

And yet Rosemary stayed on.

Why? Mr. Queen was pondering this poser as he sat one morning in the window seat of his workroom. Rosemary Haight had just come out of her brother's house, a cigarette at a disgusted angle to her red lips, clad in jodhpurs and red Russian boots and a Lana Turner sweater. She stood on the porch for a moment, slapping a crop against her boots with impatience, at odds with Wrightsville. Then she strode off into the woods behind the Wright grounds.

Later, Pat took Ellery driving; and Ellery told her about seeing the Haight woman enter the woods in a riding habit.

Pat turned into the broad concrete of Route 16, driving slowly. "Bored," she said. "Bored blue. She got Jake Bushmill the blacksmith to dig her up a saddle horse from somewhere—yesterday was her first day out, and Carmel Pettigrew saw her tearing along the dirt road toward Twin Hill like—I quote—one of the Valkyries. Carmel—silly dope!—thinks Rosemary's just too-too."

"And you?" queried Mr. Queen.

"That panther laziness of hers is an act—underneath, she's the restless type and hard as teak. A cheap wench. Or don't you think?" Pat glanced at him sidewise.

"She's terribly attractive," said Ellery evasively.

"So's a man-eating orchid," retorted Pat; and she drove in silence for eight tenths of a mile. Then she said: "What do you make of the whole thing, Ellery—Jim's conduct, Rosemary, the three letters, the visit, Rosemary's staying on when she hates it . . . ?"

"Nothing," said Ellery. But he added: "Yet."

"Ellery—look!"

They were approaching a gaudy bump on the landscape, a one-story white stucco building on whose walls oversized red lady-devils danced and from whose roof brittle cut-out flames of wood shattered the sky. The tubing of the unlit neon sign spelled out VIC CARLATTI'S *Hot Spot*. The parking lot to the side was empty except for one small car.

"Look at what?" demanded Ellery, puzzled. "I don't see anything except no customers, since the sun is shining and Carlatti's patrons don't creep out of their walls until nightfall."

"Judging from that car on the lot," said Pat, a little pale, "there's *one* customer."

Ellery frowned. "It does look like the same car."

"It is."

Pat drove up to the entrance, and they jumped out.

"It might be business, Pat," said Ellery, not with conviction.

Pat glanced at him scornfully and opened the front door.

There was no one in the chrome-and-scarlet leather interior but a bartender and a man mopping the postage-stamp dance floor. Both employees looked at them curiously.

"I don't see him," whispered Pat.

"He may be in one of those booths . . . No."

"The back room . . ."

"Let's sit down."

They sat down at the nearest table, and the bartender came over, yawning. "What'll it be, folks?"

"Cuba Libre," said Pat, nervously looking around.

"Scotch."

"Uh-huh." The bartender strolled back to his bar.

"Wait here," said Ellery. He got up and made for the rear, like a man looking for something.

"It's over that way," said the man with the mop, pointing to a door marked HE.

But Ellery pushed against a partly open red-and-gold door with a heavy brass lock. It swung noiselessly.

The room beyond was a gambling room. In a chair at the empty roulette table sprawled Jim Haight, his head on one arm on the table. A burly man with a cold cigar stub in his teeth stood half turned away from Ellery at a telephone on the far wall.

"Yeah. I said Mrs. Haight, stoopid." The man had luxuriant black brows which almost met and a gray flabby face. "Tell her Vic Carlatti."

"Stoopid" would be Alberta. Ellery stood still against the red-and-gold door.

"Mrs. Haight? This is Mr. Carlatti of the *Hot Spot*," said the proprietor in a genial bass. "Yeah . . . No, I ain't making no mistake, Mrs. Haight. It's about Mr. Haight . . . Now wait a minute. He's settin' in my back room right now, cockeyed . . . I mean drunk . . . Now don't get bothered, Mrs. Haight. Your old man's okay. Just had a couple of shots too many and passed out. What'll I do with the body?"

"Just a moment," said Ellery pleasantly.

Carlatti slewed his big head around. He looked Ellery up and down. "Hold on a second, Mrs. Haight . . . Yeah? What can I do you for?"

"You can let me talk to Mrs. Haight," said Ellery, crossing over and taking the phone from the man's furry hands. "Nora? This is Ellery Smith."

"Ellery!" Nora was frantic. "What's the matter with Jim? How is he? How did you happen to—"

"Don't be excited, Nora. Pat and I were driving past Carlatti's place, and we noticed Jim's car parked outside. We're in here now, and Jim's all right. Just had a little too much to drink."

"I'll drive right down—the station wagon—"

"You'll do nothing of the kind. Pat and I will have him home in half an hour. Don't worry, do you hear?"

"Thank you," whispered Nora, and hung up.

Ellery turned from the telephone to find Pat bending over Jim, shaking him. "Jim. Jim!"

"It's no use, girlfriend," growled Carlatti. "He's carrying a real load."

"You ought to be ashamed of yourself, getting him tight!"

"Now don't get tough, babe. He came in here under his own steam. I got a license to sell liquor. He wants to buy, he can buy. Get him outa here."

"How did you know who he was? How did you know whom to call?" Pat was fizzing with indignation.

"He's been here before; and besides, I frisked him. And don't gimme that fishy eye. Come on, pig. Blow!"

Pat gasped.

"Excuse me," said Ellery. He walked past Carlatti as if the big man were not there, and then suddenly he turned and stepped hard on Carlatti's bulldog toe. The man bellowed with pain and reached swiftly for his back pocket. Ellery set the heel of his right hand against Carlatti's chin and pushed. Carlatti's head snapped back; and as he staggered, Ellery punched him in the belly with the other hand. Carlatti groaned and sank to the floor, clutching his middle with both hands and staring up, surprised.

"Miss Pig to you," said Ellery. He yanked Jim out of his chair and got him in a fireman's grip. Pat picked up Jim's crushed hat and ran to hold the door open.

Ellery took the wheel going back.

In the open car, with the wind striking his face and Pat shaking him, Jim began to revive. He goggled glassily at them.

"Jim, whatever made you do a silly thing like this?"

"Huh?" gurgled Jim, closing his eyes again.

"In midafternoon, when you should be at the bank!"

Jim sank lower in the seat, muttering.

"Stupefied," said Ellery. There was a deep cleft between brows. His rear-vision mirror told him a car was overtaking them rapidly—Carter Bradford's car.

Pat noticed and turned. And turned back, very quickly.

Ellery slowed down to let Bradford pass. But Bradford did not pass. He slowed down alongside and honked his horn. A lean gray Yankee with a red face and jellyfish eyes sat beside him.

Obediently, Ellery pulled up at the side of the road; and Bradford stopped his car, too.

Pat said: "Why, hello, Cart," in a surprised voice. "And Mr. Dakin! Ellery, this is Chief Dakin of the Wrightsville police. Mr. Ellery Smith."

Chief Dakin said: "How do, Mr. Smith," in a polite voice, and Ellery nodded.

"Anything wrong?" asked Carter Bradford, a little awkwardly. "I noticed Jim here was—"

"Well, that's extremely efficient, Cart," said Pat warmly. "Practically Scotland Yardish, or at the very least F.B.I. Isn't it, Ellery? The Public Prosecutor and the Chief of Police—"

"There's nothing wrong, Bradford," said Ellery.

"Nothing that a bicarbonate of soda and a good night's sleep won't fix," said Chief Dakin dryly. "Carlatti's?"

"Something like that," said Ellery. "Now if you don't mind, gentlemen, Mr. Haight needs his bed—badly."

"Anything I can do, Pat . . ." Cart was flushed. "Matter of fact, I was thinking of calling you up—"

"You were thinking of calling me up."

"I mean—"

Jim stirred between Pat and Ellery, mumbling.

Pat said severely: "Jim, how do you feel?"

He opened his eyes again. They were still glassy, but something behind the glaze made Pat look at Ellery with a swift fear.

"Say, he's in a bad way, at that," said Dakin.

"Relax, now, Jim," soothed Ellery. "Go to sleep."

Jim looked from Pat to Ellery to the men in the other car, but he did not recognize any of them. The mumble became intelligible: "Wife my wife damn her oh damn wife . . ."

"Jim!" cried Pat. "Ellery, get him home!"

Ellery released his hand brake quickly. But Jim was not to be repressed. He pulled himself up and his cheeks, pale from sickness, grew scarlet.

"Rid of her!" he shouted. "Wait'n' see! I'll get rid of the bas'ard! I'll kill 'a bas'ard!"

Chief Dakin blinked, and Carter Bradford looked immensely surprised and opened his mouth to say something.

But Pat pulled Jim down savagely, and Ellery shot the convertible forward, leaving Bradford's car behind. Jim began to sob, and in the middle of a sob he suddenly fell asleep again.

Pat shrank as far from him as she could. "Did you hear what he *said*, Ellery? Did you?"

"He's crazy blind." Ellery stepped hard on the gas pedal.

"It's true, then," moaned Pat. "The letters—Rosemary . . . Ellery, I tell you Rosemary and Jim have been putting on an act! They're in cahoots to—to— And Cart and Chief Dakin heard him!"

"Pat"—Ellery kept his eyes on the road—"I haven't wanted to ask you this before, but . . . Has Nora any considerable sum of money, or property, in her own right?"

Pat moistened her lips very slowly. "Oh . . . no. It couldn't be . . . that."

"Then she has."

"Yes," Pat whispered. "By my grandfather's will. Pop's father. Nora automatically inherited a lot of money when she married, held in trust for her if and when. Grandfather Wright died soon after Lola eloped with that actor—he'd cut Lola off because of that and divided his estate between Nora and me. I get half when I marry, too—"

"How much did Nora get?" asked Ellery. He glanced at Jim. But Jim was stertorously asleep.

"I don't know. But Pop once told me it's more than Nora and I could ever spend. Oh, Lord—Nora!"

"If you start to cry," said Ellery grimly, "I'll dump you overboard. Is this inheritance to you and Nora a secret?"

"Try to keep a secret in Wrightsville," said Pat. "Nora's money . . ." She began to laugh. "It's like a bad movie. Ellery, what are we going to *do?*" She laughed and laughed.

Ellery turned Pat's car into the Hill drive. "Put Jim to bed," he muttered.

# 11

## Thanksgiving: The First Warning

The next morning Mr. Queen was knocking at Nora's door before eight.

Nora's eyes were swollen. "Thanks for—yesterday. Putting Jim to bed while I was being so silly—"

"Rubbish," said Ellery cheerfully. "There hasn't been a bride since Eve who didn't think the world was going under when hubby staggered home under his first load. Where's the erring husband?"

"Upstairs shaving." Nora's hand trembled as she fussed with the gleaming toaster on the breakfast table.

"May I go up? I shouldn't want to embarrass your sister-in-law by prowling around the bedroom floor at this hour—"

"Oh, Rosemary doesn't get up till ten," said Nora. "These wonderful November mornings! Please do—and tell Jim what you think of him!"

Ellery laughed and went upstairs. He knocked on the master-bedroom door, which was half open; and Jim called from the bathroom: "Nora? Gosh, darling, I knew you'd be my sweet baby and forgive—" His voice blurred when he spied Ellery. Jim's face was half shaved; the shaved half was pasty and his eyes puffed. "Morning, Smith. Come in."

"I just dropped by for a minute to ask you how you were feeling, Jim." Ellery draped himself against the bathroom jamb.

Jim turned, surprised. "How did *you* know?"

"How did *I* know! Don't tell me you don't remember. Why, Pat and I brought you home."

"Gosh," groaned Jim. "I wondered about that. Nora won't talk to me. Can't say I blame her. Say, I'm awfully grateful, Smith. Where'd you find me?"

"Carlatti's place on Route 16. The *Hot Spot*."

"That dive?" Jim shook his head. "No wonder Nora's sore." He grinned sheepishly. "Was I sick during the night! Nora fixed me up, but she wouldn't say a word to me. What a dumb stunt!"

"You did some pretty dumb talking on the ride home, too, Jim."

"Talking? What did I say?"

"Oh . . . something about 'getting rid of' some bastard or other," said Ellery lightly.

Jim blinked. He turned back to the mirror again. "Out of my head, I guess. Or else I was thinking of Hitler."

Ellery nodded, his eyes fixed on the razor. It was shaking.

"I don't remember a damn thing," said Jim. "Not a damn thing."

"I'd lay off the booze if I were you, Jim," said Ellery amiably. "Not that it's any of my business, but . . . well, if you keep saying things like that, people might misunderstand."

"Yeah," said Jim, fingering his shaved cheek. "I guess they would at that. Ow, my head! Never again."

"Tell that to Nora," laughed Ellery. "Well, morning, Jim."

"Morning. And thanks again."

Ellery left, smiling. But the smile vanished on the landing. It seemed to him that the door to the guest room was open a hands-breadth wider than when he had gone in to talk to Jim.

Mr. Queen found it harder and harder to work on his novel. For one thing, there was the weather. The countryside was splashy with reds and oranges and yellowing greens; the days were frost-touched now as well as the nights, hinting at early snows; nights came on swiftly, with a crackle. It was a temptation to roam back-country roads and crunch the crisp dry corpses of the leaves underfoot. Especially after sunset, when the sky dropped its curtains, lights sparkled in isolated farmhouses, and an occasional whinny or howl came from some black barn.

Wilcy Gallimard came into town with five truckloads of turkeys and got rid of them in no time.

"Yes, sir," said Mr. Queen to himself. "Thanksgiving's in the air—everywhere except at 460 Hill Drive."

Then there was Pat, whose recent habit of peering over her own shoulder had become chronic. She clung to Ellery so openly that Hermione Wright began to make secret plans in her head and even John F., who never noticed anything but flaws in mortgages and rare postage stamps, looked thoughtful . . . It made work very difficult.

But most of all it was watching Jim and Nora without seeming to that occupied Ellery's time. Things were growing worse in the Haight household.

For Jim and Nora no longer "got along." There were quarrels so bitter that their impassioned voices flew through the November air all the way across the driveway to the Wright house through closed windows. Sometimes it was about Rosemary; sometimes it was about Jim's drinking; sometimes it was about money. Jim and Nora continued to put up a brave show before Nora's family, but everyone knew what was going on.

"Jim's got a new one," reported Pat to Ellery one evening. "He's gambling!"

"Is he?" said Mr. Queen.

"Nora was talking to him about it this morning." Pat was so distressed she could not sit still. "And he admitted it—*shouted* it at her. And in the next breath asked her for money. Nora pleaded with him to tell her what was wrong; but the more Nora pleads, the angrier and harder Jim gets. Ellery, I think he's touched. I really do!"

"That's not the answer," said Ellery stubbornly. "There's a pattern here. His conduct doesn't *fit*, Patty. If only he'd talk. But he won't. Ed Hotchkiss brought him home in the cab last night. I was waiting on the porch—Nora'd gone to bed. Jim was pretty well illuminated. But when I began to pump him—" Ellery shrugged. "He swung at me . . . *Pat.*"

Pat jerked. "What?"

"He's pawning jewelry."

"Pawning jewelry! Whose?"

"I followed him at lunch today, when he left the bank. He ducked into Simpson's, on the Square, and pawned what looked to me like a cameo brooch set with rubies."

"That's Nora's! Aunt Tabitha gave it to her as a high-school graduation present!"

Ellery took her hands. "Jim has no money of his own, has he?"

"None except what he earns." Pat's lips tightened. "My father spoke to him the other day. About his work. Jim's neglecting it. You know Pop. Gentle as a lamb. It must have embarrassed him dreadfully. But Jim snapped at him, and poor Pop just blinked and walked away. And have you noticed how my mother's been looking?"

"Dazed."

"Muth won't admit anything's wrong—even to me. Nobody will, nobody. And Nora's worse than any of them! And the town—Emmy DuPré's busier than Goebbels! They're all whispering . . . I hate them! I hate the town, I hate Jim . . ."

Ellery had to put his arms around her.

Nora planned Thanksgiving with a sort of desperation—a woman trying to hold on to her world as it growled and heaved about her.

There were two of Wilcy Gallimard's fanciest toms, and chestnuts to be grated in absurd quantities, and cranberries from Bald Mountain to be mashed, and turnips and pumpkins and goodies galore . . . all requiring preparation, fuss, work, with and without Alberta Manaskas's help . . . all requiring *concentration*. And while her house filled with savory odors, Nora would brook no assistance from anyone but Alberta—not Pat, not Hermione, not even old Ludie, who went about muttering for days about "these snippy young know-it-all brides."

Hermy dabbed at her eyes. "It's the first Thanksgiving since we were married, John, that I haven't made the family dinner. Nora baby—your table's so beautiful!"

"Maybe this time," chuckled John F., "I won't have indigestion. Bring on that turkey and stuffing!"

But Nora shooed them all into the living room—things weren't quite ready. Jim, a little drawn, but sober, wanted to stay and help. Nora smiled pallidly at him and sent him after the others.

Mr. Queen strolled out to the Haight porch, so he was the first to greet Lola Wright as she came up the walk.

"Hello," said Lola. "You bum."

"Hello yourself."

Lola was wearing the same pair of slacks, the same tight-fitting sweater, the same ribbon in her hair. And from her wry mouth came the same fumes of Scotch.

"Don't look at me that way, stranger! I'm invited. Fact. Nora. Family reunion an' stuff. Kiss and make up. I'm broad-minded. But you're a bum just the same. How come no see little Lola?"

"Novel."

"Your eye," laughed Lola, steadying herself against his arm. "No writer works more than a few hours a day, if that. It's my Snuffy. You're making love to Pat. 'Sall right. You could do worse. She's even got a brain on that swell chassis."

"I could do worse, but I'm not doing anything, Lola."

"Ah, noble, too. Well, give 'em hell, brother. Excuse me. I've got to go jab my family's sensibilities." And Lola walked, carefully, into her sister's house.

Mr. Queen waited on the porch a decent interval and then followed.

He came upon a scene of purest gaiety. It took keen eyes to detect the emotional confusion behind Hermy's sweet smile, and the quivering of John F.'s hand as he accepted a Martini from Jim. Pat forced one on Ellery; so Ellery proposed a toast to "a wonderful family," at which they all drank grimly.

Then Nora, all flushed from the kitchen, hustled them into the dining room; and they dutifully exclaimed over the magazine-illustration table . . . Rosemary Haight holding on to John F.'s arm.

It happened just as Jim was dishing out second helpings of turkey.

Nora was passing her mother's plate when she gasped, and the full platter fell into her lap. The plate—Nora's precious Spode—crashed on the floor.

Jim gripped the arms of his chair.

Nora was on her feet, palms pressed against the cloth, her mouth writhing in a horrid spasm.

"Nora!"

Ellery reached Nora in one leap. She pushed at him feebly, licking her lips, white as the new cloth. Then with a cry she ran, snatching herself from Ellery's grip with surprising strength.

They heard her stumble upstairs, the click of a door.

"She's sick. Nora's sick!"

"Nora, where are you?"

"Call Doc Willoughby, somebody!"

Ellery and Jim reached the upper floor together, Jim looking around like a wild man. But Ellery was already pounding on the bathroom door.

"Nora!" Jim shouted. "Open the door! What's the matter with you?"

Then Pat got there, and the others.

"Dr. Willoughby will be right over," said Lola. "Where is she? Get out of here, you men!"

"Has she gone crazy?" gasped Rosemary.

"Break the door down!" commanded Pat. "Ellery, break it down! Jim—Pop—help him!"

"Out of the way, Jim," said Ellery. "You're a bloody nuisance!"

But at the first impact Nora screamed.

"If anyone comes in here, I'll—I'll . . . *Don't come in!*"

Hermy was making mewing sounds, like a sick cat, and John F. kept saying: "Now, Hermy. Now, Hermy. Now, Hermy."

At the third assault the door gave. Ellery catapulted into the bathroom and pounced. Nora was leaning over the basin, trembling, weak, greenish, swallowing huge spoonfuls of milk of magnesia. She turned a queerly triumphant look on him as she slumped, fainting, into his arms.

But later, when she came to in her bed, there was a scene.

"I feel like a—like an animal in a zoo! Please, Mother—get everybody out of here!"

They all left except Mrs. Wright and Jim. Ellery heard Nora from the upper-hall landing. Her tone was stridulant; the words piled on one another.

"No, no, no! I *won't* have him! I don't *want* to see him!"

"But dearest," wailed Hermy, "Dr. Willoughby—surely the doctor who brought you into the world—"

"If that old—old goat comes near me," screamed Nora, "I'll do something desperate! I'll commit suicide! I'll jump out the window!"

"Nora," groaned Jim.

"Get out of here! Mother, you, too!"

Pat and Lola went to the bedroom door and called their mother urgently. "Mother, she's hysterical. Let her alone—she'll calm down." Hermy crept out, followed by Jim, who was red about the eyes and seemed bewildered.

They heard Nora gagging inside. And crying.

When Dr. Willoughby arrived, breathless, John F. said it was a mistake and sent him away.

Ellery softly closed his door. But he knew before he turned on the light that someone was in the room.

He pressed the switch and said: "Pat?"

Pat lay on his bed in a cramped curl. There was a damp spot on the pillow, near her face.

"I've been waiting up for you." Pat blinked in the light. "What time is it?"

"Past midnight." Ellery switched the light off and sat down beside her. "How is Nora?"

"She says she's fine. I guess she'll be all right." Pat was silent for a moment. "Where did *you* disappear to?"

"Ed Hotchkiss drove me over to Connhaven."

"Connhaven! That's seventy-five miles." Pat sat up abruptly. "Ellery, what did you do?"

"I took the contents of Nora's plate over to a research laboratory. Connhaven has a good one, I discovered. And . . ." He paused. "As you say, it's seventy-five miles—from Wrightsville."

"Did you—did they—?"

"They found nothing."

"Then maybe—"

Ellery got off the bed and began to walk up and down in the dark room. "Maybe anything. The cocktails. The soup. The hors d'oeuvres. It was a long shot; I knew it wouldn't work out. Wherever she got it, though, it was in her food or drink. Arsenic. All the symptoms. Lucky she remembered to swallow milk of magnesia—it's an emergency antidote for arsenic poisoning."

"And today is . . . Thanksgiving Day," said Pat stiffly. "Jim's letter to

Rosemary—dated November twenty-eighth . . . today. 'My wife is sick.'
*My wife is sick*, Ellery!"

"Whoa, Patty. You've been doing fine . . . It could be a coincidence."

"You think so?"

"It may have been a sudden attack of indigestion. Nora's in a dither.
She's read the letters, she's seen that passage about arsenic in the toxicology book—it may all be psychological."

"Yes . . ."

"Our imaginations may be running away with us. At any rate, there's
time. If a pattern exists, this is just the beginning."

"Yes . . ."

"Pat, I promise you: *Nora won't die*."

"Oh, Ellery." She came to him in the darkness and buried her face in
his coat. "I'm so glad you're here . . ."

"Get out of my bedroom," said Mr. Queen tenderly, "before your pa
comes at me with a shotgun."

# 12

## Christmas: The Second Warning

The first snows fell. Breaths steamed in the valleys. Hermy was busy planning her Christmas baskets for the Poor Farm. Up in the hills skis were flashing, and boys watched restlessly for the ponds to freeze.

But Nora . . .

Nora and Jim were enigmas. Nora recovered from her Thanksgiving Day "indisposition," a little paler, a little thinner, a little more nervous, but self-possessed. But occasionally she seemed frightened, and she would not talk. To anyone.

Her mother tried.

"Nora, what's wrong? You can tell me—"

"Nothing. What's the matter with everybody?"

"But Jim's drinking, dear. It's all over town," groaned Hermy. "It's getting to be a—a national disgrace! And you and Jim *are* quarreling— that *is* a fact . . ."

Nora set her small mouth. "Mother, you'll simply have to let me run my own life."

"Your father's worried—"

"I'm sorry, Mother. It's my life."

"Is it Rosemary who's causing all these arguments? She's always taking Jim off and whispering to him. How long is she going to stay with you? Nora darling, I'm your mother. You can confide in your mother—"

But Nora ran away, crying.

Pat was aging visibly.

"Ellery, the three letters . . . they're still in Nora's hatbox in her closet. I looked last night. I couldn't help it."

"I know," sighed Ellery.

"You've been keeping tabs, too?"

"Yes. Patty, she's been rereading them. They show signs of being handled—"

"But why won't Nor face the truth?" cried Pat. "She knows that November twenty-eighth marked the first attack—that first letter told her so! Yet she won't have the doctor, she won't take any steps to defend herself, she refuses help . . . I can't understand her!"

"Maybe," said Ellery carefully, "Nora's afraid to face the scandal."

Pat's eyes opened wide.

"You told me how she retreated from the world when Jim left her on their scheduled wedding day several years ago. There's a deep streak of small-town pride in your sister Nora, Pat. She can't abide being talked about. If this ever came out—"

"That's it," said Pat in a wondering voice. "I was stupid not to have seen it before. She's ignoring it, like a child. Close your eyes and you won't see the bogeyman. You're right, Ellery. *It's the town she's afraid of!*"

The Monday evening before Christmas, Mr. Queen was sitting on a stump just beyond the edge of the woods, watching 460 Hill Drive. There was no moon; but it was a still night, and sounds carried crisply and far.

Jim and Nora were at it again.

Mr. Queen chafed his cold hands.

It was about money. Nora was shrill. Where was he spending his money? What had happened to her cameo brooch? "Jim, you've got to tell me. This can't go on. It can't!"

Jim's voice was a mutter at first, but then it began to rise, like lava. "Don't put me through a third degree!"

Mr. Queen listened intently for something new, a clue to conduct. He heard nothing he had not already learned. Two young people screaming at each other on a winter's night, while he sat like a fool in the cold and eavesdropped.

He rose from the stump and, skirting the fringe of woods, made for the Wright house and warmth. But then he stopped. The front door of Calamity House—how much apter the phrase seemed these days!—had slammed.

Ellery sprinted through the snow, keeping in the shadows of the big house.

Jim Haight was plowing down the walk unevenly. He jumped into his car.

Ellery ran to the Wright garage. He had an arrangement with Pat Wright: she always left the keys of her convertible in the ignition lock for his use in an emergency.

Jim's car sloshed down the Hill at a dangerous pace, and Ellery followed. He did not turn on Pat's headlights; he could see well enough by the lights of Jim's car.

Route 16 . . . Vic Carlatti's . . .

It was almost ten o'clock when Jim staggered out of the *Hot Spot* and got into his car again. By the weave and lurch of the car Ellery knew Jim was very drunk. Was he going home?

No. The turn-off to town. Going into town!

Where?

Jim skidded to a stop before a poor wooden tenement in the heart of Low Village. He reeled into the dark hallway.

A 25-watt bulb burned drearily in the hall; by its light Ellery saw Jim creep up the stairs, knock at a door with a split, paint-blistered panel.

"Jim!" Lola Wright's exclamation.

The door closed.

Ellery slipped up the stairs, feeling each step for its creaky spot before putting his full weight on it. At the landing he did not hesitate; he went swiftly to Lola's door and pressed his ear to the thin panel.

"But you got to," he heard Jim cry. "Lola, don' turn me down. 'M a desp'r't man. 'M desp'r't . . ."

"But I've told you, Jim, I haven't any money," said Lola's cool voice. "Here, sit down. You're filthy drunk."

"So I'm drunk." Jim laughed.

"What are you desperate about?" Lola was cooing now. "There—isn't that more comfortable? Come on, Jim, tell little Lola all about it . . ."

Haight began to weep. His weeping became muffled, and Ellery knew that his face was pressed to Lola's breast. Lola's maternal murmur was indistinct.

But then she gasped, as if in pain, and Ellery almost crashed through the door.

"Jim! You pushed me!"

"All 'a same! Goo-goo. Tell Lola. Oh, yeah? Take your han's off me! I'm not tellin' you anything!"

"Jim, you'd better go home now."

"Gonna gimme dough or you gonna not gimme dough?"

"But Jim, I told you . . ."

"Nobody'll gimme dough! Get in trouble, his own wife won' shell out. Know what I oughta do? Know what? I oughta—"

"What, Jim?"

"Nothin'. Nothin' . . ." His voice trailed. There was a long interval. Apparently Jim had dropped off. Curious, Ellery waited. And then he heard Lola's faint cry and Jim's awakening snort.

"I said take your han's off me!"

"Jim, I wasn't—you fell asleep—"

"You were s-searchin' me! What you lookin' for? *Huh?*"

"Jim. Don't . . . do that. You're hurting me." Lola's voice was beautifully controlled.

"I'll hurt you plen'y! I'll show you—"

Mr. Queen opened the door.

Lola and Jim were dancing on a worn patch of carpet in the middle of a poor, neat room. His arms were around her, and he was trying drunkenly to bend her backward. She had the heel of her hand under his chin. His head was far back, his eyes glaring.

"The United States Marines," sighed Mr. Queen, and he plucked Jim from Lola and sat him down on a sagging sofa. Jim covered his face with his hands. "Any damage, Lola?"

"No," panted Lola. "You *are* a one! How much did you hear?" She straightened her blouse, fussed with her hair, turned a bit away. She took a bottle of gin from the table and, as if it didn't matter, put it in a cupboard.

"Just a scuffling," said Ellery mildly. "I was coming up to pay you that long-overdue visit. What's the matter with Jim?"

"Plastered." Lola gave him her full face now. Composed. "Poor Nora! I can't imagine why he came *here*. Do you suppose the idiot's fallen in love with me?"

"You ought to be able to answer that yourself," grinned Ellery. "Well, Mr. Haight, I think you'd best say nighty-night to your attractive sister-in-law and let your old pal take you home."

Jim sat there rocking. And then he stopped rocking, and his head flopped. He was asleep doubled up, like a big rag doll with sandy hair.

"Lola," said Ellery quickly, "what do you know about this business?"

"What business?" Her eyes met his, but they told nothing.

After a moment Ellery smiled. "No hits, no runs, one error. Someday I'll fight my way out of this unmerciful fog! Night."

He slung Jim across his shoulders; Lola held the door open.

"Two cars?"

"His and mine—or rather Pat's."

"I'll drive Jim's back in the morning. Just leave it parked outside," said Lola. "And Mr. Smith—"

"Miss Wright?"

"Call again."

"Perhaps."

"Only next time"—Lola smiled—"knock."

\* \* \*

With unexpected firmness, John F. took command for the family.

"No fuss, Hermy," he said, waggling his thin forefinger at her. "This Christmas somebody else does the work."

"John Fowler Wright, what on earth—?"

"We're all going up to the mountains for Christmas dinner. We'll spend the night at the Lodge and roast chestnuts around Bill York's fire, and we'll have *fun*."

"John, that's a *silly* idea! Nora took my Thanksgiving away from me; now you want my Christmas. I won't hear of it."

But after looking into her husband's eyes, Hermy decided his command was not a whim, and she stopped arguing.

So Ed Hotchkiss was hired to drive the Christmas gifts up to Bill York's Lodge on top of Bald Mountain, with a note to Bill from John F. concerning dinner, and lodgings, and "special preparations"—old John was mighty mysterious about the whole thing, chortling like a boy.

They were to drive up to Bald Mountain in two cars directly after dinner Christmas Eve. Everything was ready—the snow chains were on the rear tires, old Ludie had already left, released for the holiday, and they were stamping about outside the Wright house waiting for Jim and Nora to join them . . . when the door of Nora's house opened and out came Rosemary Haight, alone.

"Where are Jim and Nora, for goodness' sake?" called Hermy. "We'll never get to the Lodge!"

Rosemary shrugged. "Nora's not going."

"What!"

"She says she doesn't feel well."

They found Nora in bed, still and weak and greenish, and Jim prowling aimlessly about the room.

"Nora baby!" cried Hermy.

"Sick again?" exclaimed John F.

"It's nothing," said Nora; but it was an effort for her to talk. "Just my stomach. You all go on ahead to the Lodge."

"We'll do no such thing," said Pat indignantly. "Jim, haven't you called Dr. Willoughby?"

"She won't let me." Jim said it in a lifeless voice.

"Won't *let* you! What are you—a man or a worm? What's she got to say about it? I'm going downstairs this minute—"

"Pat," faltered Nora. Pat stopped. "Don't."

"Now Nora—"

Nora opened her eyes. They burned.

"I won't have it," said Nora through her teeth. "I'm saying this for the last time. I won't have interference. Do you understand? I'm all right.

I'm—all—right." Nora bit her lip, then with an effort continued: "Now please. Go on. If I feel better in the morning, Jim and I will join you at the Lodge—"

"Nora," said John F., clearing his throat, "it's time you and I had an old-fashioned father-and-daughter talk . . ."

"*Let me alone!*" Nora screamed.

They did so.

On Christmas Day, Ellery and Pat drove up to Bald Mountain, retrieved the gifts from Bill York at the Lodge, and drove back to Wrightsville with them. They were distributed in a distinctly unhallowed atmosphere.

Hermy spent the day in her room. Pat fixed a Christmas "dinner" of leftover lamb and a jar of mint jelly, but Hermy would not come down, and John F. swallowed two mouthfuls and dropped his fork, saying he wasn't hungry. So Pat and Ellery ate alone.

Later, they walked over to see Nora. They found Nora asleep, Jim out, and Rosemary Haight curled up in the living room with a copy of *Look* and a box of chocolates. She shrugged at Pat's question about Jim. Had another fight with Nora and ran out. Nora was fine . . . weak, but getting along all right. What does one do for excitement in this one-horse town? Wrightsville! Christmas! And, petulantly, Rosemary went back to her magazine.

Pat ran upstairs to satisfy herself about Nora. When she came back, she winked urgently, and Ellery took her outside again.

"I tried to talk to her—she wasn't asleep at all. I . . . almost told her I knew about those letters! Ellery, Nora's got me frightened. She threw something at me!"

Ellery shook his head.

"She won't talk. She got hysterical again. And she's sick as a cat! I tell you," Pat whispered, "the schedule's working out. Ellery, *she was poisoned again yesterday!*"

"You're getting to be as bad as Nora," said Ellery. "Go up and take a nap, Pat. Can't a woman be sick occasionally?"

"I'm going back to Nora. I'm *not* going to leave her alone!"

When Pat had run back, Ellery took a long walk down the Hill, feeling unhappy. The day before, while the others had been upstairs with Nora, he had quietly gone to the dining room. The table had not yet been cleared of the dinner dishes. He had sampled the remains of Nora's corned-beef hash.

It had been a minute sample, but the effects were not long in making themselves known. He felt extreme stomachic pain and nausea. Very quickly, then, he had swallowed some of the contents of a bottle he had taken to carrying about with him—ferric hydroxid, with magnesia, the official arsenic antidote.

No possible doubt. Someone had mixed an arsenic compound into Nora's corned-beef hash. And only Nora's. He had tasted the hash on the other two plates.

The pattern was working out. First Thanksgiving, then Christmas. So death was scheduled for New Year's Day.

Ellery recalled his promise to Pat: to save her sister's life.

He plodded through the drifts. His mind was swirly with thoughts that seemed to take recognizable shapes, but did not.

# 13

## New Year's: The Last Supper

Nora spent four days after Christmas Eve in bed. But on the twenty-ninth of December she appeared fresh, gay . . . too gay, and announced that she was through being sick, like some old lady; that she'd spoiled the family's Christmas, but she was going to make up for it, so everybody was invited to a New Year's Eve party!

Even Jim brightened at that and clumsily kissed her. Pat, witnessing the embrace, choked up and turned away. But Nora kissed Jim back, and for the first time in weeks they looked at each other in the old, secret way of lovers.

Hermy and John F. were overjoyed by this sudden return of Nora's spirits.

"A dandy idea, Nora!" said Hermy. "Now you plan the whole thing yourself. I shan't lift a *finger*. Unless, of course, you'd like me to . . ."

"No, indeed!" smiled Nora. "It's my party, and I'm going to boss it. Oh, darling"—and Nora threw her arms about Pat—"you've been such an angel this week, and I was so mean to you . . . throwing things! Can you ever forgive me?"

"You mug," said Pat grimly, "I'd forgive you anything if you'd only keep acting this way!"

"It's a good mood for Nora to be in," Ellery said to Pat when she told him. "Who's Nora inviting?"

"The family, and the Judge Martins, and Doc Willoughby, and Nora's even going to ask Frank Lloyd!"

"Hmm. Get her to invite Carter Bradford, too."

Pat blanched. "Cart?"

"Now, now. Bury the hatchet. It's a new year—"

"But why Cart? The pig didn't even send me a Christmas card!"

"I want Bradford here New Year's Eve. And you've got to get him here if it takes crawling to do it."

Pat looked him in the eye. "If you insist—"

"I insist."

"He'll be here."

Cart told Pat over the phone that he would "try" to come—nice of her to ask him—quite a surprise, in fact—but, of course, he had numerous other "invitations"—he wouldn't want to disappoint Carmel Pettigrew—but—well—he'd "manage" to drop in. Yes—yes, count on it. I'll drop in . . .

"Oh, Cart," said Pat, despite herself, "why can't people be friends?"

But Cart had already hung up.

Editor-Publisher Frank Lloyd came early. He showed up in a vast and sulky unconviviality, greeting people in monosyllables or not at all, and at the first opportunity made for the "bar," which was a makeshift affair off the kitchen, in Nora's pantry.

One would have said Mr. Queen's interest in matters culinary that evening was unnatural. He haunted the kitchen, watching Alberta, watching Nora, watching the stove and the icebox and who came in and went out and what they did in the vicinity of anything edible or potable. And he did it all with such a self-effacement and eagerness that when Alberta left for her own New Year's Eve party at the home of some Lithuanian friends in Low Village, Nora exclaimed: "My goodness, Ellery, you *are* a homebody, aren't you? Here, stuff some olives."

And so Mr. Queen stuffed some olives, while Jim was busy in the adjacent pantry fixing drinks. From where Mr. Queen stuffed the olives, he had a perfect view of his host.

Nora served a sumptuous buffet supper, preceded by canapés and pigs-in-blankets and stuffed celery stalks and relishes and cocktails; and before long Judge Eli Martin was saying to Aunt Tabitha, who glared about her disapprovingly: "Come, come, Tabby, take a drink and oil that soul of yours. It creaks to high heaven. Here—a Manhattan—good for you!"

But John F.'s sister snarled: "Reprobate!" and read Clarice Martin a lecture on the dangers of old fools drinking. Clarice, who was drifting about like the Lady of the Lake, misty-eyed, said of course Tabitha was *perfectly* right, and went on sipping her cocktail.

Lola was not there. Nora had invited her, but Lola had said over the phone: "Sorry, sis. I have my own celebration planned. Happy New Year!"

Rosemary Haight held court in a corner, getting the men to fetch and carry for her—not out of interest in them, surely, for she seemed bored, but more as if she felt it necessary to keep in practice . . . until Pat, watching good old Doc Willoughby trotting off to replenish Rosemary's glass, said: "Why can't men see through a woman like that?"

"Maybe," said Mr. Queen dryly, "because they're stopped by the too, too solid flesh." And he strolled off to the kitchen again—in Jim's wake, Patty's troubled eyes noticed. For the dozenth time.

Gala evenings in the "nice" homes of Wrightsville were not noted for their hilarity; but Rosemary Haight, the outlander, exercised an irresistible influence for the worst. She became quite merry on numerous Manhattans, to the pointed disgust of Aunt Tabitha. Her spirits infected the men especially, so that talk became loud and laughter a little unsteady, and twice Jim had to visit the pantry to concoct new delights with rye and vermouth, and Pat had to open another bottle of maraschino cherries.

And both times Mr. Queen appeared smiling at Jim's elbow, offering to help.

There was no sign of Carter Bradford. Pat kept listening for the doorbell.

Someone turned on the radio, and Nora said to Jim: "We haven't danced since our honeymoon, darling. Come on!" Jim looked unbelieving; then a grin spread over his face, and seizing her, he danced her madly off.

Ellery went into the kitchen abruptly to mix himself a drink—his first of the evening.

It was fifteen minutes to midnight when Rosemary waved a dramatic arm and commanded: "Jim! 'Nother drink!"

Jim said pleasantly: "Don't you think you've had enough, Rosemary?" Surprisingly, Jim had drunk very little himself.

Rosemary scowled. "Get me one, killjoy!"

Jim shrugged and made for the kitchen, followed by the Judge's admonition to "mix up a mess of 'em, boy!" and Clarice Martin's giggle.

There was a door from the hall to the kitchen, and an archway from the kitchen to the butler's pantry; there was a dining-room door to the butler's pantry, too. Mr. Ellery Queen stopped at the hall door to light a cigarette. It was half open; he could see into the kitchen and into the butler's pantry.

Jim moved about the pantry, whistling softly as he got busy with the rye and vermouth.

He had just finished filling a fresh batch of glasses with Manhattans and was reaching for the bottle of maraschino cherries when someone knocked on the back door of the kitchen.

Ellery became tense, but he resisted the temptation to take his eyes off Jim's hands.

Jim left the cocktails and went to the door.

"Lola! I thought Nora said—"

"Jim." Lola sounded in a hurry. "I had to see you—"

"Me?" Jim seemed puzzled. "But Lo—"

Lola pitched her voice low; Ellery was unable to make out the words. Jim's body blocked Lola out; whatever was happening, it took only a few moments, for suddenly Lola was gone and Jim had closed the back door, crossing the kitchen a little abstractedly to return to the pantry. He plopped a cherry into each glass.

Ellery said: "More fixin's, Jim?" as Jim came through to the hall carrying the tray of full glasses carefully. Jim grinned, and they went into the living room together to be greeted by jubilant shouts.

"It's almost midnight," said Jim cheerfully. "Here's a drink for everybody to toast the New Year in."

And he went about the room with the tray, everyone taking a glass.

"Come on, Nora," said Jim. "One won't hurt you, and New Year's Eve doesn't come every night!"

"But Jim, do you really think—"

"Take this one." He handed her one of the glasses.

"I don't know, Jim—" began Nora doubtfully. Then she took it from him, laughing.

"Now you be careful, Nora," warned Hermy. "You know you haven't been well. Ooh! I'm *dizzy*."

"Souse," said John F. gallantly, kissing Hermy's hand. She slapped him playfully.

"Oh, one sip won't hurt me, Mother," protested Nora.

"Hold it!" yelled Judge Martin. "Here's the ol' New Year rolling in right now. Yip-ee!" And the old jurist's shout was drowned in a flood of horns and bells and noisemakers coming out of the radio.

"To the New Year!" roared John F., and they all drank, even Aunt Tabitha, Nora dutifully taking a sip and making a face, at which Jim howled with laughter and kissed her.

That was the signal for everybody to kiss everybody else, and Mr. Queen, struggling to keep everything in view, found himself seized from behind by a pair of warm arms.

"Happy New Year," whispered Pat, and she turned him around and kissed him on the lips.

For an instant the room, dim with candlelight, swam; then Mr. Queen grinned and stooped for another; but Pat was snatched from his arms by

Doc Willoughby, who growled: "How about me?" and Ellery found himself foolishly pecking the air.

"More!" shrieked Rosemary. " '*Nother drink!* Let's all get stinking—What the hell!" And she waved her empty glass coyly at Judge Martin. The Judge gave her a queer glance and put his arm around Clarice.

Frank Lloyd drank two cocktails quickly.

Jim said he had to go down to the cellar for another bottle of rye—he was all "out" upstairs here.

"Where's my drink?" insisted Rosemary. "What kinda joint is this? New Year's an' no drinks!" She was angry. "Who's got a drink?" Nora was passing her on her way to the radio. "Hey! Nora! *You* got a drink!"

"But Rosemary, I've drunk from it—"

"I wanna drink!"

Nora made a face and gave her unfinished cocktail to Rosemary, who tossed it down like a veteran and staggered over to the sofa, where she collapsed with a silly laugh. A moment later she was fast asleep.

"She *snores*," said Frank Lloyd gravely. "The beaushous lady snores," and he and John F. covered Rosemary with newspapers, all but her face; and then John F. recited "Horatius at the Bridge" with no audience whatever, until Tabitha, who was a little flushed herself, called him another old fool; whereupon John F. seized his sister and waltzed her strenuously about the room to the uncooperative strains of a rumba.

Everybody agreed that everybody was a little tight, and wasn't the new year *wonderful?*

All but Mr. Ellery Queen, who was again lingering at the hall door to the kitchen watching Jim Haight make cocktails.

At thirty-five minutes past midnight, there was one strange cry from the living room and then an even stranger silence.

Jim was coming out of the kitchen with a tray, and Ellery said to him: "That's a banshee, at least. What are they up to now?" And the two men hurried to the living room.

Dr. Willoughby was stooped over Rosemary Haight, who was still lying on the sofa half-covered with newspapers.

There was a tiny, sharp prickle in Mr. Queen's heart.

Doc Willoughby straightened up. He was ashen.

"John." The old doctor wet his lips with his tongue.

John F. said stupidly: "Milo, for jiminy sake. The girl's passed out. She's been . . . sick, like other drunks. You don't have to act and look as if—"

Dr. Willoughby said: "She's dead, John."

Pat, who had been the banshee, sank into a chair as if all the strength had suddenly gone out of her.

And for the space of several heartbeats the memory of the sound of the word "dead" in Dr. Willoughby's cracked bass darted about the room, in and out of corners and through still minds, and it made no sense.

"Dead?" said Ellery hoarsely. "A . . . heart attack, Doctor?"

"I think," said the doctor stiffly, "arsenic."

Nora screamed and fell over in a faint, striking her head on the floor with a thud. As Carter Bradford came briskly in.

Saying: "Tried to get here earlier—where's Pat?—Happy New Year, everybody . . . *What the devil!*"

"Did you give it to her?" asked Ellery Queen, outside the door of Nora's bedroom. He looked a little shrunken; and his nose was pinched and pointy, like a thorn.

"No doubt about it," croaked Dr. Willoughby. "Yes, Smith. I gave it to her . . . Nora was poisoned, too." He blinked at Ellery. "How did you happen to have ferric hydroxid on you? It's the accepted antidote for arsenic poisoning."

Ellery said curtly: "I'm a magician. Haven't you heard?" and went downstairs.

The face was covered with newspapers now.

Frank Lloyd was looking down at the papers.

Carter Bradford and Judge Martin were conferring in hoarse low tones.

Jim Haight sat in a chair shaking his head in an annoyed way, as if he wanted to clear it but could not.

The others were upstairs with Nora.

"How is she?" said Jim. "Nora?"

"Sick." Ellery paused just inside the living room.

Bradford and the Judge stopped talking. Frank Lloyd, however, continued to read the newspapers covering the body.

"But luckily," said Ellery, "Nora took only a sip or two of that last cocktail. She's pretty sick, but Dr. Willoughby thinks she'll pull through all right."

He sat down in the chair nearest the foyer and lit a cigarette.

"Then it was the cocktail?" said Carter Bradford in an unbelieving voice. "But of course. Both women drank of the same glass—both were poisoned by the same poison." His voice rose. "But that cocktail was Nora's! *It was meant for Nora!*"

Frank Lloyd said, still without turning: "Carter, stop making speeches. You irk the hell out of me."

"Don't be hasty, Carter," said Judge Martin in a very old voice.

But Carter said stridently: "That poisoned cocktail was meant to kill Nora. And *who mixed it? Who brought it in?*"

"Cock Robin," said the newspaper publisher. "Go way, Sherlock Holmes."

"I did," said Jim. "I did, I guess." He looked around at them. "That's a queer one, isn't it?"

"Queer one!" Young Bradford's face was livid. He went over and yanked Jim out of the chair by his collar. "You damn murderer! You tried to poison your own wife and by pure accident got your sister instead!"

Jim gaped at him.

"Carter," said Judge Martin feebly.

Carter let go, and Jim fell back, still gaping.

"What can I do?" asked the Wright County Prosecutor in a strangled voice.

He went to the phone in the foyer, stumbling past Mr. Queen's frozen knees, and asked for Chief Dakin at Police Headquarters.

# PART THREE

# 14

## Hangover

The hill was still celebrating when Chief Dakin hopped out of his rattletrap to run up the wet flags of the Haight walk under the stars of 1941. Emmeline DuPré's house was dark, and old Amos Bluefield's—the Bluefield house bore the marks of mourning in the black smudges of its window shades. But all the others—the Livingstons', the F. Henry Minikins', the Dr. Emil Poffenbergers', the Granjons', and the rest—were alive with lights and the faint cries of merriment.

Chief Dakin nodded: it was just as well. Nobody would notice that anything was wrong.

Dakin was a thin, flapping countryman with light dead eyes bisected by a Yankee nose. He looked like an old terrapin until you saw that his mouth was the mouth of a poet. Nobody ever noticed that in Wrightsville except Patricia Wright and, possibly, Mrs. Dakin, to whom the Chief combined the best features of Abraham Lincoln and God.

Dakin's passionate baritone led Mr. Bishop's choir at the First Congregational Church on West Livesey Street in High Village each Sunday. Being a temperance man, and having his woman, the Chief would chuckle, what was there left in life but song? And, in fact, Dakin was interrupted by Prosecutor Bradford's telephone call in the midst of an "at-home" New Year's Eve carol fest.

"Poison," said Dakin soberly to Carter Bradford over the body of Rosemary Haight. "Now I wonder if folks don't overdo this New Year celebrating. What kind of poison, Doc?"

Dr. Willoughby said: "Arsenic. Some compound. I can't tell you which."

"Rat-killer, hey?" Then the Chief said slowly: "I figure this kind of puts our Prosecutor in a spot, hey, Cart?"

"Awkward as hell! These people are my friends." Bradford was shaking. "Dakin, take charge, for God's sake."

"Sure, Cart," said Chief Dakin, blinking his light eyes at Frank Lloyd. "Hi, Mr. Lloyd."

"Hi yourself," said Lloyd. "Now can I go peddle my papers?"

"Frank, I told you—" began Carter peevishly.

"If you'll be so kind as not to," said Dakin to the newspaper publisher with an apologetic smile. "Thank you. Now, how come this sister of Jim Haight's swallowed rat-killer?"

Carter Bradford and Dr. Willoughby told him.

Mr. Queen, seated in his corner like a spectator at a play, watched and listened and pondered how much like a certain New York policeman Chief Dakin of Wrightsville seemed. That ingrown air of authority . . .

Dakin listened to the agitated voices of his townsfellows respectfully; only his light eyes moved—they moved over Mr. "Smith's" person three times, and Mr. "Smith" sat very still. And noted that, after the first quick glance on entering the room, Chief Dakin quite ignored Haight, who was a lump on a chair.

"I see," said Dakin, nodding. "Yes, sir," said Dakin. "Hmm," and he shambled off with his loose gait to the kitchen.

"I can't believe it," groaned Jim Haight suddenly. "It's an accident. How do I know how the stuff got into it? Maybe some kid. A window. A joke. Why, this is *murder*."

No one answered him.

Jim cracked his knuckles and stared owlishly at the filled-out newspapers on the sofa.

Red-faced Patrolman Brady came in from outdoors, a little out of breath and trying not to look embarrassed.

"Got the call," he said to no one in particular. "Gosh." He tugged at his uniform and trod softly into the kitchen after his Chief.

When the two officers reappeared, Brady was armed with numerous bottles, glasses, and odds and ends from the kitchen "bar." He disappeared; after a few moments he came back, empty-armed.

In silence Dakin indicated the various empty and half-empty cocktail glasses in the living room.

Brady gathered them one by one, using his patrolman's cap as a container, picking them up in his scarlet fingers delicately, at the rim, and storing them in the hat as if they had been fresh-laid pigeon eggs.

The Chief nodded and Brady tiptoed out.

"For fingerprints," said Chief Dakin to the fireplace. "You never can tell. And a chemical analysis, too."

"What!" exclaimed Mr. Queen involuntarily.

The Dakin glance x-rayed Mr. Queen's person for the fourth time.

"How do, Mr. Smith," said Chief Dakin, smiling. "Seems like we're forever meeting in jams. Well, twice, anyway."

"I beg pardon?" said Mr. "Smith," looking blank.

"That day on Route 16," sighed the Chief. "I was driving with Cart here. The day Jim Haight was so liquored up?"

Jim rose; he sat down. Dakin did not look at him.

"You're a writer, Mr. Smith, ain't you?"

"Yes."

"Heard tell all over town. You said 'What!' "

Ellery smiled. "Sorry. Wrightsville—fingerprints . . . It was stupid of me."

"And chem lab work? Oh, sure," said Dakin. "This ain't New York or Chicago, but the new County Courthouse building; she's got what you might call unexpected corners."

"I'm interested in unexpected corners, Chief."

"Mighty proud to know a real live writer," said Dakin. "Course, we got Frank Lloyd here, but he's more what you'd call a hick Horace Greeley." Lloyd laughed and looked around, as if for a drink. Then he stopped laughing and scowled. "Know anything about this, Mr. Smith?" asked Dakin, glancing at Lloyd's great back.

"A woman named Rosemary Haight died here tonight." Ellery shrugged. "The only *fact* I can supply. Not much help, I'm afraid, considering that the body's lying right here."

"Poisoned, Doc Willoughby says," said Dakin politely. "That's another fact."

"Oh, yes," said Ellery with humility.

And tried to become invisible as Dr. Willoughby sent him a thick-browed question. Watch yourself. Doc Willoughby is remembering that little bottle of ferric hydroxid you whipped out when Nora Haight required an antidote against arsenic poisoning and even minutes were precious . . . Will the good doctor tell the good policeman the strange fact that a stranger to the house and the people and the case carried so strange a preparation as ferric hydroxid about with him when, strangely, one woman died and another was made seriously ill by the poison for which it was the official antidote?

Dr. Willoughby turned away.

He suspects I know something involving the Wright family, thought Ellery. He's an old friend. He brought the three Wright girls into the world . . . He's uneasy. Shall I make him still uneasier by confiding that I purchased the drug because I promised Patty Wright her sister Nora wouldn't die?

Mr. Queen sighed. It was getting complicated.

"The family," said Chief Dakin. "Where they at?"

"Upstairs," said Bradford. "Mrs. Wright insists that Nora—Mrs. Haight—be moved over to the Wright house."

"This is no place for her, Dakin," said Dr. Willoughby. "Nora's pretty sick. She'll need plenty of care."

"It's all right with me," said the Chief. "If it's all right with the Prosecutor."

Bradford nodded hastily and bit his lip. "Don't you want to question them?"

"Well, now," said the Chief slowly, "I can't see the sense of making the Wrights feel worse'n they feel already. At least right now. So if you've got no objection, Cart, let's call it a night."

Carter said stiffly: "None at all."

"Then we'll have a get-together right here in this room in the mornin'," said Dakin. "You tell the Wrights, Cart. Sort of keep it unofficial."

"Are you remaining here?"

"For a spell," drawled Dakin. "Got to call in somebody to haul this *corpus* out of here. Figure I'll phone old man Duncan's parlors."

"No *morgue?*" asked Mr. Queen, despite himself.

The Dakin eyes made another inspection. "Well, no, Mr. Smith . . . Okay for you, Mr. Lloyd. Go easy on these folks in your paper, hey? This'll raise plenty of hallelujah as it is, I guess . . . No, sir, Mr. Smith. Got to use a reg'lar undertaking parlor. You see"—and the Chief sighed—"ain't never had a homicide in Wrightsville before, and I been Chief here for pretty near twenty years. Doc, would you be so kind? Coroner Salemson's up in Piny Woods on a New Year vacation."

"I'll do the autopsy," said Dr. Willoughby shortly. He went out without saying good-night.

Mr. Queen rose.

Carter Bradford walked across the room, stopped, looked back.

Jim Haight was still sitting in the chair.

Bradford said in an angry voice: "What are you sitting here for, Haight?"

Jim looked up slowly. "What?"

"You can't sit here all night! Aren't you even going up to your wife?"

"They won't let me," said Jim. He laughed and took out a handkerchief to wipe his eyes. "They won't let me."

He leaped from the chair and dashed upstairs. They heard the slam of a door—he had gone into his study.

"See you in the morning, gents," said Chief Dakin, blinking at Ellery.

They left the Chief in the untidy living room, alone with Rosemary Haight's body. Mr. Queen would like to have stayed, but there was something in Chief Dakin's eyes that discouraged company.

Ellery did not see Patricia Wright until they all gathered in the same untidy room at ten o'clock on the morning of New Year's Day . . . all except Nora, who was in her old bed in the other house, guarded by Ludie behind the closed vanes of the Venetian blinds. Dr. Willoughby had already seen her this morning, and he forbade her leaving the room or even setting foot out of bed.

"You're a sick biddy, Nora," he had said to her sternly. "Ludie, remember."

"She'll have to fight me," said old Ludie.

"But where's Mother? Where's Jim?" moaned Nora, tossing on the bed.

"We've got to . . . go out for a few minutes, Nora," said Pat. "Jim's all right—"

"Something's happened to Jim, too!"

"Don't be a worrywart," said Pat crossly, fleeing.

Ellery waylaid her on Nora's porch. "Before we go in," he said quickly, "I want to explain—"

"I don't blame you, Ellery." Pat was almost as sick-looking as Nora. "It might have been worse. It might have been . . . Nora. It almost was." She shivered.

"I'm sorry about Rosemary," said Ellery.

Pat looked at him blankly. Then she went inside.

Ellery lingered on the porch. It was a gray day, like Rosemary Haight's face: a gray day and a cold day, a day for corpses . . . Someone was missing—Frank Lloyd.

Emmy DuPré chittered by, stopped, studied Chief Dakin's car at the curb, frowned . . . walked on slowly, craning at the two houses.

A car drove up. Frank Lloyd jumped out. Then Lola Wright. They ran up the walk together.

"Nora! Is she all right?" gasped Lola. Ellery nodded. Lola dashed inside.

"I picked Lola up," said Lloyd. He was breathing heavily, too. "She was walking up the Hill."

"They're waiting for you, Lloyd."

"I thought," said the publisher, "you might think it funny." There was a damp copy of the *Wrightsville Record* in his overcoat pocket.

"I think nothing funny on mornings like this. Did Lola know?" They walked into the house.

"No. She was just taking a walk, she said. Nobody knows yet."

"They will," said Ellery dryly, "when your paper hits the streets."

"You're a damn snoop," growled Lloyd, "but I like you. Take my advice and hop the first train out."

"I like it here," smiled Ellery. "Why?"

"Because this is a dangerous town."

"How so?"

"You'll see when the news gets around. Everybody who was at the party last night will be smeared."

"There's always," remarked Mr. Queen, "the cleansing property of a clear conscience."

"That makes you apple pie." Lloyd shook his heavy shoulders. "I don't figure you."

"Why bother? For that matter, you're not a simple sum in arithmetic yourself."

"You'll hear plenty about me."

"I already have."

"I don't know," said the newspaper publisher savagely, "why I stand here in the foyer gassing with a nitwit!" He shook the floor striding into the living room.

"The poison," said Dr. Willoughby, "is arsenic trioxid, or arsenious oxid, as you prefer. 'White' arsenic."

They were sitting in a rough circle, like unbelievers at a séance. Chief Dakin stood at the fireplace, tapping his false teeth with a rolled paper.

"Go ahead, Doc," said Dakin. "What else did you find? That part's right. We checked in our own lab during the night."

"It's used in medicine mostly as an alterative or tonic," said the doctor tonelessly. "We never prescribe a bigger therapeutic dose than a tenth of a grain. There's no way of telling from the dregs of the cocktail, of course — at least with accuracy — but judging from the speed with which the poison acted, I'd estimate there were three or four grains in that glass."

"Prescribe any of that stuff recently for . . . anyone you know, Doc?" muttered Carter Bradford.

"No."

"We've established a bit more," said Chief Dakin soberly, looking around. "Most probably it was plain ordinary rat poison. And moreover, no trace of the poison was found anywheres except in that one cocktail which Mrs. Haight and her sister-in-law drank—not in the mixing glass, nor the rye whisky, nor the vermouth, nor the bottle of cherries, nor any of the other glassware."

Mr. Queen surrendered. "Whose fingerprints did you find on the poisoned-cocktail glass, Chief Dakin?"

"Mrs. Haight's. Rosemary Haight's. Jim Haight's. No others."

Ellery could see them translate silently. Nora's . . . Rosemary's . . . Jim's . . . no others. His own thoughts were admiring. Chief Dakin had not remained idle after they left him last night. He had taken the fingerprints of the corpse. He had found some object unmistakably Nora Haight's, probably in her bedroom, and had taken *her* fingerprints. Jim Haight had been in the house all night, but Ellery was willing to make a large bet that Jim had not been disturbed, either. There were plenty of *his* things in the house, too . . . Very pretty. Very considerate. It disturbed Mr. Queen powerfully—the prettiness and considerateness of Chief Dakin's methods.

He glanced over at Pat. She was watching Dakin as if the Chief had hypnotized her.

"And what did your autopsy show, Doc?" asked Dakin deferentially.

"Miss Haight died of arsenic trioxid poisoning."

"Yes, sir. Now let's get this organized," said Dakin. "If you folks don't mind?"

"Go ahead, Dakin," said John F. impatiently.

"Yes, Mr. Wright. So we know the two ladies were poisoned by that one cocktail. Now, who mixed it?"

No one said anything.

"Well, I already know. It was you, Mr. Haight. You mixed that cocktail."

Jim Haight had not shaved. There were muddy ruts under his eyes.

"Did I?" There was a frog in his throat; he cleared it several times. "If you say so—I mixed so many—"

"And who came in from the kitchen and handed out the tray of drinks?" asked Chief Dakin. "Including the one that was poisoned? You did, Mr. Haight. Am I wrong? Because that's my information," he said apologetically.

"If you're trying to insinuate—" began Hermione in an imperious voice.

"All right, Mrs. Wright," said the Chief. "Now maybe I'm wrong. But you mixed that cocktail, Mr. Haight; you handed it out, so it looks like you're the only one could have dosed it up good with rat-killer. But it only *looks* that way. *Were* you the only one? Did you leave those cocktails you were making even for a few seconds any time up to the time you brought the tray into this room last night?"

"Look," said Jim. "Maybe I'm crazy. Maybe the things that happened last night knocked my brains for a loop. What *is* this? Am I suspected of having tried to poison my wife?"

As if this had been a fresh wind in a stale room, the air became breathable again. John F.'s hand dropped from his eyes, Hermy's color came back, and even Pat looked at Jim.

"This *is* nonsense, Chief Dakin!" said Hermy coldly.

"Did you, Mr. Haight?" asked Dakin.

"Of course I brought that tray in here!" Jim got up and began to walk up and down before the Chief, like an orator. "I'd just mixed the Manhattans—that last batch—and was going to put the maraschino cherries in, but then I had to leave the pantry for a few minutes. That's it!"

"Well, now," said Dakin heartily, "*now* we're getting places, Mr. Haight. Could someone have slipped in from the living room and poisoned one of them cocktails without you knowing or seeing? While you were gone, I mean?"

The fresh wind died, and they were in choking miasma once more. *Could someone have slipped in from the living room—*

"I didn't poison that cocktail," said Jim, "so somebody *must* have slipped in."

Dakin turned swiftly. "Who left the living room while Mr. Haight was mixing that last mess of drinks in the kitchen? This is very important, please. Think hard on it!"

Ellery lit a cigarette. Someone must have noticed that he had been missing simultaneously with Jim. It was inevitable . . . But then they all began to chatter at once, and Ellery blew smoke in great clouds.

"We'll never get anywheres this way," said the Chief. "So much drinking and dancing going on, and the room dark on account of only candles being lit . . . Not," added Dakin suddenly, "that it makes much difference."

"What do you mean?" asked Pat quickly.

"I mean that ain't the important point, Miss Wright." And this time Dakin's voice was quite, quite chill. Its chill deepened the chill in the room. "The important point is: Who had control of the *distribution* of the drinks? Answer me that! Because the one who handed that cocktail out— that's *got* to be the one who poisoned it!"

Bravo, bumpkin, thought Mr. Queen. You're wasting your smartness on the desert air . . . You don't know what I know, but you've hit the essential point just the same. You ought to capitalize your talents . . .

"*You* handed 'em out, James Haight," said Chief Dakin. "No poisoner'd have dropped rat-killer in one of those drinks and left it to Almighty God to decide who'd pick up the poisoned one! No, sir. It don't make sense. *Your wife got that poisoned cocktail, and you was the one handed it to her*. Wasn't you?"

And now they were all breathing heavily like swimmers in a surf, and Jim's eyes were red liquid holes.

"Yes, I did hand it to her!" he yelled. "Does that satisfy your damn snooping disposition?"

"A-plenty," said the Chief mildly. "Only thing is, Mr. Haight, you didn't know one thing. You went out of the living room to make more drinks, or fetch another bottle, or something. You didn't know your sister, Rosemary, was going to yell for another drink, and you didn't know that your wife, who you figured would drink the whole glassful, would just take a couple of sips and then your sister would pull the glass out of her hand and guzzle the rest down. So instead of killing your wife, you killed your sister!"

Jim said hoarsely: "Of course you can't believe I planned or did anything like that, Dakin."

Dakin shrugged. "Mr. Haight, I only know what my good horse sense tells me. The facts say you, and only you, had the—what do they call it?—the opportunity. So maybe you won't have what they call motive—*I* dunno. Do you?"

It was a disarming question—man to man. Mr. Queen was quite bathed in admiration. This was finesse exquisite.

Jim muttered: "You want to know why I should try to murder my wife four months after our marriage. Go to hell."

"That's no answer. Mr. Wright, can you help us out? Do you know of any reason?"

John F. gripped the arms of his chair, glancing at Hermy. But there was no help there, only horror.

"My daughter Nora," mumbled John F., "inherited a hundred thousand dollars—her grandfather's legacy—when she married Jim. If Nora died . . . Jim would get it."

Jim sat down, slowly, looking around, around.

Chief Dakin beckoned to Prosecutor Bradford. They left the room.

Five minutes later they returned, Carter paler than pale, staring straight before him, avoiding their eyes.

"Mr. Haight," said Chief Dakin gravely, "I'll have to ask you not to try to leave Wrightsville."

Bradford's work, thought Ellery. But not from compassion. From duty. There was no legal case yet. Damning circumstances, yes; but no case.

There would be a case, though. Glancing over the whole lean, shambling countryman that was Chief of Police Dakin, Mr. Queen knew there would be a case and that, pending the proverbial miracle, James Haight was not long for the free streets of Wrightsville.

# 15

## Nora Talks

At first all Wrightsville could talk about was the fact itself. The delicious fact. A body. A corpse. At the Wrights'. *At the Wrights'!* The snooty, stuck-up, we're-better-than-you-are First Family!

*Poison.*

Imagine. Just *imagine*. Who'd have thought? And so soon after, too. Remember that wedding?

The woman. Who was she? Jim Haight's sister. Rosalie—Rose-Marie? No, Rosemary. Well, it doesn't make any difference. She's dead. I saw her once. Tricked up. You *felt* something about her. Not nice. My dear, I was telling my husband only the other day . . .

So it's murder. Rosemary Haight, that woman from heaven knows where, she got a mess of poison in a Manhattan cocktail, and it was really meant for Nora Haight. There it is right in Frank Lloyd's paper . . . Frank was *there*.

Drinking. Wild party. Fell down dead. Foaming at the mouth. Shh, the children! . . . Cinch Frank Lloyd hasn't told the *whole* story . . . Of course not. After *all*. The *Record*'s a family newspaper!

Four-sixty Hill Drive. Calamity House. Don't you remember? That story in the *Record* years ago? First Jim Haight ran away from his own wedding, leaving Nora Wright looking silly—and the house all built and furnished and everything! Then that Mr. Whozis from Where? Anyway, *he* dropped dead just as he was going to buy it from John F. Wright. And now—a *murder* in it!

Say, I wouldn't set foot in that jinxed house for all the money in John F.'s vaults!

Bess, did *you* hear? *They say* . . .

For some days Wrightsville could talk about nothing but the fact.

\* \* \*

Siege was laid, and Mr. Ellery "Smith" Queen found himself inadvertently a soldier of the defending force.

People streamed up and down the Hill like trekking ants, pausing outside the Wright and Haight houses to pick up some luscious leaf-crumb and bear it triumphantly down into the town. Emmeline DuPré was never so popular. Right next door! Emmy, what do you *know?*

Emmy told them. Emmy's porch became a hiring hall for the masses. If a face showed at a window of either house, there was a rush and a gasp.

"What's happening to us?" moaned Hermione. "No, I *won't* answer the phone!"

Lola said grimly: "We're a Chamber of Horrors. Some Madame Tussaud'll start charging admission soon!" Since the morning of New Year's Day, Lola had not left. She shared Pat's room. At night she silently washed her underwear and stockings in Pat's bathroom. She would accept nothing from her family. Her meals she took with Jim in the "unlucky" house.

Lola was the only member of the family to show herself out of doors the first few days of January. On January second she said something to Emmy DuPré which turned Emmy pale and sent her scuttling back to her porch like an elderly crab in a panic. "We're waxworks," said Lola. "Jack the Ripper multiplied by seven. Look at the damn body snatchers!"

Alberta Manaskas had vanished in a Lithuanian dither, so Lola cooked Jim's meals.

Jim said nothing. He went to the bank as usual.

John F. said nothing. *He* went to the bank. In the bank father-in-law and son-in-law said nothing to each other.

Hermy haunted her room, putting handkerchiefs to her little nose.

Nora was in a tossing fever most of the time, wailing to see Jim, being horridly sick, keeping her pillow blue with tears.

Carter Bradford shut himself up in his office at the County Courthouse. Large plain men came and went, and at certain times of the day he conferred in pointed secrecy with Chief of Police Dakin.

Through all this Mr. Queen moved silently, keeping out of everyone's way. Frank Lloyd had been right. There was talk about "that man Smith — who *is* he?" There were other remarks, more dangerous. He noted them all in his notebook, labeled "The Mysterious Stranger — a Suspect."

He was never far from Nora's room.

On the third day after the crime, he caught Patty as she came out and beckoned her upstairs to his room.

He latched the door.

"Pat, I've been thinking."

"I hope it's done you good." Pat was listless.

"When Dr. Willoughby was here this morning, I heard him talk to Dakin on the phone. Your County Coroner, Salemson, has cut his vacation short, and he's come back to town on the double. Tomorrow there will be an inquest."

"Inquest!"

"It's the law, darling."

"You mean we'll have to . . . leave the *house?*"

"Yes. And testify, I'm afraid."

"Not Nora!"

"No. Willoughby refuses to let her leave her bed. I heard him say so to Dakin."

"Ellery . . . what are they going to *do?*"

"Establish the facts for the record. Try to get at the truth."

Pat said: "The truth?" and looked terrified.

"Pat," said Ellery gravely, "you and I are at the crossroads in this labyrinth—"

"Meaning?" But she knew what he meant.

"This is no longer a potential crime. It's a crime that's happened. A woman has died—the fact that she died by accident makes no difference, since a murder was planned and a murder was executed. So the law comes into it . . ." Ellery said grimly . . . "a most efficient law, I must say . . . and from now on it's snoop, sniff, and hunt until *all* the truth is known."

"What you're trying to say, and are saying so badly," said Pat steadily, "is that we've got to go to the police with what *we* know . . . and *they* don't."

"It's within our power to send Jim Haight to the electric chair."

Patty sprang to her feet. Ellery pressed her hand.

"It can't be that clear! You're not convinced yourself! Even *I'm* not, and I'm her sister . . ."

"We're talking now about facts and conclusions from facts," said Ellery irritably. "Feelings don't enter into it—they certainly won't with Dakin, although they might with Bradford. Don't you realize you and I are in possession of four pieces of information not known to the police— four facts that convict Jim of having plotted and all but carried out the murder of Nora?"

"Four?" faltered Pat. "As many as that?"

Ellery sat her down again. She looked up at him with her forehead all tight and wrinkled. "Fact one: the three letters written by Jim and now at the bottom of Nora's hatbox next door—the three letters establishing his *anticipation of her death* at a time when she wasn't even ill! Clearly premeditation."

Pat moistened her lips.

"Fact two: Jim's desperate need for money. This fact, which *we* know because he's been pawning Nora's jewelry and demanding money of her, plus the fact *Dakin* knows—that on Nora's death Jim would come into a large inheritance—combined would fix a powerful motive."

"Yes. Yes . . ."

"Fact three: the toxicology book belonging to Jim, with its underlined section in Jim's characteristic red crayon . . . a section dealing with arsenious trioxid, the very poison with which subsequently Nora's cocktail was spiked and from which Nora nearly died.

"And fourth," Ellery shook his head, "something I alone can establish, because I had Jim under observation every moment New Year's Eve: the fact that no one but Jim *could* have put poison into the fatal cocktail, *or did*. So I'm in a position to establish that Jim not only had the *best* opportunity to poison that drink, but the *only* opportunity."

"And that doesn't even include his threat against Nora that afternoon when we brought him away from the *Hot Spot* blind drunk—when he said he was going to get rid of her. Dakin heard it, Cart heard it . . ."

"Or," added Ellery gently, "the two previous occasions on which Nora's been poisoned by arsenic—Thanksgiving and Christmas, coinciding with the dates of Jim's first two letters . . . Pretty conclusive, put together, Patty. How could anyone disbelieve, knowing all this, that Jim planned Nora's death?"

"Yet you don't believe it," said Pat.

"I didn't say that," said Ellery slowly. "I said . . ." He shrugged. "The point is: We've got to decide now. Do we talk at the inquest tomorrow, or don't we?"

Pat bit a fingernail. "But suppose Jim *is* innocent? How can I—how can you—set up as judge and jury and condemn somebody to death? Somebody you *know?* Ellery, I couldn't." Pat made faces, a distressed young woman. "Besides," she said eagerly, "he won't try it again, Ellery! Not now. Not after he killed his sister by mistake. Not after the whole thing's out and the police—I mean, *if* he did . . ."

Ellery rubbed his hands together as if they itched, walking up and down before her, frowning, scowling.

"I'll tell you what we'll do," he said at last. "We'll put it up to Nora." Pat stared. "She's the victim, Jim's her husband. Yes, let Nora make the decision. What do you say?"

Pat sat still for a moment.

Then she got up and went to the door. "Mother's asleep, Pop's at the bank, Ludie's downstairs in the kitchen, Lola's next door . . ."

"So Nora's alone now."

"And Ellery."

Ellery unlatched his door.

"Thanks for being such a swell clam—"

He opened the door.

"Taking such a personal risk—being involved—"

He gave her a little push toward the stairs.

Nora lay in a knot under the blue comforter, staring at the ceiling.

Scared through and through, thought Ellery.

"Nora." Pat went quickly to the bed, took Nora's thin hand between both her brown ones. "Do you feel strong enough to talk?"

Nora's eyes flew from her sister to Ellery, and then darted into hiding like timid birds.

"What is it? What's the matter?" Her voice was tight with pain. "Is Jim—did they—?"

"Nothing's happened, Nora," said Ellery.

"It's just that Ellery feels—I feel—it's time the three of us understood one another," said Pat. Then she cried: "Nora, please! Don't shut yourself up! Listen to us!"

Nora braced herself and pushed against the bed until she was sitting up. Pat leaned over her, and for an instant, she looked like Hermy. She drew the edges of Nora's bed jacket together.

Nora stared at them.

"Don't be frightened," said Ellery. Pat propped the pillow against Nora's shoulders and sat down on the edge of the bed and took Nora's hand again. And then in a quiet voice Ellery told Nora what he and Pat had learned—from the beginning. Nora's eyes grew larger and larger.

"I tried to talk to you," cried Pat, "but you wouldn't listen! Nora, *why?*"

Nora whispered: "Because it isn't true. Maybe at first I thought . . . But it's not. Not Jim. You don't know Jim. He's scared of people, so he acts cocky. But inside he's like a little boy. When you're alone with him. And he's weak. Much too weak to—to do what you think he did. Oh, please!"

Nora began to cry in her hands.

"I love him," she sobbed. "I've always loved Jim. I'll never believe he'd want to kill me. Never. Never!"

"But the facts, Nora—" said Ellery wearily.

"Oh, the facts!" She took her hands away; her wet eyes were blazing.

"What do I care about the facts? A woman *knows*. There's something so horribly wrong you can't make sense out of it. I don't know who tried to poison me three times, but I do know it wasn't Jim!"

"And the three letters, Nora? The letters in Jim's handwriting announcing your illness, your . . . death?"

"He didn't write them!"

"But Nora darling," said Pat, "Jim's handwriting—"

"Forged." Nora was panting now. "Haven't you ever heard of forgery? They were forged!"

"And the threat against you we heard him make, that day I told you about, when he was drunk?" asked Ellery.

"He wasn't responsible!"

No tears now. She was fighting. Ellery went over the whole damning case with her; she fought back. Not with counter-facts. With faith. With an adamant, frightening faith. And at the end Ellery was arguing with two women, and he had no ally.

"But you don't reason—" he exploded, throwing up his hands. Then he smiled. "What do you want me to do? I'm softheaded, but I'll do it."

"Don't say anything about these things to the police!"

"All right, I won't."

Nora sank back, closing her eyes.

Pat kissed her and then signaled to Ellery.

But Ellery shook his head. "I know you're pretty well pooped, Nora," he said kindly, "but as long as I'm becoming an accessory, I'm entitled to your full confidence."

"Anything," said Nora tiredly.

"Why did Jim run out on you that first time? Three years ago, just before you were to be married, when Jim left Wrightsville?"

Pat looked at her sister anxiously.

"That." Nora was surprised. "That wasn't anything. It couldn't have anything to do—"

"Nevertheless, I'd like to know."

"You'd have to know Jim. When we met and fell in love and all, I didn't realize just how independent Jim was. I didn't see anything wrong in— well, accepting help from Father until Jim got on his feet. We'd argue about it for hours. Jim kept saying he wanted me to live on his cashier's salary."

"I remember those battles," murmured Pat, "but I didn't dream they were so—"

"I didn't take them seriously enough, either. When Mother told me Father was putting up the little house and furnishing it for us as a wedding gift, I thought I'd keep it a surprise for Jim. So I didn't tell him until the day before the wedding. He got furious."

"I see."

"He said he'd already rented a cottage on the other side of town for fifty dollars a month—it was all we'd be able to afford, he said; we'd just have to learn to live on what he earned." Nora sighed. "I suppose I lost my temper, too. We . . . had a fight. A bad one. And then Jim ran away. That's all." She looked up. "That's really all. I never told Father or Mother or anyone about it. Having Jim run out on me just because of a thing like that—"

"Jim never wrote to you?"

"Not once. And I . . . thought I'd die. The whole town was talking . . . Then Jim came back, and we both admitted what fools we'd been, and here we are."

So from the very first it had been the house, thought Ellery. Queer! Wherever he turned in this case, the house was there. Calamity House . . . Ellery began to feel that the reporter who had invented the phrase was gifted with second sight.

"And these quarrels you and Jim have been having since your marriage?"

Nora winced. "Money. He's been asking for money. And my cameo, and other things . . . But that's just temporary," she said quickly. "He's been gambling at that roadhouse on Route 16—I suppose every man goes through a phase like that—"

"Nora, what can you tell me about Rosemary Haight?"

"Not a thing. I know she's dead, and it sounds an awful thing to say, but . . . I didn't like her. At all."

"Amen," said Patty grimly.

"Can't say I was smitten myself," murmured Ellery. "But I mean—do you know anything about her that might tie her in with . . . well, the letters, Jim's conduct, the whole puzzle?"

Nora said tightly: "Jim wouldn't talk about her. But I know what I felt. She was *no good*, Ellery. I don't see how she ever came to be Jim's sister."

"Well, she was," said Ellery briskly, "and you're tired, Nora. Thanks. You'd have been wholly justified in telling me to mind my own business about all this."

Nora squeezed his hand, and he left as Pat went into the bathroom to wet a towel for her sister's head.

Nothing. Utter nothing. And tomorrow the inquest!

# 16

## The Aramean

Coroner Salemson was nervous about the whole thing. Any audience more numerous than three paralyzed his vocal cords; and it is a matter of public record that the only time the Coroner opened his mouth at Town Meeting except for breathing purposes—he had asthma—was one year when J. C. Pettigrew reared up and demanded to know why the office of Coroner shouldn't be voted out of existence—Chic Salemson hadn't had a corpus to justify his salary in his nine years' tenure. And then all the Coroner could stammer was: "But suppose!"

And so now, at last, there was a corpus.

But a corpus meant an inquest, and that meant the Coroner had to sit up there in Judge Martin's court (borrowed from the County for the occasion) and preside; and that meant talk, and lots of it, before hundreds of glittering Wrightsville eyes—not to mention the eyes of Chief Dakin and Prosecutor Bradford and County Sheriff Gilfant and Lord knows who.

To make matters worse, there was John F. Wright. To think of the exalted Name linked nastily with a murder weakened the Coroner's knees; John F. was his household god.

So as Coroner Salemson rapped feebly for order in the jammed courtroom, he was a nervous, miserable, and desperate man. And all through the selection of the Coroner's Jury he became more nervous, and more miserable, and more desperate, until finally his nervousness and misery were swallowed by his desperation, and he saw what he must do to cut his ordeal short and save—if saving was possible—the honor of the Wright name.

To say that the old Coroner sabotaged the testimony deliberately would be unjust to the best horseshoe pitcher in Wright County. No, it was just that from the first the Coroner was convinced no one named Wright, or connected with anyone named Wright, could possibly have

had the least pink or brownish stain on his conscience. So obviously it
was either all a monstrous mistake, or the poor woman committed suicide or something, and strike this out, and that's just *supposing* . . . and
the result was that, to the disgust of Dakin, the relief of the Wrights, the
sad amusement of Mr. Ellery Queen and—above all—the disappointment of Wrightsville, the confused Coroner's jury brought in a harmless
verdict of "death at the hands of person or persons unknown" after several days of altercation, heat, and gavel breaking.

Chief Dakin and Prosecutor Bradford immediately retired to Bradford's office for another conference, the Wrights sped home thankfully,
and Coroner Salemson fled to his twelve-room ancestral home in the
Junction, where he locked himself in with trembling hands and got drunk
on an old bottle of gooseberry wine left over from his orphaned niece Ep-
pie's wedding to old man Simpson's son Zachariah in 1934.

*Gently, gently, into one neat six-foot hole in the ground.*
What's her name? Rosalie? Rose-Marie?
They say she was a glamour girl. The one they're burying—the one Jim
Haight poisoned by mistake—his sister . . . Who says Jim Haight . . . ?
Why, it was right there in the *Record* only yesterday! Didn't you read it?
Frank Lloyd didn't *say* so, just like that; but you know if you read between
the lines . . . Sure, Frank's sore. Sweet on Nora Wright, Frank was, and
Jim Haight cut him out. Never did like Haight. Kind of cold proposition—
couldn't look you in the eye, 'pears to me . . . So he was the one, huh?
Why don't they arrest him?
That's what I'd like to know!
*Ashes to ashes . . .*
Think there's dirty work going on?
Wouldn't be bowled over! Cart Bradford and that Patricia Wright
started necking years ago. That's Haight's sister-in-law.
Aaah, the rich always get away with murder.
Nobody's getting away with murder in Wrightsville! Not if we have to
take the law—
*Gently, gently . . .*
Rosemary Haight was buried in East Twin Hill Cemetery, not (people
were quick to remark) in West Twin Hill Cemetery, where the Wrights
had interred their dead for two hundred-odd years. The transaction was
negotiated by John Fowler Wright, acting for his son-in-law James
Haight, and Peter Callendar, sales manager of the Twin Hill Eternity Es-
tates, Inc., selling price sixty dollars. John F. handed Jim the deed to the
grave in silence as they drove back from the funeral.
The next morning Mr. Queen, rising early for purposes of his own,

saw the words "Wife Killer" printed in red school chalk on the sidewalk before Calamity House.

He erased them.

"Morning," said Myron Garback of the High Village Pharmacy.

"Morning, Mr. Garback," said Mr. Queen, frowning. "I've got a problem. I've rented a house; and there's a small greenhouse in the garden—found vegetables growing there, by George! In January!"

"Yes?" said Myron blankly.

"Well, now, I'm mighty fond of homegrown tomatoes; and there's a fine tomato plant or two in my greenhouse, only the plant's overrun with some kind of round little bug—"

"Mmmm. Yellowish?"

"That's right. With black stripes on their wings. At least," said Mr. Queen helplessly, "I think they're black."

"Eating the leaves, are they?"

"That's just what the pests are doing, Mr. Garback!"

Myron smiled indulgently. "*Doryphora decemlineata*. Pardon me. I like to show off my Latin. Sometimes known as the potato beetle, more commonly called potato bug."

"So that's all they are," said Mr. Queen with disappointment. "Potato bugs! *Dory*—what?"

Myron waved his hand. "It doesn't matter. I suppose you'll want something to discourage them, eh?"

"Permanently," said Mr. Queen with a murderous scowl.

Myron bustled off and returned with a small tin carton, which he began to wrap in the High Village Pharmacy's distinctive pink-striped wrapping paper. "This'll do the trick!"

"What's in it that discourages them?" asked Mr. Queen.

"Arsenic—arsenious oxid. About fifty percent. Technically . . ." Myron paused. "I mean, strictly speaking, it's copper aceto-arsenite in this preparation, but it's the arsenic that slaughters 'em." He tied the package, and Mr. Queen handed him a five-dollar bill. Myron turned to the cash register. "Want to be careful with that stuff, of course. It's poisonous."

"I certainly hope so!" exclaimed Mr. Queen.

"*And* five," said Myron. "Thank you. Call again."

"Arsenic, arsenic," said Mr. Queen loquaciously. "Say, isn't that the stuff I was reading about in the *Record?* I mean that murder case? Some woman swallowed it in a cocktail at a New Year's Eve party?"

"Yes," said the pharmacist. He gave Ellery a sharp look and turned away, presenting his graying nape and heavy shoulders to his customer.

"Wonder where they got it," said Mr. Queen nosily, leaning on the counter again. "You'd need a prescription, wouldn't you, from a doctor?"

"Not necessarily." It seemed to Ellery that Pharmacist Garback's voice took on an edge. "You didn't need one just now! There's arsenic in a lot of commercial preparations." He fussed with some cartons on the shaving-preparations shelf.

"But if a druggist did sell a person arsenic without a prescription—"

Myron Garback turned about hotly. "They won't find anything wrong with *my* records! That's what I told Dakin, and the only way Mr. Haight could have got it would have been when he bought—"

"Yes?" asked Ellery, breathing not at all.

Myron bit his lip. "Excuse me, sir," he said. "I really mustn't talk about it." Then he looked startled. "Wait a minute!" he exclaimed. "Aren't you the man who—?"

"No, indeed," said Mr. Queen hastily. "Good morning!" And he hurried out.

So it had been Garback's pharmacy. A something. A trail. And Dakin had picked it up. Quietly. They were working on Jim Haight—quietly.

Ellery struck out across the slippery cobbles of the Square toward the bus stop near the Hollis Hotel. An iced wind was whistling, and he put up his overcoat collar and half-turned to protect his face. As he turned, he noticed a car pull into a parking space on the other side of the Square. The tall figure of Jim Haight got out and strode quickly toward the Wrightsville National Bank.

Five small boys with strapped books swinging over their shoulders spied Jim and began to troop after him.

Ellery stopped, fascinated.

They were evidently jeering Jim, because Jim stopped, turned, and said something to them with an angry gesture. The boys backed off, and Jim turned away.

Ellery shouted.

One of the boys had picked up a stone.

He threw it, hard.

Jim went down on his face.

Ellery began to run across the Square. But others had seen the attack; and by the time he reached the other side of the Square, Jim was surrounded by a crowd. The boys had vanished.

"Let me through, please!"

Jim was dazed. His hat had fallen off. Blood oozed from a dark stain on his sandy hair.

"Poisoner!" said a fat woman. "That's him—that's the poisoner!"

"Wife killer!"

"Why don't they arrest him?"

"What kind of law have we got in this town, anyway?"

"He ought to be strung up!"

A small dark man kicked Jim's hat. A woman with doughy cheeks jumped at Jim, screaming.

"Stop that!" growled Ellery. He cuffed the small man aside, stepped between the woman and Jim, and said hastily: "Out of this, Jim. Come on!"

"What hit me?" asked Jim. His eyes were glassy. "My head—"

*"Lynch the dirty bastard!"*

"Who's the other one?"

"Get him, too!"

Ellery found himself, absurdly, fighting for his life with a group of blood-maddened savages who were dressed like ordinary people.

As he struck back, he was thinking: This is what comes of meddling. Get out of this town. It's no good.

Using his elbows, his feet, the heels of his hands, and occasionally a fist, he maneuvered the screeching crowd with him toward the bank building.

"Hit back, Jim!" he shouted. "Defend yourself!"

But Jim's hands remained at his sides. One sleeve of his overcoat had disappeared. A rivulet of blood coursed down a cheek. He let himself be pushed, poked, punched, scratched, kicked.

Then a one-woman Panzer division struck the crowd from the direction of the curb. Ellery grinned painfully over a swollen lip. Hatless, white-mittened, fighting mad.

"You cannibals! Let 'em alone!" Pat screamed.

"Ouch!"

"Serves you right, Hosy Malloy! And you—Mrs. Landsman! Aren't you ashamed? And you drunken old witch, you—Yes, I mean you, Julie Asturio! Stop it! *Stop it, I say.*"

"Attaboy, Patsy!" shouted a man from the edge of the crowd. "Break it up, folks—come on, that's no way to carry on!"

Pat burst through to the struggling men. At the same moment Buzz Congress, the bank "special," ran out and hit the crowd with himself. Since Buzz weighed two hundred and fifteen pounds, it was a considerable blow; people squawked and scattered, and between them Ellery and Pat got Jim into the bank.

Old John F. ran by them and breasted the crowd, his gray hair whipping in the wind.

"Go home, you lunatics!" roared John F. "Or I'll sail into you my-self!"

Someone laughed, someone groaned, and then, with a sort of outgoing-tidal shame, the mob ebbed away. Ellery, helping Pat with Jim, saw through the glass doors, at the curb, the big silent figure of Frank Lloyd.

There was a bitter twist to the newspaper publisher's mouth. When he saw Ellery watching him, he grinned without mirth, as if to say: "Re-member what I told you about this town?" and lumbered off across the Square.

Pat and Ellery drove Jim back to the little house on the Hill. They found Dr. Willoughby waiting for them—John F. had phoned him from the bank.

"Some nasty scratches," said Dr. Willoughby, "a few ugly bruises, and that's a deep scalp wound; but he'll be all right."

"How about Mr. Smith, Uncle Milo?" asked Pat anxiously. "He looks like a fugitive from a meat grinder, too!"

"Now, now, I'm perfectly fine," protested Ellery.

But Dr. Willoughby fixed up Ellery, too.

When the doctor had gone, Ellery undressed Jim, and Pat helped get him into bed. He immediately turned over on his side, resting his band-aged head on a limp hand, and closed his eyes.

They watched him for a moment and then tiptoed from the room.

"He didn't say a word," moaned Pat. "Not one word. All through the whole thing . . . He's like that man out of the Bible!"

"Job," said Ellery soberly. "The silent, suffering Aramean. Well, your Aramean had better stay away from town from now on!"

After that day, Jim stopped going to the bank.

# 17

## America Discovers Wrightsville

The activities of Mr. Ellery Queen during the trying month between January and February were circumambient. For, no matter in how straight a line he started, he invariably finished by finding himself back in the same place . . . and, moreover, with the realization that Chief Dakin and Prosecutor Bradford had been there before him.

Quietly, quietly.

Ellery did not tell Pat what a web was being woven in those secret investigations of the law. There was no point in making her feel worse than she felt already.

Then there was the Press.

Apparently one of Frank Lloyd's vitriolic editorials had splashed heavily enough to deposit a drop in Chicago; for early in January, and shortly after Rosemary Haight's funeral, a smartly dressed woman with a thirty-eight waistline, silver-sprayed hair, and tired eyes got off the afternoon express and had Ed Hotchkiss drive her directly to 460 Hill Drive.

The next day the readers of two hundred and fifty-nine large newspapers in the United States learned that good old Roberta was in there once again battling for love.

The leading paragraph of *Roberta's Column*, by Roberta Roberts, said:

> Today in a small American city named Wrightsville there is being enacted a fantastic romantic tragedy, with a Man and a Woman the tragic protagonists and a whole community playing the role of villain.

That was enough for the others. Roberta had her nose in something yum-yummy. Editors began to call for back numbers of the *Wrightsville*

*Record*. By the end of January a dozen first-line reporters had arrived in town to see what Bobby Roberts had dug up.

Frank Lloyd was cooperative, and the first stories that trickled back over the wires put the name of James Haight on the front page of every newspaper in America.

The out-of-town newspapermen and -women swarmed over the town, interviewing and writing and drinking straight bourbon at Vic Carlatti's *Hot Spot* and Gus Olesen's *Roadside Tavern* and making Dunc MacLean, next door to the Hollis Hotel, put in a hurry call to the liquor wholesaler.

During the day they lolled about the County Courthouse spitting on Janitor Hernaberry's spotless lobby tiles, trailing Chief Dakin and Prosecutor Bradford for stories and photographs, and generally showing no decent respect for the opinions of mankind (although they wired same faithfully to their editors).

Most of them stayed at the Hollis, commandeering cots when they could find no legitimate accommodations. Manager Brooks complained that they were turning his lobby into a "slophouse."

Later, during sessions of the trial, they spent their nights either on Route 16 or at the Bijou Theater on Lower Main, where they ganged up on young Louie Cahan, the manager, cracking Indian nuts all over the theater and catcalling whenever the hero made love to the heroine. On Grab Bag Night one of the reporters won a set of dishes (donated by A. A. Gilboon, House Furnishings, Long-Term Payments) and "accidentally on purpose," as everyone said indignantly, dropped all sixty pieces on the stage while the rest of them whistled, howled, and stamped their feet. Louie was good and sore, but what could he do?

Bitter speeches about "those newspaper tramps" and "self-constituted privileged characters" were delivered to good effect at a special meeting of the Country Club Board by Donald Mackenzie, President of the Wrightsville Personal Finance Corporation (PFC Solves Your Unpaid-Bills Problem!), and Dr. Emil Poffenberger, Dental Surgeon, 132 Upham Block, High Village.

Yet there was something infectious in their cynical high spirits, and Mr. Ellery Queen was saddened to observe how Wrightsville gradually took on an air of County Fair. New and shiny stock began to appear in the shopwindows; prices for food and lodging went up; farmers who had never before come into town on week-nights began to parade the Square and Lower Main with their square-toed, staring families; and it became impossible to find parking space within a radius of six blocks of the

Square. Chief Dakin had to swear in five new policemen to help direct traffic and keep the peace.

The unwilling author of all this prosperity barricaded himself at 460 Hill Drive and refused to see anyone but the Wrights, Ellery, and later Roberta Roberts. To the remainder of the press Jim was adamant.

"I'm still a taxpayer!" he cried to Dakin over the phone. "I've got a right to some privacy! Put a cop at my door!"

"Yes, Mr. Haight," said Chief Dakin politely; and that afternoon Patrolman Dick Gobbin, who had been an invisible watcher in plain clothes for some time, on orders put on a uniform and became visible.

And Jim went back to his cellarette.

"It's getting worse," reported Pat to Ellery. "He's drinking himself stupid. Even Lola can't do anything with him. Ellery, is it just that he's scared?"

"He's not scared at all. Goes deeper than funk, Patty. Hasn't he seen Nora yet?"

"He's ashamed to go near her. Nora's threatening to get out of bed and go over there herself, only Dr. Willoughby said if she did, he'd send her to the hospital. I slept with her last night. She cried all night."

Ellery glumly surveyed his glass of Scotch, filched from John F.'s modest, little-used bar. "Nora still thinks he's an innocent babe?"

"Of course. She wants him to fight back. She says if he'd only come over to see her, she knows she could persuade him to stand up and defend himself from these attacks. Did you see what those damn reporters are writing about Jim *now?*"

"Yes," sighed Ellery, emptying his glass.

"It's all Frank Lloyd's fault! That grump! Turning on his best friends! Pop's so furious he says he'll never speak to Frank again."

"It's better to keep out of Lloyd's way," said Ellery with a frown. "He's a large animal, and he's thoroughly aroused. An angry beast with a hysterical typewriter. I'll tell your father myself."

"Never mind. I don't think he wants to talk to . . . anybody," said Pat in a low voice. Then she burst out: "How can people be such vermin? Mom's friends—they don't call her anymore, they're whispering the vilest things behind her back, she's being impeached by two of her organizations—even Clarice Martin's stopped calling!"

"The Judge's wife," murmured Ellery. "Which suggests another interesting problem . . . Never mind. Have you seen Carter Bradford lately?"

"No," said Pat shortly.

"Patty, what do you know about this woman Roberta Roberts?"

"The only decent reporter in town!"

"Strange what different conclusions she draws from the same facts.

Did you see this?" Ellery showed Pat a Chicago newspaper, flipped back to *Roberta's Column*. A paragraph had been ringed, and Pat read it quickly:

The longer I investigate this case, the surer I feel that James Haight is a misunderstood, hounded man, a martyr to what is at best a circumstantial case and the victim of Wrightsville's mobbism. Only the woman he is alleged by Wrightsville gossips to have tried to poison is standing by her husband foursquare, with never a doubt or a backward look. More power to you, Nora Wright Haight! If faith and love still mean anything in this wretched world, your husband's name will be cleared and you will triumph over the pack.

"That's a *wonderful* tribute!" cried Pat.

"A little emotional, even for a famous *entrepreneuse* of love," said Mr. Queen dryly. "I think I'll explore this female Cupid."

But exploration only confirmed the evidence of his eyes. Roberta Roberts was heart and soul behind the struggle to get Jim a just hearing. One talk with Nora, and they became fighters in a common cause.

"If you could only get Jim to come up here for a talk," said Nora urgently. "Won't you try, Miss Roberts?"

"He'd listen to you," Pat interposed. "He said only this morning"— Pat neglected to mention his condition when he said it—"that you were the only friend he had in the world."

"Jim's a queer love," said Roberta thoughtfully. "I've had two talks with him, and I admit I haven't got anything but his confidence. Let me take another crack at the poor dope."

But Jim refused to stir from the house.

"Why, Jim?" asked the newspaperwoman patiently. Ellery was present, and Lola Wright—a more silent Lola these days.

"Lemme alone." Jim had not shaved, under the stubble his skin was gray, and he had drunk a lot of whisky.

"You can't just lie around the house like a yellow dog and let these people spit on you, Jim! See Nora. She'll give you strength, Jim. She's ill—don't you know that? Don't you care?"

Jim turned a tortured face to the wall. "Nora's in good hands. Her family's taking care of her. And I've done her enough harm already. Lemme alone!"

"But Nora believes in you, honey."

"I'm not gonna see Nora till this is all over," he muttered. "Till I'm Jim Haight again in this town, not some lousy hyena."

And he raised himself and fumbled for his glass, and drank, and sank back, and not all of Roberta's urging and prodding could rouse him again.

When Roberta had gone and Jim was asleep, Ellery said to Lola Wright: "And what's *your* angle, my dear Sphinx?"

"No angle. Somebody has to take care of Jim. I feed him and put him to bed and see that he has a fresh bottle of painkiller every once in a while." Lola smiled.

"Unconventional," said Mr. Queen, smiling back. "The two of you, alone, in this house."

"That's me," said Lola. "Unconventional Lola."

"You haven't expressed any opinion, Lola—"

"There's been too much expression of opinion," she retorted. "But if you want to know, I'm a professional underdog-lover. My heart bleeds for the Chinese and the Czechs and the Poles and the Jews and the Negroes—it's leaking practically all the time; and every time one of my underdogs is kicked, it leaks a little more. I see this poor slob suffering, and that's enough for me."

"Apparently it's enough for Roberta Roberts, too," mumbled Ellery.

"Miss Love-Conquers-All?" Lola shrugged. "If you ask me, that dame's on Jim's side so she can get in where the other reporters can't!"

# 18

## St. Valentine's Day: Love Conquers Nothing

Considering that Nora was bedridden as a result of arsenic poisoning, that John F. was finding his cronies shying away from him and transferring their business to Hallam Luck's *Public Trust Co.*, that Hermione was having the ladyfinger put on her, Pat was sticking close to Nora's bedside, and even Lola had been jolted out of her isolation—considering all this, it was wonderful how the Wrights kept bravely pretending, even among themselves, that nothing out of the ordinary had happened.

No one referred to Nora's condition except as an "illness," as if she were suffering from laryngitis or some mysterious but legal "woman's complaint." John F. talked business at his desk in his old dry way—if he attended far fewer board meetings, it was because he was "tied up" . . . obviously; and the fact that he quite disappeared from the weekly luncheons of the Chamber of Commerce at Ma Upham's was gravely excused on grounds of dyspepsia.

As for Jim—he was not mentioned at all.

But Hermy, after the first emotional storms, did some calking and sail patching. No one was going to run *her* out of town. And grimly she began to employ her telephone again. When impeachment proceedings began at her Women's Club, Madam President astounded everyone by making a personal appearance, in her smartest winter suit, and acting as if nothing had happened whatsoever. She was impeached notwithstanding; but only after various abalone ears burned and the ladies grew scarlet under the lash of Hermy's scorn. And at home she took charge as of old. Ludie, who might have been expected to snarl back, instead went about with a relieved expression.

And by the beginning of February things took on such an air of normality that Lola actually returned to her nun's flat in Low Village, and

Nora being better, Pat assumed the task of cooking Jim's meals and straightening Nora's house.

On Thursday, February thirteenth, Dr. Willoughby said that Nora could get out of bed.

There was much joy in the household. Ludie baked a gargantuan lemon-meringue pie, Nora's favorite; John F. came home early from the bank with a double armful of American Beauty roses (and where he got them, in Wrightsville, in February, he refused to say!); Pat stretched as if she were cramped and then washed her hair and did her nails, murmuring things like: "My God! How I've let myself go!" Hermy turned the radio on for the first time in weeks to hear the war news . . . It was like coming out of a restless sleep to find yourself safely awake.

Nora wanted to see Jim instantly; but Hermione refused to let her out of the house—"The first day, dear! Are you insane?"—and so Nora phoned next door. After a while she hung up, helplessly; there was no answer.

"Maybe he's gone out for a walk or something," said Pat.

"I'm sure that's what it is, Nora," said Hermy, fussing over Nora's hair. Hermy did not say that Jim was in the house that very moment—she had just glimpsed his gray face pressed against the Venetian blinds of the master bedroom.

"I know!" said Nora, with a little excitement; and she telephoned Ben Danzig. "Mr. Danzig, send me the biggest, most expensive Valentine you've got. Right away!"

"Yes, ma'am," said Ben; and in a half hour it was all over town that Nora Haight was all right again. Sending Valentines! *Is there another man, do you suppose?*

It was a gorgeous thing, quilted in pink satin and bordered with real lace, framing numerous fat Cupids and sweet with St. Valentine sentiment—Ben Danzig's most exclusive number, 99A.

Nora addressed the envelope herself, and licked the stamp and affixed it, and sent Ellery out to mail it. She was almost gay. Mr. Queen, playing Hermes to Eros, dropped the Valentine in the box at the bottom of the Hill with the uncomfortable feeling of a man who watches a battered pugilist getting to his knees after the fourth knockdown.

In the mail Friday morning there was no Valentine for Nora.

"I'm going over there," she said firmly. "This is silly. Jim's sulking. He thinks the whole world's against him. I'm going—"

Ludie came in, very stiff and scared, and said: "It's that Chief Dakin and Mr. Bradford, Miss Hermy."

"Dakin!" The color left Hermy's girlish cheeks. "For . . . me, Ludie?"

"Says he wants to be seeing Miss Nora."

Nora said: "Me?" in a quivery voice.

John F. rose from the breakfast table. "I'll handle this!" They went into the living room.

Mr. Queen left his eggs and ran upstairs. Pat yawned "Whozit?" when he rapped on her door.

"Come downstairs!"

"Whaffor?" He heard her yawn again. "Come in, come in." Ellery merely opened the door. Pat was bunched under the bedclothes, looking rosy and mussed and young again.

"Dakin and Bradford. To see Nora. I think this is it."

"Oh!" Panic. But only for a moment. "Throw me my robe, like a darling. It's arctic in here." Ellery handed it to her, turned to walk out. "Wait for me in the hall, Ellery. I mean—I want to go downstairs with you."

Pat joined him in three minutes. She held onto his arm all the way downstairs.

As they came in, Chief Dakin was saying: "Course, Mrs. Haight, you understand I've got to cover the whole ground. I'd told Doc Willoughby to let me know when you'd be up and about—"

"So kind of you," said Nora.

She was frightened almost out of her wits. You could see it. Her figure had a wooden stillness, and she looked from Dakin to Bradford and back again like a puppet being jerked by invisible hands.

"Hello," said Pat grimly. "Isn't it early for a social call, Mr. Dakin?"

Dakin shrugged. Bradford regarded her with a furious misery. He seemed thinner, almost emaciated.

"Sit down and be quiet, baby," said Hermione faintly.

"I don't know what you can expect Nora to tell you," said John F. frigidly. "Patricia, sit down!"

"Patricia?" said Pat. She sat down. "Patricia" was a bad sign. John F. hadn't called her Patricia in such a formal voice since the last time he'd used his old-fashioned razor strop on her bottom, and that had been many many years ago. Pat contrived to grasp Nora's hand.

She did not look at Bradford once; and after that first unhappy glance, Bradford did not look at her.

Dakin nodded pleasantly to Ellery. "Glad to see you, Mr. Smith. Now if we're all set— Cart, did you want to say somethin'?"

"Yes!" exploded Cart. "I wanted to say that I'm in an impossible position. I wanted to say—" He made a helpless gesture and stared out the window at the snow-covered lawn.

"Now, Mrs. Haight," said Dakin, blinking at Nora, "would you mind telling us just what happened New Year's Eve as you saw it? I've got everybody else's story—"

"Mind? Why should I mind?" It came out froggy, and Nora cleared her throat. And began to talk shrilly and rapidly, making rapid little meaningless signs with her free hand. "But I can't really tell you anything. I mean, all that I saw—"

"When your husband came around to you with the tray of cocktails, didn't he sort of pick out one special glass for you? I mean, didn't you want to take one glass and he fixed it so you took another?"

"How can I remember a thing like that?" asked Nora indignantly. "And that's a—a nasty implication!"

"Mrs. Haight." The Chief's voice was suddenly chilly. "Did your husband ever try to poison you before New Year's Eve?"

Nora snatched her hand from Pat's and jumped up. "No!"

"Nora dear," began Pat, "you mustn't get excited—"

"You're sure, Mrs. Haight?" insisted Dakin.

"Of course I'm sure!"

"There's nothing you can tell us about the fights you and Mr. Haight been having?"

"Fights!" Nora was livid now. "I suppose it's that horrible DuPré creature—or—"

The "or" was so odd even Carter Bradford turned from the window. Nora had uttered the word with a sudden sickish emphasis and glared directly at Ellery. Dakin and Bradford glanced quickly at him, and Pat looked terrified. Mr. and Mrs. Wright were hopelessly lost.

"Or what, Mrs. Haight?" asked Dakin.

"Nothing. Nothing! Why don't you let Jim alone?" Nora was crying hysterically now. "All of you!"

Dr. Willoughby came in with his big man's light step; Ludie's face, white and anxious, peered over his shoulder, then vanished.

"Nora," he said with concern, "crying again? Dakin, I warned you—"

"Can't help it, Doc," said the Chief with dignity. "I got my job to do, and I'm doing it. Mrs. Haight, if there's nothing you can tell us that helps your husband—"

"He didn't do it, I tell you!"

"Nora," said Dr. Willoughby insistently.

"Then I'm afraid we got to do it, Mrs. Haight."

"Do what, for heaven's sake?"

"Arrest your husband."

"Arrest—Jim?" Nora began to laugh, her hands in her hair. Dr. Willoughby tried to take her hands in his, but she pushed him away. Behind the glasses her pupils were dilated. "But you can't arrest Jim! He didn't do anything! You haven't a thing on him—!"

"We've got plenty on him," said Chief Dakin.

"I'm sorry, Nora," mumbled Carter Bradford. "It's true."

"Plenty on him," whispered Nora. Then she screamed at Pat: "I knew too many people knew about it! That's what comes of taking strangers into the house!"

"Nora!" gasped Pat. "Darling . . ."

"Wait a moment, Nora," began Ellery.

"Don't *you* talk to me!" Nora shrieked. "You're against him because of those three letters! They wouldn't arrest Jim if you hadn't told them about the letters—!"

Something in Ellery's gaze seemed to penetrate her hysteria, and Nora broke off with a gasp, swaying against Dr. Willoughby, an enormous new fear leaping into her eyes. She looked quickly at Dakin, at Bradford, saw the astonishment, then the flash of exultation. And she backed up against the broad chest of the doctor and froze there, her hand to her mouth, sick with realization.

"What letters?" demanded Dakin.

"Nora, what letters?" cried Bradford.

"No! I didn't mean—"

Carter ran over to her and seized her hand. "Nora! *What letters?*" he asked fiercely.

"No," groaned Nora.

"You've got to tell me! If there are letters, you're concealing evidence—"

"Mr. Smith! What do you know about this?" demanded Chief Dakin.

"Letters?" Ellery looked astonished, and shook his head.

Pat rose and pushed Bradford. He staggered back. "You let Nora alone," said Pat in a passionate voice. "You Judas!"

Her violence kindled an answering violence. "You're not going to presume upon my friendship! Dakin, search this house and the house next door!"

"Should have done it long ago, Cart," said the Chief mildly. "If you hadn't been so blamed set—" He disappeared.

"Carter," said John F. in very low tones, "you're never to come here again. Do you understand?"

Bradford looked as if he were going to cry.

And Nora collapsed in Dr. Willoughby's arms with a moan like a sick cat.

*   *   *

With Bradford's frigid permission Nora was taken upstairs to her bedroom by Dr. Willoughby. Hermy and Pat hurried along with them, helpless and harried.

"Smith." Bradford did not turn.

"Save your breath," advised Mr. Queen politely.

"I know it's no use, but I've got to warn you—if you're contributing to the suppression of evidence . . ."

"Evidence?" echoed Mr. Queen, as if he had never heard the word before.

"Those letters!"

"What *are* these letters you people are talking about?"

Cart spun around, his mouth working. "You've been in my way ever since you came here," he said hoarsely. "You've wormed your way into this house, alienated Pat from me—"

"Here, here," said Ellery kindly. "Mind your verbs."

Cart stopped, his hands two fists. Ellery went to the window. Chief Dakin was deep in conversation with little Dick Gobbin, the patrolman, on the Haight porch . . . The two policemen went into the house.

Fifteen minutes later Messrs. Queen and Bradford were still standing in the same positions.

Pat came in with a noise.

Her face shocked them.

She went directly to Ellery. "The most awful thing's happened." And she burst into tears.

"Pat! For heaven's sake!"

"Nora—Nora is—" Pat's voice blurred and shook.

Dr. Willoughby said from the doorway: "Bradford?"

"What's happened?" asked Bradford tensely.

And then Chief Dakin came in, unknowing, and his face was like a mask. He was carrying Nora's hatbox and the fat tan book with the neat gilt title, Edgcomb's *Toxicology.*

Dakin stopped. "Happened?" he asked quickly. "What's this?"

Dr. Willoughby said: "Nora Haight is going to have a baby. In about five months."

And then there was no sound at all but Pat's exhausted sobs against Ellery's chest.

"No . . ." said Bradford in a wincing voice. "That's . . . too much." And with a queer begging gesture toward Chief of Police Dakin he stumbled out. They heard the front door slam.

"I won't be responsible for Mrs. Haight's life," said Dr. Willoughby harshly, "if she's put through any more scenes like the one just now. You can call in Wright County's whole medical fraternity to confirm what I just said. She's pregnant, in an extremely nervous condition; she has a naturally delicate constitution to begin with—"

"Look, Doc," said Dakin, "it ain't my fault if—"

"Oh, go to hell," said Dr. Willoughby. They heard him climbing furiously back up the stairs.

Dakin stood still in the middle of the room, Nora's hatbox in one hand and Jim's book on poisons in the other.

Then he sighed and said: "But it *ain't* my fault. And now these three letters in Mrs. Haight's hatbox and this medical book with the arsenic part all marked up—"

"All right, Dakin," said Ellery. His arms tightened about Pat.

"These three letters," said Dakin doggedly. "They practically make our case. And finding 'em in Mrs. Haight's closet . . . Looks mighty odd to me. I don't get this—"

Pat cried: "Doesn't that convince you? Would Nora have kept those letters if she thought Jim was trying to poison her? Are you all so stupid—"

"So you did know about the letters," said the Chief, blinking. "I see. And you're in on this, too, Mr. Smith. Not that I blame you. I got a family, too, and it's good to be loyal to friends. I got nothing against Jim Haight, or you Wrights . . . But I got to find the facts. If Jim Haight's innocent, he'll be acquitted, never you worry . . ."

"Go away, please," said Ellery.

Dakin shrugged and left the house, taking his evidence with him. He looked angry and bitter.


At eleven o'clock that morning, February fourteenth, the day of St. Valentine, when all Wrightsville was giggling over comic cards and chewing candy out of heart-shaped boxes, Chief of Police Dakin returned to 460 Hill Drive with Patrolman Charles Brady, nodded to Patrolman Dick Gobbin, and Patrolman Dick Gobbin knocked on the front door.

When there was no answer, they went in.

They found Jim Haight snoring on the living-room sofa in a mess of cigarette butts, dirty glasses, and half-empty whisky bottles.

Dakin shook Jim, not ungently, and finally Jim snorted. His eyes were all red and glassy.

"Hunh?"

"James Haight," said Dakin, holding out a blue-backed paper, "I hereby arrest you on the charge of the attempted murder of Nora Wright Haight and the murder of Rosemary Haight."

Jim screwed up his eyes, as if he could not see well.

Then he reddened all over his face. He shouted: "No!"

"Better come without a fuss," said Dakin; and he walked out with a quick, relieved step.

Charles Brady said later to the reporters at the Courthouse: "Seemed like Haight just caved in. Never saw anything like it. You could just see the fella sort of fold up, in pieces, like a contraption. I says to Dick Gobbin: 'Better take that side of him, Dick, he's gonna collapse,' but Jim Haight, he just made a kind of shoving motion at Dick, and I'll be doggone if he don't start to laugh— all folded up! An' he says, so you could hardly hear him through the laughin'—an' let me tell you fellas, the stink of booze was enough to send you higher'n a kite—he says: 'Don't tell my wife.' And he comes along nice and quiet. Now wasn't that a crazy thing for a fella to say who's just been arrested for murder? 'Don't tell my wife.' Facin' a murder rap an' thinkin' of sparin' his wife's feelin's! How could anybody keep it from her, anyway? Don't tell my wife! I tell you the fella's a nut."

All Patrolman Gobbin said was: "G-o-b-b-i-n. That's right, fellas. Hey, this'll give my kids a real kick!"

# PART FOUR

# 19

## War of the Worlds

Feb. 17, 1941

Mr. Boris Connell
News & Features Syndicate
Press Ass'n Bldg.
Chicago, Ill.

Dear Boris:

Double Mickeys to you for that hot wire, but perhaps your celebrated news nose has been misled by the tons of garbage my fellow "journalists" have been slinging back from Wrightsville.

I believe Jim Haight is innocent, and I'm going to say so in my column till I have no column.

In my naïve way I still believe a man is innocent until he's proved guilty. Jim Haight has been condemned to death by all the smart lads and lassies sent here by their editors to dish out a Roman holiday for the great American mob. Somebody has to have principles. So I'm elected—plurality, one vote.

And Wrightsville's in an ugly mood. People here talk about nothing else. Their talk is pure Fascism. It's going to be "fun" watching them pick an "unbiased" jury.

To appreciate what's happening, you've got to realize that only two months ago John F. and Hermione Wright were the lares and penates of this community. Today, they and their three swell daughters are untouchables—and everybody's scrambling to pick up the first stone. A slew of former Wright "admirers" and "friends" have been looking for a soft spot to jab the knife in, and are they jabbing! It's enough to make even me sick, and you know I've seen pretty nearly everything in the way of human meanness, malice, and downright cussedness.

It's a war of two worlds. The decent little world is hopelessly outclassed in armament, numbers, and about everything but guts and morale. The Wrights have a few real friends who are sticking by—Judge Eli Martin, Dr. Milo Willoughby, a visiting writer named Ellery Smith. (Ever hear of him? *I* haven't!) Together they're putting up a propaganda battle. The Wrights are magnificent—in the face of everything, they're bunched solidly behind Jim Haight. Even this girl Lola Wright, who's been on the outs with her family for years, has moved back home; or at least she's there constantly. They're all fighting not only for Nora's husband but for her unborn child as well. Despite the tripe I dish out for my "public" every day, I still believe in some fundamental decencies, and that little tyke can use a powerful voice!

Let me tell you something. I was in Jim's cell today in the County Courthouse, and I said to him: "Jim, did you know your wife is going to have a baby?"

He just sat down on his cell bunk and started to bawl, as if I'd hit him where a lady shouldn't.

I haven't been able to see Nora yet, though I may get Dr. Willoughby's permission in a day or so. (I mean, since Jim's arrest.) Nora's collapsed, and she can't see anyone but her family. How would you like to be in her shoes? And if *she's* behind Jim— the man who's supposed to have plotted her death—then there's really something to fight for.

I know this is wasted time and paper, Boris, since your blood is composed of nine parts bourbon and one part club soda; so this is positively my last "explanation." From now on, if you want to know what's really happening in Wrightsville on the Haight murder case, read my column.

And if you get nasty and break my contract before it runs out, I'll sue the N & F Syn and I'll keep suing it till I take away everything but that expensive bridgework behind your ruby lips.

As ever,
Roberta Roberts

Roberta Roberts did not quite know the facts.

Two days after Jim's arrest, Hermione Wright called a council of war. She closed the upstairs drawing-room doors with a grim bang. It was Sunday, and the family had just returned from church—Hermy had insisted that they attend services. They all looked weary from the ordeal.

"The question," began Hermy, "is what to do."

"What can we do, Muth?" asked Pat tiredly.

"Milo"—Hermy took Doc Willoughby's big puffy hand—"I want you to tell us the truth. How is Nora?"

"She's a sick girl, Hermy, a very sick girl."

"That's not enough, Milo! How sick?"

Dr. Willoughby's eyes shifted. "Hard to say. She's dangerously nervous, excited, unstrung. Naturally her pregnancy isn't helping. Jim's arrest, thinking about the trial—she's got to be kept calmed down. Medicine alone won't do it. But if her nerves can be brought back to normal—"

Hermy patted his big hand absently. "Then there's no question of what we've got to do."

"When I see how worn-out Nora is—" said John F. in despair. "She's begun to look the way she used to. How are we going—"

"There's one way, John," said Hermy tightly. "It's for all of us to get behind Jim and fight for him!"

"When he's ruined Nora's life?" cried John F. "He's been bad luck to her from the day he came to Wrightsville!"

"John"—Hermy's voice was steel-lined—"Nora wants it that way, and more important, for her health's sake she's got to *have* it that way. So it's going to be that way."

"All *right*," John F. almost shouted.

"John!" He subsided, muttering. "And another thing. Nora mustn't know."

"Mustn't know what?" demanded Pat.

"That we don't mean it." Hermy's eyes began to redden up. "Oh, that man! If Nora weren't his wife—"

Doc Willoughby said: "So you think the boy's guilty, Hermione?"

"Think! If I'd known before about those three horrible letters, that medical book . . . Of course I think he's guilty!"

"The dirty dog," muttered John F. "He ought to be shot down, like a dirty dog."

"I don't know," moaned Pat. "I just don't."

Lola was smoking a cigarette. She flipped it into the fireplace viciously. "Maybe I'm crazy," she snapped, "but I find myself feeling sorry for the twerp, and I don't usually spare any sympathy for murderers."

"Eli, what's your opinion?" asked Hermy.

Judge Martin's sleepy face was grave.

"I don't know what young Bradford's got in the way of evidence. It's a highly circumstantial case. But on the other hand there's not a single fact I know of to cast doubt on the circumstances. I'd say Jim is in for a rough time."

"Took generations to build up the Wright name," mumbled John F., "and one day to tear it down!"

"There's been enough damage done already," sighed Pat. "When your own family runs out on you—"

"What's this?" demanded Lola.

"Aunt Tabitha, Lo. I thought you knew. She's closed up her house and gone to Los Angeles for a 'visit' to Cousin Sophy's."

"That Zombie still around?"

"Tabitha makes me sick!" said Hermione.

"You can't blame her so much, Hermy," said John F. feebly. "You know how she hates scandal—"

"I know I shan't run away, John! Nobody in this town's going to see me with *my* head hanging."

"That's what I told Clarice," chuckled Judge Martin. Then he rubbed his dry cheeks, like a cricket. "Clarice would have come, Hermione, only—"

"I understand," said Hermy quietly. "Bless you for standing by us, Eli—you, and Milo, and you, Mr. Smith. You more than anyone. After all, Judge Martin and Dr. Willoughby are lifelong friends. But you're practically a stranger to us, and Patricia's told me how loyal you've been . . ."

"I've wanted to thank you, Smith," said John F. awkwardly, "but I think you know how hard it is—"

Ellery looked uncomfortable. "Please. Don't think about me at all. I'll help all I can."

Hermy said in a low voice: "Bless you . . . Now that things have come out in the open, we'll completely understand, though, if you decide to leave Wrightsville—"

"I'm afraid I couldn't even if I wanted to," smiled Ellery. "The Judge will tell you I'm practically an accessory to the crime."

"Suppressing evidence," grinned Judge Eli. "Dakin will have the hounds after you if you try to run away, Smith."

"So you see? I'm stuck," said Mr. Queen. "Let's say no more about it."

Pat's hand stole into Ellery's and squeezed, hard.

"Then if we all understand one another," declared Hermione in a firm tone, "we're going to hire the best lawyer in the state to defend Jim. We're going to show Wrightsville a united front!"

"And if Jim's found guilty, Muth?" asked Pat quietly.

"We'll have done our best, dear. In the long run, such a verdict, hard as it seems, would be the best solution to our problem—"

"What a vile thing to say," snapped Lola. "Mother, that's not right or fair. You say that because you're convinced Jim's guilty. You're as bad as the rest of this town. Best solution—!"

"Lola, do you realize that if it were not for the intervention of Providence," Hermy cried, "your sister would be a corpse this very minute?"

"Let's not quarrel," said Pat wearily.

Lola lit another cigarette, looking angry.

"And if Jim's acquitted," said Hermy stiffishly, "I'm going to insist that Nora divorce him."

"Mother!" Now Pat was shocked. "Even if a jury finds Jim *innocent*, you'll still believe he's guilty?"

"Now Hermy, that's not right," said Judge Martin.

"I mean he's not the right man for my Nora," said Hermy. "He's brought her nothing but grief. Nora will divorce that man if *I've* got anything to say about it!"

"You won't," said Doc Willoughby dryly.

Lola kissed her mother on the cheek. Ellery heard Pat gasp, and guessed that history had just been made.

"You old Trojan," laughed Lola. "When you get there, you'll insist on running Heaven. Imagine—*you* urging a divorce!" And she added grimly: "Why didn't you feel that way about *my* divorce from Claude?"

"This isn't . . . the same," said Hermy, embarrassed. And suddenly Mr. Queen saw a bright, bright light. There was an old antagonism between Hermione Wright and her daughter Lola that cut deep into their personalities. Pat was too young to have been a cause of irritation. But Nora— Nora had always been the preferred, Nora had always stood between Hermione and Lola emotionally, an innocent rope in a psychological tug-of-war.

Hermy was saying to Judge Martin: "We'll need an extra-fine lawyer for Jim, Eli. Whom can you suggest?"

"Will I do?" asked Judge Martin.

John F. was startled. "Eli! You?"

"But Uncle Eli," protested Pat, "I thought—it's your court—I thought you'd have to sit—"

"In the first place," said the old jurist dryly, "that's not possible. I'm involved. I was present on the scene of the crime. I am known to have strong ties with the Wright family. Legally and ethically, I can't sit on this case." He shook his head. "Jim will be tried before Judge Newbold. Newbold's a complete outsider."

"But you haven't pleaded a case in fifteen years, Eli," said John F. suspiciously.

"Of course, if you're afraid I won't do—" He smiled at their protestations. "I forgot to mention that I'm retiring from the Bench, so . . . "

"You old fraud," growled Dr. Willoughby. "John, Eli's quitting the Bench just to defend this case!"

"Now Eli, we can't let you do that," said John F.

"Nonsense," said the Judge gruffly. "Don't go getting any sentimental ideas. Was going to retire anyway. Old Has-been Martin. Itching to get to work again, instead of dozing my life away in a robe. If you want a has-been in your corner, we won't say any more about it."

Hermy burst into tears and ran from the room.

# 20

## No Time for Pride

The next morning Pat rapped on Ellery's door, and he opened it to find her dressed for the street.

"Nora wants to see you." She looked around the room curiously. Ludie had already done the room, but it was briskly littered again, as if Ellery had been hard at work for some time.

"Right with you." Ellery looked fatigued. He fussed with some pencil-scrawled papers on the desk; the typewriter carriage held a sheet. He slipped the cover over the portable and, putting the papers in a desk drawer, locked it. The key he dropped casually into his pocket, and put on his jacket.

"Working?" asked Pat.

"Well . . . yes. This way out, Miss Wright." Mr. Queen walked her out of his room and locked the door.

"Your novel?"

"In a way." They went down to the second floor.

"What does 'in a way' mean?"

"Yes and no. I've been . . . you might call it reconnoitering." Ellery looked her over. "Going out? You look cute."

"I've a special reason for looking cute this morning," murmured Pat. "In fact, I'll have to look irresistible."

"You do. But where are you going?"

"Can't a girl have any secrets from you, Mr. Queen?" Pat stopped him outside Nora's room and looked him in the eye. "Ellery, you've been going over your notes on the case, haven't you?"

"Yes."

"Find anything?" she asked eagerly.

"No."

"Damn!"

"It's a queer thing," grumbled Ellery, putting his arm around her. "Something's been annoying me for weeks. Flying around in my skull. Can't catch it . . . I thought it might be a fact—something trivial—that I'd overlooked. You know, I . . . well, I based my novel on you people— the facts, the events, the interrelationships. So everything's in my notes that's happened." He shook his head. "But I can't put my finger on it."

"Maybe," frowned Pat, "it's a fact you don't *know*."

Ellery held her off at arm's length. "That," he said slowly, "is very likely. Do *you* know anything that—"

"You know if I did, I'd tell you, Ellery."

"I wonder." Then he shrugged and said: "Well! Let's go in and see Nora."

Nora was sitting up in bed, reading the *Wrightsville Record*. She was thinner, unhealthy-looking. Ellery was shocked to see how transparent the skin of her hands had grown.

"I always say," grinned Mr. Queen, "that the test of a woman's attractiveness is—how does she look in bed of a winter's morning."

Nora smiled wanly and patted the bed. "Do I pass?"

*"Summa cum laude,"* said Ellery, sitting down beside her.

Nora looked pleased. "Most of it's powder, lipstick—yes, and a dab of rouge on each cheek—and of course this ribbon in my hair is a help. Charming liar! Patty darling, sit down."

"I really have to be going, Nor. You two can talk—"

"But Pats, I want you to hear this, too."

Pat glanced at Ellery; he blinked, and she sat down in the chintz-covered chair on the other side of the bed. She seemed nervous, and Ellery kept watching her as Nora talked.

"First," said Nora, "I owe you an apology."

"Who, me?" said Ellery, astonished. "For what, Nora?"

"For having accused you of telling the police about those three letters and the toxicology book. Last week. When Chief Dakin said he was going to arrest Jim and I lost my head."

"You see? I'd forgotten it. You do the same."

Nora took his hand. "It was a malicious thought. But for the moment I couldn't imagine who'd told them but you. You see, I thought they knew—"

"You weren't responsible, Nora," said Pat. "Ellery understands that."

"But there's something else," cried Nora. "I can apologize for a nasty thought, but I can't wipe out what I did to Jim." Her lower lip quivered. "If not for me, they'd never have found out about those letters!"

"Nor dear," said Pat, leaning over her, "you know you mustn't. If you keep crying, I'll tell Uncle Milo and he won't let you have *any* company."

Nora sniffled with her handkerchief to her nose. "I don't know why I didn't burn them. Such a stupid thing—to keep them in that hatbox in my closet! But I had some idea I'd be able to find out who really wrote them. I was sure Jim hadn't—"

"Nora," said Ellery gently, "forget it."

"But I practically handed Jim over to the police!"

"That isn't true. Don't forget Dakin came here last week *prepared* to arrest Jim. Questioning you beforehand was just a formality."

"Then you think those letters and the book don't make any essential difference?" asked Nora eagerly.

Ellery got up from the bed and looked out the window at the winter sky. "Well . . . not too much."

"You're lying to me!"

"Mrs. Haight," said Pat firmly, "you've had enough company for one morning. Ellery, scram."

Ellery turned around. "This sister of yours, Pat, will suffer more from doubt than from knowledge. Nora, I'll tell you exactly what the situation is."

Nora gripped her comforter with both hands.

"If Dakin was prepared to arrest Jim *before* he knew about the letters and the toxicology book, then obviously he and Carter Bradford thought they had a good case." Nora made a tiny sound. "*With* the letters and the book, therefore, they just as obviously have a better case. Now that's the truth, you've got to face it, you've got to stop accusing yourself, you've got to be sensible and get well again, you've got to stand by Jim and give him courage." He leaned over her and took her hand. "Jim needs your strength, Nora. You have a strength he lacks. He can't face you, but if he knows you're behind him, never wavering, having faith—"

"Yes," breathed Nora, her eyes shining, "I have. Tell him I have."

Pat came around the bed and kissed Ellery on the cheek.

"Going my way?" asked Ellery as they left the house.

"Which way is that?"

"Courthouse. I want to see Jim."

"Oh. I'll drive you down."

"Don't go out of your way—"

"I'm going to the Courthouse, too."

"To see Jim?"

"Don't ask me questions!" cried Pat a little hysterically.

They drove down the Hill in silence. There was ice on the road, and the chains sang cheerfully. Wrightsville looked nicely wintry, all whites and reds and blacks, no shading; it had the country look, the rich and simple cleanliness, of a Grant Wood painting.

But in town there were people, and sloppy slush, and a meanness in the air; the shops looked pinched and stale; everybody was hurrying through the cold; no one smiled. In the Square they had to stop for traffic; a shopgirl recognized Pat and pointed her out with a lacquered fingernail to a pimpled youth in a leather storm-breaker. They whispered excitedly as Pat kicked the gas pedal.

On the Courthouse steps Ellery said: "Not *that* way, Miss Wright," and steered Pat around to the side entrance.

"What's the idea?" demanded Pat.

"The press," said Mr. Queen. "Infesting the lobby. I assume we'd rather not answer questions."

They took the side elevator.

"You've been here before," said Pat slowly.

"Yes."

Pat said: "I think I'll pay Jim a visit myself."

The County Jail occupied the two topmost floors of the Courthouse. As they stepped out of the elevator into the waiting room, an odor of steam and Lysol rushed into their noses, and Pat swallowed hard. But she managed a smile for the benefit of Wally Planetsky, the officer on duty.

"If it ain't Miss Pat," said the officer awkwardly.

"Hullo, Wally. How's the old badge?"

"Fine, fine, Miss Pat."

"Wally used to let me breathe on his badge and shine it up when I was in grade school," Pat explained. "Wally, don't stand there shifting from one foot to the other! You know what I'm here for."

"I guess," muttered Wally Planetsky.

"Where's his cell?"

"Judge Martin's with him, Miss Pat. Rules say only one visitor at a time—"

"Who cares about the rules? Take us to my brother-in-law's cell, Wally!"

"This gentleman a reporter? Mr. Haight, he won't see any reporters excepting that Miss Roberts."

"No, he's a friend of mine and Jim's."

"I guess," muttered Planetsky again; and they began a long march, interrupted by unlocking of iron doors, locking of iron doors, steps on concrete, unlocking and locking and steps through corridors lined with man-sized birdcages; and at each step the odor of steam and Lysol grew stronger, and Pat grew greener, and toward the last she clung tightly to Ellery's arm. But she kept her chin up.

"That's it," murmured Ellery; and she swallowed several times in succession.

Jim sprang to his feet when he spied them, a quick flush coming to his sallow cheeks; but then he sat down again, the blood draining away, and said hoarsely: "Hello there. I didn't know you were coming."

"Hello, Jim!" said Pat cheerily. "How are you?"

Jim looked around his cell. "All right," he said with a vague smile.

"It's clean, anyway," grunted Judge Martin, "which is more than you could say about the *old* County Jail. Well, Jim, I'll be on my way. I'll drop in tomorrow for another talk."

"Thanks, Judge." Jim smiled the same vague smile up at the Judge.

"Nora's fine," said Pat with an effort, as if Jim had asked.

"That's swell," said Jim. "Fine, uh?"

"Yes," said Pat in a shrill voice.

"That's swell," said Jim again.

Mercifully, Ellery said: "Pat, didn't you say you had an errand somewhere? There's something I'd like to say to Jim in private."

"Not that it will do you the least good," said Judge Martin in an angry tone. It seemed to Ellery that the old jurist's anger was assumed for the occasion. "This boy hasn't the sense he was born with! Come along, Patricia."

Pat turned her pale face to Ellery, mumbled something, smiled weakly at Jim, and fled with the Judge. Keeper Planetsky relocked the cell door after them, shaking his head.

Ellery looked down at Jim; Jim was studying the bare floor of his cell.

"He wants me to talk," mumbled Jim suddenly.

"Well, why not, Jim?"

"What could I say?"

Ellery offered him a cigarette. Jim took it; but when Ellery held a lighted match up, he shook his head and slowly tore the cigarette to shreds.

"You could say," murmured Ellery between puffs, "you could say that you didn't write those three letters or underline that paragraph on arsenic."

For an instant Jim's fingers stopped tormenting the cigarette; then they resumed their work of destruction. His colorless lips flattened against his face in something that was almost a snarl.

"Jim." Jim glanced at him and then away. "Did you really plan to poison Nora?"

Jim did not even indicate that he had heard the question.

"You know, Jim, often when a man is guilty of a crime, he's much better off telling the truth to his lawyer and friends than keeping quiet. And when he's not guilty, it's actually criminal to keep quiet. It's a crime against himself."

Jim said nothing.

"How do you expect your family and friends to help you when you won't help yourself?"

Jim's lips moved.

"What did you say, Jim?"

"Nothing."

"As a matter of fact, in this case," said Ellery briskly, "your crime of silence isn't directed half so much against yourself as it is against your wife and the child that's coming. How can you be so far gone in stupidity or listlessness that you'd drag them down with you, too?"

"Don't say that!" said Jim hoarsely. "Get out of here! I didn't ask you to come! I didn't ask Judge Martin to defend me! I didn't ask for anything! I just want to be let alone!"

"Is that," asked Ellery, "what you want me to tell Nora?"

There was such misery in Jim's eyes as he sat, panting, on the edge of his cell bunk that Ellery went to the door and called Planetsky.

All the signs. Cowardice. Shame. Self-pity . . . But that other thing, the stubbornness, *the refusal to talk about anything*, as if in the mere act of self-expression there were *danger* . . .

As Ellery followed the guard down the eye-studded corridor, a cell exploded in his brain with a great and disproportionate burst of light. He actually stopped walking, causing old Planetsky to turn and look at him in surprise. But then he shook his head and strode on again. He'd almost had it that time—by sheer divination. Maybe the next time . . .

Pat drew a deep breath outside the frosted-glass door on the second floor of the County Courthouse, tried to see her reflection, poked nervously at her mink hat, tried out a smile or two, not too successfully, and then went in.

Miss Billcox looked as if she were seeing a ghost.

"Is the Prosecutor in, Billy?" murmured Pat.

"I'll . . . see, Miss Wright," said Miss Billcox, and fled.

Carter Bradford came out to her himself, in a hurry.

"Come in, Pat." He looked tired and astonished. He stood aside to let her pass, and as she passed, she heard his uneven breathing. O Lord, she thought. Maybe. Maybe it isn't too late.

"Working?" His desk was covered with legal papers.

"Yes, Pat." He went around his desk to stand behind it. One sheaf of bound papers lay open—he closed it surreptitiously and kept his hand on it as he nodded toward a leather chair. Pat sat down and crossed her knees.

"Well," said Pat, looking around, "the old office—I mean the new office—doesn't seem to have changed, Cart."

"About the only thing that hasn't."

"You needn't be so careful about that legal paper," smiled Pat. "I haven't got X-ray eyes."

He flushed and removed his hand.

"There isn't a shred of Mata Hari in my makeup."

"I'm *not*—" Cart began angrily. Then he pushed his fingers through his hair in the old, old gesture. "Here we are, scrapping again. Pat, you look simply delicious."

"It's nice of you to say so," sighed Pat, "when I really am beginning to look my age."

"Look your age! Why, you're—" Cart swallowed hard. Then he said, as angrily as before: "I've missed you like hell."

Pat said rigidly: "I suppose I've missed you, too." Oh, dear! That wasn't what she had meant to say at all. But it was hard, facing him this way, alone in a room together for the first time in so long—hard to keep from feeling . . . feelings.

"I dream about you," said Cart with a self-conscious laugh. "Isn't that silly?"

"Now, Cart, you know perfectly well you're just saying that to be polite. People don't dream about people. I mean in the way *you* mean. They dream about animals with long noses."

"Maybe it's just before I drop off." He shook his head. "Dreaming or not dreaming, it's always the same. Your face. I don't know why. It's not such a wonderful face. The nose is wrong, and your mouth's wider than Carmel's, and you've got that ridiculous way of looking at people sidewise, like a parrot—"

And she was in his arms, and it was just like a spy drama, except that she hadn't planned the script exactly this way. *This* was to come after—as a reward to Cart for being a sweet, obliging, self-sacrificing boy. She hadn't thought of herself at all, assuming regal stardom. Certainly this pounding of her heart wasn't in the plot—not with Jim caged in a cell six stories above her head and Nora lying in bed across town trying to hold on to something.

His lips were on hers, and he was pressing, pressing.

"Cart. No. Not yet." She pushed. "Darling. Please—"

"You called me darling! Damn it, Pat, how could you play around with me all these months, shoving that Smith fellow in my face—"

"Cart," moaned Pat, "I want to talk to you . . . first."

"I'm sick of talk! Pat, I want you so blamed much—" He kissed her mouth; he kissed the tip of her nose.

"I want to talk to you about Jim, Cart!" cried Pat desperately.

She felt him go cold in one spasm.

He let her go and walked to the wall with the windows that overlooked the Courthouse plaza, to stare out without seeing anything—cars or people or trees or Wrightsville's gray-wash sky.

"What about Jim?" he asked in a flat voice.

"Cart, look at me!" Pat begged.

He turned around. "I can't do it."

"Can't look at me? You are!"

"Can't withdraw from the case. That's why you came here today, isn't it—to ask me?"

Pat sat down again, fumbling for her lipstick. Her lips. Blobbed. Kiss. Her hands were shaking, so she snapped the bag shut. "Yes," she said, very low. "More than that. I wanted you to resign the Prosecutor's office and come over to Jim's defense. Like Judge Eli Martin."

Cart was silent for so long that Pat had to look up at him. He was staring at her with an intense bitterness.

But when he spoke, it was with gentleness. "You can't be serious. The Judge is an old man, your father's closest friend. And he wouldn't have been able to sit on this case, anyway. But I was elected to this office only a short time ago. I took an oath that means something to me. I hate to sound like some stuffed shirt of a politician looking for votes—"

"Oh, but you do!" flared Pat.

"If Jim's innocent, he'll go free. If he's guilty— You wouldn't want him to go free if he's guilty, would you?"

"He's *not* guilty!"

"That's something the jury will have to decide."

"You've decided already! In your own mind, you've condemned him to death!"

"Dakin and I have had to collect the facts, Pat. We've *had* to. Don't you understand that? Our personal feelings can't interfere. We both feel awful about this thing . . ."

Pat was near tears now and angry with herself for showing it. "Doesn't it mean anything to you that Nora's whole life is tied up in this 'thing,' as you call it? That there's a baby coming? I know the trial can't be stopped, but I wanted *you* on our side. I wanted you to help, not hurt!"

Cart ground his teeth together.

"You've said you love me," cried Pat. "How could you love me and still—" Horrified, she heard her own voice break and found herself sobbing. "The whole town's against us. They stoned Jim. They're slinging mud at us. Wrightsville, Cart! A Wright founded this town. We were all born here—not only us kids, but Pop and Muth and Aunt Tabitha and the Bluefields and . . . I'm not the spoiled brat you used to neck in the back of your lizzie at the Grove in Wrightsville Junction on Saturday nights! The whole world's gone to pot, Cart. I've grown old watching it. Oh, Cart, I've no pride left—no defenses. Say you'll help me! I'm afraid!"

She hid her face, giving up the emotional battle. Nothing made any sense—what she'd just said, what she was thinking. Everything was drowning, gasping, struggling in tears.

"Pat," said Cart miserably, "I can't. I just can't."

That did it. She was drowned now, dead, but there was a sort of vicious other-life that made her spring from the chair and scream at him.

"You're nothing but a selfish, scheming politician! You're willing to see Jim die, and Pop, and Mother, and Nora, and me, and everyone suffer, just to further your own career! Oh, this is an *important* case. Dozens of New York and Chicago and Boston reporters to hang on your every word! Your name and photo—Young Public Prosecutor Bradford—brilliant—says this—my duty is—yes—no—off the record . . . You're a hateful, shallow *publicity hound!*"

"I've gone all through this in my mind, Pat," Cart replied with a queer lack of resentment. "I suppose I can't expect you to see it my way—"

Pat laughed. "Insult to injury!"

"If I don't do this job—if I resign or step out—someone else will. Someone who might be a lot less fair to Jim. If I prosecute, Pat, you can be sure Jim will get a square deal—"

She ran out.

And there, on the side of the corridor opposite the Prosecutor's door, waiting patiently, was Mr. Queen.

"Oh, *Ellery!*"

Ellery said gently: "Come home."

# 21

## Vox Pops

"Ave, Caesar!" wrote Roberta Roberts at the head of her column under the dateline of March fifteenth.

> He who is about to be tried for his life finds even the fates against him. Jim Haight's trial begins on the Ides of March before Judge Lysander Newbold in Wright County Courthouse, Part II, Wrightsville, U.S.A. This is chance, or subtlety . . . Kid Vox is popping furiously, and it is the impression of cooler heads that the young man going on trial here for the murder of Rosemary Haight and the attempted murder of Nora Wright Haight is being prepared to make a Roman holiday.

And so it seemed.

From the beginning there was a muttering undertone that was chilling. Chief of Police Dakin expressed himself privately to the persistent press as "mighty relieved" that his prisoner didn't have to be carted through the streets of Wrightsville to reach the place of his inquisition, since the County Jail and the County Courthouse were in the same building.

People were in such an ugly temper you would have imagined their hatred of the alleged poisoner to be inspired by the fiercest loyalty to the Wrights.

But this was odd, because they were equally ugly toward the Wrights. Dakin had to assign two county detectives to escort the family to and from the Courthouse. Even so, jeering boys threw stones, the tires of their cars were slashed mysteriously and the paint scratched with nasty words; seven unsigned letters of the "threat" variety were delivered by a nervous Postman Bailey in one day alone. Silent, John F. Wright turned them over to Dakin's office; and Patrolman Brady himself caught the Old

Soak, Anderson, standing precariously in the middle of the Wright lawn in bright daylight, declaiming not too aptly to the unresponding house Mark Antony's speech from Act III, Scene I of *Julius Caesar*. Charlie Brady hauled Mr. Anderson to the town lockup hastily, while Mr. Anderson kept yelling: "O parm me thou blee'n' piece of earth that I am meek an' zhentle with theshe—hup!—bushers!"

Hermy and John F. began to look beaten. In court, the family sat together, in a sort of phalanx, with stiff necks if pale faces; only occasionally Hermy smiled rather pointedly in the direction of Jim Haight, and then turned to sniff and glare at the jammed courtroom and toss her head, as if to say: "Yes, we're all in this together, you miserable rubbernecks!"

There had been a great deal of mumbling about the impropriety of Carter Bradford's prosecuting the case. In an acid editorial Frank Lloyd put the *Record* on record as "disapproving." True, unlike Judge Eli Martin, Bradford had arrived at the fatal New Year's Eve party *after* the poisoning of Nora and Rosemary, so he was not involved either as participant or as witness. But Lloyd pointed out that "our young, talented, but sometimes emotional Prosecutor has long been friendly with the Wright family, especially one member of it; and although we understand this friendship has ceased as of the night of the crime, we still question the ability of Mr. Bradford to prosecute this case without bias. Something should be done about it."

Interviewed on this point before the opening of the trial, Mr. Bradford snapped: "This isn't Chicago or New York. We have a close-knit community here, where everybody knows everybody else. My conduct during the trial will answer the *Record*'s libelous insinuations. Jim Haight will get from Wright County a forthright, impartial prosecution based solely upon the evidence. That's all, gentlemen!"

Judge Lysander Newbold was an elderly man, a bachelor, greatly respected throughout the state as a jurist and trout fisherman.

He was a square, squat, bony man who always sat on the Bench with his black-fringed skull sunk so deeply between his shoulders that it seemed an outgrowth of his chest.

His voice was dry and careless; he had the habit, when on the Bench, of playing absently with his gavel, as if it were a fishing rod; and he never laughed.

Judge Newbold had no friends, no associates, and no commitments except to God, country, Bench, and the trout season.

Everybody said with a sort of relieved piety that "Judge Newbold is just about the best judge this case could have." Some even thought he was *too* good. But they were the ones who were muttering.

Roberta Roberts baptized these grumblers "the Jimhaighters."

It took several days to select a jury, and during these days Mr. Ellery Queen kept watching only two persons in the courtroom—Judge Eli Martin, defense counsel, and Carter Bradford, Prosecutor.

And it soon became evident that this would be a war between young courage and old experience. Bradford was working under a strain. He held himself in one piece, like a casting; there was a dogged something about him that met the eye with defiance and yet a sort of shame. Ellery saw early that he was competent. He knew his townspeople, too. But he was speaking too quietly, and occasionally his voice cracked.

Judge Martin was superb. He did not make the mistake of patronizing young Bradford, even subtly; that would have swung the people over to the prosecution. Instead, he was most respectful of Bradford's comments. Once, returning to their places from a low-voiced colloquy before Judge Newbold, the old man was seen to put his hand affectionately on Carter's shoulder for just an instant. The gesture said: You're a good boy; we like each other; we are both interested in the same thing—justice; and we are equally matched. This is all very sad, but necessary. The People are in good hands.

The People rather liked it. There were whispers of approval. And some were heard to say: After all, old Eli Martin—he *did* quit his job on the Bench to defend Haight. Can't get around that! Must be pretty convinced Haight's innocent . . . And others replied: Go on. The Judge is John F. Wright's best friend, that's why . . . Well, I don't know . . .

The whole thing was calculated to create an atmosphere of dignity and thoughtfulness, in which the raw emotions of the mob could only gasp for breath and gradually expire.

Mr. Ellery Queen approved.

Mr. Queen approved even more when he finally examined the twelve good men and true. Judge Martin had made the selections as deftly and surely as if there were no Bradford to cope with at all. Solid, sober male citizens, as far as Ellery could determine. None calculated to respond to prejudicial appeals, with one possible exception, a fat man who kept sweating; most seemed anxiously thoughtful men, with higher-than-average intelligence. Men of the decent world, who might be expected to understand that a man can be weak without being criminal.

For students of the particular, the complete court record of *People* vs. *James Haight* is on file in Wright County—day after day after day of question and answer and objection and Judge Newbold's precise rulings. For that matter, the newspapers were almost as exhaustive as the court stenographer's notes.

The difficulty with detailed records, however, is that you cannot see the tree for the leaves.

So let us stand off and make the leaves blur and blend into larger shapes. Let us look at contours, not textures.

In his opening address to the jury, Carter Bradford said that the jury must bear in mind continuously one all-important point: that while Rosemary Haight, the defendant's sister, was murdered by poison, her death was not the true object of defendant's crime. The true object of defendant's crime was to take the life of defendant's young wife, Nora Wright Haight—an object so nearly accomplished that the wife was confined to her bed for six weeks after the fateful New Year's Eve party, a victim of arsenic poisoning.

And yes, the State freely admits that its case against James Haight is circumstantial, but murder convictions on circumstantial evidence are the rule, not the exception. The only direct evidence possible in a murder case is an eyewitness's testimony as to having witnessed the murder at the moment of its commission. In a shooting case, this would have to be a witness who actually saw the accused pull the trigger and the victim fall dead as a result of the shot. In a poisoning case, it would have to be a witness who actually saw the accused deposit poison in the food or drink to be swallowed by the victim and, moreover, who saw the accused hand the poisoned food or drink *to* the victim.

Obviously, continued Bradford, such "happy accidents" of persons witnessing the Actual Deed must be few and far between, since murderers understandably try to avoid committing their murders before an audience. Therefore nearly all prosecutions of murder are based on circumstantial rather than direct evidence; the law has wisely provided for the admission of such evidence, otherwise most murderers would go unpunished.

But the jury need not flounder in doubts about *this* case; here the circumstantial evidence is so clear, so strong, so indisputable, that the jury must find James Haight guilty of the crime as charged beyond any reasonable doubt whatsoever.

"The People will prove," said Bradford in a low, firm tone, "that James Haight planned the murder of his wife a minimum of five weeks before he tried to accomplish it; that it was a cunning plan, depending upon a series of poisonings of increasing severity to establish the wife as subject to attacks of 'illness,' and supposed to culminate in a climactic poisoning as a result of which the wife was to die.

"The People will prove," Bradford went on, "that these preliminary poisonings did take place on the very dates indicated by the schedule James Haight had prepared with his own hand; that the attempted murder of Nora Haight and the accidental murder of Rosemary Haight did take place on the very date indicated by that same schedule.

"The People will prove that on the night under examination, James Haight and James Haight alone mixed the batch of cocktails among whose number was the poisoned cocktail; that James Haight and James Haight alone handed the tray of cocktails around to the various members of the party; that James Haight and James Haight alone handed his wife the poisoned cocktail from the tray and even urged her to drink it; that she did drink of that cocktail and fell violently ill of arsenic poisoning, her life being spared only because at Rosemary Haight's insistence she gave the rest of the poisoned cocktail to her sister-in-law after having merely sipped . . . a circumstance James Haight couldn't have foreseen.

"The People will prove," Bradford went on quietly, "that James Haight was in desperate need of money; that he demanded large sums of money of his wife while under the influence of liquor, and sensibly, she refused; that James Haight was losing large sums of money gambling; that he was taking other illicit means of procuring money; that upon Nora Haight's death her estate, a large one as the result of an inheritance, would legally fall to the defendant, who is her husband and heir-at-law.

"The People," concluded Bradford in a tone so low he could scarcely be heard, "being convinced beyond reasonable doubt that James Haight did so plan and attempt the life of one person in attempting which he succeeded in taking the life of another, an innocent victim—the People demand that James Haight pay with his own life for the life taken and the life so nearly taken."

And Carter Bradford sat down to spontaneous applause, which caused the first of Judge Newbold's numerous subsequent warnings to the spectators.

In that long dreary body of testimony calculated to prove Jim Haight's sole Opportunity, the only colorful spots were provided by Judge Eli Martin in cross-examination.

From the first the old lawyer's plan was plain to Ellery: to cast doubt, doubt, doubt. Not heatedly. With cool humor. The voice of reason . . . Insinuate. Imply. Get away with whatever you can and to hell with the rules of cross-examination.

Ellery realized that Judge Martin was desperate.

"But you can't be *sure?*"

"N-no."

"You didn't have the defendant under observation *every moment?*"

"Of course not!"

"The defendant *might* have laid the tray of cocktails down for a moment or so?"

"No."

"Are you *positive?*"

Carter Bradford quietly objects: the question was answered. Sustained. Judge Newbold waves his hand patiently.

"Did you *see* the defendant prepare the cocktails?"

"No."

"Were you in the living room *all* the time?"

"You know I was!" This was Frank Lloyd, and he was angry. To Frank Lloyd, Judge Martin paid especial attention. The old gentleman wormed out of the newspaper publisher his relationship with the Wright family — his "peculiar" relationship with the defendant's wife. He had been in love with her. He had been bitter when she turned him down for James Haight. He had threatened James Haight with bodily violence. Objection, objection, objection. But it managed to come out, enough of it to reawaken in the jury's minds the whole story of Frank Lloyd and Nora Wright — after all, that story was an old one to Wrightsville, and everybody knew the details!

So Frank Lloyd became a poor witness for the People; and there was a doubt, a doubt. The vengeful jilted "other" man. Who knows? Maybe —

With the Wright family, who were forced to take the stand to testify to the actual events of the night, Judge Martin was impersonal — and cast more doubts. On the "facts." Nobody actually *saw* Jim Haight drop arsenic into the cocktail. Nobody could be *sure* . . . of anything.

But the prosecution's case proceeded, and despite Judge Martin's wily obstructions, Bradford established: that Jim alone mixed the cocktails; that Jim was the only one who could have been certain the poisoned cocktail went to Nora, his intended victim, since he handed each drinker his or her cocktail; that Jim pressed Nora to drink when she was reluctant.

And the testimony of old Wentworth, who had been the attorney for John F.'s father. Wentworth had drawn the dead man's will. Wentworth testified that on Nora's marriage she received her grandfather's bequest of a hundred thousand dollars, held in trust for her until that "happy" event.

And the testimony of the five handwriting experts, who agreed unanimously, despite the most vigorous cross-examination by Judge Martin, that the three unmailed letters addressed to Rosemary Haight, dated Thanksgiving, Christmas, and New Year's, and announcing far in advance of those dates the "illnesses" of Nora Haight, the third actually an-nouncing her "death"—agreed unanimously that these damning letters were in the handwriting of the defendant, beyond any doubt whatever. For several days the trial limped and lagged while huge charts were set up in the courtroom and Judge Martin, who had obviously boned up, de-bated the finer points of handwriting analysis with the experts . . . unsuc-cessfully.

Then came Alberta Manaskas, who turned out a staunch defender of the public weal. Alberta evinced an unsuspected volubility. And, to judge from her testimony, her eyes, which had always seemed dull, were sharper than a cosmic ray; and her ears, which had merely seemed large and red, were more sensitive than a photoelectric cell.

It was through Alberta that Carter Bradford brought out how, as the first letter had predicted, Nora took sick on Thanksgiving Day; how Nora had another, and worse, attack of "sickness" on Christmas Day. Alberta went into clinical detail about these "sicknesses."

Judge Martin rose to his opportunity.

Sickness, Alberta? Now what kind of sickness would you say Miss Nora had on Thanksgiving and Christmas?

Sick! Like in her belly. *(Laughter.)*

Have *you* ever been sick like in your—uh—belly, Alberta?

Sure! You, me, everyone. *(Judge Newbold raps for order.)* Like Miss Nora?

Sure!

*(Gently)*: *You've* never been poisoned by arsenic, though, have you, Alberta?

Bradford, on his feet.

Judge Martin sat down smiling. Mr. Queen noticed the sweat fringing his forehead.


Dr. Milo Willoughby's testimony, confirmed by the testimony of Coroner Chic Salemson and the testimony of L. D. ("Whitey") Magill, State Chemist, established that the toxic agent which had made Nora Haight ill, and caused the death of Rosemary Haight, was arsenious acid, or arsenic trioxid, or arsenious oxid, or simply "white arsenic"—all names for the same deadly substance.

Henceforth prosecutor and defense counsel referred to it simply as "arsenic."

Dr. Magill described the substance as "colorless, tasteless, and odor-less in solution and of a high degree of toxicity."

Q. *(by Prosecutor Bradford)*—It is a powder, Dr. Magill?

A.—Yes, sir.

*Q.*—Would it dissolve in a cocktail or lose any of its effectiveness if taken that way?

*A.*—Arsenic trioxid is very slightly soluble in alcohol, but since a cocktail is greatly aqueous, it will dissolve quite readily. It is soluble in water, you see. No, it would lose none of its toxicity in alcohol.

*Q.*—Thank you, Dr. Magill. Your witness, Judge Martin.

Judge Martin waives cross-examination.

Prosecutor Bradford calls to the stand Myron Garback, proprietor of the High Village Pharmacy, Wrightsville.

Mr. Garback has a cold; his nose is red and swollen. He sneezes frequently and fidgets in the witness chair. From the audience Mrs. Garback, a pale Irishwoman, watches her husband anxiously.

Being duly sworn, Myron Garback testifies that "sometime" during October of 1940—the previous October—James Haight had entered the High Village Pharmacy and asked for "a small tin of Quicko."

*Q.*—What exactly is Quicko, Mr. Garback?

*A.*—It is a preparation used for the extermination of rodents and insect pests.

*Q.*—What is the lethal ingredient of Quicko?

*A.*—Arsenic trioxid. *(Sneeze. Laughter. Gavel.)*

Mrs. Garback turns crimson and glares balefully about.

*Q.*—In highly concentrated form?

*A.*—Yes, sir.

*Q.*—Did you sell the defendant a tin of this poisonous preparation, Mr. Garback?

*A.*—Yes, sir. It is a commercial preparation, requiring no prescription.

*Q.*—Did the defendant ever return to purchase more Quicko?

*A.*—Yes, sir, about two weeks later. He said he'd mislaid the can of stuff, so he'd have to buy a new can. I sold him a new can.

*Q.*—Did the defendant— I'll rephrase the question. What did the defendant say to you, and what did you say to the defendant, on the occasion of his first purchase?

*A.*—Mr. Haight said there were mice in his house, and he wanted to kill them off. I said I was surprised, because I'd never heard of house mice up on the Hill. He didn't say anything to that.

Cross-examination by Judge Eli Martin:

*Q.*—Mr. Garback, how many tins of Quicko would you estimate you sold during the month of October last?

*A.*—That's hard to answer. A lot. It's my best-selling rat-killer, and Low Village is infested.

*Q.*—Twenty-five? Fifty?

*A.*—Somewhere around there.

*Q.*—Then it's not unusual for customers to buy this poisonous preparation—purely to kill rats?

*A.*—No, sir, not unusual at all.

*Q.*—Then how is it you remembered that Mr. Haight purchased
some—remembered it *for five months?*

*A.*—It just stuck in my mind. Maybe because he bought two tins so
close together, and it was the Hill.

*Q.*—You're positive it was two cans, two weeks apart?

*A.*—Yes, sir. I wouldn't say it if I wasn't.

*Q.*—No comments, please; just answer the question. Mr. Garback, do
you keep records of your Quicko sales, listed by customer?

*A.*—I don't have to, Judge. It's legal to sell—

*Q.*—Answer the question, Mr. Garback. Have you a written record of
James Haight's alleged purchases of Quicko?

*A.*—No, sir, but—

*Q.*—Then we just have your word, relying on your memory of two incidents you allege to have occurred five months ago, that the defendant
purchased Quicko from you?

*Prosecutor Bradford:* Your Honor, the witness is under oath. He has
answered Counsel's question not once, but several times. Objection.

*Judge Newbold:* It seems to me witness has answered, Judge. Sustained.

*Q.*—That's all, thank you, Mr. Garback.

Alberta Manaskas is recalled to the stand. Questioned by Mr. Bradford, she testifies that she "never seen no rats in Miss Nora's house." She
further testifies that she "never seen no rat-killer, neither."

On cross-examination, Judge Martin asks Alberta Manaskas if it is not
true that in the tool chest in the cellar of the Haight house there is a large
rat trap.

*A.*—Is there?

*Q.*—That's what I'm asking you, Alberta.

*A.*—I guess there is, at that.

*Q.*—If there are no rats, Alberta, why do you suppose the Haights
keep a rat trap?

*Prosecutor Bradford:* Objection. Calling for opinion.

*Judge Newbold:* Sustained. Counsel, I'll have to ask you to restrict
your cross-examination to—

*Judge Martin (humbly):* Yes, Your Honor.

\* \* \*

Emmeline DuPré, under oath, testifies that she is a Dramatic and Dancing Teacher residing at Number 468 Hill Drive, Wrightsville, "right next door to Nora Wright's house."

Witness testifies that during the previous November and December she "happened to overhear" frequent quarrels between Nora and James Haight. The quarrels were about Mr. Haight's heavy drinking and numerous demands for money. There was one markedly violent quarrel, in December, when Miss DuPré heard Nora Haight refuse to give her husband "any more money." Did Miss DuPré "happen to overhear" anything to indicate why the defendant needed so much money?

*A.*—That's what shocked me so, Mr. Bradford—

*Q.*—The Court is not interested in your emotional reactions, Miss DuPré. Answer the question, please.

*A.*—Jim Haight admitted he'd been gambling and losing plenty; and that's why he needed money, he said.

*Q.*—Was any name or place mentioned by either Mr. or Mrs. Haight in connection with the defendant's gambling?

*A.*—Jim Haight said he'd been losing a lot at the *Hot Spot*, that scandalous place on Route 16—

*Judge Martin:* Your Honor, I move that this witness's entire testimony be stricken out. I have no objection to give-and-take in this trial. Mr. Bradford has been extremely patient with me, and it is an admittedly difficult case, being so vaguely circumstantial—

*Mr. Bradford:* May I ask Counsel to restrict his remarks to his objection and stop trying to influence the jury by characterizing the case?

*Judge Newbold:* The Prosecutor is right, Counsel. Now what is your objection to this witness's testimony?

*Judge Martin:* No attempt has been made by the People to fix the times and circumstances under which witness allegedly overheard conversations between defendant and wife. Admittedly witness was not present in the same room or even in the same house. How, then, did she "overhear"? How can she be sure the two people *were* the defendant and his wife? Did she see them? Didn't she see them? I hold—

*Miss DuPré:* But I heard all this with my own ears!

*Judge Newbold:* Miss DuPré! Yes, Mr. Bradford?

*Mr. Bradford:* The People have put Miss DuPré on the stand in an effort to spare defendant's wife the pain of testifying to the quarrels—

*Judge Martin:* That's not my point.

*Judge Newbold:* No, it is not. Nevertheless, Counsel, I suggest you cover your point in cross-examination. Objection denied. Proceed, Mr. Bradford.

Mr. Bradford proceeds, eliciting further testimony as to quarrels be-

tween Jim and Nora. On cross-examination, Judge Martin reduces Miss
DuPré to indignant tears. He brings out her physical position relative to
the conversationalists—crouched by her bedroom window in darkness
listening to the voices floating warmly across the driveway between her
house and the Haight house—confuses her in the matter of dates and
times involved, so that she clearly contradicts herself several times.

The spectators enjoy themselves.

Under oath, J. P. Simpson, proprietor of Simpson's Pawnshop in the
Square, Wrightsville, testifies that in November and December last,
James Haight pledged various items of jewelry at Simpson's Pawnshop.

*Q.*—What kind of jewelry, Mr. Simpson?

*A.*—First one was a man's gold watch—he took it off his chain to
pawn it. Nice merchandise. Fair price—

*Q.*—Is this the watch?

*A.*—Yes, sir. I remember givin' him a fair price—

*Q.*—Placed in evidence.

*Clerk:* People's exhibit thirty-one.

*Q.*—Will you read the inscription on the watch, Mr. Simpson?

*A.*—The what? Oh. "To—Jim—from—Nora."

*Q.*—What else did the defendant pawn, Mr. Simpson?

*A.*—Gold and platinum rings, a cameo brooch, and so on. All good
merchandise. Very good loan merchandise.

*Q.*—Do you recognize these items of jewelry I now show you, Mr.
Simpson?

*A.*—Yes, sir. They're the ones he pawned with me. Gave him mighty
fair prices—

*Q.*—Never mind what you gave him. These last items are all women's
jewelry, are they not?

*A.*—That's right.

*Q.*—Read the various inscriptions. Aloud.

*A.*—Wait till I fix my specs. "N.W."—"N.W."—"N.W.H."—"N.W."

Nora's jewelry is placed in evidence.

*Q.*—One last question, Mr. Simpson. Did the defendant ever redeem
any of the objects he pawned with you?

*A.*—No, sir. He just kept bringing me new stuff, one at a time, an' I
kept givin' him fair prices for 'em.

Judge Martin waives cross-examination.

Donald Mackenzie, President of the Wrightsville Personal Finance
Corporation, being duly sworn, testifies that James Haight had borrowed

considerable sums from the PFC during the last two months of the preceding year.

*Q.* — On what collateral, Mr. Mackenzie?

*A.* — None.

*Q.* — Isn't this unusual for your firm, Mr. Mackenzie? To lend money without collateral?

*A.* — Well, the PFC has a *very* liberal loan policy, but of course we usually ask for collateral. Just business, you understand. Only, since Mr. Haight was Vice-President of the Wrightsville National Bank and the son-in-law of John Fowler Wright, the company made an exception in his case and advanced the loans on signature only.

*Q.* — Has the defendant made any payments against his indebtedness, Mr. Mackenzie?

*A.* — Well, no.

*Q.* — Has your company made any effort to collect the moneys due, Mr. Mackenzie?

*A.* — Well, yes. Not that we were worried, but— Well, it was five thousand dollars, and after asking Mr. Haight several times to make his stipulated payments and getting no satisfaction, we—I finally went to the bank to see Mr. Wright, Mr. Haight's father-in-law, and explained the situation, and Mr. Wright said he hadn't known about his son-in-law's loan, but of course he'd make it good himself, and I wasn't to say anything about it—to keep it confidential. I would have, too, only this trial and all—

*Judge Martin:* Objection. Incompetent, irrelevant—

*Q.* — Never mind that, Mr. Mackenzie. Did John F. Wright repay your company the loan in full?

*A.* — Principal and interest. Yes, sir.

*Q.* — Has the defendant borrowed any money since January the first of this year?

*A.* — No, sir.

*Q.* — Have you had any conversations with the defendant since January the first of this year?

*A.* — Yes. Mr. Haight came in to see me in the middle of January and started to explain why he hadn't paid anything on his loan—said he'd made some bad investments—asked for more time and said he'd surely pay back his debt. I said to him that his father-in-law'd already done that.

*Q.* — What did the defendant say to that?

*A.* — He didn't say a word. He just walked out of my office.

Judge Martin cross-examines.

*Q.* — Mr. Mackenzie, didn't it strike you as strange that the Vice-President of a banking institution like the Wrightsville National Bank, and the son-in-law of the President of that bank, should come to *you* for a loan?

*A.* — Well, I guess it did. Only I figured it was a confidential matter, you see —

*Q.* — In a confidential matter, without explanations or collateral, on a mere signature, you still advanced the sum of five thousand dollars?

*A.* — Well, I knew old John F. would make good if —

*Mr. Bradford:* Your Honor —

*Judge Martin:* That's all, Mr. Mackenzie.

Not all the evidence against Jim Haight came out in the courtroom.

Some of it came out in Vic Carlatti's, some in the Hollis Hotel Tonsorial Parlor, some in Dr. Emil Poffenberger's dental office in the Upham Block, some in Gus Olesen's *Roadside Tavern*, and at least one colorful fact was elicited from the bibulous Mr. Anderson by a New York reporter, the scene of the interview being the pedestal of the Low Village World War Memorial, on which Mr. Anderson happened to be stretched out at the time.

Emmeline DuPré heard the Luigi Marino story through Tessie Lupin. Miss DuPré was having her permanent done in the Lower Main Beauty Shop where Tessie worked, and Tessie had just had lunch with her husband, Joe, who was one of Luigi Marino's barbers. Joe had told Tessie, and Tessie had told Emmy DuPré, and Emmy DuPré . . .

Then the town began to hear the other stories, and old recollections were raked over for black and shining dirt. And when it was all put together, Wrightsville began to say: Now there's something funny going on. Do you suppose Frank Lloyd was right about Carter Bradford's being the Wrights' friend and all? Why doesn't he put Luigi and Dr. Poffenberger on the stand? And Gus Olesen? And the others? Why, this all makes it plain as day that Jim Haight wanted to kill Nora! He *threatened* her all over town!

Chief Dakin was tackled by Luigi Marino before court opened one morning when the Chief came in for a quick shave. Joe Lupin listened from the next chair with both hairy ears.

"Say, Chefe!" said Luigi in great excitement. "I been lookin' all over for-a you! I just remember something hot!"

"Yeah, Luigi? Once over, and take it easy."

"Las' Novemb'. Jim-a Haight, he come in here one day for I should cut-a his hair. I say to Mist' Haight, 'Mist' Haight, I feel-a fine. You know what? I'm-a gonna get hitched!' Mist' Haight he say that's-a good, who's-a the lucky gal? I say: 'Francesca Botigliano. I know Francesca from the ol' countree. She been workin' by Saint-a Louey, but I proposea in a lett' an' now Francesca she's-a comin' to Wrights-a-ville to be Mrs. Marino—I send-a her the ticket an' expense-a mon' myself. Ain't that something?' You remember I get-a married, Chefe . . ."

"Sure, Luigi. Hey, take it easy!"

"So what-a does Mist' Haight say? He say: 'Luigi, nev' marry a poor gal! There ain't-a no per-cent-age in it!' You see? He marry that-a gal Nora Wright for her mon'! You get-a Mist' Bradford put me on-a stand. I'll tell-a dat story!"

Chief Dakin laughed.

But Wrightsville did not. To Wrightsville it seemed logical that Luigi's story should be part of the trial testimony. It would show that he married Nora Wright for her money. If a man would marry a woman for her money, he'd poison her for it, too . . . Those ladies of Wrightsville who were so unfortunate as to have lawyers in the family heard a few pointed remarks about "admissible" testimony.

Dr. Poffenberger had actually gone to Prosecutor Bradford before the trial and offered to testify.

"Why, Haight came to me last December, Cart, suffering from an abscessed wisdom tooth. I gave him gas, and while he was under the influence of the gas, he kept saying: 'I'll get rid of her! I'll get rid of her!' And then he said: 'I need that money for myself. I want that money for myself!' Doesn't that prove he was planning to kill her and why?"

"No," said Bradford wearily. "Unconscious utterances. Inadmissible testimony. Go way, Emil, and let me work, will you?"

Dr. Poffenberger was indignant. He repeated the story to as many of his patients as would listen, which was practically all of them.

Gus Olesen's story reached the Prosecutor's ears by way of Patrolman Chris Dorfman, Radio Division (one car). Patrolman Chris Dorfman had "happened" to drop into Gus Olesen's place for a "coke" (*he* said), and Gus, "all het up," had told him what Jim Haight had once said to him, Gus, on the occasion of a "spree." And now Patrolman Chris Dorfman was all het up, for he had been wondering for weeks how he could muscle into the trial and take the stand and get into the papers.

"Just what is it Haight is supposed to have said, Chris?" asked Prosecutor Bradford.

"Well, Gus says Jim Haight a couple of times drove up to the *Tavern* cockeyed and wanting a drink, and Gus says he'd always turn him down. Once he even called up Mrs. Haight and asked her to come down and get her husband, he was raisin' Cain, plastered to the ears. But the thing Gus remembers that I think you ought to get into your trial, Mr. Bradford, is when one night Haight was in there, drunk, and he kept ravin' about wives, and marriage, and how lousy it all was, and then he said: 'Nothin' to do but get rid of her, Gus. I gotta get rid of her quick, or I'll go nuts. She's drivin' me nuts!' "

"Statements under the influence of liquor," groaned Cart. "Highly questionable. Do you want me to lose this case on reversible error? Go back to your radio car!"

Mr. Anderson's story was simplicity itself. With dignity he told the New York reporter: "Sir, Mr. Haight an' I have quaffed the purple flagon on many an occasion together. Kindred spirits, you understand. We would meet in the Square an' embrace. Well do I recall that eventful evening in 'dark December,' when 'in this our pinching cave,' we discoursed 'the freezing hours away'! *Cymbeline*, sir; a much-neglected masterwork . . ."

"We wander," said the reporter. "What happened?"

"Well, sir, Mr. Haight put his arms about me and he said, Quote: 'I'm going to kill her, Andy. See 'f I don't! I'm going to kill her dead!' "

"Wow," said the reporter, and left Mr. Anderson to go back to sleep on the pedestal of the Low Village World War Memorial.

But this luscious morsel, too, Prosecutor Bradford refused; and Wrightsville muttered that there was "something phony," and buzzed and buzzed and buzzed.

The rumors reached Judge Lysander Newbold's ears. From that day on, at the end of each court session, he sternly admonished the jury not to discuss the case with anyone, not even among themselves.

It was thought that Eli Martin had something to do with calling the rumors to Judge Newbold's attention. For Judge Martin was beginning to look harried, particularly in the mornings, after breakfast with his wife. Clarice, who served in her own peculiar way, was his barometer for readings of the temper of Wrightsville. So a fury began to creep into the courtroom, and it mounted and flew back and forth between the old lawyer and Carter Bradford until the press began to nudge one another with wise looks and say "the old boy is cracking."

Thomas Winship, head cashier of the Wrightsville National Bank, testified that James Haight had always used a thin red crayon in his work at the bank, and produced numerous documents from the files of the bank, signed by Haight in red crayon.

The last exhibit placed in evidence by Bradford—a shrewd piece of timing—was the volume Edgcomb's *Toxicology*, with its telltale section marked in red crayon . . . the section dealing with arsenic.

This exhibit passed from hand to hand in the jury box, while Judge Martin looked "confident" and James Haight, by the old lawyer's side at the defense table, grew very pale and was seen to glance about quickly, as if seeking escape. But the moment passed, and thenceforward he behaved as before—silent, limp in his chair, his gray face almost bored.

At the close of Friday's session, March the twenty-eighth, Prosecutor Bradford indicated that he "might be close to finished," but that he would know better when court convened the following Monday morning. He thought it likely the People would rest on Monday.

There was an interminable conversation before the Bench, and then Judge Newbold called a recess until Monday morning, March the thirty-first.

The prisoner was taken back to his cell on the top floor of the Courthouse, the courtroom emptied, and the Wrights simply went home. There was nothing to do but wait for Monday . . . and try to cheer Nora up.

Nora lay on the chaise longue in her pretty bedroom, plucking the roses of her chintz window drapes. Hermy had refused to let her attend the trial; and after two days of tears, Nora had stopped fighting, exhausted.

She just plucked the roses from the drapes.

But another thing happened on Friday, March the twenty-eighth. Roberta Roberts lost her job.

The newspaperwoman had maintained her stubborn defense of Jim Haight in her column throughout the trial—the only reporter there who had not already condemned "God's silent man," as one of the journalistic wits had dubbed him, to death.

On Friday, Roberta received a wire from Boris Connell in Chicago, notifying her that he was "yanking the column."

Roberta telegraphed a Chicago attorney to bring suit against News & Features Syndicate.

But on Saturday morning there was no column.

"What are you going to do now?" asked Ellery Queen.

"Stay on in Wrightsville. I'm one of those pesky females who never give up. I can still do Jim Haight some good."

She spent the whole of Saturday morning in Jim's cell, urging him to speak up, to fight back, to strike a blow in his own defense. Judge Martin was there, quite pursy-lipped, and Ellery; they heard Roberta's vigorous plea in silence.

But Jim merely shook his head or made no answering gesture at all—a figure bowed, three-quarters dead, pickled in some strange formaldehyde of his own manufacture.

# 22

## Council of War

The whole weekend stood between them and Monday. So on Saturday night Nora invited Roberta Roberts and Judge Eli Martin to dinner to "talk things over" with the family.

Hermione wanted Nora to stay in bed, because of her "condition"; but Nora said: "Oh, Mother, it will do me lots more good to be up on my feet and going through some motions!" So Hermy wisely did not press the point.

Nora was beginning to thicken noticeably about the waist; her cheeks were puffy and unhealthy-looking suddenly, and she walked about the house as if her legs were stuffed with lead. When Hermione questioned Dr. Willoughby anxiously, he said that "Nora's getting along about as well as we can expect, Hermy." Hermy didn't dare ask him any more questions. But she rarely left Nora's side, and she would go white if she saw Nora try to lift so much as a long biography.

After dinner, which was tasteless and uneasy, they all went into the living room. Ludie had tightly flapped the blinds and lit a fire.

They sat before it with the uncomfortable stiffness of people who know they should say something but cannot think of what. There was no solace anywhere, not even in the friendly flames. It was impossible to relax — Nora was too much there.

"Mr. Smith, you haven't said much tonight," remarked Roberta Roberts at last.

Nora looked at Ellery beseechingly, but he avoided her eyes.

"There hasn't been too much to say, has there?"

"No," the newspaperwoman murmured. "I suppose not."

"As I see the problem before us, it's not intellectual or emotional, but legal. Faith isn't going to acquit Jim, although it may bolster his spirits. Only facts can get him off."

"And there aren't any!" cried Nora.

"Nora dearest," moaned Hermy, "please. You heard what Dr. Willoughby said about getting upset."

"I know, Mother, I know." Nora glanced eagerly at Judge Eli Martin, whose long fingers were bridged before his nose as he glowered at the fire. "How does it look, Uncle Eli?"

"I wouldn't want to deceive you, Nora." The old jurist shook his head. "It looks just as bad as it possibly can."

"You mean Jim hasn't got a chance?" she wailed.

"There's always a chance, Nora," said Roberta Roberts.

"Yes," sighed the Judge. "You can never tell about a jury."

"If there was only something we could *do*," said Hermy helplessly.

John F. burrowed more deeply into his smoking jacket.

"Oh, you people!" cried Lola Wright. "Moaning the blues! I'm sick of this sitting around, wringing our hands—" Lola flung her cigarette into the flames with disgust.

"So am I," said Pat between her teeth. "Sick as the devil."

"Patricia darling," said Hermy, "I'm sure you'd better stay out of this discussion."

"Of course, Momsy," said Lola with a grimace. "*Your* baby. You'll never see Pat as anything but a long-legged brat who wouldn't drink her nice milk and kept climbing Emmy DuPré's cherry tree!"

Pat shrugged. Mr. Ellery Queen regarded her with suspicion. Miss Patricia Wright had been acting peculiarly since Thursday. Too quiet. Over-thoughtful for a healthy extrovert. As if she were brewing something in that fetching skull-pan of hers. He started to say something to her but lit a cigarette instead. The Gold Rush of '49, he thought, started with a battered pan in a muddy trickle of water. Who knows where the Fact may be found?

"Ellery, what *do* you think?" pleaded Nora.

"Ellery's been mulling over the case looking for a loophole," Pat explained to Judge Martin.

"Not legally," Ellery hastened to explain as the Judge's brows went up. "But I've been handling crime facts so long in fiction that I've—uh—acquired a certain dexterity in handling them in real life."

"If you juggle *these* with any success," growled the old lawyer, "you're a magician."

"Isn't there *anything?*" Nora cried.

"Let's face it, Nora," said Ellery grimly. "Jim's in a hopeless position. You'd better prepare yourself . . . I've gone over the whole case. I've sifted every grain of evidence in the hopper. I've weighed every known fact. I've reexamined each incident a dozen times. And I haven't found a loophole. There's never been so one-sided a case against a defendant. Carter Bradford and Chief Dakin have built a giant, and it will take a miracle to topple it over."

"And I," said Judge Eli dryly, "am no Goliath."

"Oh, I'm prepared all right," said Nora with a bitter laugh. She twisted about violently in her chair and dropped her face on her arms.

"Sudden movements!" said Hermy in an alarmed voice. "Nora, you've *got* to be careful!" Nora nodded without raising her head.

And silence entered, to fill the room to bursting.

"Look here," said Ellery at last. He was a black man against the flames. "Miss Roberts, I want to know something."

The newspaperwoman said slowly: "Yes, Mr. Smith?"

"You've lost your column because you chose to buck public opinion and fight for Jim Haight."

"This is still a free country, thank God," said Roberta lightly. But she was sitting very still.

"Why have you taken such a remarkable interest in this case—even to the point of sacrificing your job?"

"I happen to believe Jim Haight is innocent."

"In the face of all the evidence against him?"

She smiled. "I'm a woman. I'm psychic. That's two reasons."

"No," said Ellery.

Roberta got to her feet. "I'm not sure I like that," she said clearly. "What are you trying to say?"

The others were frowning. There was a something in the room that crackled more loudly than the burning logs.

"It's too beautiful," mocked Mr. Queen. "Too, too beautiful. Hard-boiled newspaperwoman renounces livelihood to defend total stranger who—all the facts and all the world agree—is guilty as Cain. There's an excuse for Nora—she's in love with the man. There's an excuse for the Wrights—they want their son-in-law cleared for the sake of their daughter and grandchild. But what's yours?"

"I've told you!"

"I don't believe you."

"You don't. What am I supposed to do—care?"

"Miss Roberts," said Ellery in a hard voice, "what are you concealing?"

"I refuse to submit to this third degree."

"Sorry! But it's plain you do know something. You've known something from the time you came to Wrightsville. What you know has *forced* you to come to Jim's defense. *What is it?*"

The newspaperwoman gathered her gloves and silver-fox coat and bag. "There are times, Mr. Smith," she said, "when I dislike you very much . . . No, please, Mrs. Wright. Don't bother." She went out with a quick step.

Mr. Queen stared at the space she had just vacated. "I thought," he said apologetically, "I might be able to irritate it out of her."

"I think," said Judge Martin reflectively, "I'll have a heart-to-heart talk with that female."

Ellery shrugged. "Lola."

"Me?" said Lola, surprised. "What did I do, teacher?"

"You've concealed something, too."

Lola stared. Then she laughed and lit a cigarette. "You *are* in a Scotland Yard mood tonight, aren't you?"

"Don't you think the time has come," smiled Mr. Queen, "to tell Judge Martin about your visit to the back door of Nora's house just before midnight New Year's Eve?"

"Lola!" gasped Hermy. "You were *there?*"

"Oh, it's nothing at all, Mother," said Lola impatiently. "It hasn't a thing to do with the case. Of course, Judge, I'll tell you. But as long as we're being constructive, how about the eminent Mr. Smith getting to work?"

"At what?" asked the eminent Mr. Smith.

"My dear Smarty-Pants, you know a lot more than you've let on!"

"Lola," said Nora, in despair. "Oh, all this wrangling—"

"Don't you think," cried Pat, "that if there were something Ellery could do, he'd do it?"

"I dunno," said Lola critically, squinting at the culprit through her cigarette smoke. "He's a tough 'un to figure."

"Just a minute," said Judge Martin. "Smith, if you know anything at all, I want to put you on the stand!"

"If I thought going on the stand for you would help, Judge," protested Ellery, "I'd do it. But it won't. On the contrary, it would hurt—a lot."

"Hurt Jim's case?"

"It would just about cement his conviction."

John F. spoke for the first time. "You mean you *know* Jim is guilty, young man?"

"I didn't say that," growled Ellery. "But my testimony would make things look so black against him—it would establish so clearly that no one but Jim could have poisoned that cocktail—that you wouldn't be able to shake it with the Supreme Court to help you. *I mustn't take the stand.*"

"Mr. Smith."

Chief Dakin, alone . . .

"Sorry to bust in this way, folks," said the police chief gruffly, "but this was one subpoena I had to serve myself."

"Subpoena? On me?" asked Ellery.

"Yes, sir. Mr. Smith, you're summoned to appear in court Monday morning to testify for the People in the case of People Against James Haight."

# PART FIVE

# 23

## Lola and the Check

"I got one, too," murmured Lola to Ellery Queen in the courtroom Monday morning.

"Got one what?"

"A summons to testify today for the beloved People."

"Strange," muttered Mr. Queen.

"The pup's got something up his sleeve," said Judge Martin. "And what's J.C. doing in court?"

"Who?" Ellery looked about.

"J. C. Pettigrew, the real-estate man. There's Bradford whispering to him. J.C. can't know anything about this case."

Lola said in a strangled voice: "Oh, nuts," and they stared at her. She was very pale.

"What's the matter, Lola?" asked Pat.

"Nothing. I'm sure it can't possibly—"

"Here's Newbold," said Judge Martin, hastily standing up. "Remember, Lola, just answer Carter's questions. Don't volunteer information. Maybe," he whispered grimly as the bailiff shouted to the courtroom to rise, "maybe I've got a trick or two myself on cross-examination!"

J. C. Pettigrew sat down in the witness chair shaking and swabbing his face with a blue polka-dot handkerchief, such as the farmers around Wrightsville use.

Yes, his name is J. C. Pettigrew, he is in the real-estate business in Wrightsville, he's been a friend of the Wrights for many years—his daughter Carmel is Patricia Wright's best friend.

(Patricia Wright compresses her lips. Her "best friend" has not telephoned since January first.)

There was an aqueous triumph about Carter Bradford this morning.

His own brow was slick with perspiration, and he and J.C. kept up a duet of handkerchiefs.

*Q.*—I hand you this canceled check, Mr. Pettigrew. Do you recognize it?

*A.*—Yep.

*Q.*—Read what it says.

*A.*—The date—December thirty-first, nineteen-forty. Then it says: Pay to the order of cash, one hundred dollars. Signed J. C. Pettigrew.

*Q.*—Did you make out this check, Mr. Pettigrew?

*A.*—I did.

*Q.*—On the date specified—the last day of last year, the day of New Year's Eve?

*A.*—Yes, sir.

*Q.*—To whom did you give this check, Mr. Pettigrew?

*A.*—To Lola Wright.

*Q.*—Tell us the circumstances of your giving Miss Lola Wright this check for a hundred dollars, please.

*A.*—I sort of feel funny about . . . I mean, I can't help if . . . Well, last day of the year, I was just cleaning up at my office in High Village when Lola come in. Said she was in a bad spot, and she'd known me all her life, and could I let her have a hundred dollars. I saw she was worried—

*Q.*—Just tell us what she said and you said.

*A.*—Well, that's all, I guess. I gave it to her. Oh, yes. She asked for cash. I said I didn't have any cash to spare, and it was past banking hours, so I'd give her a check. She said: "Well, if it can't be helped, it can't be helped." So I made out a check, she said thanks, and that's all. Can I go now?

*Q.*—Did Miss Wright tell you what she wanted the money for?

*A.*—No, sir, and I didn't ask her.

The check was placed in evidence, and when Judge Martin, who had been about to demand the deletion of all J.C.'s remarks, turned the check over and saw what was written on the other side, he blanched and bit his lip. Then he waved his hand magnanimously and declined to cross-examine.

J.C. stumbled and almost fell, he was so anxious to get off the stand. He sent Hermy a sickly smile. His face was steaming, and he kept swabbing it.

Lola Wright was nervous as she took the oath; but her gaze was defiant, and it made Carter Bradford flush.

He showed her the check in evidence.

"Miss Wright, what did you do with this check when you received it from J. C. Pettigrew on December thirty-first last?"

"I put it in my purse," said Lola. There were titters. But Judge Martin frowned, so Lola sat up straighter.

"Yes, I know," said Carter, "but to whom did you give it?"

"I don't remember."

Foolish girl, thought Ellery. He's got you. Don't make things worse by being difficult.

Bradford held the check up before her. "Miss Wright, perhaps this will refresh your memory. Read the endorsement on the back, please."

Lola swallowed. Then she said in a low voice: " 'James Haight.' "

At the defense table James Haight unaccountably seized that instant to smile. It was the weariest smile imaginable. Then he sank into apathy again.

"Can you explain how James Haight's endorsement appears on a check you borrowed from J. C. Pettigrew?"

"I gave it to Jim."

"When?"

"That same night."

"Where?"

"At the house of my sister Nora."

"At the house of your sister Nora. Have you heard the testimony here to the effect that you were not present at the house of your sister Nora during the New Year's Eve party?"

"Yes."

"Well, were you or weren't you?"

There was something in Bradford's voice that was a little cruel, and Pat writhed in her seat in front of the rail, her lips saying: "I hate you!" almost aloud.

"I did stop at the house for a few minutes, but I wasn't at the party."

"I see. Were you invited to the party?"

"Yes."

"But you didn't go?"

"No."

"Why not?"

Judge Martin objected, and Judge Newbold sustained him. Bradford smiled.

"Did anyone see you but your brother-in-law, the defendant?"

"No. I went around to the back door of the kitchen."

"Then did you *know* Jim Haight was in the kitchen?" asked Carter Bradford quickly.

Lola grew pink. "Yes. I hung around outside in the backyard till I saw, through the kitchen window, that Jim came in. He disappeared in the butler's pantry, and I thought there might be someone with him. But after a few minutes I decided he was alone, and knocked. Jim came out of the pantry to the kitchen door, and we talked."

"About what, Miss Wright?"

Lola glanced at Judge Martin in a confused way. He made as if to rise, then sank back.

"I gave Jim the check."

Ellery was leaning far forward. So that had been Lola's mission! He had not been able to overhear, or see, what had passed between Jim and Lola at the back door of Nora's kitchen that night.

"You gave him the check," said Bradford courteously. "Miss Wright, did the defendant ask you to give him money?"

"No!"

Ellery smiled grimly. Liar—of the genus white.

"But didn't you borrow the hundred dollars from Mr. Pettigrew for the purpose of giving it to the defendant?"

"Yes," said Lola coolly. "Only it was in repayment of a debt I owed Jim. I owe everybody, you see—chronic borrower. I'd borrowed from Jim some time before, so I paid him back, that's all."

And Ellery recalled that night when he had trailed Jim to Lola's apartment in Low Village, and how Jim had drunkenly demanded money and Lola had said she didn't have any . . . Only it wasn't true that on New Year's Eve, Lola had repaid a "debt." Lola had made a donation to Nora's happiness.

"You borrowed from Pettigrew to pay Haight?" asked Carter, raising his eyebrows. (*Laughter.*)

"The witness has answered," said Judge Eli.

Bradford waved. "Miss Wright, did Haight ask you for the money you say you owed him?"

Lola said, too quickly: "No, he didn't."

"You just decided suddenly, on the last day of the year, that you'd better pay him back—without any suggestion from him?"

Objection. Argument. At it again.

"Miss Wright, you have only a small income, have you not?" Objection. Argument. Heat now. Judge Newbold excused the jury. Bradford said sternly to Judge Newbold: "Your Honor, it is important to the People to show that this witness, herself in badly reduced circumstances, was nevertheless somehow induced by the defendant to get money for him, thus indicating his basic character, how desperate he was for money—all part of the People's case to show his gain motive for the poisoning."

The jury was brought back. Bradford went at Lola once more, with savage persistence. Feathers flew again; but when it was over, the jury was convinced of Bradford's point, juries being notoriously unable to forget what judges instruct them to forget.

But Judge Martin was not beaten. On cross-examination, he sailed in almost with joy.

"Miss Wright," said the old lawyer, "you have testified in direct examination that on the night of New Year's Eve last you called at the back door of your sister's house. What time was that visit, do you recall?"

"Yes. I looked at my wristwatch, because I had a—a party of my own to go to in town. It was just before midnight—fifteen minutes before the New Year was rung in."

"You also testified that you saw your brother-in-law go into the butler's pantry, and after a moment or two you knocked and he came out to you, and you talked. Where exactly did that conversation take place?"

"At the back door of the kitchen."

"What did you say to Jim?"

"I asked him what he was doing, and he said he was just finishing mixing a lot of Manhattan cocktails for the crowd. He'd about got to the maraschino cherries when I knocked, he said. Then I told him about the check—"

"Did you see the cocktails he referred to?"

The room rustled like an agitated aviary, and Carter Bradford leaned forward, frowning. This was important—this was the time the poisoning must have taken place. After that ripple of sound, the courtroom was very still.

"No," said Lola. "Jim had come from the direction of the pantry to answer the door, so I know that's where he'd been mixing the cocktails. From where I was standing, at the back door, I couldn't see into the pantry. So of course I couldn't see the cocktails, either."

"Ah! Miss Wright, had someone sneaked into the kitchen from the main hall or the dining room while you and Mr. Haight were talking at the back door, would you have been able to see that person?"

"No. The door from the dining room doesn't open into the kitchen; it leads directly into the pantry. And while the door from the hall does open into the kitchen and *is* visible from the back door, I couldn't see it, because Jim was standing in front of me, blocking my view."

"In other words, Miss Wright, while you and Mr. Haight were talking—Mr. Haight with his back to the rest of the kitchen, you unable to see most of the kitchen because he was blocking your view—someone *could* have slipped into the kitchen through the hall door, crossed to the pantry, and retraced his steps without either of you being aware of what had happened or who it had been?"

"That's correct, Judge."

"Or someone could have entered the pantry through the dining room during that period, and neither you nor Mr. Haight could have seen him?"

"Of course we couldn't have seen him. I told you that the pantry is out of sight of—"

"How long did this conversation at the back door take?"

"Oh, five minutes, I should think."

"That will be all, thank you," said the Judge triumphantly.

Carter Bradford climbed to his feet for a redirect examination. The courtroom was whispering, the jury looked thoughtful, and Carter's hair looked excited. But he was very considerate in manner and tone.

"Miss Wright, I know this is painful for you, but we must get this story of yours straight. *Did* anyone enter the pantry either through the kitchen or the dining room while you were conversing at the back door with Jim Haight?"

"I don't know. I merely said someone could have, and we wouldn't have known the difference."

"Then you can't really say that someone *did?*"

"I can't say someone did, but by the same token I can't say someone didn't. As a matter of fact, it might very easily have happened."

"But you *didn't* see anyone enter the pantry, and you *did* see Jim Haight come out of the pantry?"

"Yes, but—"

"And you saw Jim Haight go back into the pantry?"

"No such thing," said Lola with asperity. "I turned around and went away, leaving Jim at the door!"

"That's all," said Carter softly; he even tried to help her off the stand, but Lola drew herself up and went back to her chair haughtily.

"I should like," said Carter to the Court, "to recall one of my previous witnesses. Frank Lloyd."

As the bailiff bellowed: "Frank Lloyd to the stand!" Mr. Ellery Queen said to himself: "The build-up."

Lloyd's cheeks were yellow, as if something were rotting his blood. He shuffled to the stand, unkempt, slovenly, tight-mouthed. He looked once at Jim Haight, not ten feet away from him. Then he looked away, but there was evil in his green eyes.

He was on the stand only a few minutes. The substance of his testimony, surgically excised by Bradford, was that he now recalled an important fact which he had forgotten in his previous testimony. Jim Haight had not been the only one out of the living room during the time he was mixing the last batch of cocktails before midnight. There had been one other.

*Q.*—And who was that, Mr. Lloyd?

*A.*—A guest of the Wrights'. Ellery Smith.

You clever animal, thought Ellery admiringly. And now I'm the animal, and I'm trapped . . . What to do?

*Q.*—Mr. Smith left the room directly after the defendant?

*A.*—Yes. He didn't return until Haight came back with the tray of cocktails and started passing them around.

This is it, thought Mr. Queen.

Carter Bradford turned around and looked directly into Ellery's eyes.

"I call," said Cart with a snap in his voice, "Ellery Smith."

# 24

## Ellery Smith to the Stand

As Mr. Ellery Queen left his seat, and crossed the courtroom foreground, and took the oath, and sat down in the witness chair, his mind was not occupied with Prosecutor Bradford's unuttered questions or his own unuttered answers.

He was reasonably certain what questions Bradford intended to ask, and he was positive what answers he would give. Bradford knew, or guessed, from the scene opened up to him by Frank Lloyd's delayed recollection, what part the mysterious Mr. "Smith" had played that bitter night. So one question would lead to another, and suspicion would become certainty, and sooner or later the whole story would have to come out. It never occurred to Ellery that he might frankly lie. Not because he was a saint, or a moralist, or afraid of consequences; but because his whole training had been in the search for truth, and he knew that whereas murder will not necessarily out, the truth must. So it was more practical to tell the truth than to tell the lie. Moreover, people expected you to lie in court, and therein lay a great advantage, if only you were clever enough to seize it.

No, Mr. Queen's thoughts were occupied with another question altogether. And that was: How turn the truth, so damning to Jim Haight on its face, to Jim Haight's advantage? That would be a shrewd blow, if only it could be delivered; and it would have the additional strength of unexpectedness, for surely young Bradford would never anticipate what he himself, now, on the stand, could not even imagine.

So Mr. Queen sat waiting, his brain not deigning to worry, but flexing itself, exploring, dipping into its deepest pockets, examining all the things he knew for a hint, a clue, a road to follow.

Another conviction crept into his consciousness as he answered the first few routine questions about his name and occupation and connection with the Wright family, and so on; and it arose from Carter Bradford himself.

Bradford was disciplining his tongue, speaking impersonally; but there was a bitterness about his speech that was not part of the words he was uttering. Cart was remembering that this lean and quiet-eyed man theoretically at his mercy was, in a sense, an author of more than books—he was the author of Mr. Bradford's romantic troubles, too.

Patty's personality shimmered between them, and Mr. Queen remarked it with satisfaction; it was another advantage he held over his inquisitor. For Patty blinded young Mr. Bradford's eyes and drugged his quite respectable intelligence. Mr. Queen noted the advantage and tucked it away and returned to his work of concentration while the uppermost forces of his mind paid attention to the audible questions.

And suddenly he saw how he could make the truth work for Jim Haight!

He almost chuckled as he leaned back and gave his whole mind to the man before him. The very first pertinent question reassured him—Bradford was on the trail, his tongue hanging out.

"Do you recollect, Mr. Smith, that we found the three letters in the defendant's handwriting as a result of Mrs. Haight's hysterical belief that you had told us about them?"

"Yes."

"Do you also recall two unsuccessful attempts on my part that day to find out from you what you knew about the letters?"

"Quite well."

Bradford said softly: "Mr. Smith, today you are on the witness stand, under oath to tell the whole truth. I now ask you: Did you know of the existence of those three letters before Chief Dakin found them in the defendant's house?"

And Ellery said: "Yes, I did."

Bradford was surprised, almost suspicious.

"When did you first learn about them?"

Ellery told him, and Bradford's surprise turned into satisfaction.

"Under what circumstances?" This was a rapped question, tinged with contempt. Ellery answered meekly.

"Then you knew Mrs. Haight was in danger from her husband?"

"Not at all. I knew there were three letters saying so by implication."

"Well, did you or did you not believe the defendant wrote those letters?"

Judge Martin made as if to object, but Mr. Queen caught the Judge's eye and shook his head ever so slightly.

"I didn't know."

"Didn't Miss Patricia Wright identify her brother-in-law's handwriting for you, as you just testified?"

Miss Patricia Wright, sitting fifteen feet away, looked murder at them both impartially.

"She did. But that did not make it so."

"Did you check up yourself?"

"Yes. But I don't pretend to be a handwriting expert."

"But you must have come to some conclusion, Mr. Smith?"

"Objection!" shouted Judge Martin, unable to contain himself. "His conclusion."

"Strike out the question," directed Judge Newbold.

Bradford smiled. "You also examined the volume belonging to the defendant, Edgcomb's *Toxicology*, particularly pages seventy-one and seventy-two, devoted to arsenic, with certain sentences underlined in red crayon?"

"I did."

"You knew from the red-crayon underlining in the book that if a crime *were* going to be committed, death by arsenic poisoning was indicated?"

"We could quarrel about the distinction between certainty and probability," replied Mr. Queen sadly, "but to save argument—let's say I knew; yes."

"It seems to me, Your Honor," said Eli Martin in a bored voice, "that this is an entirely improper line of questioning."

"How so, Counsel?" inquired Judge Newbold.

"Because Mr. Smith's thoughts and conclusions, whether certainties, probabilities, doubts, or anything else, have no conceivable bearing upon the facts at issue."

Bradford smiled again, and when Judge Newbold asked him to limit his questions to events and conversations, he nodded carelessly, as if it did not matter.

"Mr. Smith, were you aware that the third letter of the series talked about the 'death' of Mrs. Haight as if it had occurred on New Year's Eve?"

"Yes."

"During the New Year's Eve party under examination, did you keep following the defendant out of the living room?"

"I did."

"You were keeping an eye on him all evening?"

"Yes."

"You watched him mix cocktails in the pantry?"

"Yes."

"Now do you recall the last time before midnight the defendant mixed cocktails?"

"Distinctly."

"Where did he mix them?"

"In the butler's pantry off the kitchen."

"Did you follow him there from the living room?"

"Ycs, by way of the hall. The hall leads from the foyer to the rear of the house. He entered the kitchen and went into the pantry; I was just behind him but stopped in the hall, beside the door."

"Did he see you?"

"I haven't the faintest idea."

"But you were careful not to be seen?"

Mr. Queen smiled. "I was neither careful nor careless. I just stood there beside the half-open hall door to the kitchen."

"Did the defendant turn around to look at you?" persisted Bradford.

"No."

"But *you* could see *him?*"

"Clearly."

"What did the defendant do?"

"He prepared some Manhattan cocktails in a mixing glass. He poured some into each of a number of clean glasses standing on a tray. He was reaching for the bottle of maraschino cherries, which had been standing on the pantry table, when there was a knock at the back door. He left the cocktails and went out into the kitchen to see who had knocked."

"That was when Miss Lola Wright and the defendant had the conversation just testified to?"

"Yes."

"The tray of cocktails left in the butler's pantry were visible to you all during the period in which the defendant conversed with Lola Wright at the kitchen back door?"

"Yes, indeed."

Carter Bradford hesitated. Then he asked flatly: "Did you see anyone go near those cocktails between the time the defendant left them in the pantry and the time he returned?"

Mr. Queen replied: "I saw no one, because there wasn't anyone."

*"The pantry remained absolutely empty during that period?"*

"Of organic life—yes."

Bradford could scarcely conceal his elation; he made a brave but unsuccessful effort. On the mourners' bench inside the railing the Wrights turned stone-faced.

"Now, Mr. Smith, did you see the defendant return to the pantry after Lola Wright left?"

"I did."

"What did he do?"

"He dropped a maraschino cherry from the bottle into each cocktail, using a small ivory pick. He picked up the tray in both hands and carefully walked through the kitchen toward the door at which I was standing. I acted casual, and we went into the living room together, where he immediately began distributing the glasses to the family and guests."

"On his walk from the pantry to the living room with the tray, did anyone approach him except yourself?"

"No one."

Ellery waited for the next question with equanimity. He saw the triumph gather in Bradford's eyes.

"Mr. Smith, wasn't there something else you saw happen in that pantry?"

"No."

"Nothing else happened?"

"Nothing else."

"Have you told us *everything* you saw?"

"Everything."

*"Didn't you see the defendant drop a white powder into one of those cocktails?"*

"No," said Mr. Queen. "I saw nothing of the sort."

"Then on the trip from the pantry to the living room?"

"Both Mr. Haight's hands were busy holding the tray. He dropped no foreign substance of any kind into any of the cocktails at any time during their preparation or while he carried the tray into the living room."

And then there was an undercurrent jabber in the room, and the Wrights glanced at one another with relief while Judge Martin wiped his face and Carter Bradford sneered almost with sound.

"Perhaps you turned your head for two seconds?"

"My eyes were on that tray of cocktails continuously."

"You didn't look away for even a second, eh?"

"For even a second," said Mr. Queen regretfully, as if he wished he had, just to please Mr. Bradford.

Mr. Bradford grinned at the jury—man to man—and at least five jurors grinned back. Sure, what could you expect? A friend of the Wrights'. And then everybody in town knew why Cart Bradford had stopped seeing Pat Wright. This Smith bird had a case on Patty Wright. So . . .

"And you didn't see Jim Haight drop arsenic into one of those cocktails?" insisted Mr. Bradford, smiling broadly now.

"At the risk of seeming a bore," replied Mr. Queen with courtesy, "no, I did not." But he knew he had lost with the jury; they didn't believe him.

He knew it, and while the Wrights didn't know it yet, Judge Martin did; the old gentleman was beginning to sweat again. Only Jim Haight sat unmoved, unchanged, wrapped in a shroud.

"Well, then, Mr. Smith, answer this question: Did you see anyone else who had the *opportunity* to poison one of those cocktails?"

Mr. Queen gathered himself; but before he could reply, Bradford snapped: "In fact, did you see anyone else who *did* poison one of those cocktails—anyone other than the defendant?"

"I saw no one else, but—"

"In other words, Mr. Smith," cried Bradford, "the defendant James Haight was not only in the *best* position, but he was in the *only* position, to poison that cocktail?"

"No," said Mr. Smith. And then *he* smiled.

You asked for it, he thought, and I'm giving it to you. The only trouble is, I'm giving it to myself, too, and that's foolishness. He sighed and wondered what his father, Inspector Queen, no doubt reading about the case in the New York papers and conjecturing who Ellery Smith was, would have to say when he discovered Mr. "Smith's" identity and read about this act of puerile bravado.

Carter Bradford looked blank. Then he shouted: "Are you aware that this is perjury, Smith? You just testified that no one else entered the pantry! No one approached the defendant while he was carrying the cocktails into the living room! Allow me to repeat a question or two. *Did* anyone approach the defendant during his walk to the living room with the tray?"

"No," said Mr. Queen patiently.

"*Did* someone else enter the pantry while the defendant was talking to Lola Wright at the back door?"

"No."

Bradford was almost speechless. "But you just said—! Smith, who but James Haight *could* have poisoned one of those cocktails, by your own testimony?"

Judge Martin was on his feet, but before he could get the word "Objection" out of his mouth, Ellery said calmly: "*I could.*"

There was a wholesale gasp before him and then a stricken silence. So he went on: "You see, it would have been the work of ten seconds for me to slip from behind the door of the hall, cross the few feet of kitchen to the pantry unobserved by Jim or Lola at the back door, drop arsenic into one of the cocktails, return the same way . . ."

And there was Babel all over again, and Mr. Queen looked down upon the noisemakers from the highest point of his tower, smiling benignly.

He was thinking: It's full of holes, but it's the best a man can do on short notice with the material at hand.

Over the shouting, and Judge Newbold's gavel, and the rush of reporters, Carter Bradford bellowed in triumph: *"Well, DID you poison that cocktail, Smith?"*

There were several instants of quiet again, during which Judge Martin's voice was heard to say feebly: "I object ⸺ " and Mr. Queen's voice topped the Judge's by adding neatly: "On constitutional grounds⸺"

Then hell broke loose, and Judge Newbold broke his gavel off at the head, and roared to the bailiff to clear the damn courtroom, and then he hog-called a recess until the next morning and practically ran into his chambers, where it is presumed he applied vinegar compresses to his forehead.

# 25

## The Singular Request of Miss Patricia Wright

By the next morning several changes had taken place.

Wrightsville's attention was temporarily transferred from one Jim Haight to one Ellery Smith.

Frank Lloyd's newspaper came out with a blary edition reporting the sensational facts of Mr. Smith's testimony; and an editorial which said, in part:

> The bombshell of Mr. Smith's testimony yesterday turns out to be a dud. There is no possible case against this man. Smith had no possible motive. He had not known Nora or James Haight or any of the Wrights before he came to Wrightsville last August. He has had practically no contact with Mrs. Haight, and less than that with Rosemary Haight. Whatever his reason for the quixotic nature of his farcical testimony yesterday — and Prosecutor Bradford is to be censured for his handling of the witness, who obviously led him on — it means nothing. Even if Smith were the only other person aside from Jim Haight who could have poisoned the fatal cocktail on New Year's Eve, he could not possibly have been sure that that one poisoned cocktail would reach Nora Haight, whereas Jim Haight could have and, in effect, did. Nor could Smith have written the three letters, which are indisputably in the handwriting of James Haight. Wrightsville and the jury can only conclude that what happened yesterday was either a desperate gesture of friendliness on Smith's part or a cynical bid for newspaper space by a writer who is using Wrightsville as a guinea pig.

The first thing Bradford said to Ellery on the stand the next morning was: "I show you the official transcript of your testimony yesterday. Will you please begin to read?"

Ellery raised his brows, but he took the transcript and read: " 'Question: What is your name? Answer: Ellery Smith—' "

"Stop right there! That *is* what you testified, isn't it—that your name is Ellery Smith?"

"Yes," said Ellery, beginning to feel cold.

"Is Smith your real name?"

Ho hum, thought Ellery. The man's a menace. "No."

"An assumed name, then?"

"Order in the court!" shouted the bailiff.

"Yes."

"What is your real name?"

Judge Martin said quickly: "I don't see the point of this line of questioning, Your Honor. Mr. Smith is not on trial—"

"Mr. Bradford?" said Judge Newbold, who was looking curious.

"Mr. Smith's testimony yesterday," said Bradford with a faint smile, "raised a certain logical question about what the People allege to have been the defendant's unique opportunity to poison the cocktail. Mr. Smith testified that he himself was in a position to have poisoned the cocktail. My examination this morning, then, must necessarily include an examination of Mr. Smith's character—"

"And you can establish Mr. Smith's character by bringing out his true name?" asked Judge Newbold, frowning.

"Yes, Your Honor."

"I think I'll allow this, Counsel, pending testimony."

"Will you please answer my last question," said Bradford to Ellery. "What is your real name?"

Ellery saw the Wrights looking bewildered—all but Pat, who was biting her lip with vexation as well as perplexity. But it was quite clear to him that Bradford had been busy through the intervening night. The name "Queen" carried no theoretical immunity against a charge of murder, of course; but as a practical measure its revelation would banish from the minds of the jury any notion that its well-known bearer could have had anything to do with the crime.

The jig was up.

Ellery Queen sighed and said: "My name is Ellery Queen."

Judge Martin did his best, under the circumstances. The punctuality of Bradford's timing became evident. By putting Ellery on the stand, Bradford had given the defense a handhold to an important objective. But the objective was lost in the revelation of Ellery's true identity.

Judge Martin hammered away at the anvil of one point.

"Mr. Queen, as a trained observer of criminal phenomena, you were interested in the possibilities of this case?"

"Immensely."

"That is why you kept James Haight under unrelaxing observation New Year's Eve?"

"That, and a personal concern for the Wright family."

"You were watching for a possible poisoning attempt on Haight's part?"

"Yes," said Ellery simply.

*"Did you see any such attempt on Haight's part?"*

"I did not!"

"You saw James Haight make no slightest gesture or motion which might have concealed a dropping of arsenic into one of the cocktail glasses?"

"I saw no such gesture or motion."

"And you were watching for that, Mr. Queen?"

"Exactly."

"That's all," said Judge Martin in triumph.

The newspapers all agreed that Mr. Ellery Queen, who was in Wrightsville seeking material for a new detective story, had seized upon this hell-sent opportunity to illuminate the cause of dark letters with some national publicity.

And Bradford, with a grim look, rested for the people.

The weekend intervened, and everybody involved in the case went home or to his hotel room or, as in the case of the out-of-town newspaperpeople, to their cots in the lobby of the Hollis; and all over town people were agreeing that it looked black for Jim Haight, and why shouldn't it—he did it, didn't he?

The roadhouses and taverns were jammed over the weekend, and there was considerable revelry.

On Friday night, however, the unofficial committee for the defense of James Haight met again in the Wright living room, and the atmosphere was blue with despair.

Nora said to Ellery, to Judge Martin, to Roberta Roberts: "What do you think?"—painfully and without hope; and all they could do was shake their heads.

"Queen's testimony would have helped a great deal more," growled old Judge Eli, "if that jury weren't so dad-blamed set on Jim's guilt. No, Nora, it looks bad, and I'm not going to tell you anything different."

Nora stared blindly into the fire.

"To think that you've been Ellery Queen all along," sighed Hermy. "I suppose there was a time when I'd have been thrilled, Mr. Queen. But I'm so washed-out these days—"

"Momsy," murmured Lola, "where's your fighting spirit?"

Hermy smiled, but she excused herself to go upstairs to bed, her feet dragging.

And after a while John F. said: "Thanks, Queen," and went off after Hermy, as if Hermy's going had made him a little uneasy.

And they sat there without speaking for a long time, until Nora said: "At least, Ellery, what you saw confirms Jim's innocence. That's something. It ought to mean *something*. Heavens," she cried, "they've got to believe *you!*"

"Let's hope they do."

"Judge Martin," said Roberta suddenly. "Monday's your day to begin howling. What are you going to howl about?"

"Suppose you tell me," said Judge Martin.

Her glance fell first. "I have nothing to tell that could help," she said in a faint voice.

"Then I *was* right," murmured Ellery. "Don't you think others might make better judges—"

Something crashed. Pat was on her feet, and the sherry glass from which she had been sipping lay in little glittery fragments in the fireplace, surrounded by blue flames.

"What's the matter with *you?*" demanded Lola. "If this isn't the screwiest family!"

"I'll tell you what's the matter with me," panted Pat. "I'm through sitting on my—sitting around and imitating Uriah Heep. I'm going to *do* something!"

"Patty," gasped Nora, looking at her younger sister as if Pat had suddenly turned into a female Mr. Hyde.

Lola murmured: "What in hell are you babbling about, Patticums?"

"I've got an idea!"

"The little one's got an idea," grinned Lola. "I had an idea once. Next thing I knew I was divorcing a heel and everybody began to call me an amptray. Siddown, Snuffy."

"Wait a moment," said Ellery. "It's possible. What idea, Pat?"

"Go ahead and be funny," said Pat hotly. "All of you. But I've worked out a plan, and I'm going through with it."

"What kind of plan?" demanded Judge Martin. "I'll listen to anyone, Patricia."

"Will you?" jeered Pat. "Well, I'm not talking. You'll know when the time comes, Uncle Eli! You've got to do just one thing—"

"And that is?"

"To call me as *the last witness for the defense!*"

The Judge began in bewilderment: "But what—?"

"Yes, what's stewing?" asked Ellery quickly. "You'd better talk it over with your elders first."

"There's been too much talk already, Grandpa."

"But what do you think you're going to accomplish?"

"I want three things." Pat looked grim. "Time, last crack at the witness stand, and some of your new Odalisque Parfum, Nora . . . Accomplish, Mr. Queen? *I'm going to save Jim!*"

Nora ran out of the room, using her knitting as a handkerchief.

"Well, I will!" said Pat, exasperated. And she added, in a gun-moll undertone: "I'll show that Carter Bradford!"

# 26

## Juror Number 7

"We will take," said old Eli Martin to Mr. Queen in the courtroom Monday morning, as they waited for Judge Newbold to enter from chambers, "what the Lord provides."

"Meaning what?" asked Ellery.

"Meaning," sighed the lawyer, "that unless Providence intercedes, my old friend's son-in-law is a fried squab. If what I've got is a defense, may God help all petitioners for justice!"

"Legally speaking, I'm a blunderbuss. Surely you've got some sort of defense?"

"Some sort, yes." The old gentleman squinted sourly at Jim Haight, sitting nearby with his head on his breast. "I've never had such a case!" he exploded. "Nobody tells me anything—the defendant, the Roberts woman, the family . . . Why, even that snippet Patricia won't talk to me!"

"Patty . . ." said Ellery thoughtfully.

"Pat wants me to put her on the stand, and I don't even know what for! This isn't law, it's lunacy."

"She went out mysteriously Saturday night," murmured Ellery, "and again last night, and she came home very late both times."

"While Rome burns!"

"She'd been drinking Martinis, too."

"I forgot you're something of a sleuth. How did you find that out, Queen?"

"I kissed her."

Judge Martin was startled. "Kissed her? You?"

"I have my methods," said Mr. Queen, a whit stiffly. Then he grinned. "But this time they didn't work. She wouldn't tell me what she'd been doing."

"Odalisque Parfum," sniffed the old gentleman. "If Patricia Wright thinks a sweet *odeur* is going to divert young Bradford . . . He looks un-diverted to me this morning. Doesn't he to you?"

"An immovable young man," agreed Mr. Queen uneasily.

Judge Martin sighed and glanced over at the row of chairs inside the railing, where Nora sat with her little chin raised high and a pallid face between her mother and father, her gaze fixed beggingly upon her husband's motionless profile. But if Jim was conscious of her presence, he made no sign. Behind them the courtroom was jammed and whispery.

Mr. Queen was furtively scanning Miss Patricia Wright. Miss Patricia Wright had an Oppenheim air this morning—slitted eyes, and a certain enigmatic expression about the mouth Mr. Queen had kissed in the interests of science the night before . . . in vain. Perhaps not quite in vain . . .

He became aware that Judge Eli was poking his ribs. "Get up, get up. You ought to know something about courtroom etiquette! Here comes Newbold."

"Good luck," said Ellery absently.

The first witness Judge Martin called to testify in defense of Jim Haight was Hermione Wright.

Hermy crossed the space before the Bench and mounted the step to the witness chair if not quite like royalty ascending the throne, then at least like royalty ascending the guillotine. On being sworn, she said "I do" in a firm, if tragic, voice.

Clever, thought Ellery. Putting Hermy on the stand. Hermy, mother of Nora. Hermy, who of all persons in the world except Nora should be Jim Haight's harshest enemy—Hermy to testify for the man who had tried to kill her daughter!

The courtroom and jury were impressed by the dignity with which Hermy met all their stares. Oh, she was a fighter! And Ellery could detect the pride on the faces of her three daughters, a queer shame on Jim's, and the faint admiration of Carter Bradford.

The old lawyer led Hermione skillfully through the night of the crime, dwelling chiefly on the "gaiety" of the occasion, how happy everyone had been, how Nora and Jim had danced together like children, and incidentally, how much Frank Lloyd, who had been Bradford's chief witness to the events of the evening, had had to drink; and the Judge contrived, through Hermy's helpless, "confused" answers, to leave the impression with the jury that no one there could possibly have said for certain what had happened so far as the cocktails were concerned, let alone Frank Lloyd—unless it was Mr. Ellery Queen, who'd had only one drink before the fatal toast to 1941.

And then Judge Martin led Hermione around to a conversation she had had with Jim shortly after Jim and Nora returned from their honey-moon—how Jim had confided in his mother-in-law that Nora and he sus-pected Nora was going to have a baby, and that Nora wanted it to be kept a secret until they were "sure," except that Jim said he was so happy he couldn't keep it in any longer, he had to tell someone, and Hermy wasn't to let on to Nora that he'd blabbed. And how ecstatic Jim had been at the prospect of being father to Nora's child—how it would change his whole life, he said, give him a fresh push toward making a success of himself for Nora and the baby—how much he loved Nora . . . more every day.

Carter Bradford waived cross-examination with almost a visible kind-liness.

But there was a little whiff of applause as Hermy stepped off the wit-ness stand.

Judge Martin called up a roll of character witnesses as long as Judge Newbold's face. Lorrie Preston and Mr. Gonzales of the bank, Brick Miller the bus driver, Ma Upham, young Manager Louie Cahan of the Bijou, who had been one of Jim's bachelor cronies, Miss Aikin of the Carnegie Library—that *was* a surprise, as Miss Aikin had never been known to say a kind word about anybody, but she managed to say several about Jim Haight despite the technical limitations of "character" testi-mony—chiefly, Ellery suspected, because Jim had patronized the Library in the old days and broken not a single one of Miss Aikin's numerous rules . . . The character witnesses were so many, and so socially diversi-fied, that people were surprised. They hadn't known Jim Haight had so many friends in town.

But that was exactly the impression Judge Martin was trying to make. And when John F. clambered to the stand and said simply and directly that Jim was a good boy and the Wrights were behind him heart and soul, people remarked how old John F. looked—"aged a lot these past couple of months, John F. has"—and a tide of sympathy for the Wrights began to creep up in the courtroom until it was actually lapping Jim Haight's shoes.

During the days of this character testimony, Carter Bradford main-tained a decent respect for the Wrights—just the proper note of deference and consideration, but a little aloof, as if to say: "I'm not going to badger your people, but don't expect my relationship with your family to influ-ence my conduct in this courtroom one iota!"

Then Judge Martin called Lorenzo Grenville.
Lorenzo Grenville was a drippy-eyed little man with hourglass cheeks

and a tall Hoover collar, size sixteen, out of which his neck protruded like a withered root.

He identified himself as a handwriting expert.

Mr. Grenville agreed that he had sat in the courtroom from the beginning of the trial, that he had heard the testimony of the People's experts regarding the authenticity of the handwriting in the three letters alleged to have been written by the defendant; that he had had ample opportunity to examine said letters, also undisputed samples of the defendant's true handwriting; and that in his "expert" opinion there was grave reason to doubt James Haight's authorship of the three letters in evidence.

"As a recognized authority in the field of handwriting analysis, you do not believe Mr. Haight wrote the three letters?"

"I do not." (The Prosecutor leers at the jury, and the jury leers back.)

"Why don't you believe so, Mr. Grenville?" asked the Judge.

Mr. Grenville went into punctilious detail. Since he drew almost exactly opposite conclusions from the identical data which the jury had heard the People's experts say proved Jim Haight *had* written those letters, several jurymen were not unnaturally confused, which contented Judge Martin.

"Any other reasons for believing these letters were not written by the defendant, Mr. Grenville?"

Mr. Grenville had many which, edited, became a question of composition. "The phrasing is stilted, unnatural, and is not like the defendant's ordinary letter style at all." Mr. Grenville cited chapter and verse from Haight letters in evidence.

"Then what is your opinion, Mr. Grenville, as to the authorship of the three letters?"

"I am inclined to consider them forgeries."

Mr. Queen would have felt reassured, but he happened to know that a certain defendant in another case *had* written a check which Mr. Lorenzo Grenville just as solemnly testified to be a forgery. There was no slightest doubt in Ellery's mind about the Haight letters. They *had* been written by Jim Haight, and that's all there was to it. He wondered what Judge Martin was up to with the unreliable Mr. Grenville.

He found out at once. "Is it your considered opinion, Mr. Grenville," purred Judge Eli, "that it would be easy, or difficult, to forge Mr. Haight's handwriting?"

"Oh, very easy," said Mr. Grenville.

"Could *you* forge Mr. Haight's handwriting?"

"Certainly."

"Could you forge Mr. Haight's handwriting *here and now?*"

"Well," said Mr. Grenville apologetically, "I'd have to study the hand-writing a while—say two minutes!"

Bradford was on his feet with a bellow, and there was a long, inaudible argument before Judge Newbold. Finally, the Court allowed the demonstration, the witness was provided with pen, paper, ink, and a photostatic copy of one of Jim Haight's acknowledged samples of handwriting—it happened to be a personal note written to Nora by Jim on the Wrightsville National Bank stationery and dated four years before—and the courtroom sat on the edge of its collective seat.

Lorenzo Grenville squinted at the photostat for exactly two minutes.

Then, seizing the pen, he dipped it into the ink, and with a casual air wrote swiftly on the blank paper.

"I'd do better," he said to Judge Martin, "if I had my own pens to work with."

Judge Martin glanced earnestly at what his witness had written and then, with a smile, passed the sheet around the jury box, together with the photostat of Jim's undisputed handwriting. From the amazement on the jurors' faces as they compared the photostat with Grenville's forgery, Ellery knew the blow had told.

On cross-examination, Carter Bradford had only one question to ask the witness.

"Mr. Grenville, how many years has it taken you to learn the art of forging handwriting?"

It seemed Mr. Grenville had spent his whole life at it.

Victor Carlatti to the stand. Yes, he is the owner of a roadhouse on Route 16 called the *Hot Spot*. What sort of establishment is it? A night-club.

*Q.*—Mr. Carlatti, do you know the defendant, James Haight?

*A.*—I've seen him around.

*Q.*—Has he ever visited your nightclub?

*A.*—Yeah.

*Q.*—Drinking?

*A.*—Well, a drink or two. Once in a while. It's legal.

*Q.*—Now, Mr. Carlatti, there has been testimony here that James Haight allegedly admitted to Mrs. Haight that he had "lost money gambling" in your establishment. What do you know about this?

*A.*—It's a dirty lie.

*Q.*—You mean James Haight has never gambled in your nightclub?

*A.*—Sure he never. *Nobody* ever—

*Q.*—Has the defendant borrowed any money from you?

*A.*—He nor nobody else.

*Q.*—Does the defendant owe you a single dollar?

*A.*—Not a chip.

*Q.*—As far as you know, has the defendant ever "lost" any money in your establishment? Gambling or any other way?

*A.*—Maybe some broad may have took him to the cleaners while he was feeling happy, but he never shelled out one cent in my place except for drinks.

*Q.*—You may cross-examine, Mr. Bradford.

Mr. Bradford murmurs, "With pleasure," but only Judge Eli hears him, and Judge Eli shrugs ever so slightly and sits down.

Cross-examination by Mr. Bradford:

*Q.*—Carlatti, is it against the law to operate a gambling parlor?

*A.*—Who says I operate a gambling parlor? Who says?

*Q.*—Nobody "says," Carlatti. Just answer my question.

*A.*—It's a dirty frame. Prove it. Go ahead. I ain't gonna sit here and take no double-cross—

*Judge Newbold:* The witness will refrain from gratuitous remarks, or he will lay himself open to contempt. Answer the question.

*A.*—What question, Judge?

*Q.*—Never mind. Do you or do you not run roulette, faro, craps, and other gambling games in the back room of your so-called "nightclub"?

*A.*—Am I supposed to answer dirty questions like that? It's an insult, Judge. This kid ain't dry behind the ears yet, and I ain't gonna sit here and take—

*Judge Newbold:* One more remark like that—

*Judge Martin:* It seems to me, Your Honor, that this is improper cross. The question of whether the witness runs a gambling establishment or not was not part of the direct examination.

*Judge Newbold:* Overruled!

*Judge Martin:* Exception!

*Mr. Bradford:* If Jim Haight did owe you money lost at your gambling tables, Carlatti, you'd have to deny it, wouldn't you, or face prosecution on a charge of running a gambling establishment?

*Judge Martin:* I move that question be stricken—

*A.*—What is this? All of a sudden all you guys are getting angels. How do you think I been operating—on my sex appeal? And don't think no hick judge can scare Vic Carlatti. I got plenty of friends, and they'll see to it that Vic Carlatti ain't going to be no fall guy for some old goat of a judge and some stinker of a D.A.—

*Judge Newbold:* Mr. Bradford, do you have any further questions of this witness?

*Mr. Bradford:* I think that will be quite sufficient, Your Honor.

*Judge Newbold:* Clerk, strike the last question and answer. The jury will disregard it. The spectators will preserve the proper decorum, or the room will be cleared. Witness is held in contempt of court. Bailiff, take charge of the prisoner.

Mr. Carlatti puts up his dukes as the bailiff approaches, roaring: "Where's my mouthpiece? This ain't Nazzee Goimany!"

When Nora took the oath and sat down and began to testify in a choked voice, the court was like a church. She was the priestess, and the people listened to her with the silent unease of a sinning congregation confronted by their sins . . . Surely the woman Jim Haight had tried to do in would be against him?

But Nora was not against Jim. She was for him, every cell in her. Her loyalty filled the courtroom like warm air.

She made a superb witness, defending her husband from every charge. She reiterated her love for him and her unquestioning faith in his innocence. Over and over. While her eyes kept coming back to the object of her testimony, those scant few feet away, who sat with his face lowered, wearing a dull red mask of shame, blinking at the tips of his unpolished shoes.

The idiot might be more cooperative! thought Mr. Queen angrily.

Nora could give no factual evidence to controvert the People's case. Judge Martin, who had put her on the stand for her psychological value, did not touch upon the two poisoning attempts preceding New Year's Eve; and in a genuine act of kindness, Carter Bradford waived cross-examination and the opportunity to quiz her on those attempts. Perhaps Bradford felt he would lose more in goodwill by grilling Nora than by letting her go.

Mr. Queen, a notorious skeptic, could not be sure.

Nora was to have been Judge Martin's last witness; and indeed he was fumbling with some papers at the defense table, as if undecided whether to proceed or not, when Pat signaled him furiously from inside the railing, and the old gentleman nodded with a guilty, unhappy look and said: "I call Patricia Wright to the stand."

Mr. Queen sat forward in the grip of a giant tension he could not understand.

Obviously at a loss where to begin, Judge Martin began a cautious reconnaissance, as if seeking a clue. But Pat took the reins out of his hands almost at once. She was irrepressible—deliberately, Ellery knew; but why? What was she driving at?

As a defense witness, Pat played squarely into the hands of the People.

The more she said, the more damage she did to Jim's cause. She painted her brother-in-law as a scoundrel, a liar—told how he had humiliated Nora, stolen her jewelry, squandered her property, neglected her, subjected her to mental torment, quarreled with her incessantly . . .

Before she was half through, the courtroom was sibilating, Judge Martin was perspiring like a coolie and trying frantically to head her off, Nora was gaping at her sister as if she were seeing her for the first time, and Hermy and John F. slumped lower and lower in their seats, like two melting waxworks.

Judge Newbold interrupted Pat during a denunciation of Jim and an avowal of her hatred for him.

"Miss Wright, are you aware that you were called as a witness for the defense?"

Pat snapped: "I'm sorry, Your Honor. But I can't sit here and see all this hush-hush going on when we all know Jim Haight is guilty—"

"I move—" began Judge Martin in an outraged bellow.

"Young woman—" began Judge Newbold angrily.

But Pat rushed on. "And that's what I told Bill Ketcham only last night—"

*"What!"*

The explosion came from Judge Newbold, Eli Martin, and Carter Bradford simultaneously. And for a moment the room was plunged in an abyss of surprise; and then the walls cracked, and Bedlam piled upon Babel, so that Judge Newbold pounded with his third gavel of the trial, and the bailiff ran up and down shushing people, and in the press row someone started to laugh as realization came, infecting the whole row, and the row behind that.

"Your Honor," said Judge Martin above the din, "I want it to go on record here and now that the statement made by my witness a moment ago comes to me as an absolute shock. I had no faintest idea that—"

"Just a moment, just a moment, Counsel," said Judge Newbold in a strangled voice. "Miss Wright!"

"Yes, Your Honor?" asked Patty in a bewildered way, as if she couldn't imagine what all the fuss was about.

"Did I hear you correctly? Did you say you told *Bill Ketcham* something last night?"

"Why, yes, Your Honor," said Pat respectfully. "And Bill agreed with me—"

"I object!" shouted Carter Bradford. "She's got it in for me! This is a put-up job—!"

Miss Wright turned innocent eyes on Mr. Bradford.

"One moment, Mr. Bradford!" Judge Newbold leaned far forward on the Bench. "Bill Ketcham agreed with you, did he? What did he agree with you about? What else happened last night?"

"Well, Bill said Jim was guilty, all right, and if I'd promise to"—Pat blushed—"well, if I'd promise him a certain something, he'd see to it that Jim got what was coming to him. Said he'd talk to the others on the jury, too—being an insurance man, Bill said, he could sell anything. He said I was his dream girl, and for me he'd climb the highest mountain—"

"Silence in the court!" bellowed Judge Newbold.

And there was silence.

"Now, Miss Wright," said Judge Newbold grimly, "are we to understand that you had this conversation last night with the William Ketcham who is Juror Number 7 in this trial?"

"Yes, Your Honor," said Pat, her eyes wide. "Is anything wrong with that? I'm sure if I had known—"

The rest was lost in uproar.

"Bailiff, clear the room!" screamed Judge Newbold.


"Now, then," said Judge Newbold. "Let's have the rest of it, if you please!"—so frigidly that Pat turned *café au lait* and tears appeared in the corners of her eyes.

"W-we went out together, Bill and I, last Saturday night. Bill said we oughtn't to be seen, maybe it wasn't legal or something, so we drove over to Slocum to a hot spot Bill knows, and—and we've been there every night since. I said Jim was guilty, and Bill said sure, he thought so, too—"

"Your Honor," said Judge Martin in a terrible voice, "I move—"

"Oh, you do!" said Judge Newbold. "Eli Martin, if your reputation weren't . . . You there!" he roared at the jurist. "Ketcham! Number 7! Get up!"

Fat Billy Ketcham, the insurance broker, tried to obey, half hoisted himself, fell back again, and finally made it.

He stood there in the rear row of the jury box, swaying a little, as if the box were a canoe.

"William Ketcham," snarled Judge Newbold, "have you spent every evening since last Saturday in the company of this young woman? Did you promise her to influence the rest of the jury—Bailiff! Chief Dakin! *I want that man!*"

Ketcham was trapped in the main aisle after knocking over two fellow jurors and scattering the people inside the rail like a fat tom charging a brood of chicks.

When he was hauled up before Judge Newbold, he chattered: "I didn't m-mean any harm, J-Judge—I d-didn't think I was doing wrong,

Judge—I s-swear to you—everybody knows the s-sonofabitch is guilty—"

"Take this man in custody," whispered Judge Newbold. "Bailiff, station guards at the doors. There will be a five-minute recess. Jury, remain where you are. No one now present is to leave the courtroom!" And Judge Newbold groped for his chambers.

"That," said Mr. Queen while they waited, "is what comes of not locking juries in. It's also," he added to Miss Patricia Wright, "what comes of scatterbrained brats meddling in grown-up people's affairs!"

"Oh, Patty, how could you?" wept Hermione. "And that impossible Ketcham man, too! I warned you he'd make improper advances if you encouraged him. You remember, John, how he used to pester Patty for dates—"

"I also remember," said John F. wildly, "where my old hairbrush is!"

"Look," said Pat in a low voice, "Jim was in a bad spot, wasn't he? All right! So I worked on Fat Billy, and he drank a lot of Martinis, and I let him make a pass or two at me . . . Go ahead and l-look at me as if I were a loose woman!" And Miss Wright began to cry. "Just the same, I did something none of *you* has been able to do—watch and see!"

"It's true," said Ellery hastily, "that we had nothing to look forward to but a conviction."

"If only . . ." began Nora, a great bright hope on her pale face. "Oh, Patsy, you're mad, but I love you!"

"And is Cart's face r-red," blubbered Pat. "Thinks he's smart . . ."

"Yes," pointed out Mr. Queen dryly. "But look at Judge Martin's."

Old Eli Martin came over to Pat, and he said: "Patricia, you've placed me in the most embarrassing position of my life. I don't care about that, or the ethics of your conduct, so much as I do about the fact that you probably haven't helped Jim's chances, you've hurt them. No matter what Newbold says or does—and he really hasn't any choice—everybody will know you did this deliberately, and it's bound to bounce back on Jim Haight."

And Judge Martin stalked away.

"I suppose," said Lola, "you can't scratch an ex-judge without stuffiness leaking out. Don't you worry, Snuffles! You gave Jim a zero-hour reprieve. It's better than he deserves, the dumb ox!"

"I wish to state in preamble," said Judge Newbold coldly, "that in all my years on the Bench I have encountered no more flagrant, disgraceful example of civic irresponsibility.

"William Ketcham!" He transfixed Juror Number 7, who looked as if he were about to faint, with a stern and glittering eye. "Unfortunately, there is no statutory offense with which you can be charged, unless it can be shown that you have received property or value of some kind. For the time being, however, I order the Commissioner of Jurors to strike your name from the panel of jurors, and never so long as you are a resident of this State will you be permitted to exercise your privilege of serving on a jury."

William Ketcham's expression said that he would gladly relinquish many more appreciated rights for the privilege of leaving the courtroom that very instant.

"Mr. Bradford"—Carter looked up, thin-lipped and black-angry— "you are requested to investigate the conduct of Patricia Wright with a view toward determining whether she willfully and deliberately sought to influence Juror Number 7. If such intention can be established, I ask you to draw an indictment charging Patricia Wright with the appropriate charge—"

"Your Honor," said Bradford in a low voice, "the only conceivable charge I can see would be corrupting a juror; and to establish corruption, it seems to me necessary to show consideration. And in this case it doesn't seem as if there was any consideration—"

"She offered her body!" snapped Judge Newbold.

"I did not!" gasped Pat. "He asked for it, but I didn't—"

"Yes, Your Honor," said Bradford, blushing, "but it is a moot point whether that sort of thing constitutes legal consideration—"

"Let's not get entangled, Mr. Bradford," said Judge Newbold coldly. "The woman is clearly guilty of embracery if she attempted to influence a juror improperly, whether she gave any consideration or not!"

"Embracery? What's that?" muttered Pat.

But no one heard her except Mr. Queen, who was chuckling inside.

"Also," continued Judge Newbold, slamming a book down on a heap of papers, "I shall recommend that in future trials coming under the jurisdiction of this court, juries shall be locked in, to prevent a recurrence of this shameful incident.

"Now." He glared at Billy Ketcham and Pat, and then at the jury. "The facts are clear. A juror has been influenced in a manner prejudicial to the rights of the defendant to a fair trial. This by the admission of both parties involved.

"If I permitted this trial to continue, it could only bring an appeal to a superior court which must, on the record, order a new trial. Consequently, to save further and needless expense, I have no choice. I regret the inconvenience and waste of time caused the remaining members of the jury; I deplore the great expense of this trial already incurred by Wright County.

"Much as I regret and deplore, however, the facts leave me no recourse but to declare People Against James Haight a mistrial. I do so declare, the jury is discharged with the apology and thanks of the Court, and the defendant is remanded to the custody of the Sheriff until the date for a new trial can be set.

"Court is adjourned!"

# 27

## Easter Sunday: Nora's Gift

The invading press retreated, promising to return for the new trial; but Wrightsville remained, and Wrightsville chortled and raged and buzzed and gossiped until the very ears of the little Buddha clock on Pat's dresser were ringing.

William Ketcham, by a curious inversion, became the town hero. The "boys" stopped him on street corners to slap his back, he sold five insurance policies he had long since given up, and, as confidence returned, he related some "details" of his relationship with Miss Patricia Wright on the critical nights in question which, when they reached Pat's ears by way of Carmel Pettigrew (who was phoning her "best friend" again), caused Miss Wright to go downtown to Mr. Ketcham's insurance office in the Bluefield Block, grasp Mr. Ketcham firmly by the collar with the left hand, and, with the right, slap Mr. Ketcham's right cheek five ringing times, leaving assorted marks in the damp white flesh.

"Why five?" asked Mr. Queen, who had accompanied Miss Wright on the excursion and had stood by, admiring, while she cleansed her reputation.

Miss Wright flushed. "Never mind," she said tartly. "It was—exact—retribution. That lying, bragging—!"

"If you don't watch out," murmured Mr. Queen, "Carter Bradford will have another indictment to draw against you—this one for assault and battery."

"I'm just waiting," said Pat darkly. "But he won't. He knows better!"

And apparently Cart did know better, for nothing more was heard from him about Pat's part in the debacle.

Wrightsville prepared for the Easter holidays. The Bon Ton did a New York business in dresses and spring coats and shoes and underwear and bags, Sol Gowdy put on two "extras" to help in his Men's Shop, and the Low Village emporia were actually crowded with mill and factory customers.

Mr. Ellery Queen shut himself up in his quarters on the top floor of the Wright house and, except for meals, remained incommunicado. Anyone looking in on him would have been puzzled. He was doing exactly nothing visible to the uninitiated eye. Unless it was to consume innumerable cigarettes. He just sat still in the chair by the window and gazed out at the spring sky, or patrolled the room with long strides, head bent, puffing like a locomotive.

Oh, yes. If you looked hard, you could see a mass of notes on his desk—a mess of a mass, for the papers were scattered like dead leaves in autumn. And indeed the wind of Ellery's fury had scattered them so. They lay there discarded and a mockery.

So there was nothing exciting in *that* direction.

Nor anywhere else, except possibly in Nora's.

It was strange about Nora. She had stood up so gallantly under the stresses of the arrest and trial that everyone had begun taking her for granted. Even Hermione thought of nothing but Nora's "condition" and the proper care of the mother, and there old Ludie was of infinitely more practical use. Old Ludie said a woman was a woman, and she was made to have babies, and the less fuss you made over Nora's "condition," the better off they'd both be—Nora *and* the little one. Eat good plain food, with plenty of vegetables and milk and fruit, don't go gallivantin', go easy on the candy and do plenty of walking and mild exercise, and the good Lord would do the rest. Ludie had incessant quarrels about it with Hermione, and at least one memorable tiff with Dr. Willoughby.

But the pathology of the nervous system was so much Sanskrit to Ludie; and while the others were better informed, only two persons close to Nora suspected what was going to happen, and at least one of them was helpless to avert the catastrophe. That was Mr. Queen, and he could only wait and watch. The other was Doc Willoughby, and the doctor did all he could—which meant tonic and daily examinations and advice, all of which Nora ignored.

Nora went to pieces of a sudden. On Easter Sunday, just after the family returned from church, Nora was heard laughing in her bedroom. Pat, who was fixing her hair in her own room down the hall and was nearest, got there first, alarmed by a queer quality in Nora's laughter. She found her sister in a swollen heap on the floor, rocking, laughing her head off while her cheeks changed from red to purple to yellow-ivory. Her eyes were spumy and wild, like a sea storm.

They all ran in then and, among them, managed to drag Nora onto the bed and loosen her clothes, while she laughed and laughed as if the tragedy of her life were the greatest joke in the world. Ellery telephoned Dr. Willoughby and set about with the assistance of Pat and Lola to arrest Nora's hysteria. By the time the doctor arrived, they had managed to stop the laughter, but Nora was shaking and white and looked about her with frightened eyes.

"I can't—understand—it," she gasped. "I was—all right. Then— everything . . . Ooh, I *hurt*."

Dr. Willoughby chased them all away. He was in Nora's room for fifteen minutes. When he came out, he said harshly: "She's got to be taken to the hospital. I'll arrange it myself."

And Hermy clutched at John F., and the girls clung to each other, and nobody said anything while a big hand took hold of them and squeezed.

The Wrightsville General Hospital was understaffed for the day, since it was Easter Sunday and a holiday. The ambulance did not arrive for three quarters of an hour, and for the first time within the memory of John F. Wright, Dr. Milo Willoughby was heard to swear—a long, loud, imagistic curse, after which he clamped his jaws together and went back to Nora.

"She'll be all right, Hermy," said John F.; but his face was gray. If Milo swore, it was bad!

When the ambulance finally came, the doctor wasted no time in further anathema. He had Nora whisked out of the house and away, leaving his car at the Wright curb to accompany her in the ambulance.

They glimpsed Nora's face for an instant as the interns carried her downstairs on a stretcher. The skin lay in coils that jerked this way and that, as if they had a life of their own. The mouth was twisted into a knot, and the eyes were opalescent with agony.

Mercifully, Hermione did not see that face; but Pat did, and she said to Ellery in flat horror: "She's in horrible pain, and she's scared to death, Ellery! Oh, Ellery, do you think—?"

"Let's be getting over to the hospital," said Ellery.

He drove them.

There was no private pavilion at the Wrightsville General, but Doc Willoughby had a corner of the Women's Surgical Ward screened off and Nora put to bed there. The family were not admitted to the ward; they had to sit in the main waiting room off the lobby. The waiting room was gay with Easter posies and sad with the odor of disinfectant. It sickened Hermy, so they made her comfortable on a mission-wood settee, where she lay with tightly closed eyes. John F. just pottered about, touching a flower now and then, and saying once how nice it felt to have the spring here again. The girls sat near their mother. Mr. Queen sat near the girls. And there was nothing but the sound of John F.'s shoes whispering on the worn flowered rug.

And then Dr. Willoughby came hurrying into the waiting room, and everything changed—Hermy opened her eyes, John F. stopped exploring, the girls and Ellery jumped up.

"Haven't much time," panted the doctor. "Listen to me. Nora has a delicate constitution. She's always been a nervy girl. Strain, aggravation, worry, what she's gone through—the poisoning attempts, New Year's Eve, the trial—she's very weak, very badly run-down . . ."

"What are you trying to say, Milo?" demanded John F., clutching his friend's arm.

"John, Nora's condition is serious. No point in keeping it from you and Hermy. She's a sick girl." Dr. Willoughby turned as if to hurry away.

"Milo—wait!" cried Hermy. "How about the . . . baby?"

"She's going to have it, Hermy. We've got to operate."

"But—it's only six months!"

"Yes," said Dr. Willoughby stiffly. "You'd better all wait here. I've got to get ready."

"Milo," said John F., "if there's anything—money— I mean, get anybody—the best—"

"We're in luck, John. Henry Gropper is in Slocum visiting his parents over Easter, classmate of mine, best gynecologist in the East. He's on his way over now."

"Milo—" wailed Hermy.

But Dr. Willoughby was gone.

And now the waiting began all over again, in the silent room with the sun beating in and the Easter posies approaching their deaths fragrantly.

John F. sat down beside his wife and took her hand. They sat that way, their eyes fixed on the clock over the waiting-room door. Seconds came and went and became minutes. Lola turned the pages of a *Cosmopolitan* with a torn cover. She put it down, took it up again.

"Pat," said Ellery, "over here."

John F. looked at him, Hermy looked at him, Lola looked at him. Then Hermy and John F. turned back to the clock, and Lola to the magazine.

"Where?" Pat's voice was shimmering with tears.

"By the window. Away from the family."

Pat trudged over to the farthest bank of windows with him. She sat down on the window seat and looked out.

He took her hand. "Talk."

Her eyes filled. "Oh, Ellery—"

"I know," he said gently. "But you just talk to me. Anything. It's better than choking on the words inside, isn't it? And you can't talk to *them*, because they're choking, too." He gave her a cigarette and held a match up; but she just fingered the cigarette, not seeing it or him. He snuffed the flame between two fingers and then stared at the fingers.

"Talk . . ." said Pat bitterly. "Well, why not? I'm so confused. Nora lying there—her baby coming prematurely—Jim in jail a few squares away—Pop and Mother sitting here like two old people . . . *old*, Ellery. They *are* old."

"Yes, Patty," murmured Ellery.

"And we were so happy before," Pat choked. "It's all like a foul dream. It can't be us. We were—*everything* in this town! Now look at us. Dirtied up. Old. They spit on us."

"Yes, Patty," said Ellery again.

"When I think of how it happened . . . How *did* it happen? Oh, I'll never face another holiday with any gladness!"

"Holiday?"

"Don't you realize? Every last awful thing that's happened—happened on a holiday! Here's Easter Sunday—and Nora's on the operating table. When was Jim arrested? On St. Valentine's Day! When did Rosemary die, and Nora get so badly poisoned? On New Year's Eve! And Nora was sick—poisoned—on Christmas Day, and before that on Thanksgiving Day . . ."

Mr. Queen was looking at Pat as if she had pointed out that two plus two adds up to five. "No. On that point I'm convinced. It's been bothering me for weeks. But it's coincidence. Can't be anything else. No, Patty . . ."

"Even the way it started," cried Patty. "It started on Hallowe'en! Remember?" She stared at the cigarette in her fingers; it was pulpy ruin now. "If we'd never found those three letters in that toxicology book, everything might have been different, Ellery. *Don't* shake your head. It might!"

"Maybe you're right," muttered Ellery. "I'm shaking my head at my own stupidity—" A formless something took possession of his mind in a little leap, like a struck spark. He had experienced that sensation once more—how long ago it seemed!—but now the same thing happened. The spark died; and he was left with a cold, exasperating ash which told nothing.

"You talk about coincidence," said Pat shrilly. "All right, call it that. I don't care what you call it. Coincidence, or fate, or just rotten luck. But if Nora hadn't accidentally dropped those books we were moving that Hallowe'en, the three letters wouldn't have tumbled out and they'd probably be in the book still."

Mr. Queen was about to point out that the peril to Nora had lain not in the letters but in their author; but again a spark leaped, and died, and so he held his tongue.

"For that matter," Pat sighed, "if the most trivial thing had happened differently that day, maybe none of this would have come about. If Nora and I hadn't decided to fix up Jim's new study—if we hadn't opened that box of books!"

"*Box* of books?" said Ellery blankly.

"I brought the crate up myself from the cellar, where Ed Hotchkiss had put it when he cabbed Jim's stuff over from the railroad station after Jim and Nora got back from their honeymoon. Suppose I hadn't opened that box with a hammer and screwdriver? Suppose I hadn't been able to *find* a screwdriver? Or suppose I'd waited a week, a day, even another hour . . . Ellery, what's the matter?"

For Mr. Queen was standing over her like the judgment of the Lord, a terrible wrath on his face; and Patty was so alarmed she shrank back against the window.

"Do you mean to sit there and tell me," said Mr. Queen in an awful quietude, "that those books—the armful of books Nora dropped—those books were *not* the books usually standing on the living-room shelves?" He shook her, and she winced at the pressure of his fingers on her shoulder. "Pat, answer me! You and Nora weren't merely transferring books from the living-room bookshelves to the new shelves in Jim's study upstairs? You're *sure* the books came from that box in the cellar?"

"Of course I'm sure," said Pat shakily. "What's the matter with you? A nailed box. I opened it myself. Why, just a few minutes before you came in that evening, I'd lugged the empty wooden box back to the cellar, with the tools and wrapping paper and mess of bent nails—"

"It's . . . fantastic," said Ellery.

One hand groped for the rocker near Pat. He sat down, heavily.

Pat was bewildered. "But I don't get it, Ellery. Why all the dramatics? What difference can it make?"

Mr. Queen did not answer at once. He just sat there, pale and growing perceptibly paler, nibbling his nails. And the fine lines about his mouth deepened and became hard, and there appeared in his silvery eyes a baffled something that he concealed very quickly—almost as quickly as it showed itself.

"What difference?" He licked his lips.

"Ellery!" Pat was shaking *him* now. "Don't act so mysterious! What's wrong? Tell me!"

"Wait a minute." She stared at him and waited.

He just sat.

Then he muttered: "If I'd only *known*. But I couldn't have . . . Fate. The fate that brought me into that room five minutes late. The fate that kept you from telling me all these months. The fate that concealed the essential fact!"

"But Ellery—"

"Dr. Willoughby!"

They ran across the waiting room. Dr. Willoughby had just blundered in. He was in his surgical gown and cap, his face mask around his throat like a scarf.

There was blood on his gown and none in his cheeks.

"Milo?" quavered Hermione.

"Well, well?" croaked John F.

"For God's sake, Doc!" cried Lola.

Pat rushed up to grab the old man's thick arm.

"Well," said Dr. Willoughby in a hoarse voice, and he stopped.

Then he smiled the saddest smile and put his arm around Hermy's shoulder, quite dwarfing her. "Nora's given you a real Easter present . . . Grandma."

"Grandma," whispered Hermy.

"The baby!" cried Pat. "It's all *right?*"

"Fine, fine, Patricia. A perfect little baby girl. Oh, she's very tiny—she'll need the incubator—but with proper care she'll be all right in a few weeks."

"But Nora," panted Hermy. "My Nora."

"How is Nora, Milo?" demanded John F.

"Is she out of it?" Lola asked.

"Does she know?" cried Pat. "Oh, Nor must be so happy!"

Dr. Willoughby glanced down at his gown, began to fumble at the spot where Nora's blood had splattered.

"Damn it all," he said. His lips were quivering.

Hermione screamed.

"Gropper and I—we did all we could. We couldn't help it. We worked over her like beavers. But she was carrying too big a load. John, don't look at me that way . . ."

The doctor waved his arms wildly.

"Milo—" began John F. in a faint voice.

"She's dead, that's all!"

He ran out of the waiting room.

# PART SIX

# 28

## The Tragedy on Twin Hill

He was looking at the old elms before the new Courthouse. The old was being reborn in multitudes of little green teeth on brown gums of branches; and the new already showed weather streaks in its granite, like varicose veins.

There is sadness, too, in spring, thought Mr. Ellery Queen.

He stepped into the cool shadows of the Courthouse lobby and was borne aloft.

"No time for visitors to be visitin'," said Wally Planetsky sternly. Then he said: "Oh. You're that friend of Patty Wright's. It's a hell of a way to be spendin' the Easter Sunday, Mr. Queen."

"How true," said Mr. Queen. The keeper unlocked an iron door, and they trudged together into the jail. "How is he?"

"Never saw such a man for keepin' his trap shut. You'd think he'd taken a vow."

"Perhaps," sighed Mr. Queen, "he has . . . Anyone been in today to see him?"

"Just that newspaperwoman, Miss Roberts."

Planetsky unlocked another door, locked it carefully behind them.

"Is there a doctor about?" asked Ellery unexpectedly.

Planetsky scratched his ear and opined that if Mr. Queen was feelin' sick . . .

"Is there?"

"Well, sure. We got an infirmary here. Young Ed Crosby—that's Ivor Crosby the farmer's son—he's on duty right now."

"Tell Dr. Crosby I may need him in a very little while."

The keeper looked Ellery over suspiciously, shrugged, unlocked the cell door, locked it again, and shuffled away.

Jim was lying on his bunk, hands crossed behind his head, examining the graph of sky blue beyond bars. He had shaved, Ellery noted; his clean shirt was open at the throat; he seemed at peace.

"Jim?"

Jim turned his head. "Oh, hello, there," he said. "Happy Easter."

"Jim—" began Ellery again, frowning.

Jim swung his feet to the concrete floor and sat up to grip the edge of his bunk with both hands. No peace now. Fear. And that was strange . . . No, logical. When you came to think of it. When you *knew*.

"Something's wrong," said Jim. He jumped to his feet. "Something's wrong!"

Ellery grimaced. This was the punishment for trespassing. This was the pain reserved for meddlers.

"I'm all for you, Jim—"

"What is it?" Jim made a fist.

"You've got a great deal of courage, Jim—"

Jim stared. "She's . . . It's Nora."

"Jim, Nora's dead."

Jim stared, his mouth open.

"I've just come from the hospital. The baby is all right. A girl. Premature delivery. Instruments. Nora was too weak. She didn't come out of it. No pain. She just died, Jim."

Jim's lips came together. He turned around and went back to his bunk and turned around again and sat down, his hands reaching the bunk before he reached it.

"Naturally, the family . . . John F. asked me to tell you, Jim. They're all home now, taking care of Hermione. John F. said to tell you he's terribly sorry, Jim."

Stupid, thought Ellery. A stupid speech. But then he was usually the observer, not a participant. How did one go about drawing the agony out of a stab to the heart? Killing without hurting—for as much as a second? It was a branch of the art of violence with which Mr. Queen was unacquainted.

He sat helplessly on the contraption which concealed Wright County's arrangement for the physical welfare of its prisoners, and thought of symbolism.

"If there's anything I can do—"

That wasn't merely stupid, thought Ellery angrily; that was vicious. Anything he could do! Knowing what was going on in Jim's mind!

Ellery got up and said: "Now, Jim. Now wait a minute, Jim—"

But Jim was at the bars like a great monkey, gripping two of them, his thin face pressed as hard between two adjacent ones as if he meant to force his head through and drag his body after it.

"Let me out of here!" he kept shouting. "Let me out of here! Damn all of you! I've got to get to Nora! Let me out of here!"

He panted and strained, his teeth digging into his lower lip and his eyes hot and his temples bulging with vessels.

"Let me out of here!" he screamed.

A white froth sprang up at the corners of his mouth.

When Dr. Crosby arrived with a black bag and a shaking Keeper Planetsky to open the door for him, Jim Haight was flat on his back on the floor and Mr. Queen knelt on Jim's chest holding Jim's arms down, hard, and yet gently, too.

Jim was still screaming, but the words made no sense.

Dr. Crosby took one look and grabbed a hypodermic.

Twin Hill is a pleasant place in the spring. There's Bald Mountain off to the north, almost always wearing a white cap on its green shoulders, like some remote Friar Tuck; there's the woods part in the gulley of the Twins, where boys go hunting woodchuck and jackrabbit and occasionally scare up a wild deer; and there are the Twins themselves, two identical humps of hill all densely populated with the dead.

The east Twin has the newer cemeteries—the Poor Farm burial ground pretty far down, in the scrub, the old Jewish cemetery, and the Catholic cemetery; these are "new" because not a headstone in the lot bears a date earlier than 1805.

But the west Twin has the really old cemeteries of the Protestant denominations, and there you can see, at the very bald spot of the west Twin, the family plot of the Wrights, the first Wright's tomb—Jezreel Wright's—in its mathematical center. Of course, the Founder's grave is not exposed to the elements—that wind off Bald Mountain does things to grass and topsoil. John F.'s grandfather had built a large mausoleum over the grave—handsome it is, too, finest Vermont granite, white as Patty Wright's teeth. But inside there's the original grave with its little stick of headstone; and if you look sharp, you can still make out the scratches on the stone—the Founder's name, a hopeful quotation from the Book of Revelation, and the date 1723.

The Wright family plot hogs pretty nearly the whole top of the west Twin. The Founder, who seems to have had a nice judgment in all business matters, staked out enough dead land for his seed and his seed's seed to last for eternity. As if he had faith that the Wrights would live and die in Wrightsville unto Judgment Day.

The rest of the cemetery, and the other burial grounds, simply took what was left. And that was all right with everyone, for after all didn't the Founder found? Besides, it made a sort of showplace. Wrightsvillians were forever hauling outlanders up to Twin Hill, halfway to Slocum Township, to exhibit the Founder's grave and the Wright plot. It was one of the "sights."

The automobile road ended at the gate of the cemetery, not far from the boundary of the Wright family plot. From the gate you walked—a peaceful walk under trees so old you wondered they didn't lie down and ask to be buried themselves out of plain weariness. But they just kept growing old and droopier. Except in spring. Then the green hair began sprouting from their hard black skins with a sly fertility, as if death were a great joke.

Maybe the graves so lush and thick all over the hillside had something to do with it.

Services for Nora—on Tuesday, April the fifteenth—were private. Dr. Doolittle uttered a few words in the chapel of Willis Stone's Eternal Rest Mortuary, on Upper Whistling Avenue in High Village. Only the family and a few friends were present—Mr. Queen, Judge and Clarice Martin, Dr. Willoughby, and some of John F.'s people from the bank. Frank Lloyd was seen skulking about the edge of the group, straining for a glimpse of the pure, still profile in the copper casket. He looked as if he had not taken his clothes off for a week or slept during that time. When Hermy's eye rested on him, he shrank and disappeared . . . Perhaps twenty mourners in all.

Hermy was fine. She sat up straight in her new black, eyes steady, listening to Dr. Doolittle; and when they all filed past the bier for a last look at Nora, she merely grew a little paler and blinked. She didn't cry. Pat said it was because she was all cried out. John F. was a crumpled, red-nosed little derelict. Lola had to take him by the hand and lead him away from the casket to let Mr. Stone put the head section in place.

Nora had looked very calm and young. She was dressed in her wedding gown.

Just before they went out to the funeral cars, Pat slipped into Mr. Stone's office. When she came back, she said: "I just called the hospital. Baby's fine. She's growing in that incubator like a little vegetable."

Pat's lips danced, and Mr. Queen put his arm about her.

Looking back on it, Ellery saw the finer points of Jim's psychology. But that was after the event. Beforehand it was impossible to tell, because Jim acted his part perfectly. He fooled them all, including Ellery.

Jim came to the cemetery between two detectives, like an animated sandwich. He was "all right." Very little different from the Jim who had sat in the courtroom—altogether different from the Jim Ellery had sat upon in the cell. There was a whole despair about him so enveloping that he had poise and self-control, even dignity.

He marched along steadily between his two guards, ignoring them, looking neither to right nor to left, on the path under the aged trees up to the top of the hill where the newly turned earth gaped, like a wound, to receive Nora. The cars had been left near the gate.

Most of Wrightsville watched from a decent distance—let us give them that. But they were there, silent and curious; only occasionally someone whispered, or a forefinger told a story.

The Wrights stood about the grave in a woebegone group, Lola and Pat pressing close to Hermione and their father. John F.'s sister, Tabitha, had been notified, but she had wired that she was ill and could not fly to the funeral from California, and the Lord in His wisdom taketh away, and perhaps it was all for the best, may she rest in peace, your loving sister, Tabitha. John F. made a wad out of the wire and hurled it blindly; it landed in the early morning fire Ludie had lit against the chill in the big old house.

So it was just the immediate family group, and Ellery Queen, and Judge Eli Martin and Clarice and Doc Willoughby and some others; and, of course, Dr. Doolittle.

When Jim was brought up, a mutter arose from the watchers; eyes became very sharp for this meeting; this was very nearly "the best part of it." But nothing remarkable happened. Or perhaps it did. For Hermy's lips were seen to move, and Jim went over to her and kissed her. He paid no attention to anyone else; after that he just stood there at the grave, a thin figure of loneliness.

During the interment service a breeze ran through the leaves, like fingers; and indeed, Dr. Doolittle's voice took on a lilt and became quite musical. The evergreens and lilies bordering the grave stirred a little, too.

Then, unbelievably, it was over, and they were shuffling down the walk, Hermy straining backward to catch a last glimpse of the casket which could no longer be seen, having been lowered into the earth. But the earth had not yet been rained upon it, for that would have been bestial; that could be done later, under no witnessing eyes but the eyes of the gravediggers, who were a peculiar race of people. So Hermy strained, and she thought how beautiful the evergreens and the lilies looked and how passionately Nora had detested funerals.

The crowd at the gate parted silently.

Then Jim did it.

One moment he was trudging along between the detectives, a dead man staring at the ground; the next he came alive. He tripped one of his guards. The man fell backward with a thud, his mouth an astonished O even as he fell. Jim struck the second guard on the jaw, so that the man fell on his brother officer and they threshed about, like wrestlers, trying to regain their feet.

In those few seconds Jim was gone, running through the crowd like a bull, bowling people over, spinning people around, dodging and twisting . . .

Ellery shouted at him, but Jim ran on.

The detectives were on their feet now, running, too, revolvers out uselessly. To fire would mean hitting innocent people. They pushed through, cursing and ashamed.

And then Ellery saw that Jim's madness was not madness at all. For a quarter way down the hill, past all the parked cars, stood a single great car, its nose pointed away from the cemetery. No one was in it; but the motor had been kept running, Ellery knew, for Jim leaped in and the car shot forward at once.

By the time the two detectives reached a clear space and fired down the hill, the big limousine was a toy in the distance. It was careening crazily and going at a great speed.

And after another few moments, the detectives reached their own car and took up the chase, one driving, the other still firing wildly. But Jim was well out of range by this time, and everyone knew he had a splendid chance of escaping. The two cars disappeared.

For some moments there was no sound on the hillside but the sound of the wind in the trees.

Then the crowd shouted and swept over the Wrights and their friends, and automobiles began flying down the hill in merry clouds of dust, as if this were a paid entertainment and their drivers were determined not to miss the exciting climax.

Hermy lay on the living-room settee, and Pat and Lola were applying cold vinegar compresses to her head while John F. turned the pages of one of his stamp albums with great deliberation, as if it were one of the most important things in the world. He was in a corner by the window to catch the late afternoon light. Clarice Martin was holding Hermy's hand tightly in an ecstasy of remorse, crying over her defection during the trial and over Nora and over this last shocking blow. And Hermy—Hermy the Great!—was comforting her friend!

Lola slapped a new compress so hard on her mother's forehead that Hermy smiled at her reproachfully. Pat took it away from her angry sister and set it right.

At the fireplace Dr. Willoughby and Mr. Queen conversed in low tones.

Then Judge Martin came in from outdoors.

And with him was Carter Bradford.

Everything stopped, as if an enemy had walked into camp. But Carter ignored it. He was quite pale but held himself erect; and he kept from looking at Pat, who had turned paler than he. Clarice Martin was frankly frightened. She glanced quickly at her husband, but Judge Eli shook his head and went over to the window to seat himself by John F. and watch the fluttering pages of the stamp album, so gay with color.

"I don't want to intrude, Mrs. Wright," said Carter stiffishly. "But I had to tell you how badly I feel about—all this."

"Thank you, Carter," said Hermy. "Lola, stop babying me! Carter, what about"—Hermy swallowed—"Jim?"

"Jim got away, Mrs. Wright."

"I'm *glad*," cried Pat. "Oh, I'm so very glad!"

Carter glanced her way. "Don't say that, Patty. That sort of thing never winds up right. Nobody 'gets away.' Jim would have been better . . . advised to have stuck it out."

"So that you could hound him to his death, I suppose! All over again!"

"Pat." John F. left his stamp album where it was. He put his thin hand on Carter's arm. "It was nice of you to come here today, Cart. I'm sorry if I was every harsh with you. How does it look?"

"Bad, Mr. Wright." Carter's lips tightened. "Naturally, the alarm is out. All highways are being watched. It's true he got away, but it's only a question of time before he's captured—"

"Bradford," inquired Mr. Queen from the fireplace, "have you traced the getaway car?"

"Yes."

"Looked like a put-up job to me," muttered Dr. Willoughby. "That car was in a mighty convenient place, and the motor was running!"

"Whose car is it?" demanded Lola.

"It was rented from Homer Findlay's garage in Low Village this morning."

"Rented!" exclaimed Clarice Martin. "By whom?"

"Roberta Roberts."

Ellery said: "Ah," in a tone of dark satisfaction, and nodded as if that were all he had wanted to know. But the others were surprised.

Lola tossed her head. "Good for her!"

"Carter let me talk to the woman myself just now," said Judge Eli Martin wearily. "She's a smart female. Insists she hired the car just to drive to the cemetery this morning."

"And that she left the motor running by mistake," added Carter Bradford dryly.

"And was it a coincidence that she also turned the car about so that it pointed down the hill?" murmured Mr. Queen.

"That's what I asked her," said Carter. "Oh, there's no question about her complicity, and Dakin's holding her. But that doesn't get Jim Haight back, nor does it give us a case against this Roberts woman. We'll probably have to let her go." He said angrily: "I never did trust that woman!"

"She visited Jim on Sunday," remarked Ellery reflectively.

"Also yesterday! I'm convinced she arranged the escape with Jim then."

"What difference does it make?" Hermy sighed. "Escape—no escape—Jim won't ever escape." Then Hermy said a queer thing, considering how she had always claimed she felt about her son-in-law and his guilt. Hermy said: "Poor Jim," and closed her eyes.

The news arrived at ten o'clock that same night. Carter Bradford came over again, and this time he went directly to Pat Wright and took her hand. She was so astonished she forgot to snatch it away.

Carter said gently: "It's up to you and Lola now, Pat."

"What . . . on earth are you talking about?" asked Pat in a shrill tight voice.

"Dakin's men have found the car Jim escaped in."

"*Found* it?"

Ellery Queen rose from a dark corner and came over into the light. "If it's bad news, keep your voices down. Mrs. Wright's just gone to bed, and John F. doesn't look as if he could take any more today. Where was the car found?"

"At the bottom of a ravine off Route 478A, up in the hills. About fifty miles from here."

"Lord," breathed Pat, staring.

"It had crashed through the highway rail," growled Carter, "just past a hairpin turn. The road is tricky up there. Dropped about two hundred feet—"

"And Jim?" asked Ellery.

Pat sat down in the love seat by the fireplace, looking up at Cart as if he were a judge about to pronounce doom.

"Found in the car." Cart turned aside. "Dead." He turned back and looked humbly at Pat. "So that's the end of the case. It's the end, Pat . . ."

"Poor Jim," whispered Pat.

*     *     *

"I want to talk to you two," said Mr. Queen.

It was very late. But there was no time. Time had been lost in the nightmare. Hermione had heard, and Hermione had gone to pieces. Strange that the funeral of her daughter should have found her strong and the news of her son-in-law's death weak. Perhaps it was the crushing tap after the heavy body blows. But Hermy collapsed, and Dr. Willoughby spent hours with her trying to get her to sleep. John F. was in hardly better case: he had taken to trembling, and the doctor noticed it and packed him off to bed in a guest room while Lola assisted with Hermy and Pat helped her father up the stairs . . . Now it was over, and they were both asleep, and Lola had locked herself in, and Dr. Willoughby had gone home, sagging.

"I want to talk to you two," said Mr. Queen.

Carter was still there. He had been a bed of rock for Hermy this night. She had actually clung to him while she wept, and Mr. Queen thought this, too, was strange. And then he thought: No, this is the rock, the last rock, and Hermy clings. If she lets go, she drowns, they all drown. That is how she must feel.

And he repeated: "I want to talk to you two."

Pat was suspended between worlds. She had been sitting beside Ellery on the porch, waiting for Carter Bradford to go home. Limply and far away. And now Carter had come out of the house, fumbling with his disreputable hat and fishing for some graceful way to negotiate the few steps of the porch and reach the haven of night shadows beyond, on the lawn.

"I don't think there's anything you can have to say that I'd want to hear," said Carter huskily; but he made no further move to leave the porch.

"Ellery—don't," said Pat, taking his hand in the gloom.

Ellery squeezed the cold young flesh. "I've got to. This man thinks he's a martyr. *You* think you're being a heroine in some Byronic tragedy. You're both fools, and that's the truth."

"Good night!" said Carter Bradford.

"Wait, Bradford. It's been a difficult time and an especially difficult day. And I shan't be in Wrightsville much longer."

"Ellery!" Pat wailed.

"I've been here much too long already, Pat. Now there's nothing to keep me—nothing at all."

"Nothing . . . at all?"

"Spare me your tender farewells," snapped Cart. Then he laughed sheepishly and sat down on the step near them. "Don't pay any attention to me, Queen. I'm in a fog these days. Sometimes I think I must be pretty much of a drip."

Pat gaped at him. "Cart—*you?* Being humble?"

"I've grown up a bit these past few months," mumbled Cart.

"There's been a heap of growing up around here these past few months," said Mr. Queen mildly. "How about you two being sensible and proving it?"

Pat took her hand away. "Please, Ellery—"

"I know I'm meddling, and the lot of the meddler is hard," sighed Mr. Queen. "But just the same, how about it?"

"I thought you were in love with her," said Cart gruffly.

"I am."

"Ellery!" cried Pat. "You never *once*—"

"I'll be in love with that funny face of yours as long as I live," said Mr. Queen wistfully. "It's a lovely funny face. But the trouble is, Pat, that you're not in love with *me*."

Pat stumbled over a word, then decided to say nothing.

"You're in love with Cart."

Pat sprang from the porch chair. "What if I was! Or am! People don't forget hurts and burns!"

"Oh, but they do," said Mr. Queen. "People are more forgetful than you'd think. Also, they have better sense than we sometimes give them credit for. Emulate them."

"It's impossible," said Pat tightly. "This is no time for silliness, anyway. You don't seem to realize what's happened to us in this town. We're pariahs. We've got a whole new battle on our hands to rehabilitate ourselves. And it's just Lola and me now to help Pop and Muth hold their heads up again. I'm not going to run out on them now, when they need me most."

"I'd help you, Pat," said Cart inaudibly.

"Thanks! We'll do it on our own. Is that all, Mr. Queen?"

"There's no hurry," murmured Mr. Queen.

Pat stood there for a moment, then she said good-night in an angry voice and went into the house. The door huffed. Ellery and Carter sat in silence for some time.

"Queen," said Cart at last.

"Yes, Bradford?"

"This isn't over, is it?"

"What do you mean?"

"I have the most peculiar feeling you know something I don't."

"Oh," said Mr. Queen. Then he said: "Really?"

Carter slapped his hat against his thighs. "I won't deny I've been pig-headed. Jim's death has done something to me, though. I don't know why it should, because it hasn't changed the facts one iota. He's still the only one who could have poisoned Nora's cocktail, and he's still the only one who had any conceivable motive to want her to die. And yet . . . I'm not so sure anymore."

"Since when?" asked Ellery in a peculiar tone.

"Since the report came in that he was found dead."

"Why should that make a difference?"

Carter put his head between his hands. "Because there's every reason to believe the car he was driving didn't go through that rail into the ravine by accident."

"I see," said Ellery.

"I didn't want to tell that to the Wrights. But Dakin and I both think Jim drove that car off the road deliberately." WOW (MB, August 7, 2011)

Mr. Queen said nothing.

"And somehow that made me think—don't know why it should have— Well, I began to wonder. Queen!" Carter jumped up. "For God's sake, tell me if you know! I won't sleep until I'm sure. *Did Jim Haight commit that murder?*"

*"No."*

Carter stared at him. "Then who did?" he asked hoarsely.

Mr. Queen rose, too. "I shan't tell you."

"Then you do know!"

"Yes," sighed Ellery.

"But Queen, you can't—"

"Oh, but I can. Don't think it's easy for me. My whole training rebels against this sort of—well, connivance. But I like these people. They're nice people, and they've been through too much. I shouldn't want to hurt them anymore. Let it go. The hell with it."

"But you can tell, Queen!" implored Cart.

"No. You're not sure of yourself; not yet, Bradford. You're rather a nice chap. But the growing-up process—it's been retarded." Ellery shook his head. "The best thing you can do is forget it and get Patty to marry you. She's crazy in love with you."

Carter grasped Ellery's arm so powerfully that Ellery winced. "But you've *got* to tell me!" he cried. "How could I . . . knowing that any-one . . . any *one* of them . . . might be . . . ?"

Mr. Queen frowned in the darkness.

"Tell you what I'll do with you, Cart," he said at last. "You help these people get back to normal in Wrightsville. You chase Patty Wright off her feet. Wear her down.

"But if you're not successful, if you feel you're not making any headway, wire me. I'm going back home. Send me a wire in New York, and I'll come back. And maybe what I'll have to say to you and Patty will solve your problem."

"Thanks," said Carter Bradford hoarsely.

"I don't know that it will," sighed Mr. Queen. "But who can tell? This has been the oddest case of mixed-up people, emotions, and events I've ever run across. Good-bye, Bradford."

# 29

## The Return of Ellery Queen

This, thought Mr. Ellery Queen as he stood on the station platform, makes me an admiral all over again. The second voyage of Columbus . . .

He glanced moodily at the station sign. The tail of the train that had brought him from New York was just disappearing around the curve at Wrightsville Junction three miles down the line. He could have sworn that the two small boys swinging their dirty legs on the hand truck under the eaves of the station were the same boys he had seen—in another century!—on his first arrival in Wrightsville.

Gabby Warrum, the station agent, strolled out to stare at him. Ellery waved and made hastily for Ed Hotchkiss's cab, drawn up on the gravel.

As Ed drove him "uptown," Ellery's hand tightened in his pocket about the telegram he had received the night before. It was from Carter Bradford, and it said simply: COME. PLEASE.

He had not been away long—a matter of three weeks or so—but just the same it seemed to him that Wrightsville had changed. Or perhaps it would be truer to say that Wrightsville had changed *back*. It was the old Wrightsville again, the town he had come into so hopefully the previous August, nine months ago. It had the same air of unhurried peace this lovely Sunday afternoon. Even the people seemed the old people, not the maddened horde of January and February and March and April.

Mr. Queen made a telephone call from the Hollis Hotel, then had Ed Hotchkiss drive him up the Hill. It was late afternoon, and the birds were whizzing and chirping at a great rate around the old Wright house. He paid Ed off, watched the cab chug down the Hill, and then strolled up the walk.

The little house next door—the house of Nora and Jim—was shuttered up; it looked opaque and ugly in its blindness. Mr. Queen felt a tremor in his spine. That *was* a house to avoid.

He hesitated at the front steps of the big house and listened. There were voices from the rear gardens. So he went around, walking on the grass.

He paused in the shadow of the oleander bush, where he could see them without being seen.

The sun was bright on Hermy, joggling a brand-new baby carriage in an extremely critical way. John F. was grinning, and Lola and Pat were making serious remarks about professional grandmothers and how about giving a couple of aunts a chance to practice, for goodness' sake? The baby would be home from the hospital in just a couple of weeks!

Mr. Queen watched, unobserved, for a long time. His face was very grave. Once he half turned away, as if he meant to flee once and for all. But then he saw Patricia Wright's face again and how it had grown older and thinner since last he had seen it, and so he sighed and set about making an end of things. After five minutes of delicate reconnaissance he managed to catch Pat's eye while the others were occupied—caught her eye and put his finger to his lips, shaking his head in warning.

Pat said something casual to her family and strolled toward him. He backed off, and then she came around the corner of the house and flew into his arms.

"Ellery! Darling! Oh, I'm so *glad* to see you! When did you come? What's the mystery for? Oh, you bug—I *am* glad!" She kissed him and held him close, and for a moment her face was the gay young face he had remembered.

He let her sprinkle his shoulder, and then he took her by the hand and drew her toward the front of the house. "That's your convertible at the curb, isn't it? Let's go for a ride."

"But Ellery, Pop and Muth and Lola—they'll be heartbroken if you don't—"

"I don't want to disturb them now, Patty. They look really happy, getting ready for the baby. How is she, by the way?" Ellery drove Pat's car down the Hill.

"Oh, wonderful. Such a clever little thing! And do you know? She looks just like—" Pat stopped. Then she said quietly: "Just like Nora."

"Does she? Then she must be a beautiful young lady indeed."

"Oh, she is! And I'll swear she knows Muth! Really, I mean it. We can't *wait* for her to come home from the hospital. Of course, Mother won't let *any* of us touch little Nora—that's her name, you know—when we visit her—we're there practically *all* the time! except that I sneak over there alone once in a while when I'm not supposed to . . . Little

Nora is going to have Nora's old bedroom—ought to see how we've fixed it up, with ivory furniture and gewgaws and big teddy bears and special nursery wallpaper and all. Anyway, the little atom and I have secrets . . . Well, we do! . . . Of course, she's out of the incubator . . . and she gurgles at me and hangs on to my hand for dear life and *squeezes*. She's so fat, Ellery, you'd laugh!"

Ellery laughed.

"You're talking like the old Patty I knew—"

"You think so?" asked Pat in a queer voice.

"But you don't *look*—"

"No," said Pat. "No, I don't. I'm getting to be an old hag. Where are we going?"

"Nowhere in particular," said Ellery vaguely, turning the car south and beginning to drive toward Wrightsville Junction.

"But tell me! What brings you back to Wrightsville? It must be us— couldn't be anyone else! How's the novel?"

"Finished."

"Oh, grand! Ellery, you never let me read a word of it. How does it end?"

"That," said Mr. Queen, "is one of my reasons for coming back to Wrightsville."

"What do you mean?"

"The end," he grinned. "I've ended it, but it's always easy to change the last chapter—at least, certain elements not directly concerned with mystery plot. You might be of help there."

"Me? But I'd love to! And—oh, Ellery. What am I thinking of? I haven't thanked you for that magnificent gift you sent me from New York. And those wonderful things you sent Muth, and Pop, and Lola. Oh, Ellery, you shouldn't have. We didn't do anything that—"

"Oh, bosh. Seeing much of Cart Bradford lately?"

Pat examined her fingernails. "Oh, Cart's been around."

"And Jim's funeral?"

"We buried him next to Nora."

"Well!" said Ellery. "You know, I feel a thirst coming on. How about stopping in somewhere for a long one, Patty?"

"All right," said Pat moodily.

"Isn't that Gus Olesen's *Roadside Tavern* up ahead? By gosh, it is!"

Pat glanced at him, but Ellery grinned and stopped the car before the tavern, and helped her out, at which she grimaced and said men in Wrightsville didn't do things like that, and Ellery grinned again, which made Pat laugh; and they walked into Gus Olesen's cool place arm in arm, laughing together; and Ellery walked her right up to the table where

Carter Bradford sat waiting in a coil of knots, and said: "Here she is, Bradford. C.O.D."

"Pat," said Cart, his palms flat on the table.

"Cart!" cried Pat.

"Good morrow, good morrow," chanted a cracked voice; and Mr. Queen saw old Anderson the Soak, seated at a nearby table with a fistful of dollar bills in one hand and a row of empty whisky glasses before him.

"Good morrow to you, Mr. Anderson," said Mr. Queen; and while he nodded and smiled at Mr. Anderson, things were happening at the table; so that when he turned back, there was Pat, seated, and Carter seated, and they were glaring at each other across the table. So Mr. Queen sat down, too, and said to Gus Olesen: "Use your imagination, Gus."

Gus scratched his head and got busy behind the bar.

"Ellery"—Pat's eyes were troubled—"you tricked me into coming here with you."

"I wasn't sure you'd come, untricked," murmured Mr. Queen.

"*I* asked Queen to come back to Wrightsville, Pat," said Cart hoarsely. "He said he'd— Pat, I've tried to see you. I've tried to make you understand that we can wipe the past out, that I'm in love with you and always was and always will be, and that I want to marry you more than anything in the world—"

"Let's not discuss *that* anymore," said Pat. She began making pleats in the skirt of the tablecloth.

Carter seized a tall glass Gus set down before him; and Pat did, too, with a sort of gratitude for the diversion; and they sat in silence for a while, drinking and not looking at each other.

At his table old Anderson had risen, one hand on the cloth to steady himself, and he was chanting:

> "I believe a leaf of grass is no less than the journeywork of the stars,
> And the pismire is equally perfect, and a grain of sand, and the egg of the wren,
> And the tree toad is a chef-d'oeuvre of the highest,
> And the running blackberry would adorn the parlors of heaven—"

"Siddown, Mr. Anderson," said Gus Olesen gently. "You're rockin' the boat."

"Whitman," said Mr. Queen, looking around. "And very apt."

Old Anderson leered, and went on:

"And the narrowest hinge in my hand puts to scorn all machinery,

And the cow, crunching with depressed head, surpasses any statue,

And a mouse is miracle enough to stagger sextillions of infidels!"

And with a courtly bow the Old Soak sat down again and began to pound out rhythms on the table. "I was a poet!" he shouted. His lips waggled. "And l-look at me now . . ."

"Yes," said Mr. Queen thoughtfully. "That's very true indeed."

"Here's your poison!" said Gus at the next table, slopping a glass of whisky before Mr. Anderson. Then Gus looked very guilty and, avoiding the startled eyes of Pat, went quickly behind his bar and hid himself in a copy of Frank Lloyd's *Record*.

Mr. Anderson drank, murmuring to himself in his gullet.

"Pat," said Mr. Queen, "I came back here today to tell you and Carter who was really responsible for the crimes Jim Haight was charged with."

"Oh," said Patty, and she sucked in her breath.

"There are miracles in the human mind, too. You told me something in the hospital waiting room the day Nora died—one little acorn fact—and it grew into a tall tree in my mind."

" 'And a mouse,' " shouted Mr. Anderson exultantly, " 'is miracle enough to stagger sextillions of infidels!' "

Pat whispered: "Then it wasn't Jim after all . . . Ellery, no! Don't! Please! No!"

"Yes," said Ellery gently. "That thing is standing between you and Cart. It's a question mark that would outlive you both. I want to erase it and put a period in its place. Then the chapter will be closed, and you and Cart can look each other in the eye again with some sort of abiding faith." He sipped his drink, frowning. "I hope!"

"You hope?" muttered Cart.

"The truth," said Ellery soberly, "is unpleasant."

"Ellery!" cried Pat.

"But you're not children, either of you. Don't delude yourselves. It would stand between you even if you married . . . the uncertainty of it, the not-knowing, the doubt and the night-and-day question. It's what's keeping you apart and what has kept you apart. Yes, the truth is unpleasant. But at least it *is* the truth, and if you know the truth, you have knowledge; and if you have knowledge, you can make a decision with durability . . . Pat, this is surgery. It's cut the tumor out or die. Shall I operate?"

Mr. Anderson was singing "Under the Greenwood Tree" in a soft croak, beating time with his empty whisky glass.

Patty sat up perfectly straight, her hands clasped about her glass. "Go ahead . . . Doctor."

And Cart took a long swallow and nodded.


Mr. Queen sighed.

"Do you recall, Pat, telling me in the hospital about the time I came into Nora's house—last Hallowe'en—and found you and Nora transferring books from the living room to Jim's new study upstairs?" Pat nodded wordlessly. "And what did you tell me? That the books you and Nora were lugging upstairs you had just removed from a *nailed box*. That you'd gone down into the cellar just a few minutes before I dropped in, seen the box of books down there all nailed up, exactly as Ed Hotchkiss had left it when he cabbed it from the station weeks and weeks before . . . *seen the box intact and opened it yourself.*"

"A box of books?" muttered Carter.

"That box of books, Cart, had been part of Jim's luggage which he'd shipped from New York to Wrightsville when he came back to Wrightsville to make up with Nora. He'd checked it at the Wrightsville station, Cart. It was at the station all the time Jim and Nora were away on their honeymoon; it was brought to the new house only on their return, stored down in the cellar, and on Hallowe'en, Pat found that box still intact, still nailed up, stilled unopened. That was the fact I hadn't known— the kernel fact, the acorn fact, that told me the truth."

"But how, Ellery?" asked Pat, feeling her head.

"You'll see in a moment, honey. All the time, I'd assumed that the books I saw you and Nora handling were merely being transferred from the living-room bookshelves to Jim's new study upstairs. I thought they were *house books*, books of Jim's and Nora's that had been in the house for some time. It was a natural assumption—I saw no box on the living-room floor, no nails—"

"I'd emptied the box and taken the box, nails, and tools down to the cellar just before you came in," said Pat. "I told you that in the hospital that day."

"Too late," growled Ellery. "When I came in, I saw no evidence of such a thing. And I'm not a clairvoyant."

"But what's the point?" frowned Carter Bradford.

"One of the books in the wooden box Patty opened that Hallowe'en," said Ellery, "was Jim's copy of Edgcomb's *Toxicology*."

Cart's jaw dropped. "The marked passage about arsenic!"

"Not only that, but it was from between two pages of that volume that the three letters fell out."

This time Cart said nothing. And Pat was looking at Ellery with deep quotation marks between her eyebrows.

"Now, since the box had been nailed up in New York and sent to General Delivery, Wrightsville, where it was held, and the toxicology book with the letters in it was found by us directly after the box was unpacked—the letters fell out as Nora dropped an armful of books quite by accident—then the conclusion is absolutely inescapable: *Jim could not possibly have written those three letters in Wrightsville.* And when I saw that, I saw the whole thing. The letters *must* have been written by Jim in New York—*before* he returned to Wrightsville to ask Nora for the second time to marry him, *before* he knew that Nora would accept him after his desertion of her and his three-year absence!"

"Yes," mumbled Carter Bradford.

"But don't you see?" cried Ellery. "How can we now state with such fatuous certainty that the sickness and death Jim predicted for his 'wife' in those three letters *referred to Nora?* True, Nora was Jim's wife when the letters were found, *but she was NOT his wife, nor could Jim have known she would BE his wife, when he originally wrote them!*"

He stopped and, even though it was cool in Gus Olesen's taproom, he dried his face with a handkerchief and took a long pull at his glass. At the next table, Mr. Anderson snored.

Pat gasped: "But Ellery, if those three letters didn't refer to Nora, then the whole thing—the whole thing—"

"Let me tell it my way," said Mr. Queen in a harsh voice. "Once doubt is raised that the 'wife' mentioned in the three letters was Nora, then two facts that before seemed irrelevant simply shout to be noticed. One is that the letters bore *incomplete dates.* That is, they marked the month, and the day of the month, *but not the year.* So the three holidays—Thanksgiving, Christmas, and New Year's—which Jim had written down on the successive letters as marking the dates of his 'wife's' illness, more serious illness, and finally death, might have been the similar dates of one, two, or even three years before! Not 1940 at all, but 1939, or 1938, or 1937 . . .

"And the second fact, of course, was that not once did any of the letters refer to *the name Nora;* the references were consistently to '*my wife.*'

"If Jim wrote those letters in New York—before his marriage to Nora, before he even knew Nora would marry him—then Jim could not have been writing about *Nora's* illness or *Nora's* death. And if we can't believe this—an assumption we all took for granted from the beginning of the case—then the whole structure which postulated *Nora* as Jim's intended poison victim collapses."

"This is incredible," muttered Carter. "Incredible."

"I'm confused," moaned Patty. "You mean—"

"I mean," said Mr. Queen, "that Nora was never threatened, Nora was never in danger . . . *Nora was never meant to be murdered.*"

Pat shook her head violently and groped for her glass.

"But that opens up a whole new field of speculation!" exclaimed Carter. "If Nora wasn't meant to be murdered—ever, at all—"

"What are the facts?" argued Ellery. "A woman did die on New Year's Eve: Rosemary Haight. When we thought Nora was the intended victim, we said Rosemary died by accident. But now that we know Nora *wasn't* the intended victim, surely it follows that Rosemary did NOT die by accident—*that Rosemary was meant to be murdered from the beginning?*"

"Rosemary was meant to be murdered from the beginning," repeated Pat slowly, as if the words were in a language she didn't understand.

"But Queen—" protested Bradford.

"I know, I know," sighed Ellery. "It raises tremendous difficulties and objections. But with Nora eliminated as the intended victim, it's the only logical explanation for the crime. So we've got to accept it as our new premise. Rosemary was *meant* to be murdered. Immediately I asked myself: Did the three letters have anything to do with Rosemary's death?

"Superficially, no. The letters referred to the death of Jim's wife—"

"And Rosemary was Jim's sister," said Pat with a frown.

"Yes, and besides Rosemary had shown no signs of the illnesses predicted for Thanksgiving Day and Christmas Day. Moreover, since the three letters can now be interpreted as two or three years old or more, they no longer appear necessarily criminal. They can merely refer to the natural death of a previous wife of Jim's—not Nora, but *a first wife whom Jim married in New York* and who died there some New Year's Day between the time Jim ran out on Nora and the time he came back to marry Nora."

"But Jim never said anything about a first wife," objected Pat.

"That wouldn't prove he hadn't had one," said Cart.

"No," nodded Ellery. "So it all might have been perfectly innocent. Except for two highly significant and suspicious factors: first, that the letters were written but never mailed, as if no death *had* occurred in New York; and second, that a woman did actually die in Wrightsville on New Year's Day of 1941, as written by Jim in his third and last letter a long time before it happened. Coincidence? My gorge rises at the very notion.

"No, I saw that there must be *some* connection between Rosemary's death and the three letters Jim wrote—he did write them, of course; poor Judge Eli Martin's attempt to cast doubt on their authenticity during the trial was a brave but transparent act of desperation."

Mr. Anderson woke up, looking annoyed. But Gus Olesen shook his head. Mr. Anderson tottered over to the bar. " 'Landlord,' " he leered, " 'fill the flowing bowl until it does run over!' "

"We don't serve in bowls, and besides, Andy, you had enough," said Gus reprovingly.

Mr. Anderson began to weep, his head on the bar; and after a few sobs, he fell asleep again.

"What connection," continued Mr. Queen thoughtfully, "is possible between Rosemary Haight's death and the three letters Jim Haight wrote long, long before? And with this question," he said, "we come to the heart of the problem. For with Rosemary the intended victim all along, the use of the three letters can be interpreted as a stupendous blind, a clever deception, *a psychological smoke screen to conceal the truth from the authorities!* Isn't that what happened? Didn't you and Dakin, Bradford, instantly dismiss Rosemary's death as a factor and concentrate on Nora as the intended victim? But that was just what Rosemary's murderer would want you to do! You ignored the actual victim to look for murder motives against the ostensible victim. And so you built your case around Jim, who was the only person who could possibly have poisoned *Nora*, and never for an instant sought the real criminal—*the person with the motive and opportunity to poison Rosemary.*"

Pat was by now so bewildered that she gave herself up wholly to listening. But Carter Bradford was following with a savage intentness, hunched over the table and never taking his eyes from Ellery's face.

"Go on!" he said. "Go on, Queen!"

"Let's go back," said Mr. Queen, lighting a cigarette. "We now know Jim's three letters referred to a hidden, a never-mentioned, a first wife. If this woman died on New Year's Day two or three years ago, why didn't Jim mail the letters to his sister? More important than that, why didn't he disclose the fact to you or Dakin when he was arrested? Why didn't Jim tell Judge Martin, his attorney, that the letters didn't mean Nora, for use as a possible defense in his trial? For if the first wife were in all truth dead, it would have been a simple matter to corroborate—the attending physician's affidavit, the death certificate, a dozen things.

"*But Jim kept his mouth shut.* He didn't by so much as a sober word indicate that he'd married another woman between the time he and Nora broke up almost four years ago and the time he returned to Wrightsville to marry her. Why? Why Jim's mysterious silence on this point?"

"Maybe," said Pat with a shiver, "because he'd actually planned and carried out the murder of his first wife."

"Then why didn't he mail the letters to his sister?" argued Cart. "Since he'd presumably written them for that eventuality?"

"Ah," said Mr. Queen. "The very counterpoint. So I said to myself: Is it possible that the murder Jim had planned of his first wife *did not take place at the time it was supposed to?*"

"You mean she was alive when Jim came back to Wrightsville?" gasped Pat.

"Not merely alive," said Mr. Queen; he slowly ground out the butt of his cigarette in an ashtray. "She followed Jim here."

"The first *wife?*" Carter gaped.

"She came to *Wrightsville?*" cried Pat.

"Yes, but not as Jim's first wife. Not as Jim's any-wife."

"Then who—?"

"*She came to Wrightsville,*" said Ellery, "*as Jim's sister.*"

Mr. Anderson came to life at the bar and began: "Landlord—"

"Go home," said Gus, shaking his head.

"Mead! Nepenthe!" implored Mr. Anderson.

"We don't carry that stuff," said Gus.

"As Jim's sister," whispered Pat. "The woman Jim introduced to us as his sister, Rosemary, *wasn't his sister at all?* She was his *wife?*"

"Yes." Ellery motioned to Gus Olesen. But Gus had the second round ready. Mr. Anderson followed the tray with gleaming eyes. And no one spoke until Gus returned to the bar.

"But Queen," said Carter, dazed, "how in hell can you know *that?*"

"Well, whose word have we that the woman who called herself Rosemary Haight was Jim Haight's sister?" demanded Ellery. "Only the word of Jim and Rosemary, and they're both dead . . . However, that's not how I know she was his first wife. I know that because I know who really killed her. And knowing who really killed her, it just isn't possible for Rosemary to have been Jim's sister. The only person she could have been, the only person against whom the murderer had motive, was Jim's first wife; as you'll see."

"But Ellery," said Pat, "didn't you tell me yourself that day, by comparing the woman's handwriting on Steve Polaris's trucking receipt with the handwriting on the flap of the letter Jim received from 'Rosemary Haight,' that that proved the woman *was* Jim's sister?"

"I was wrong," said Mr. Queen, frowning. "I was stupidly wrong. All that the two signatures proved, really, was that *the same woman had written them both*. That meant only that the woman who showed up here was the same woman who wrote Jim that letter which disturbed him so. I was misled by the fact that on the envelope she had signed the name 'Rosemary Haight.' Well, she was just using that name. I was wrong, I was stupid, and you should have caught me up, Patty. Let's drink?"

"But if the woman who was poisoned New Year's Eve was Jim's first wife," protested Carter, "why didn't Jim's real sister come forward after the murder? Lord knows the case had enough publicity!"

"If he had a sister," mumbled Patty. "If he had one!"

"Oh, he had a sister," said Ellery wearily. "Otherwise, why should he have written those letters to one? When he originally penned them, in planning the murder of his then-wife—the murder he didn't pull off—he expected those letters to give him an appearance of innocence. He expected to send them to his real sister, Rosemary Haight. It would have to be a genuine sister to stand the searchlight of a murder investigation, or he'd really be in a mess. So Jim had a sister, all right."

"But the papers!" said Pat. "Cart's right, Ellery. The papers were full of news about 'Rosemary Haight, sister of James Haight,' and how she *died* here in Wrightsville. If Jim had a real sister, Rosemary, surely she'd have come lickety-split to Wrightsville to expose the mistake?"

"Not necessarily. But the fact is—Jim's sister *did* come to Wrightsville, Patty. Whether she came to expose the mistake I can't say; but certainly, after she'd had a talk with her brother, Jim, she decided to say nothing about her true identity. I suppose Jim made her promise to keep quiet. And she's kept that promise."

"I don't follow, I don't follow," said Cart irritably. "You're like one of those fellows who keep pulling rabbits out of a hat. You mean the real Rosemary Haight's been in Wrightsville all these months, calling herself by some other name?"

Mr. Queen shrugged. "Who helped Jim in his trouble? The Wright family, a small group of old friends whose identities, of course, are unquestionable, myself, and . . . one other person. And that person a woman."

"Roberta!" gasped Pat. *"Roberta Roberts, the newspaperwoman!"*

"The only outsider of the sex that fits," nodded Ellery. "Yes, Roberta Roberts. Who else? She 'believed' in Jim's innocence from the start, she fought for him, she sacrificed her job for him, and at the end—in desperation—she provided the car by which Jim escaped his guards at the cemetery. Yes, Roberta's the only one who *could* be Jim's sister, from the facts; it explains all the peculiarities of her conduct. I suppose 'Roberta Roberts' has been her professional name for years. But her real name is Rosemary Haight!"

"So that's why she cried so at Jim's funeral," said Pat softly. And there was no sound but the swish of Gus Olesen's cloth on the bar and Mr. Anderson's troubled muttering.

"It gets clearer," growled Cart at last. "But what I don't understand is why Jim's first wife came to Wrightsville *calling* herself Jim's sister."

"And why," added Pat, "Jim permitted the deception. It's mad, the whole thing!"

"No," said Ellery, "it's frighteningly sane, if you'll only stop to think. You ask why. I asked why, too. And when I thought about it, I saw what must have happened." He drank deeply of the contents of the frosty glass. "Look. Jim left almost four years ago on the eve of his wedding to Nora, as a result of their quarrel about the house. He went to New York, I should suppose desperately unhappy. But remember Jim's character. An iron streak of independence—that's usually from the same lode as stubbornness and pride. They kept him from writing to Nora, from coming back to Wrightsville, from being a sensible human being; although, of course, Nora was as much to blame for not understanding how much standing on his own feet meant to a man like Jim.

"At any rate, back in New York, Jim's life—as he must have thought—blasted, Jim ran into this woman. We all saw something of her—a sultry, sulky wench, quite seductive . . . especially attractive to a man licking the wounds of an unhappy love affair. On the rebound, this woman hooked Jim. They must have been miserable together. Jim was a good solid boy, and the woman was a fly-by-night, selfish and capable of driving a man quite mad with exasperation. She must have made his life intolerable, because Jim wasn't the killing type and still he did finally plan to kill her. The fact that he planned each detail of her murder so carefully, even to writing those letters to his sister *in advance*—a silly thing to do!—shows how obsessed he became with the necessity of being rid of her."

"I should think," said Pat in a sick voice, "that he could have divorced her!"

Ellery shrugged again. "I'm sure that if he could have, he would. Which leads me to believe that, at first, she wouldn't give him a divorce. The leech, genus *Homo*, sex female. Of course, we can't be sure of anything. But Cart, I'm willing to lay you odds that if you followed the trail back, you'd discover (a) that she refused to give him a divorce, (b) that he then planned to murder her, (c) that she somehow got wind of his plans, was frightened, ran away from him, causing him to abandon his plans, and (d) that she later informed him that she had got a divorce!

"Because what follows makes all that inevitable. We know that Jim was married to one woman—we know that subsequently he came rushing back to Wrightsville and asked *Nora* to marry him. He would only have done that if *he thought he was free of the first*. But to think so, she must have given him reason. So I say she told him she'd got a divorce.

"What happened? Jim married Nora; in his excited emotional state he completely forgot about those letters which had been lying in the toxicology book for heaven knows how long. Then the honeymoon, Jim and Nora returned to Wrightsville to take up their married life in the little house . . . and the trouble began. Jim received a letter from his 'sister.' Remember that morning, Patty? The postman brought a letter, and Jim read it and was tremendously agitated, and then later he said it was from his 'sister' and wouldn't it be proper to ask her up to Wrightsville for a visit . . ."

Pat nodded.

"The woman who turned up claiming to be Jim's sister—and whom he accepted as his sister and introduced as his sister—was, we now know, not his sister at all but his first wife.

"But there's a more factual proof that the letter was from the first wife . . . the business of the identical signatures on the charred flag of the letter Jim received and on Steve Polaris's receipt for the visitor's luggage. So it *was* the first wife who wrote to Jim, and since Jim could scarcely have relished the idea of her coming to Wrightsville, it must have been *her* idea, not his, and that's what her letter to him was about.

"But why did she write to Jim and appear in Wrightsville as Jim's sister at all? In fact, why did Jim permit her to come? Or, if he couldn't keep her from coming, why did he connive at the deception after her arrival and keep it a secret until her death and *still* afterward? There can be only one reason: *she had a powerful hold over him.*

"Confirmation of that? Yes. Jim was 'squandering' lots of money—and mark that his squandering habits coincided in point of time with the arrival of his first wife in Wrightsville! Why was he pawning Nora's jewelry? Why did he borrow five thousand dollars from the Wrightsville Personal Finance Corporation? Why did he keep bleeding Nora for cash? Why? Where did all that money go? Gambling, you said, Cart. And tried to prove it in court—"

"But Jim himself admitted to Nora that he gambled the money away, according to the testimony," protested Carter.

"Naturally if his secret first wife was blackmailing him, he'd have to invent an excuse to Nora to explain his sudden appetite for huge sums of cash! The fact is, Cart, you never did *prove* Jim was losing all that money gambling in Vic Carlatti's *Hot Spot*. You couldn't find a single eyewitness to his gambling there, or you'd have produced one. The best you could get was an eavesdropper who overheard *Jim* say to Nora that he'd been gambling! Yes, Jim drank a lot at the *Hot Spot*—he was desperate; but he wasn't gambling there.

"Still, that money was going somewhere. Well, haven't we postulated a woman with a powerful hold on him? Conclusion: *he was giving Rosemary that money*—I mean, the woman who called herself Rosemary, the woman who subsequently died on New Year's Eve. He was giving it on

demand to the cold-blooded creature he had to continue calling his sister—the woman he'd actually been married to!"

"But what could the hold on him have been, Ellery?" asked Pat. "It
must have been something terrific!"

"Which is why I can see only one answer," said Ellery grimly. "It fits
into everything we know like plaster of Paris into a mold. Suppose the
woman we're calling Rosemary—the first wife—*never did get a divorce?* Suppose she'd only fooled Jim into believing he was free? Perhaps by showing him forged divorce papers? Anything can be procured
for money! Then the whole thing makes sense. Then Jim, when he'd
married Nora, had committed *bigamy.* Then he was in this woman's
clutches for good . . . She warned Jim in advance by letter and then came
to Wrightsville posing as his sister so that she could blackmail him on the
spot without exposing her true identity to Nora and the family! So now
we know why she posed as his sister, too. If she exposed her real status,
her power over Jim was gone. She wanted money, not revenge. It was
only by holding a *threat* of exposure over Jim's head that she would be
able to suck him dry. To do that, she had to pretend to be someone
else . . .

"And Jim, caught in her trap, had to acknowledge her as his sister, had
to pay her until he went nearly insane with despair. Rosemary knew her
victim. For Jim couldn't let Nora learn the truth—"

"No," moaned Pat.

"Why not?" asked Carter Bradford.

"Once before, when Jim ran out on her, he'd humiliated Nora frightfully in the eyes of her family and the town—the town especially. There
are no secrets or delicacies, and there is much cruelty, in the
Wrightsvilles of this world; and if you're a sensitive, inhibited, self-
conscious Nora, public scandal can be a major tragedy and a curse to
damn your life past regeneration.

"Jim saw what his first defection had done to Nora, how it had driven
her into a shell, made her over into a frightened little person half-crazy
with shame, hiding from Wrightsville, from her friends, even from her
family. If a mere jilting at the altar did that to Nora, what wouldn't the
shocking revelation that she'd married a bigamist do to her? It would
drive her mad; it might even kill her.

"Jim realized all that . . . The trap Rosemary laid and sprung was sa-
tanic. Jim simply couldn't admit to Nora or let her find out that she was
not a legally married woman, that their marriage was not a true marriage,
and that their coming child . . . Remember Mrs. Wright testified that Jim
knew almost as soon as it happened that Nora was going to have a baby."

"This," said Carter hoarsely, "is damnable."

Ellery sipped his drink and then lit a fresh cigarette, frowning at the incandescent end for some time. "It gets more difficult to tell, too," he murmured at last. "Jim paid and paid, and borrowed money everywhere to keep the evil tongue of that woman from telling the awful truth which would have unbalanced Nora or killed her."

Pat was close to tears. "It's a wonder poor Jim didn't embezzle funds at Pop's bank!"

"And in drunken rages Jim swore that he'd 'get rid of her'—that he'd 'kill her'—and made it plain that he was speaking of his 'wife.' Of course he was. He was speaking of the only legal wife he had—the woman calling herself Rosemary Haight and posing as his sister. When Jim foolishly made those alcoholic threats, *he never meant Nora at all*."

"But it seems to me," muttered Cart, "that when he was arrested, facing a conviction, to keep quiet *then*—"

"I'm afraid," replied Mr. Queen with a sad smile, "that Jim in his way was a great man. He was willing to die to make up to Nora for what he had done to her. And the only way he could make up to her was to pass out in silence. He unquestionably swore his real sister, Roberta Roberts, to secrecy. For to have told you and Chief Dakin the truth, Cart, Jim would have had to reveal Rosemary's true identity, and that meant revealing the whole story of his previous marriage to her, the divorce-that-wasn't-a-divorce, and consequently Nora's status as a pregnant, yet unmarried, woman. Besides, revealing the truth wouldn't have done *him* any good, anyway. For Jim had infinitely more motive to murder Rosemary than to murder Nora. No, he decided the best course was to carry the whole sickening story with him to the grave."

Pat was crying openly now.

"And," muttered Mr. Queen, "Jim had still another reason for keeping quiet. The biggest reason of all. A heroic, an epic, reason. I wonder if you two have any idea what it is."

They stared at him, at each other.

"No," sighed Mr. Queen, "I suppose you wouldn't. The truth is so staggeringly simple that we see right through it, as if it were a pane of glass. It's two-plus-two, or rather two-minus-one; and those are the most difficult calculations of all."

A bulbous organ the color of fresh blood appeared over his shoulder, and they saw that it was only Mr. Anderson's wonderful nose.

"*O vita, misero longa! felici brevis!*" croaked Mr. Anderson. "Friends, heed the wisdom of the ancients . . . I suppose you are wondering how I, poor wretch, am well-provided with lucre this heaven-sent day. Well, I am a remittance man, as they say, and my ship has touched port today. *Felici brevis!*" And he started to fumble for Patty's glass.

"Why don't you go over there in the corner and shut up, Andy?" shouted Cart.

"Sir," said Mr. Anderson, going away with Pat's glass, " 'the sands are number'd that make up my life; Here must I stay, and here my life must end.' " He sat down at his table and drank quickly.

"Ellery, you can't stop now!" said Pat.

"Are you two prepared to hear the truth?"

Pat looked at Carter, and Carter looked at Pat. He reached across the table and took her hand.

"Shoot," said Carter.

Mr. Queen nodded. "There's only one question left to be answered— the most important question of all: who really poisoned Rosemary?

"The case against Jim had shown that he alone had opportunity, that he alone had motive, that he alone had control of the distribution of the cocktails and therefore was the only one who could have been positive the poisoned cocktail reached its intended victim. Further, Cart, you proved that Jim had bought rat poison and so could have had arsenic to drop into the fatal cocktail.

"All this is reasonable and, indeed, unassailable—*if* Jim meant to kill Nora, to whom he handed the cocktail. But now we know Jim never intended to kill Nora at all!—that the real victim from the beginning was meant to be Rosemary and only Rosemary!

"So I had to refocus my mental binoculars. Now that I knew *Rosemary* was the intended victim, was the case just as conclusive against Jim as when Nora was believed to be the victim?

"Well, Jim still had opportunity to poison the cocktail; with Rosemary the victim, he had infinitely greater motive; he still had a supply of arsenic available. BUT—with Rosemary the victim, did Jim control the *distribution* of the fatal cocktail? Remember, he handed the cocktail subsequently found to contain arsenic to *Nora* . . . Could he have been sure the poisoned cocktail would go to *Rosemary?*

"*No!*" cried Ellery, and his voice was suddenly like a knife. "True, he'd handed Rosemary a cocktail previous to that last round. But that previous cocktail had not been poisoned. In that last round *only Nora's cocktail*—the one that poisoned both Nora and Rosemary—had arsenic in it! If *Jim* had dropped the arsenic into the cocktail he handed Nora, how could he know that *Rosemary* would drink it?

"He couldn't know. It was such an unlikely event that he couldn't even dream it would happen . . . imagine it, or plan it, or count on it. Actually, *Jim was out of the living room*—if you'll recall the facts—*at the time Rosemary drank Nora's cocktail.*

"So this peripatetic mind had to query: Since *Jim* couldn't be sure Rosemary would drink that poisoned cocktail, who *could* be sure?"

Carter Bradford and Patricia Wright were pressing against the edge of the table, still, rigid, not breathing.

Mr. Queen shrugged. "And instantly—two minus one. Instantly. It was unbelievable, and it was sickening, and it was the only possible truth. Two minus one—one. Just one . . .

"Just one other person had opportunity to poison that cocktail, for just one other person handled it before it reached Rosemary!

"Just one other person had motive to kill Rosemary and could have utilized the rat poison for murder which Jim had bought for innocent, mice-exterminating purposes . . . perhaps at someone else's suggestion? Remember he went back to Myron Garback's pharmacy a second time for another tin, shortly after his first purchase of Quicko, telling Garback he had 'mislaid' the first tin? How do you suppose that first tin came to be 'mislaid'? With what we now know, isn't it evident that it wasn't mislaid at all, but was stolen and stored away by the only other person in Jim's house with motive to kill Rosemary?"

Mr. Queen glanced at Patricia Wright and at once closed his eyes, as if they pained him. And he stuck the cigarette into the corner of his mouth and said through his teeth: *"That person could only have been the one who actually handed Rosemary the cocktail on New Year's Eve."*

Carter Bradford licked his lips over and over.

Pat was frozen.

"I'm sorry, Pat," said Ellery, opening his eyes. "I'm frightfully, terribly sorry. But it's as logical as death itself. And to give you two a chance, I had to tell you both."

Pat said faintly: "Not Nora. Oh, *not Nora!*"

# 30

## The Second Sunday in May

"A drop too much to drink," said Mr. Queen quickly to Gus Olesen. "May we use your back room, Gus?"

"Sure, sure," said Gus. "Say, I'm sorry about this, Mr. Bradford. That's good rum I used in those drinks. And she only had one—Andy took her second one. Lemme give you a hand—"

"We can manage her all right, thank you," said Mr. Queen, "although I do think a couple of fingers of bourbon might help."

"But if she's sick—" began Gus, puzzled. "Okay!"

The Old Soak stared blindly as Carter and Ellery helped Pat, whose eyes were glassy chips of agony, into Gus Olesen's back room. They set her down on Gus's old horsehair black leather couch; and when Gus hurried in with a glass of whisky, Carter Bradford forced her to drink. Pat choked, her eyes streaming; then she pushed the glass aside and threw herself back on the tufted leather, her face to the wall.

"She feels fine already," said Mr. Queen reassuringly. "Thanks, Gus. We'll take care of Miss Wright."

Gus went away, shaking his head and muttering that that was good rum—he didn't serve rat poison like that chiseling grease-ball Vic Carlatti over at the *Hot Spot*.

Pat lay still. Carter stood over her awkwardly. Then he sat down and took her hand. Ellery saw her tanned fingers go white with pressure. He turned away and strolled over to the other side of the room to examine the traditional Bock Beer poster. There was no sound at all, anywhere.

Until he heard Pat murmur: "Ellery."

He turned around. She was sitting up on the couch again, both her hands in Carter Bradford's; he was holding on to them for dear life, almost as if it were he who needed comforting, not she. Ellery guessed that in those few seconds of silence a great battle had been fought, and won.

He drew a chair over to the couch and sat down facing them.

"Tell me the rest," said Pat steadily, her eyes in his. "Go on, Ellery. Tell me the rest."

"It doesn't make any difference, Patty darling," mumbled Cart. "Oh, you know that. You know it."

"I know it, Cart."

"Whatever it was, darling—she was sick. I guess she was always a neurotic, always pretty close to the borderline."

"Yes, Cart. Tell me the rest, Ellery."

"Pat, do you remember telling me about dropping in to Nora's a few days after Rosemary arrived, in early November, and finding Nora 'trapped' in the serving pantry?"

"You mean when Nora overheard Jim and Rosemary having an argument?"

"Yes. You said you came in at the tail end and didn't hear anything of consequence. And that Nora wouldn't tell you what she'd overheard. You said Nora had the same kind of look on her face as that day when those three letters tumbled out of the toxicology book."

"Yes . . ." said Pat.

"That must have been the turning point, Pat. That must have been the time when Nora learned the whole truth—by pure accident, she learned from the lips of Jim and Rosemary themselves that Rosemary wasn't his sister but his wife, that she herself was not legally married . . . the whole sordid story."

Ellery examined his hands. "It . . . unbalanced Nora. In a twinkling her whole world came tumbling down, and her moral sense and mental health with it. She faced a humiliation too sickening to be faced. And Nora was emotionally weakened by the unnatural life she'd been leading for the years between Jim's sudden desertion and her marriage to him . . . Nora slipped over the line."

"Over the line," whispered Pat. Her lips were white.

"She planned to take revenge on the two people who, as her disturbed mind now saw it, had shamed her and ruined her life. She planned to kill Jim's first wife, the hated woman who called herself Rosemary. She planned to have Jim pay for the crime by using the very tools he'd manufactured for a similar purpose years before and which were now, as if by an act of Providence, thrust into her hand. She must have worked it out slowly. But work it out she did. She had those three puzzling letters that were puzzling no longer. She had Jim's own conduct to help her create the illusion of his guilt. And she found in herself a great strength and a great cunning; a talent, almost a genius, for deceiving the world as to her true emotions."

Pat closed her eyes, and Carter kissed her hand.

"Knowing that we knew about the letters—you and I, Pat—Nora deliberately carried out the pattern of the three letters. She deliberately swallowed a small dose of arsenic on Thanksgiving Day so that it would seem to us Jim was following his schedule. And recall what she did immediately after showing symptoms of arsenic poisoning at the dinner table? She ran upstairs and gulped great quantities of milk of magnesia which, as I told you later that night in my room, Pat, is an emergency antidote for arsenic poisoning. Not a well-known fact, Patty. *Nora had looked it up.* That doesn't prove she poisoned herself, but it's significant when you tack it onto the other things she did.

"Patty, must I go on? Let Carter take you home—"

"I want the whole thing," said Pat. "This moment, Ellery. Finish."

"That's my baby," said Carter Bradford huskily.

"I said 'the other things she did,' " said Ellery in a low tone. "Recall them! If Nora was as concerned over Jim's safety as she pretended, would she have left those three incriminating letters to be found in her hatbox? Wouldn't any wife who felt as she claimed to feel about Jim have burned those letters instantly? But no—*Nora saved them* ... Of course. She knew they would turn out to be the most damning evidence against Jim when he was arrested, and she made sure they survived to be used against him. As a matter of cold fact, how *did* Dakin eventually find them?"

"Nora . . . Nora called our attention to them," said Cart feebly. "When she had hysterics and mentioned the letters, which we didn't even know about—"

"Mentioned?" cried Ellery. "Hysterics? My dear Bradford, that was the most superb kind of acting! She pretended to be hysterical; she pretended that *I* had already told you about the letters! In saying so, she established the existence of the letters for your benefit. A terrible point, that one. But until I knew that Nora was the culprit, it had no meaning for me." He stopped and fumbled for a cigarette.

"What else, Ellery?" demanded Pat in a shaky voice.

"Just one thing. Pat, you're sure— You look ill."

"What else?"

"Jim. *He was the only one who knew the truth*, although Roberta Roberts may have guessed it. Jim knew *he* hadn't poisoned the cocktail, so he *must* have known only Nora could have.

"*Yet Jim kept quiet.* Do you see why I said before that Jim had a more sublime reason for martyrizing himself? *It was his penance, his self-imposed punishment.* For Jim felt himself to have been completely responsible for the tragedy in Nora's life—indeed, for driving Nora into murder. So he was willing to take his licking silently and without complaint, as if that would right the wrong! But agonized minds think badly. Only . . . Jim couldn't *look* at her. Remember in the courtroom? Not once. He wouldn't, he couldn't look at her. He wouldn't see her, or talk to her, before, during, or after. That would have been too much. For after all, she *had*—" Ellery rose. "I believe that's all I'm going to say."

Pat sank back on the couch to rest her head against the wall.

Cart winced at the expression on her face. So he said, as if somehow it softened the blow and alleviated the pain: "But Queen, isn't it possible that Nora and Jim together, *as accomplices—?*"

Ellery said rapidly: "If they'd been accomplices, working together to rid themselves of Rosemary, would they have deliberately planned the crime in such a way that Jim, one of the accomplices, would turn out to be the only possible criminal? No. Had they combined to destroy a common enemy, they would have planned it so that *neither* of them would be involved."

And then there was another period of quiet, behind which tumbled the waters of Mr. Anderson's voice in the taproom. His words all ran together, like rivulets joining a stream. It was pleasant against the malty odor of beer.

And Pat turned to look at Cart; and, oddly, she was smiling. But it was the wispiest, lightest ghost of a smile.

"No," said Cart. "Don't say it. I won't hear it."

"But Cart, you don't know what I was going to say—"

"I do! And it's a damned insult!"

"Here—" began Mr. Queen.

"If you think," snarled Cart, "that I'm the kind of heel who would drag a story like this out for the edification of the Emmy DuPrés of Wrightsville, merely to satisfy my sense of 'duty,' then you're not the kind of woman I want to marry, Pat!"

"I couldn't marry you, Cart," said Pat in a stifled voice. "Not with Nora—not with my own sister—a . . . a . . ."

"She wasn't responsible! She was sick! Look here, Queen, drive some sense into— Pat, if you're going to take that stupid attitude, I'm through— I'll be damned if I'm not!" Cart pulled her off the sofa and held her to him tightly. "Oh, darling, it isn't Nora, it isn't Jim, it isn't your father or mother or Lola or even you I'm really thinking of . . . Don't think I haven't visited the hospital. I—I have. I saw her just after they took her out of the incubator. She glubbed at me, and then she started to bawl, and— Damn it, Pat, we're going to be married as soon as it's decent, and we're going to carry this damn secret to the grave with us, and we're going to adopt little Nora and make the whole damn thing sound like some impossible business out of a damn book—that's what we're going to do! Understand?"

"Yes, Cart," whispered Pat. And she closed her eyes and laid her cheek against his shoulder.

When Mr. Ellery Queen strolled out of the back room, he was smiling, although a little sadly.

He slapped a ten-dollar bill down on the bar before Gus Olesen and said: "See what the folks in the back room will have, and don't neglect Mr. Anderson. Also, keep the change. Goodbye, Gus. I've got to catch the train for New York."

Gus stared at the bill. "I ain't dreaming, am I? You ain't Santa Claus?"

"Not exactly, although I just presented two people with the gift of several pounds of baby, complete down to the last pearly toenail."

"What is this?" demanded Gus. "Some kind of celebration?"

Mr. Queen winked at Mr. Anderson, who gawped back. "Of course! Hadn't you heard, Gus? Today is Mother's Day!"

THE END

*Finished re-reading this stunner at 9:00PM on August 6 2011.*
*WOW*

# CAT OF MANY TAILS

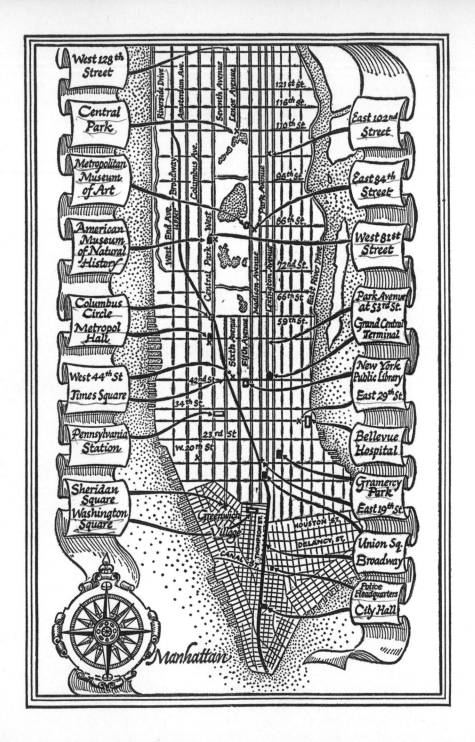

# 1

The strangling of Archibald Dudley Abernethy was the first scene in a nine-act tragedy whose locale was the City of New York.

Which misbehaved.

Seven and one-half million persons inhabiting an area of over three hundred square miles lost their multiple head all at once. The storm center of the phenomenon was Manhattan, that "Gotham" which, as the *New York Times* pointed out during the worst of it, had been inspired by a legendary English village whose inhabitants were noted for their foolishness. It was a not entirely happy allusion, for there was nothing jocular in the reality. The panic seizure caused far more fatalities than the Cat; there were numerous injured; and what traumata were suffered by the children of the City, infected by the bogey fears of their elders, will not be comprehended until the psychiatrists can pry into the neuroses of the next generation.

In the small area of agreement in which the scientists met afterward, several specific indictments were drawn. One charged the newspapers. Certainly the New York press cannot disclaim some responsibility for what happened. The defense that "we give John Public the news as it happens, how it happens, and for as long as it happens," as the editor of the *New York Extra* put it, is plausible but fails to explain why John Public had to be given the news of the Cat's activities in such necrotic detail, embellished by such a riches of cartoonical crape and obituary embroidery. The object of this elaborate treatment was, of course, to sell more newspapers—an object which succeeded so admirably that, as one circulation manager privately admitted, "We really panicked 'em."

Radio was named codefendant. Those same networks which uttered approving sounds in the direction of every obsessionist who inveighed against radio mystery and crime programs as being the First Cause of hysteria, delinquency, seclusive behavior, *idée fixe*, sexual precocity, nailbiting, nightmare, enuresis, profanity, and other antisocial ills of juvenile America saw nothing wrong in thoroughly airing the depredations of the Cat, with sound effects . . . as if the sensational were rendered harmless by the mere fact of its being not fiction. It was later charged, not without justice, that a single five-minute newscast devoted to the latest horror of the strangler did more to shatter the nerves of the listening population than all the mystery programs of all the networks percussively put together. But by that time the mischief was done.

Others fished deeper. There were certain elements in the Cat's crimes, they said, which plucked universal chords of horror. One was the means employed. Breath being life and its denial death, their argument ran, the pattern of strangulation was bound to arouse the most basic fears. Another was the haphazard choice of victims—"selection by caprice," they termed it. Man, they stated, faces death most equably when he thinks he is to die for some purpose. But the Cat, they said, picked his victims at random. It reduced the living to the level of the subhuman and gave the individual's extinction no more importance or dignity than the chance crushing of an ant. This made defenses, especially moral defenses, impossible; there was nowhere to hide; therefore panic. And still a third factor, they went on, was the total lack of recognition. No one lived who saw the terrorizer at his chill and motiveless work; he left no clues to his age, sex, height, weight, coloration, habits, speech, origin, even to his species. For all the data available, he might well have been a cat—or an incubus. Where nothing was to be perceived, the agitated imagination went berserk. The result was a Thing come true.

And the philosophers took the world view, opening casements to the great panorama of current events. *Weltanschauung!* they cried. The old oblate spheroid was wobbling on its axis, trying to resist stresses, cracking along faults of strain. A generation which had lived through two global conflicts; which had buried millions of the mangled, the starved, the tortured, the murdered; which rose to the bait of world peace through the bloody waters of the age and found itself hooked by the cynical barb of nationalism; which cowered under the inexplicable fungus of the atomic bomb, not understanding, not wishing to understand; which helplessly watched the strategists of diplomacy plot the tactics of an Armageddon that never came; which was hauled this way and that, solicited, exhorted, suspected, flattered, accused, driven, unseated, inflamed, abandoned, never at peace, never at rest, the object of pressures and contrary forces by the night and the day and the hour—the real victims of the universal War of Nerves . . . it was no wonder, the philosophers said, that such a generation should bolt screaming at the first squeak of the unknown. In a world that was desensitized, irresponsible, threatened and threatening, hysteria was not to be marveled at. It had attacked New York City; had it struck anywhere in the world, the people of that place would have given way. What had to be understood, they said, was that the people had welcomed panic, not surrendered to it. In a planet shaking to pieces underfoot it was too agonizing to remain sane. Fantasy was a refuge and a relief.

But it remained for an ordinary New Yorker, a 20-year-old law student, to state the case in language most people could understand. "I've just been reading up on Danny Webster," he said. "In one case he was mixed up in, trial of a fellow named Joseph White, Webster tossed this one over the plate: *Every unpunished murder takes away something from the security of every man's life.* I figure when you live in our cockeyed kind of world, when some boogyman they call the Cat starts sloughing folks right and left and nobody can get to first base on it, and as far as Joe Schmo can see this Cat's going to keep right on strangling the population till there's not enough customers left to fill the left field bleachers at Ebbets Field—or am I boring you and by the way whatever happened to Durocher?" The law student's name was Gerald Ellis Kollodny and he made the statement to a Hearst reporter on sidewalk-interview assignment; the statement was reprinted in the *New Yorker*, the *Saturday Review of Literature*, and *Reader's Digest; M-G-M News* invited Mr. Kollodny to repeat himself before its cameras; and New Yorkers nodded and said that was just about how it had stacked up.

*A time capsule of publications in The United States in the late 1940s.*

# 2

August 25 brought one of those simmering subtropical nights in which summer New York specializes. Ellery was in his study stripped to his shorts, trying to write. But his fingers kept sliding off the keys and finally he turned off his desk light and padded to a window.

The City was blackly quiet, flattened by the pressures of the night. Eastward thousands would be drifting into Central Park to throw themselves to the steamy grass. To the northeast, in Harlem and the Bronx, Little Italy, Yorkville; to the southeast, on the Lower East Side and across the river in Queens and Brooklyn; to the south, in Chelsea, Greenwich Village, Chinatown—wherever there were tenements—fire escapes would be crowded nests in the smother, houses emptied, streets full of lackadaisical people. The parkways would be bug trails. Cars would swarm over the bridges— Brooklyn, Manhattan, Williamsburg, Queensborough, George Washington, Triborough—hunting a breeze. At Coney Island, Brighton, Manhattan Beach, the Rockaways, Jones Beach, the sands would be seeded by millions of the sleepless turned restlessly to the sea. The excursion boats would be scuttling up and down the Hudson and the ferries staggering like overloaded old women to Weehawken and Staten Island.

Heat lightning ripped the sky, disclosing the tower of the Empire State Building. A huge photographic process; for the shutterflash of a citysized camera taking a picture of the night.

A little to the south hung a bright spume. But it was a mirage. Times Square would be sweltering under it; the people would be in Radio City Music Hall, the Roxy, the Capitol, the Strand, the Paramount, the State— wherever there was a promise of lower temperatures.

Some would seek the subways. The coupled cars kept their connecting doors open and when the trains rushed along between stations there was a violent displacement of the tunnel air, hellish but a wind. The choice position was in the front doorway of the head car beside the motorman's cubicle. Here the masses would be thickest, swaying in a grateful cata-lepsy.

In Washington Square, along Fifth Avenue, 57th Street, upper Broad-way, Riverside Drive, Central Park West, 110th Street, Lexington Av-enue, Madison, the busses would accept the few and spurn the many and they would rush up and down, north and south, east and west, chasing their tails like . . .

Ellery blundered back to his desk, lit a cigaret.

No matter where I start, he thought, I wind up in the same damned place.

That Cat's getting to be a problem.

He tilted, embracing his neck. His fingers slithered in the universal ooze and he tightened them, thinking that he could stand an over-all tightening. Nonskid thoughts. A new lining job on the will.

The Cat.

Ellery smoked, crookedly.

A great temptation.

In the Wrightsville Van Horn case Ellery had run into stunning treach-ery. He had found himself betrayed by his own logic. The old blade had turned suddenly in his hand; he had aimed at the guilty with it and it had run through the innocent. So he had put it away and taken up his type-writer. As Inspector Queen said, ivory tower stuff.

Unhappily, he had to share his turret with an old knight who jousted daily with the wicked. Inspector Richard Queen of the New York Police Department being also the unhorsed champion's sire, it was a perilous proximity.

"I don't want to hear about a case," Ellery would say. "Just let me be."

"What's the matter?" his father would jeer. "Afraid you might be tempted?"

"I've given all that up. I'm not interested any longer."

But that was before the Cat strangled Archibald Dudley Abernethy.

He had tried to ignore the murder of Abernethy. And for some time he had succeeded in doing so. But the creature's round little face with its round little eyes had an annoying way of staring out at him from his morning newspaper.

In the end he had brought himself up to date.

It was interesting, an interesting case.

He had never seen a less meaningful face. It was not vicious, or kind, or sly, or stupid; it was not even enigmatic. It was nothing, a rotundity, a 44-year-old fetus-face; one of nature's undeveloped experiments.

Yes, an interesting homicide.

And then the second strangling.

And the third.

And . . .

The apartment door *blupped!*

"Dad?"

Ellery jumped, banging his shin. He limped hurriedly to the living room.

"Hi there." Inspector Queen already had his jacket and necktie off; he was removing his shoes. "You look cool, son."

The Inspector looked gray.

"Tough day?" It was not the heat. The old man was as weatherproof as a desert rat.

"Anything on the ice, Ellery?"

"Lemonade. Quarts of it."

The Inspector shuffled into the kitchen. Ellery heard the icebox open and close. "By the way, congratulate me."

"Congratulate you on what?"

"On being handed today," said his father, reappearing with a frosty glass, "the biggest pig in the poke of my alleged—I say alleged—career." He threw his head back and drank. Throat showing, he looked even grayer.

"Fired?"

"Worse."

"Promoted."

"Well," said the Inspector, seating himself, "I'm now top dog in the Cat chase." *clever*

"The Cat."

"You know, the Cat?"

Ellery leaned against the study jamb.

"The Commissioner called me in," said the Inspector, folding his hands about the glass, "and he told me he'd had the move under consideration for some time. He's creating a special Cat squad. I'm in full charge. As I said, top dog."

"Caninized." Ellery laughed.

"Maybe you find this situation full of yuks," said his father, "but as for me, give me liberty and lots of it." He drained what was left in the glass. "Ellery, I damn near told the Commissioner to his face today that Dick Queen's too old a bird to be handed a deal like this. I've given the P.D. a pretty full lifetime of faithful service. I deserve better."

"But you took it."

"Yes, I took it," said the Inspector, "and God help me, I even said, 'Thanks, Commissioner.' And then I got the feeling," he went on in a worried way, "that he had some angle he wasn't putting on the line and, son, I wanted to duck out even more. I can still do it."

"You talking about quitting?"

"Well, I'm just talking. Anyway, you can't say you don't come by it honestly."

"Ourrrrch." Ellery went to one of the living room windows. "But it's not my brawl," he complained to New York. "I played around a little, that's all. For a long time I was lucky. But when I found out I was using loaded dice—"

"I see your point. Yes. And this crap game's for keeps."

Ellery turned around. "Aren't you exaggerating?"

"Ellery, this is an emergency."

"Oh, come."

"I said," said the old man, "an emergency."

"A few murders. Granted they're puzzling. That's hardly a new twist. What's the percentage of unsolved homicides? I don't understand you, Dad. I had a reason for quitting; I'd taken on something and I flubbed it, causing a death or two by the way. But you're a pro. This is an assignment. The responsibility for failure, if you fail, is the Commissioner's. And suppose these stranglings aren't solved—"

"My dear philosopher," said the Inspector, rolling the empty glass between his palms, "if these stranglings aren't solved, and damned quickly, something's going to pop in this man's town."

"Pop? In New York? How do you mean?"

"It hasn't really got going yet. Just signs. The number of phone calls to Headquarters asking for information, instructions, reassurance, anything. The increase in false alarm police calls, especially at night. The jitters of the men on duty. A little more all-around tension than there ought to be. A . . ." the Inspector groped with his glass . . . "a sort of concentration of interest on the part of the public. They're too interested. It isn't natural."

"Just because an overheated cartoonist—"

"Just because! Who cares a hoot in Hell Gate what's caused it? It's on its way, Ellery. Why is the only smash hit on Broadway this summer that ridiculous murder farce, *The Cat?* Every critic in town panned it as the smelliest piece of rat cheese to hit New York in five years, and it's the only show doing business. Winchell's latest is 'Cat-Astrophes.' Berle turned down a cat joke, said he didn't think the subject was funny. The pet shops report they haven't sold a kitten in a month. They're beginning to see the Cat in Riverdale, Canarsie, Greenpoint, the East Bronx, Park Row, Park Avenue, Park Plaza. We're starting to find alley cats strangled with cords all over the city. Forsythe Street. Pitkin Avenue. Lenox. Second. Tenth. Bruckner Boulevard—"

"Kids."

"Sure, we've even caught some of them at it. But it's a symptom, Ellery. A symptom of something that scares the stiffener out of me, and I'm man enough to admit it."

"Have you eaten anything today?"

"Five murders and the biggest city in the world gets the shakes! Why? How do you explain it?"

Ellery was silent.

"Come on," said the Inspector sarcastically. "You won't endanger your amateur standing."

But Ellery was only thinking. "Maybe," he said, "maybe it's the strange feel of it. New York will take fifty polio cases a day in its stride, but let two cases of Asiatic cholera break out and under the right conditions you might have mass hysteria. There's something alien about these stranglings. They make indifference impossible. When a man like Abernethy can get it, anyone can get it." He stopped. The Inspector was staring at him.

"You seem to know a lot about it."

"Just what I've happened to catch in the papers."

"Like to know more? Worm's eye view?"

"Well . . ."

"Sit down, son."

"Dad—"

"Sit down!"

Ellery sat down. After all, the man was his father.


"Five murders so far," said the Inspector. "All in Manhattan. All stranglings. Same kind of cord used in each."

"That tussah silk number? Indian silk?"

"Oh, you know that."

"The papers say you've got nowhere trying to trace them."

"The papers are correct. It's a strong, coarse-fibered silk of—so help me—Indian jungle origin, and it's the only clue we have."

"What?"

"I repeat: not a single cursed other clue. Nothing! Nothing, Ellery. No prints. No witnesses. No suspects. No motives. There isn't a thing to work on. The killer comes and goes like a breeze, leaving only two things behind, a corpse and a cord. The first victim was—"

"Abernethy, Archibald Dudley. Aged 44. Three-room apartment on East 19th Street near Gramercy Park. A bachelor left alone by the death of his invalid mother a few years ago. His father, a clergyman, died in 1922. Abernethy never worked a lick in his life. Took care of mama and afterward of himself. 4-F in the war. Did his own cooking, housekeeping. No apparent interests. No entangling alliances. No anything. A colorless, juiceless nonentity. Has the time of Abernethy's death been fixed more accurately?"

"Doc Prouty is pretty well satisfied he was strangled around midnight of June 3. We have reason to believe Abernethy knew his killer; the whole setup smacked of an appointment. We've eliminated relatives; they're scattered to hell and gone and none of them could have done it. Friends? Abernethy didn't have any, not one. He was the original lone wolf."

"Or sheep."

"As far as I can see, we didn't miss a trick," said the Inspector morosely. "We checked the super of the building. We checked a drunk janitor. Every tenant in the house. Even the renting agent."

"I understand Abernethy lived off the income from a trust—"

"Handled by a bank for umpty years. He had no lawyer. He had no business—how he occupied his time since his mother's death God only knows; we don't. Just vegetated, I guess."

"Tradesmen?"

"All checked off."

"Barber, too?"

"You mean from the killer's getting behind his sweet petit point chair?" The Inspector did not smile. "He shaved himself. Once a month he got a haircut in a shop off Union Square. He'd gone there for over twenty years and they didn't even know his name. Just the same we checked the three barbers. And no dice."

"You're convinced there was no woman in Abernethy's life?"

"Positive."

"And no man?"

"No evidence that he was even a homo. He was a small fat skunk egg. No hits, no runs, no errors."

"One error. At least one." Inspector Queen started, but then his lips tightened. Ellery sloshed a little in his chair. "No man can be the total blank the facts make out Abernethy to have been. It's just not possible. And the proof that it's not is that he was murdered. He had a feeble life of *some* sort. He did *something*. All five of them did. What about Violette Smith?"

"Violette Smith," said the Inspector, closing his eyes. "Number 2 on the Cat's hit parade. Strangled just nineteen days after Abernethy—date, June 22, sometime between 6 P.M. and midnight. Unmarried. 42. Lived alone in a two-room apartment on the top floor of a bug trap on West 44th, over a *pizzeria*. Side entrance, walkup. Three other tenants in the building besides the restaurant downstairs. Had lived at that address six years. Before that on 73rd and West End Avenue. Before that on Cherry Street in the Village, where she'd been born.

"Violette Smith," said the Inspector without opening his eyes, "was the opposite of Archie Abernethy in just about every conceivable way. He was a hermit, she knew everybody around Times Square. He was a babe in the woods, she was a she-wolf. He'd been protected by mama all his life, the only protection she knew was the kind she had to pay. Abernethy had no vices, Violette had no virtues. She was a dipso, a reefer addict, and she'd just graduated to the hard stuff when she got hers. He never earned a penny in his life, she made her living the hard way."

"Sixth Avenue mostly, I gather," said Ellery.

"Not true. Violette never worked the pavements. Her hustling was on call; she had a mighty busy phone.

"Whereas in Abernethy's case," the Inspector droned on, "we had nothing to work on, in Violette's we hit the jackpot. Normally, when a woman like her gets knocked off, you check the agent, the girl friends, the clients, the dope peddler, the mobster who's always in the background somewhere—and somewhere along the line you hit the answer. Well, this setup was normal enough; Vi had a record of nine arrests, she'd done some time, she was tied up with Frank Pompo, all the rest of it. Only nothing got anywhere."

"Are you sure—"

"—it was a Cat job? As a matter of fact, at first we weren't. If not for the use of the cord—"

"Same Indian silk."

"The color was different. Pinkish, a salmony kind of color. But the silk was that tussah stuff, all right, same as in Abernethy's case, only his was blue. Of course, when the third one came along, and the fourth and fifth, the pattern was clear and we're sure now the Smith woman was one of the series. The more we dig in the surer we get. The picture, atmosphere, are the same. A killer who came and went and didn't even leave a shadow on a windowshade."

"Still—"

But the old man was shaking his head. "We've worked the vine overtime. If Violette was slated to go we'd get some hint of it. But the stools don't know a thing. It's not that they've clammed up; they just don't know.

"She wasn't in any trouble. This definitely wasn't a crackdown for holding out, or anything like that. Vi was in the racket for a living and she was smart enough to play ball without a squawk. She took shake-downs as part of the hazards of the business. She was well-liked, one of the old reliables."

"Over 40," said Ellery. "In a wearing profession. I don't suppose—"

"Suicide? Impossible."

Ellery scratched his nose. "Tell me more."

"She wasn't found for over thirty-six hours. On the morning of June 24 a girl friend of hers who'd been trying to reach her by phone a whole day and night climbed the stairs, found Violette's door shut but not locked, went in—"

"Abernethy's body was found seated in an easychair," said Ellery. "Exactly how was the Smith woman found?"

"Her flat was a bedroom and sitting room—kitchenette was one of those wall-unit jobs. She was found on the floor in the doorway between the two rooms."

"Facing which way?" asked Ellery quickly.

"I know, I know, but there was no way of telling. She was all bunched up. Might have fallen from any position."

"Attacked from which direction?"

"From behind, same as Abernethy. And the cord knotted."

"Oh, yes, there's that."

"What?"

"The cord was knotted in Abernethy's case, too. It's bothered me."

"Why?" The Inspector sat up.

"Well . . . there's a sort of finality about it."

"A what?"

"Decorative, but was it necessary? You'd hardly let go till your victim was dead, would you? Then why the knot? In fact, it would be pretty hard to tie a knot while the victim was strangling. It suggests that the knots were tied after they were dead."

His father was staring.

"It's like putting a bow on a package that's quite adequately wrapped. The extra—I almost said the artistic—touch. Neat, satisfying. Satisfying a . . . what would you say? a passion for completeness? finality? Yes, so damned final."

"What in the world are you talking about?"

"I'm not sure," said Ellery mournfully. "Tell me—was there a sign of forcible entry?"

"No. The general opinion is that she expected her killer. Like Aber-nethy."

"Posing as a client?"

"Could be. If he was, it was only to get in. The bedroom wasn't dis-

turbed and while she was found wearing a wrapper, she had a slip and
panties on underneath. The testimony is she nearly always wore a negligee when she was home. But it could have been anybody, Ellery. Someone she knew well or someone she didn't know so well or even someone
she didn't know at all. It wasn't hard," said the Inspector, "to make Miss
Smith's acquaintance."

"The other tenants—"

"Nobody heard a thing. The restaurant people didn't even know she
existed. You know how it is in New York."

"Ask no questions and mind your own business."

"While the lady upstairs is getting herself dead."

The Inspector got up and fussed to a window. But immediately he returned to his chair, scowling. "In other words," he said, "we drew a blank
in the Smith case, too. Then—"

"Question. Did you find any connection between Abernethy and Violette Smith? Any at all?"

"No."

"Go on."

"Cometh Number 3," said the Inspector in a sort of liturgical mutter.
"Rian O'Reilly, 40-year-old shoe salesman, living with his wife and four
kids in a Chelsea tenement. Date, July 18; twenty-six days after the
Smith murder.

"O'Reilly's kill," the Inspector said, "was so damn . . . so damn discouraging. Here was a hardworking fellow, good husband, crazy father,
struggling to keep his head above water and having a tough time of it. To
keep his family going O'Reilly held down two jobs, a full-timer in a
lower Broadway shoe store, a night relief job in a shop on Fulton and
Flatbush across the river in Brooklyn. He'd have managed to scrape
along if he hadn't run into such hard luck. One of his children got polio
two years ago. Another one got pneumonia. Then his wife splashed herself with hot paraffin putting up grape jelly and he paid a skin specialist
for a year trying to heal her burn. On top of that another kid was run over
by a hit-and-run driver who was never identified and spent three months
in a hospital. O'Reilly'd borrowed the limit against his $1000 insurance
policy. His wife had hocked her measly engagement ring. They'd had a
'39 Chevvy—O'Reilly sold it to pay doctors' bills.

"O'Reilly liked his nip now and then, but he gave up drinking. Even
beer. He held himself down to ten cigarets a day, and he'd been a heavy
smoker. His wife put up box lunches and he didn't eat supper till he got
home, usually after midnight. In the past year he'd suffered a lot from
toothache, but he wouldn't go to a dentist, said he didn't have time for
such foolishness. But he'd toss around some at night, his wife said."

The heat flowed through their windows. Inspector Queen wiped his face with a ball of handkerchief.

"O'Reilly was no Saturday night Irishman. He was a little guy, thin and ugly, with heavy eyebrows that made him look worried even when he was dead. He used to tell his wife he was a physical coward, but she thought he'd had plenty of guts. I guess he did, at that. He was born in Hell's Kitchen and his life was one long battle. With his drunk of a father and with the street hoodlums when he was a boy, and after that with poverty and sickness. Remembering his old man, who used to beat his mother up, O'Reilly tried to make up for it to his own wife and children. His whole life was his family.

"He was wild about classical music. He couldn't read a note and he'd never had a lesson, but he could hum snatches of a lot of operas and symphonies and during the summer he tried to take in as many of the free Sunday concerts in Central Park as he could. He was always after his kids to tune in WQXR, used to say he thought Beethoven would do them a lot more good than *The Shadow*. One of his boys has a talent for the violin; O'Reilly finally had to stop his lessons. The night that happened, Mrs. O'Reilly said, he cried like a baby all night.

"This was the man," said Inspector Queen, watching his curling toes, "whose strangled body was found early in the morning of July 19 by the janitor of the building. The janitor was mopping the entrance hall down when he noticed a heap of clothes in the dark space behind the stairway. It was O'Reilly, dead.

"Prouty fixed the time of death as between midnight and 1 A.M. of the 18th-19th. Obviously, O'Reilly was just coming home from his night job in Brooklyn. We checked with the store and the time he left jibed, sure enough, with his movements if he'd gone directly home and been attacked as he entered the house on his way upstairs. There was a lump on the side of his head—"

"The result of a blow, or from a fall?" asked Ellery.

"We're not sure. A blow seems more likely, because he was dragged—there are rubberheel scrapes on the marble—from just inside the front door to the spot under the stairs where the janitor found him. No struggle, and nobody heard anything." The Inspector pinched his nose so hard the tip remained whitish for a few seconds. "Mrs. O'Reilly had been up all night waiting for her husband, afraid to leave the kids alone in the apartment. She was just going to phone the police—they held on to their phone, she said, because O'Reilly always said suppose one of the kids got sick in the middle of the night?—when the cop the janitor'd called came up to give her the bad news.

"She told me she'd been scared and nervous ever since the Abernethy murder. 'Rian had to come home from Brooklyn so late,' she said. 'I kept at him to quit the night job, and then when that woman on West 44th Street was choked to death too I nearly went out of my mind. But Rian only laughed. He said nobody'd bother to kill *him*, he wasn't worth killing.' "

Ellery planted his elbows on his naked knees and his face secretively between his hands.

The Inspector said, "Seems like it's getting hotter," and Ellery mumbled something. "It's against nature," complained the Inspector. He took off his shirt and undershirt and he plastered them with a smack against the back of his chair. "Leaving a widow and four children, with what was left of his insurance going to pay for his burial. I understand his priest is trying to do something, but it's a poor parish and O'Reilly's heirs are now enjoying City relief."

"And now his kids will be listening to *The Shadow* if they can hang on to their radio." Ellery rubbed his neck. "No clues."

"No clues."

"The cord."

"Same silk, blue."

"Knotted at the back?"

"Knotted at the back."

"Plenty of rhyme," muttered Ellery. "But where's the reason?"

"You tell O'Reilly's widow."

And Ellery was quiet. But after a while he said, "It was about that time that the cartoonist was inspired. I remember the unveiling of the Cat. He jumped out at you from the editorial page of the *Extra* . . . such as it was and is. One of the great monsters of cartoonical time. The man should get the Pulitzer prize for Satanism. A diabolical economy of line; the imagination fills in what the artist leaves out. Guaranteed to share your bed. *How Many Tails Has the Cat?* asks the caption. And we count three distinct appendages, curling at the ends back upon themselves. Not thick true tails, you understand. More like cords. Ending in nooselike openings just right for necks . . . which aren't there. And one cord bears the number 1, and the second cord the number 2, and the third cord the number 3. No *Abernethy, Smith*, or *O'Reilly*. He was so right. The Cat is quantitative. It's numbers that equalize all men, the Founding Fathers and Abe Lincoln to the contrary notwithstanding. The Cat is the great leveler of humanity. It's no accident that his claws are shaped like sickles."

"Sweet talk, but the point is the day after August 9 there was the Cat again," said the Inspector, "and he'd grown a fourth tail."

"And I remember that, too," nodded Ellery.

"Monica McKell. August 9. Twenty-two days after O'Reilly."

"The perennial debutante. A mere 37 and going strong."

"Park and 53rd. Café society. A table jumper they got to calling Leaping Lena."

"Or in the more refined phrase of Lucius Beebe—Madcap Monica."

"That's the one," said the Inspector. "Also known as McKell's Folly, McKell being her old man, the oil millionaire, who told me Monica was the only wildcat he'd never brought in. But you see he was proud of her. She was wild, all right—cut her teeth on a gin bottle, came out during Prohibition, and her favorite trick when she was tight was to get behind the bar and outmix the bartender. They say she mixed the best Martini in New York, drunk or sober. She was born in a penthouse and died in the subway. Downhill all the way.

"Monica never married. She once said that the only unrelated male she'd ever known that she could stand having around for any length of time was a horse named Leibowitz, and the only reason she didn't marry him, she said, was that she doubted she could housebreak him. She was engaged a dozen times, but at the last minute she'd take a walk. Her father would yell, and her ma, who's a handkerchief-twister, would get hysterics, but it was no deal. They had high hopes about Monica's last engagement—it looked as if she was really going to marry this Hungarian count—but the Cat put a crimp in that."

"In the subway," said Ellery.

"Sure, how did she get there. Well, it was this way. Monica McKell was the biggest booster the New York subway system ever had. She'd ride it every chance she got. She told Elsa Maxwell it was the only place a girl could get the feel of people. She took a particular delight in dragging her escorts there, especially when they were in tails.

"Funny," said the Inspector, "that it should have been the subway that did her in. Monica was out clubbing that night with Snooky—her count—and a bunch of their friends. They wound up in some Village dive, and around a quarter of four in the morning Monica got tired tending bar and they decided to call it a night. They began piling into cabs— all except Monica, who stood her ground and argued that if they really believed in the American way they'd all go home in the subway. The others were game, but the count got his Hungarian up—he was also tanked on vodka-and-Cokes—and said something like if he wanted to smell peasants he'd have stayed in Hungary and he'd be damned if he'd lower himself, into the ground or any other way, and she could bloody well go home in the subway herself if she wanted to so bad. And she did.

"And she did," said the Inspector, licking his lips, "and she was found a little after 6 A.M. lying on a bench near the tailpiece of the platform of the Sheridan Square station. A trackwalker found her. He called a cop and the cop took one look and went green. There was the salmon-colored silk cord around her neck."

The Inspector got up and went into the kitchen and came back with the pitcher of lemonade. They drank in silence and then the Inspector put the pitcher back in the icebox.

When he returned, Ellery said with a frown, "Was there time for—?"

"No," said the Inspector. "She'd been dead about two hours. That would place the murder attack at around 4 A.M. or a little later, just about time for her to have walked over to Sheridan Square from the night club and maybe wait around a few minutes—you know how the trains run at that hour of the morning. But Count Szebo was with the others until at least 5:30. They all stopped in at an allnight hamburger place on Madison and 48th on their way uptown. Every minute of his time is accounted for well past the murder period. Anyway, what would the point have been? Old man McKell had contracted to settle a hot million on Szebo when the knot was tied—excuse me, that was a bad figure of speech. I mean the count would have strangled himself before he'd lay a finger to that valuable throat. He doesn't have a Hungarian pretzel.

"In Monica McKell's case," said the Inspector, shaking his head, "we were able to trace her movements right up to the entrance of the Sheridan Square station. A nighthawk cab spotted her about halfway to the station from the club, pulled up alongside. She was on foot, alone. But she laughed and said to the hack, 'You've got me wrong, my friend. I'm a poor working girl and I've just got a dime to get home on,' and she opened her gold mesh bag and showed him; there was nothing in it but a lipstick, a compact, and a dime, he said. And she marched off down the street, the hack said, the diamond bracelet on her arm sparkling under the street lights. Swinging along like a movie star, was the way he put it. Actually, she was wearing a gold lamé creation designed like a Hindu sari, with a jacket of white mink thrown over it.

"And another cab driver parked near the station saw her cross the Square and disappear down the steps. She was still on foot, still alone.

"There was no one on duty at the change booth at that hour. Presumably she put her dime in the turnstile and walked down the platform to the end bench. A few minutes later she was dead.

"Her jewelry, her bag, her jacket weren't touched.

"We've found no evidence that anybody else was on the platform with her. The second cab driver picked up a fare right after he saw Monica go down the subway steps, and apparently he was the only one around. The Cat may have been waiting on the platform; the Cat may have followed Monica down from the street after ducking into doorways to avoid being seen by the two cab drivers; or the Cat may have got off at Sheridan

Square from an uptown train and found her there—there's nothing to tell. If she put up a battle, there's no sign of it. If she screamed, no one heard it. And that was the end of Monica McKell—born in New York, died in New York. From penthouse to subway. Downhill all the way."

After a long time Ellery said, "A girl like that must have been mixed up in a thousand pulp story plots. I've heard a lot of scandal . . ."

"I am now," sighed his father, "the world's foremost authority on the Mysteries of Monica. I can tell you, for instance, that she had a burn scar just under the left breast that she didn't get from falling on a hot stove. I know just where she was, and with whom, in February of 1946 when she disappeared and her father had us and the FBI chasing our tails looking for her, and despite what the papers said at the time her kid brother Jimmy had nothing to do with it—he'd just got out of the Service and he was having his own troubles readjusting to civilian life. I know how Monica came to get the autographed photo of Legs Diamond that's still hanging on her bedroom wall, and it's not for the reason you'd think. I know why she was asked to leave Nassau the year Sir Harry Oakes was murdered, and who asked her. I even know something J. Parnell Thomas never found out— that she was a card-carrying member of the Communist Party between 1938 and 1941, when she quit to become a Christian Fronter for four months, and then jumped that to take a course in Yoga Breathing Exercises under a Hollywood swami named Lal Dhyana Jackson.

"Yes, sir, I know everything there is to know about Leaping Lena, or Madcap Monica," said the Inspector, "except how she came to be strangled by the Cat . . . I can tell you this, Ellery. If when the Cat walked up to her on that subway platform he said, 'Excuse me, Miss McKell, I'm the Cat and I'm going to strangle you,' she probably moved over on the bench and said, 'How perfectly thrilling. Sit down and tell me more.' "

Ellery jumped up. He took a turn around the living room, busily, like a runner limbering up. Inspector Queen watched the sweat roll down his back.

"And that," said the Inspector, "is where we're hung up."

"Nothing—?"

"Not a bastardly thing. I suppose," the old man said angrily, "I can't blame McKell Senior for offering $100,000 reward, but all it's done is give the papers another angle to play up and flood us with a barrage of happy gas from ten thousand crackpots. And it hasn't been any help having McKell's high-priced prima donna dicks underfoot, either!"

"What about the current mouse?"

"Number 5?" The Inspector cracked his knuckles, clicking off integers in a bitter arithmetic. "Simone Phillips, 35, lived with a younger sister in a coldwater flat on East 102nd Street." He grimaced. "This mouse couldn't even rustle her own cheese. Simone'd had something wrong with her spine since childhood and she was paralyzed from the waist down. Spent most of her life in bed. What you might call a pushover."

"Yes." Ellery was sucking a piece of lemon and making a face. "Doesn't seem cricket, somehow. Even from the Cat."

"It happened last Friday night. August 19. Ten days after the McKell woman. Celeste—the younger sister—fixed Simone up, turned on the radio for her, and left for a neighborhood movie. Around 9 o'clock."

"Pretty late?"

"She went for just the main feature. Celeste said Simone hated being left alone, but she simply had to get out once a week—"

"Oh, this was routine?"

"Yes. The sister went every Friday night—her only recreation, by the way. Simone was helpless and Celeste was the only one she had. Anyway, Celeste got back a little after 11. She found the paralytic strangled. Salmon-colored silk cord tied around her neck."

"The crippled woman could hardly have let anyone in. Weren't there any signs—?"

"Celeste never locked the apartment door when she had to leave Simone. Simone was deathly afraid of gas leaks and fires, afraid she'd be caught helpless in bed sometime when her sister wasn't there. Leaving the door unlocked eased her mind. For the same reason they had a phone, which they certainly couldn't afford."

"Last Friday night. Almost as hot as tonight," mused Ellery. "In that district the people would all be congregated on the stoop, hanging out the windows. Do you mean to tell me no one saw anything?"

"There's so much testimony to the effect that no stranger entered the building through the front entrance between 9 and 11 that I'm convinced the Cat got in through the rear. There's a back door leading out to a court, and the court is accessible from one of a half-dozen different directions, the backs of other houses and the two side streets; it runs right through. The Phillips flat is on the ground floor, rear. The hall is dark, has only a 25-watt light. That's the way he got in, all right, and out again. But we've been over the square block a dozen times, inside the buildings and out, and we haven't turned up a thing."

"No screams."

"If she did yell, nobody paid any attention to it. You know what a tenement district's like on a hot night—kids out on the street till all hours and screams a dime a dozen. But my hunch is she didn't make a sound. I've never seen such fright on a human face. Paralysis on top of paralysis. She didn't put up the scrawniest kind of scrap. Wouldn't surprise me if she just sat there with her mouth open, pop-eyed, while the Cat took his cord and tied it around her neck and pulled it tight. Yes, sir, this was his easiest strike."

The Inspector pulled himself to his feet. "Simone was very fat from the waist up. The kind of fat that gives you the feeling that if you poked it you'd go clear through to the other side. As if she had no bones, no muscle."

"*Musculus*," said Ellery, sucking the lemon. "Little mouse. The shrunken little mice of the mouse. Little atrophies."

"Well, she'd been parked in that bed over twenty-five years." The old man trudged to one of the windows. "Sure is a scorcher."

"Simone, Celeste."

"What?" said the Inspector.

"Their names. So Gallic. Maternal poetry? And if not, how come 'Phillips'?"

"Their father was French. The family name was originally Phillippe, but he Anglicized it when he came to America."

"Mother French, too?"

"I think so, but they were married in New York. Phillips was in the import-export business and he made a fortune during the First World War. He dropped it all in the '29 crash and blew his brains out, leaving Mrs. Phillips penniless."

"With a paralyzed child. Tough."

"Mrs. Phillips managed by taking in sewing. They made out fine, Celeste says—in fact, she was enrolled as a freshman in N.Y.U. downtown when Mrs. Phillips died of pleurisy-pneumonia. That was five years ago."

"Must have been even tougher. For Celeste."

"It couldn't have been a peach parfait. Simone needed constant attention. Celeste had to quit school."

"How'd she manage?"

"Celeste has a modeling job in a dress shop her mother did business with. Afternoons and all day Saturday. She has a beautiful figure, dark coloring—pretty goodlooking number. She could make a lot more somewhere else, she told me, but the store isn't far from their home and she couldn't leave Simone alone too long. I got the impression Celeste was pretty much dominated by Simone and this was confirmed by the neighbors. They told me Simone nagged at Celeste all the time, whining and complaining and making the younger sister, who they all think is a saint, run her legs off. Probably accounts for her beatup look; she really was dragging her chin when I saw her."

"Tell me," said Ellery. "On Friday night last did this saintly young character go to the movies alone?"

"Yes."

"Does she usually?"

The Inspector looked surprised. "I don't know."

"Might pay to find out." Ellery leaned far forward to smooth out a wrinkle in the rug. "Doesn't she have a boy friend?"

"I don't think so. I gather she hasn't had much opportunity to meet men."

"How old is this Celeste?"

"23."

"Ripe young age.—The cord *was* tussah silk?"

"Yes."

The rug was now smooth.

"And that's all you have to tell me?"

"Oh, there's lots more, especially about Abernethy, Violette Smith, and Monica McKell."

"What?"

"I'll be happy to open the files to you."

Ellery was silent.

"Want to go over them?" asked his father.

"You found no connection among any of the five victims."

"Not a particle."

"None of them knew any of the others."

"As far as we can tell."

"They had no common friends, acquaintances, relatives?"

"So far we haven't hit any."

"Religious affiliation?" asked Ellery suddenly.

"Abernethy was a communicant of the Episcopal Church—in fact at one time, before his father died, he was studying for the ministry. But he gave that up to take care of his mother and if he attended church it wasn't on a regular basis. Certainly there's no record that he ever went after his mother died.

"Violette Smith's family are Lutherans. As far as we know, she herself went to no church. Her family threw her out years ago.

"Monica McKell—all the McKells—Presbyterian. Mr. and Mrs. McKell are very active in church affairs and Monica—it sort of surprised me—was quite religious.

"Rian O'Reilly was a devout Roman Catholic.

"Simone Phillips came of French Protestants on both sides, but she herself was interested in Christian Science."

"Likes, dislikes, habits, hobbies . . ."

The Inspector turned from the window. "What?"

"I'm fishing for a common denominator. The victims form a highly conglomerate group. Yet there must be some quality, some experience, some function they shared . . ."

"There's not a single indication that the poor mutts were tied up any way at all."

"As far as you know."

The Inspector laughed. "Ellery, I've been on this merry-go-round since the first ride and I tell you there's as much sense in these killings as there was in a Nazi crematorium.

"The murders haven't followed any time pattern or recognizable sequence. The intervals between the various crimes have been nineteen days, twenty-six, twenty-two, ten. It's true that they all occurred at night, but that's when cats walk, isn't it?

"The victims came from all over the City. East 19th near Gramercy Park. West 44th between Broadway and Sixth. West 20th near Ninth. Park and 53rd, in this case the victim actually getting it under Sheridan Square in Greenwich Village. And East 102nd.

"Economically? Upper crust, middle class, the poor. Socially? You find a pattern that includes an Abernethy, a Violette Smith, a Rian O'Reilly, a Monica McNell, and a Simone Phillips.

"Motive? Not gain. Not jealousy. Not anything *personal*.

"There's nothing to indicate that these have been sex crimes, or that a sex drive is even behind it.

"Ellery, this is killing for the sake of killing. The Cat's enemies are the human race. Anybody on two legs will do. If you ask me, that's what's really cooking in New York. And unless we clamp the lid on this—this *homicide*, it's going to boil over."

"And yet," said Ellery, "for an undiscriminating, unselective, blood-lusting and mankind-hating brute, I must say the Cat shows a nice appreciation of certain values."

"Values?"

"Well, take time. The Cat uses time the way Thoreau did, as a stream, to go fishing in. To catch Abernethy in his bachelor apartment he'd have to run the risk of being seen or heard entering or leaving, because Abernethy was an early-to-bed man. What's more, Abernethy rarely had a visitor, so that going to his door at a normal hour might have aroused a neighbor's curiosity. So what does the Cat do? He contrives to get Abernethy to agree to an appointment at an hour when the building's settled down for the night. To accomplish this called for the considerable feat of making an ossified bachelor change a habit of years' standing. In other words, the Cat weighed the difficulties against the time and he chose in favor of the time.

"In Violette Smith's case, whether it was done by appointment or as a result of careful study of her business practices, you can't deny that the Cat did pick a *time* when a very busy lady was in her flat alone.

"O'Reilly? Most vulnerable when he came home from his Brooklyn night job. And there was the Cat lying in wait in the downstairs hall. Nicely timed, wouldn't you say?"

The Inspector listened without comment.

"Monica McKell? A woman obviously running away from herself. And that kind of woman—from that kind of background—loses herself in crowds. She was always surrounded by people. It's no accident that she adored the subway. Monica must have presented a problem. Still— the Cat caught her alone, in a place and at a time which were most favorable for his project. How many nights did he trail her, I wonder, watching for just the right *moment?*

"And Simone, the paralytic. Easy pickings once he got to her. But how to get to her without being seen? Crowded tenement, the summer—day-time was out of the question, even when Celeste was away at work. But at night her sister is always with her. Always? Well, not exactly. On Friday nights the annoying Celeste goes to the movies. And Simone is strangled when? On a Friday night."

"You finished?"

"Yes."

Inspector Queen was remote. "Very plausible," he said. "Very convincing. But you're arguing from the premise that the Cat picks his people in advance. Suppose I argue from the premise that he does nothing of the sort?—a premise, incidentally, that's borne out by the total lack of connection among the victims.

"Then the Cat happened to be prowling on West 44th Street one night, picked a likely-looking building at random, chose the top floor apartment because it was closer to a roof getaway, pretended to be a salesman for nylons or French perfume—anything to get in—and that was the end of somebody whose name happened to be Violette Smith, call girl.

"On the night of July 18 he was feeling the urge again and chance took him to the Chelsea district. It was around midnight, his favorite hunting hour. He follows a tired-looking little guy into a hall and that's the end of a hard-working Irishman named O'Reilly. It might just as well have turned out to be William Miller, a shipping clerk who came home from a date with a Bronx girl around 2 A.M. and walked up the stairs under which O'Reilly's body was lying, still warm.

"In the early morning hours of August 9 the Cat was on the loose in the Village. He spotted an unescorted woman, walking. He followed her to the Sheridan Square subway and that was the end of Well-Known New York Socialite, who should have stuck to her twelve-cylinder job.

"And on the night of August 19 he was up around 102nd Street hankering after another neck, and he got into a nice dark court and pussy-footed around till he saw through a ground floor window a fat young woman lying in a bed, alone. And that was the end of Simone Phillips.

"Now tell me something—anything—that says it didn't happen that way."

"Abernethy?"

"You left Abernethy out," said Ellery. "Abernethy the Vague. Admittedly not a hard thing to do. But he *is* dead, he *was* strangled with one of those silk cords, and didn't you yourself say it was by appointment?"

"I said the whole setup smacked of an appointment. But we don't *know* it. Something could have made him sit up past his usual bedtime that night, maybe a radio program, or he fell asleep in the easychair. The Cat could have been in the building on the loose and seen the light under Abernethy's door and knocked—"

"At which Abernethy let him in?"

"All he'd have to have done was unlock the door."

"An Abernethy? At midnight?"

"Or maybe he'd forgotten to check his spring latch and the Cat just walked in, releasing it on his way out."

"Then why didn't Archibald use his lungs? Or run? How is it he permitted the Cat to get behind him while he sat in his chair?"

"He might have been—like Simone Phillips—scared stiff."

"Yes," said Ellery, "I suppose that's possible."

"I know," muttered the Inspector. "The Abernethy thing doesn't conform. Nothing conforms." He shrugged. "I'm not saying you're not right, Ellery. But you see what we're up against. And the whole blasted thing's in my lap now. It would be bad enough if that's all I had to worry about. But he's not through; you know that. There's going to be another one, and another one after that, until we catch him or he drops dead from overexercise. How can we prevent it? There aren't enough cops in the U.S. to make every nook and cranny of a city like New York murderproof. We can't even be sure he'll keep restricting his activities to Manhattan. And the other boroughs know it. They're getting identical reactions from the public in the Bronx, Brooklyn, Queens, Richmond. Hell, it's being felt on Long Island, in Westchester, Connecticut, New Jersey, all the commuter places. Sometimes I think it's a bad dream. Ellery—"

Ellery's lips parted.

"Don't answer till I'm finished. You feel that you failed in the Van Horn case and that because you failed two people went to their deaths. Lord knows I've tried to help you get it out of your system. But I guess nobody can talk away another man's conscience . . . I've had to sit by and watch you crawl into a hole while you kept swearing by the beards of all the Prophets that you'd never mix into another case.

"But son," said the old man, "this is a special kind of deal. This one is tough. It's tough not only on its own merits—which are tough enough—but because of the atmosphere it's creating. This isn't just a matter of clearing up a few murders, Ellery. It's a race against—against citywide collapse. And don't make with the eyebrow; I tell you it's coming. It's only a question of time. Just one murder in the wrong place . . . Nobody downtown's out to rob me of the glory; not in this one. They're all feeling sorry for the old duck. Let me tell you something." The Inspector stared down at 87th Street, bracing himself against the window frame. "I mentioned earlier that I thought the Commissioner had an angle in putting me at the head of this special Cat squad. The boss thinks you're a screwball, but he's often asked me when you're going to snap out of the sulks and get back to using the crazy talents God gave you. Well, my opinion, Ellery, is that he's put me on the spot deliberately."

"For what reason?"

"To force you into the case."

"You're not serious!"

His father looked at him.

"But he wouldn't do a thing like that." Ellery's face was dark. "Not to you. That's the dirtiest kind of slap in the face."

"To stop these stranglings, son, I'd do a lot worse. Anyway, what's the odds? You're no superman. Nobody expects miracles. It's even a sort of insult to you. In an emergency people will try anything, even tough old eggs like the Commissioner."

"Thanks," mumbled Ellery. "That sets me up. It really does."

"Kidding aside. It would hit me pretty hard to think that when I needed you most you let me down. Ellery, how about getting into this?"

"You," said the son, "are an extremely clever old man."

The Inspector grinned.

"Naturally if I thought I could help out in a thing as serious as this I'd . . . But, damn it, Dad, I feel virginal. I want to and I don't want to. Let me sleep on it. I'd be no use to you or anybody in my present state."

"Fair enough," said his father briskly. "Good grief, I've been making speeches. How do these politicians do it? How about some more lemonade, son, with a shot of gin in it to take the bite off?"

"In my case, it'll take more than a shot."

"Motion seconded."

But neither meant it.

\* \* \*

The inspector sat down at the kitchen table with a groan, thinking that with Ellery the usual psychology was a waste of breath. The Cat and Ellery seemed two twinges of the same pain.

He leaned back against the tiled wall, tipping his chair.

The blasted heat . . .

He opened his eyes to find the Police Commissioner of the City of New York leaning over him.

"Dick, Dick," the Commissioner was saying. "Wake up."

Ellery was in the kitchen doorway, still in his shorts.

The Commissioner was hatless and the gabardine around his armpits was soaked.

Inspector Queen blinked up at him.

"I told them I'd notify you in person."

"Notify me about what, Commissioner?"

"The Cat's got another tail."

"When?" The old man licked his lips.

"Tonight. Between 10:30 and midnight."

"Where?" He brushed past them, darted into the living room, grabbed at his shoes.

"Central Park, not far from the 110th Street entrance. In some bushes behind a rock."

"Who?"

"Beatrice Willikins, 32, single, sole support of an aged father. She'd taken him to the Park for some air and left him on a bench to go looking for water. She never came back and finally he called a Park patrolman. The patrolman found her a couple of hundred feet away, strangled. Salmon-colored silk cord. Purse not touched. Hit over the head from behind and signs of dragging into the bushes. The strangulation took place there, probably while she was unconscious. No superficial indication of rape."

"No, Dad," said Ellery. "Those are wet. Here's a fresh shirt and undershirt."

"Bushes, Park," said the Inspector rapidly. "That's a break. Or is it? Prints on the ground?"

"So far, nothing. But Dick," said the Commissioner, "something new's been added."

The Inspector looked at him. He was trying to button his shirt. Ellery did it for him.

"Beatrice Willikins lived at West 128th Street."

"West," said the Inspector mechanically, sticking an arm into the jacket Ellery was holding up. Ellery was staring at the Commissioner.

"Near Lenox."

*"Harlem?"*

The Commissioner swabbed his neck. "This one might do it, Dick. If someone lost his head."

Inspector Queen ran to the door. He was very pale. "This means all night, Ellery. You go to bed."

But Ellery was saying, "This one might do what if someone lost his head, Commissioner?"

"Push the button that blows New York higher than Hiroshima."

"Come on, Commissioner," said the Inspector impatiently from the foyer.

"Wait." Ellery was looking politely at the Commissioner, and the Commissioner was looking just as politely at him. "If you'll give me three minutes, I'll go with you."

# 3

The Sixth Tail of the Cat, which went on display on the morning of August 26, offered a delicate departure from the mode. Where its five fellows were hairlines enclosing white space, this tail was solidly inked in. Thus New York City was informed that the Cat had crossed the color line. By the glowing encirclement of one black throat, to the seven million pale necks already within the orbit of the noose were joined five hundred thousand others.

It was notable that, while Inspector Queen occupied himself in Harlem with Beatrice Willikins's demise, the Mayor called a dawn press conference at City Hall which was attended by the Police Commissioner and other officials.

"We are convinced, gentlemen," said the Mayor, "that there is no race angle to Beatrice Willikins's murder. The one thing we've got to avoid is a repetition of the kind of tension that brought on the so-called Black Ides of March in 1935. A trivial incident and a false rumor resulted in three deaths, thirty-odd people hospitalized for bullet wounds, and over two hundred others treated for injuries, cuts, and abrasions. Not to mention property damage amounting to more than $2,000,000."

"I was under the impression, Mr. Mayor," remarked a reporter for one of the Harlem newspapers, "that—to quote from the report of the bi-racial commission appointed by Mayor La Guardia to investigate the riot—it was caused by 'resentments against racial discrimination and poverty in the midst of plenty.' "

"Of course," replied the Mayor quickly. "There are always underlying social and economic causes. Frankly, that's what we're a little apprehensive about. New York is a melting pot of every race, national origin, and creed under the sun. One out of every fifteen of our fellow New Yorkers is Negro. Three out of every ten are Jewish. There are more Italians in

New York City than in Genoa. More Germans than in Bremen. More Irish than in Dublin. We've got Poles, Greeks, Russians, Spaniards, Turks, Portuguese, Chinese, Scandinavians, Filipinos, Persians—everything. That's what makes us the greatest city on earth. But it also keeps us on the lid of a volcano. Postwar tensions haven't helped. These stranglings have made the whole City nervous and we don't want anything foolish to touch off public disorders. Naturally, that last remark is off the record.

"Gentlemen, our most sensible course is to treat these murders, uh, as routine. Non-sensationally. They're a bit off the beaten path and they present some rather tough problems, but we have the finest crime-investigating agency in the world, we're working on the murders night and day, and the break may be expected at any time."

"Beatrice Willikins," said the Commissioner, "was strangled by the Cat. She was Negro. The five other victims have all been white. That's the thing for you boys to emphasize."

"Our angle might be, Commissioner," said the reporter for the Harlem paper, "that the Cat is a firm democratic believer in civil rights."

In the shout that followed, an atmosphere was created which enabled the Mayor to close the conference without disclosing that the latest murder was giving the head of the new Cat squad a very bad time.

They were sitting around in the squad room of the main Harlem precinct weighing reports on Beatrice Willikins. The investigation on the scene, in the Park, had yielded nothing. The ground behind the boulder was rocky and if the Cat had left the print of his pads on it the first confusion following the discovery of the young woman's body had scuffed it out. An inch-by-inch examination of the grass, soil, and paths in the vicinity of the boulder produced only two hairpins, both identified as coming from the victim's head. Laboratory analysis of certain particles scraped from under the victim's fingernails, at first thought to be coagulated blood or bloody tissue, proved that they consisted principally of lip rouge, of a shade popular with Negro women and which matched exactly the rouge still on the dead girl's lips. There was no trace of the weapon with which the Cat had struck her head and the bruise gave no clue to its nature; it could only be described by that most inconclusive of terms, "blunt instrument."

As for the catch of the police dragnet, thrown around the area within minutes of the body's discovery, it consisted of a great many citizens of both colors and sexes and all ages, uniformly overheated, excited, frightened, and guilty-looking; none, however, gave off precisely the whiff for which Ellery's nostrils were sniffing. It took the entire night to screen them. At the end, with echoes of bedlam still in their ears, the police had only two likely fish, a white and a black, the white an unemployed jazz trumpet player 27 years old found lying on the grass smoking a marijuana cigaret, the black a skinny, undersized runner for a Lenox Avenue drop. The Negro, a middleaged man, was caught in the act of peddling the numbers. Each was stripped to the skin and thoroughly examined without result. The policy employee was released when Negro detectives rounded up witnesses who accounted for his whereabouts for an hour preceding the general crime period, and for some time after that; at which everyone, remembering the Black Ides, looked happy. The white musician was taken to Headquarters for further questioning. But, as Inspector Queen remarked, it didn't look promising: if he was the Cat, he had been in New York on June 3, June 22, July 18, August 9, and August 19; whereas the trumpet player claimed to have left New York in May and returned only five days before. He said he had been employed during that period on a round-the-world luxury boat. He had described the boat, the captain, the purser, and the other members of the ship's orchestra; and, in some detail, several feminine passengers.

So they tackled it from the other end and hoisted the victim to the scales. Which tipped depressingly on the side of rectitude and good works.

Beatrice Willikins had been a responsible member of the Negro community, belonging to the Abyssinian Baptist Church and active in many of its groups. Born and raised in Harlem, and educated at Howard University, she had been employed by a child welfare agency and her work had been exclusively with the underprivileged and delinquent children of Harlem.

She had contributed sociological articles to *Journal of Negro Education* and poetry to *Phylon*. Occasional freelance pieces under her byline had appeared in the *Amsterdam-Star News, Pittsburgh Courier*, and the Atlanta *Daily World*.

Beatrice Willikins's associations had been impeccable. Her friends were Negro educators, social workers, writers, and professional people. Her work had taken her from Black Bohemia to San Juan Hill; she had come in frequent contact with dope peddlers, pimps, the streetwalkers of "The Market Place"; Puerto Ricans, Negro Moslems, French Africans, Black Jews, darkskinned Mexicans and Cubans, Negroid Chinese and Japanese. But she had gone among them as a friend and healer, unresented and unmolested. The police of Harlem had known her as a quietly determined defender of juvenile delinquents.

"She was a fighter," the precinct captain told Inspector Queen, "but she wasn't any fanatic. I don't know of anybody in Harlem, white or black, who didn't respect her."

In 1942 she had been engaged to a young Negro physician named
Lawrence Caton. Dr. Caton had gone into the Army and he had been killed
in Italy. Her fiancé's death had apparently sealed off the girl's emotional
life; there was no record that she had ever gone out with another man.

The Inspector took a Negro lieutenant aside, and the detective nodded
and went over to the bench on which the girl's father was seated, beside
Ellery.

"Pap, who do you figure did the girl in?"

The aged man mumbled something.

"What?"

"He says," said Ellery, "that his name is Frederick Willikins and his
father was a slave in Georgia."

"That's fine, that's okay, Pap, but what man was she messing around
with? White man?"

The old man stiffened. They could see him struggle with something.
Finally he drew back his brown skull, like a snake, and struck.

The Negro detective stooped and wiped the old man's spittle from his
shoe.

"I guess old Pappy here figures I insulted him. On two counts."

"It's important." The Inspector moved toward the bench.

"Better let me, Inspector," said the detective. "He's got a spitting eye."
He stooped over the old man again. "Okay, Pap, your daughter was a gal
in a million. Now you want to bring down the wrath on the one who give
it to her, don't you?"

He mumbled again.

"I think he said, Lieutenant," said Ellery, "something about the Lord
providing."

"Not in Harlem," said the detective. "Pap, you keep your mind on this.
All we want to know is, did your girl Bea know some white?"

The old man did not answer.

"It's all this pale hide around here," said the Negro lieutenant apologetically. "Pap, who was he? What did he look like? Bea ever tell a white
skin off?"

The brown skull drew back again.

"Better save that juice," growled the lieutenant. "Come on, Pappy, all
I want is one answer to one question. Bea had a phone. Did a white man
keep calling her up?"

The withered lips drew back in a tormented grin. "She has truck with a
white, I kill her with my own two hands." Then he shrank into the corner
of the bench.

"Say."

But the Inspector was shaking his head. "He's 80 if he's a day, Lieutenant. And look at his hands. All crippled up with arthritis. He couldn't strangle a sick kitten."

Ellery got up. "There's nothing here. I need a few hours' sleep, Dad. And so do you."

"You go on along home, Ellery. If I get a chance I'll stretch out on a cot upstairs. Where will you be tonight?"

"At Headquarters," said Ellery. "With those files."

On the morning of August 27 the Cat was at his old stand on the editorial page of the *New York Extra* doing a brisk business in fear. But business can be brisker, and during the day the circulation manager of the *Extra* earned a bonus, the reason for which became evident on the morning of the 28th. In that issue the Cat moved over to Page 1, cartoonically speaking, on a longterm lease; a new tenancy so successful that by midmorning not a copy was to be found on any news stand in the City.

And, as if to celebrate his leasehold, he waved a new tail.

It was ingenious. At first glance—there was no caption—the picture advertised a new horror: There were the six numbered tails and the giant-sized seventh, a scratchline arrogance. The reader seized the paper and hunted in vain among the headlines. Puzzled, he returned to the drawing; whereupon he saw it as it was, the noose shaped by the great tail numbered 7 being no noose at all but a question mark.

In the places of authority there was sharp disagreement as to precisely which question the question mark marked. The *Extra*'s editor, in an interesting telephone conversation with the Mayor on the afternoon of the 28th, protested in a wide-eyed tone of voice that the question was, obviously, *Is the Cat going to claim a seventh victim?*—a logical, ethical, public-service, newsworthy query, the editor said, arising smack from the facts of record. The Mayor replied carbolically that it seemed to him, and to a great many other New Yorkers who had seen the cartoon and who were even now harrying the City Hall and Police Headquarters telephone operators, that the question it posed was, crudely and brutally, *Who's going to be the Cat's seventh victim?*—executed, moreover, in a drooling-whiskered, chop-licking style which was distinctly not in the public service, quite the contrary, and which he, the Mayor, might have expected from an opposition newspaper which was incapable of subordinating dirty politics to the public interest. The editor retorted that he, the Mayor, ought to know, as he was lugging around a rather large bundle of soiled laundry himself, and the Mayor shouted, "What do you mean by that slanderous remark?," at which the editor replied that he yielded to no man in his admiration for the rank and file of New York's Finest but everybody who knew the score knew that the Mayor's appointee, the present Commissioner, was an old party firehorse who couldn't catch a pop fly let alone a desperate criminal, and if the Mayor was so deletedly concerned about the public interest why didn't he appoint somebody sharp to the top police post?—then maybe the people of the City of New York could go back to sleeping nights. What was more, this was a suggestion the *Extra* intended to toss off in its lead editorial tomorrow—"in the public interest, Mr. Mayor, you understand." With which the editor of the *Extra* hung up to receive a circulation report that left him glowing.

He glowed too soon.

As the Mayor angrily sniffed the green carnation in his lapel, the Commissioner said, "Jack, if you want my resignation—"

"Don't pay any attention to that rag, Barney."

"It has a lot of readers. Why not cross it up before that editorial hits the streets tomorrow?"

"By firing you? I'll be damned if I will." And the Mayor added thoughtfully, "And damned if I won't, too."

"Exactly," said the Commissioner, lighting a cigar. "I've given the whole situation a lot of thought. Jack, what New York needs in this crisis is a hero, a Moses, somebody who'll capture their imaginations and—"

"Distract their attention?"

"Well . . ."

"Come on, Barney, what's on your mind?"

"Well, you appoint this fellow something like . . . well, like Special Cat Catcher for the Mayor."

"Pied Piper of Gotham, hm?" muttered His Honor. "No, that was rats. We've got plenty of those, too."

"No connection with the P.D. A roving assignment. Sort of advisory. And you could break the story just too late for the *Extra* to yank that editorial."

"Don't you mean, Barney," murmured the Mayor, "that you want me to appoint a fall guy who'll absorb all the heat and take all the raps, while you and the Department get off the spot and back to everyday operations?"

"Well, it's a fact," said the Commissioner, looking critically at his cigar, "that the men, from the brass down, have been thinking more of headlines than results—"

"Suppose this fellow," asked the Mayor, "beats you to the Cat?"

The Commissioner laughed.

Rather abruptly, the Mayor said, "Barney, whom did you have in mind?"

"A real glamor boy, Jack. Native New Yorker, no political ax to grind, nationally known as a crime investigator, yet he's a civilian. He can't refuse, because I softened him up first by dropping the whole hot potato in his old man's lap."

The Mayor slowly brought his swivel chair back to the vertical.

The Commissioner nodded.

The Mayor reached for his private line. "Barney," he said, "this time I think you've outfoxed yourself. Oh, Birdy. Get me Ellery Queen."

"I'm overcome, Mr. Mayor," said Ellery. "But certainly my qualifications—"

"I can't think of a better man to become Special Investigator for the Mayor. Should have thought of it long ago. I'll be frank with you, Mr. Queen—"

"Yes," said Ellery.

"Sometimes a case comes along," said the Mayor, one eye on his Police Commissioner, "that's so off the trail, so eccentric, it licks even the finest cop. I think this Cat business needs the kind of special talents you've demonstrated so brilliantly in the past. A fresh and unorthodox approach."

"Those are kind words, Mr. Mayor, but wouldn't a thing like this create hard feeling on Centre Street?"

"I think I can promise you, Mr. Queen," said His Honor dryly, "the full co-operation of the Department."

"I see," said Ellery. "I suppose my father—"

"The only one I've discussed this with is the Commissioner. Will you accept?"

"May I take a few minutes to think it over?"

"I'll be waiting here at my office for your call."

Ellery hung up.

"Special Investigator to the Mayor," said the Inspector, who had been listening on the extension. "They're really getting fussed."

"Not about the Cat," Ellery laughed. "The case is getting too torrid to the touch and somebody's looking for a potential burnt sacrifice to stand up and take the heat."

"The Commissioner . . ."

"He's really played that angle, hasn't he?"

The Inspector scowled. "Not the Mayor, Ellery. The Mayor's a politician, but he's also an honest man. If he fell for this, it's for the reason he gave you. Why not do it?"

Ellery was silent.

"All this would do is make it official . . ."

"And tougher."

"What you're afraid of," said his father deliberately, "is being committed."

"Well, I'd have to see it through."

"I hate to get personal, but doesn't that make two of us? Ellery, the move might be important in another way."

"How?"

"Just the act of your taking this job might scare the Cat off. Thought of that?"

"No."

"The publicity alone—"

"I meant no, it won't."

"You underestimate your rep."

"You underestimate our kitty. I have the feeling," said Ellery, "that nothing can scare him off."

His voice conveyed such a burdensome knowledge that the Inspector started. "For a second there you had me thinking . . ." But then he said slowly, "*Ellery, you've spotted something.*"

Between them lay the archaeology of murder. Detail photographs of the victims, full and side views. General views of the scenes of the crimes, interiors, exteriors, closeups, from various angles. Cross-sketchings, neatly compass-directed and drawn to specified scale. The file of appurtenant fingerprints. A whole library of reports, records, assignments, details of work complete with notations of time, place names, addresses, findings, questions and answers and statements and technical information. And, on a separate table, *res gestae* evidence, the originals.

Nowhere in this classified heterogeneity had a recognizable clue been discovered.

In a sharper tone the Inspector said, "Have you?"

Ellery said, "*Maybe.*"

The Inspector opened his mouth.

"Don't ask me any more, Dad. It's something, but where it may lead . . ." Ellery looked unhappy. "I've spent forty-eight hours on this. But I want to go over it again."

Inspector Queen said into his phone, "Get the Mayor. Tell him Ellery Queen."

He sounded at peace for the first time in twelve weeks.

The news burst upon the City with a roar that soothed even the Police Commissioner. The noise was largely jubilant. The Mayor's mail increased fivefold and the City Hall switchboard was unable to handle the volume of telephone calls. Commentators and columnists approved. It was noted that within twenty-four hours the gross number of false alarm police calls had been reduced by half and the strangulation of alley cats all but stopped. A small section of the press scoffed, but its collective voice was too feeble to register against the applause. As for the *New York Extra*, Ellery's appointment caught it with the issue containing its editorial blast all but run off; and although in a follow up edition the paper excoriated the Mayor for "undermining the morale of the finest police force in the world," the Mayor's announcement took the sting out of the charge.

"Mr. Queen's appointment," the Mayor's handout had said in part, "in no way conflicts with, weakens, or is an expression of lack of confidence in, the regular police authority. The homicide record of the New York Police Department speaks for itself. But in view of the rather peculiar nature of this particular series of homicides, I have felt it advisable to enlist the aid of an expert who has specialized in unusual crimes. The suggestion that Ellery Queen be appointed Special Investigator came from the Police Commissioner himself, with whom Mr. Queen will work in the closest co-operation."

The Mayor repeated his statement over the air the same night.

At City Hall, after the swearing-in ceremony, punctuated by flashlight shots of the Mayor and Ellery Queen, of Ellery Queen and the Police Commissioner, of the Police Commissioner and the Mayor, and of the Mayor, the Police Commissioner, and Ellery Queen, Ellery read a prepared statement.

"The Cat has been at large in Manhattan for almost three months. In that period he has murdered six people. The file on six homicides weighs just about as much as the responsibilities I have accepted in taking this post. But while I have a great deal of catching up to do, I am sufficiently familiar with the facts to feel justified in stating even at this time that the case can and will be solved and the killer caught. Whether he will be caught before he commits another murder remains, of course, to be seen. But if the Cat should claim another victim tonight, I ask everyone to bear in mind that more New Yorkers are killed by automobiles in one day on our streets than the Cat has killed in three months."

Immediately he finished reading the statement, Ellery was asked by the reporter for the *Extra* if he was not already "withholding information": "Did you mean by saying 'I am sufficiently familiar with the facts to feel justified in stating that the case will be solved' that you've got a hot lead?"

Ellery smiled faintly and said: "I'll stand on my statement as read."

In the next few days his course was puzzling. He did not act like a man who has found something. He did not act at all. He retired to the Queen apartment and remained invisible to the public eye. As for the

public ear, he took his telephone off the cradle, leaving Inspector
Queen's direct line to Headquarters as his sole contact with the City. The
Queen front door he kept locked.

It was not quite what the Commissioner had planned, and Inspector
Queen heard rumblings of his discontent. But the old man merely continued to lay reports before Ellery as they came in, without comment or
question. One of these concerned the marijuana-smoking trumpet player
detained in the Beatrice Willikins investigation: the musician's story had
been substantiated and he had been released. Ellery scarcely glanced at
the report. He balanced on his coccyx chainsmoking as he studied the lu-
nar topography of his study ceiling, that epic issue between the Queens
and their wily landlord. But the Inspector knew that Ellery was not thinking of the unattainable calcimine. *a white or tinted wash of glue, whiting or*

During the evening of August 31, however, Ellery was back at the reports. Inspector Queen was about to leave his office after another day
which had contrived to be both full and empty when his private line came
to life and he picked up the phone to hear his son's voice.

"I've been going over the reports on the cords again—"

"Yes, Ellery."

"I was thinking of a possible way to determine the Cat's manual pref-
erence."

"What do you have in mind?"

"The technique worked out years ago on the Continent by the Belgian,
Goddefroy, and others."

"With rope?"

"Yes. The surface fibers will lie in the direction opposite to that of the
pulling or other motions involving friction."

"Well, sure. We've settled a few hanging cases that way where the
question was suicide or murder. What of it?"

"The Cat loops the silk cord around his victim's neck from behind.
Before he can start pulling and tightening the noose, he's got to cross the
ends over each other. Theoretically, therefore, there ought to be a point of
friction where the noose crosses itself at the nape of the neck.

"In two of these cases, O'Reilly and Violette Smith, the neck photos
show that during the stranglings—before knots were tied—the two ends
of the cord did make contact in crossing."

"Yes."

"All right. He's pulling with both hands, one to each end of the cord,
in opposite directions. But unless he's ambidextrous, he's not pulling
with equal force. One hand will tend to hold, while the other—his favored hand—will tend to pull. In other words, if he's righthanded the end
of the cord held by his left hand ought to show a point of friction, and the

*Zinc white, and water used esp. on plastered surfaces*

end of the cord held by his right hand ought to show a line of friction. Vice versa if he's lefthanded. Tussah silk is coarse-fibered. There may be observable effects."

"It's a thought," muttered the Inspector.

"Call me back when you find out, Dad."

"I don't know how long it'll take. The lab's been overworked and it's late. You'd better not wait up. I'll stick around here till I find out."

The Inspector made several telephone calls, leaving word that he was to be notified the moment a finding was made. Then, because he had had a couch hauled into his office several weeks before, he stretched out on it thinking he would close his eyes for just a few minutes.

When he opened them, the September 1 sun was pouring in speckled splendor through his dusty windows.

One of his phones was ringing.

He tottered over to his desk.

"What happened to you?" asked Ellery.

"I lay down for a cat nap last night and the next thing I knew the phone was ringing."

"I was about to call a policeman. What about those cord findings?"

"I haven't . . . Wait, the report's on my desk. Damn it, why didn't they wake me?" After a moment, the Inspector said: "Inconclusive."

"Oh."

"Their opinion is that O'Reilly and the Smith woman thrashed about from side to side during the attacks just enough to make the Cat alternate his pull from one hand to the other and back. In a sort of seesaw movement. Maybe O'Reilly was only stunned and fought back. Anyway, there's no point of friction determinable. What slight friction areas are detectable in the silk are about equally divided between right and left."

"And there you are." But then Ellery said in an altogether different tone, "Dad, come right home."

"Home? I'm just starting my day, Ellery."

"Come home."

The Inspector dropped the phone and ran.

"What's up?" Inspector Queen was breathing hard from his sprint up the stairs.

"Read these. They came in this morning's mail."

The Inspector sat down slowly in the leather armchair. One envelope bore the brash imprint of the *New York Extra*, the address typewritten; the other was small, pinkish, and secretive-looking and it had been addressed by hand.

From the *Extra* envelope he took a slip of yellow scratch-pad paper.

DEAR E.Q.—What did you do, rip out your phone? Or are you looking for the Cat in Bechuanaland? I've been up to your place six times in the past couple of days and no answer.

I've got to see you.

JAMES GUYMER MCKELL

P.S. Known to the trade as "Jimmy Leggitt." Leg-It, get it? Call me at the *Extra*.

J.G.M.

"Monica McKell's kid brother!"

"Read the other one."

The notepaper of the second letter matched the envelope. This was elegance unaccustomed, a yearning after effect. The hand was hurried and a bit wretched.

DEAR MR. QUEEN,

I have been trying to reach you by telephone ever since the radio announced your appointment as Special Investigator of the Cat murders.

Can you possibly see me? This is *not* an attempt to get your autograph.

*Please.*

Sincerely,<br>CELESTE PHILLIPS

"Simone Phillips's sister." The Inspector laid the two letters down on an endtable, carefully. "Going to see them?"

"Yes. I phoned the Phillips girl at her home and I reached McKell at his paper. They both sound pretty young. I've seen some of McKell's stuff on the Cat cases under the name of Leggitt, but nothing that connected him personally with any of them. Did you know Leggitt and McKell were the same man?"

"No." The Inspector seemed disturbed by his ignorance. "I've seen him, of course, but in the McKell home on Park Avenue. I suppose being a legman is the thing to do just now in his set. Did they say what they wanted?"

"Celeste Phillips said she'd rather tell me in person. I told McKell if it was an interview he was after for that ragbag he works for I'd heave him out on his ear, but he assured me it was personal."

"Both in the same morning," muttered the Inspector. "Did either mention the other?"

"No."

"When are they due?"

"I violated a cardinal rule of the Manual. I'm seeing them at the same time. 11 o'clock."

"Five of! I've got to shower, shave, and get into clean clothes." The old man, hurrying to his bedroom, added over his shoulder, "Hold them here. By force, if you have to."

When the refurbished man emerged, his son was gallantly applying the flame of a lighter to a cigaret held by two slim gloved fingers to two female lips of distinction. She was sleekly modish from her hairdo to her shoetips, but young—the New York woman as she would like to be, but not quite grown up to it. The Inspector had seen girls like her on Fifth Avenue in the late afternoons, alone and unapproachable, the healthy raw material of youth covered by a patina of chic. But she was never upper crust; there was no boredom in her. *Vogue* just graduated from *Seventeen*, and very beautiful.

The Inspector was confused. It was Celeste Phillips. But what had happened to her?

"Hello, Miss Phillips." They shook hands; her grip was quick, withdrawing. She wasn't expecting me, he thought; Ellery didn't say I was home. "I almost didn't recognize you." It was incredible; less than two weeks. "Please sit down."

Over her shoulder as she turned he glimpsed Ellery being quizzical. The Inspector recalled his description of Simone Phillips's sister and he shrugged in reply. It was impossible to see this spick-and-span girl against the smeary background of the flat on 102nd Street. Yet she still lived there; Ellery had reached her there. Inspector Queen decided that it was the clothes. Probably borrowed for the occasion from that dress shop she models in, he thought. The rest was makeup. When she got home and returned the finery and washed her face she would be again the Cinderella he remembered. Or would she? He was really not so sure. The sunny shallows under her bright black eyes, which had replaced the purple deeps he remembered, would not blot off with a towel. And certain planes then in her face had . . . been buried with her sister?

*By the pricking of my thumbs . . .*

"Don't let me interrupt anything," said the Inspector with a smile.

"Oh, I was just telling Mr. Queen how impossible the apartment situation still is." Her fingers were unclasping and reclasping the catch on her bag with a life of their own.

"You're intending to move?" At the Inspector's glance the fingers flew to a stop.

"As soon as I can find another place."

"Yes, you'll be starting a new life," the Inspector nodded. "Most peo-ple do. In cases like this." Then he said, "Did you get rid of the bed?"

"Oh, no. I sleep in it." She said very quickly, "I've been sleeping on a cot for years. Simone's bed is so comfortable. She'd want me to. And then . . . I'm not afraid of my sister, you see."

"Well," said Ellery. "That's a good healthy attitude. Dad, I'd just about got round to the point of asking Miss Phillips why she wanted to see me."

"I want to help, Mr. Queen." She had a *Vogue* voice this morning, too. So careful.

"Help? In what way?"

"I don't know. I don't even know . . ." She covered her distress with a *Vogue* smile. "I don't understand it myself. Sometimes you feel you just have to do something. You don't know why."

"Why did you come, Miss Phillips?"

She twisted in the chair. But then she snapped forward and she was no longer a figure in a magazine but a very young woman stripped all but bare. "I pitied my sister terribly. She was a cripple in more ways than one. Anybody would be, chained to a bed so long. Absolutely helpless. I hated myself for not being a cripple, too. I always felt so *guilty*.

"How can I explain it?" she cried. "Simone wanted to live. She was, oh, greedy about it. She was interested in everything. I had to tell her how people in the streets looked, what the sky was like on a cloudy day, the garbage men, the lines of wash across the court. She kept the radio going from morning to night. She had to know all about the movie stars and the society people, who was getting married, who was getting di-vorced, who was having a baby. When I went out with some man, which wasn't too often, I had to tell her what he said, how he said it—what his line was, the passes he made, how I felt about the icky phase of going out.

"And she hated me. She was jealous. When I came home from work I used to wipe the makeup off before I stepped into the house. I never . . . dressed or undressed in front of her if I could help it. Only—she'd make me. She seemed to like being jealous; she'd get a kick out of it.

"And then there were other times when she'd cry and I knew she loved me very much.

"She was right," Celeste Phillips said in a hard voice. "There was no justice in her being a cripple. It was a punishment she didn't deserve and she was determined not to give up. She wanted to live much more than I do. Much more.

"Killing her wasn't—wasn't *fair*.

"I want to help find the one who killed her. I don't understand it and I can't believe yet that it really happened to us—to her . . . I've got to be part of his punishment. I can't just stand around doing nothing. I'm not afraid or kittenish or silly. Let me help, Mr. Queen. I'll carry your briefcase, run errands, type letters, answer your phone—anything. Whatever you say. Whatever you think I can do."

She looked down at her white doeskins, blinking angrily.

The Queens kept looking at her.

"I'm really awfully, terribly sorry," said a voice, "but I rang and rang—"

Celeste jumped up and ran to the window. A long wrinkle ran like a crack from one shoulder to the opposite hip and the young man in the doorway seemed spellbound by it. As if he half-expected a shell to fall off.

He said again, "I can't tell you how sorry," not taking his eyes from her back, "but I lost a sister by that route myself. I'll come back later."

Celeste said, "Oh!" and she turned around, quickly.

They stared at each other across the room.

Ellery said, "Miss Phillips and—I gather—Mr. McKell."

"Ever see New York the way it's going to look the day after God Almighty strikes us all dead because He's sick and tired of us?—I mean, Wall Street on Sunday morning?" Jimmy McKell was saying to Celeste Phillips ten minutes later. As far as he was concerned, the Almighty had already begun, with the Queens. "Or Big Liz coming up the bay? Or the mid-Hudson from the Yonkers ferry in June? Or Central Park from a Central Park South penthouse looking north any old time? Ever taste a *bagel? Halvah?* Chopped liver with chicken fat and a slice of black radish? *Shish kebab?* Anchovy *pizza?*"

"No," said Celeste primly.

"This is ridiculous." He waved his absurd arms. He looks like young Abe Lincoln, thought Ellery. All length and enthusiasm, awkward and lovely. An ugly, humorous mouth and eyes not so frank as his voice. His brown suit was positively disreputable. 25 or 26. "And you call yourself a New Yorker, Celeste?"

Celeste stiffened. "Maybe, *Mister* McKell, being poor all my life has something to do with it." She has the French heritage of middleclass propriety, Ellery thought.

"You sound like my saintly father in reverse," said James Guymer McKell. "He never ate a *bagel*, either. Are you anti-Semitic?"

"I'm not anti-anything," gasped Celeste.

"Some of my father's best friends are anti-Semitic," said young Mc-

Kell. "Listen, Celeste, if we're going to be friends you've got to understand that my father and I—"

"I've got my own tender heart to thank for this," said Celeste coldly. "That and the fact that my sister—"

"And mine."

She said, flushing, "I'm sorry."

Jimmy McKell flung a grasshopper leg up and over. "I live on a legman's stipend, my girl, and not because I like it, either. It's that or go into oil with my father. I wouldn't go into oil if I was—if I was a Portuguese sardine."

Celeste looked suspicious but interested.

"I thought, McKell," remarked the Inspector, "that you lived with your people in that Park Avenue museum."

"Yes," smiled Celeste. "How much board do you pay?"

"Eighteen bucks a week," said Jimmy, "just about enough to buy the butler's cigars. And I don't know that I'm getting my money's worth. For my silken flop, with running hot toddies, I have to take long sermons on class distinction, a Communist in every garage, how we must rebuild Germany, what this country needs is a Big Businessman in the White House, my-boy-marry-into-Steel, and that grand old favorite, The Unions Be Damned. The only reason I stay to take it is that I'm kind of sentimental about my mother. And now that Monica . . ."

"Yes?" said Ellery.

Jimmy McKell looked around. "What? Say, I've kind of forgotten what I came for, haven't I? It's that old debbil sex again. Pin-up GI McKell, they used to call me."

"Tell me about your sister," said Celeste suddenly, pinching her skirt forward.

"Monica?" He pulled a cigaret with the texture of a prune from his pocket, and a large match. Celeste covertly watched him light up and lean forward in a jackknife, one eye cocked against the smoke, his elbows on his shanks and an overgrown hand tossing the match stump up and down. Jimmy Stewart and Gregory Peck, Celeste thought. And— yes—the teeniest dash of Raymond Massey around the mouth. Young- wise and boy-old. Homely and sweet. Probably had every woman in New York running after him. "A good joe. Everything they said about Monica was true, yet they never got to know her. Least of all father or mother. It was her own fault; she was misery-misery-misery inside, and she put up a front to cover it that was tougher to get through than a tank trap. Monica could be mean, and cruel, and toward the end she was getting worse."

He tossed the match into an ashtray. "Father had always spoiled her

I like it that the authors wrote of these fine actors.

mP
August 3
2011

rotten. He taught her what power was and he gave her his own contempt for people. His attitude toward me's always been different; he made me toe the line from the start. We used to have some pretty rough times. Monica was a grown woman when I was still in knee pants, and it was Monica who slugged it out with father in my defense. He never could stand up to Monica.

"Mother was always afraid of her."

Jimmy hooked a garter-revealing leg over the arm of the chair. "My sister grew up—as long as you're asking—without a slum kid's chance to find out what she really wanted out of life. Whatever it was, it wasn't what she had, and that's what made my father into an even meaner old man than he'd ordinarily have been, because in his view she had everything. I found out by spending three years in the Army as a doughfoot, two of them crawling around the Pacific mosquito parks on my belly. Monica never did find out. The only outlet she had was kicking the rules in the pants. And all the time, underneath, she was scared and mixed up . . . It's a funny deal, Celeste," said Jimmy suddenly, staring at her.

"Yes . . . Jimmy?"

"I know a lot about you." She was startled at that. "I've been covering the Cat cases since the Abernethy murder—I get special privileges at the Bastille because they find me useful for dirt-digging purposes in the upper crust. I actually talked to you after your sister was murdered."

"You did? I didn't . . ."

"Naturally. I was just one of the vultures, and you were pretty numb. But I remember thinking at the time that you and I had a lot in common. We were both way out of our class and we both had sisters who were cripples and whom we loved and understood and who got the same nasty, sickening deal."

"Yes."

"I've been meaning to look you up when you'd had a chance to unpack the bags under your eyes and get your defenses up a little. I was thinking about you when I walked up those stairs."

Celeste looked at him.

"Cross my heart and hope to die in the oil business." Jimmy grinned, but only for an instant. He turned abruptly to Ellery. "I run off at the mouth, Queen, but only when I'm with fellow-workers. I'm a great lover of humanity and it comes out here. But I also know how and when to button up. I was interested—as a reporter—when Abernethy, Violette, and O'Reilly were knocked off; when my own sister got it, it got personal. I've got to be on the inside in this cat race. I'm no boy genius, but I've learned to toddle around this town and I think you can use me. If my newspaper connection rules me out, I'll quit today. Myself, I think it's an advantage; gives me entree I wouldn't have otherwise. But that's strictly up to you. Maybe before you say no I ought to go on record before witnesses that I wouldn't write anything for that lousy bedsheet I work for that you nixed. Do I get the job?"

Ellery went to the mantelpiece for a pipe. He took a long time filling it.

"That makes two questions, Mr. Queen," said Celeste in a tense voice, "you haven't answered."

Inspector Queen said, "Excuse us a minute. Ellery, I'd like to talk to you."

Ellery followed his father into the study and the Inspector shut the door. "You're not considering it."

"Yes."

"Ellery, for God's sake. Send them home!"

Ellery lit his pipe.

"Are you out of your mind? A couple of hopped-up kids. And they're both connected with the case!"

Ellery puffed.

"Look here, son. If it's help you want, you've got the entire Department on call. We've got a flock of ex-GI's who'd give you everything this youngster could and a lot more—they're trained men. If you want a pretty girl, there's at least three I can think of right now in the Policewomen's Bureau who'd give the Phillips number a run for her money. And they're trained too."

"But they're not," said Ellery thoughtfully, "connected with the case."

The Inspector blinked. Ellery grinned and went back to the living room.

"Very unorthodox," he said. "I'm inclined to go for it."

"Oh, Mr. Queen."

"What did I tell you, Celeste?"

The Inspector snarled from the doorway, "Ellery, I've got to phone my office," and he slammed the door.

"But it might be dangerous."

"I know some judo," said Jimmy helpfully.

"It's not funny, McKell. Maybe very dangerous."

"Listen, son." Jimmy was growling. "The little folks we kids played tag with in New Guinea didn't wrap a cord around your neck. They cut it. But you'll notice mine is still in one piece. Of course, Celeste here— that's different. Inside work, I'd say. Something exciting, useful, and safe."

"How about Celeste's speaking for herself, Jimmy?"

"Go on, Miss Alden."

"I'm scared," said Celeste.

"Sure you are! That's what I—"

"I was scared when I walked in and I'll be scared when I walk out. But being scared won't stop me from doing anything I can to help catch Simone's murderer."

"Well, now," began Jimmy.

"No," she said. Distinctly.

Jimmy reddened. He mumbled, "My mistake," and dug another refugee cigaret from his pocket.

"And we've got to have something else understood," said Ellery, as if nothing had happened. "This is no fraternity of rollicking companions, like the Three Musketeers. I'm Big Chief Plotto and I take nobody into my confidence. I give unexplained orders. I expect them to be carried out without protest, without questions, in confidence . . . and without consultation even between yourselves."

They looked up at that.

"Perhaps I should have made that part of it clear first. You're not coworkers in this little QBI. Nothing as cosy as that. You're accountable always and solely to me, what I give you to do is your personal assignment, not to be communicated to each other or anyone else; and for the support of this declaration I expect you to pledge your lives, your fortunes, and your sacred honor if any. If you feel you can't join me under these conditions, say so now and we'll write this session off as a pleasantly wasted hour."

They were silent.

"Celeste?"

She clutched her bag. "I said I'd do anything. I accept."

But Ellery persisted. "You won't question your instructions?"

"No."

"No matter what they happen to be?"

"No."

"No matter how unpleasant or incomprehensible?"

"No," said Celeste.

"And you agree not to disclose your instructions to anyone?"

"I agree, Mr. Queen."

"Even to Jimmy?"

"To anybody."

"Jimmy?"

"You're a tougher boss than the human oak knot who holds down the city desk at the *Extra*."

"Amusing," smiled Ellery, "but it doesn't answer my question."

"I'm in."

"On those precise terms?"

"Yes, sir."

Ellery looked at them for a moment.

"Wait here."

He went quickly into his study, shutting the door.

As Ellery began to write on a tablet, his father came in from his bedroom. The old man stood at the desk watching, his lips pushed out.

"Anything new downtown, Dad?" murmured Ellery, writing.

"Just a call from the Commissioner asking—"

"Asking what?"

"Just asking."

Ellery tore the sheet off the pad, put it into a plain envelope, sealed the envelope, and wrote on its face, "J."

He began to write on another sheet.

"Nothing at all, hm?"

"Oh, it's not all Cat," said the Inspector, watching. "Murder on West 75th and Amsterdam. Double header. Betrayed wife trails hubby to apartment and lets both sinners have it. With a pearl-handled job, .22."

"Anybody I know?" Ellery cheerfully tore the second sheet off the pad.

"Dead woman was a nightclub dancer, Oriental numbers a specialty. Dead man was a wealthy lobbyist. Wife's a society woman prominent in church affairs."

"Sex, politics, society, and religion," said Ellery as he sealed the second envelope. "What more could anyone ask?" He wrote on the envelope, "C."

"It'll take the heat off for a few days, anyway." As Ellery got up his father demanded, "What's that you just wrote?"

"Instructions to my 87th Street Irregulars."

"You're really going through with this Hollywood damfoolery?"

Ellery went back to the living room.

The Inspector paused in the doorway again, bitterly.

To Celeste Ellery handed the sealed envelope marked "C," to Jimmy the sealed envelope marked "J."

"No, don't open them now. Read, destroy, and report back to me here when you're ready."

Celeste was a little pale as she tucked her envelope into her bag. Jimmy crammed his into his outside pocket, but he kept his hand there.

"Going my way, Celeste?"

"No," said Ellery. "Leave separately. You first, Jimmy."

Jimmy jammed his hat on and loped out.

To Celeste the room seemed empty.

"When do I go, Mr. Queen?"

"I'll tell you."

Ellery went to one of the windows. Celeste settled back again, opened her bag, took out a compact. The envelope she did not touch. After a while she replaced the compact and shut her bag. She sat looking at the dark fireplace. Inspector Queen, in the study doorway, said nothing at all.

"All right, Celeste."

About five minutes had passed. Celeste left without a word.

"Now," exploded the Inspector, "will you tell me what you wrote in those damned notes?"

"Sure." Ellery was watching the street. "As soon as she comes out of the house."

They waited.

"She stopped to read the note," said the Inspector.

"And there she goes." Ellery strolled over to the armchair. "Why, Dad," he said, "in Celeste's note I instructed her to find out all she can about Jimmy McKell. In Jimmy's note I instructed him to find out all he can about Celeste Phillips."

Ellery relit his pipe, puffing placidly.

"You conniver," breathed his father. "The one thing I didn't think of, and the only thing that makes sense."

"If Heaven drops a date, the wise man opens his mouth. Chinese proverb."

The Inspector launched himself from the jamb, steaming around the room like Scuffy the Tugboat.

"Beautiful," he chortled. "They'll have to head for each other like two—" He stopped.

"Cats?" Ellery took the pipe from his mouth. "That's just it, Dad. I don't know. This could be brutal. But we can't take chances. We simply mustn't."

"Oh, it's ridiculous," snapped the old man. "A couple of romantic kids."

"I thought I detected the inspectorial nose twitch once or twice during Celeste's true confession."

"Well, in this business you suspect everybody at least once. But when you stop to think about it, you—"

"You what? We don't know a thing about the Cat. The Cat may be male, female, 16, 60, white, black, brown, or purple."

"I thought you told me a few days ago that you'd spotted something. What was it, a mirage?"

"Irony really isn't your long suit, Dad. I didn't mean something about the Cat himself."

The Inspector shrugged. He started for the door.

"I meant something about the Cat's operations."

The old man pulled up, turned around.

"What did you say?"

"The six murders have certain elements in common."

"Elements in *common?*"

Ellery nodded.

"How many?" The Inspector sounded choked.

"At least three. I can think of a fourth, too."

His father ran back. "What, son? What are they?"

But Ellery did not answer.

After a moment the Inspector hitched his trousers up and, very pale, marched out of the room.

"Dad?"

"What?" His angry voice shot in from the foyer.

"I need more time."

"For what? So he can wring a few more necks?"

"That was below the belt. You ought to know these things can't be rushed sometimes."

Ellery sprang to his feet. And he was pale, too. "Dad, they mean something. They must! But what?"

# 4

Ellery was nervy that weekend. For hours he occupied himself with compass, ruler, pencil, graph paper. Plotting the curves of statistical mysteries. Finally he hurled his co-ordinates into the fireplace and sent them up in smoke. Inspector Queen, coming upon him that broiling Sunday apparently warming himself at a fire, made the feeble remark that if he had to live in purgatory he was going to do something about lowering the temperature.

Ellery laughed disagreeably. "There are no fans in hell."

And he went into his study and made a point of closing the door.

But his father followed.

"Son."

Ellery was standing at his desk. Glaring down at the case. He had not shaved for three days; under the rank stubble his skin was green and mortal.

Looks more like a vegetable gone to seed than a man, thought his father. And he said again, "Son."

"Dad, I'd better give up."

The Inspector chuckled. "You know you won't. Feel like talking?"

"If you can suggest a cheerful topic of conversation."

The Inspector turned on the fan. "Well, there's always the weather. By the way, heard from your—what did you call those two—Irregulars?"

Ellery shook his head.

"How about a walk in the Park? Or a bus ride?"

"Nothing new?" muttered Ellery.

"Don't bother shaving. You won't meet anybody you know; the City's half-empty. What do you say, son?"

"That's another thing." Ellery looked out. There was a crimson hem on the sky. It brushed the buildings. "This damned weekend."

"Now look," said his father. "The Cat's operated strictly on working days. No Saturday, no Sunday, and he bypassed the only holiday since he got going, Fourth of July. So we don't have to get the jitters about the Labor Day weekend."

"You know what New York's like on Labor Day night." The buildings bloodied. Twenty-four hours from now, he thought. "Bottlenecks at every road, bridge, tunnel, terminal. Everybody cramming back into town at the same time."

"Come on, Ellery! Let's take in a movie. Or, I'll tell you what. We'll rustle up a revue. I wouldn't mind seeing a leg show tonight."

Ellery failed to smile. "I'd only take the Cat with me. You go on and enjoy yourself, Dad. I'd be no fun at all."

The Inspector, a sensible man, went.

But he did not go to a leg show.

With the assistance of a busman, he went downtown to Police Headquarters instead.

The dark turned cherry-colored in the heat as the French blades swished toward his neck. He held himself ready. He was calm, even happy. The tumbril below was jammed with cats knitting solemnly with silk cords of blue and salmon-pink and nodding their approval. A small cat, no larger than an ant, sat just under his nose looking up at him. This cat had black eyes. As he all but felt the flick of the knife and the clean and total pain across his neck it seemed to him the night lifted and a great light flew over everything.

Ellery opened his eyes.

His cheek throbbed where something on the desk had corrupted it and he was wondering that the screeching agony of the dream persisted past its borders when it occurred to him that the telephone in his father's bedroom was ringing in a nasty monotone.

He got up and went into the bedroom and turned on the light.

1:45.

"Hello." His neck ached.

"Ellery." The Inspector's voice stung him awake. "I've been ringing for ten minutes."

"I fell asleep at my desk. What's up, Dad? Where are you?"

"Where would I be on this line? I've been hanging around all evening. Still dressed?"

"Yes."

"Meet me right away at the Park-Lester apartment house. It's on East 84th between Fifth and Madison."

1:45 A.M. It is therefore Labor Day. The 25th of August to the 5th of

September. Eleven days. Eleven is one more than ten. Between Phillips, Simone, and Willikins, Beatrice, it was ten days. One more than ten makes . . .

"Ellery, you there?"

"Who is it?" His neck ached abominably.

"Ever hear of Dr. Edward Cazalis?"

"Cazalis?"

"Never mind—"

*"The psychiatrist?"*

"Yes."

"Impossible!"

You crept along the catwalk of a rationale while the night split into a billion tinsel fragments.

"What did you say, Ellery?"

He felt hung up in far space. Lost.

"It couldn't be Dr. Cazalis." He mustered his forces.

The Inspector's voice said craftily, "Now what would make you say a thing like that, son?"

"Because of his age. Cazalis can't be the seventh victim. It's out of the question. There's a mistake somewhere."

*"Age?"* The old man floundered. "What the devil has Cazalis's age got to do with anything?"

"He must be in his mid-60s. It can't be Cazalis. It's not in the scheme."

"What scheme?" His father was shouting.

"It's not Dr. Cazalis, is it? If it's Dr. Cazalis . . ."

"It just happens it isn't!"

Ellery sighed.

"It's Cazalis's wife's niece," said the Inspector peevishly. "She's Lenore Richardson. The Park-Lester is where the Richardsons live. The girl, her father and mother."

"Do you know how old she was?"

"Late or middle 20s, I think."

"Not married?"

"I don't think so. I have very little information. I've got to hang up now, Ellery. Get a move on."

"I'll be right there."

"Wait. How did you know Cazalis wasn't—?"

Just across the Park, Ellery was thinking, staring at the phone on the cradle. He had already forgotten having put it there.

The phone book.

He ran back to the study, grabbed the Manhattan directory.

Richardson.

*Richardson Lenore 12½ E 84.*

There was also a *Richardson Zachary 12½ E 84* listed at the same number.

Ellery went about shaving and changing his clothes in a blissful nirvana.

Later, it was possible to synthesize his nightlong impressions into one complex. The night itself was a jumble. Faces flowed and crossed and hung apart; fragments of things said, voices broken, tears shed, looks passed, men coming, telephones ringing, pencils writing; doors, a chaise, a photograph, photographers, measurements, sketches, a small bluish fist, the dangle of a silk cord, a gold Louis XVI clock on an Italian marble fireplace, an oils nude, a torn book jacket . . .

But Ellery's mind was a machine. The unselective evidence of his senses stoked it, and after a while out came a product.

Tonight's production, by a squirrel instinct, Ellery stored away, sensing a future need.

The girl herself told him nothing. He could see what she might have been, but only from a photograph; the flesh, hardened at the supreme moment of the struggle not to die, was the usual meaningless petrifaction. She had been small and cuddlesome, with soft brown curly hair. Her nose was saucy and her mouth—from the photograph—had been pettish. She was manicured and pedicured and her hair had been recently set. The lingerie under her pongee negligee was expensive. The book she had been reading at the pounce of the Cat was a tattered reprint of *Forever Amber*. The remains of an orange and a few cherry pits lay on the inlaid occasional table beside the chaise. On the table also were a bowl of fruit, a silver cigaret box, an ashtray with fourteen lipstick-tipped butts in it, and a silver table lighter in the shape of an armored knight.

In the withering lividity of death the girl looked 50; in the photograph, a recent one, untouched 18. She had been 25 and an only child.

Ellery dismissed Lenore Richardson as a regrettable intrusion.

The living told more.

They were four: the father and mother of the murdered girl; the girl's aunt—Mrs. Richardson's sister—Mrs. Cazalis; and the eminent Dr. Cazalis.

There was no family fellowship in their grief. This Ellery found stimulating, and he studied them carefully one by one.

The mother passed what was left of the night in uncurbed hysterics. Mrs. Richardson was a superb woman of middle age, rather too fashionably gowned, and overjeweled. Ellery thought he discovered in her a chronic anxiety, unrelated to her sorrow; like the frown of a colicky infant. She was apparently the kind of woman who hoards life like a miser. The gold of her youth having tarnished, what little remained she kept gilding and packaging in extravagant self-delusion. Now she writhed and shrieked as if, in losing her daughter, she had found something long mislaid. *Incredibly pungent writing! Woowee! (MP) August 3 2011*

The father, a gray little rigid man of 60, looked like a jeweler, or a librarian. Actually, he was the head of Richardson, Leeper & Company, one of the oldest wholesale dry-goods houses in New York. Ellery had passed the Richardson, Leeper & Company building often in his prowls about the City. It stood nine stories high on half a square block on Broadway and 17th Street. The firm was known for its old-fashioned merchant virtues: sternly nonunionized, run on the benevolent-patron system, with employees who tottered comfortably along in the traces until they dropped. Richardson would be unswervingly honest, unalterably stubborn, and as narrow as a straight line. This was all quite beyond him. He could only sit by himself in a corner glancing bewilderedly from the tormented woman in the evening gown to the tumbled little mountain range under the blanket.

Richardson's sister-in-law was much younger than his wife; Ellery judged Mrs. Cazalis to be early-fortyish. She was pallid, slender, tall, and self-contained. Unlike her older sister, she had found her orbit; her eyes went often to her husband. She had a submissive quality Ellery had found frequently in the wives of brilliant men. This was a woman whose marriage was the sum of existence to her, in a pitifully arithmetic way. In a society composed largely of Mrs. Richardsons, Mrs. Cazalis would tend to have few friends and few social interests. She comforted her middleaged sister as a mother might soothe a child in a tantrum; it was only during Mrs. Richardson's wilder vocalisms that the younger woman's ministrations took on an edge of rebuke and resentment. It was as if she felt herself cheapened and cheated. There was a virginal, unthawed sensitivity in her, a chill delicacy of feeling, which recoiled from her sister's exhibitionism. *Another strong paragraph. My the writers had to be keen observers of human nature. (MP) August 3 2011*

It was during one of these moments that an amused male voice said in Ellery's ear, "I see you've noticed it."

Ellery turned quickly. It was Dr. Cazalis, big and stoop-shouldered and powerful, with cold milky eyes and masses of icegray hair; a glacier of a man. His voice was deliberate and carried a musical undertone of cynicism. Ellery had heard somewhere that Dr. Cazalis had an unusual history for a psychiatrist; meeting the man for the first time, he was disposed to acceptance of the report. He must be 65, Ellery thought, possibly older; in semi-retirement, taking only a few cases, chiefly women, and those on a selective basis—it all added up to failing health, the declining phase of a medical career, the coronary age; and yet Dr. Cazalis seemed, aside from a certain restlessness of his large thick surgeon's hands, a vigorous and functioning personality; certainly not a man to spare himself. It was a puzzle, not the less interesting for its irrelevance. His rather encyclopedic eyes were unavoidable. He sees everything, thought Ellery, and he tells exactly nothing; or what he tells is automatically conditioned by what he thinks his hearer ought to know.

"Noticed what, Dr. Cazalis?"

"The difference between my wife and her sister. Where Lenore was concerned, my sister-in-law was criminally inadequate. She was afraid of the child, jealous and overindulgent. Alternated between pampering and screaming at her. And in the sulks ignored Lenore entirely. Now Della's in a panic, overwhelmed by feelings of guilt. Clinically speaking, mothers like Della wish for the death of their young and when it happens they set up a terrified howl for forgiveness. Her grief is for herself."

"It seems to me Mrs. Cazalis is as aware of that as you are, Doctor."

The psychiatrist shrugged. "My wife's done what she could. We lost two babies in the delivery room within four years of our marriage and Mrs. Cazalis was never able to have another. She transferred her affections to Della's child and it compensated each of them—I mean my wife and Lenore—for her own lack. It couldn't be complete, of course; for one thing, the biological but otherwise inadequate mama is always a problem. Essentially," said the doctor dryly, glancing over at the sisters, "essentially unsatisfactory even in mourning. The mother beats her breast and the aunt suffers in silence. I was rather fond of the little chicken," said Dr. Cazalis suddenly, "myself." He walked away.

By 5 A.M. they had the facts orderly. Such as there were.

The girl had been home alone. She was to have accompanied her father and mother to a party in Westchester at the home of one of Mrs. Richardson's friends, but Lenore had begged off. ("She was due for her mensis," Mrs. Cazalis told Inspector Queen. "Lenore always had a hard time. She told me in the morning over the phone that she wouldn't be able to go. And Della was cross with her.") Mr. and Mrs. Richardson had left for Westchester shortly after 6 o'clock; it was a dinner party. One of the two domestics, the cook, was away for the holiday, having left Saturday afternoon to visit her family in Pennsylvania. The other, a maid, had been given the night off by Lenore herself; since she did not sleep in, she was not expected until morning.

The Cazalises, who lived eight blocks away, at Park Avenue and 78th

Street, had been worried about Lenore all evening. At 8:30 Mrs. Cazalis had telephoned. Lenore had said she was "in the usual crampy dumps" but otherwise all right and that her aunt and uncle were not to "throw fits" about her. But when Mrs. Cazalis learned that Lenore had characteristically failed to eat anything, she had gone over to the Richardson apartment, prepared a warm meal, forced Lenore to eat it, made the girl comfortable on the chaise in the living room, and had spent perhaps an hour with her niece afterward, talking.

Lenore had been depressed. Her mother, she had told her aunt, had been hounding her to "get married and stop running from one man to another like a stupid high school girl." Lenore had been deeply in love with a boy who was killed at St.-Lô, a poor boy of Jewish origin of whom Mrs. Richardson had violently disapproved; "Mother doesn't understand and she won't let him alone even when he's dead." Mrs. Cazalis had let the girl pour out her troubles and then had tried to get her to bed. But Lenore said "with all this pain" she would stay up reading; the heat was bothering her, too. Mrs. Cazalis had urged her not to stay up too late, had kissed her good night, and left. It was about 10 P.M. She had last seen her niece reclining on the chaise, reaching for a book, and smiling.

At home, Mrs. Cazalis had wept, her husband had soothed her, and he had sent her to bed. Dr. Cazalis was staying up over an involved case history and he had promised his wife he would call Lenore before turning in, "as the chances are Della and Zach won't be rolling in till 3 or 4 in the morning." At a few minutes past midnight the doctor had phoned the Richardson apartment. There was no answer. Five minutes later he tried again. There was an extension in Lenore's bedroom so that even if she had gone to sleep the repeated rings of the phone should have aroused her. Disturbed, Dr. Cazalis had decided to investigate. Without awakening his wife, he had walked over to the Park-Lester and found Lenore Richardson on the chaise with the salmon-colored silk cord imbedded in her flesh, dead of strangulation.

His in-laws had still not returned. Except for the dead girl, the apartment was empty. Dr. Cazalis had notified the police and, finding the telephone number of Mrs. Richardson's Westchester friends on the foyer table—"I left it for Lenore in case she felt sick and wanted me to come home," sobbed Mrs. Richardson—he had notified them that something had "happened" to Lenore. He had then phoned his wife to come at once, as she was, in a taxi. Mrs. Cazalis had hurried over with a long coat thrown over her night gown to find the police already there. She collapsed, but by the time the Richardsons arrived she had recovered sufficiently to take charge of her sister—"for which," muttered Inspector Queen, "she ought to get the Nobel peace award."

The usual variation on the theme, thought Ellery. Chips of incident and accident, the death-colored core remaining. The non-crackable nut.

("I took one look at the silk cord around her neck," said Dr. Cazalis, "and I recall only one coherent thought. 'The Cat.' ")

Pending daylight examination of the terrace and roof—the living room French doors had stood open all evening—they were inclined to the belief that the Cat had gained entrance boldly through the front door by way of the self-service penthouse elevator. Mrs. Cazalis recalled having tried the front door from the foyer on her way out at 10 o'clock and, at that time, the door was locked; but on her husband's arrival about 12:30 A.M. the door was wide open, held ajar by a doorstop. Since the doorstop revealed the dead girl's fingerprints, it was evident that Lenore had propped the apartment door open after her aunt's departure, probably to encourage some slight circulation of air; it was a stifling night. The night doorman remembered Mrs. Cazalis's arrival and departure and Dr. Cazalis's arrival after midnight; but he admitted that he had slipped out several times in the course of the evening to get a cold bottle of beer at the delicatessen at 86th Street and Madison Avenue and that, even while he was on duty in the lobby, a prowler could have got past him unnoticed: "It's been a hot night, half the tenants are out of town, and I snoozed on the lobby settee on and off the whole evening." He had seen and heard nothing out of the ordinary.

Neighbors had heard no screams.

The fingerprint men turned up nothing of interest.

Dr. Prouty of the Medical Examiner's office was unable to fix the time of death more accurately than the limits defined by Mrs. Cazalis's departure and her husband's arrival.

The strangling cord was of tussah silk.

"Henry James would have called it," said Dr. Cazalis, "the fatal futility of facts."

They were sitting around at dawn in the wreckage of the night over cold ginger ale and beer. Mrs. Cazalis had prepared a platter of cold chicken sandwiches to which no one applied but Inspector Queen, and he only under Ellery's bullying. The body had been removed on the official order; the sinister blanket was gone; a breeze blew from the penthouse terrace. Mrs. Richardson was asleep in her bedroom under sedation.

"With all respect to the Great Casuist," replied Ellery, "it's not the futility of facts that's fatal, Doctor, but their scarcity."

"In seven murders?" cried the doctor's wife.

"Seven multiplied by zero, Mrs. Cazalis. Well, perhaps not quite, but it's very difficult."

Inspector Queen's jaws were going mechanically. He seemed not to be listening.

"What can I do!"

They were startled. Lenore's father had been still so long.

"I've got to do something. I can't just sit here. I have a great deal of money . . ."

"I'm afraid money won't do it, Mr. Richardson," said Ellery. "Monica McKell's father had the same idea. His offer of $100,000 reward on August 10 hasn't even been threatened. It's simply increased the work of the police."

"How about turning in, Zach?" suggested Dr. Cazalis.

"She didn't have an enemy in the world. Ed, you know that. Everyone was mad about her. Why did this . . . why did he pick Lenore? She was all I had. Why my daughter?"

"Why anybody's daughter, Mr. Richardson?"

"I don't care about the others. What do we pay our police for!"

Richardson was on his feet, his cheeks cerise.

"Zach."

He sagged, and after a moment he mumbled something and went out very quietly.

"No, dear, let him go," said the psychiatrist quickly to his wife. "Zach has that sturdy Scotch sense of the fitness of things and life is very precious to him. But I've got to worry about you. Your eyes are dropping out of your head. Come on, darling, I'll take you home."

"No, Edward."

"Della's asleep—"

"I won't go without you. And you're needed here." Mrs. Cazalis took her husband's paw. "Edward, you are. You can't stay out of this now. Tell me you'll do something."

"Certainly. I'll take you home."

"I'm not a child!"

The big man sprang to his feet. "But what can I do? These people are trained to this sort of thing. I wouldn't expect them to walk into my office and tell me how to treat a patient!"

"Don't make me seem stupid, Edward." Her voice had sharpened. "You can tell these gentlemen what you've told me so many times. Your theories—"

"Unfortunately, that's all they are. Now let's be sensible. You're going home this—"

"Della needs me." The taut voice was stretching.

"Darling." He seemed startled.

"You know what Lenore meant to me." Mrs. Cazalis broke. "You know, you know!"

"Of course." His glance warned Ellery and Inspector Queen off. "Lenore meant a great deal to me, too. Now stop, you'll make yourself very ill."

"Edward, you know what you said to me!"

"I'll do what I can. You've got to cut this out, dearest. Stop it." Gradually, in his arms, her sobs subsided.

"But you haven't promised."

"You needn't go home. I think you're right. Della will need you. Use the guest room, dear. I'll give you something to make you sleep."

"Edward, promise!"

"I promise. Now I'm putting you to bed."

When Dr. Cazalis returned, he looked apologetic. "I should have seen those hysterics coming on."

"I'd welcome a good old-fashioned emotional binge myself right now," murmured Ellery. "By the way, Doctor, which theories was Mrs. Cazalis referring to?"

"Theories?" Inspector Queen looked around. "Who's got theories?"

"Why, I suppose I have," said Dr. Cazalis, seating himself and reaching for a sandwich. "Say, what are those fellows doing out there, anyway?"

"Examining the terrace and roof. Tell me about these theories of yours, Doctor." The Inspector took one of Ellery's cigarets; he never smoked cigarets.

"I suppose everybody in New York has one or two," smiled the psychiatrist. "The Cat murders would naturally not pass a psychiatrist by. And even though I don't have the inside information at your disposal—"

"It wouldn't add much to what you've read."

Cazalis grunted. "I was about to say, Inspector, that I'm sure it wouldn't make any material difference. Where it seems to me you people have gone off is in applying to these murders the normal investigatory technique. You've concentrated on the victims—admittedly the sensible methodology in ordinary cases, but in this one exactly wrong. In this case you stand a better chance concentrating on the murderer."

"How do you mean?"

"Isn't it true that the victims have had nothing in common?"

"Yes?"

"Their lives crossed nowhere?"

"As far as we can tell."

"Take my word for it, you'll never find a significant point of contact.

The seven seem unrelated because they are unrelated. At no time did they stand a greater chance of interrelationship than if the murderer had shut his eyes and opened the telephone directory, let's say, to seven different pages at random, determined to kill the forty-ninth person listed in the second column of each page."

Ellery stirred.

"We have, then," continued Dr. Cazalis, swallowing the last of his sandwich, "seven persons dying by the same hand who have no inter-identity or contiguity. What does this mean in practical terms? A series of apparently *indiscriminate* acts of violence. To the trained mind, this spells psychosis. I say 'apparently' indiscriminate, by the way, because the conduct of the psychotic appears unmotivated only when judged in the perspective of reality—that is, by more or less healthy minds viewing the world as it is. The psychotic has his motivations, but they proceed from distorted views of reality and falsification of facts.

"My opinion, based on an analysis of the data available to me, is that the Cat—damn that cartoonist! an infamous libel on a very well-balanced beast!—suffers from what we call a systematized delusional state, a para-noid psychosis."

"Well, naturally," said the Inspector, who seemed disappointed, "one of our first theories was that the killer's insane."

"Insanity is the popular and legal term," said Dr. Cazalis with a shrug. "There are any number of individuals who, though not insane in a legal sense, are nevertheless subjects of a psychosis. I suggest we stick to the medical terminology."

"Psychotic, then. We've checked the mental hospitals time and again without result."

"Not all psychotics are institutionalized, Inspector Queen," said the psychiatrist dryly. "That's exactly my point. If, for example, the Cat is a paranoid psychotic of the schizophrenic type, he may well be as normal in appearance and behavior—to the untrained eye—as any of us. He might remain unsuspected for a long time, during which he could do plenty of damage."

"I never yet talked to one of you birds," said the Inspector wearily, "that I didn't come away with my chin dragging."

"I gather, Dad," said Ellery, "that Dr. Cazalis has more to disseminate than gloom. Go on, Doctor."

"I was merely going to suggest the alternative, which is that he may be undergoing treatment, or may have been recently under treatment, by a private doctor. It would seem to me whoever's committing these crimes is a local product, all seven murders having taken place in Manhattan, so a good place to start checking would be right in the borough here. It would mean, obviously, getting the co-operation of every man in the field. Each one, being briefed on what to look out for, could comb his own records for patients, either current or discharged, who might be possibilities; and those possibilities would have to be questioned by trained people for clinical clues as well as investigated by you people in the routine way. It might be a total frost, of course, and there'd be a dickens of a lot of work—"

"It's not the work," muttered Inspector Queen. "It's the trained personnel that's bothering me."

"Well, I'd be glad to do what I could to help. You heard my wife! I don't have many patients these days—" the psychiatrist made a face— "I'm tapering off to retirement—so it wouldn't work any special hardship on me."

"Handsome offer, Dr. Cazalis." The Inspector rubbed his mustache. "I'll admit this has opened up a field we haven't scratched. Ellery, what do you think?"

"By all means," said Ellery promptly. "It's a constructive suggestion and might well lead straight to our man."

"Do I detect the faintest note of doubt?" smiled Dr. Cazalis. His powerful fingers were drumming on the table.

"Perhaps."

"You don't agree with my analysis."

"Not entirely, Doctor."

The psychiatrist stopped drumming.

"I'm not convinced that the crimes are indiscriminate."

"Then you have information I haven't."

"No. I base my opinion on the same data, I'm sure. But, you see, there's a pattern in these crimes."

"Pattern?" Cazalis stared.

"The murders have a number of elements in common."

"Including this one?" rasped the Inspector.

"Yes, Dad."

Dr. Cazalis began to drum again. "I take it you don't mean consistency of method—the cords, strangling—"

"No. I mean elements common to the seven victims. I'm convinced they signify a plan of some sort, but what it arises from, what its nature is, where it's going . . ." Ellery's eyes clouded.

"Sounds interesting." Dr. Cazalis was studying Ellery surgically. "If you're right, Mr. Queen, I'm wrong."

"We may both be right. I have the feeling we are. 'Though this be madness, yet there is method in 't.' " They laughed together. "Dad, I'd emphatically recommend that Dr. Cazalis's suggestion be followed up, and right away."

"We're breaking every rule in the book," groaned his father. "Doctor, would you consider taking full charge?"

"I? Of the psychiatric end?"

"That's right."

Dr. Cazalis's fingers stopped exercising. But they remained, as it were, available.

"This is going to be as big a selling as a medical job. It won't work unless every doctor in the field co-operates. With you heading that phase of the investigation—with your reputation and professional connections, Doctor—it's a guarantee of thorough coverage I don't think we'd get another way. As a matter of fact," said the Inspector thoughtfully, "it wouldn't be a bad arrangement for other reasons. The Mayor's already appointed my son special investigator. We're covering the official end. With you in charge of a medical inquiry, it would give us a three-pronged offensive. Maybe," said the Inspector, exhibiting his denture, "maybe we'd even turn up a little something."

He said abruptly, "I'd have to get confirmation of this downtown, Dr. Cazalis, but something tells me the Mayor and the Commissioner will be very happy about the whole thing. Pending an okay, can I tell them you're available?"

The psychiatrist threw up his hands. "What was that line from a movie I once saw? 'Bilked by my own chicanery!' All right, Inspector, I'm hooked. What's the procedure?"

"Where you going to be later today?"

"Depends on how Della and Zach behave themselves. Either here or at home, Inspector. This morning I'm going to try to get a few hours' sleep."

"Try?" Ellery stretched, rising, "In my case it won't be the least problem."

"Sleeping is always a problem with me. I'm a chronic insomniac—a symptom which is generally part of the clinical picture," said the psychiatrist with a smile, "of dementia, general paresis, and so on, but don't tell my patients. I keep well supplied with sleeping pills."

"I'll phone you this afternoon, Dr. Cazalis."

Cazalis nodded to the Inspector and strolled out.

The Queens were silent. The men working on the terrace were beginning to drift away. Sergeant Velie was crossing the terrace in the sun.

"What do you think?" asked the Inspector suddenly.

"Think? About what, Dad?"

"Cazalis."

"Oh. — Very solid citizen."

"Yes, isn't he."

"Nothing doing," said Sergeant Velie. "No sign of a damn thing, Inspector. He got in by that penthouse elevator, all right."

"The only thing is," mumbled the Inspector, "I wish he'd stop those finger exercises of his. Makes me nervous.—Oh, Velie. Knock off and get some shuteye."

"What about those newspaper guys?"

"They've probably ganged up on Dr. Cazalis. Run interference for him and tell them I'll be right there. With my own pet line of double talk."

The sergeant nodded and clumped off, yawning.

"How about you, Dad?"

"I'll have to go downtown first. You going home now?"

"If I can get away in one piece."

"Wait in the hall closet. I'll decoy 'em into the living room here and then you can make the break."

They parted rather awkwardly.

When Ellery woke up he found his father perched on the edge of the bed, looking at him.

"Dad. What time is it?"

"Past 5."

Ellery stretched. "Just pull in?"

"Uh-huh."

"Anything new in crime?"

"P.m. shows nothing so far. The cord's a washout. It's the other six continued."

"How's the atmosphere? Safe?"

"I wouldn't say so." Inspector Queen hugged himself as if he were cold. "They're really laying into this one. Every line into Headquarters and City Hall jammed. The papers have taken the gloves off and they're yelping for blood. Whatever good the announcement of your appointment did has gone up the flue with the murder of the Richardson girl. When I walked into the Mayor's office with the Commissioner this morning to confer on the Cazalis thing His Honor practically kissed me. Phoned Cazalis then and there. First thing he said over the phone was, 'Dr. Cazalis, when can you hold a press conference?' "

"Cazalis going to do it?"

"He's doing it right this minute. And going on the air tonight."

"I must be a great disappointment to His Honor." Ellery laughed.

"Now hit the sack or you'll be a candidate for a medical conference yourself."

The Inspector failed to move.

"There's something else?"

"Ellery." The old man pulled up his left leg and began slowly to untie his shoelace. "There's been some nasty talk downtown. I wouldn't ask you this except that if I'm to keep taking it on the chin I've got to know what round it is."

"Ask me what?"

"I want you to tell me what you've spotted." He began on the other shoe. "For my own information, you understand," he explained to the shoe. "Or let me put it another way. If I'm to keep singeing my pants I want to know what the hell I'm sitting on."

It was a kind of declaration of independence, conceived in grievance and delivered for just cause.

Ellery looked unhappy.

He reached for a cigaret and an ashtray and lay back with the tray balanced on his chest.

"All right," he said. "From your standpoint I'm a disloyal dispenser of nothing and from your standpoint I suppose I am. Now let's see whether what I've been holding out on you could prove of the slightest utility to you, me, the Mayor, the Commissioner, or the shade of Poe.

"One: Archibald Dudley Abernethy was 44 years old. Violette Smith was 42 years old. Rian O'Reilly was 40 years old. Monica McKell was 37 years old. Simone Phillips was 35 years old. Beatrice Willikins was 32 years old. Lenore Richardson was 25 years old. 44, 42, 40, 37, 35, 32, 25."

The Inspector was staring.

"Each victim's been younger than the victim preceding. That's why I was so positive Dr. Cazalis couldn't have been Number 7; he's older than any of them. To have been seventh on the list he'd have to have been under 32, the sixth victim's age . . . that is, if there was a descending-age pattern. And it turned out that Number 7, the Richardson girl, was 25, and I was right. There *is* a descending-age pattern. Mathematically irregular differences, but they're always younger, younger."

The old man gripped his right shoe. "We didn't see that. Nobody saw it."

"Well, it's one of those exasperating little fragments of sense in a jumble. Like the hidden-face puzzles. You look and look, and suddenly there it is. But what does it mean? It's sense, all right, but what sense? It springs from a cause, but what cause? It can't conceivably be the result of coincidence; not seven! And yet the longer you examine it, the less it seems to signify. Can you think of a single satisfactory reason why any-

one should go to the trouble of killing successively younger people—
who haven't the faintest connection with one another? I can't."

"It's a poser, all right," his father muttered.

"It's true I might announce tonight that no New Yorker 25 years old or
older has anything to worry about because the Cat's going down the actu-
arial tables and he's passed Age 25 . . ."

"Very funny," said the Inspector feebly. "It sounds like—like something out of Gilbert and Sullivan. They'd all think you were crazy and if
they thought you were sane it would only pack all the anxiety down into
the—the lower brackets."

"Something like that," nodded Ellery. "So I kept it to myself.

"Two." He crushed the cigaret out and cradled his head, staring at the
ceiling. "Of the seven victims, two have been male, five female. Until
this last one, the victims have been 32 years old or older. Well past the
minimum age of consent, wouldn't you say?"

"The what?"

"I mean, we live in a connubial society. All the roads of our culture
lead to the American Home, which is not conceived as the citadel of
celibacy; if the point requires any proof, we have only to consider, gentlemen, the delicious sense of naughtiness we get out of the mere phrase
'bachelor apartment.' Our women spend their maidenhood catching a
husband and the rest of their lives trying to hold on to him; our men
spend their entire boyhood envying their father and consequently can't
wait when they grow up to marry the next best thing to their mother. Why
do you suppose the American male is obsessed with the mammae? What
I'm trying to say—"

"Well, for heaven's sake, say it!"

"—is that if you picked seven American adults at random, all of them
over 25 years of age, six of them over 32, what are the odds that all but
one of them will be unmarried?"

"O'Reilly," said the Inspector in an awed voice. "By God, O'Reilly
was the only one."

"Or you could put it another way. Of the two men, Abernethy was a
bachelor and O'Reilly was married. That seems to cancel out the men.
But of the five women, all have been single! When you stop to think of it,
that's really remarkable. Five women between the ages of 42 and 25 and
not one of them succeeded in the great American rat race. As in the case
of the descending ages, coincidence is unthinkable. Then the Cat deliberately chooses—among his female victims, at least—only unmarried
ones. Why? Inform me."

Inspector Queen gnawed his nails. "The only thing I can think of is
that he dangles the marriage bait in order to get in close. But—"

"But that just isn't the explanation, right. No such Lothario's turned up, or the slightest trace of one.

"Of course, I could have cried the glad tidings to Mrs. New York that the only females who need fear the embrace of the Cat are virgins, misogamists, and Lesbians, but—"

"Go on," snarled his father.

"Three: Abernethy was strangled with a blue silk cord, Violette Smith with a salmon-colored one, O'Reilly blue, Monica McKell salmon, Simone Phillips salmon, Beatrice Willikins salmon, Lenore Richardson salmon. There's even a report on that."

Mumbled the Inspector: "I'd forgotten that."

"One color for the males, another for the females. Consistently. Why?"

After a time the Inspector said, rather timidly: "The other day, son, you mentioned a fourth point . . ."

"Oh. Yes. They *all* had phones."

His father rubbed an eye.

"In a way, the very prosiness of the point makes it the most provocative. To me, anyway. Seven victims, seven phones. Even Simone, the poor cripple. They all had phones or, where the subscriber was someone else—as in the cases of Lenore Richardson, Simone Phillips, and Monica McKell—they had separate listings in the directory; I checked.

"I don't know the figures, but I should imagine there's a ration of some twenty-five phones in the United States per hundred population. One out of four. In the big urban centers, like New York, the percentage may be greater. Let's say in New York one out of three. Yet of the seven victims tagged by the Cat, not one, not two, not four, but all seven had phones.

"The first explanation to suggest itself is that the Cat picks his dainties out of the phone book. Pure lottery. But in a lottery the odds against picking seven victims successively each of whom turns out to be younger than the last would be literally incalculable. Then the Cat makes his selections on some other basis.

"Still, all his victims are listed in the Manhattan directory. Those phones are a point, a point."

Ellery set the ashtray on his night table and swung his legs off the bed to squat, mourner-fashion. "It's damnable," he moaned. "If there were one break in the sequence—one victim older than the last, one woman strangled who was married or who'd ever been married, one man found necktied in salmon—or heliotrope!—one who didn't have a phone . . . Those points in common exist for *reasons*. Or maybe," said Ellery, sitting up suddenly, "or maybe the points in common exist for the *same* reason. A sort of great common denominator. The Rosetta stone. One key to all the doors. Do you know, that would be nice."

But Inspector Queen was mumbling as he stripped. "That getting-younger business. When you think of it . . . Two years' difference in age between Abernethy and Violette. Two years between Vi and O'Reilly. Three years between O'Reilly and McKell's sister. Two years between her and Celeste's sister. Three years between her and Beatrice Willikins. Two and three. Never more than three. In six cases. And then—"

"Yes," said Ellery, "and then Lenore Richardson and we find a jump in the age differential from a previous maximal three to seven . . . That haunted me all last night."

And now the Inspector was denuded, his little sexagenarian hide impaled on the point of a needle.

"What's haunting me," he mumbled, "is who's next?"

Ellery turned away.

"And that's all you had, son?"

"That's all I *have*."

"I'm going to bed." The little naked man shuffled out.

# 5

Inspector Queen overslept. He came galloping out at 9:45 Tuesday morning like a late starter under the whip, but when he saw who was having coffee with Ellery he slowed to a walk which neatly ended at the breakfast table.

"Well, look who's among us," beamed the Inspector. "Good morning, McKell."

"Morning, Inspector," said Jimmy McKell. "On your way to the abattoir?"

"Mmmmmmmmmch," inhaled the Inspector. "I think I'll have a slup or two of the life-giving mocha myself." He pulled out a chair and sat down. "Morning, son."

"Morning, morning," said Ellery absently, reaching for the coffeepot. "Jimmy came up with the papers."

"Do people still read?"

"Cazalis's interview."

"Oh."

"Goodnaturedly but firmly neutral. The calm voice of organized knowledge. We promise nothing. But one has the feeling that an Osirian hand directed by a radiant eye has taken over. The Mayor must be in the eleventh heaven."

"I thought it was seven," said Jimmy McKell.

"Not in the Egyptian cosmography, Jimmy. And there is something Pharaonic about Cazalis. 'Soldiers, from these pyramids forty centuries look down upon you.' "

"Napoleon."

"In Egypt. Cazalis is soothing syrup to the general. Simply wonderful for morale."

"Don't mind him," grinned the Inspector, reading the paper. "You'll

never win . . . Say, this is pretty good medicine at that. You given up journalism, McKell? I didn't spot you among the rest of the scavengers yesterday."

"The Richardson deal?" Jimmy looked secretive. "Yesterday was Labor
Day. My day. I'm a working stiff."

"Took off, eh?"

"Who labors best and so on," said Ellery. "Or was it in line of duty,
Jimmy?"

"Something like that."

"You had a date with Celeste Phillips."

Jimmy laughed. "And not just yesterday. It's been one sweet journey
through time. You give the most interesting assignments, dearie. You
should have been a city editor."

"I take it you two have been getting along."

"We manage," replied Jimmy, "to tolerate each other."

"Nice girl," nodded the Inspector. "Son, that tasted like a refill."

"Ready to talk about it, Jimmy?"

"Say, it's getting to be my favorite subject."

"Let's have another all around." Ellery poured, amiably.

"I don't know what you two witch doctors are up to," said Jimmy, "but
I'm happy to report that this is a wench of exceptional merit, and in my cir-
cles I'm known as Iconoclast McKell, Female Images a Specialty." He fingered his cup. "All kidding aside, I feel like a heel."

"Heeling is a hard profession," said Ellery. "Would you mind itemizing
the assignment's virtues, as you found them?"

"Well, the gal has looks, brains, personality, guts, ambition—"

"Ambition?"

"Celeste wants to go back to college. You know she had to quit in
her freshman year to take care of Simone. When Simone's mother died
back in—"

"Simone's mother?" Ellery frowned. "You make it sound as if Simone's
mother wasn't Celeste's mother."

"Didn't you know that?"

"Know what?"

"That Celeste wasn't the daughter of Mrs. Phillips?"

"You mean those two weren't sisters?" The Inspector's cup rattled.

Jimmy McKell looked from Queen to Queen. He pushed his chair back.
"I don't know that I'm fond of this," he said. "In fact, I know damn well
I'm not."

"Why, what's the matter, Jimmy?"

"You tell me!"

"But there's nothing to tell," said Ellery. "I asked you to find out what you could about Celeste. If we now have something new on her—"

"*On* her?"

"I mean about her, something we didn't know, why, you've only justified my confidence in you."

"May we dispense with the horse droppings, sleuth?"

"Jimmy, sit down."

"I want to know what cooks!"

"Why all the heat?" growled Inspector Queen. "You'll have me thinking in a minute . . ."

"Right." Jimmy sat down suddenly. "There's nothing to think. Simone was Celeste's third cousin or something. Celeste's parents were killed in a gas stove explosion when she was a baby. Mrs. Phillips was her only relative in New York and took her in. That's all there is to it. When Mrs. Phillips died, Celeste naturally took care of Simone; they always considered each other sisters. I know a hell of a lot of real sisters who wouldn't have done what Celeste did!"

"Even speaking not Delphically," said Ellery, "so do I."

"What?"

"Go on, Jimmy."

"She's crazy to get a college education—it half-killed her when she had to give it up at Mrs. Phillips's death. The books that kid's read! Deep stuff— philosophy, psychology—why, Celeste knows more right now than I do, and I've got a Princeton sheepskin acquired by sweat, oil, and grand larceny. Now that Simone's gone, the kid's free to live her own life again, go back to school and make something of herself. She's going to enroll this week in Washington Square College for the fall semester. She wants a B.A., majoring in English and philosophy, and then she'll go on to graduate work. Maybe teach."

"She must want it a great deal to cut out a program like that for herself on a night school basis."

"Night school? Who said anything about night school?"

"We still live in a competitive economy, Jimmy. Or," said Ellery cheerfully, "were you thinking of taking that problem off her hands?"

"Maybe," said the Inspector with a wink, "maybe that question is irrelevant, immaterial, and none of our business."

Jimmy gripped the table. "Are you crumbums suggesting—?"

"No, no, Jimmy. With benefit of clergy, of course."

"Oh. Well . . . let's leave me out of it." His homely face was angry and watchful.

"She can't work as a model daytimes and go to day college too, Jimmy," said Ellery.

"She's giving up that job."

"Really?" said the Inspector.

"Oh," said Ellery, "she's got herself a night job."

"No job at all!"

"I'm afraid," said Ellery mournfully, "I lost you somewhere back in the third canto. No job at all? How is she going to support herself?"

"With Simone's nestegg!" Jimmy was shouting now.

"Nestegg?"

"What er . . . what nestegg would that be, Jimmy?" asked the Inspector.

"Look." Jimmy inflated his chest. "You asked me to do a dirty chore and I've done it. I don't understand this, any of it. But assuming you're a big wheel in the gray cell department, Queen, and I'm just a little screw rattling around, will you tell me what the devil difference any of this makes?"

"No more difference than the truth ever makes."

"Sounds profound, but I suspect a gimmick."

"McKell." Inspector Queen was grim. "I've had a lot of men working on this case and I've been in it myself up to my Adam's apple. This is the first I've heard about Simone Phillips's leaving anybody anything but a lower back ache. Why didn't Celeste tell us?"

"Because she only found it last week! Because it's got nothing to do with the murder!"

"Found it?" murmured Ellery. "Where?"

"She was cleaning out Simone's junk. There was an old wooden table clock, a French deal that was a family heirloom or something—it hadn't run for ten years and Simone would never let Celeste have it fixed, kept it on a shelf over her bed. Well, when Celeste took it down last week it slipped out of her hands and cracked open like an egg on the floor. There was a big roll of bills inside, bound with a rubber band."

"Money? I thought Simone—"

"So did Celeste. The money had been left by Simone's father. There was a note in his handwriting bound in with the bills. According to the note, written just before he committed suicide, from the date on it, he managed to save $10,000 out of the wreckage when he dropped his fortune in the '29 market crash. He left the ten grand to his wife."

"And Celeste knew nothing about it?"

"Mrs. Phillips and Simone never mentioned it to her. Most of the dough is there, about $8600. Celeste thinks the missing $1400 went toward Simone's doctors' bills in the early days, when Mrs. Phillips still had hopes she could be cured. Certainly Simone knew all about it, because she had fits if Celeste went anywhere near the clock. Well, now the money is Celeste's and it's going to make life tolerable for her for a while. And that's the great big mysterious story," said Jimmy with out-thrust jaw, "the moral of which—if you ask me—is that, invalid or no invalid, Simone was a first-class drip. Imagine letting that poor kid nurse her in that Black Hole of Calcutta and shag her legs off trying to support both of them when all the time Simone had almost nine grand stashed away! What was she keeping it for, the junior prom? . . . What's the matter? Why the steely looks?"

"What do you think, Dad?"

"Any way you slice it, Ellery, it's a motive."

"*Motive?*" said Jimmy.

"The first one we've found." The Inspector went to a window, looking unhappy.

Jimmy McKell began to laugh. But then he stopped laughing.

"I wondered last week if there might have been a motive," said Ellery, thoughtfully. "When she came here."

"*Celeste?*"

Ellery did not reply.

"I know," said Jimmy. "This is something out of H. G. Wells. An unknown gas drifts into the earth's atmosphere out of interstellar space and everybody in the world goes fay. Including the great Ellery Queen. Why, Queen," he snarled, "she came here to help you *find* the killer of Simone!"

"Who, it develops, wasn't her sister and had deliberately held her in peonage for years."

"Give me air. Sweet, sane air!"

"I'm not saying it's so, Jimmy. But by the same token can you say it isn't?"

"Damned right I can! That kid is as pure as I was till I stumbled into this Siberian Casbah this morning and got polluted! Besides, I thought you were looking for the Cat—seven-times strangler!"

"Ellery." Inspector Queen came back to the table. He had apparently fought an engagement with himself and won it. Or lost it. "It's out of the question. Not that girl."

"Now there's a man," shouted Jimmy, "who's still got one toenail on the ground!"

Ellery stared into his cooling coffee. "Jimmy, have you ever heard of the ABC theory of multiple murder?"

"The *what?*"

"X wants to kill D. X's motive isn't apparent, but if he killed D in the ordinary way the police investigation would disclose eventually that the only person, or the most likely person, with motive to kill D was X. X's problem is, How can he kill D and gain his object without having his motive stand out? X sees that one way to accomplish this is by surrounding D's murder with a smokescreen of other murders, deliberately committed with the same technique in order to tie them up as a series of interrelated crimes.

Consequently, X first murders A, B, and C . . . wholly innocent people, you understand, with whom he's not in the least involved. Only then does he murder D.

"The effect of this is to make the murder of D appear as merely a single link in a chain of crimes. The police will not be looking for someone with motive against D, they will look for someone with motive against A, B, C, *and* D. But since X had no motive whatever for murdering A, B, and C, his motive against D is either overlooked or ignored. At least, that's the theory."

"How to become a detective in one easy lesson," said Jimmy McKell. "In a series of murders, last one with motive is It and leave my fee in the hypodermic needle, please."

"Not quite," said Ellery, without rancor. "X is smarter than that. To stop at the one murder which incriminates him, he realizes, is to bring it into exactly the prominence he has been trying to avoid by making it one of a series. Therefore X follows the relevant murder of D with the irrelevant murders of E, F, and G—and H and I and J, if necessary. He kills as many nonsignificant persons as he feels will successfully obfuscate his motive against the significant one."

"Pushing my way through the thicket of scholarly language," grinned Jimmy, "I now get it. This 23-year-old she-gorilla with the detachable chassis, this fiend in human form, strangles Abernethy, the Smith babe, O'Reilly, Monica, Beatrice Willikins, and little Lenore Richardson just so she can sandwich in the bumpoff of her crippled cousin Simone. Queen, have you seen a good doctor lately?"

"Celeste gave up five years of her life to Simone," said Ellery patiently. "She faced the prospect of giving up—how many more? Ten? Twenty? Simone might have lived on and on. Evidently Celeste had given her excellent care; the medical report indicates no bedsores, for example, the prevention of which in such cases requires constant attention.

"But Celeste wants desperately to make something of herself. Celeste would like to get away from the cheerless and limiting environment to which Simone's existence condemns her. Celeste is also young, pretty, and hot-blooded, and her life with Simone is frustrating emotionally. On top of all this, Celeste finds one night—not last week, but last May, let's say—a young fortune, which Simone has kept a secret from her all these years and possession of which would enable Celeste to satisfy her needs and wants for a considerable period. Only one thing stands in the way of possessing it—and putting it to use—and that's her cousin Simone. She can't bring herself to leave a helpless invalid—"

"So she kills her," chuckled Jimmy. "Along with six other folks."

"We've obviously hypothesized a person of confused motivations and personality—"

"I take it back. You don't need a checkup, Queen. You need a checkdown. From the scalp."

"Jimmy, I haven't said Celeste killed Simone and the others. I haven't even indicated an opinion as to its likelihood. I'm putting the known facts together in one possible way. In a shambles that's already seen seven people slaughtered and for all we know may eventually include a great many more, would you have me ignore Celeste simply because she's young and attractive?"

"Attractive. If what you're 'hypothesizing' about Celeste is true, she's a maniac."

"Read yesterday's interview with Dr. Edward Cazalis, Noted Psychiatrist. A maniac—of a very deceptive type—is exactly what Noted Psychiatrist is looking for, and I must say he makes out a convincing case."

"*I* am the type maniac," said Jimmy through his large teeth, "who can take just so much sanity. Watch out below!" And he went over the breakfast table as if it were the edge of a pool.

But Ellery was on his feet and to one side rather more quickly, and Jimmy McKell landed on his nose in a splash of tepid coffee.

"I must say that was silly, Jimmy. Are you all right?"

"Leggo, you character assassin!" yelled Jimmy, swinging.

"Here, sonny-boy." The Inspector caught Jimmy's arm. "You've been reading too many of Ellery's books."

Jimmy shook off the Inspector's hand. He was livid. "Queen, you get somebody else to do your stooling. I'm through. And what's more, I'm going to tell Celeste what she's up against. Yes, and how you suckered me into collecting your garbage for you! And if she upchucks at the mere proximity of McKell, it'll be no more than the yokel deserves!"

"Please don't do that, Jimmy."

"Why not?"

"Our agreement."

"Produce it in writing. What did you buy, Mephisto—my soul?"

"No one forced you into this, Jimmy. You came to me, offered your services, I accepted them on explicit conditions. Remember that, Jimmy?"

Jimmy glowered.

"Granted it's a quadrillion-to-one shot. Just on that remote possibility, will you keep your mouth shut?"

"Do you know what you're asking me to do?"

"Keep your promise."

"I'm in love with her."

"Oh," said Ellery. "That's really too bad."

The Inspector exclaimed: "So soon?"

Jimmy laughed. "Did they clock it in your day, Inspector?"

"Jimmy. You haven't answered my question."

When the doorbell rang.

The Queens looked at each other quickly.

"Who is it?" called the Inspector.

"Celeste Phillips."

But it was James Guymer McKell who reached the door first, swooping down like a stork.

"Jimmy. You didn't tell me you were—"

His long arms dropped around her.

"Jimmy." She struggled, laughing.

"I want you to be the last to know," snarled Jimmy McKell. "I love you."

"Jimmy, what . . . !"

He kissed her angrily on the lips and took off, sailing down the stairs.

"Come in, Celeste," said Ellery.

Celeste went crimson. She came in fumbling for her compact. Her lipstick was smeared and she kept looking at it in her mirror.

"I don't know what to say. Is Jimmy plastered? This early in the morning?" She laughed, but she was embarrassed and, Ellery thought, a little scared.

"Looked to me," said the Inspector, "as if he knew just what he was doing. Hey, Ellery?"

"Looked to *me* like the basis for a nuisance charge."

"*All* right," laughed Celeste, eying the repairs. "But I really don't know what to say." She was dressed less modishly this morning, but it was a new dress. Her own, thought Ellery. Bought with Simone's money.

"It's a situation not covered by Miss Post. I imagine James will go into it in detail at the first opportunity."

"Sit down, Miss Phillips, sit down," said the Inspector.

"Thank you. But what's the matter with him? He seemed upset. Is anything wrong?"

"First time I told a girl I loved her, I found myself making pleats in her father's best derby. Ellery, were you expecting Miss Phillips this morning?"

"No."

"You told me to come when I had something to report, Mr. Queen." Her black eyes were troubled. "Why did you ask me to find out everything I could about Jimmy McKell?"

"Remember our compact, Celeste?"

She looked down at her manicured nails.

"Now, Ellery, don't be a fuddy-duddy before your time," said the Inspector genially. "A kiss cancels all contracts. Why, Miss Phillips, there's no mystery about it. Jimmy McKell is a newspaperman. This might have been a dodge for him to get in on the inside of the Cat case, beat other reporters to news breaks. We had to be sure Jimmy's interest was personal, as he claimed. Do you find him a straightshooter?"

"He's simply drearily honest. If that's what you're worried about . . ."

"Well, that's that, isn't it?" beamed the Inspector.

"But as long as you're here, Celeste," said Ellery, "you may as well tell us the rest."

"I really can't add anything to what Jimmy told you about himself last week. He's never got along with his father and, since he got out of the Service, they hardly speak each other because Jimmy insists on living his own life. He really does pay his father $18 a week for board." Celeste giggled. "Jimmy says he's going to make it $75 as soon as the lawyers unwind all the red tape."

"Lawyers?"

"Oh, that business of his grandfather's estate."

"His grandfather," said the Inspector. "Now, let's see. That would be . . ."

"Mrs. McKell's father, Inspector. He was a very rich man who died when Jimmy was 13. Jimmy and his sister were their mother's father's only grandchildren and he left a big estate for them in trust. The income from the estate was to start being paid when each grandchild reached the age of 30. Monica'd been collecting her share for seven years, but Jimmy wasn't due to start for five years more, or whenever it is. The only thing is, now Jimmy will get the whole thing, because under his grandfather's will if one of the two grandchildren died the entire estate — principal and income — was to go to the survivor at once. There's millions in the estate and Jimmy's sick about the whole thing, I mean the way it's coming to him. Through Monica's death and all . . . what's the matter?"

Ellery was looking at his father. "How was that missed?"

"I don't know. None of the McKells said a word about an existing trust from an outside source. Of course, we'd have found out eventually."

"Found out *what?*" asked Celeste fretfully.

Neither man answered.

After a moment she got up. "Do you mean . . ."

"The fact is," said Ellery, "the death of Monica McKell means a fortune to her brother, who lives on a reporter's salary. It's what's known in our depressing profession, Celeste, as a motive."

*"Motive."*

Rage reshaped her. It was an alteration that began deep inside, like the first tiny release of energy in the heart of an explosive. Then it burst, and Celeste sprang.

Even as he felt the rip of her fingernails, Ellery thought absurdly: Like a cat.

"To usc mc to trap him!"

She kept screaming as Ellery seized the clawing hand and his father came up fast from behind.

"To think Jimmy'd do a thing like that! To *think* it! I'm going to tell him!"

Sobbing, she wrenched away and ran.

They saw Jimmy McKell step out of the basement areaway as thc front door burst open and Celeste Phillips flew out. He must have said something, because the girl whirled, looking down. Then she ran down the brownstone steps and hurled herself at him. She was crying and talking wildly. When she stopped, he said something to her very quietly and she put her hand to her mouth.

Then a cab veered inquiringly toward the curb and Jimmy held the door open and Celeste crept in. He got in after her and the cab raced off.

"End of an experiment," sighed Ellery. "Or the beginning of one."

Inspector Queen grunted. "Do you believe that baloney you sliced for McKell about ABC, D, X, and what have you?"

"It's possible."

"That somebody connected with only one of the seven murders is behind all of them as a coverup?"

"It's possible."

"I know it's possible! I asked you if you believe it."

"Can you be certain someone connected with only one of the seven murders isn't behind all of them?"

The Inspector shrugged.

Ellery tossed the stained handkerchief on the sofa. "As far as Celeste and Jimmy are concerned, the way they came to me logically admitted of suspicion. The fact that each one has just disclosed information damaging to the other, viewed without sentiment and on its own merits, only enlarges the suspicion area. Still, I'm willing to go on belief—I don't believe either is the Cat, no. There's a factor that goes beyond logic. Or maybe," said Ellery, "maybe I'm rusty. Do you suppose that could be it?"

"You're not convinced."

"Are you?"

"You'll be questioning me next!"

"Or myself."

The Inspector reached for his hat, scowling. "I'm going downtown."

# 6

The Cazalis phase of the investigation ran into shoal water immediately.

As originally charted by Dr. Cazalis, the psychiatric inquiry was to be a fishing expedition of all the specializing physicians in the local field, a sort of grand fleet sailing under a unified command. But it became evident that the expedition would have to be remapped. Each specialist, it appeared, was his own captain, guarding his nets and lines and the secrets of his fishing grounds with Japanese zeal. He regarded his catch as his exceptional property and no other fisher should have them.

To the credit of most, their scruples were largely ethical. The sanctity of the physician-patient confessional could not, *in propria persona*, be invaded even by other physicians. Dr. Cazalis surmounted the first obstacle by proposing the adoption of a published-case history technique. Each psychiatrist was to go through his files, select his possibilities on the broadest base, and make transcripts in which all identifying allusions were to be altered, leaving only the initials of the patient for reference. This suggestion was approved. When the case histories came in a five-doctor central board, headed by Dr. Cazalis, was to go to work. The board was to consider each history, rejecting those which in the consultative view were unlikely. By this method many persons would be screened out while being spared the violation of their privacy.

Here, however, agreement went aground.

How were the remaining cases to be treated? Anonymity could be preserved only so far. Then names must be disclosed.

The inquiry almost foundered on this reef.

For therapeutic reasons the type and class of suspect Dr. Cazalis's plan involved could not be handled as the police handled the daily haul of the dragnet, even assuming that the problem of protecting the confidences of the consulting room could be solved. Inspector Queen was directing and co-ordinating the activities of over three hundred detectives under orders to stop at nothing. Since early June each morning's lineup had been crowded not merely with dope addicts, alcoholics, old sex offenders, and criminal psychopaths with penal or institutional records but also with vagrants, prowlers, "suspicious characters" of all descriptions—a category which in three months had swollen alarmingly from the internal pressures of the case. In the high prevailing temperature, civil rights had tended to shrink as official frustration expanded. There had been typhoons of protest from all quarters. The courts had been showered with writs. Citizens had howled, politicians had roared, judges had thundered. But the investigation was plunging ahead in the teeth of all this. Dr. Cazalis's colleagues would have been reluctant to submit their patients to normal police procedures; how, they demanded, could they be expected to turn their patients over to the authorities in this stormy, overheated atmosphere? To many of their charges even an ordinary questioning session would raise dangers. These people were under treatment for mental and emotional disorders. The work of months or years might be undone in an hour by detectives callously intent only on finding a connection between the suspect and the Cat.

There were other difficulties. The patients originated for the most part in the prominences of the cultural geography. Many were socially well-known or came from well-known families. The arts and sciences were heavily represented, the theatrical world, business, finance, even politics. Democracy or no democracy, said the psychiatrists, such people could not be thrown into the lineup as if they were poolroom loiterers or park prowlers. How were they to be questioned? How far might the questions go? Which questions should be avoided and who was to decide? And who was to do the questioning, and when, and where?

The whole thing, they said, was impossible.

It took the better part of the week to work out a plan satisfactory to the majority. The solution took shape when it was recognized that no single *modus operandi* was practicable. There would have to be a separate plan, as it were, for each patient.

Accordingly a list of key questions, carefully composed so as to conceal their origin and objective, was drawn up by Dr. Cazalis and his board in collaboration with Inspector Queen. Each doctor co-operating received a confidential copy of this list. The individual physician was to do his own questioning, in his own office, of those patients on his suspect roll whom he considered it therapeutically risky to turn over to others. He agreed to file reports of these sessions with the board. Patients who in the judgment of their doctors could be safely interviewed by others were to be handled directly by the board at any one of their several offices. The police were not to come into contact with any patient except in the final stage of the medical inquiry, and then only where the findings compelled it. Even at this point the procedure was to emphasize the protection of the patient rather than the overriding hunt for damaging facts. Wherever possible in these cases the investigation was to proceed around the suspect instead of through him.

To the police it was a clumsy and irritating plan; but as Dr. Cazalis, who had begun to look haggard, pointed out to the Police Commissioner and Inspector Queen, the alternative was no investigation at all. The Inspector threw up his hands and his superior said politely that he had been looking forward to a rather more alluring prospect.

So, it appeared, had the Mayor. At an unhappy meeting in City Hall, Dr. Cazalis was inflexible: there were to be no further interviews with the press on his part or on the part of anyone associated with him in the psychiatric phase of the investigation. "I gave my professional word on that, Mr. Mayor. Let one patient's name leak to the newspapers and the whole thing will blow up in my face."

The Mayor replied with a plaintive, "Yes, yes, Dr. Cazalis, I hadn't thought it through, I'm sure. Good luck, and keep right on it, won't you?"

But when the psychiatrist had left, the Mayor remarked bitterly to his private secretary, "It's that damned Ellery Queen business all over again. By the way, Birdy, whatever happened to that fellow?"

What had happened was that the Mayor's Special Investigator had taken to the streets. Ellery might have been seen these days—and he was seen, by various Headquarters men—at eccentric hours lounging on the sidewalk across from the building on East 19th Street where Archibald Dudley Abernethy had come to an end, or standing in the hall outside the ex-Abernethy apartment, which was now occupied by a Guatemalan member of the United Nations secretariat and his wife, or wandering about Gramercy Park and Union Square; silently consuming *pizza* in the Italian restaurant on West 44th Street over which Violette Smith had flirted successfully with death, or leaning against the banister of the top floor hall listening to a piano stammer along behind the apartment door to which was thumbtacked a large sign:

THIS IS IT—YES!!!!
ALL SQUARES, VISITING
FIREMEN, EAR BENDERS,
PEARL DIVERS, AND
PEEPING TOMS
*KEEP OUT!!*

SONG WRITER AT WORK!!

poking about beneath the staircase in the lobby of a Chelsea tenement at the spot where the body of Rian O'Reilly had been found; sitting on a bench at the end of the Sheridan Square subway-station platform, uptown side, with the shade of Madcap Monica McKell; prowling beneath the washlines in a certain rear court on East 102nd Street and never once catching a glimpse of the emancipated cousin of fat little Simone Phillips; standing before the brassrailed stoop of a house on West 128th Street in a swarm of dark children, or strolling down Lenox Avenue among brown and saffron people to the 110th Street entrance to Central Park, or sitting on a park bench not far from the entrance or on the nearby boulder which had been the rock, if not the salvation, of Beatrice Willikins; or trudging along East 84th Street from Fifth Avenue to Madison past the canopied entrance of the Park-Lester and up Madison and back again to circumviate the block, or taking the private elevator in the Park-Lester's neighbor to a boarded-up penthouse whose occupants were away for the summer to stare frankly across the parapet at the terrace beyond which Lenore Richardson had gripped *Forever Amber* in the convulsion of strangulation.

Ellery rarely spoke to anyone on these excursions.

They took place by day as well as by night, as if he wished to view the sites in both perspectives.

He returned to the seven localities again and again. Once he was picked up by a detective who did not know him and spent several hours as a suspicious character in the nearest precinct house before Inspector Queen hurried in to identify him.

Had he been asked what he was about, the Mayor's Special Investigator would have been at a loss for a communicable reply. It was difficult to put into words. How materialize a terror, much more see him whole? This was one whose feet had whispered over pavements, displacing nothing larger than molecules. You followed his trackless path, sniffing upwind, hopefully.

All that week the eighth tail of the Cat, the now familiar question mark, hooked and held the eye of New York.

Ellery was walking up Park Avenue. It was the Saturday night after Lenore Richardson's murder and he was drifting in a vacuum.

He had left the night life of the City behind. In the 70s only piles of articulated stone kept him company, and an occasional goldbraided doorman.

At 78th Street Ellery paused before the royal blue-awninged house where the Cazalises lived. The ground-floor Cazalis apartment, with its private office entrance directly off the street, showed lights, but the vanes of the Venetian blinds were closed and Ellery wondered if Dr. Cazalis and his fellow-psychiatrists were at work behind them. Brewing the potion, stirring the caldron; wrapping truth in darkness. They would never find the Cat in their co-wizards' notes. He did not know how he knew this, but he knew it.

He walked on and some time later found himself turning into 84th Street.

But he passed the Park-Lester without breaking the rhythm of his torpor.

At the corner of 84th and Fifth, Ellery stopped. It was still early, the evening was warm, but the Avenue was a nervous emptiness. Where were the Saturday night arm-in-arm strollers? Even the automobile traffic seemed lighter. And the busses whined by carrying remarkably few passengers.

Facing him across Fifth Avenue was the Metropolitan Museum of Art, a broadbeamed old lady sitting patiently in darkness.

He crossed over on the green light and began to walk uptown along the old lady's flank. Beyond her lay the black and silent Park.

They're beginning to stick to the well-lighted areas, he thought. *O comfort-killing night, image of Hell.* No friendly darkness now. Especially here. In this part of the jungle the beast had pounced twice.

He almost cried out at the touch on his arm.

"Sergeant."

"I tailed you for two blocks before I recognized you," said Sergeant Velie, falling into step.

"On duty tonight?"

"Naw."

"Then what are you doing around here?"

"Oh . . . just walking around." The big fellow said carelessly, "I'm baching it these days."

"Why, where's your family, Velie?"

"Sent the wife and kid to my mother-in-law's for a month."

"To Cincinnati? Is Barbara-Ann—?"

"No, Barbsy's okay. And as far as school is concerned," said Sergeant Velie argumentatively, "she can catch up any time. She's got her ma's brains."

"Oh," said Ellery; and they ambled on in silence.

After a long time the Sergeant said, "I'm not intruding on anything, I trust?"

"No."

"I mean, I thought you might be on the prowl." The Sergeant laughed.

"Just going over the Cat's route. For the umpteenth time. Backwards, Sergeant. Richardson, Lenore, to Willikins, Beatrice. Number 7 to Number 6. East 84th to Harlem. The Lord's anointed to His unshorn lamb. One mile or so between and the Cat jumps it by way of the moon. Do you have a light?"

They stopped under a street lamp and the Sergeant struck a match.

"Talking about the Cat's route," he said. "You know, Maestro, I've been giving this case a lot of thought."

"Thanks, Velie."

They crossed 96th Street.

"I long ago gave up," the Sergeant was saying—"I'm speaking only for Thomas Velie, you understand—gave up trying to get anywhere on this carrousel. My personal opinion is when the Cat's knocked off it will be by dumb-bunny luck. Some rookie cop'll walk up to a drunk bent over like he's regretting the whole thing and bingo, it'll be the Cat tying a bow in the latest neck. But just the same," said the Sergeant, "you can't help figuring the angles."

"No," said Ellery, "you certainly can't."

"Now I don't know what your impression is, and of course this is all off the record, but I got busy the other night with a map of Manhattan and environs that I traced off my kid's geography book and I started spotting in the locations of the seven homicides. Just for the hell of it." The Sergeant's voice lowered. "Well, sir, I think I got something."

"What?" asked Ellery. A couple were passing, the man arguing and pointing to the Park and the woman shaking her head, walking very fast. The Sergeant stopped abruptly; but Ellery said, "It's all right, Velie. That's only a Saturday night date with ideas."

"Yeah," said the Sergeant sagely, "sex suckers all men."

But they did not move until they saw the man and woman climb into a southbound bus.

"You'd got something, Velie."

"Oh! Yeah. I put a heavy dot on each location on the map, see. The first one—Abernethy's, East 19th—I marked that one 1. The second one—Violette Smith's, on West 44th off Times Square—I mark 2. And so forth."

"You," said Ellery, "and that *Extra* cartoonist."

"Then when I've got all seven spotted and numbered, I begin drawing lines. A line from 1 to 2. A line from 2 to 3. Et cetera. And what do you think?"

"What?"

*"It's got a kind of a design."*

"Really? No, wait, Sergeant. The Park gives me nothing tonight. Let's strike crosstown." They crossed 99th and began to make their way east through the dark and quiet street. "Design?"

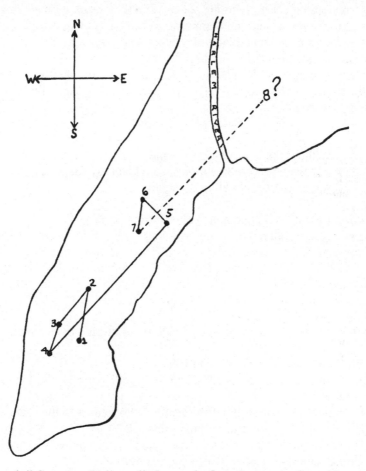

"Look." Sergeant Velie pulled a wad of tracing paper from his pocket and unfolded it on the corner of 99th and Madison. "It's a kind of double-circular movement, Maestro. Straight up from 1 to 2, sharp down again but westerly from 2 to 3, keeps going southwest to 4, then what? Sharp up again. A long one this time, crossing the 1–2 line. Up, down, over, and up again. Now look! Now it starts all over again! Oh, not at exactly the same angles, of course, but close enough to be interesting, hmmm? Again it's up and over from 5 to 6—northwesterly—then sharp down to 7 . . ." The Sergeant paused. "Let me show you something. If you as-

sume there's a sort of scheme behind this, if you continue that same circular movement, what do you find?" The Sergeant pointed to his dotted
line. "You can predict just about where Number 8's going to come! Maestro, I'd almost bet the next one's in the Bronx." He folded his piece of
paper, restored it carefully to his pocket, and they resumed their eastward
way. "Maybe up around the beginning of the Grand Concourse. Around
Yankee Stadium or some place like that." And after a few moments, the
Sergeant asked, "What do you think?"

Ellery frowned at the passing sidewalk. "There's a little thing that
comes out of *The Hunting of the Snark*, Sergeant," he said, "that's always
stuck in my mind.

> "He had bought a large map representing the sea,
>     Without the least vestige of land:
>   And the crew were much pleased when they found it to be
>     A map they could all understand."

"I don't get it," said Sergeant Velie, staring at him.

"I'm afraid we all have our favorite maps. I had one recently I was extremely attached to, Sergeant. It was a Graph of Intervals. The intervals
between the various murders expressed in number of days. The result
was something that looked like a large question mark lying flat on its
face. It was a lesson in humility. I burned it, and I advise you to do the
same with yours."

After that, the Sergeant just strode along, muttering occasionally.

"Why look where we are," said Ellery.

The Sergeant, who had been acting dignified, started as he glanced up
at the street sign.

"So you see, Sergeant, it's the detective who returns to the scene of the
crime. Drawn by a sort of horizontal gravity."

"Drawn by my garter belt. You knew just where you were going."

"Unconsciously, maybe. Shall we press our luck?"

"Last one in is a dirty name," said the Sergeant, unbending; and they
plunged into the noisy breakers of 102nd Street.

"I wonder how my female ex-Irregular is getting along."

"Say, I heard about that. That was a pretty smart trick."

"Not so smart. The shortest collaboration on record.—Hold it, Velie."

Ellery stopped to fish for a cigaret. The Sergeant dutifully struck a
match, saying, "Where?"

"In that doorway behind me. Almost missed him."

The flame snuffed out and Sergeant Velie said in a loud voice, "Darn it all, old man, let's get on over here," and they moved around a frantic hopscotch game toward the building line. The big man grinned. "Hell, it's Piggott." He struck another match near the doorway and Ellery bent over.

"Evening, evening," said the detective from somewhere. "I saw you two amateurs coming a block away."

"Is there a law against it?" demanded Sergeant Velie. "What are you working tonight, Piggo? Yeah, I'll have one." He took a cigaret from Ellery.

"Watch it! Here he comes."

Ellery and the Sergeant jumped into the doorway beside the Headquarters man. A tall fellow had come out of an unlighted vestibule halfway up the street, on their side. He began pushing his way through the children.

"I've been tailing him all night," said the detective.

"On whose orders, Piggott?"

"Your old man's."

"How long has this been going on?"

"All week. Hesse and I are divvying him."

"Didn't the Inspector tell you?" asked Sergeant Velie.

"I've hardly seen him this week."

"It's nothing exciting," said the detective. "Just satisfying the taxpayers, the Inspector said."

"How's he been spending his time?"

"Walking and standing still."

"Up here much?"

"Till last night."

"What's he been up to in that vestibule tonight?"

"Watching the entrance of the girl's house across the street."

Ellery nodded. Then he said, "Is she home?"

"We all pulled in here about a half hour ago. She spent the evening in the 42nd Street Library. Reference Room. So that's where we were, too. Then he tailed her here, and I tailed him, and here we are."

"Hasn't he gone in there?"

"No, sir."

"He hasn't approached her, spoken to her?"

"Hell, she didn't know he was following her. It's been kind of like a Humphrey Bogart movie, at that. Johnson's been tailing *her*. He's been in the back court across the street since we pulled in here."

"Sounds like a Canarsie clambake." Then the Sergeant said swiftly, *"Piggo, get lost."*

The tall man was coming directly toward their doorway.

*※ = yippee to read THIS name!*
*August 4, 2011*

"Well, well," said Ellery, stepping out. "Hi."

"I thought I'd save you some wear and tear." Jimmy McKell stood innerbraced, looking from Ellery to Sergeant Velie and back again. Behind them, the doorway was empty. "What's the significant idea?"

"Idea?" said Ellery, considering it.

"I saw you two rubberheels sneak into this doorway. What are you doing, watching Celeste Phillips?"

"Not me," said Ellery. "Were you, Sergeant?"

"I wouldn't do a thing like that," said the Sergeant.

"Very funny." Jimmy McKell kept looking at them. "Why don't you ask me what I'm doing here?"

"All right, Jimmy. What are you doing here?"

"The same thing you are." Jimmy excavated a cigaret, brushed off the linty detritus, and stuck it like a flag between his lips. His tone was amiable, however. "Only my angle is maybe different. I'm told there's somebody doing the town collecting necks. Now that woman has one of the prettiest head supports in Christendom." He lit the cigaret.

"Protecting her, huh?" said the Sergeant. "You play long shots, reporter."

"Two-Million-to-One McKell, they call me." Jimmy tossed the match; it glanced off Velie's ear. "Well, I'll be seeing you. If that's my kismet." He began to walk away.

"Jimmy, wait."

"For what?"

"What do you say we drop in on her?"

Jimmy sauntered back. "For what?"

"I've been meaning to have a talk with you two."

"For what?"

"You're both entitled to an explanation, Jimmy."

"You don't have to explain anything to me. My nose knows."

"No kidding."

"I'm not. It really does."

"I don't blame you for being griped—"

"Hell, who's griped? What's a little thing like being suspected of seven murders? I mean between pals?" He stepped close all at once and Sergeant Velie stirred. Jimmy's lips were out. "Queen, that was the most two-faced, poisonous deal since the days of the Medicis. To sick me onto Celeste and Celeste onto me. I ought to boff you for that."

The Sergeant said, "Here."

"Take that ham hock off me."

"It's all right, Sergeant." Ellery was preoccupied and morose. "But Jimmy, I had to make some test."

"Some test is right."

"Yes, it was on the silly side. But you both came to me at such a convenient moment. I couldn't close my eyes to the possibility that one of you—"

"Is the Cat." Jimmy laughed.

"We're not dealing with normality."

"Do I look abnormal? Does Celeste?"

"Not to my eyes, no. But then I don't have psychiatric vision." Ellery grinned. "And dementia, for example, is a youthful disease."

"Praecox McKell. Well, they called me a lot worse in the late Hot War."

"Jimmy, I never really believed it. I don't believe it now."

"But there's always the mathematical chance."

"Come on, let's drop in on Celeste."

"I take it if I refuse," said Jimmy, not budging, "Charley the Anthropoid here will pinch me?"

"I'll pinch you," said Sergeant Velie. "Where it hurts."

"See what I mean?" said Jimmy bitterly. "We're just not compatible." And he strode away, breaking up the hopscotch game and pursued by the curses of little children.

"Let him go, Velie."

After a few moments Detective Piggott's voice said, "There goes my bread and butter. Night, Brother Elks." When they looked around, Piggott was gone.

"So he's been watching Celeste to save her from the Cat," said Ellery as they began to cross the street.

"In a swine's eyeball."

"Oh, Jimmy means it, Sergeant. At least he thinks he does."

"What is he, feebleminded?"

"Hardly." Ellery laughed. "But he's suffering from a severe attack of what our friend Cazalis might call—though I doubt it—confusional inanity. Otherwise known as the love psychosis."

The Sergeant grunted. They stopped before the tenement and he looked around casually. "You know what I think, Maestro?"

"After that double wingback map of Manhattan of yours I wouldn't even attempt a guess."

"Go ahead and horse," said the Sergeant. "But I think you put a bee in his buzzer."

"Explain."

"I think McKell thinks maybe Celeste *is* the Cat."

Ellery glanced up at the behemoth as if he had never really seen him before.

"You know what I think, Velie?"

"What?"

"I think you're right." And, looking slightly ill, he said, "Let's go in."

The hall was cheaply dim and pungent. A boy and a girl jumped apart as Ellery and Velie walked in; they had been clutching each other in the shadows beside the staircase. "Oh, *thank* you, I had such a lovely time," said the girl, running up the stairs. The boy smirked. "I ain't complaining, Carole." He slouched out, winking at the two men.

A door at the rear stood open, a line of wash clipping its upper corner to the dark sky.

"Piggott said Johnson was out there, Maestro."

"Not any more Johnson isn't," said a voice from under the stairs. "I got an old camp chair in here, Sarge."

" 'Lo, Johnson," said the Sergeant, not turning. "How's the trick?"

"With those two juvenile delinquents that were just here it was colossal. You calling on C.P.?"

"Is she still up?" Ellery asked the darkness.

"There's the light under her door, Mr. Queen."

"That door there," said the Sergeant.

"Alone, Johnson?"

"Uh-huh." There was a yawn.

Ellery went over and knocked on the door. Sergeant Velie moved to one side, out of range.

After a moment, Ellery knocked again.

"Who is it?" She sounded frightened.

"Ellery Queen. Please open, Celeste."

They heard her undo the latch chain very slowly.

"What do you want?"

In the box of light she stood bristling. One hand clutched a large book to her breast. It looked like an old book, one fingered with respect.

*Survey of English Literature—First Year.*

Saturday night on East 102nd Street. A voom with the Venerable Bede. Bebop with *Beowulf*. Holding hands with Hakluyt's *Divers Voyages*. Jive print in double columns, kneedeep in footnotes.

She blocked his view of the room. He had never seen this room, only photographs.

She was dressed in a full black pleated skirt and a tailored white blouse and her hair was disordered, as if she had had her fists in it as she read. There was blue ink on one finger. What he could make out of her face was a little shocking. The violet stains had spread and her skin was blotchy, cupped to bitter heads.

"May I come in?" asked Ellery with a smile.

"No. What do you want?"

"In this neighborhood, Maestro," said Sergeant Velie, "you couldn't run for your life."

Celeste took a quick look out. She immediately withdrew her head. "I remember *him*."

Sergeant Velie stiffened.

"Haven't you done enough damage?"

"Celeste—"

"Or did you come to arrest me? Not that I'd put it past you. I suppose Jimmy McKell and I were accomplices. We strangled all those people together. Each of us pulling on one end of the silk cords."

"Celeste, if you'll let me—"

"You've spoiled everything. *Everything*."

The door slammed in his face. They heard the furious turn of the key, the lash of the latch chain.

"Each on one end," mused Sergeant Velie. "Think that's such a crosseyed idea? Did anybody take that into consideration? Two of them?"

Ellery muttered, "They've had a blowup."

"Sure, last night. It was just terrible," said Johnson's voice cheerfully. "He says she suspected him of being the Cat and she says nonono it's him who suspected *her* of being the Cat. Then they both deny it like mad. Going at it hot and heavy—I was out in the court there and I was afraid they'd collect a crowd and I'd have to fade. Well, sir, she starts bawling like she means it and what does he do but say a naughty word and damn near bust the hinges off the door blasting his way out."

"Love's sweet young stuff," said the Sergeant. "Do you suppose it could have been an act? Maybe they're wise to you, Johnson. Hey, Maestro. Where you going?"

Ellery sounded miserable. "Home."

All during the week following Ellery had a sense of marking time. Nothing occurred of the least interest. He saw the reports on Jimmy McKell and Celeste Phillips; they had made up, they had quarreled again, they had made up again. Other reports had all but stopped coming in. One morning Ellery dropped in to view the lineup performance. As entertainment it was depressing, and it told nothing, but he experienced the satisfaction of a man who has performed a duty. He did not go again. He cleverly refrained from venturing below Centre Street and the good Magistrate at City Hall seemed to have forgotten his existence, for which Ellery was abysmally grateful. He saw little of his father and he purposely avoided asking questions about the progress of Dr. Cazalis's investigation . . . And the Cat's eighth tail remained a question mark on the front page of the *Extra*.

Even the newspapers were marking time.

It was curious. The *status quo ante* in American journalism is not a standing still; it is a going backward. A Page 1 story remains there only so long as it grows. Let it stop growing and it finds itself on Page 6, and it will continue this oblivious process until it backs right out of the paper. But the Cat story blandly bucked the rule. If it got nowhere, neither did it lose headway. It rode anchor on the front page. It was news even when it was not.

In a way, it was more news when it was not than when it was, when the Cat lay napping in his den than when he padded out to hunt another neck. His inactivity exerted a special attraction, horrid and hypnotic: the magnetism of suspense. It was like a smolder between bursts of flame. If, as Jefferson said, newspapers "serve to carry off noxious vapors and smoke," the New York press could only obey the physics of the times.

It was during these intervals that the public nervousness was most remarkable. The waiting was worse than the event. When the Cat killed, people were actually relieved for a few days, in a semi-hysterical way; they and theirs were safe once more. But their dread was not destroyed; it was merely becalmed. Relief soon wore off, suspense surfaced again, the night anxieties, the counting of the days, the pitching wonder as to who would be next.

It was no use pitting the mathematical improbabilities against the individual's fears. The psychological laws of lottery ruled, the only difference being that in this policy game the prize was not money but extinction. Tickets were free to all New Yorkers, and each holder knew in his heart that he would win at the next drawing.

So the week wore on.

Ellery was thankful to see the week end; by Saturday it had become insupportable. His absurd Graph of Intervals persisted in haunting him. Between Victims 1 and 2, nineteen days; between Victims 2 and 3, twenty-six days; between Victims 3 and 4, twenty-two days; between Victims 4 and 5—Monica McKell to Simone Phillips—the teasing, inexplicable drop to ten days; between Victims 5 and 6, the further drop to six days; and then the reascending curve of eleven days between Victims 6 and 7. Was this the beginning of a new upward spiral? Were the intervals leveling off? It was now the twelfth day after the strangling of Mrs. Cazalis's niece.

In the uncertainty, each moment excreted fear.

Ellery spent that Saturday chasing police calls. It was the first time he had used any of the vague powers conferred on him by the Mayor's appointment. He was not even sure it would work. But when he commandeered a car with a police radio, a black seven-passenger limousine with no identifying insignia occupied by a plainclothes chauffeur and his plainclothes companion showed up promptly. Most of the time Ellery slumped low in the tonneau listening to interminable accounts of "real baffling cases." Each detective was the size of Sergeant Velie and each was equipped with inexhaustible lungs.

Ellery kept wondering on and off through the long tiresome day what had happened to his father. No one seemed to know where Inspector Queen was; he had left the apartment before Ellery rose, he had not been to Headquarters, he had not called in.

They roared with open siren from the Battery to the Harlem River, from Riverside Drive to First Avenue. They were in on the breakup of a teenage street fight in San Juan Hill and the arrest of a cocaine addict caught trying to slip a forged prescription by an alert Yorkville pharmacist. They visited the scenes of holdups, traffic accidents, minor assaults; on the agenda in order were a queue-pulling match off Chatham Square, an attempted rape in a Hell's Kitchen hallway, the case of a getaway car in a Third Avenue pawnshop robbery. They witnessed the bloodless capture of a meek gangster in Little Italy wanted for questioning in an old homicide, the escape of a Lithuanian cook from a Little Hungary restaurant where he had suddenly gone berserk. There were four suicides—above the average for such a short period, the detectives explained, but it had been a bad summer: one in the Bowling Green subway station, an elderly Brooklynite who had thrown himself in the path of an incoming IRT express; another a Herald Square window-jumping case, a girl registered in a hotel from Chicopee Falls, Mass., identified as an eloper; another a gas range job in a Rivington Street tenement, a woman and a baby; the fourth an alcoholic case in the West 130s who had slashed his wrists. There were two homicide calls: the first, shortly before noon, a knifing in a Harlem poolroom; the second, at 6:30, a woman beaten to death with a Stillson wrench in the East 50s by her husband, an advertising agency executive. This last aroused some interest in the detectives since it involved another man, a Broadway character, and they were disposed to linger; but Ellery waved them on.

There were no strangulations, with or without cords.

"Just another day," said the detective at the wheel as he slid the squad car into 87th Street. He sounded apologetic.

"Why not keep going tonight?" suggested the other detective as Ellery got out. "Saturday night's always lively, Mr. Queen, and maybe it's the Cat's night out."

"By the twitching of my left ventricle," said Ellery, "I can tell it isn't.
Doesn't matter, anyway—I can always read about it in the papers. Will
you boys join me in a friendly glass?"

"Well, now," said the driver.

But the other detective said, "Give your old woman a break for once,
Frank. And I've got a long haul, Mr. Queen. Out to Rockville Center.
Thanks just the same."

Upstairs, Ellery found a note from his father.

It was a scribble marked 7 *P.M.*

   EL—Been phoning since 5. Dashed home to leave this note.
Meet me at Cazalis's the minute you get in. Big powwow set for
7:30.

   7:35.
   Ellery ran.

When the uniformed maid ushered him into the Cazalis living room,
the first person he saw was the Mayor of the City of New York. That har-
rowed servant of the people was lying back in an easy-chair, hands
clasped about a tall glass, glaring at a bust of Sigmund Freud above
Ellery's head.

The Police Commissioner, seated beside the Mayor, was studying the
fume of his cigar.

Dr. Cazalis sat on a Turkish divan, bolstered by silk pillows. His wife
held on to his hand.

At a window stood Inspector Queen, cocooned in silence.

The air was chill.

"Don't tell me, please," said Ellery. "It's a washout."

No one replied. Mrs. Cazalis rose and prepared a Scotch-and-soda,
which Ellery accepted with genuine gratitude.

"Ellery, where have you been today?" But the Inspector failed to
sound as if he cared.

"Out chasing radio calls. Don't be misled, Mr. Mayor," said Ellery.
"It's the first time since I took over. Hereafter I'll do my special investigating from an armchair—that is, if there *is* a hereafter?"

The Mayor's glance touched him briefly, almost with loathing. "Sit
down, Queen, sit down."

"Nobody's answered my question."

"It wasn't a question, it was a statement," said Dr. Cazalis from the
pillows. "And as a statement it exactly states the case."

"Sit down, Queen," snapped the Mayor again.

"Thank you, Mr. Mayor. I'll keep my father company." Ellery was startled by Dr. Cazalis's appearance. His pale eyes were inflamed and his skin was plowed so raw that Ellery thought of floodwater soil eroded into gullies; the glacier had given way. And he recalled Cazalis's remark about his insomnia. "Doctor, you look depreciated."

"There's been considerable wear and tear."

"He's worn out," said Mrs. Cazalis shrilly. "He drives himself so. No more sense than an infant. He's been at this day and night since . . ."

Her husband squeezed her hand. "The whole psychiatric attack, Mr. Queen, is a fizzle. We've got exactly nowhere."

Inspector Queen said curtly: "This week I've been working close to Dr. Cazalis, Ellery. We wound up today. There were a number of possibilities. We ran every one of them down."

"Quietly, you understand," said the Mayor bitterly. "No toes stepped on. Not a word in the papers."

"Well," said Dr. Cazalis, "it was a long chance at best. My fault entirely. It seemed a notion at the time."

"At the time, Edward? Isn't it still?" Mrs. Cazalis was regarding her husband in a puzzled way.

"Humpty Dumpty, dear."

"I don't understand."

"I take it, Queen," said the Mayor, "you haven't got to first base?"

"I never took the bat off my shoulder, Mr. Mayor."

"I see." Here goes a Special Investigator, thought Ellery. "Inspector Queen, what's your feeling?"

"We have a very tough case, Mr. Mayor. In the usual murder investigation, the range of suspicion is limited. The husband, the 'friend,' the handyman, the rival, the enemy, and so on. Motive begins to stick out. The field narrows. Opportunity narrows it even further. We've got human material to work on. Sooner or later in even the most complicated case we make a rap stick. But in this one . . . How are you going to narrow the field? Where do you start? No connection among the victims anywhere. No suspects. No clues. Every murder a dead end. The Cat could be anybody in New York."

"You can still say that, Inspector?" cried the Mayor. "After all these weeks?"

The Inspector's lips thinned. "I'm ready to hand in my shield right now."

"No, no, Inspector, I was just thinking aloud." The Mayor glanced at his Police Commissioner. "Well, Barney, where do we go from here?"

The Commissioner tapped a long ash very carefully into a tray. "When you get right down to it, there's no place we can go. We've done, and we're doing, everything humanly possible. I could suggest a new Police Commissioner, Jack, but I doubt if that would satisfy anybody except the *Extra* and the other crowd, and I'm Irish enough to believe it wouldn't necessarily bag your Cat, either."

The Mayor waved, impatiently. "The question is, *are* we doing everything possible? It seems to me where we may have gone off is in assuming that the Cat is a New Yorker. Suppose he comes from Bayonne? Stamford? Yonkers? He may be a commuter—"

"Or a Californian," said Ellery.

"What? What was that?" exclaimed the Mayor.

"A Californian, or an Illinoisan, or a Hawaiian."

"The Mayor said irritably, "Queen, I can't see that that sort of talk gets us anywhere. The point is, Barney, have we done anything outside the City?"

"Everything we can."

"We've had every community within a radius of fifty miles of the City alerted for at least six weeks," said the Inspector. "From the start they've been requested to keep their eyes peeled for psychos. But so far—"

"Jack, until we get a concrete reason for believing otherwise, nobody can crucify us for concentrating on Manhattan."

"My personal opinion," added the Inspector, "has been all along that he's a Manhattanite. To me this Cat smells local."

"Besides, Jack," said the Commissioner with a certain dryness, "our jurisdiction ends at the City limits. After that we've got a tin cup in our hands and take what the saints provide."

The Mayor set his glass down with a little bang and went over to the fireplace. Ellery was nuzzling his Scotch with a faraway look, the Commissioner was back at his cigar examination, Dr. Cazalis and Inspector Queen were blinking at each other across the room to keep awake, and Mrs. Cazalis sat like a grenadier.

The Mayor turned suddenly. "Dr. Cazalis, what are the chances of extending your psychiatric investigation to include the entire metropolitan area?"

"Manhattan is the concentration point."

"But there are other psychiatrists outside?"

"Oh, yes."

"What about them?"

"Well . . . it would take months, and then you wouldn't get anything like satisfactory coverage. Even here, in the heart of things, where I exert a pretty direct professional influence, I haven't been able to get better than 65 or 70 per cent of the men in the field to co-operate. If the survey were extended to Westchester, Long Island, Connecticut, New Jersey . . ." Dr. Cazalis shook his head. "As far as I personally am concerned, Mr. Mayor, it would be pretty much out of the question. I haven't either the strength or the time to tackle such a project."

Mrs. Cazalis's lips parted.

"Won't you at least continue covering Manhattan, then, Dr. Cazalis? The answer may well lie in the files of one of the 30 or 35 per cent you say refused to play along. Won't you keep after those people?"

Dr. Cazalis's fingers pumped rapidly. "Well, I've been hoping . . ."

"Edward, you're not giving up. You're not!"

"*Et tu, darling?* I thought I had no more sense than an infant."

"I mean for going at it the way you have. Ed, how can you stop altogether? Now?"

"Why, dear, simply by doing so. I was paranoid to attempt it."

She said something in such a low tone that Dr. Cazalis said, "What, dear?"

"I said what about Lenore!"

She was on her feet.

"Darling." Dr. Cazalis scrambled off the divan. "All this tonight's upset you—"

"Tonight? Did you think I wasn't upset yesterday? And the day before?" She sobbed into her hands. "If Lenore had been your sister's child . . . had meant as much to you as she did to me . . ."

"I think, gentlemen," said the Mayor quickly, "we've imposed on Mrs. Cazalis's hospitality long enough."

"I'm sorry!" She was really trying to stop. "I'm so sorry. Edward, let me go. Please. I want to . . . get something."

"Tell you what, darling. Give me twenty-four hours' sleep, a two-inch T-bone when I wake up, and I'll tackle it where I left off. Good enough?"

She kissed him suddenly. Then, murmuring something, she hurried out.

"I submit, gentlemen," said the Mayor, "that we owe Mrs. Cazalis a few dozen roses."

"My only weakness," laughed the psychiatrist. "I never could resist the diffusion of the female lachrymal glands."

"Then, Doctor," said Ellery, "you may be in for a bad time."

"How's that, Mr. Queen?"

"If you'll run over the ages of the seven victims, you'll find that each victim has been younger than the one preceding."

The Commissioner's cigar almost fell out of his mouth.

The Mayor went brick-red.

"The seventh victim, Doctor—your wife's niece—was 25 years old. If any prediction is possible in this case, it's that Victim Number 8 will be under 25. Unless you're successful, or we are, we may soon be investigating the strangulation of children." Ellery set his glass down. "Would you say good night to Mrs. Cazalis for me?"

# 7

The so-called "Cat Riots" of September 22–23 marked the dread appearance in New York City of *mobile vulgus* for the first time since the Harlem disorders of almost fifteen years before. But in this case the mob was predominantly white; as a wry vindication of the Mayor's dawn press conference of the previous month, there was no "race angle." The only racial fears involved were the primitive ones of all mankind.

Students of mob psychology found the Cat Riots interesting. If in one sense the woman whose hysterical outburst set off the panic in Metropol Hall exerted the function of the inevitable *meneur*—the leader each mob tends to throw up, who starts the cheering or the running away—if the hysterical woman represented the fuse which sparked the explosion, she in her turn had been ignited by the inflammatory Citizens' Action Teams which had sprung up all over the Greater City during the immediately preceding Four Days and whose activities were responsible for her presence in the Hall. And no one could say with certainty who originally inspired those groups; at least no individual responsibility was ever determined.

The shortlived movement which came to be known as the Four Days (although from inception to culminating riot it spanned six days) was first publicly taken note of early on Monday, September 19, in the late morning editions of the newspapers.

An "association of neighbors" had been formed over the past weekend on the Lower East Side under the name of "The Division Street Vigilantes." At an organizing meeting held Saturday night a series of resolutions had been drawn up in the form of a "Declaration" which was ratified "in full convention assembled" on the following afternoon. Its "Preamble" asserted "the right of lawabiding American citizens, in the failure of regular law enforcement," to band together "for common security." Anyone in the prescribed neighborhood was eligible to join. World War II veterans were especially solicited. Various patrols were to be set up: a Streets Patrol, a Roofs Patrol, an Alleys Patrol. There was a separate Unit Patrol for each dwelling or other building in the area. The function of the patrols was "to stand guard against the marauder who has been terrorizing the City of New York." (There was some intra-organizational protest against the use of "fancy language," but the language stood when the Resolutions Committee pointed out that "on Division Street and around here we're supposed to be a bunch of pigs.") Discipline was to be military. Patrolmen were to be equipped with flashlights, armbands, "and available weapons of defense." A 9 P.M. curfew for children was to be enforced. Street level lighting was to be maintained until daybreak; special arrangements were being made with landlords of dwellings and stores.

In the same news story was noted the simultaneous formation of three similar organizations, apparently unconnected with one another or with the Division Street Vigilantes. One was in the Murray Hill section and called itself "The Murray Hill Committee of Safety." Another took in the area between West 72nd Street and West 79th Street and was named "The West End Minutemen." The third centered in Washington Square, "The Village Home Guard."

Considering the differences among the three groups culturally, socially, and economically, their avowed purposes and operating methods were astonishingly similar to those of the Division Street Vigilantes.

Editorials that morning commented on "the coincidence of four widely separated communities getting the same idea over the same weekend" and wondered "if it is so much of a coincidence as it appears." The anti-Administration papers blamed the Mayor and the Police Commissioner and used phrases like "the traditional American way" and "the right to defend the American home." The more responsible journals deplored the movement and one of them was "confident that the traditional good humor of New York will laugh these well-meaning but overexcited people back to their senses." Max Stone, editorial writer of the leading liberal paper, wrote: "This is fascism on the sidewalks of New York."

By 6 P.M. Monday the newscasters were reporting to their audiences that "at least three dozen action committees have sprung up in scattered neighborhoods of the five boroughs since the announcement this morning of the organization of the Division Street, Murray Hill, West End Avenue, and Greenwich Village groups."

The late evening editions of the newspapers were able to say that "the idea is spreading like an old-fashioned prairie fire. By press time the number of action committees was over a hundred."

By Tuesday morning the count was reported as "hundreds."

The term "Citizens' Action Teams" seems to have first appeared in a Tuesday *Extra* story on the amazing citywide phenomenon. The story was bylined "Jimmy Leggitt." The phrase took hold when Winchell, Lyons, Wilson, and Sullivan noted in their columns that its initials spelled "cat." And CATs they remained.

At an emergency meeting in the Mayor's office Monday night, the Police Commissioner expressed himself as being in favor of "taking tough police measures to stop this thing dead in its tracks. We can't have every Joe, Moe, and Schmo in town a selfappointed cop. It's anarchy, Jack!" But the Mayor shook his head. "You're not going to put out a fire by passing a law against it, Barney. We can't stop this movement by force; it's out of the question. What we've got to do is try to control it."

At his press conference Tuesday morning the Mayor said with a smile, "I repeat that this Cat thing has been exaggerated far out of proportion and there is absolutely no basis for public alarm with the Police Department working on it twenty-four hours a day. These groups will function much more in the public interest with the advice and assistance of the authorities. The Police Commissioner and his various heads of department will be on hand all day today to receive delegations of these groups with the end in view of systematizing and co-ordinating their activities, in much the way that the splendid ARP groups operated during the War."

Disturbingly, the groups did not appear to be received.

On Tuesday night the Mayor went on the air. He did not in the slightest impugn the integrity and good intentions of the people forming home defense groups, but he felt sure all reasonable people would agree that the police power of the greatest city in the world could not be permitted to be usurped by individual citizens, no matter how honest or well-intentioned, in defiance of legal authority. "Let it not be said that the City of New York in the fifth decade of the twentieth century resorted to frontier town vigilante law." The dangers implicit in this sort of thing were recognized by all, he was certain, as far exceeding any possible threat of one homicidally inclined psychotic. "In the old days, before the establishment of official police systems, night patrols of citizens were undoubtedly necessary to protect communities from the robberies and murders of the criminal element; but in the face of the record of New York's Finest, what justification is there for such patrols today?" He would regret, the Mayor stated, having to resort to countermeasures in the all-over public interest. He knew such a step would prove unnecessary. "I urge all already functioning groups of this nature, and groups in the process of organizing, to get in touch immediately with their police precincts for instructions."

By Wednesday morning the failure of the Mayor's radio appeal was apparent. The most irresponsible rumors circulated in the City: that the National Guard had been called out, that the Mayor had made an emergency-flight personal appeal to President Truman in the White House, that the Police Commissioner had resigned, that in a clash between a Washington Heights CAT patrol and police two persons had been killed and nine injured. The Mayor canceled all appointments for the day and remained in continuous conference. Top officials of the Police Department were unanimous in favor of presenting ultimatums to the CAT groups: Disband at once or face arrest. The Mayor refused to sanction such action. No disorders had been reported, he pointed out; apparently the groups were maintaining internal discipline and restricting themselves to their avowed activities. Besides, the movement by now embraced too many people for such measures. "They might lead to open clashes and we'd have riots all over the City. That might mean calling for troops. I'll exhaust every peaceful means before I lay New York open to that."

By midafternoon Wednesday word came that "the central committee" of "the combined Citizens' Action Teams of New York City" had engaged the vast and windy Metropol Hall on Eighth Avenue for "a monster mass meeting" Thursday night. Immediately after, the Mayor's secretary announced a delegation of this committee.

They filed in, a little nervous but with stubborn looks on their faces. The Mayor and his conferees regarded the deputation with curiosity. They seemed a cross-section of the City's people. There were no sharp or shady faces among them. The spokesman, a tall man in his 30s with the look of a mechanic, identified himself as "Jerome K. Frankburner, veteran."

"We've come here, Mr. Mayor, to invite you to talk at our mass meeting tomorrow night. Metropol Hall seats twenty thousand people, we'll have a radio and television setup, and everybody in the City will be sitting in. It's democracy, it's American. What we'd like you to tell us, Mr. Mayor, is what you've done to stop the Cat and what plans you and your subordinates have for the future. And if it's straight talk that makes sense we guarantee that by Friday morning there won't be a C.A.T. in business. Will you come?"

The Mayor said, "Would you gentlemen wait here?" and he took his people into a private office next door.

"Jack, don't do it!"

"Why not, Barney?"

"What can we tell them that we haven't told them a hundred times already? Let's ban the meeting. If there's trouble, crack down on their leaders."

"I don't know, Barney," said one of the Mayor's advisers, a power in the Party. "They're no hoodlums. These people represent a lot of good votes. We'd better go easy."

There were other expressions of opinion, some siding with the Police Commissioner, some with the Party man.

"You haven't said anything, Inspector Queen," said the Mayor suddenly. "What's your opinion?"

"The way I see it," replied Inspector Queen, "it's going to be mighty tough for the Cat to stay away from that meeting."

"Or to put it another way," said the Mayor—"although that's a very valuable thought, Inspector—I was elected on a people's platform and I'm going to stay on it."

He opened the door and said, "I'll be there, gentlemen."

The events of the night of September 22 began in an atmosphere of seriousness and responsibility. Metropol Hall was filled by 7 P.M. and an overflow crowd gathered which soon numbered thousands. But there was exemplary order and the heavy concentration of police had little to do. The inevitable enterprising notions distributor had sent hawkers out to peddle ticklers with a cat's head on the end and oversized C.A.T. lapel buttons of cardboard, and others were peddling orange-and-black cats' heads with grisly expressions which were recognizably advance stocks of Hallowe'en gimcrackery, but there were few buyers in the crowd and the police hustled the vendors along. There were noticeably few children and an almost total absence of horseplay. Inside the Hall people were either quiet or spoke in whispers. In the streets around the Hall the crowds were patient and well-behaved; too patient and too well-behaved, according to old hands of the Traffic Division, who would have welcomed, it appeared, a few dozen drunks, a rousing fistfight or two, or a picket line of Communist demonstrators. But no drunks were visible, the people were strangely passive, and if Communists were among them it was as individuals.

The Traffic brass, testing the wind, put in a call for more mounted police and radio-patrol cars.

A noose dropped quietly around the entire area at 8 P.M. Between 51st and 57th Streets south to north, and between Seventh and Ninth Avenues east to west, solid lines of police appeared to screen off each intersection. Automobile traffic was detoured. Pedestrians were permitted to penetrate the police lines entering the area, but none were allowed to leave before identifying themselves and answering certain questions.

Throughout the district hundreds of plainclothesmen circulated.

Inside the Hall there were hundreds of others.

Among them was one Ellery Queen.

On the platform sat the central committee of the combined Citizens' Action Teams of New York. They were a polyglot group in which no single face stood out; they might have been a jury in a courtroom, and they all wore the intent but self-conscious expressions of jurymen. The Mayor and his official party occupied the seats of honor—"which means," as the Mayor remarked behind his hand to Dr. Edward Cazalis, "where they can keep an eye on us." The speaker's rostrum was flanked with massed American flags. Radio and public address microphones clustered before it. The television people were set up and waiting.

The meeting was opened at 9 P.M. by Jerome K. Frankburner, acting chairman of the evening. Frankburner wore a GI uniform. On the breast of his tunic glittered several decorations, and his sleeve carried an impressive weight of overseas stripes. Above the military figure hung a grim face. He spoke without notes, quietly.

"This is the voice of a New Yorker," Frankburner began. "It doesn't matter what my name is or where I live. I'm speaking for hundreds of New York neighborhood groups who have organized to protect our families and our neighbors' families from a citywide menace. Lots of us fought in the last war and we're all lawabiding Americans. We represent no self-seeking group. We have no axes to grind. You won't find any chiselers, racketeers, or Commies among us. We're Democrats, Republicans, Independents, Liberals, Socialists. We're Protestants, Catholics, Jews. We're whites and we're Negroes. We're business people, white collar people, laboring people, professional people. We're second-generation Americans and we're fourth-generation Americans. We're New York.

"I'm not going to make a speech. We're not here to listen to me. All I want to do is ask a few questions.

"Mr. Mayor, people are being murdered right and left by some lunatic. It's almost four months since the Cat got going and he's still on the prowl. All right, you can't catch him or you haven't been able to yet. Meanwhile what protection do we have? I'm not saying anything against our police. They're a hardworking bunch like the rest of us. But the people of New York ask you: What have our police done about it?"

A sound went through the Hall and met another from outdoors. It was very little, a distant flutter of thunder, but in the Hall and throughout the surrounding streets police nervously fingered their clubs and tightened ranks and on the platform beside the speaker the Mayor and his Police Commissioner were seen to go a little pale.

"To the last man and woman," said Frankburner, a ring coming into his voice, "we're against vigilante law. But we're asking you, Mr. Mayor, what other recourse we have. My wife or my mother might be feeling that silk cord around her throat tonight, and the police wouldn't be in on it till it was all over but the funeral arrangements.

"Mr. Mayor, we've invited you here tonight to tell us what plans you and the law-enforcement authority have for giving us the protection we feel we haven't got.

"Ladies and gentlemen, His Honor, the Mayor of New York."

The mayor spoke for a long time. He spoke in a sober, neighborly way, exercising his considerable charm and knowledge of the City's people. He traced the history of the New York Police Department, its growth, its gigantic organization, its complexity. He cited the record of its eighteen thousand men and women in guarding law and maintaining order. He gave some reassuring statistics on homicide arrests and convictions. He went into the legal and social aspects of vigilantism and its threats to democratic institutions, its tendency to degenerate from original high purposes to mob rule and the satisfaction of the worst passions of the lowest elements. He pointed to the dangers—violence begetting violence, leading to military intervention, to martial law, and to the suppression of civil liberties, "the first step on the road to fascism and totalitarianism."

"And all this," the Mayor said goodhumoredly, "because temporarily we have failed to locate a single homicidal maniac in the haystack of a city of over seven and one-half millions of people."

But the Mayor's speech, for all its ease and sanity and persuasiveness, was not eliciting those little signs and responses by which veteran public speakers gauge the success or failure of their exertions. This audience gave no signs and responses whatever. It simply sat, or stood, listening. A multibreathing, unstirred entity waiting for something . . . a loosening word.

The Mayor knew it; his voice took on an edge.

His party knew it; they whispered to one another on the platform with exaggerated ease, conscious of the eyes, the television cameras.

Rather abruptly, the Mayor asked the Police Commissioner to give an accounting of the specific measures already taken and "being planned" for the apprehension of the Cat.

As the commissioner approached the rostrum, Ellery rose in the audience and began to walk down the central aisle toward the press section, scanning the ranks of human heads.

He spotted Jimmy McKell shortly after the Commissioner began to speak.

McKell twisted about in his seat, glaring at a girl three rows behind him. The girl, pink, was looking at the Commissioner.

Celeste Phillips.

Ellery could not have said what thought, feeling, intuition kept him in the vicinity. Perhaps it was merely the sight of familiar faces.

He dropped to his heels in the aisle at the end of Celeste's row.

He was uneasy. There was something in the air of Metropol Hall that affected him unpleasantly. He saw that others were in the grip of the same disquiet. A sort of mass autointoxication. The crowd breathing its own poisons.

And then he knew what it was.

Fear.

The crowd breathing its own fear. It came out of people in invisible droplets, loaded down the air.

What had seemed patience, passivity, expectancy . . . nothing but fear.

They were not listening to the voice of the man on the platform.

They were listening to the inner voice of fear.

*"THE CAT!"*

It came as the Commissioner turned a page of his notes in the silence.

He looked up very quickly.

The Mayor, Dr. Cazalis, half-rose.

Twenty thousand heads turned.

It had been a woman's scream, pitched to a rare level and held there. It raised the flesh.

A group of men were pushing their way with flailing arms through the standees at the rear of the Hall.

The Commissioner began to say: "Get that woman qui—"

*"THE CAT!"*

A little eddy of noise began to spin; another; another. A man rose from his seat, a woman, a couple, a group. Craning.

"Ladies and gentlemen, please be seated. Just a hyster—"

*"THE CAT!"*

"Please!" The Mayor, on the rostrum beside the Commissioner. "Please! Please!"

People were running along the side aisles.

At the rear, a fight was going on.

*"THE CAT!"*

Somewhere upstairs a man's voice bellowed. It was choked off, as if he were being throttled.

"Take your seats! Officers!"

Bluecoats materialized all over the auditorium.

The disturbance at the rear was now a yeasty corruption, eating into the main aisle, nibbling at the seats.

*"THE CAT!"*

A dozen women began to scream.

*"HE'S HERE!"*

Like a stone, it smashed against the great mirror of the audience and the audience shivered and broke. Little cracks widened magically. Where masses had sat or stood, gaps appeared, grew rapidly, splintered in crazy directions. Men began climbing over seats, using their fists. People went down. The police vanished. Trickles of shrieks ran together. Metropol Hall became a great cataract obliterating human sound.

On the platform the Mayor, Frankburner, the Commissioner, were shouting into the public address microphones, jostling one another. Their voices mingled; a faint blend, lost in the uproar.

The aisles were logjammed, people punching, twisting, falling toward the exits.

Overhead a balcony rail snapped; a man fell into the orchestra. People were carried down the balcony staircases. Some slipped, disappeared. At the upstairs fire exits hordes struggled over a living, shrieking carpet.

Suddenly the whole contained mass found vents and shot out into the streets, into the frozen thousands, in a moment boiling them to frenzy, turning the area about Metropol Hall into a giant frying pan. Its ingredients sizzled over the police lines, melting men, horses, machines, overflowing the intersections and pouring uptown and down, toward Broadway and toward Ninth Avenue—a smoking liquid that burned everything in its path.

Ellery remembered shouting Jimmy McKell's name as the stampede began, remembered pointing to a petrified Celeste Phillips, trying himself to buck the wall of flesh which pushed him back. He managed to struggle on to a seat, keep his footing there. He saw Jimmy fight his way slowly over three rows, reach the terrified girl, seize her waist. Then they were sucked into the mass and Ellery lost them.

He devoted himself thereafter to keeping off the floor.

A long time afterward he found his father helping the Mayor and the Commissioner direct rescue operations. They had no time for more than a few words. Both were hatless, bleeding, in tatters; all that was left of the Inspector's jacket was the right sleeve. No, he had not seen McKell or the Phillips girl. Or Dr. Cazalis. His eye kept stealing toward the neat and lengthening line of the dead. Then the Inspector was called away and Ellery plodded back into Metropol Hall to help with the casualties. He was one of an impromptu army: police, firemen, ambulance doctors, Red Cross workers, volunteers from the streets. Sirens kept up their outcry, silencing the moans of the injured.

Other horrors took shape as reports kept pouring in. The mob in fleeing had accidentally broken some shop windows in the side streets between Eighth Avenue and Broadway. Looting had begun, led by hoodlums, loiterers, kid gangs. Bystanders who had tried to interfere had been beaten; shopkeepers had been assaulted and in some instances knifed. For a long time the looting had threatened to get out of hand; there was a furious hour as theaters emptying into Broadway had fed the chaos. Hotels had locked their doors. But the police drove patrol cars into the mobs, mounted patrolmen charged concentrations of rioters, and gradually they were dispersed. Hundreds of stores had sustained broken windows and rifled stocks as far south as 42nd Street. Polyclinic Hospital was bedding the injured in corridors; Red Cross emergency first-aid stations had been set up throughout the Times Square area. Ambulances were speeding into the district from as far north as Fordham Hospital. Lindy's, Toots Shor's, Jack Dempsey's, other restaurants in the vicinity were sending coffee and sandwiches to the relief workers.

At 4:45 A.M. one Evarts Jones, an attorney, handed the following statement to the press:

> I am authorized by Jerome K. Frankburner, chairman of tonight's disastrous meeting, and by the central committee of the so-called CATs of Greater New York City, to announce that all units will be immediately disbanded and organized patrol activities will cease.
>
> Mr. Frankburner and the committee speak for all citizens who joined in this well-meant but ill-advised popular movement when they express their great sorrow and profound regret over what occurred in Metropol Hall last night.

Pressed by reporters for a personal statement, Frankburner shook his head. "I'm too punchy to say anything. What can anybody say? We were dead wrong. The Mayor was dead right."

At dawn the Cat Riots were quelled and the Four Days were a bloody paragraph in the unwritten almanacs.

Later, the Mayor in silence distributed the statistics of the night's disorders to the press.

*The Dead*
| | |
|---|---|
| Women | 19 |
| Men | 14 |
| Children | 6 |
| TOTAL | 39 |

*Seriously Injured*
| | |
|---|---|
| Women | 68 |
| Men | 34 |
| Children | 13 |
| TOTAL | 115 |

*Minor Injuries, Fractures, Abrasions, etc.*
| | |
|---|---|
| Women | 189 |
| Men | 152 |
| Children | 10 |
| TOTAL | 351 |

*Arrested on Charges of Looting, Unlawful Assemblage, Inciting to Violence, etc.*

127 persons (including minors)

*Property Damage (estimated)*

$4,500,000

The woman whose screams touched off the panic and the rioting that followed, said the Mayor, was trampled to death. Her name was Mrs. Maybelle Legontz, 48, a widow, childless. Her body was identified at 2:38 A.M. by a brother, Stephen Chorumkowski, steamfitter, of 421 West 65th Street. Persons in the audience in the immediate vicinity of Mrs. Legontz had testified that to the best of their recollection she had not been attacked or molested by anyone; but the standees had been packed together and an accidental nudge by some bystander may have exploded her nervous fears.

Mrs. Legontz had a medical history of neurasthenia, a condition which first appeared following the death of her husband, a sand-hog, of the "bends."

There was no possibility that she had been the Cat.

It had been, the Mayor agreed with the reporters, one of the worst out-

breaks in New York's history, perhaps the worst since the draft riots of
1863.

Ellery found himself in the milky darkness seated on one of the
benches of Rockefeller Plaza. There was no one else in the Plaza but
Prometheus. Ellery's head was dancy and the chill of the New York
morning against the torn places on his hands and face was deliciously
personal, keeping him in a rare consciousness.

Prometheus spoke from his watery niche in the sunken court and
Ellery took a certain comfort in his company.

"You're wondering how it came about," began the golden giant, "that
this beast in human form you call the Cat has been able, through the mere
bawling of his name, to drive thousands of men out of their heads and
send them like frightened animals to an animal death.

"I'm so old I don't recall where I originally came from, except that it's
supposed to have been without women—which I find very unconvinc-
ing—but I seem to remember that I found it necessary to bring men the
gift of fire. If I really did that, I'm the founder of civilization, so I feel
qualified to make certain extended remarks on the late unpleasantness.

"The truth is, what happened last night had nothing to do with the Cat
at all.

"The world today reminds me of the very old days, when religions
were being born. I mean, modern society resembles primitive society to
an amusing degree. There's the same concentration on democratic gov-
ernment, for example, while certain of your number who claim to be in
touch with higher powers push to the top to rule. You make the same
virtue out of common names and common bloods, investing both with
mystic mumbo jumbo. In sexual affairs, your women are equally overre-
spected and kept inside a convenient cage of sanctity, while important affairs are arrogated to themselves by your males. You've even reverted to
food taboos in your worship of diets and vitamins.

"But I find the most interesting similarity," continued Prometheus, apparently impervious to the cold dawn which was making Ellery rattle like
an old gourd, "in the way you react to your environment. The crowd, not
the individual, is the thinking unit. And the thinking power of a crowd, as
last night's unfortunate events demonstrated, is of an extremely low order. You're bursting with ignorance, and ignorance breeds panicky fears.
You're afraid of nearly everything, but most of all you're afraid of personal contact with the problems of your time. So you're only too happy
to huddle together inside the high magic wall of tradition and let your
leaders manipulate the mysteries. They stand between you and the terrors
of the unknown.

"But once in a while your priests of power fail you and suddenly you're left to face the unknown in person. Those on whom you relied to bring you salvation and luck, to shield you from the mysteries of life and of death, no longer stand between you and the dreadful darkness. All over your world the magic wall has crumbled, leaving your people paralyzed on the edge of the Pit.

"In such a state of affairs," said Prometheus, "is it to be wondered at that a single hysterical voice, screaming a single silly taboo, can frighten thousands into running away?"

Ellery awoke on the bench to pain and an early sun burnishing his tutor. There were people in the Plaza and automobiles were rushing by. It seemed to him that someone was making an unlawful lot of noise and he got up angrily.

The cries were coming from the west, hoarse and exultant.

Boy's voices, booming in the canyons.

Ellery limped up the steps, crossed the street, and made his way stiffly toward Sixth Avenue.

There's no hurry, he thought. They're peddling the obituary of C.A.T. So many dead, so many injured, so many dollars' worth of wreckage. Read all about it.

No, thank you. Hot Coffee would do nicely instead.

Ellery limped along trying not to think at all.

But bubbles kept bobbing up.

Obituary of C.A.T. Obituary of *Cat* . . . now that would be something. Obituary of Cat. Come seven.

Our wishes lengthen as our sun declines.

Ellery laughed.

Or as another immortal observer put it, I should of stood in bed. *whee! s4ll mp*

Brother Q, you're through. Only you had to rise from the dead. To chase a Cat.

What next?

What do you do?

Where do you look?

How do you look?

In the fresh shadow of the Music Hall marquee the boy's mouth was going through an acrobatic exercise under his popping eyes.

Never an ill wind, thought Ellery as he watched the pile of papers dwindle.

And he began to pass, to cross Sixth Avenue for his coffee, when a shouted syllable made sense and something on top of the heap flew up and lodged in his brain.

Ellery fumbled for a coin. The coin felt cold.

*"Extra."*

He stood there being elbowed right and left.

There was the familiar Cat, but he had an eighth tail and it was not a question mark.

# 8

Her name was Stella Petrucchi. She lived with her family on Thompson Street, less than half a mile below Washington Square. She was 22 years of age; of Italian parentage; of the Roman Catholic faith.

For almost five years Stella Petrucchi had been employed as a stenographer in the same law office on Madison Avenue and 40th Street.

Her father had been in the United States for forty-five years. He was a wholesale fish merchant in Fulton Market. He came from Livorno. Stella's mother was also from the province of Toscana.

Stella was the sixth of seven children. Of her three brothers, one was a priest and the other two were in business with George Petrucchi. Of her three sisters, the eldest was a nun of the Carmelite order, one was married to an Italian cheese and olive oil importer, the third was a student at Hunter College. All the Petrucchi children but the priest, who was the eldest, had been born in New York City.

They had thought at first that Stella was part of the immortal debris littering the vicinity of Metropol Hall, overlooked in the streetcleaning. But the silk cord around the girl's neck gave her the special distinction conferred by the Cat and they found that when they pulled her head back by the tumbled black hair and exposed her throat.

A pair of patrolmen had run across her body a block and a half from Metropol Hall at just about the time the Mayor was giving reporters the statistics of the carnage. It was lying on the cement of an alley between two stores, ten feet from the Eighth Avenue sidewalk.

She had been strangled, said the Medical Examiner's man, some time before midnight.

The identification was made by Father Petrucchi and the married sister, Mrs. Teresa Bascalone. Mr. and Mrs. George Petrucchi collapsed on being informed of the tragedy.

A man, Howard Whithacker, 32, who gave a West 4th Street rooming house address, was closely questioned.

Whithacker was a very tall, lean, blackhaired man with closely set diamond black eyes, a horny skin, and Gothic cheekbones. He looked considerably older than the age he gave.

His occupation, he stated, was "unsuccessful poet." On being pressed, he grudgingly admitted that he "kept body and soul together" by working as a counterman in a Greenwich Avenue cafeteria.

Whithacker said that he had known Stella Petrucchi for sixteen months. They had met in the cafeteria late one night the previous spring. She had been out on a date and had stopped in with her escort at two in the morning. The escort, "a deep Bronx troglodyte with handpainted mermaids on his tie," had jeered at Whithacker's midwestern speech. Whithacker had picked up a baked apple from the counter between them, leaned over, and crammed the apple into the offending mouth. "After that, Stella used to drop in almost every night and we became kind of friendly."

He denied angrily having had an affair with the girl. When this line of questioning persisted, he became quite violent and had to be subdued. "She was a pure, sweet soul," he yelled. "Sex with her was out of the question!"

Whithacker talked reluctantly about his background. He hailed from Beatrice, Nebraska. His people were farmers; the original stock had been Scotch—a great-grandfather had come up out of Kentucky in 1829 in a group of Campbellites. There was Pawnee blood in the family and a splatter of Bohemian and Danish. "I'm one of the percentage Americans," said Howard Whithacker. "All decimal points. You know?" At home, he said, he attended the Disciples of Christ church.

He was a graduate of the University of Nebraska.

At the beginning of the war he had enlisted in the Navy, "winding up in the Pacific. I was blown into the water by a kamikaze who darn near made it. My ears still ring sometimes. It had a remarkable effect on my poetry."

After the war, finding Beatrice confining, he went to New York—"financed by my brother Duggin, who thinks I'm poetry's gift to Gage County, Nebraska."

His sole published work since his arrival two years before consisted of a verse entitled "Corn in the Coral." It had appeared in Greenwich Village's newspaper, the *Villager*, in the spring of 1947; Whithacker produced a greasy clipping to prove it. "My brother Duggin is now convinced I'm not another John Neihardt. However," he said, "I have received considerable encouragement from fellow-poets in the Village, and of course

Stella adored me. We have regular 3 A.M. poetry-reading sessions in the cafeteria. I live Spartanly but adequately. The death of Stella Petrucchi leaves an empty pigeonhole in my heart; she was a dear child without a brain cell in her head."

He denied indignantly having taken money from her.

As to the events of the night of September 22, Whithacker stated that Thursday night being his night off, he had met Stella outside her office building to take her to the Metropol Hall mass meeting. "A cat poem had been taking shape in my mind for some time," he explained. "It was important that I attend. Stella, of course, always looked forward to our Thursday nights together."

They had walked crosstown, stopping in at an Eighth Avenue spaghetti house "owned by a cousin of Stella's father. I discussed the Citizens' Action Teams movement with Mr. Ferriquancchi and we were both surprised to find that the subject made Stella extremely nervous. Ignazio said we oughtn't to go if Stella felt that way and I offered to go alone, but Stella said no, she wanted to go, at last somebody was doing something about the murders. She said she asked the Virgin Mother every night to keep everyone she knew safe."

They had managed to get into Metropol Hall and had found downstairs seats well to the front of the auditorium.

"When the stampede started, Stella and I tried to hold on to each other, but the damn cattle tore us apart. The last I saw of her she was being carried off in a crowd of lunatics, screaming something at me. But I couldn't hear. I never saw her alive again."

Whithacker had been lucky, suffering no more than a torn pocket and some pummeling.

"I crowded with a few other people in a doorway across from the Hall to keep out of harm's way. When the worst was over I started searching for Stella. I couldn't find her among the dead or injured at the Hall so I began looking along Eighth Avenue, the side streets, Broadway. I wandered around all night."

Whithacker was asked why he had not telephoned to the Petrucchis; the family had been up all night frantic over Stella's failure to come home. They had not known about her appointment with him.

"That's the reason. They didn't know about me. Stella said it was better that way. She said they were strict Catholics and it would only cause a ruckus if they found out she was going around with a non-Catholic. She didn't mind her father's cousin Ignazio knowing about us, she said, because Mr. Ferriquancchi is anti-Papist and nobody in the Petrucchi family has anything to do with him anyway."

At 7:30 A.M. Whithacker had returned to Metropol Hall for another checkup, intending to telephone the Petrucchis "despite their religious scruples" if this last effort to locate Stella failed.

At his first question he was seized by the police.

"I must have passed the entrance to that alley a dozen times during the night," Howard Whithacker said. "But it was dark, and how was I to know Stella was laid out in there?"

Whithacker was held "for further questioning."

"No," Inspector Richard Queen told reporters, "we have absolutely nothing on him. But we want to check his story, and so on." The "and so on" was taken by the press—correctly—to refer both to related matters in the recent past and to a certain interesting wildness of eye, manner, and speech in Stella Petrucchi's friend.

There was no medical evidence of rape or attempted rape.

The girl's purse was missing; but it was found later, its contents intact, in the debris of the Hall. A gold religious medal on a fine chain about her neck had not been touched.

The strangling cord was of the familiar tussah silk, dyed salmon-pink. It had been knotted at the nape exactly as in the previous cases. Laboratory examination of the cord turned up nothing of significance.

It seemed clear that Stella Petrucchi had taken refuge in the alley after being hurled into the street with the rest of the Metropol audience. But whether the Cat had been waiting for her in the alley, or had entered with her, or had followed her in, there was no way of telling.

The probability was that she had suspected nothing until the clutch of the silk. She might well have entered the alley at the Cat's invitation, assuming he caught up with her and offered to "protect" her from harm at the hands of the mob.

As usual, he had left no trail.

It was past noon when Ellery pulled himself up the stairs to find the door of the Queen apartment unlocked. Wondering, he went in; and the first thing he saw on entering his bedroom was a torn nylon stocking dangling from the seat of his ladderback chair. Over one of the chair posts was hooked a white brassière.

He bent over his bed and shook her.

Her eyes popped open.

"You're all right."

Celeste shuddered. "Don't *ever* do that again! For a split century I thought it was the Cat."

"Is Jimmy . . . ?"

"Jimmy's all right, too."

Ellery found himself sitting on the edge of his bed; the back of his neck throbbed again. "I've often dreamed about this situation," he said, rubbing it.

"What situation?" She stretched her long legs stiff under the sheet, moaning, "Oh, I ache."

"I know," said Ellery. "This all happened in a *The New Yorker*, Peter Arno drawing."

"What?" said Celeste sleepily. "Is it still today?"

Her black hair coursed over his pillow in sweet poetic streams. "But exhaustion," Ellery explained, "is the enemy of poetry."

"*What?* You look kind of dilapidated. Are *you* all right?"

"I will be once I get the hang of sleeping again."

"I am sorry!" Celeste clutched the sheet to her and sat up quickly. "I wasn't really awake. Er, I'm not . . . I mean, I didn't want to poke around in your bureau . . ."

"You cad," said a stern voice. "Would you boot out an unclothed maiden?"

"Jimmy!" said Celeste happily.

Jimmy McKell was in the bedroom doorway, one arm about a large, mysterious-looking paper sack.

"Well," said Ellery. "The McKell. Indestructible, I see."

"I see you made it, too, Ellery."

They grinned at each other. Jimmy was wearing one of Ellery's most cherished sports jackets, which was too small for him, and Ellery's newest tie.

"Mine were torn clean off me," explained Jimmy. "How you feeling, woman?"

"Like September Morn at an American Legion convention. *Would* you two step into the next room?"

In the living room Jimmy scowled. "You look beat, old-timer. What's with the Petrucchi girl?"

"Oh, you know about that."

"Heard it on your radio this morning." Jimmy set the sack down. "What's in that bag?"

"Some hardtack and pemmican. Your larder'd run dry. Have you eaten anything, bud?"

"No."

"Neither have we. Hey, Celeste!" Jimmy shouted. "Never mind making with the clothes. Rustle us some breakfast!"

Celeste laughed from Ellery's bathroom.

"You two seem awfully gay," remarked Ellery, feeling for the arm-chair.

"Funny how it hits you." Jimmy laughed, too. "You get mixed up in something like last night's fandango and all of a sudden everything drops into the slot. Even stupidity. I thought I'd seen everything in the Pacific, but I hadn't. The war was murder, all right, but organized. You wear a uniform and you carry a gun and you take great big orders and somebody cooks your chow and you kill or get killed, all according to the book. But last night . . . tooth and claw. Man stripped to the bloody bones. Disintegration of the tribe. Every fellow-cannibal your enemy. It's good to be alive, that's all."

"Hello, Celeste," said Ellery.

Her clothes were macerated and although she had evidently brushed them and applied pins to secret parts, they looked like hardening lava. Her legs were rowdy; she carried her stockings.

"I don't suppose you'd have an old pair of nylons around, Mr. Queen?"

"No," said Ellery gravely. "My father, you know."

"Oh, dear. Well! I'll fix you men something in a jiffy," and Celeste went into the kitchen with the sack.

"Superior, hey?" Jimmy stared at the swinging door. "You'll note, Brother Queen, that the lady made no apology for her appearance. Definitely superior."

"How'd you two manage to keep together last night?" asked Ellery, closing his eyes.

"Now don't cork off on us, Ellery." Jimmy began setting the drop-leaf table. "Why, the fact is we didn't."

"Oh?" said Ellery, opening one eye.

"We lost each other right after I got to her. She doesn't remember how she got out, and neither do I. We kept hunting for each other all night. I found her around 5 A.M. sitting on the steps of Polyclinic Hospital, bawling."

Ellery closed the eye.

"How do you like your bacon, Mr. Queen?" called Celeste.

Jimmy said, "Are you there?" and Ellery mumbled something. "Curly and wet, he says! — What, Ellery?"

"The last word," said Ellery, "was 'bawling.' "

"Her eyes out. I tell you, I was touched. Anyway, we had some coffee at an allnight joint and then we went looking for you. But you'd disappeared. We thought you'd probably got out all right and gone home, so we came up here. Nobody home, so I said to Celeste, 'He won't mind,' and I climbed up the fire escape. For an eye, Ellery, you're very careless about your windows."

"Go on," said Ellery, when Jimmy stopped.

"I don't know if I can explain it. Why we came, I mean. I don't think Celeste and I said two dozen words to each other after we clutched this morning. I think we both realized your position for the first time and we wanted to tell you we've been a couple of firstclass *schlemihls* and didn't quite know how to do it." Jimmy straightened a spoon. "This thing is awfully gross," he said to the spoon. "The war all over again. In another form. The individual doesn't mean a damn. Human dignity gets flushed down the drain. You have to get up to your elbow in muck to hold on to it. I didn't see that till last night, Ellery."

"Neither did I." Celeste was in the kitchen doorway with a piece of toast in one hand and a buttery knife in the other. Ellery thought, Piggott and Johnson lost them last night; they must have. "You were right, Mr. Queen. After what we saw last night you were right."

"About what, Celeste?"

"About suspecting Jimmy and me. Jimmy and me or anybody."

"I guess what we wanted to hear you say was 'Come back, all is forgiven,' " grinned Jimmy. But then he began on the cutlery again.

"So you waited here for me."

"When we heard the news we knew what was keeping you. I made Celeste get into your bed—she was dead on her feet—and I parked on the sofa in here. Anything to connect the Petrucchi girl with the others?"

"No."

"What about this cornhusker-poet character? What's his name?"

"Whithacker?" Ellery shrugged. "Dr. Cazalis seems interested in him and they're going to examine him carefully."

"I'm one hell of a newspaperman." Jimmy banged a spoon down. "All right, I'll say it. Do you want us back?"

"I don't have anything for you to do, Jimmy."

"For me!" cried Celeste.

"Or for you."

"You don't want us back."

"I do. But I have no work for you." Ellery got up, groping for a cigaret. But his hands dropped. "I don't know where to turn. That's the truth. I'm absolutely hung up."

Jimmy and Celeste looked swiftly at each other. Then Jimmy said, "You're also absolutely pooped. What you need is to slice a herring with Morpheus. Hey, Celeste! *The coffee!*"

Ellery awoke to the sound of a loud voice.

He switched on the night light.

8:12.

The voice was driving. Ellery crawled out of bed, pulled on his robe and slippers, and hurried to the living room.

The voice was the radio's. His father was lying back in the armchair. Jimmy and Celeste crouched on the sofa in a nest of newspapers.

"You two still here?"

Jimmy grunted. His long chin was nuzzling his chest and Celeste kept rubbing her drawnup bare leg in a reassuring way.

The Inspector was all bones and gray wilt.

"Dad—"

"Listen."

"— reported tonight," said the voice. "A third-rail short circuit on the BMT subway at Canal Street caused a panic and forty-six persons were treated for injuries. Trains out of Grand Central Terminal and Pennsylvania Station are running from ninety minutes to two hours behind schedule. The parkways out of the City are a solid double line of cars as far north as Greenwich and White Plains. Traffic is clogged for a large area around the Manhattan approaches to the Holland and Lincoln Tunnels and the George Washington Bridge. Nassau County authorities report that traffic conditions on the major Long Island parkways are out of control. New Jersey, Connecticut, and upstate New York police report—"

Ellery snapped the radio off.

"What is it?" he asked wildly. "War?" His glance flew to the windows, as if he expected to see a flaming sky.

"New York's turned Malay," said Jimmy with a laugh. "The *amok*. They'll have to rewrite the psychology books." He began to get up, but Celeste pulled him back.

"Fighting? Panic?"

"That Metropol Hall business last night was just the beginning, Ellery." The Inspector was fighting something, nausea or rage. "It snapped a vital part. Started a sort of chain reaction. Or maybe it was the Petrucchi murder on top of the panic and riot—that was bad timing. Anyway, it's all over the City. Been spreading all day."

"They're running," said Celeste. "Everybody's running."

"Running where?"

"Nobody seems to know. Just running."

"It's the Black Death all over again," said Jimmy McKell. "Didn't you know? We're back in the Middle Ages. New York is now the pesthole of the Western Hemisphere, Ellery. In two weeks you'll be able to shoot hyenas in Macy's basement."

"Shut up, McKell." The old man's head rolled on the back of his chair. "There's a lot of disorder, son, a lot. Looting, holdups . . . It's been particularly bad on Fifth Avenue, 86th around Lexington, 125th, upper Broadway, and around Maiden Lane downtown. And traffic accidents, hundreds of traffic accidents. I've never seen anything like it. Not in New York."

Ellery went to one of the windows. The street was empty. A fire engine screamed somewhere. The sky glowed to the southwest.

"And they say," began Celeste.

"Who says?" Jimmy laughed again. "Well, that's the point, my friends, whereupon today I'm proud to be one of the capillaries in the circulation system of organized opinion. We've really swung it this time, comrades." He kicked a drooping newspaper. "Responsible journalism! And the blessed radio—"

"Jimmy," said Celeste.

"Well, old Rip's got to hear the news, hasn't he? He's slept through history, Miss Phillips. Did you know, sir, that there's a citywide quarantine? It's a fact. Or is it? That all schools will be shut down indefinitely— O happy day? That Father Knickerbocker's chickens are to be evacuated to camps outside the metropolitan area? That all flights from La Guardia, Newark, and Idlewild have been nixed? That the Cat's made of extremely green cheese?"

Ellery was silent.

"Also," said Jimmy McKell, "Beldame Rumor hath it that the Mayor's been attacked by the Cat, that the FBI's taken over Police Headquarters, that the Stock Exchange positively will not open its doors tomorrow—and that's a fact, seeing that tomorrow's Saturday." Jimmy unfolded himself. "Ellery, I went downtown this afternoon. The shop is a madhouse. Everybody's busy as little beavers denying rumors and believing every new one that comes in. I stopped on my way back to see if Mother and Father were maintaining their equilibrium and do you know what? I saw a Park Avenue doorman get hysterics. Brother, that's the end of the world." He swiped his nose backhandedly, glaring. "It's enough to make you cancel your membership in the human race. Come on, let's all get drunk."

"And the Cat?" Ellery asked his father.

"No news."

"Whithacker?"

"Cazalis and the psychiatrists have been working on him all day. Still are, far as I know. But they're not doing any backbends. And we didn't find a thing in his West 4th Street flop."

"Do I have to do it all by myself?" demanded Jimmy, pouring Scotch. "None for you, Celeste."

"Inspector, what's going to happen now?"

"I don't know," said the Inspector, "and what's more, Miss Phillips, I don't think I give an Irish damn." He got up. "Ellery, if Headquarters calls, I've gone to bed."

The old man shuffled out.

"Here's to the Cat," said Jimmy, lofting his glass. "May his giblets wither."

"If you're going to start toping, Jimmy," said Celeste, "I'm going home. I'm going home anyway."

"Right. To mine."

"Yours?"

"You can't stay up in that foul nest of underprivilege alone. And you may as well meet Father now and get it over with. Mother, of course, will be nightingale soup."

"It's sweet of you, Jimmy," Celeste was all olive-pink. "But just impossible."

"You can sleep in Queen's bed but you can't sleep in mine! What is this?"

She laughed, but she was angry. "It's been the ghastliest and most wonderful twenty-four hours of my life, darling. Don't spoil it."

"Spoil it! Why, you proletarian snob!"

"I can't let your parents think I'm some dead-end kid to be taken in off the streets."

"You are a snob."

"Jimmy." Ellery turned from the fireplace. "Is it the Cat you're worrying about?"

"Always. But this time the rabbits, too. It's a breed that bites."

"You can stop worrying about the Cat, at any rate. Celeste is safe."

Celeste looked bewildered.

Jimmy said, "The hell you say."

"For that matter, so are you." Ellery explained the diminishing-age pattern of the murders. When he had finished he packed a pipe and lit it, watching them, and all the time they stood peering at him as if he were performing a minor miracle.

"And nobody saw that," muttered Jimmy. "Nobody."

"But what does it mean?" Celeste cried.

"I don't know. But Stella Petrucchi was 22; and you and Jimmy being older than that, the Cat's passed your age groups by." Just relief, he thought, wondering why he was disappointed.

"May I print that, Ellery?" Jimmy's face fell. "I forgot. *Noblesse oblige.*"

"Well, I think," said Celeste defiantly, "that people ought to be told, Mr. Queen. Especially now, when they're so frightened."

Ellery stared at her. "Wait a minute."

He went into his study.

When he returned he said, "The Mayor agrees with you, Celeste. Things are very bad . . . I'm holding a press conference at 10 o'clock tonight and I'm going on the air with the Mayor at 10:30. From City Hall. Jimmy, don't double-cross me."

"Thanks, pal. This descending-age business?"

"Yes. As Celeste says, it ought to quiet some fears."

"You don't sound hopeful."

"It's a question which can be more alarming," said Ellery, "danger to yourself or danger to your children."

"I see what you mean. I'll be right back, Ellery. Celeste, come on." He grabbed her arm.

"Just put me in a cab, Jimmy."

"Are you going to be pork-headed?"

"I'll be as safe on 102nd Street as on Park Avenue."

"How about compromising in a—I mean on a hotel?"

"Jimmy, you're wasting Mr. Queen's time."

"Wait for me, Ellery. I'll go downtown with you."

They went out, Jimmy still arguing.

Ellery shut the door after them carefully. Then he went back to the radio, turned it on, and sat down on the edge of the chair, like an audience.

But at the first blat of the newscaster he leaped, throttled the voice, and hurried to his bedroom.

It was afterward said that the press conference and radio talk of the Mayor's Special Investigator on that topsyturvy night of Friday, September 23, acted as a brake on the flight of New Yorkers from the City and in a matter of hours brought the panic phase of the case to a complete stop. Certainly the crisis was successfully passed that night and never again reached a peak. But what few realized who were following the complex psychology of the period was that something comparably undesirable replaced it.

As people straggled back to the City in the next day or so, it was remarked that they no longer seemed *interested* in the Cat case. The cataract of telephone calls and in-person inquiries which had kept City Hall, Police Headquarters, and precincts all over the City swamped for almost four months ebbed to a trickle. Elected officials, who had been under continuous bombardment from their constituents, discovered that the siege had unaccountably lifted. For once, to their relief, ward politicians found their clubhouses deserted. *Vox populi*, which had kept the correspondence columns of the newspapers in an uproar, sank to a petty whisper.

An even more significant phenomenon was observed.

On Sunday, September 25, churches of all denominations throughout the City suffered a marked drop in attendance. While this fall from grace was deplored by the clergy, it was almost unanimously regarded by lay observers as an agreeable evil, considering "the recent past." (Already the panic had dwindled to the size of a footnote in the City's history, so dramatic was the change.) The unusually heavy church attendance during the summer, these observers said, had been inspired largely by Cat-generated fears and a panic flight to spiritual reassurance; the sudden wholesale defection could only mean that the panic was over, the pendulum had swung to the other extreme. Shortly, they predicted, church attendance would find itself back in the normal rhythm.

On all sides responsible people were congratulating one another and the City on "the return to sanity." It was recognized that the threat to the City's young people had to be guarded against, and special measures were planned, but everyone seemed to feel—in official quarters—that the worst was over.

It was almost as if the Cat had been caught.

But there were contrary signs to be seen by those who were not blinded by sheer relief.

During the week beginning Saturday, September 24, *Variety* and Broadway columnists began to report an extraordinary increase in night club and theater attendance. The upswing could not be ascribed to seasonal change; it was too abrupt. Theaters which had not seen a full house all summer found themselves under the pleasant compulsion to rehire laidoff ushers and haul out ropes and S.R.O. signs. Clubs which had been staggering along were regarding their jammed dance floors with amazement; the famous ones were haughtily turning people away again. Broadway bars and eating places sprang to jubilant life. Florist shops, candy shops, cigar stores were crowded. Liquor stores tripled their sales. Scalpers, barkers, and steerers began to smile again. Bookmakers rubbed their eyes at the flow of bets. Sports arenas and stadiums reported record receipts and new attendance marks. Pool rooms and bowling alleys put on extra employees. The shooting galleries on Broadway, 42nd Street, Sixth Avenue were mobbed.

Overnight, it seemed, show business and its feedline subsidiaries began to enjoy boomtime prosperity. Times Square from sundown to 3 A.M. was roaring and impassable. Taxi drivers were saying, "It's just like the war all over again."

The phenomenon was not restricted to midtown Manhattan. It was simultaneously experienced by the entertainment districts of downtown

Brooklyn, Fordham Road in the Bronx, and other localities throughout the five boroughs.

That week, too, advertising agency executives were bewildered by advance reports from their radio-polling services. At a time when most major radio shows had returned to the air to begin the fall and winter broadcasting cycles and an appreciable rise in listener-response should have become apparent, the advance ratings unaccountably dropped in the metropolitan area. All networks were affected. The independent stations with local coverage had Pulse and BMB make hasty special surveys and discovered that the bottom had fallen out of their program-response and listener-circulation tables. The most significant figures of all—in all surveys—were those showing the percentage of sets-in-use. They were unprecedentedly small.

A parallel drop was noted in television surveys.

New Yorkers were not listening to the radio and watching the telecasts.

Account executives and broadcasting company vice-presidents were busy preparing explanations to their clients, chiefly masochistic. The truth seemed to have occurred to none of them, which was that radio and television sets could not be turned on in the home by people who were not there or who, if they were, were absent spiritually.

Police were puzzled by the abrupt rise in drunkenness and disorderly conduct cases. Routine raids on gambling houses bagged huge takes and a type of burgher clientele not ordinarily found throwing its money away. Marijuana and narcotics cases took a disturbing jump. The Vice Squad was compelled to put on a co-ordinated drive in an attempt to curb the sudden spread and acceleration of prostitution activities. Muggings, car thefts, holdups, common assaults, sex offenses increased sharply. The rise in juvenile delinquency was especially alarming.

And of peculiar interest was the reappearance all over the City of strangled alley cats.

It was evident to the thoughtful few that what had seemed a healthy loss of interest in the Cat case on the part of New Yorkers was not that at all. Fear had not died; the City was still in the mob mood and mob psychology was still at the panic stage; it had merely taken a new form and direction. People were now in flight from reality on a psychic rather than a physical level. But they were still fleeing.

On Sunday, October 2, an unsurprisingly large number of clergymen took as their texts Genesis XIX, 24–25. It was natural to cite Sodom and Gomorrah that day, and brimstone and fire were generously predicted. The ingredients of moral disintegration were all present in the melting pot, bubbling to the boil. The only trouble was that those whom the les-

son would most have profited were atoning for their wickedness in a less
godly fashion, elsewhere.

By a sly irony the ninth life of the Cat proved the crucial one.
For the break in the case came with the ninth murder.

The body was found a few minutes after 1 A.M. on the night of September 29–30, exactly one week after the Cat Riots and less than two
miles from the site of Stella Petrucchi's murder. It lay sprawled in deep
shadows on the steps of the American Museum of Natural History, at
77th Street and Central Park West. A sharpeyed patrolman spotted it on
his rounds.

Death was by strangulation. A cord had been employed, of tussah silk,
dyed blue as in the cases of Archibald Dudley Abernethy and Rian
O'Reilly.

According to a driver's license found in his untouched wallet, his
name was Donald Katz, he was 21 years old, and he lived on West 81st
Street. The address proved to be an apartment house between Central
Park West and Columbus Avenue. His father was a dentist, with offices at
Amsterdam Avenue and West 71st Street near Sherman Square. The family was of the Jewish faith. The victim had an elder sister, Mrs. Jeanne
Immerson, who lived in the Bronx. Donald was enrolled in extension
courses in radio and television engineering. He had been, it seemed, a
bright quixotic boy given to quick enthusiasms and dislikes; he had had
many acquaintances and few friends.

The father, Dr. Morvin Katz, officially identified the body.

It was from Dr. Katz that police learned about the girl his son had been
out with that evening. She was Nadine Cuttler, 19, of Borough Park,
Brooklyn, a student at the New York Art Students' League. Brooklyn detectives picked her up during the night and she was brought to Manhattan
for questioning.

She fainted on viewing the body and it was some time before she
could give a coherent story.

Nadine Cuttler said that she had known Donald Katz for almost two
years. "We met at a Palestine rally." They had had "an understanding" for
the past year, during which period they had seen each other three or four
times a week. "We had practically nothing in common. Donald was interested in science and technology, and I in art. He was politically undeveloped; not even the war taught him anything. We didn't even agree about
Palestine. I don't know why we fell in love."

The previous evening, Miss Cuttler stated, Donald Katz had met her at
the Art Students' League after her classes and they had walked down
Seventh Avenue from 57th Street, stopping in at Lum Fong's for a chow

mein dinner. "We fought over the check. Donald had juvenile ideas about this being a man's world, and that women ought to stay home and have babies and smooth their husbands' brows when the men came home after an important day, and all that sort of thing. He got very angry with me because I pointed out to him that it was my turn to pay. Finally, I let him pay the check just to avoid a scene in public."

Afterward, they had gone dancing in a little Russian night club on 52nd Street, The Yar, across from 21 and Leon and Eddie's.

"It was a place we liked very much and often went to. They knew us there and we called Maria and Lonya and Tina and the others by their first names. But last night it was crowded and after a while we left. Donald had had four vodkas and didn't touch any of the *zakuska*, so when we hit the air he got lightheaded. He wanted to go clubbing, but I said I wasn't in the mood and instead we strolled back uptown on Fifth Avenue. When we got to Fifth and 59th, Donald wanted to go into the Park. He was feeling very . . . gay; the drinks hadn't worn off. But it was so dark in there, and the Cat . . ."

At this point Nadine Cuttler broke down.

When she was able to continue, the girl said: "I found myself awfully nervous. I don't know why. We'd often talked about the Cat murders and neither of us ever felt a personal threat, I'm sure of it. We just couldn't seem to take it seriously, I mean really seriously. Donald used to say the Cat was anti-Semitic because in a City with the biggest Jewish population in the world he hadn't strangled a single Jew. Then he'd laugh and contradict himself and say the odds were the Cat was Jewish because of that very fact. It was a sort of joke between us which I never thought very funny, but you couldn't take offense at anything Donald said, not really, he . . ."

She had to be recalled to her story.

"We didn't go into the Park. We walked crosstown on Central Park South, sticking to the side of the street where the buildings are. On the way Donald seemed to sober up a bit; we talked about the murder of the Petrucchi girl last week and the Cat Riots and the stampede out of the City, and we agreed it was a funny thing but it was usually the older people who lost their heads in a crisis while the young ones, who had most to lose, kept theirs . . . Then, when we got to Columbus Circle, we had another quarrel."

Donald had wanted to take her home, "even though we'd had an absolute compact for months that on weeknight dates I'd go back to Brooklyn by myself. I was really exasperated with him. His mother didn't like him to get in late; it was the only basis on which I allowed myself to see him so often. Why didn't I let him, why didn't I let him?"

Nadine Cuttler cried again and Dr. Katz quieted her, saying that she had nothing to condemn herself for, that if it was Donald's fate to become a victim of the Cat nothing would have changed the result. The girl clung to his hand.

There was little more to her story. She had refused to let the boy accompany her to Brooklyn and she had urged him to hop a cab and go right home, because "he was looking sick and besides I didn't like the idea of his being alone on the streets in that condition. That made him even madder. He didn't even . . . kiss me. The last I saw of him was when I was going down the subway steps. He was standing at the top talking to somebody, I think a taxi driver. That was about 10:30."

The taxi driver was found. Yes, he remembered the young couple's tiff. "When the girl sails off down the steps I open my door and say to this kid, 'Better luck next time, Casanova. Come on, I'll take you home.' But he was sore as a boil. 'You can take your cab and shove it,' he says to me. 'I'm walking home.' And he crosses the Circle and turns into Central Park West. Headed uptown. He was pretty rocky on his pins."

It seemed clear that Donald Katz had tried to carry out his intention, walking uptown along the west side of Central Park West from Columbus Circle for almost a mile to 77th Street—just four blocks short of his home. There seemed no question but that the Cat had followed him all the way, perhaps had followed the couple all evening, although nothing developed from inquiries made at Lum Fong's and The Yar, and the taxi driver could not recall having seen anyone acting suspiciously as Donald Katz left him. The Cat had undoubtedly bided his time, waiting for an opportunity to pounce. The opportunity had come at 77th Street. On the steps of the Museum, at the spot where Donald was found, there was a mess of regurgitated matter; some of it was on Donald's coat. Apparently as he was passing the Museum his intoxication reached the stage of nausea and Donald had sat down on the steps in a dark place and he had been ill.

And the Cat had approached him from the side and got behind him as he sat retching.

He had struggled violently.

Death occurred, said the Medical Examiner, between 11 P.M. and midnight.

No one heard screams or choked cries.

The most thorough examination of the body, the clothing, the strangling cord, and the scene turned up nothing of importance.

"As usual," said Inspector Queen at the dawn's early light, "the Cat's left not a clue."

\* \* \*

But he had.

The fateful fact emerged obliquely during the morning of the 30th in the Katz apartment on West 81st Street.

Detectives were questioning the family, going through the familiar motions of trying to establish a connection between Donald Katz and the persons involved in the previous eight murders.

Present were the boy's mother and father; their daughter; the daughter's husband, Philbert Immerson. Mrs. Katz was a lean brown-eyed woman of bitter charm; her face was undressed by weeping. Mrs. Immerson, a chubby young woman without her mother's mettle, sobbed throughout the interview; Ellery gathered from something Mrs. Immerson said that she had not got along with her young brother. Dr. Katz sat by himself in a corner, as Zachary Richardson had sat on the other side of Central Park three and a half weeks before; he had lost his son, there would be no others. Donald's brother-in-law, a balding young man with a red mustache, wearing a sharp gray business suit, stood away from the others as if to avoid being noticed. He had freshly shaved; his stout cheeks were perspiring under the talcum.

Ellery was paying little attention to the automatic questions and the surcharged replies; he was dragging himself about these days and it had been a particularly depleting night. Nothing would come of this, he felt sure, as nothing had come of any of the others. A few slight alterations in the pattern—Jewish instead of Christian, seven days since the last one instead of seventeen, or eleven, or six—but the bulk features were the same: the strangling cord of tussah silk, blue for men, salmon-pink for women; the victim unmarried (Rian O'Reilly was still the baffling single exception); the victim listed in the telephone directory—Ellery had checked that immediately; and the ninth victim younger than the eighth who had been younger than the seventh who had been . . .

"—no, I'm positive he didn't know anybody of that name," Mrs. Katz was saying. Inspector Queen was being perversely insistent about Howard Whithacker, who had disappointed the psychiatrists. "Unless, of course, this Whithacker was somebody Donald met in training camp."

"You mean during the war?" asked the Inspector.

"Yes."

"Your son in the war, Mrs. Katz? Wasn't he too young?"

"No. He enlisted on his eighteenth birthday. The war was still on."

The Inspector looked surprised. "Germany surrendered in May, I think it was, of 1945—Japan in August or September. Wasn't Donald still 17 in 1945?"

"I ought to know my own son's age!"

"Pearl." Dr. Katz stirred in his corner. "It must be that driving license."

The Queens both made the slightest forward movement.

"Your son's license, Dr. Katz," said Inspector Queen, "gives his birth date as March 10, 1928."

"That's a mistake, Inspector Queen. My son made a mistake putting down the year on his application and never bothered to have it corrected."

"You mean," asked Ellery, and he found himself clearing his throat, "you mean Donald was *not* 21 years old, Dr. Katz?"

"Donald was 22. He was born on March 10, 1927."

"22," said Ellery.

"22?" The Inspector sounded froggy, too. "Ellery. Stella Petrucchi."

Abernethy, 44. Violette Smith, 42. Rian O'Reilly, 40. Monica McKell, 37, Simone Phillips, 35. Beatrice Willikins, 32. Lenore Richardson, 25. Stella Petrucchi, 22. Donald Katz . . . 22.

*For the first time the diminishing-age sequence had been broken.*

Or had it?

"It's true," Ellery said feverishly in the hall, "it's true that up to now the age drop's been in years. But if we found . . ."

"You mean this Katz boy might still be younger than Stella Petrucchi," mumbled his father.

"In terms of months. Suppose the Petrucchi girl had been born in January of 1927. That would make Donald Katz two months younger."

"Suppose Stella Petrucchi was born in *May* of 1927. That would make Donald Katz two months *older*."

"I don't want to think about that. That would . . . What month *was* she born in?"

"I don't know!"

"I don't remember seeing her exact birth date on any report."

"Wait a minute!"

The Inspector went away.

Ellery found himself pulling a cigaret to pieces. It was monstrous. Fat with meaning. He knew it.

The secret lay here.

But what secret?

He tried to contain himself as he waited. From somewhere he heard the Inspector's voice, in tones of manhood. God bless the shade of Alexander Graham Bell. What secret?

Suppose it turned out that Donald Katz had been older than Stella

Petrucchi. By so little as one day. Suppose. What could it mean? What *could it* mean?

"Ellery."

"Well!"

"March 10, 1927."

"What?"

"Father Petrucchi says his sister Stella was born on March 10, 1927."

*"The same day?"*

They glared at each other.

Later they agreed that what they did was reflexive; on its merits it promised nothing. Their inquiry was a sort of conditioned response, the detective organism reacting to the stimulus of another uncomprehended fact by calling into play the nerves of pure habit. The futility of any conscious consideration of the identical-natal day phenomenon was too painfully apparent. In lieu of explanation—even of reasonable hypothesis—the Queens went back to fundamentals. Never mind what the fact might mean; first, was it a fact?

Ellery said to his father, "Let's check that right now," and the Inspector nodded and they went down into West 81st Street and climbed into the Inspector's car and Sergeant Velie drove them to the Manhattan Bureau of Vital Records and Statistics of the Department of Health.

Neither man uttered a sound on the ride downtown.

Ellery's head hurt. A thousand gears were trying to mesh and failing to do so. It was maddening, because he could not rid himself of the feeling that it was all so very simple. He was sure there was a rhythmic affinity in the facts but they were not functioning through a silly, aggravating failure of his perceptive machinery.

Finally, he shut the power off and was borne blankminded to their destination.

"The original birth certificates," said Inspector Queen to the Registrar of Records. "No, we don't have the certificate numbers. But the names are Stella Petrucchi, female, and Donald Katz, male, and the date of birth in each case is, according to our information, March 10, 1927. Here, I've written the names down."

"You're sure they were both born in Manhattan, Inspector?"

"Yes."

The Registrar came back looking interested. "I see they were not only born on the same day, but—"

"March 10, 1927? In both cases?"

"Yes."

"Wait, Dad. Not only born on the same day, but what?"

"But the same doctor delivered them."

Ellery blinked.

"The same . . . doctor delivered them," said his father.

"May I see those certificates, please?" Ellery's voice was cracked again.

They stared at the signatures. Same handwriting. Both certificates signed:

*Edward Cazalis M.D.*

"Now, son, let's take it easy," Inspector Queen was saying, his hand muffling the phone. "Let's not jump. We don't know a thing. We're just bumbling around. We've got to go slow."

"I'll go as I damn please. Where's that list?"

"I'm getting it. They're getting it for me—"

"Cazalis, Cazalis. Here it is! Edward Cazalis. I told you it was the same one!"

"He delivered babies? I thought—"

"Started his medical career in the practice of obstetrics and gynecology. I knew there was something queer about his professional history."

"1927. He was still doing O.B. work as late as 1927?"

"Later! Here. It says—"

"Yes, Charley!"

Ellery dropped the medical directory. His father began writing as he listened. He wrote and wrote. It seemed as if he would never stop writing.

Finally, he did.

"Got 'em all?"

"Ellery. It just isn't reasonable that *all* of them—"

"Would you please get the original birth certificates," Ellery said, handing the Inspector's paper to the Registrar, "of the people listed here?"

"Dates of birth . . ." The Registrar ran his eye down the list. "All Manhattan-born?"

"Most of them. Maybe all of them. Yes," said Ellery, "I think all of them. I'm sure of it."

"How can you be 'sure' of it?" snarled his father. "What do you mean, 'sure'? We know about some of them, but—"

"I'm sure of it. All born in Manhattan. Every last one. See if I'm wrong."

The Registrar went away.

They kept walking around each other like two dogs.

The clock on the wall crept along.

Once the Inspector said in a mutter: "This could mean . . . You know this could mean . . ."

Ellery turned around, baring his teeth. "I don't want to know what this 'could' mean. I'm sick of thinking of 'possibilities.' First things first, that's my motto. I just invented it. One thing per time. Step by step. B follows A, C follows B. One and one make two, and that's the limit of my arithmetic until I have to add two more."

"Okay, son, okay," said the Inspector; after that he muttered to himself.

And then the Registrar came back.

He was looking baffled, inquisitive, and uneasy.

Ellery set his back against the office door. "Give it to me slowly, please. One at a time. Start with Abernethy. Abernethy, Archibald Dudley—"

"Born May 24, 1905," said the Registrar. Then he said, "Edward Cazalis, M.D."

"Interesting. Interesting!" said Ellery. "Smith. Violette Smith."

"Born February 13, 1907," said the Registrar. "Edward Cazalis, M.D."

"Rian O'Reilly. Is good old Rian O'Reilly there, too?"

"They're all here, Mr. Queen. I really . . . Born December 23, 1908. Edward Cazalis, M.D."

"And Monica McKell?"

"July 2, 1912. Edward Cazalis, M.D. Mr. Queen . . ."

"Simone Phillips."

"October 11, 1913. Cazalis."

"Just 'Cazalis'?"

"Well, of course not," snapped the Registrar. "Edward Cazalis, M.D. See here, I really don't see the point of going through this name by name, Inspector Queen. I said they're all here—"

"Give the boy his head," said the Inspector. "He's been reined in a long time."

"Beatrice Willikins," said Ellery. "I'm especially interested in Beatrice Willikins. I should have seen it, though. Birth is the universal experience along with death; the two have always played footsie under God's table. Why didn't I see that at once? Beatrice Willikins."

"April 7, 1917. The same doctor."

"The same doctor," nodded Ellery. He was smiling, a forbidding smile. "And that was a Negro baby, and it was the same doctor. A Hippocratic physician, Cazalis. The god of the maternity clinic, no doubt, on alternate Wednesdays. Come all ye pregnant, without regard for color or creed, fees adjusted according to the ability to pay. And Lenore Richardson?"

"January 29, 1924. Edward Cazalis, M.D."

"And that was the carriage trade. Thank you, sir, I believe that completes the roll. I take it these certificates are the untouchable trust of the Department of Health of the City of New York?"

"Yes."

"If anything happens to them," said Ellery, "I shall personally come down here with a derringer, sir, and shoot you dead. Meanwhile, no word of this is to get out. No whisper of a syllable. Do I make myself clear?"

"I don't mind telling you," began the Registrar stiffly, "that I don't like either your tone or your attitude, and—"

"Sir, you address the Mayor's Special Investigator. I beg your pardon," said Ellery, "I'm higher than the much-abused kite. May we use your office and your telephone for a few minutes—alone?"

The Registrar of Records went out with a bang.

But immediately the door opened and the Registrar stepped back into his office, shut the door with care, and said in a confidential tone, "A doctor who would go back to murder the people he himself brought into the world—why, gentlemen, he's nothing but a lunatic. How in hell did you let him weasel his way into your investigation?"

And the Registrar stamped out.

"This isn't," said the Inspector, "going to be easy."

"No."

"There's no evidence."

Ellery nibbled a thumbnail on the Registrar's desk.

"He'll have to be watched night and day. Twenty-four out of twenty-four. We've got to know what he's doing every minute of every hour of the day."

Ellery continued to nibble.

"There mustn't be a tenth," said the Inspector, as if he were explaining something abstruse, top-secret, and of global importance. Then he laughed. "That cartoonist on the *Extra* doesn't know it but he's run out of tails. Let me get to that phone, Ellery."

"Dad."

"What, son?"

"We've got to have the run of that apartment for a few hours." Ellery took out a cigaret.

"Without a warrant?"

"And tip him off?"

The Inspector frowned.

"Getting rid of the maid ought to present no problem. Pick her day off.

No, this is Friday and the chances are she won't be off till the middle of next week. I can't wait that long. Does she sleep in?"

"I don't know."

"I want to get in there over the weekend, if possible. Do they go to church?"

"How should I know? That cigaret won't draw, Ellery, because you haven't lit it. Hand me the phone."

Ellery handed it to him. "Whom are you going to put on him?"

"Hesse. Mac. Goldberg."

"All right."

"Police Headquarters."

"But I'd like to keep this thing," said Ellery, putting the cigaret back into his pocket, "exclusive and as far away from Centre Street as you can manage it."

His father stared.

"We really don't know a thing . . . Dad."

"What?"

Ellery uncoiled from the desk. "Come right home, will you?"

"You going *home?*"

But Ellery was already closing the door.

Inspector Queen called from his foyer, "Son?"

"Yes."

"Well, it's all set—" He stopped.

Celeste and Jimmy were on the sofa.

"Hello," said the Inspector.

"We were waiting for you, Dad."

His father looked at him.

"No, I haven't told them yet."

"Told us what?" demanded Jimmy.

"We know about the Katz boy," began Celeste. "But—"

"Or has the Cat walked again?"

"No." Ellery scrutinized them. "I'm ready," he said. "How about you?"

"Ready for what?"

"To go to work, Celeste."

Jimmy got up.

"Sit down, Jimmy." Jimmy sat down. "This time it's the McCoy."

Celeste grew quite pale.

"We're on the trail of something," said Ellery. "Exactly what, we're still not sure. But I think I can say that for the first time since the Cat got going there's something encouraging to work on."

"What do I do?" asked Jimmy.

"Ellery," said the Inspector.

"No, Dad, it's safer this way. I've thought it over very carefully."

"What do I do?" asked Jimmy again.

"I want you to get me a complete dossier on Edward Cazalis."

"Cazalis?"

"Dr. Cazalis?" Celeste was bewildered. "You mean—"

Ellery looked at her.

"Sorry!"

"Dossier on Cazalis," said Jimmy. "And?"

"Don't jump to conclusions, please. As I said, we don't know where we are . . . Jimmy, what I want is an intimate sketch of his life. Trivial details solicited. This isn't just a *Who's Who* assignment. I could do that myself. As a working newspaperman you're in a perfect position to dig up what I want, and without arousing suspicion."

"Yes," said Jimmy.

"No hint to anyone about what you're working on. That goes in spades for your people at the *Extra*. When can you start?"

"Right away."

"How long will it take you?"

"I don't know. Not long."

"Do you suppose you could have a good swatch of it for me by . . . say . . . tomorrow night?"

"I can try." Jimmy rose.

"By the way. Don't go near Cazalis."

"No."

"Or anyone connected with him closely enough so that word might get back to him that somebody's asking questions about him."

"I understand." Jimmy lingered.

"Yes?" said Ellery.

"What about Celeste?"

Ellery smiled.

"Got you, got you," said Jimmy, flushing. "Well, folks . . ."

"Celeste has nothing to do yet, Jimmy. But I do want you to go home, Celeste, pack a bag or two, and come back here to live."

"What?" said the Inspector and Jimmy together.

"That is, Dad, if you have no objection."

"Er, no. None at all. Glad to have you, Miss Phillips. The only thing is," said the Inspector, "if I'm to get any rest I'd better stake out *my* bed right now. Ellery, if there's a call—anything at all—be sure and wake me." And he retreated to his bedroom rather hurriedly.

"Live *here*, you said," said Jimmy.

"Yes."

"Sounds tasty, but is it kosher?"

"Mr. Queen." Celeste hesitated.

"On second thought," said Jimmy, "this is a very delicate situation. It raises all sorts of possible conflicts."

"I'm going to need you, Celeste—when I do—on a moment's notice." Ellery frowned. "I can't predict when it will be. If it's late at night and you weren't at my fingertips—"

"No, sir," said Jimmy, "I can't say I'm wild about this development."

"Will you be quiet and let me think?" cried Celeste.

"I should tell you, too, that it may be quite dangerous."

"So taking it all in all," said Jimmy, "I don't think it's such a hot idea, darling. Do you?"

Celeste ignored him.

"I'll say it's dangerous! It's also downright immoral! What will people say?"

"Oh, muffle it, Jimmy," said Ellery. "Celeste, if my plans work out you're going to be right up there on the razor's edge. Now's the time for you to jump off. If you're going to do any jumping at all."

Celeste rose. "When do I move in?"

Ellery grinned. "Sunday night will do."

"I'll be here."

"You'll have my room. I'll bed down in the study."

"I hope," said Jimmy bitterly, "you'll both be very happy."


He watched Jimmy boost Celeste rudely into a taxi and then shamble angrily up the street.

Ellery began wandering about the living room.

He felt exhilarated. Jumpy.

Finally, he sat down in the armchair.

The hand that cut the cord.

Tightened it.

*The end flows from the beginning.*

The circular madness of paranoia.

God in the fingertips.

Was it possible?

Ellery had the feeling that he sat on the brink of a vast peace.

But he had to wait.

From some stronghold he had to summon the reserve to wait.

# 9

Inspector Queen phoned home a little after noon on Saturday to announce that everything was arranged for the following day.

"How long will we have?"

"Long enough."

"The maid?"

"She won't be there."

"How did you work it?"

"The Mayor," said Inspector Queen. "I got His Honor to invite the Cazalises for Sunday dinner."

Ellery shouted. "How much did you have to tell the Mayor?"

"Not very much. We communicated mostly by telepathy. But I think he's impressed with the necessity of not letting our friend go too soon after the brandy tomorrow. Dinner's called for 2:30 and there are going to be bigshot guests in afterward. Once Cazalis gets there, the Mayor says, he'll stay there."

"Brief me."

"We're to get a buzz the minute Cazalis sets foot in the Mayor's foyer. On the signal we shoot over to the apartment and get in through the service door by way of the basement and a back alley. Velie will have a duplicate key ready for us by tomorrow morning. The maid won't be back till late; she gets every other Sunday off and it happens tomorrow is her off-Sunday. The building help are being taken care of. We'll get in and out without being seen. Have you heard from Jimmy McKell?"

"He'll be up around ninish."

Jimmy showed up that night needing a shave, a clean shirt, and a drink, "but I can dispense with the first two items," he said, "providing Number 3 is produced forthwith," whereupon Ellery planted the decanter, a bottle of seltzer, and a glass at Jimmy's elbow and waited at least ten seconds before he made an encouraging sound in his throat.

"I'll bet the seismograph at Fordham is going crazy," said Jimmy. "Where do you sphinxes want it from?"

"Anywhere?"

"Well," said Jimmy, admiring his glass in the light, "the story of Edward Cazalis is kind of lopsided. I couldn't find out much about his family background and boyhood, just a few details. Seems he got away from home early—"

"Born in Ohio, wasn't he?" said the Inspector. He was measuring three fingers of Irish whiskey with care.

"Ironton, Ohio, 1882," nodded Jimmy McKell. "His father was a laborer of some sort—"

"Ironworker," said the Inspector.

"Whose report is this, anyway?" demanded Jimmy. "Or am I being checked up on?"

"I just happen to have a few facts, that's all," said the Inspector, holding his glass up to the light, too. "Go on, McKell."

"Anyway, Papa Cazalis was descended from a French soldier who settled in Ohio after the French and Indian War. About Mama I couldn't find out." Jimmy looked at the old gentleman belligerently, but when that worthy downed his whiskey without saying anything Jimmy continued. "Your hero was one of the youngest of fourteen ill-fed, ill-clothed, and ill-housed brats. A lot of them died off in childhood. The survivors and their descendants are strewn around the Middle West landscape. As far as I can tell, your Eddie's the only one who made anything of himself."

"Any criminals in the family?" asked Ellery.

"Sir, don't asperse the rank and file of our glorious heritage," said Jimmy, pouring another drink for himself. "Or are you taking a refresher course in sociology? I couldn't find anything special in that line." He said suddenly, "What are you digging for?"

"Keep going, Jimmy."

"Well, Edward seems to have been a very hep cookie. Not a prodigy, you understand. But precocious. And very ambitious. Poor but honest, he burned the midnight oil, worked his industrious little fingers to the bone, and got a southern Ohio hardware king all hopped up about him; in fact, he became this tycoon's protégé. A real Horatio Alger character. Up to a point, that is."

"What do you mean by that?"

"Well, in my book young Eduardo was something of a heelo. If there's anything worse than a rich snob, it's a poor one. The hardware hidalgo, whose name was William Waldemar Gaeckel, lifted the bloke clean out of his lousy environment, scrubbed him up, got him some decent clothes, and sent him away to a fancy prep school in Michigan . . . and there's no record that Cazalis ever went back to Ironton even on a visit. He ditched pa and ma, he ditched Tessie, Steve, and the other fifty thousand brothers and sisters, and after old Gaeckel sent him proudly to New York to study medicine he ditched Gaeckel, too—or maybe Mr. G. got wise to him; anyway, they had no further relations. Cazalis got his M.D. from Columbia in 1903."

"1903," murmured Ellery. "Aged 21. One of fourteen children, and he became interested in obstetrics."

"Very funny," grinned Jimmy.

"Not very." Ellery's voice was chill. "Any information on the obstetrical specialty?"

Jimmy McKell nodded, looking curious.

"Let's have it."

Jimmy referred to the back of a smudged envelope. "Seems that back in those days medical schools weren't standardized. In some the courses were two years, in others four, and there weren't any obstetrical or gynecological internships or residencies . . . it says here. Very few men did obstetrics or gynecology exclusively, and those who did became specialists mostly by apprenticeship. When Cazalis graduated from Columbia— with honors, by the way—he hooked onto a New York medico named Larkland—"

"John F.," said the Inspector.

"John F.," nodded Jimmy. "East 20s somewhere. Dr. Larkland's practice wasn't entirely O.B. and gyne but it was apparently enough to keep Cazalis with him about a year and a half. Then in 1905 Cazalis started his own specializing practice—"

"Just when in 1905?"

"February. Larkland died that month of cancer, and Cazalis took over his practice."

Then Archibald Dudley Abernethy's mother had been old Dr. Larkland's patient and young Cazalis had inherited her, thought Ellery. It soothed him. Clergymen's wives in 1905 were not attended by 23-year-old physicians except in extraordinary circumstances.

"Within a few years," continued Jimmy, "Cazalis was one of the leading specialists in the East. As I get the picture, he'd moved in on the ground floor and by 1911 or '12, when the specialty had become defined, he had one of the biggest practices in New York. He wasn't a money-grubber, I understand, although he made pots. He was always more interested in the creative side of his profession, pioneered a couple of new techniques, did a lot of clinic work, and so on. I've got lots of dope here on his scientific achievements—"

"Skip it. What else?"

"Well, there's his war record."

"World War I."

"Yes."

"When did he go in?"

"Summer of 1917."

"Interesting, Dad. Beatrice Willikins was born on April 7 that year, the day after Congress declared war on Germany. Must have been one of Cazalis's last deliveries before getting into uniform." The Inspector said nothing. "What about his war record?"

"Tops. He went into the Medical Corps as a captain and came out a full colonel. Surgery up front—"

"Ever wounded?"

"No, but he did spend a few months in a French rest area in '18, and in early '19 after the war ended. Under treatment for—I quote—'exhaustion and shell shock.' "

Ellery glanced at his father, but the Inspector was pouring his fourth, fifth, and sixth finger of whiskey.

"Apparently it wasn't anything serious." Jimmy glanced at his envelope. "He was sent home from France as good as new and when he was mustered out—"

"In 1919."

"—he went back to his specialty. By the end of 1920 he'd worked up his practice again and was going great guns."

"Still doing obstetrics and gynecology exclusively?"

"That's right. He was then in his late 30s, approaching his prime, and in the next five years or so he really hit the top." Jimmy hauled out another envelope. "Let's see . . . yes, 1926. In 1926 he met Mrs. Cazalis through her sister, Mrs. Richardson—and married her. She was one of the Merigrews of Bangor. Old New England family—blood transparent, blue, and souring, but I'm told she was a genetic sport, very pretty, if you went for Dresden china. Cazalis was 44 and his bride was only 19, but apparently he had Dresden china ideas; it seems to have been an epic romance. They had a fancy wedding in Maine and a long honeymoon. Paris, Vienna, and Rome.

"I find," said Jimmy McKell, "I find nothing to indicate that the Cazalises have been anything but happily married—in case you're interested. No whisper about him, in spite of all the ladies in his medical life, and for Mrs. Cazalis there's never been any man but her husband.

"They ran into hard luck, though. In 1927 Mrs. Cazalis had her first baby and early in 1930 her second—"

"And lost both in the delivery room," nodded Ellery. "Cazalis mentioned that the night I met him."

"He felt terrible about it, I'm told. He'd taken fanatical care of his wife during both pregnancies and he'd done the deliveries himself— what's the matter?"

"Cazalis was his wife's obstetrician?"

"Yes." Jimmy looked at them both. Inspector Queen was now at the window, pulling at his fingers behind his back.

"Isn't that unethical?" asked the Inspector casually. "A doctor delivering his own wife?"

"Hell, no. Most doctors don't do it because they're emotionally involved with the woman in labor. They doubt their ability to maintain— where's that note?—to maintain 'the necessary objective, detached professional attitude.' But many doctors do, and Dr. Edward Cazalis of the Tearing Twenties was one of them."

"After all," said the Inspector to Ellery, as if Ellery were arguing the point, "he was a big man in his field."

"The type man," said Jimmy, "so supremely egocentric he'd maybe become a psychiatrist. Hm?"

"I don't think that's quite fair to psychiatrists," laughed Ellery. "Any data on the two babies he lost?"

"All I know about it is that both births were toughies and that after the second Mrs. Cazalis couldn't have any more children. I gathered that they were both breeches."

"Go on."

The Inspector came back and sat down with his bottle.

"In the year 1930, a few months after they lost their second child, we find Cazalis having a breakdown."

"Breakdown," said Ellery.

"Breakdown?" said the Inspector.

"Yes. He'd been driving himself, he was 48—his collapse was attributed to overwork. By this time he'd been practicing obstetrical and gynecological medicine for over twenty-five years, he was a wealthy man, so he gave up his practice and Mrs. Cazalis took him traveling. They went on a world cruise—you know the kind, through the Canal up to Seattle, then across the Pacific—and by the time they reached Europe Cazalis was practically well again. Only, he wasn't. While they were in Vienna— this was early in '31—he had a setback."

"Setback?" said Ellery sharply. "You mean another breakdown?"

" 'Setback' was the word. It was nerves again, or mental depression or something. Anyway, being in Vienna, he went to see Béla Seligmann and—"

"Who's Béla Seligmann?" demanded Inspector Queen.

"Who's Béla Seligmann, he says. Why, Béla Seligmann is—"

"There was Freud," said Ellery, "and there's Jung, and there's Seligmann. Like Jung, the old boy hangs on."

"Yes, he's still around. Seligmann got out of Austria just in time to observe *Anschluss* from an honored bleacher seat in London, but he went back to Vienna after the little cremation ceremony in the Berlin Chancellery and I believe he's still there. He's over 80 now, but in 1931 he was at the height of his powers. Well, it seems Seligmann took a great interest in Cazalis, because he snapped him out of whatever was wrong with him and aroused in the guy an ambition to become a psychiatrist."

"He studied with Seligmann?"

"For four years—one under par, I'm told. Cazalis spent some time in Zürich, too, and then in 1935 the Cazalises returned to the States. He put in over a year getting hospital experience and early in 1937—let's see, that would have made him 55—he set himself up in the practice of psychiatry in New York. The rest is history." Jimmy laced his flagging glass.

"That's all you got, Jimmy?"

"Yes. No." Jimmy referred hastily to his last envelope. "There's one other item of interest. About a year ago—last October—Cazalis broke down again."

"Broke down?"

"Now don't go asking me for clinical details. I don't have access to medical records. Maybe it was plain pooping out from overwork—he has a racehorse's energy and he's never spared himself. And, of course, he was 66. It wasn't much of a breakdown but it must have scared him, because he started to whittle down his practice. I understand he hasn't taken a new case in a year. He's polishing off the patients under treatment and transferring long-termers to other men when he can. I'm told that within a short time he'll be retiring." Jimmy tossed his collection of disreputable envelopes on the table. "End of report."

The envelopes lay there.

"Thanks, Jimmy," said Ellery in a curiously final voice.

"Is it what you wanted?"

"What I wanted?"

"Well, expected."

Ellery said carefully, "It's a very interesting report."

Jimmy set his glass down. "I take it you shamans want to be alone."

Neither man replied.

"Never let it be said," said Jimmy, picking up his hat, "that a McKell couldn't recognize a brush."

"Fine job, McKell, just fine," said the Inspector. "Night."

"Keep in touch with me, Jimmy."

"Mind if I drift in with Celeste tomorrow night?"

"Not in the least."

"Thanks! Oh." Jimmy paused in the foyer. "There's one little thing."

"What's that?"

"Let me know when you clap him in irons, will you?"

When the door closed Ellery sprang to his feet.

His father poured another drink. "Here, have one."

But Ellery mumbled, "That touch of so-called shell shock in the first war. Those recurring breakdowns. And in middle age the obvious attempt to compensate for something in that sudden, apparently unprepared-for interest in psychiatry. It fits, it fits."

"Drink it," said his father.

"Then there's the whole egocentric pattern. It's unusual for a man of 50 to begin studying psychiatry, to set up in practice at 55, and to make a success of it to boot. His drive must be gigantic.

"Look at his early history. A man who set out to prove something to— whom? himself? society? And who wouldn't let anything stand in his way. Who used every tool that came to hand and tossed it aside when it outlived its immediate usefulness. Professionally ethical always, but in the narrowest sense; I'm sure of it. And then marriage to a girl less than half his age—and not just any girl; it had to be a Merigrew of Maine.

"And those two tragic confinements, and . . . guilt. Guilt, decidedly: immediately that first breakdown. Overwork, yes; but not his body. His conscience."

"Aren't you doing an awful lot of guessing?" asked Inspector Queen.

"We're not dealing with clues you can put on a slide. I wish I knew more!"

"You're spilling it, son."

"The conflicts set in, and from then on it's a question of time. A gradual spreading of the warp. A sickening, a corruption of the whole psychic process—whatever the damned mechanism is. Somewhere along the line a personality that was merely paranoid in potential crossed over and became paranoid in fact. I wonder . . ."

"You wonder what?" asked his father when Ellery paused.

"I wonder if in either of those deliveries the infant died of strangulation."

"Of *what?*"

"Umbilical. The umbilical cord wound around its neck."

The old man stared.

Suddenly he bounced to his feet.

"Let's go to bed."

They found the white index card marked *Abernethy, Sarah-Ann* within twenty seconds of opening the file drawer labeled *1905–10*. It was the eleventh card in the file. A blue card was clipped to it marked *Abernethy, Archibald Dudley, m., b. May 24, 1905, 10:26 A.M.*

There were two old-fashioned filing cabinets of walnut, each containing three drawers. Neither had locks or catches, but the storage closet in which they found the cabinets had to be unlocked, a feat Sergeant Velie performed without difficulty. It was a large closet filled with the memorabilia and bric-a-brackery of the Cazalis household; but on the side where the cabinets stood were also a glass case of obstetrical and surgical instruments and a worn medical bag.

The records of his psychiatric practice were housed in modern steel cabinets in his inner office. These cabinets were locked.

The Queens, however, spent all their time in the crowded, musty-smelling closet.

Mrs. Abernethy's card recorded an ordinary case history of pregnancy. Archibald Dudley's recorded the data of birth and infant development. It was evident that Dr. Cazalis had provided the customary pediatric care of the period.

Ninety-eight white cards later they ran across one marked *Smith, Eulalie* to which was clipped a pink card marked *Smith, Violette, f., b. Feb. 13, 1907, 6:55 P.M.*

One hundred and sixty-four cards beyond the Smith cards they found entries for *O'Reilly, Maura B.* and *O'Reilly, Rian, m., b. Dec. 23, 1908, 4:36 A.M.* Rian O'Reilly's card was blue.

In less than an hour they located the cards of all nine of the cat's victims. There was no difficulty. They were arranged in chronological order in the drawers, each drawer was labeled with its year-sequence, and it was simply a matter of going through the drawers card by card.

Ellery sent Sergeant Velie for the Manhattan telephone directory. He spent some time with it.

"It's so damnably logical," complained Ellery, "once you have the key. We couldn't understand why the Cat's victims should be successively younger when there was no apparent connection among them. Obviously, Cazalis simply followed the chronology of his records. He went back to the beginning of his medical practice and systematically worked his way forward."

"In forty-four years a lot had changed," said the Inspector thoughtfully. "Patients had died off. Children he'd brought into the world had grown up and moved to other localities. And it's nineteen years at a minimum since he had any medical contact with any of them. So most of these cards must be as obsolete as the dodo."

"Exactly. Unless he was willing or prepared to undertake a complicated search, he couldn't hope to make a clean sweep. So he'd tend to concentrate on the cards bearing names most easily traced. Since he'd had a Manhattan practice, the obvious reference was to the Manhattan phone book. Undoubtedly he began with the first card in his files. It's a Sylvan Sacopy, a boy born to a Mrs. Margaret Sacopy in March of 1905. Well, neither name is to be found in the current Manhattan directory. So he went on to the second card. Again no luck. I've checked every name on the first ten listings and not one is to be found in the Manhattan book. Abernethy's was the first card with a current listing. And Abernethy was the first victim. And while I haven't checked all the names on the ninety-seven cards between Abernethy and Violette Smith, I've taken enough of a sampling to indicate that Violette Smith became the Cat's second victim for exactly the same reason: despite the fact that her card is Number 109, she had the misfortune to be Number 2 in the phone book checkback. There's no doubt in my mind that the same thing is true of all the others."

"We'll check."

"Then there was the baffling business of the non-marital status of all but one of the victims. Now that we know how Cazalis picked them, the answer is childishly clear. Of the nine victims, six were women and three were men. Of the three men, one was married and two were not—but Donald Katz was a youngster: it was a reasonable average. But of the six women not one was married. Why were the female victims consistently single? Because when a woman marries *her name changes!* The only women Cazalis could trace through the phone book were those whose names had remained the same as the names appearing on his case cards.

"And the curious color note that ran through the crimes," continued Ellery. "That was the most obvious clue of all, damn it. Blue cords for males, salmon-pink for females. Maybe it was the salmony cast of the pink that threw me off. But salmon *is* a shade of pink, and pink and blue are the traditional colors for infants."

"It's a sentimental touch," muttered his father, "I could do without."

"Sentimental nothing—it's as significant as the color of hell. It indicates that deep in the chasm of his mind Cazalis regards his victims as infants still. When he strangled Abernethy with a blue cord he was really strangling a boy baby . . . using a cord to return him to limbo? The umbilical symbolism was there from the start. The murderous colors of childbirth."

From somewhere in the apartment came the peaceful sounds of drawers opening.

"Velie," said the Inspector. "God, if only some of those cords are here."

But Ellery said, "And that tantalizing gap between Victims 6 and 7— Beatrice Willikins to Lenore Richardson. Up to that point the age differential between successive victims was never more than three years. Suddenly, seven."

"The war—"

"But he was back in practice by 1919 or '20, and Lenore Richardson was born in '24."

"Maybe he couldn't locate one born during those years."

"Not true. Here's one, for instance, born in September 1921, Harold Marzupian. It's in the directory. Here's another, January 1922, Benjamin Treudlich. And he's in the directory. I found at least five others born before 1924, and there are undoubtedly more. Still, he bypassed them to strike at Lenore Richardson, 25. Why? Well, what happened between the murders of Beatrice Willikins and Lenore Richardson?"

"What?"

"It's going to sound stuffy, but the fact is that between those two homicides the Mayor appointed a Special Investigator to look into the Cat murders."

The Inspector raised his brows.

"No, think about it. There was an enormous splash of publicity. My name and mission were talked and written about sensationally. My appointment couldn't fail to have made an impression on the Cat. He must have asked himself what the sudden turn of events meant to his chances of continuing his murder spree with safety. The newspapers, you'll recall, spread out the whole hog. They rehashed old cases of mine, spectacular solutions—Superman stuff. Whether the Cat knew much about me before that, you may be sure he read everything that was printed and listened to everything that was broadcast afterwards."

"You mean he was scared of you?" grinned Inspector Queen.

"It's much more likely," Ellery retorted, "that he welcomed the prospect of a duel. Remember that we're dealing with a special kind of madman— a man trained in the science of the human mind and personality and at the same time a paranoiac in full flight, with systematized delusions of his own greatness. A man like that would likely consider my appearance in the investigation a challenge; and it's borne out by that seven-year jump from Willikins to Richardson."

"How so?"

"What's the outstanding fact about the Richardson girl in relation to Cazalis?"

"She was his wife's niece."

"So Cazalis deliberately skipped over any number of available victims to murder his own niece, knowing that this would draw him into the case naturally. Knowing he'd be bound to meet me on the scene. Knowing that under the circumstances it would be a simple matter to get himself drawn into the investigation as one of the investigators. Why did Mrs. Cazalis insist on her husband's offering his services? Because he'd often 'discussed' his 'theories' about the Cat with her! Cazalis had prepared the way carefully by playing on his wife's attachment to Lenore even before Lenore's murder. If Mrs. Cazalis hadn't brought the subject up, he would have volunteered. But she did, as he knew she would."

"And there he was," grunted the Inspector, "on the inside, in a position to know just what we were doing—"

"In a position to revel in his own power." Ellery shrugged. "I told you I was rusty. I was aware all along of the possibility of such a move on the Cat's part. Didn't I suspect Celeste and Jimmy of exactly that motive? Couldn't get it out of my mind. And all the while there was Cazalis—"

"No cords."

They jumped.

But it was only Sergeant Velie in the closet doorway.

"They ought to be here, Velie," snapped the Inspector. "How about those steel files in his office?"

"We'd have to get Bill Devander down to open them. I can't. Not without leaving traces."

"How much time do we have?" The Inspector pulled on his watch chain.

But Ellery was pinching his lip. "To do the job properly would take more time than we have today, Dad. I doubt that he keeps the cords here, anyway. Too much danger that his wife or the maid might find them."

"That's what I said," said Sergeant Velie heatedly. "I said to the Inspector—remember?—I said, Inspector, he's got 'em stashed in a public locker some place . . ."

"I know what you said, Velie, but they might also be right here in the apartment. We've got to have those cords, Ellery. The D.A. told me the other day that if we could connect a find of the same type of blue and pink cords with some individual, he'd be willing to go into court pretty nearly on that alone."

"We can give the D.A.," said Ellery suddenly, "a much better case."

"How?"

Ellery put his hand on one of the walnut filing cabinets.

"All we have to do is put ourselves in Cazalis's place. He's certainly not finished—the cards on Petrucchi and Katz took him only as far as March 10, 1927, and his obstetrical records extend over three years beyond that."

"I don't quite get it," complained the Sergeant.

But the Inspector was already at work on the drawer labeled 1927–30.

The birth card following Donald Katz's was pink and it recorded the name "Rhutas, Roselle."

There was no Rhutas listed in the directory.

The next card was blue. "Finkleston, Zalmon."

There was no such name in the directory.

Pink. "Heggerwitt, Adelaide."

"Keep going, Dad."

The Inspector took out another card. "Collins, Barclay M."

"Plenty of Collinses . . . But no Barclay M."

"The mother's card gives her Christian name as—"

"It doesn't matter. All his victims have had personal listings in the phone book. I checked a few parents' names before, where the victim wasn't listed, and I found two in the book; there must be lots of others. But he passed those up, I imagine because it would have increased the amount of investigating he'd have to do and by that much increased the risk. So far at least he's taken only directly traceable cases. What's the next card?"

"Frawlins, Constance."

"No."

Fifty-nine cards later the Inspector read, "Soames, Marilyn."

"How do you spell that?"

"S-o-a-m-e-s."

"S-o-a . . . Soames. Here it is! Soames, Marilyn!"

"Let me see that!"

It was the only Soames listed. The address was 486 East 29th Street.

"Off First Avenue," muttered the Inspector. "Within spitting distance of Bellevue Hospital."

"What are the mother's and father's names? On the white card?"

"Edna L. and Frank P. Father's occupation given as 'postal employee.' "

"Could we get a quick check on Marilyn Soames and her family? While we're waiting here?"

"It's getting late . . . I'll ring the Mayor first, make sure he hangs on to Cazalis. Velie, where's the phone?"

"There's a couple in his office."

"No household phone?"

"In a phone closet off the foyer."

The Inspector went away.

When he returned, Ellery said, "They're not calling back here, are they?"

"What do you think I am, Ellery?" The Inspector was peevish. "We'd be in a fine mess if we answered a personal call! I'm calling them back in half an hour. Velie, if the phone rings out there don't answer it."

"What do you think *I* am!"

They waited.

Sergeant Velie kept tramping about the foyer.

The Inspector kept pulling out his watch.

Ellery picked up the pink card.

*Soames, Marilyn, f., b. Jan. 2, 1928, 7:13 A.M.*

Add to population of Manhattan one female. Vital statistics of a birth. Recorded by the hand of death.

| | |
|---|---|
| Onset of labor | *Natural* |
| Position at delivery | *L.O.T.* |
| Duration of labor | *10 hrs.* |
| Normal | *Normal* |
| Anaesthesia | *Morphine-scopalamine* |
| Operative | *Forceps* |
| Crede—prophylaxis | *Crede* |
| Period gestation | *40 wks.* |
| Respiration | *Spontaneous* |
| Method of resuscitation | *None* |
| Injuries at birth | *None* |
| Congenital anomalies | *None* |
| Medication p-n. | *None* |
| Weight | *6 lbs. 9 oz.* |
| Length | *49 cm.* |

And so on, unto the tenth day. *Behavior of Baby . . . Type of supplemental or complemental feeding . . . Disturbances noted: Digestive, Respiratory, Circulatory, Genito-urinary, Nervous system, Skin, Umbilicus . . .*

A conscientious physician. Death was always conscientious. Digestive. Circulatory. Umbilicus. Especially umbilicus. *The place where the extraembryonic structures are continuous with those of the body proper of the embryo*, anatomical and zoological definition. *To which is attached the umbilical cord connecting the fetus of the mammal with the placenta . . . Jelly of Wharton . . . Epiblastic epithelium . . .* No mention of tussah silk.

But that was to come twenty-one years later.

Meanwhile, pink cards for females, blue cards for males.

Systematized. The scientific mumbo jumbo of parturition.

It was all down here on a card in faded pen-marks. God's introductory remarks on another self-contained unit of moist, red, squirming life.

And even as the Lord giveth, He taketh away.

When the inspector set the telephone down he was a little pale. "Mother's name Edna, nee Lafferty. Father's name Frank Pellman Soames, occupation post office clerk. Daughter Marilyn is a public stenographer. Aged 21."

Tonight, tomorrow, next week, next month. Marilyn Soames, aged 21, occupation public stenographer, of 486 East 29th Street, Manhattan, would be plucked from the files of Dr. Edward Cazalis by the hand that had pulled her into the world and he would begin measuring her for a salmon-pink cord of tussah silk.

And he would set out on his quest, cord in hand, and later the cartoonist of the *New York Extra* would sharpen his pens and refashion his Cat to wave a tenth tail and an eleventh in the form of a question mark.

"Only this time we'll be waiting for him," Ellery said that night in the Queen living room. "We're going to catch him with a cord in his hands as close to the actual instant of attack as we can safely manage. It's the only way we can be sure of slapping the Cat label on him so that it sticks."

Celeste and Jimmy were both looking frightened.

From his armchair Inspector Queen kept watching the girl.

"Nothing's been left to chance," said Ellery. "Cazalis has been under twenty-four-hour observation since Friday, Marilyn Soames since late this afternoon. We're getting hourly reports on Cazalis's movements in a special office at Police Headquarters, where Sergeant Velie and another man are on continuous duty. These two officers are instructed to call us on our private line the moment a suspicious movement on Cazalis's part is phoned in.

"Marilyn Soames knows nothing of what's going on; no one in her family does. To let them in on it would only make them nervous and their actions might get Cazalis suspicious. Then we'd have the whole thing to do over again or it might scare him off permanently—or for a very long time. We can't afford to wait. We can't afford to miss.

"We're getting hourly reports on the girl, too. We're almost completely set."

"Almost?" said Jimmy.

The word hung among them in a peculiarly unpleasant way.

"Celeste, I've been holding you in reserve," said Ellery. "For the most important and certainly the riskiest job of all. As an alternate to Jimmy. If Cazalis's next available victim had turned out to be male, I had Jimmy. Female—you."

"What job would that be?" asked Jimmy cautiously.

"My original idea was to substitute one of you for the next victim indicated by Cazalis's files."

And there was McKell, out of the cubist tangle of his arms and legs and glaring down at Ellery. "The answer is no. You're not going to turn this woman into a slaughterhouse beef. I won't have it—me, McKell!"

"I told you we should have locked this character up as a public nuisance, Ellery." The Inspector snapped, "Sit down, McKell."

"I'll stand up and you'll like it!"

Ellery sighed.

"You're so cute, Jimmy," said Celeste. "But I'm not going to run out no matter what Mr. Queen has in mind. Now won't you sit down and mind your own business like a lambie-pie?"

"No!" roared Jimmy. "Do you enjoy the prospect of getting your silly neck wrung? Even this vast intellect here can have his off-days. Besides, when was he ever human? I know all about *him*. Sits in this control tower of his and fiddles with little dials. Talk about delusions of grandeur! If he runs your neck into Cazalis's noose, what's the difference between him and Cazalis? They're both paranoiacs! Anyway, the whole idea is plain damn imbecility. How could you fool Cazalis into thinking you were somebody else? Who are you, Mata Hari?"

"You didn't let me finish, Jimmy," said Ellery patiently. "I said that was my original notion. But on second thought I've decided it's too dangerous."

"Oh," said Jimmy.

"Not for Celeste—she'd have been as well protected as Marilyn Soames is going to be—but for the sake of the trap. The Soames girl is going to be his objective; he's going to scout her, as he's scouted the others; it's safest to string along with her."

"I might have known even your reason for *not* making Cat bait out of her would be non-human!"

"Then what's my job, Mr. Queen?—Jimmy, shut up."

"As I said, we have every reason to believe Cazalis makes some sort of preliminary investigation of his victims. Well, we've got Marilyn covered every time she steps out of the Soames flat. But obviously with detectives we can only work from outside. That takes care of physical protection, but it doesn't give us a line on—for example—telephone calls.

"We could tap Cazalis's phones, on the chance that he'll try to contact Marilyn or her family from his home. But Cazalis is informed as well as shrewd, and the public's been made conscious of official wiretapping in the past year or two—the technique, what to listen for, have been well publicized; we can't chance Cazalis's getting suspicious. Besides, it's unthinkable that he'd be foolish enough to use his own phones for such a purpose; that he's cautious as well as daring is proved by his operations. So if he tries a phone approach it will undoubtedly be from a public booth somewhere, and that we can't prepare for.

"We could tap the Soames phone, but here again we can't run the risk of arousing the family's suspicions; too much depends on the Soameses behaving normally in the next few weeks.

"Or Cazalis may not phone at all. He may try a correspondence contact."

"It's true we've found no evidence of approaches by letter in previous cases," put in the Inspector, "but that doesn't mean there haven't been any; and even if he's never done it before, that's no guarantee he won't do it now."

"So a letter under an assumed name is possible," said Ellery. "And while we could intercept the United States mail . . ." Ellery shook his head. "Let's say it just wouldn't be practicable.

"In either event, our safest course is to plant somebody we can trust in the Soames household. Somebody who'll live with the family on a round-the-clock basis for the next two or three weeks."

"And that's me," said Celeste.

"Will somebody please tell me," came a choked voice from the sofa, "if this is or is not a nightmare concocted by Dali, Lombroso, and Sax Rohmer?"

But no one paid any attention to him. Celeste was frowning. "Wouldn't he recognize me, though, Mr. Queen? From the time when he—?"

"Scouted Simone?"

"And from those pictures of me in the papers afterward."

"I rather think he concentrated on Simone and didn't pay too much attention to you, Celeste. And I've checked the file on your newspaper photos and they're uniformly execrable. Still, it's possible he'd recognize you—yes. If he saw you, Celeste. But we'd make very sure," smiled

Ellery, "that he didn't. This would be strictly an inside job and you'd never come out on the streets except under rigidly controlled conditions."

Ellery glanced at his father, and the Inspector got up.

"I don't mind telling you, Miss Phillips," began Inspector Queen, "that I've been dead set against this. This job calls for a trained operative."

"But," said Jimmy McKell bitterly.

"But two facts exist which made me let Ellery change my mind. One is that for years you nursed a paralyzed invalid. The other is that one of the younger children in the Soames family—there are four, with Marilyn—a boy of 7, broke his hip a month ago and he was brought home from the hospital only last week in a cast.

"We've had a medical report on this boy. He's got to stay in bed and he's going to need a lot of care for the next few weeks. A trained nurse isn't necessary, but a practical nurse is. We've already had an intermediary in touch with the family doctor, a Dr. Myron Ulberson, and it turns out that Dr. Ulberson has been trying to find a practical nurse for the child but so far hasn't had any luck." The Inspector shrugged. "The boy's accident could be a great break for us, Miss Phillips, if you felt qualified to act the part of a practical nurse in a broken hip case."

"Oh, yes!"

"Besides being fed, washed, and amused," said Ellery, "the boy will need massages, I understand, and care of that sort. Do you think you could handle it, Celeste?"

"I did exactly that kind of nursing for Simone, and Simone's doctor often told me I was better than a lot of trained nurses he knew."

The Queens looked at each other, and the Inspector waved.

"Tomorrow morning, Celeste," said Ellery crisply, "you'll be taken to see Dr. Ulberson. He knows you're not a working practical nurse and that your presence in the Soames household is required for a highly secret purpose not connected with the ostensible one. Dr. Ulberson's been very tough—we had to get a high official of the City to give him personal reassurances that this is all in the interests of the Soames family. Just the same, he's going to test you unmercifully."

"I know how to move patients in bed, give hypos—I'll satisfy him, I know I will."

"Just turn on some of that charm," growled Jimmy. "The kind you befogged me with."

"I'll do it on merit, McKell!"

"I have a hunch you will," said Ellery. "By the way, you'd better not use your real name, even with Dr. Ulberson."

"How about McKell?" sneered McKell. "In fact, how about changing your name to McKell and to hell with this lady-dick opium dream?"

"One more crack out of you, McKell," snapped the Inspector, "and I'll personally escort you to the door on the end of my foot!"

"Okay, if you're going to be that selfish," muttered Jimmy; and he curled up on the sofa like an indignant sloth.

Celeste took his hand. "My real family name is Martin, pronounced the French way, but I could use it as just plain English-sounding Martin—"

"Perfect."

"—and then Mother Phillips used to call me Suzanne. It's my middle name. Even Simone called me Sue sometimes."

"Sue Martin. All right, use that. If you satisfy Dr. Ulberson, he'll recommend you to Mr. and Mrs. Soames as a live-in nurse and you can go right to work. You will charge, of course, the prevailing practical nurse fee, whatever it happens to be. We'll find that out for you."

"Yes, Mr. Queen."

"Stand up a minute, Miss Phillips," said Inspector Queen.

Celeste was surprised. "Yes?"

The Inspector looked her up and down.

Then he walked around her.

"At this point," said Jimmy, "they usually whistle."

"That's the trouble," rasped the Inspector. "Miss Phillips, I suggest you deglamorize yourself. Meaning no disrespect to the highly important profession of practical nursing, if you look like a practical nurse I look like Olivia de Havilland."

"Yes, Inspector," said Celeste, blushing.

"No makeup except a little lipstick. And not too vivid."

"Yes, sir."

"Simplify your hairdo. Take off your nail polish and clip your nails. And wear your plainest clothes. You've got to make yourself look older and more—more tired-looking."

"Yes, sir," said Celeste.

"Do you have a white uniform?"

"No—"

"We'll get you a couple. And some white stockings. How about low-heeled white shoes?"

"I have a pair that will do, Inspector."

"You'll also need a practical nurse's bag, equipped, which we'll provide."

"Yes, sir."

"How about a pearlhandled heater?" suggested Jimmy. "No eye-ette genuine without one."

But when they ignored him he got up and went to the Scotch decanter.

"Now as to this detective business," said Ellery. "Aside from nursing the Soames boy, you're to keep your eyes and ears open at all times. Marilyn Soames operates her stenographic business from home—she does manuscript typing and that sort of thing; that's why she has a phone in her name. Marilyn's working at home is another break; it will give you an opportunity to get friendly with her. She's only two years your junior and, from the little we've been able to learn so far, a nice, serious-minded girl."

"Gads," said Jimmy from the cellaret. "You have just described Operative 29-B." But he was beginning to sound proud.

"She seldom goes out socially, she's interested in books—very much your type, Celeste, even physically. Best of all, she's mad about her kid brother, the sick boy, so you'll have something in common right off."

"You're to pay particular attention to phone calls," said the Inspector.

"Yes, find out the substance of every conversation, especially if the caller is a stranger to the Soameses."

"And that goes whether the call is for Marilyn or anyone else."

"I understand, Inspector."

"You'll have to manage to read every letter Marilyn gets, too," Ellery said. "The whole family's mail, if possible. In general, you're to observe everything that happens in the household and to report it to us in detail. I want daily reports as a matter of routine."

"Do I report by phone? That might be hard."

"You're not to use the phone there except in an emergency. We'll arrange meeting places in the neighborhood of East 29th and First and Second Avenues. A different spot each night."

"Me, too," said Jimmy.

"At a certain time each night after Stanley's gone to sleep—you'll have to set the time for us after you get in and find out more about the setup—you'll go out for a walk. Establish the habit the very first night, so that the family comes to take your nightly absences as a matter of course. If something should come up to prevent your leaving the house at the agreed time, we'll wait at the meeting place till you can get away, even if it means waiting all night."

"Me, too," said Jimmy.

"Any questions?"

Celeste pondered. "I can't think of any."

Ellery looked at her rather nakedly, Jimmy thought. "I can't stress too much how important you may be in this thing, Celeste. Of course, the break may come from outside and you won't be involved at all, which is what we're all hoping. But if it doesn't, you're our Trojan filly. Everything may then depend on you."

"I'll do my best," said Celeste in a smallish voice.

"By the way, how do you feel about this?"

"Just . . . fine."

"We'll go over all this again in greater detail after you've seen Dr. Ulberson tomorrow." Ellery put an arm around her. "You'll stay here tonight as we arranged."

And Jimmy McKell snarled, *"Me, too!"*

# 10

Celeste would have felt better about having to play female Janus in the Soames household if she had found Marilyn's father a burly lecher, Mrs. Soames a shrew, Marilyn a slut, and the youngsters a pack of street rats. But the Soameses turned out insidiously nice.

Frank Pellman Soames was a skinny, squeezed-dry-looking man with the softest, burriest voice. He was a senior clerk at the main post office on Eighth Avenue at 33rd Street and he took his postal responsibilities as solemnly as if he had been called to office by the President himself. Otherwise he was inclined to make little jokes. He invariably brought something home with him after work—a candy bar, a bag of salted peanuts, a few sticks of bubble gum—to be divided among the three younger children with Rhadamanthine exactitude. Occasionally he brought Marilyn a single rosebud done up in green tissue paper. One night he showed up with a giant charlotte russe, enshrined in a cardboard box, for his wife. Mrs. Soames was appalled at his extravagance and said she just wouldn't eat it, it would be too selfish, but her husband said something to her in a sly *sotto voce* and she blushed. Celeste saw her put the little carton carefully away in the ice chest. Marilyn said that in charlotte russe season her parents always got "whispery." Next morning, when Celeste went to the chest for some milk for Stanley's breakfast, she noticed that the box was gone.

Marilyn's mother was one of those naturally powerful women whose strength drains off in middle age, leaving raw debility behind. She had led a back-breaking, penny-balancing life and she had not had time to spare herself; besides, she was going through a trying menopause. "I've got change of life, falling of the room rent, varicose veins, and bad feet," Mrs. Soames said to Celeste with grim humor, "but I'd like to see the Sutton Place lady who can bake a better berry pie," adding, "when there's money for berries." Often she had to lie down from weakness, but it was impossible to keep her in bed during the day for longer than a few minutes. "You know what Dr. Ulberson said, Edna," her husband would say anxiously. "Oh, you and your Dr. Ulberson," she would snort. "I've got the week's wash to do." Mrs Soames was obsessive on the subject of her laundry. She would never let Marilyn touch it. "You girls these days expect soap to do your scrubbing for you," she would say scornfully. But to Celeste Mrs. Soames once said, "She'll have wash enough to do in her life." Mrs. Soames's single self-indulgence was the radio. There was only one machine in the house, a small table model which usually occupied the center of the catchall shelf above the kitchen range; this Mrs. Soames had placed with a sigh at little Stanley's bedside. When Celeste ruled that Stanley might listen to the radio for no more than two hours a day, at selected times—and selected those times which did not conflict with his mother's favorite programs—Mrs. Soames looked guiltily grateful. She never missed Arthur Godfrey, she told Celeste, or *Stella Dallas, Big Sister*, and *Double or Nothing*. And she confided that "when our ship comes in, Frank's going to get me a television set," adding dryly, "At least, that's what Frank says. He's that sure one of those Irish Sweepstakes tickets he's always buying will come through."

Stanley was the youngest child, a thin little boy with blazing eyes and an imagination which ran to mayhem and gore. In the very beginning he was suspicious of Celeste and she could get hardly a word out of him. But late that first day, when she was giving his bony body a massage, he suddenly said: "You a real nurse?" "Well, sort of," smiled Celeste, although her heart skipped a beat. "Nurses stick knives into you," Stanley said glumly. "Whoever told you a story like that?" "Yitzie Frances Ellis, that's my teacher." "Stanley, she didn't. And where did you get that awful nickname of 'Yitzie' for a perfectly nice lady teacher?" "The principal calls her that," said Stanley indignantly. *"Yitzie?"* "The principal calls Miss Ellis Yitzie-Bitzie when nobody's around." "Stanley Soames, I don't believe a single—" But Stanley had screwed his little head about, his eyes bugging with horror. "Lie still! What's the matter?" "You know something, Miss Martin?" whispered Stanley. Celeste heard herself whispering back, "What, Stanley, what?" *"I got green blood."* After that, Celeste digested Master Stanley's remarks, revelations, and confidences with great quantities of salt. She often had to exercise considerable judgment to distinguish fact from fancy.

Stanley was thoroughly familiar with the Cat. He told Celeste solemnly that he *was* the Cat.

Between her patient and Marilyn there were two other children: Eleanor, 9, and Billie, 13. Eleanor was a large calm child with an unhur-

ried attitude toward life; her rather plain features were illuminated by a
pair of remarkably direct eyes, and Celeste hastened to make friends with
her. Billie was in junior high, a fact which he accepted philosophically.
He was clever with his hands and the apartment was always turning up
things he had built for his mother out of "nothing," as Mrs. Soames said.
But his father seemed disappointed. "We'll never make a student out of
Billie. His heart isn't in it. All he does is hang around garages after
school learning about motors. He can't wait till he's old enough to get his
working papers and learn some mechanical trade. The scholars in my
family are the girls." Billie was in the weedy age, "a regular Ichabod
Crane," as Mr. Soames put it. Frank Soames was something of a reader;
he generally had his nose buried in some library book and he owned a
prize shelf of decrepit volumes which he had hoarded from young manhood—Scott, Irving, Cooper, Eliot, Thackeray—authors whom Billie
characterized as "squares"; Billie's reading was restricted almost entirely
to comic books, which he acquired in wholesale quantities by some complex barter-system incomprehensible to his father. Celeste liked Billie—
his overgrown hands, his rather furtive voice.

And Marilyn was a darling; Celeste fell in love with her immediately.
She was a tall girl, not pretty: her nose was a little broad and her cheekbones were pitched too steep; but her dark eyes and hair were lovely and
she carried herself with a defiant swing. Celeste understood her secret
sorrow: the necessity of earning a living to help her father carry the
weight of the family's needs had kept her from going on from high
school to the higher education she craved. But Marilyn was no com-
plainer; outwardly she was even serene. Celeste gathered that she had another, independent life, a vicarious one: through her work she kept in
touch with a sort of malformed, teasing shadow of the creative and intellectual world. "I'm not the best manuscript typist in the business," she
told Celeste. "I get too blamed interested in what I'm typing." Nevertheless, she had built up a good clientele. Through a former high school
teacher she had got in with a young playwrights' group whose art was, if
nothing else, prolific; one of her accounts was a Columbia full professor
who was engaged in writing a monumental work of scholarship, "a psychological outline of world history"; and her best client was a famous
journalist author who, Mr. Soames said proudly, swore by her—"and
sometimes at me," added Marilyn. Her earnings were capricious and the
importance of maintaining them kept Marilyn a little on the grim side.
For the sake of her father's self-esteem she preserved the fiction that her
co-producing role in the family was a temporary one, "to tide us over the
high prices." But Celeste knew that Marilyn knew there would be no escape for many years, if ever. The boys would grow up, marry, and move

off; there was Eleanor's education to provide for—Marilyn was firm that Eleanor should go to college, "she's really a genius. You ought to read the poetry she writes right now, at 9"; Mrs. Soames was headed for invalidism; Frank Soames was not a well man. Marilyn knew her fate and was prepared for it. Because of this she discouraged the romantic advances of several men who were pursuing her, "at least one of them," Marilyn said with a laugh, "with honorable intentions." Her most persistent pursuer was the journalist author—"he's *not* the one. Every time I have to call for a new chapter—he writes in longhand—or deliver one I've typed, he chases me around his apartment with an African war club he picked up in his travels. It's supposed to be a gag, but it's gagging on the level. One of these days I'm going to stop running and poke him one. I'd have done it long ago if I hadn't needed his work." But Celeste suspected that one of these days Marilyn would stop running and not poke him one. She persuaded herself that the experience would do Marilyn good; Marilyn was a passionate girl who had kept herself, Celeste was sure of it, rigidly chaste. (It also occurred to the sophisticate that this was true of a certain Celeste Phillips as well; but at this point Miss Phillips dropped the whole subject out of her thoughts.)

The Soameses lived in a two-bedroom, five-room apartment in an ancient walkup; because they needed three sleeping rooms, the "front room" had been converted into a third bedroom, and this room served both as the girls' bedroom and Marilyn's workshop. "Marilyn ought to have her own room," sighed Mrs. Soames, "but what can we do?" Billie had rigged up a partition—a drape on a long curtain pole—to cut off part of the room for Marilyn's "office"; here she had her work table, her typewriter, her stationery, her telephone; there was a modest illusion of separate quarters. The arrangement was also necessary because Marilyn often had to work at night and Eleanor went to bed early.

The location of the telephone prompted Celeste to make an ulterior suggestion. When she arrived to take up her duties she found Stanley occupying his own bed in the boys' room. On the plea that she could not very well share a bedroom with a boy as big as Billie—and obviously she had to be within call of her patient during the night—Celeste moved Stanley into the front bedroom, to Eleanor's bed, and Eleanor moved to the boys' room. "You're sure this won't interfere with you?" Celeste asked Marilyn anxiously; she was feeling wretched about the whole thing. But Marilyn said she had trained herself to work under impossible conditions: "With a boy like Stanley in the house you either learn how to turn your ears off or you cut your throat." Marilyn's easy reference to "throat" made Celeste sick; on her third day she became aware that she had been unconsciously avoiding that part of Marilyn's generous anatomy. It was a strong throat, and in the days that followed it became for Celeste a sort of symbol, a link between the lives of all of them and the death that waited outside. She trained herself to look at it.

The transfer of Eleanor to Stanley's bed created a problem and sharpened Celeste's feeling of guilt. Mrs. Soames said it was "not good" for brother and sister to share a bedroom at Eleanor's and Billie's ages. So Billie was sent to his parents' room and Mrs. Soames moved over to the boys' room to sleep with Eleanor. "I feel as if I've created a revolution," Celeste wailed, "upsetting your lives this way." And when Mrs. Soames said, "Why, Miss Martin, don't give a thought to us. We're so grateful you could come nurse our baby," Celeste felt like the most callous doubledealing spy. There was a small portion of consolation for her in the thought that the bed she had to sleep on in the front room, an antique cot borrowed from a neighbor, was as hard as the floor of a flagellant's cave. On this she did penance for her chicanery. She almost angrily rejected the family's offer of any one of their own beds in exchange.

"It's so mean," Celeste moaned to the Queens and Jimmy during their second-night rendezvous in a First Avenue areaway. "They're so sweet about everything I feel like a criminal."

"I told you she's too peasant-like for this job," jeered Jimmy; but in the dark he was nibbling her fingertips.

"Jimmy, they're the nicest people. And they're all so grateful to me. If they only knew!"

"They'd smother you with onions," said Jimmy. "Which reminds me . . ."

But Ellery said, "What's the mail situation, Celeste?"

"Marilyn goes downstairs for it first thing in the morning. Mr. Soames leaves the house before the first delivery—"

"We know that."

"She keeps her current correspondence in a wire basket on her desk. I won't have any trouble reading it," said Celeste in a trembly voice. "Last night I managed to do it in the middle of the night, when Marilyn and Stanley were asleep. There are opportunities during the day, too. Sometimes Marilyn has to go out in connection with her work."

"We know that, too," said the Inspector grimly. Marilyn Soames's unpredictable excursions, sometimes in the evening, were keeping them all on the edge of ulcers.

"Even if she doesn't, she always eats lunch in the kitchen. I can even read her mail while Stanley's awake, because of the heavy curtain."

"Wonderful."

"I'm glad you think s-so!" And Celeste found herself irrigating Jimmy's dusty-blue tie.

But when she returned to the Soames flat she had color in her cheeks and she told Marilyn that the walk had done her oceans of good, really it had.

Their meeting time was set by Celeste at between 10 and 10:15. Stanley was not tucked in for the night much before 9, she said, and he rarely fell asleep until 9:30 or so. "Being in bed all the time he doesn't need so much sleep. I can't leave till I'm sure he's dropped off, and then too I've been helping with the supper dishes."

"You mustn't overdo that, Miss Phillips," said the Inspector. "They'll get suspicious. Practical nurses don't—"

"Practical nurses are human beings, aren't they?" sniffed Celeste. "Mrs. Soames is a sick woman who slaves all day and if I can save her some work by doing the supper things I'm going to do it. Would it put me out of the spy union if I told you I also pitch in to the housework? Don't worry, Inspector Queen, I shan't give anything away. I'm quite aware of what's at stake."

The Inspector said feebly that he just thought he'd mention it, that was all, and Jimmy reeled off some verse that he said he had made up but which sounded remarkably like one of the Elizabethan things.

So they met at 10 o'clock or a little later, each night in a different place by prearrangement the night before. For Celeste, at least, it took on the greenish cast of fantasy. For twenty-three and a half hours a day she worked, ate, spied, and slept among the Soameses; the half hour away was a flight to the moon. Only Jimmy's presence made it bearable; she had come to dread the taut, questioning faces of the Queens. She had to brace herself as she walked along the dark street to the appointed spot, waiting for the signal of Jimmy's soft wolf-whistle. Then she would join them in the doorway, or under the store awning, or just inside the alley— wherever the agreed rendezvous was—and she would report the increasingly pleasant monotonies of the past twenty-four hours and answer questions about the Soames mail and the telephone calls, all the while clinging to Jimmy's hand in the darkness; and then, feeling the pull of Jimmy's eyes, she would run back to what had come to signify for her the endearing sanity of the little Soames world.

She did not attempt to tell them how much the aroma of Mrs. Soames's rising bread reminded her of Mother Phillips or of how, by some witchery, Marilyn had become the best of remembered Simone.

And of how frightened, how icily frightened, she was during every moment of every waking hour, and beyond.

To tell any of them.

Especially Jimmy.

\*　\*　\*

They speculated interminably. Beyond meeting Celeste each night, there was nothing else to do.

Over and over they came back to the reports on Cazalis. They were exasperating. He was acting exactly as if he were Dr. Edward Cazalis, Noted Psychiatrist, and not a cunning paranoiac bent on satiating his appetite for death. He was still working with his board on occasional private case histories sent in by psychiatric stragglers. He even attended a meeting called by the Mayor at which the Queens were present. At this meeting Cazalis was studied closely by men trained in the art of dissimulation; but it was a question who was the best actor present. The psychiatrist was affably discouraging; he said again that he and his board were wasting their time; they had cracked a few of their reluctant colleagues but the remainder were adamant and nothing was to be expected of them. (And Inspector Queen reported to the Mayor with a garmented face that in the trickle of suspects turned over by Dr. Cazalis and his coworkers there was exactly none who could be the Cat.) "Haven't you fellows made any progress at all on your end?" Cazalis asked the Inspector. When the Inspector shook his head, the big man smiled. "It's probably someone from outside the metropolitan area."

Ellery thought it unworthy of him.

But he was looking poorly these days, and that was provocative; thinned out, fallen in, the ice of his hair crumbling. His heavy face was sludgy and cracked; he had developed twitches under both eyes; his large hands, when they were not drumming on the nearest object, kept drifting about his person as if seeking an anchorage. Mrs. Cazalis, who was in miserable attendance, said that the work her husband had done for the City had taken too much out of him, it was her fault for having pounded at him to continue investigating. The doctor patted his wife's hand. He was taking it easy, he said; what bothered him was that he had failed. A young man "rises above failure," he said, an old man "sinks under it." "Edward, I want you to go away." But he smiled. He was considering a long rest, he said. As soon as he tied off certain "loose ends" . . .

Was he mocking them?

The metaphor remained with them.

Or had he become suspicious and was uncertainty or the fear of detection strong enough to check the continuing impulse to kill?

He might have caught sight of one of his pursuers. The detectives were sure he had not.

Still, it was possible.

Or had they left a trace of their visit to his apartment? They had worked systematically, touching and moving nothing until they had fixed in their memories the exact position and condition of each object to be touched and moved. And afterward they had restored each object to its original place.

Still, again, he may have noticed something wrong. Suppose he had set a trap? He might have had a little signal for himself, a trivial thing, unnoticeable, in the storage closet or in one of the drawers. A psychotic of a certain type might have taken such a precaution. Elaborately. They were dealing with a man whose brilliance overlapped his psychosis. In certain flights he might be prescient.

It was possible.

Dr. Cazalis's movements were as innocent as those of a man walking across a field under the sunny sky. A patient or two a day in his office, chiefly women. An occasional consultation with other psychiatrists. Long nights when he did not step out of his apartment. Once a visit with Mrs. Cazalis to the Richardsons'. Once a concert at Carnegie, when he listened to the Franck symphony with open eyes and clenched hands; and then, curl-lipped and calm, listening with enjoyment to Bach and Mozart. Once a social evening with some professional friends and their wives.

At no time did he venture near East 29th Street and First Avenue.

It was possible.

That was the canker.

Anything was *possible.*

By the tenth day after the strangulation of Donald Katz, and in the sixth day of "Sue Martin's" practical-nursing career, they were sweating. They spent most of their time now in the report room at Police Headquarters. In silence. Or, when the silence became intolerable, snapping at one another with a querulousness that made silence a relief.

What was digging new hollows in Inspector Queen's face was the thought that Cazalis might be outwaiting them. Madmen had been known to exercise extraordinary patience. Sooner or later—Cazalis might be thinking—they would conclude that he had reached the end of his string . . . if only he did nothing long enough. Then they would call off their watchdogs. Sooner or later.

Was that what Cazalis was waiting for?

If, of course, he knew he was being watched.

Or, if he foresaw that this was one case in which the watchers would never be withdrawn, he might deliberately be waiting until he tired them into carelessness. And then . . . an opening. And he would slip into the clear.

With a tussah silk cord in his pocket.

Inspector Queen kept harrying his operatives until they hated him.

Ellery's brain performed more desperate acrobatics. Suppose Cazalis *had* set a trap in his storage closet. Suppose he *did* know someone had been looking through his old files. Then he knew they had exposed the heart of his secret. Then he knew they knew how he chose his victims.

In such case it would not be overcrediting Cazalis's acumen to say that he would also guess their plan. He had merely to do what Ellery was now doing: to put himself in the adversary's place.

Then Cazalis would know that they had gone beyond Donald Katz to Marilyn Soames, and that with Marilyn Soames they had baited a trap for him.

If I were Cazalis, said Ellery, what would I do then? I would give up all thought of snaring Marilyn Soames. Instantly. He said, I would go to my old obstetrical records and I would move on from Marilyn Soames's card to the card of the next regularly indicated victim. Or, to play it even safer, I would skip the next regularly indicated victim to the one follow-ing, on the chance that the enemy had taken out insurance as well. Which we haven't done . . .

Ellery writhed. He could not forgive himself. There was no excuse, he kept saying. To have failed to take the precaution of searching Cazalis's cards past Marilyn Soames to the next-indicated victim, and the next, and the next, and protecting them all—even if it meant going to the end of the file and having to guard a hundred young people all over the City . . .

If these premises were sound, Cazalis might even now be waiting for the detectives trailing him to relax their vigilance. And when they did, the Cat would slink out to strangle a tenth, unknown victim at his leisure, laughing all the while at the detectives he knew were guarding Marilyn Soames.

Ellery became quite masochistic about it.

"The best we can hope for," he groaned, "is that Cazalis makes a move toward Marilyn. The worst, that he's already moved against some-one else. If that happens, we won't know about it till it's over. Unless we can keep Cazalis at the other end of the tail, Dad. We've got to hang on to him! How about assigning a few extra men . . . ?"

But the Inspector shook his head. The more men, the greater the chance of giving the game away. After all, there was no *reason* to believe that Cazalis suspected anything. The trouble was that they were getting too nervous.

"Who's nervous?"

"You are! And so am I!—though I wasn't till you started your old fancy mental gymnastics!"

"Tell me it couldn't happen that way, Dad."

"Then why not go after those records again?"

Well, muttered Ellery, they were better off stringing along with what they had. Let well enough alone. Watchful waiting. Time will tell.

"The master of the original phrase," snarled Jimmy McKell. "If you ask me, your morale is showing. Doesn't anybody give a slup in bloody borsch what happens to my girl?"

That reminded them that it was time to go uptown for the nightly meeting with Celeste.

They jostled one another getting through the door.

The night of Wednesday, October 19, was uncharitable. The three men huddled in the alley entrance between two buildings on the south side of East 29th Street, near Second Avenue. There was a cutting wet wind and they kept up a little dance as they waited.

10:15.

It was the first time Celeste had been late.

They kept yapping at one another. Swearing at the wind. Jimmy would poke his head out of the alley and say under his breath, "Come onnnnnn, Celeste!" as if she were a horse.

The lights of Bellevue over on First Avenue were no comfort.

The reports on Cazalis that day had been discouraging. He had not left his apartment. Two patients had called during the afternoon, both young women. Della and Zachary Richardson had shown up at 6:30 on foot; apparently for dinner, as by 9 P.M., the time of the last report the Queens had received before leaving Headquarters, they had still not come out.

"It's nothing, Jimmy," Ellery kept saying. "Cazalis is safe for the night. Can't mean a thing. She just couldn't get away—"

"Isn't that Celeste now?"

She was trying not to run and not succeeding. She would walk, faster and faster, then break into a trot, then slow down suddenly, then run. Her black cloth coat kept flopping around her like birds.

It was 10:35.

"Something's up."

"What could be?"

"She's late. Naturally she'd hurry." Jimmy whistled the signal; it came out all dry and blowy. "Celeste—"

"Jimmy." She was gulping.

"What is it?" Ellery had her by both arms.

"He phoned."

The wind had dropped and her words shrilled through the alley. Jimmy shouldered Ellery aside, put his arms around her. She was trembling.

"There's nothing to be scared of. Stop shaking."

She began to cry.

They waited. Jimmy kept tumbling her hair.

Finally, she stopped.

Inspector Queen said instantly: "When?"

"A few minutes past 10. I was just leaving—out in the hall with my hand on the doorknob—when I heard the phone ring. Marilyn was in the dining room with Billie and Eleanor and their father and mother and I was nearest to the front room. I ran and got to the phone first. It was . . . I know it was. I heard his voice over the radio the day he gave his press conference and talk. It's low and musical and at the same time sort of sharp."

"Cazalis," said the Inspector. "You mean this was Dr. Edward Cazalis's voice, Miss Phillips?" He said it as if he did not believe it at all and as if it were of the greatest importance to corroborate his disbelief.

"I tell you it was!"

"Well, now," said the Inspector. "Just from hearing it on the radio." But he moved closer to Celeste.

"What did he say?" This was Ellery. "Word for word!"

"I said hello, and he said hello, and then he gave me the Soames phone number and asked if that was the number and I said yes. He said, 'Is this the public stenographer, Marilyn Soames, speaking?' It was his voice. I said no and he said, 'Is Miss Soames in—it is *Miss* Soames, isn't it, not Mrs.? I believe she's the daughter of Edna and Frank Soames.' I said yes. Then he said, 'I want to talk to her, please.' By that time Marilyn was in the room so I handed her the phone and hung around pretending I had to fix my slip."

"Checking up," muttered the Inspector. "Making sure."

"Go on, Celeste!"

"Give her a chance, will you!" growled Jimmy.

"I heard Marilyn say yes once or twice and then she said, 'Well, I am kind of piled up, but if it's that kind of deal I'll try to get it out for you by Monday, Mr.—What was your name again, sir?' When he told her, Marilyn said, 'I'm sorry, would you mind spelling that?' and she spelled it after him."

"The name."

"Paul Nostrum. N-o-s-t-r-u-m."

"Nostrum." Ellery laughed.

"Then Marilyn said yes, she could call for the manuscript tomorrow, and she asked him where she was to pick it up. He said something and Marilyn said, 'I'm tall and dark and I have a mashed nose and I'll be wearing a cloth coat, big white and black checks, you can't miss it, and a beanie. How about you?' and after he answered she said, 'Well, then maybe you'd better do all the looking, Mr. Nostrum. I'll be there. Good night,' and she hung up."

Ellery shook her. "Didn't you get the address, the time?"

Jimmy shook Ellery. "Give her a chance, I said!"

"Wait, wait." Inspector Queen pushed them both aside. "Did you get any other information, Miss Phillips?"

"Yes, Inspector. When Marilyn hung up I said as offhandedly as I could, 'New client, Marilyn?' and she said yes, she wondered how he knew about her, some writer she did work for must have recommended her. 'Nostrum' had said he was a writer in from Chicago with his new novel to see his publisher, that he'd had to revise his last few chapters and he needed then retyped in a hurry. He hadn't been able to get a hotel accommodation and he was staying with 'friends,' so he'd meet her to-morrow at 5:30 in the lobby of the Astor to give her his manuscript."

"Lobby of the Astor!" Ellery was incredulous. "He couldn't have picked a busier spot at a busier hour in the whole City of New York."

"You're sure it's the Astor, Miss Phillips."

"That's what Marilyn said."

They were silent.

Finally, Ellery shrugged. "No use beating our brains out —"

"No, indeed, for time will tell," said Jimmy. "Meanwhile what happens to our heroine? Does Celeste stay in that rat cage? Or does she show up at the Astor tomorrow in a checked coat, garnished with parsley?"

"Idiot." Celeste rested her head on his arm.

"Celeste stays where she is. This is just his opening move. We'll play along."

The Inspector nodded. "What time did you say he made that call?" he asked Celeste.

"It was just about five minutes past 10, Inspector Queen."

"You go on back to the Soameses'."

Ellery squeezed her hand. "Stick to that phone, Celeste. If there's a call tomorrow from 'Paul Nostrum'—or anyone else—changing the time and place of Marilyn's appointment, that's one of the emergencies I mentioned. Phone Police Headquarters immediately."

"All right."

"Ask for Extension 2-X," said the Inspector. "That's a code signal that will put you right through to us." The old man patted her arm awkwardly. "You're a good girl."

"Good, shmood," muttered Jimmy. "Give me a kiss."

They watched her walk down the windy street, not moving until she disappeared in the entrance of 486.

Then they ran toward Third Avenue, where the squad car was parked.

\*   \*   \*

According to Sergeant Velie, Detective Goldberg's 10 P.M. report had stated that at 9:26 Mr. and Mrs. Richardson, accompanied by Dr. and Mrs. Cazalis, had left the Cazalis apartment house. The two couples had strolled up Park Avenue. According to Detective Young, Goldberg's partner, Cazalis had been in high spirits; he had laughed a great deal. The four had turned west on 84th Street, crossed Madison Avenue, and they had stopped before the Park-Lester. Here the couples separated, the Cazalises walking back to Madison, turning north, and stopping in at a drugstore on the corner of 86th Street. They sat at the counter and were served hot chocolates. This was at two minutes of 10, and at 10 o'clock Goldberg had telephoned his hourly report from a coffee shop across the street.

Ellery glanced at the wall clock. "Ten after 11. What about the 11 o'clock report, Sergeant?"

"Wait," said Sergeant Velie. "Goldie called in again at 10:20. A special."

The Sergeant seemed to be expecting exclamation and excitement, for he paused dramatically.

But Ellery and Jimmy McKell were doodling on pads at opposite sides of the desk and all that the Inspector said was, "Yes?"

"Goldberg said he'd no sooner got off the phone in the coffee shop at 10 when Young signaled him from across the street and Goldie walked over and saw Mrs. Cazalis sitting at the soda counter—all by her lonesome. Goldie thought he was seeing things because he doesn't spot Cazalis any place and he says to Young, Where's our man, where's our man? Young points to the back of the drugstore and Goldie sees Cazalis in a booth back there, phoning. Young told Goldberg that right after Goldie left Cazalis looked at his watch like he'd all of a sudden remembered something. Young said it was a great big take and it looked like a phony to him, Cazalis putting on an act to fool his wife. He said a few words— like he was excusing himself—got off the stool, and goes to the back. He looks up a number in one of the phone books on the rack, then he goes into the booth and makes a call. Time of entry into booth: 10:04."

"10:04," said Ellery. "10:04."

"That's what I said," said the Sergeant. "Cazalis is on the phone around ten minutes. Then he comes back to Mrs. Cazalis, drinks the rest of his hot chocolate, and they leave.

"They took a cab, Cazalis giving the hack his home address. Young tailed them in another cab and Goldie went into the drugstore. He'd noticed that the directory Young said Cazalis had looked a name up in was open on the stand, and he wanted a gander at it because nobody had used it after Cazalis. It turned out to be the Manhattan book, and it was open at the pages with . . ." Velie paused impressively, . . . "with the S-O names."

"The S-O names," said Inspector Queen. "Did you hear that, Ellery? The S-O names." His denture was showing.

"Would you think," said Jimmy, drawing a set of fangs, "that a kindly old gent like that could look so much like a Brontosaurus?"

But the Inspector said genially, "Go on, Velie, go on."

"There's nothing more," said Sergeant Velie with dignity. "Goldberg said he thought that rated a hurry-up special report, so he phoned right in before leaving to go back to Park Avenue after Young."

"Goldberg was so right," said the Inspector. "And the 11 o'clock report?"

"The Cazalises went right home. At ten minutes to 11 their lights were out. Unless the doc is figuring on a sneak tonight, after his old woman is in dreamland—"

"Not tonight, Sergeant, not tonight," said Ellery, smiling; "5:30 tomorrow, at the Astor."

They saw him enter the Astor lobby through the 44th Street doorway. The time was 5:05 and they had already been there an hour. Detective Hesse was close on his tail.

Cazalis was dressed in a dark gray suit, a rather seedy dark topcoat, and a stained gray hat. He came in with several other people, as if he were one of their group, but well in the transverse corridor at the rear of the lobby he took himself off, bought a copy of the *New York Post* at the cigar counter, stood for a few moments glancing at the front page, and then began a strolling tour of the lobby. Moving a few feet at a time, with long pauses between.

"Making sure she hasn't come yet," said the Inspector.

They were on the balcony of the mezzanine, well hidden.

Cazalis kept circulating. The lobby was crowded and it was hard to keep him in sight. But Hesse had taken a central position; he had to move very little, and they knew he would not lose his man.

There were six other Headquarters men planted in the lobby.

When Cazalis had completed his tour, he edged alongside five people, men and women, who were standing near the Broadway entrance talking and laughing. He held an unlighted cigaret.

On the steps outside they caught an occasional glimpse of the broad back and accented waistline of Detective Zilgitt. He was a Negro and one of the most valuable men at Headquarters; Inspector Queen had especially detailed him to work with Hesse for the day. Zilgitt, who was a

modest dresser, had rigged himself out in sharp clothes for his assignment; he looked like a Broadway character waiting for a heavy date.

At 5:25 Marilyn Soames arrived.

She came hurrying into the lobby, out of breath. She paused by the
florist's shop to look around. She wore a big-checked cloth coat and a little felt cap. She carried an old simulated-leather briefcase.

Detective Johnson walked in, passed her, and mingled with the crowd.
But he kept within fifteen feet of her. Detective Piggott entered the
florist's shop from Broadway; he took some time buying a carnation. He
had a perfect view of both Marilyn and Cazalis through the glass walls of
the shop. A little later he sauntered out into the lobby and stopped almost
at the girl's elbow, looking around as if for a familiar face. She glanced at
him doubtfully and seemed about to speak to him; but when his glance
passed over her she bit her lip and looked elsewhere.

Cazalis had spotted her instantly.

He began to read his newspaper. Leaning against the wall, the cigaret
between his fingers still unlighted.

From where the Queens stood watching they could see his glance
fixed on her face above his paper.

Marilyn had begun scanning the area within her orbit from the side of
the lobby opposite to which Cazalis stood. Her glance searched slowly.
When it had all but completed its half-circle, just as it was about to reach
him, Cazalis lowered his newspaper, murmured something to one of the
men in the group by his side, and the man produced a packet of matches,
struck a match, and held the flame to the tip of Cazalis's cigaret. For that
moment Cazalis looked like one of the group.

Marilyn's glance passed him as if he were invisible.

He inched back. Now he stood with the group between them, studying
her frankly.

The Soames girl remained where she was until 5:40. Then she moved
off, walking around the lobby and searching among the men who were
seated. A few smiled and one said something to her. But she frowned and
walked on.

As she walked, Cazalis followed.

He made no attempt to get close to her.

At times he even stood still, his eyes taking up the hunt.

He seemed to be committing her to memory—her gait, the swing of
her body, the plain strong profile.

He was flushed now, breathing heavily. As if he were tremendously
excited.

By ten minutes to 6 she had gone completely around the lobby and returned to her original position near the florist's shop. Cazalis passed her.

It was the closest he had come to her—he could have touched her, and Johnson and Piggott could have touched him. She actually studied his face. But this time his glance was elsewhere and he passed her briskly, as if he were going somewhere. Apparently he had given her a false description of himself, or no description at all.

He paused in the nearest doorway.

It was just inside the entrance where Detective Zilgitt waited. Zilgitt glanced at him casually and moved off the steps.

The girl's foot began tapping. She did not look behind her and Cazalis was able to study her without subterfuge.

At 6 o'clock Marilyn straightened up and with determination began to push toward the bell captain's desk.

Cazalis remained where he was.

A few moments later a bellboy began to call: "Mr. Nostrum. Mr. Paul Nostrum."

Immediately Cazalis went down the steps, crossed the sidewalk, and got into a taxicab. As the cab moved away from the curb into the Broadway traffic, Detective Hesse jumped into the next cab at the stand.

At 6:10 Marilyn Soames, looking very angry, left the Astor and walked with long strides down Broadway toward 42nd Street.

Johnson and Piggott were just behind her.

"Marilyn was fit to be tied," Celeste reported that night. "I almost kissed her when she got home, I was so relieved. But she was so mad at being stood up she didn't notice. Mr. Soames said writers were temperamental and she'd probably get a bouquet of flowers from him as an apology, but Marilyn snapped that she wasn't going to be blarneyed out of it, he was probably drunk in some bar and if he phoned again she'd meet him just so she could tell him where to get off." The Inspector was annoying his mustache. "Where on earth did he go from the Astor?"

"Home." Ellery seemed disturbed, too. "Where is Marilyn, Celeste? She hasn't gone out again, has she?"

"She was so mad she had supper and went right to bed."

"I'd better take a walk around and tell the boys to keep an extra eye out tonight," muttered the Inspector.

They watched him hurry down the street.

Finally Celeste pushed away from Jimmy. "Do you think he'll phone again, Mr. Queen?"

"I don't know."

"What was the idea today?"

"He's had to play this one differently. Marilyn doesn't go out to work, hasn't a predictable routine. He's probably too cagey to hang around here day after day hoping to catch a glimpse of her, so he had to use a trick to get a good look."

"That's . . . right, isn't it. He didn't know what Marilyn looked like."

"Not since he spanked her rosy bottom," said Jimmy. "Now can I have five minutes alone in this palatial hallway with my future wife? Before the bell tolls, Fairy Godfather, and I turn into a pumpkin."

But Celeste said, "When do you think he'll . . ."

"It won't be long." Ellery sounded remote. "Any night now, Celeste."

And they were quiet.

"Well," said Celeste at last.

Jimmy stirred.

"I'd better be getting back."

"Keep checking the phone calls. And pay particular attention to Marilyn's mail."

"Right."

"You've got to give me my five lousy minutes!" wailed Jimmy. Ellery stepped out into the street.

Inspector Queen came back before Jimmy and Celeste were finished in their hallway.

"Everything all right, Dad?"

"They're scratching fleas."

Afterwards, the three men went back to Headquarters. The latest word, delivered in Detective Goldberg's 11 P.M. report, was that the Cazalises were entertaining a large number of people who had arrived in chauffeur-driven limousines. The party, Goldberg had said, was gay. Once, prowling in the court, he had heard the boom of Cazalis's laugh, accompanied by a chatter of crystal. "The doc," Goldberg had said, "sounded just like Santa Claus."

Friday. Saturday. Sunday.

And nothing.

The Queens were scarcely on speaking terms. Jimmy McKell found himself functioning as part peacemaker, part interpreter. He suffered the usual fate of middlemen; sometimes they both turned on him. He was beginning to wear a haunted look himself.

Even Sergeant Velie was antisocial. When he spoke at all it was in an animal growl.

Once an hour the telephone rang. Then they all leaped.

The messages varied, but their gist was the same.

Nothing.

They began to share a common loathing for the report room, which was only surpassed by their loathing for one another.

Then, on Monday, October 24, the Cat moved.

The announcement came from Detective MacGayn, who was Hesse's partner on the regular day trick. MacGayn called only a few minutes after his hourly report, in considerable excitement, to say that their man was taking a powder. Several suitcases had just been carried out of the Cazalis apartment by the doorman. Hesse had overheard him instruct a taxi driver to wait as he had "some people going to Penn Station to catch a train." Hesse was set to follow in another cab; MacGayn had run to phone in the news.

Inspector Queen instructed MacGayn to go immediately to Pennsylvania Station, locate Hesse and their man, and then wait at the 31st Street entrance nearest Seventh Avenue.

The squad car screamed uptown.

Once Ellery said angrily, "It isn't possible. I don't believe it. It's a trick."

Otherwise, there was no conversation.

On order, the driver cut his siren out at 23rd Street.

MacGayn was waiting for them. He had just found Hesse. Dr. and Mrs. Cazalis were standing in a crowd at the gate of a Florida train. They had been joined by Mr. and Mrs. Richardson. The gate was not yet open. Hesse was standing by.

They made their way cautiously into the station.

From the windows of the south waiting room MacGayn pointed out the Cazalis-Richardson group and, nearby, Hesse.

"Take Hesse's place," said Inspector Queen. "And send him here."

Hesse walked in briskly a few moments later.

Ellery kept his eyes on Cazalis.

"What's going on?" demanded the Inspector.

Hesse was worried. "I don't know, Inspector. There's something off-beat, but they're a little in the clear out there and I can't get close enough to listen in. His wife keeps arguing with him and he keeps smiling and shaking his head. The luggage has gone down. The Richardsons', too."

"Oh, so they're also going," said Ellery.

"Looks like it."

He was not wearing Thursday's disreputable topcoat. His coat looked new and fashionable, he wore a smart Homburg, a small 'mum in his lapel.

"If he ever wiggles out of this one," remarked Jimmy McKell, "he can always make himself a tidy zloty by posing as a Man of Distinction."

But Ellery muttered, "Florida."

The gate opened and the crowd began squeezing through.

Inspector Queen seized Hesse's arm. "Get down there after him and stick. Take MacGayn and if anything happens send him back up. We'll be waiting at the gate."

Hesse hurried away.

The gate had opened late; train-departure time, according to the figures posted above the gate, was only ten minutes off.

"It's all right, Ellery," said the Inspector. "They won't pull out on time." His tone was paternal.

Ellery looked wild.

They strolled out into the shed and mingled with the people gathering before a gate marked *Philadelphia Express: Newark-Trenton-Philadelphia.* The stairway to the Florida train was two gates away. They kept glancing from the gateway to the big clocks.

"I told you," said the Inspector.

"But why Florida? Suddenly!"

"He's called Operation Necktie off," said Jimmy.

"No."

"Don't you want him to?"

"Who says he's called it off?" Ellery scowled. "He's given up on the Soames girl, granted. Spotted something Thursday, maybe. Or figured she was too tough. Or this might be a trick to put us off guard, if he suspects something. After all, we don't know how much he knows. We don't know anything! . . . If he doesn't suspect, this may mean he's gone on to somebody else—"

"Somebody who he found out is vacationing in Florida," nodded Inspector Queen.

Jimmy said, "New York papers please copy. Dateline Miami, Palm Beach, or Sarasota. *Cat Hits Florida.*"

"It could be," said Ellery. "But somehow I can't get myself to believe it. It's something else. Some other trick."

"What do you need, diagrams? I'll bet he's got those silk cords in his bags. What are you waiting for?"

"We can't chance it." Inspector Queen looked dour. "We just can't. If we have to we'll work through the Florida locals. We'll have him watched down there and set him up on his return to New York. It means doing the whole thing over again."

"The hell it does! Not with Celeste, Old Sleuth. I can't wait that long, see?"

And just then MacGayn came running out of the gateway making frantic signals. The trainman was looking at his watch.

"MacGayn—"

"Get back, he's coming back up!"

"What?"

*"He's not going!"*

They scuttled into the thick of the crowd.

Cazalis appeared.

Alone.

He was smiling.

He cut diagonally across the shed toward the corner marked *Taxicabs* with the happy stride of a man who has accomplished something.

Hesse shuffled after him studying a timetable.

As he walked he rubbed his left ear; and MacGayn wriggled through the crowd and began to saunter along behind.

When they got back to the report room at Headquarters they found a message from MacGayn.

Their man had cabbed directly home.

Now they could look back on the four weeks just past and see what had undoubtedly happened. Cazalis had outsmarted himself. Ellery pointed out that in murdering his wife's niece and insinuating himself into the Cat case as a psychiatric consultant Cazalis had seriously hobbled himself. He had not foreseen the demands on his time; he had failed to take into account the white light in which he would have to operate. Before his murder of Lenore Richardson he had had only to deceive a submissive, trusting wife; in semi-retirement, he had moved very nearly at will and in satisfactory shadows. But now he was crippled. He had made himself accountable to officialdom. He was linked with a board of fellow-psychiatrists. Colleagues were communicating with him about their patients. His failing health was causing Mrs. Cazalis to take sharper notice of his activities. And there was the little family matter involving the Richardsons which he could scarcely ignore.

"He strangled Stella Petrucchi and Donald Katz under difficulties," said Ellery. "Conditions were not as favorable to him in those two murders as in the previous ones. Undoubtedly he had to run bigger risks, invent more lies to account for his absences at least in the Katz case; how he managed it in the Petrucchi case, especially on the night of the murder itself, after the Cat Riot, I'd love to know. It's reasonable to suppose that his wife, the Richardsons, began to ask embarrassing questions.

"Significantly, it's those three who've gone to Florida.

"Hesse saw Mrs. Cazalis 'arguing' with Cazalis at the gate to the train. It's an argument that must have started days ago, when Cazalis first suggested the Florida trip. Because it's a certainty Cazalis was the one who suggested it, or who saw to it that the suggestion was made.

"I'm inclined to think he worked it through his sister-in-law. Mrs. Richardson was his logical tool. In her Cazalis had an excellent argument for his wife, who must have been hard to persuade: Della could stand a rest and a change of scene after what had 'happened,' she leaned heavily on her sister, and so on.

"However Cazalis managed it, he got the Richardsons to leave town and his wife to accompany them. Unquestionably he explained his inability to go with them on the double ground of his remaining patients and his promise to the Mayor to clean up his end of the investigation.

"Anything to get his wife and in-laws out of the way.

"Anything to give himself freedom of movement."

Jimmy said, "There's still the maid."

"He's given her the week off," said the Inspector.

"And now they're all out of the way," nodded Ellery, "he has unlimited opportunity and mobility, and the Cat can really go to work on the delightful problem of Marilyn Soames."

And he did. Cazalis went to work on Marilyn Soames as if getting his noose around her throat was of the utmost importance to his peace of mind and he could no longer hold himself in.

He was so eager he was careless. He went back to his shabby topcoat and old felt hat; he added a motheaten gray wool muffler and scuffed shoes; but otherwise he neglected to alter his appearance and it was child's play to keep track of him.

And he went hunting in daylight.

It was evident that he felt completely secure.

He left his apartment early on Tuesday morning, just after Detectives Hesse and MacGayn took over from Goldberg and Young. He left by way of the service entrance, slipping out into the side street and walking rapidly toward Madison Avenue as if his destination lay westward. But at Madison he veered south and walked all the way down to 59th Street. On the southeast corner he looked casually around. Then he jumped into a parked taxicab.

The taxi headed east. Hesse and MacGayn followed in separate cabs to minimize the danger of losing him.

When Cazalis's cab turned south on Lexington Avenue the detectives tensed. It kept going south but as it did it worked its way farther eastward until it reached First Avenue.

It went straight down First Avenue to 28th Street.

Here Cazalis's taxi made a four-corner turn and drew up before Belle-vue Hospital.

Cazalis got out, paid his driver. Then, briskly, he began to stride toward the hospital entrance.

The cab drove off.

Immediately Cazalis stopped, looking after the cab. It turned a corner, heading west.

He retraced his steps and walked rapidly toward 29th Street. His muffler was high around his neck and he had pulled the snapbrim of his hat over his eyes as low as it would go without looking grotesque.

His hands were in the pockets of his topcoat.

At 29th he crossed over.

He walked past 486 slowly, looking the entrance over but without stopping or changing his pace.

Once he looked up. It was a four-story building of dirty tan brick.

Once he glanced back.

A postman was trudging into 490.

Cazalis continued to amble up the street. Without pausing he strolled around the corner into Second Avenue.

But then he reappeared, coming back at a fast clip, as if he had forgotten something. Hesse barely had time to step into a doorway. MacGayn was watching from a hallway across the street, out of sight. They knew that at least one of the detectives assigned to guard Marilyn Soames was in 486, probably at the rear of the downstairs hall, in the gloom behind the staircase. Another was on MacGayn's side of the street somewhere.

There was no danger.

No danger at all.

Still, their palms kept sweating.

Cazalis strode past the house, glancing in as he passed. The postman was now in the vestibule of 486, slipping mail into the letter boxes.

Cazalis stopped before 490, looking at the number inquiringly. He fumbled in an inner pocket and produced an envelope which he consulted elaborately, glancing from time to time at the house number above the entrance, like a collector of some sort.

The postman emerged from 486, shuffled up the street, turned into 482.

Cazalis walked directly into 486.

Detective Quigley in the hall saw him look over the letter boxes.

He studied the Soames box briefly. The paper name plate bore the name *Soames* and the apartment number 3*B*. There was mail in the box. He made no attempt to touch the box.

Quigley was having a bad time. The mail was delivered at the same time every morning and it was Marilyn Soames's habit to come downstairs for it within ten minutes of the regular delivery.

Quigley fingered his holster.

Suddenly Cazalis opened the inner door and walked into the hall.

The detective crouched in the blackest corner behind the stairs.

He heard the big man's step, saw the thick legs pass and disappear. He did not dare make the slightest movement.

Cazalis walked up the hall, opened the back door. The door closed quietly.

Quigley shifted his position.

Hesse ran in and joined him under the stairs.

"In the court."

"Casing it." Then Hesse whispered, "Somebody coming down the stairs, Quig."

"The girl!"

She went into the vestibule, unlocked the Soames box.

Marilyn wore an old bathrobe; her hair was in curlers.

She took out the mail, stood there shuffling letters.

They heard the snick of the rear door.

Cazalis, and he saw her.

The men said afterward they expected the Cat case to be written off then and there. The setup was ideal: the victim in the vestibule in a bathrobe, bound to come back into the gloomy hall in a matter of seconds; no one about; the street outside almost deserted; the court for an emergency getaway.

They were disappointed. Hesse said, "Hell, he'd probably have tried to drag her behind the stairs, the way he did O'Reilly over in Chelsea. Where Quigley and I were parked. The crazy bastard must have had a premonition."

But Ellery shook his head. "Habit," he said. "And caution. He's a night worker. Probably didn't even have a cord along."

"I wish we had as standard equipment X-ray eyes," mumbled Inspector Queen.

Cazalis stood there at the end of the hall, pale eyes burning.

In the vestibule Marilyn was reading a letter. Her flattish nose, her cheekbones, chin, were tacked against the glass of the street door.

She stood there three minutes.

Cazalis did not move.

Finally, she opened the inner door and ran upstairs.

The old boards rattled.

Hesse and Quigley heard him let his breath go.

Then Cazalis walked down the hall.

Dejected. Furious. They could tell by the slope of his thick shoulders, the mauls of his fists.

He went out into the street.

He was back after dark, watching the entrance to 486 from a hallway across the street.

Until a quarter of 10.

Then he went home.

"Why didn't you jump him?" cried Jimmy McKell. "And end this Grand Guignol? You'd have found a cord in his pocket!"

"Maybe we would and maybe we wouldn't," said the Inspector. "He's trying to fix her habits. This may go on for a couple of weeks. She's a toughie for him."

"He'd certainly have one of those cords on him!"

"We can't be sure. We'll just have to wait. Anyway, an actual attack will put him away. A cord might slip. We can't risk anything." Jimmy heard Ellery's teeth grinding.

Cazalis prowled about the neighborhood all day Wednesday; with the night, he settled down in a doorway across the street again.

But at ten minutes to 10 he left.

"He must be wondering if she ever leaves that house," said the Inspector that night, when Celeste reported.

"I'm beginning to wonder myself," rapped Ellery. "Celeste, what the devil is Marilyn doing?"

"Working." Celeste sounded muffled. "On a rush job for one of her playwright customers. She says she won't be finished with it till Saturday or Sunday."

"He'll go nuts," said the McKell voice.

No one laughed, least of all the quipster.

Their nightly meetings in the dark had taken on the weightless flow of dreams. Nothing was real but the unreality they watched. They were conscious only occasionally that the City ground and grumbled somewhere below. Life was buried under their feet; they marked time above it, a treadmill experience.

On Thursday he repeated himself. Only this time he gave up at two minutes past 10.

"Later each night."

Jimmy was fretful. "At this rate, Ellery, he'll be seeing Celeste leave the house. I won't have that."

"He's not after me, Jimmy." But Celeste was sounding shrill.

"It's not that," said Ellery. "It's the regularity. If he spots Celeste coming out every night at the same time, he may get curious."

"We'd better change the time, son."

"Let's do it this way: Celeste, those third-floor windows are in the Soameses' front room, aren't they? The room where Stanley is?"

"Yes."

"From now on don't leave until 10:15, and then only under certain conditions. Is your wristwatch accurate?"

"It keeps very good time."

"Let's synchronize." Ellery struck a match. "I have 10:26 exactly."

"I'm about a minute and a half off."

He struck another match. "Fix it." When she did, he said, "From now on be at one of those front windows every night between 10:10 and 10:15. We'll meet you, starting tomorrow night, somewhere along First Avenue in the immediate neighborhood—tomorrow night let's make it in front of that empty store near the corner of 30th."

"We met there Sunday night."

"Yes. If between 10:10 and 10:15 you see a light flash three times from one of the doorways or alleys across from 486—we'll use a pocket pencil flash—that will mean Cazalis has left for the night and you can come down and make your report. If you see no signal, stay upstairs. It will mean he's still around. If he should leave between 10:10 and 10:25 you'll get the signal between 10:25 and 10:30. If there's no signal in those five minutes, he'll still be around; stay put. We'll operate on the same system till he leaves. Watch for a signal every fifteen minutes. All night if necessary."

By MacGayn's 5 P.M. report Friday Cazalis had still not left his apartment. It puzzled them. He did not leave until dusk. Friday night it was necessary to keep Celeste waiting until 11:15. Ellery flashed the signal himself and trailed her to the rendezvous.

"I thought that flash would never come." Celeste was white. "He's gone?"

"Gave up a few minutes ago."

"I tried to get a call in all afternoon and evening but Stanley was demanding and fidgety today—he's much better—and Marilyn stuck to her typewriter . . . He phoned a little after 1 P.M."

They pressed around her in the dark.

"Paul Nostrum again. Apologized for having stood her up at the Astor, said he was taken sick suddenly and that he's been laid up till today. He wanted her to meet him . . . tonight." Celeste was trying to sound steady. "I've been leaping."

"What did Marilyn say to him?"

"She refused. Said she was all tied up on a special piece of work and he'd have to get somebody else. Then he tried to date her."

"Go on!" Inspector Queen's voice was shaky.

"She just laughed and hung up."

Jimmy drew her away.

"He's getting impatient, Dad."

"That maid of his comes back Monday."

They milled a little.

"Celeste."

Celeste came back, Jimmy protesting.

"How much did she actually tell him about the work she's doing?"

"She said she couldn't possibly be finished before tomorrow night, probably Sunday, and then she'd have to deliver it—" Celeste caught her breath. Then she said in the queerest way, "Deliver it. She did say . . ."

"This weekend," said Ellery.

The Saturday sky was overcast; a glum rain fell intermittently on the City all day. It stopped at dusk and a fog settled over the streets.

The Inspector cursed and passed the word around: he did not consider an act of God sufficient excuse for failure to keep their man covered. "If necessary, take chances. But stick with him." He added, gratuitously: "Or else."

It was a bad day.

The whole day was bad. During the morning Detective Hesse was seized with cramps. MacGayn put in a hurry call. "Hesse has to knock off. He's writhing. Step on it, he's all alone over there." By the time Hagstrom reached Park Avenue MacGayn was gone. "I don't know where," gasped Hesse. "Cazalis came out at 11:05 and walked off toward Madison, MacGayn covering him. Put me in a cab before I foul myself up." It took Hagstrom over an hour to locate MacGayn and his quarry. Cazalis had merely gone to a restaurant. He returned to his apartment immediately afterward.

But a little past 2 found Cazalis leaving in his working clothes, by way of the court. He headed for East 29th Street.

Then, shortly before 4 o'clock, Marilyn Soames walked out of 486. Celeste Phillips was with her.

\* \* \*

The two girls hurried west on 29th Street.

The fog had not yet come down; it was still drizzling. But the sky was threatening to black out.

Visibility was poor.

Cazalis moved. He moved in a glide, very rapidly. His hands were in his pockets. He kept to the opposite side of the street. MacGayn, Hagstrom, Quigley, the Queens, Jimmy McKell followed. Singly, in pairs.

Jimmy kept mumbling, "Is Celeste out of her mind? The fool, the fool."

The Inspector was mumbling, too. A rather stronger characterization.

They could see Cazalis's rage. It told in his pace. He would lunge ahead, then walk, then trot, then come to a dead stop. As he followed the girls his head thrust itself forward.

"Like a cat," said Ellery. "There's the Cat."

"She's out of her mind," whispered Jimmy.

"She's out of mine!" Inspector Queen was close to tears. "We set him up—we set him up all this time. His tongue is hanging out. He'd have tried it in this bad light sure. And she . . ."

The girls turned into Third Avenue and entered a stationery store. The man in the store began wrapping reams of paper, other articles.

It was growing quite dark.

Cazalis was beyond caution. He stood eagerly in the rain on one of the corners of Third Avenue and 29th Street before a drugstore window. The lights came on as he stood there, but he did not move.

The head was still thrust forward.

Ellery had to hang on to Jimmy's arm.

"He won't try anything while Celeste is with her. Too many people on the streets, Jimmy. Too much traffic. Take it easy."

The girls came out of the store. Marilyn carried a large package.

She was smiling.

They walked back the way they had come.

For a moment, fifty feet from the tenement, it looked as if Cazalis were going to take the plunge. The drizzle had thickened and the girls were running for the vestibule, laughing. Cazalis gathered himself, actually jumped into the gutter.

But a car drove up to the curb before 490 and three men got out. They stood on the opposite pavement, shouting to one another in the rain, arguing hotly about something.

Cazalis stepped back.

The girls disappeared into 486.

He walked heavily down the street, stepped into a hallway opposite the Soames building.

Goldberg and Young arrived to take over from MacGayn and Hagstrom.

They worked in close, for the fog had descended.

Cazalis lingered all evening, not moving except to change hallways when someone headed for the one he occupied.

Once he chose Young's, and the detective was within fifteen feet of him for over a half hour.

A few minutes after 11 o'clock he gave up. His bulky figure plunged along in the fog, chin on his breast. They saw him pass from their own observation post near Second Avenue and, a few seconds later, Goldberg and Young.

The three vanished going west.

With some grimness, Inspector Queen insisted on flashing the all-clear signal to Celeste himself.

The meeting place for the night was a dimwalled bar-and-grill on First Avenue between 30th and 31st Streets. They had used it once before; it was crowded, smoky, and mindful of the rights of man.

Celeste came in and sat down and without waiting for anything she said, "I couldn't help it. When she ran out of onionskin second sheets and said she was walking over to Third Avenue for some, I almost died. I knew he wouldn't dare try anything if somebody was with her. Now give me ten demerits."

Jimmy glared. "Are you out of your everloving mind?"

"Did he follow us?" She was bloodless tonight, very nervous. Ellery idly noticed her hands. They were cracked and red; her nails were chewed-looking. There was something else about her, too, but it insisted on being elusive.

What was it?

"He followed you," said the Inspector. Then he said, "Miss Phillips, nothing would have happened to her." He said, "Miss Phillips, this case has cost the City of New York I don't know how many tens of thousands of dollars and months of work. Today by acting like an irresponsible moron you undid every last bit of it. We may never get as good a chance again. It could mean not getting him at all. Today he was desperate. If she'd been alone, he'd have jumped. I can't tell you how put out I am with you. In fact, Miss Phillips, I'm not being irreverent when I say I wish to God Almighty I'd never seen or heard of you."

Jimmy started to get up.

Celeste pulled him down, rested her cheek on his shoulder. "Inspector, I just couldn't find the strength to let her walk out into that street alone. What do I do now?"

The old man raised his glass of beer with shaking hands and drained it. "Celeste." *What was it?*

"Yes, Mr. Queen." Jimmy's clutch tightened and she smiled up at him.

"You're not to do that again."

"I can't promise that, Mr. Queen."

"You did promise it."

"I'm so sorry."

"We can't pull you out now. We can't disturb the status quo. He may try another trick tomorrow."

"I wouldn't leave. I couldn't."

"Won't you promise not to interfere?"

Jimmy touched her face.

"This may all be over by tomorrow night. He hasn't the remotest chance of hurting her. She's covered, so is he. Let him get that cord out, make one move toward her, and he'll be jumped by four armed men. Did Marilyn finish the play she's typing?"

"No, she was too exhausted tonight. She has a few more hours' work on it tomorrow. She says she's going to sleep late, so that means she won't have it done till late afternoon."

"She's to deliver it immediately?"

"The writer is waiting for it. It's overdue now."

"Where does he live?"

"The Village."

"Weather forecast for tomorrow is more rain. It will be dark or almost dark when she leaves the house. He'll make his pitch either on East 29th Street or in the Village. One day more, Celeste, and we can bury this with the rest of our bad dreams. Won't you let her go alone?"

"I'll try."

*What was it?*

Inspector Queen snarled, "Another beer!"

"You're making this awfully tough, Celeste. Did you leave Marilyn all right?"

"She's gone to bed. They all have. Mr. and Mrs. Soames and Billie and Eleanor are going to church early tomorrow."

"Good night." Ellery's chin was angular. "I'd hate to think you let us down."

Jimmy said, "Cheese it. The aborigine."

The waiter slapped a beer down before the Inspector. He lisped, "What's for the lady?"

"Nothing," said Jimmy. "Remove yourself."

"Listen, pally, this is a going concern. She drinks, or you do your smooching someplace else."

Jimmy slowly uncoiled. "Listen yourself, no-brow—"

The Inspector barked, "On your way."

The waiter looked surprised and backed off.

"Go on back, baby," crooned Jimmy. "I would have a word or two with our associates here."

"Jimmy, kiss me?"

"Here?"

"I don't care."

He kissed her. The waiter glowered from afar.

Celeste ran.

The fog swallowed her.

Jimmy got up to lean over the Queens with a bitter expression. He opened his mouth.

But Ellery said, "Isn't that Young?" He was squinting through the murk.

They jerked about like rabbits.

The detective was in the open doorway. His glance darted along the bar, from booth to booth. There were deep yellowish lines around his mouth.

Ellery laid a bill on their table.

They got up.

Young spotted them. He was breathing through his mouth.

"Now listen, Inspector, listen." There was sweat on his upper lip. "It's this goddam fog, you can't see your hand in front of your face in this goddam fog. Goldberg and I were right on his tail when all of a sudden he doubled back on us. Back east. Back here. Like he got the urge again and decided to make a night of it. He looked crazy-mad. I don't know if he saw us or not. I don't think so." Young inhaled. "We lost him in the fog. Goldie's out there roaming around, looking for him. I've been looking for you."

"He headed back here and you lost him."

Inspector Queen's cheeks were damp and hardening plaster.

*Now I remember.*

"That checked coat," said Ellery mechanically.

"What?" said his father.

"She was so upset tonight she put it on instead of her own. *He's loose and Celeste is out there in Marilyn's coat.*"

They tumbled after Jimmy McKell into the fog.

# 11

They heard Celeste's shriek as they sprinted along First Avenue between 30th and 29th Streets.

A man was running toward them from the 29th Street corner waving them back wildly.

"Goldberg . . ."

Not on 29th Street, then. It was here, along First Avenue.

The scream gurgled. It gurgled again, like a song.

"That alley!" yelled Ellery.

It was a narrow opening between the 29th Street corner building and a block of stores. The alley was nearer to Goldberg but Jimmy McKell's praying mantis legs got him there first.

He vanished.

A radio-patrol car tore up, its headlights splashing against the fog. Inspector Queen shouted something and the car backed and lurched to train its brights and side light on the alley entrance.

As they dashed in, Johnson and Piggott skidded around the corner with drawn guns.

Sirens began sawing away on 29th, 30th, Second Avenue.

An ambulance shot diagonally across First Avenue from Bellevue.

In the boiling fog the girl and the two men were struggling casually. Staggered: Celeste, Cazalis, Jimmy; caught in the molecular path of a slow motion projection. Celeste faced them, arched; a bow in the arms of a bowman. The fingers of both hands were at her throat defending it; they had deliberately trapped themselves between her neck and the pinkish cord encircling it. Blood sparkled on her knuckles. Behind Celeste, gripping the ends of the noose, swayed Cazalis, bare head wrenched back by Jimmy McKell's stranglehold; the big man's tongue was between his teeth, eyes open to the sky in a calm expressionless glare. Jimmy's free hand was trying to claw Cazalis's clutch loose from the cord. Jimmy's lips were drawn back; he looked as if he were laughing.

Ellery reached them a half-step before the others.

He smashed Cazalis directly behind the left ear with his fist, inserted his arm between Jimmy and Cazalis and smacked Jimmy's chin with the heel of his hand.

"Let go, Jimmy, let go."

Cazalis slid to the wet concrete, his eyes still open in that curious glare. Goldberg, Young, Johnson, Piggott, one of the patrolmen, fell on him. Young kneed him; he doubled under them, screeching like a woman.

"That wasn't necessary," said Ellery. He kept nursing his right hand.

"I've got a trick knee," said Young apologetically. "In a case like this it goes pop! like that."

Inspector Queen said, "Open his fist. As if he were your mother. I want that cord smoking hot."

An intern in an overcoat was kneeling by Celeste. Her hair glittered in a puddle. Jimmy cried out, lunging. Ellery caught him by the collar with his other hand.

"But she's dead!"

"Fainted, Jimmy."

Inspector Queen was scrutinizing the pink cord with love. It was made of thick, tough silk. Tussah.

He said, "How's the girl, Doctor, hm?" as he eyed the noose dangling from his upheld hand.

"Neck's lacerated some, mostly at the sides and back," replied the ambulance doctor. "Her hands got the worst pressure. Smart little gal."

"She looks dead, I tell you."

"Shock. Pulse and respiration good. She'll live to tell this to her grandchildren till it's coming out of their ears." Celeste moaned. "She's on her way out of it now."

Jimmy sat down in the wet of the alley.

The Inspector was snaking the silk cord carefully into an envelope. Ellery heard him humming "My Wild Irish Rose."

They had Cazalis's hands manacled behind his back. He was lying on his soaked right side with his knees drawn up, staring through Young's big legs at an overturned trash can a few feet away. His face was dirty and gray, his eyes seemed all whites.

The Cat.

He lay in a cage whose bars were the legs of men, breathing ponderously.

The Cat.

They were taking it easy, waiting for the intern to get finished with Celeste Phillips; joking and laughing. Johnson, who disliked Goldberg, offered Goldberg a cigaret; Goldberg had lost his pack somewhere. Goldberg accepted it companionably and struck a match for Johnson, too, who said, "Thanks, Goldie." Piggott was telling about the time—it was during a train wreck—when he had been cuffed to a homicidal maniac for fourteen solid hours: "I was so jittery I smacked him on the jaw every ten minutes to keep him quiet." They guffawed.

Young was complaining to the patrolman, "Hell, I was on the Harlem run for six years. Up there you use your knee first and ask questions afterward. Shiv artists. The whole bastardly lot of 'em."

"I don't know," said the patrolman doubtfully. "I've known some that were white men. You take Zilgitt."

"What difference does it make?" Young glanced down at their prisoner. "He's squirrel bait, anyway. Where there's no sense there's no feeling."

The man lying at their feet had his mouth going a little, as if he were chewing on something.

"Hey," said Goldberg. "What's he doing that for?"

"Doing what?" Inspector Queen shouldered in, alarmed.

"Look at his mouth, Inspector!"

The Inspector dropped to the concrete and grasped Cazalis's jaw.

"Watch it, Inspector," someone laughed. "They bite."

The mouth opened docilely. Young flashed a light into it over Inspector Queen's shoulder.

"Nothing," said the Inspector. "He was chewing on his tongue."

Young said, "Maybe the Cat's got it," and most of them laughed again.

"Hurry it up, Doctor, will you?" said the Inspector.

"In a minute." The intern was wrapping Celeste in a blanket; her head kept lolling.

Jimmy was trying to fend off the other ambulance man. "Scatter, scatter," he said. "Can't you see McKell is in conference?"

"McKell, you've got blood all over your mouth and chin."

"I have?" Jimmy felt his chin, looked at his fingers with surprise.

"Mister, you bit halfway through your lower lip."

"Come onnnnn, Celeste," crooned Jimmy. Then he yelped. The ambulance man kept working on his mouth.

It had turned colder suddenly, but no one seemed to notice. The fog was thinning rapidly. There was a star or two.

Ellery was sitting on the trash can. "My Wild Irish Rose" was going patiently in his head, like a hurdy-gurdy. Several times he tried to turn it off but it kept going.

There was another star.

The back windows of the surrounding buildings were all bright and open; it was very cheerful. Crammed with heads and shoulders. Box seats. Arena, that was it. The pit. *It.* They couldn't possibly see *It*, but they could hope, couldn't they? In New York, hope dwells in every eye. A dwindling old building. A sidewalk excavation. An open manhole. A traffic accident. *What was it? What's happened? Who got hit? Is it gangsters? What are they doing down there?*

It didn't matter.

*The Cat's in his Hell, all's right with the world.*

New York papers please copy.

"Jimmy, come here."

"Not now."

"*Extra,*" called Ellery, with significance. "Don't you want a bonus?"

Jimmy laughed. "Didn't I tell you? They fired me last week."

"Get to a phone. They'll make you editor."

"The hell with them."

"It's worth a million to them."

"I've got a million."

Ellery rocked on the trash can. The screwball was really a card. Swell kid, Jimmy. Ellery laughed again, wondering why his hand felt so queer.

The third floor windows at the rear of 486 East 29th were all filled, too.

*They don't know. The name of Soames goes down in history and they're sitting up there wondering whose name they'll read in the papers.*

"Here she is," announced the intern. "Greetings, Miss, and may I be the first to congratulate you?"

Her bandaged hands went to her throat.

Jimmy mumbled to the other one, "Will you get the devil off my lip? Baby, it's me. It's all over. *Fini.* Jimmy, baby. Remember me?"

"Jimmy."

"She recognizes me! All over, baby."

"That horrible . . ."

"It's all over."

*My Wiiiiiild Irish Rooooose . . .*

"I was hurrying along First Avenue."

"Practically a grandmother. This iodine dispenser said so."

"He pulled me in as I passed. I saw his face and then it was dark. My neck."

"Save it, save your strength for a little later, Miss Phillips," said the Inspector genially.

"All over, baby."

"The Cat. Where is he? Jimmy, where is he?"

"Now stop shaking. Lying right over there. Just an alley cat. See? Look. Don't be afraid."

Celeste began to cry.

"It's all over, baby." Jimmy had his arms around her and they rocked together in a little puddle.

*Wonder where they think Celeste is. Down here "helping out," probably. Clara Barton stuff . . . And is it not a battlefield? The battle of First Avenue. After sending McKell's Marauders out on cavalry reconnaissance, General Queen feinted with Phillips's Corps and engaged the enemy with his Centre Str . . .* Ellery thought he spied the dark head of Marilyn Soames among the other heads, but then he untwisted his neck and rubbed the back of it. *What was in that beer?*

"Okay, Doc, okay," the Inspector was saying. "Over here now."

The intern stooped over Cazalis, looked up. "Who did you say this is?" he asked sharply.

"He got a hard one in the groin. I don't want to move him till you say it's all right."

"This man is Dr. Edward Cazalis, the psychiatrist!"

Everybody laughed.

"Thanks, Doc," said Detective Young, winking at the others. "We're beholden to you."

They laughed again.

The intern flushed. After a while he got to his feet. "Hold him up and he'll make it. Nothing serious."

"Upsadaisy!"

"Say, I'll bet he was pulling a fakeroo all the time."

"Young, you better practice up that knee action."

"Watch him, watch him."

He was making a strong effort to move his legs, mincing along half on his toes like a student ballet dancer, his knees not quite supporting him.

"Don't look," Jimmy said. "It's not the least bit important."

"It is. I want to. I promised my—" But then Celeste shuddered and looked away.

"Keep that street out there cleared." The Inspector looked around. "Hold it." The procession stopped and Cazalis seemed grateful. "Where's Ellery?"

"Over there, Inspector."

"Hey."

"What's the matter with him?"

*My Wiiiiild lr . . .*

The trash can clattered and rolled a few feet.

"He's hurt."
"Doctor!"
The intern said, "He passed out. His hand is fractured. Easy . . ."

Easy. Easy does it, a mere five months' worth of sniff and dig and hunt and plot—twenty-one weeks of it; to be exact, twenty-one weeks and one day, one hundred and forty-eight days from a soft rap on the door of an East 19th Street apartment to a hard smash to a man's head in a First Avenue alley; from Abernethy, Archibald Dudley to Phillips, Celeste, alias Sue Martin, Girl Spy; from Friday, June 3, to Saturday, October 29; point four-o-four per cent of a single year in the life of the City of New York, during which period one of the City's numerous hatchetmen cut down the population of the Borough of Manhattan by nine lives although, to be sure, there was that little matter of the Metropol Hall panic and the rioting that followed; in the sum, however, statistical chicken feed lost in Bunyan's barnyard, and what was all the excitement about?

Easy does it.

Easy does it, for the Cat sat in a hard chair under photographic light and he was not the tails-lashing chimera of the broken metropolitan dream but a tumbledown old man with shaking hands and an anxious look, as if he wanted to please but was not quite sure what was required of him. They had found a second salmon-pink cord of tussah silk on his person and at the rear of one of the locked filing cabinets in his Park Avenue office a cache of two dozen others of which more than half were dyed the remembered blue; he had instructed them where to look and he had picked out the right key for them from the assortment in his key case. He said he had had the cords for many years; since late in 1930, when he was on a tour around the world after retiring from his obstetrical practice. In India a native had sold him the cords, representing them to be old strangling cords of thuggee origin. Later, before putting them away, he had dyed them blue and pink. Why had he saved them all these years? He looked bewildered. No, his wife had never known about them; he had been alone when he purchased them in the bazaar and he had kept them hidden afterward . . . His head slanted readily to their questions and he answered in a courteous way, although there were stretches when he became uncommunicative or slightly erratic. But the rambling episodes were few; for the most part he caught the pertinent past in brilliant focus, sounding quite like the Dr. Cazalis they had known.

His eyes, however, remained unchanged, staring, lenslike.

Ellery, who had come there directly from Bellevue Hospital with Celeste Phillips and Jimmy McKell, sat to one side, his right hand in a splint, listening and saying nothing. He had not yet run down; he still had a feeling of unreality. The Police Commissioner and the District Attorney were also present; and at a little past 4:30 A.M. the Mayor hurried in, paler than the prisoner.

But the grimy old man in the chair seemed not to see any of them. It was a deliberate avoidance, they all felt, dictated by a kind of tact. They knew how plausible such madmen could be.

In the main, his account of the nine murders was remarkable for its detail. Barring his few lapses from clarity, which might well have resulted from pain, confusion, emotional and physical exhaustion—had they not known what he really was—his confession was excellent.

His least satisfactory reply came in response to Ellery's only contribution to the night's inquisition.

When the prisoner had nearly concluded, Ellery leaned forward and asked: "Dr. Cazalis, you've admitted that you hadn't seen any of these people since their infancy. As individuals, therefore, they couldn't possibly have meant anything to you. Yet obviously you had something against them. What was it? Why did you feel you had to kill them?"

*Because the conduct of the psychotic appears unmotivated only when judged in the perspective of reality—that is, by more or less healthy minds viewing the world as it is . . .*

Said Dr. Cazalis.

The prisoner twisted in his chair and looked directly at the source of Ellery's voice, although because of the lights beating on his bruised face it was plain that he could not see beyond them.

"Is that Mr. Queen?" he asked.

"Yes."

"Mr. Queen," said the prisoner in a friendly, almost indulgent tone, "I doubt that you're scientifically equipped to understand."

Sunday's morning was full-grown when they got away from the reporters. Jimmy McKell sprawled in a corner of the taxi with Celeste in his arms and in the other corner Ellery pampered his immobilized hand, looking out the window on his side not for reasons of delicacy but because he wanted to see through it.

The City looked different this morning.

Felt, smelled, sounded different.

New.

The air had a tune in it. Maybe it was the churchbells. Churches were bellowing their wares downtown and up, East Side to West. *Adeste fideles!* Come and get it!

In the residential sections delicatessens, bakeries, newsstands, drugstores were busy opening.

An El train went bucketing by somewhere.

A newsboy, bluepawed.

Occasionally an early riser appeared, rubbing his hands together, walking smartly.

At taxi stands cabs stood parked. Bootleg radios going. Drivers intent.

People began collecting around them.

New York was stretching.

Waking up.

# 12

New York awoke and for a week or two the ugly vision tarried. Had radio's celebrated planetary invasion of Earth been real, people would have stood in long lines afterward to view the Martian remains and wonder at their gullibility. Now that the monster was localized in a cage, where it could be seen, heard, pinched, reported, read about, even pitied, New York queued up. The clarity of hindsight engaged the facts of postmortem and out of it came citywide conversation pieces in shame, a safe and even enjoyable exercise for all. The Cat was merely a demented old man; and what was one lunatic against a city? File and forget; Thanksgiving was coming.

New York laughed.

Still, like his British cousin from Cheshire, the Cat lingered in his grin after the rest of him had vanished. It was not the grin of the old man in the cell; that old man did not grin. It was the grin of the dream monster. And there were the children, with shorter memories but fresher senses. Parents had still to contend with nightmares. Not excluding their own.

Then, on the morning after Armistice Day, the body of a young girl later identified as Reva Xavinzky, of Flushing, was found in various places about Jamaica Bay. She had been ravished, mutilated, dismembered, and decapitated. The familiar horrors of this case, its recognizably atrocious details, instantly diverted public attention; and by the time the murderer, an ex-Army deserter with a typical history of the sexual psychopath, was caught, the diversion—at least insofar as adults were concerned—was complete. Thereafter the word "cat" raised no grislier image in the mind's eye of the average New Yorker than that of a small domestic animal characterized by cleanliness, independence, and a useful appetite for mice. (That the case of Reva Xavinzky performed a like service for younger New York may be questioned; but most parents seemed to feel that with Thanksgiving and Christmas hovering, the Cat would be supplanted in their children's dreams by turkey and Santa Claus. And perhaps they were right.)

There was a minority with special interests, however, who hung on. For some—certain City officials, reporters, psychiatrists, the families of the Cat's victims—this was a matter of duty, or specific assignment, or professional or personal implication. For others—the sociologists, the psychologists, the philosophers—the capture of the nine-times murderer signalized the opportunity to launch a socio-scientific investigation of the City's behavior since early June. The second groups were wholly unconcerned with Edward Cazalis; the first were concerned with no one else.

The prisoner had retreated to a sullen phase. He refused to talk, he refused to exercise, for a time he refused to eat; he appeared to exist only for the visits of his wife, for whom he called constantly. Mrs. Cazalis, accompanied by her sister and brother-in-law, had flown back from Florida on October 30. She had refused to believe the reports of her husband's arrest as the Cat, protesting to reporters in Miami and New York that "there's some mistake. It can't be. My husband is innocent." But that was before her first meeting with him. She emerged from it deathly pale, shaking her head to the press, going directly to the home of her sister. She was there for four hours; then she returned to her own apartment.

It was noted in those first excited days after the monster's capture that it was his mate who took the full impact of the City's animus. She was pointed out, jeered at, followed. Her sister and brother-in-law vanished; no one could or would say where they had gone. Her maid deserted her and she was unable to engage another. She was asked to vacate her apartment by a management that made it frantically clear they would use every means within their power to evict her if she resisted. She did not resist; she placed her household furnishings in storage and moved to a small downtown hotel; and when the hotel management discovered who she was the next morning, she was asked to leave. This time she found quarters in a lugubrious rooming house on Horatio Street in the Village; and it was here that her eldest brother, Roger Braham Merigrew of Bangor, Maine, located her.

Merigrew's visit to his sister did not outlast the night. He had come accompanied by a shadlike man carrying a briefcase; when the two emerged from the Horatio Street building at 3:45 in the morning and found the reporters waiting, it was Merigrew's companion who covered his factor's escape and gave the statement which appeared in the newspapers later that day. "As Mr. Merigrew's attorney I am authorized to state the following: Mr. Merigrew has attempted for several days to persuade his sister, Mrs. Cazalis, to rejoin her kin in Maine. Mrs. Cazalis refused.

So Mr. Merigrew flew down to renew his appeal in person. Mrs. Cazalis still refuses. There is nothing further Mr. Merigrew can do, therefore he is returning home. That's all there is to this." Asked by reporters why Mr. Merigrew did not remain by his sister's side in New York, the Maine attorney snapped, "You'll have to ask Mr. Merigrew that." Later, a Bangor paper managed to get a few words from Merigrew. He said, "My sister's husband is insane. There's no call to stand by a murdering lunatic. It's not fair to us, the publicity and so on. Any further statements will have to come from my sister." The Merigrews owned large conservative business interests throughout New England.

So Mrs. Cazalis faced her ordeal alone, living in a squalid Village room, dogged by reporters, visiting her husband, and growing daily wilder-eyed and more silent.

She engaged the famous attorney, Darrell Irons, to defend her husband. Irons was uncommunicative, but it was rumored that he was having his hands full. Cazalis, it was said, "refused" to be defended and would not co-operate with the psychiatrists Irons sent endlessly to his cell. Stories began to circulate of maniacal rages, attempted physical violence, incoherent ravings on the part of the prisoner; those who knew Darrell Irons stated that he had inspired them and that most likely, therefore, they were not true. It was clear what Irons's defense would be, for the District Attorney seemed determined to prosecute Cazalis as a man who knew the nature and quality of his acts, who had demonstrated in his daily life even during the period of his crimes his capacity to act rationally and who therefore, under the legal definition, must be considered "sane," no matter what he may have been under the medical definition. The District Attorney set considerable store, it was said, by the prisoner's conversation with the Mayor's Special Investigator and Inspector Richard Queen of Police Headquarters on the night of the Lenore Richardson investigation, when he had outlined his "theory" of the Cat case as pointing to a psychotic pure and simple. This had been the calculated act of a calculating murderer, the D.A. was said to hold, purposely turning the investigation into a channel of "gibbering idiocy" the more effectually to divert attention from the responsible mentality behind the stranglings.

A dramatic trial was forecast.

Ellery's interest in the case flagged early. He had lived with it far too long at too steep a pitch to experience anything but exhaustion after the events of the night of October 29–30. He found himself trying not merely to forget the past but to dodge the present. The present, at least, would not be evaded; it insisted on applying pomp to circumstance. There were Athenian honors, press and radio-television interviews, a hundred invitations to address civic groups and write articles and investigate unsolved crimes. He managed to back away from most of these with approximate grace. The few he could not avoid left him irritable and profane. "What's the matter with you?" demanded his father. "Let's say," snapped Ellery, "that success has gone to my head." The Inspector puckered; he was no stranger to migraine, either. "Well," he said cheerfully, "at least this time it's not caused by failure."

Ellery continued to fling himself from chair to chair.

One day he decided he had located the infection. It was the boil of pressure. But not of the past or the present; of the future. He was not finished. On the morning of January 2, in one of the larger courtrooms under the gray dome of the Supreme Court building in Foley Square, a Mr. Justice-Somebody would make his blackrobed entrance from chambers and one Edward Cazalis, alias the Cat, would go on trial charged with murder. And in this trial one Ellery Queen, Special Investigator to the Mayor, would be a major witness for the people. There would be no release for him until that ordeal was passed. Then he could go about his business purged of the whole corrupting mess.

Why the trial should cause him such twinges Ellery did not attempt to diagnose. Having discovered—as he thought—the source of his malady, he adjusted his psychic screws to the inevitable and turned to other matters. By this time Reva Xavinzky had been collated and the spotlight probed elsewhere. He was able almost to relax. Even to think about getting back to writing. The novel he had neglected since August 25 lay in its lonely grave. He exhumed it and was surprised to find it as alien as any tax roll papyrus dug out of the Nile delta after three thousand years. Once, long ago, he had labored greatly on this, and now it had the historic smell of shards. *Look on my Works, ye Mighty, and despair!* Despairing, Ellery dropped the primitive effort of his pre-Cat days into the fire.

And sat him down to compose a newer wonder.

But before he could settle his feet on the bottom drawer, there was an agreeable interruption.

Jimmy McKell and Celeste Phillips were being wed and it seemed that Mr. Queen, in his single person, was to constitute the wedding party.

"Exclusive," grinned Jimmy. "By McKell."

"Jimmy means," sighed Celeste, "that his father hit the roof and won't come."

"He's biting the Chippendale," said Jimmy, "because his hitherto invincible weapon—disownery? disownment?—has turned to womanish water in his hand, now that I'm buckled into Grandfather's millions. And

Mother'd no sooner got over sopping up the tears than she started planning a twenty-thousand guest wedding. So I said the hell with it—"

"And we've got our license, we've taken our Wassermanns—"

"Successfully," added Jimmy, "so would you hand my bride over to
me in City Hall at 10:30 tomorrow morning, Mr. Q?"

They were married between the Arthur Jackson Beals of Harlem and
the Cary G. Cohens-to-be of Brownsville, Brooklyn; the City Clerk did
them distinguished honor by going no more than half so rapidly as usual;
Mr. Queen bussed the bride with a fervent "At last!"; and afterward there
were only eighteen reporters and cameramen waiting for them in the hall.
Mrs. James Guymer McKell exclaimed that she couldn't imagine how in
the world they had all known, because she and Jimmy hadn't breathed a
word to anyone but Ellery . . . and her groom growled an invitation to his
ex-fellow-journalists to hoist a few on him, whereupon the augmented
party set out for La Guardia Airport and the wedding luncheon was imbibed in a cocktail lounge, with Parlay Phil Gonachy of the *Extra* crying
the square dance which somehow followed. At the climax of a thunderous quadrille the Airport police appeared, causing certain strict constitutionalists among the working guests to defend with camera, bottle, and
bar stool the sacred freedom of the press and enabling the happy couple
to slip away with their sponsor.

"Whither do you fly with your unravished bride?" inquired Mr. Queen
in a slightly wobbly tone. "Or is said question none of my olfactory business?"

"It is entirely *comme il faut*," replied Mr. McKell with the grandeur of
one who has also given generous lip service to the sacraments of Reims
and Epernay, "since we fly nowhither," and he steered his bride gallantly
exitward.

"Then why La Guardia?"

"A ruse to mislead those roistering anteaters. Equerry!"

"We're spending our honeymoon at the Half-Moon Hotel," confided
the bride with a blush as a cab rushed up. "You're positively the only one
who knows *that*."

"Mrs. McKell, I shall guard your secret with my honor."

"Mrs. McKell," murmured Mrs. McKell.

"All my life," said her husband in a whisper that shot heads around
twenty feet away, "I have yearned for a winter's honeymoon among the
frolicking Polar Bears of Coney Island." And Mr. McKell yelled to the
apprehensive hack, "Okay, White Fang. Mush!"

Ellery observed their exhaust fondly as they rode off into the smog.

*   *   *

After that he found it joy to settle down to work. Ideas for a new mystery novel flowed like the wedding party's champagne; the only problem was to keep a sober judgment.

One morning Ellery looked around to find Father Christmas breathing down his neck. And he saw with some astonishment that New York's Yule was to be white; overnight, 87th Street sparkled. A Samoyed rolling in the snow across the street made him think of arctic huskies; and thus he was reminded of the James McKells and their Coney Island honeymoon among the curious tribe of New Yorkers who called themselves the Polar Bears. Ellery grinned, wondering why he had not heard from Jimmy and Celeste. Then it occurred to him that he had, and he began looking through his deserted mail, an accumulation of several weeks.

He found Jimmy's note in the middle of the heap.

We like it, Ellery. We *like* it.

If you have a mind to crack a friendly jeroboam for auld lang syne, the McKells are receiving in the back room of Kelly's Bar on East 39th at 2 P.M. tomorrow for all of the tribe of Jurgen. We still haven't found an apartment and are bedding down with various disreputable characters. I *won't* take my *wife* to a hotel.

JAMES

P.S. If you don't show, we'll see you at the Assizes.
P.P.S. Mrs. McK. sends love.

J.

The postmark was ten days old.

The McKells and Christmas . . . This called for heroism.

A half hour later Ellery was up to his armpits in lists, and a half hour after that he was sallying forth in galoshes.

Fifth Avenue was already a speckled swamp. The plows were still working in the side streets but along the Avenue they had toiled all night like beetles rolling dung and the brown-splattered snowpiles challenged the ability of jaywalkers and squeezed motor traffic into an impossible bottleneck.

A white Christmas, everybody was saying, shuffling through the slush, sneezing and coughing.

At Rockefeller Center Noel was being caroled and in the Plaza, dwarfed by a hundred-foot tree raped from some Long Island estate, the skaters were whizzing along to a determined version of "Jingle Bells."

Santas in wrinkled red suits clanged at almost every corner, shivering. Shop windows were faery glimpses into the magic wood of advertising. And everywhere people slipped and sloshed, and Ellery slipped and sloshed with them, wearing the glazed frown by which you may know all New Yorkers in the last week before Christmas.

He dodged in and out of great stores, trampling on little children, pushing and being pushed, clawing at merchandise, shouting his name and address, writing out checks—until, in midafternoon, his master list was reduced to a single uncrossed-off name.

But beside that name stood a large, repulsive question mark.

The McKells were the nice problem. Ellery had not sent them a wedding gift in view of the uncertainty surrounding their future habitat. At the time he had thought that by Christmas they would surely be settled, whereupon he could combine the nuptial gift with the seasonal; and here was the annual Miracle and neither the problem of the McKells' residence nor the nature of his gifts to them had been solved. He had kept an eye alerted for inspiration all day. Silver? Glass? Silk?—no, not silk, definitely not silk. Ceramic? He saw a glossy Bubastis and shuddered. Native wood carving, something primitive? An antique? Nothing came, nothing at all.

Until, in late afternoon, Ellery found himself on 42nd Street between Fifth and Sixth Avenues. Before Stern's a Salvation Army lass, a strapping soldier of charity, sang hymns accompanied by a bluing comrade at a portable organ set down in the slush.

The organ made tinkly sounds in the treble and for a moment sounded like a musicbox.

Musicbox.

Musicbox!

They were originally a fad of French exquisites, dispensing snuff to little metallic tunes, but centuries of delight had made them currency in the realm of childhood and their pure elfishness purchased smiles from lovers.

Ellery dropped a dollar in the tambourine and considered his idea excitedly. Something special . . . featuring the Wedding March . . . yes, that was a must . . . inlays of precious woods, mother-of-pearl, cunning stonework . . . a big one, artfully made. An import, of course. The most delicate pieces came from central Europe . . . Swiss. A Swiss musicbox of the most elaborate craftsmanship would be expensive, but hang the expense. It would become a household treasure, a little chest of golden sentiment unawed by the McKell millions, to be kept at their beside until they were eigh—

Swiss.

Swiss?

Switzerland!

*ZÜRICH!*

In a twinkling musicboxes, Wedding Marches, Christmas itself were forgotten.

Ellery waded wildly across 42nd Street and dashed through the side entrance into the New York Public Library.

For a point in his plot-in-progress had been bothering him for days. It concerned certain phobias. Ellery was postulating a significant relationship (of such is the kingdom of mystery writers) among morbid fear of crowds, of darkness, and of failure. Just how he had come to juxtapose these three phobias plotwise he did not know; it was his impression that he had read about their interrelationship, or heard about it, somewhere. But research had failed to turn up the source. It was holding him up.

And now Zürich. Zürich on the Limmat, Athens of Switzerland.

Zürich rang that bell!

For now Ellery remembered having either read or been told that in Zürich, at some recent international meeting of psychoanalysis, precisely such a phobic relationship had been the subject of a paper.

Search in the foreign periodical section of the Library rewarded him in less than an hour.

The source was a *Zürcher* scientific journal, one of a pile Ellery was leafing through as he exercised his stiffened German. The entire issue was given over to the proceedings of the convention, which had lasted ten days, and all scientific papers read before it were reprinted in full. The paper he was interested in bore the alarming title of *Ochlophobia, Nyctophobia, and Ponophobia*; but when he glanced through it he found it to contain exactly what he was looking for.

He was about to go back to the beginning to start rereading carefully when an italic note at the end of the article caught his eye.

A familiar name.

*—Paper read by Dr. Edward Cazalis of the United States . . .*

Of course! It was Cazalis who had been responsible for the birth of the idea. Ellery recalled it all now. It had come up during that September night in the Richardson apartment, in the first hours of the on-scene investigation of Lenore's murder. There had been a lull and Ellery had found himself in conversation with the psychiatrist. They had talked about Ellery's fiction and Dr. Cazalis had remarked with a smile that the field of phobias offered Ellery's craft rich stores of material. On being pressed, Cazalis had mentioned work he himself had done on "ochlophobia and nyctophobia" in relation to the development of "ponophobia"; in fact, Ellery remembered his saying, he had read a paper on the subject at a convention in Zürich. And Cazalis had talked for a little about his findings, until they were interrupted by the Inspector and recalled to the sorry business of the night.

Ellery made a face. The brief conversation had sunk into his unconscious under the weight of events, to emerge two months later under pressure, its source forgotten. *Sic semper* the "original" idea.

It was an irony of coincidence that Cazalis should prove responsible for it.

Smiling, Ellery glanced at the footnote again.

*—Paper read by Dr. Edward Cazalis of the United States at the night session of 3rd June. This paper was originally scheduled for presentation at 10 P.M. However, the preceding speaker, Dr. Naardvoessler of Denmark, exceeded his allotted time and did not conclude the reading of his paper until 11:52 P.M. A motion to adjourn was withdrawn when President Dr. Jurasse of France, Chairman of the Convention, asserted that Dr. Cazalis had attended all the sessions patiently awaiting the Convention's pleasure and that, notwithstanding the lateness of the hour, in view of the fact that this was the concluding session of the Convention, the distinguished Members present should extend the adjournment hour to enable Dr. Cazalis to present his paper. This was done* viva voce, *Dr. Cazalis presented his paper, concluding at 2:03 A.M., and the Convention was adjourned for the year by President Dr. Jurasse as of 2:24 A.M. 4th June.*

Still smiling, Ellery flipped the journal to the front cover and glanced at the year of issue.

Now he did not smile. Now he sat staring at the last digit of the date as it grew rapidly larger, or as he himself rapidly shrank.

*"Drink Me."*

He felt—if it could be called feeling—like Alice.

The *Zürcher* rabbit-hole.

And the Looking-Glass.

How did you get out?

At last Ellery got up from the table and made his way to the information desk outside the main reading rooms.

He crouched over copies of *Who's Who* and the latest annual roster of the American Psychiatric Association.

*Who's Who* . . . Cazalis, Edward.

The national roster of the American Psychiatric Association . . . Caza-
lis, Edward.
In each case a single Cazalis, Edward.
In each case the same Cazalis, Edward.
It was really not to be borne.

Ellery returned to his Zürich journal.
He turned the pages slowly.
Calmly.
*Anyone watching me is saying: There's a man who's sure of himself.*
*He turns pages calmly. Knows just what's what.*

There it was.

> Dr. Fulvio Castorizo, Italy
> Dr. John Sloughby Cavell, Great Britain
> Dr. Edward Cazalis, United States

Of course he'd be listed.
And that old man? Had he been present?
Ellery turned the page.

> Dr. Walther Schoenzweig, Germany
> Dr. Andrés Selborán, Spain
> Dr. Béla Seligmann, Austria

Someone tapped Ellery on the shoulder.
"Closing time, sir."
The room was empty.
*Why hadn't they caught it?*
He trudged into the hall. A guard directed him to the staircase when he
made the wrong turn.
*The District Attorney knows his business. His office is topnotch. They're*
*old hands.*
He supposed they had backtracked from Katz, Donald, to Petrucchi,
Stella, past Richardson, Lenore, to Willikins, Beatrice, the way growing
fainter as they retreated in time until, at the five-months-ago mark, it had
disappeared or become impassable. But that wouldn't have stopped
them. They probably had one or two or even three others they hadn't
been able to fix. It would actually not seem necessary to fix each one. Not
in so many murders. Not over such a long period in such a peculiar case
where the identity of the victim was a detail hardly meriting notice. Six,

say, would do the District Attorney nicely. Plus the caught-in-the-act attempt on Celeste-Phillips-thinking-she-was-Marilyn-Soames and the minute-to-minute evidence of his Soames stalk in the days preceding the attempt.

Ellery walked uncertainly up Fifth Avenue. The weather had turned very cold and the slush had frozen in serrated little icehills of dirty gray, rutted and pocked, a relief map of nowhere on which he teetered along.

*This will have to be done from home . . . I've got to have a place where I can sit and feel safe.*

*When the ax falls.*

*Executions brought to your door.*

*At no extra charge.*

He stopped at a shop window through which a faceless angel with a needlethin torch was trying to fly, and he looked at his watch.

*In Vienna it's the middle of the night.*

*Then I can't go home.*

*Not yet.*

*Not till it's time.*

He drew back from the thought of facing his father like a turtle rapped on the nose.


Ellery let himself in at a quarter of 4 in the morning.

On the tips of his toes.

The apartment was dark except for a night light in the majolica lamp on the living room table.

He felt refrigerated. The mercury had dropped to five above in the streets and the apartment was only a little less icy.

His father was snoring. Ellery went to the bedroom door and shut it, thievishly.

Then he stole into his study and turned the key. He did not remove his overcoat. Switching on the desk light, he sat down and drew the telephone to him.

He dialed the operator and asked for the Overseas Operator.


There were difficulties.

It was almost 6 o'clock. The steam had just begun to rattle the radiators and he kept his eye apprehensively on the door.

The Inspector was a 6 o'clock riser.

Finally, he got through.

Ellery prayed that his father oversleep as he waited for the Vienna operator to settle matters at her end.

"Here is your party, sir."

"Professor Seligmann?"

"*Ja?*"

It was an old, old voice. Its bass cracked and a little peevish.

"My name is Ellery Queen," said Ellery in German. "You do not know me, Herr Professor—"

"Incorrect," said the aged voice in English, Oxonian English with a Viennese accent. "You are an author of *romans policiers*, and out of guilt feelings for the many crimes you commit on paper you also pursue malefactors in life. You may speak English, Mr. Queen. What do you want?"

"I hope I haven't caught you at an inopportune moment—"

"At my age, Mr. Queen, all moments are inopportune except those devoted to speculations about the nature of God. Yes?"

"Professor Seligmann, I believe you are acquainted with the American psychiatrist, Edward Cazalis."

"Cazalis? He was my pupil. Yes?" There was nothing in the voice, nothing at all.

*Is it possible he doesn't know?*

"Have you seen Dr. Cazalis in recent years?"

"I saw him in Zürich earlier this year. Why do you ask?"

"On which occasion, Herr Professor?"

"At an international convention of psychoanalysis. But you do not tell me why, *mein Herr*."

"You don't know the trouble Dr. Cazalis is in?"

"Trouble? No. What is this trouble?"

"I can't explain now, Professor Seligmann. But it's of the greatest importance that you give me exact information."

The line wheezed and keened and for a moment Ellery thought: *Let us pray*.

But it was only the mysterious defects of the transoceanic process coming up through Professor Seligmann's silence.

He heard the old voice again.

Growling this time.

"Are you Cazalis's friend?"

*Am I?*

"Yes, I'm Cazalis's friend," said Ellery.

"You hesitate. I do not like this."

"I hesitated, Professor Seligmann," said Ellery carefully, "because friendship is a word I weigh."

He thought he had lost, but there was a faint chuckle in his ear and the old man said: "I attended the last few days of the Zürich meeting. Cazalis was present. I heard him read his paper on the night of the last session and I kept him up until long past dawn afterward in my hotel room telling him how absurd I thought it was. Are you answered, Mr. Queen?"

"You have an excellent memory, Herr Professor."

"You question it."

"Forgive me."

"I am reversing the usual process of senescence. My memory is apparently the last to go." The old voice sharpened. "You may rely on the accuracy of the information."

"Professor Seligmann—"

There was a word, but it was swallowed up by such a howl of atmospheric expletive that Ellery snatched the receiver from his ear.

"Herr Professor Seligmann?"

"Yes. Yes. Are you—?" But then he faded, bolting into space. Ellery cursed. Suddenly the line was clear.

"Herr Queen! Yes?"

"I must see you, Professor Seligmann."

"About Cazalis?"

"About Cazalis. If I fly to Vienna at once, will you see me?"

"You would be coming to Europe for this alone?"

"Yes."

"Come."

*"Danke schön. Auf Wiedersehen."*

But the old man had already broken the connection.

Ellery hung up.

*He's so damned old. I hope he lasts.*

His European flight was a bother from beginning to end. There was trouble about his visa, long talks with the State Department, much questioning and headshaking and form-filling. And passage seemed an impossibility; everyone was flying to Europe, and everyone who flew was a person of terrestrial importance. Ellery began to realize what a very small tuber he was in the vast potato patch of world affairs.

He spent Christmas in New York after all.

The Inspector was magnificent. Not once in those days of pacing did he question the purpose of Ellery's trip. They merely discussed ways and means and the impediments.

But the Inspector's mustache grew noticeably ragged.

On Christmas Day Ellery cabled Professor Seligmann that he was being delayed by transportation and other nuisances but that he expected clearance at any hour.

The hour arrived late on December 28, in time to save the crumbs of Ellery's sanity.

Exactly how his father managed it Ellery never learned, but at dawn on December 29 he found himself on a conspicuously special plane in the company of persons of obvious distinction, all of whom were unmistakably bound on missions of global gravity. He had no idea where the plane was going or when it was scheduled to arrive. He heard murmurs of "London," "Paris," and such, but he could detect no Strauss waltzes, and to judge from the pursed blankness that met his worried inquiries the *Wiener Wald* was something in Moscow.

Neither his nails nor his stomach survived the Atlantic crossing.

When they did touch soil, it was fog-choked and British. Here a mysterious delay occurred. Three and a half hours later they took off again and Ellery sank into a doze. When he awoke it was to no thunder of motors. He sat in a great hush. As far as he could make out through his window, they had landed on an Arctic ice field; his very corpuscles were frozen. He nudged his companion, a U.S. Army officer. "Tell me, Colonel. Is our destination Fridtjof Nansen Land?"

"This is France. Where you going?"

"Vienna."

The colonel pushed out his lips and shook his head.

Ellery doggedly began to work his glaciated toes. Just as the first motor exploded, the co-pilot tapped his shoulder.

"Sorry, sir. Your space is required."

"What!"

"Orders, sir. Three diplomats."

"They must be very thin," said Ellery bitterly, getting up. "What happens to the bum?"

"You'll be put up at the field, sir, till they can find space for you on another ship."

"Can't I stand? I promise not to sit on anybody's lap and I'll gladly drop off over the Ringstrasse by parachute."

"Your bag's already off, sir. If you don't mind . . ."

Ellery spent thirty-one hours in a whistling billet, surrounded by the invisible Republic of France.

When he did reach Vienna, it was by way of Rome. It seemed impossible, but here he was on a frozen railway station with his bag and a little Italian priest who had unaccountably clung to him all the way from Rome and a sign somewhere that said *Westbahnhof*, which was certainly in Vienna, so he was in Vienna.

On New Year's Day.

Where was Professor Seligmann?

Ellery began to worry about the Viennese fuel situation. He had a frostbitten recollection of engine trouble, a forced landing after tumbling over and over among the stars like a passenger on a space ship out of control, and a miserable railway train; but his chief memory was of the cold. As far as Ellery could make out, Europe was in the Second Ice Age; and he fully expected to locate Professor Seligmann imbedded in the heart of a glacier, like a Siberian mastodon, in a perfect state of preservation. He had telephoned Seligmann from Rome, giving the old man such information as he had had about his Italian plane's scheduled arrival. But he had not foreseen the journey through outer space and the groaning aftermath of the miserable train. Seligmann was probably getting pneumonia at . . . which airfield had that been?

The hell with it.

Two figures approached, crunching the icy platform. But one was a saber-toothed porter and the other a *Schwester* of some Austrian Roman Catholic order and neither satisfied Ellery's conception of a world-famous psychoanalyst.

The *Schwester* hurried the little Italian priest away and the saber-toothed porter came dashing up, full of colloquialisms and bad breath. Ellery found himself engaged in a battle of unconquerable tongues. Finally he left his bag in the fellow's charge, although not with confidence; the porter looked exactly like Heinrich Himmler. And he went sleuthing for a telephone. An excited female voice answered. "Herr Kavine? But is not Herr Professor with you? *Ach*, he will die in the cold! He must meet you. You are to wait, Herr Kavine, to wait where you are. *Westbahnhof?* Herr Professor will find you. He said it!"

*"Bitte schön,"* muttered Herr Kavine, feeling like Landru; and he returned to the platform and the glacial epoch. And waited again, stamping, blowing on his fingers, and catching only every fifth word of the porter's. Probably the coldest winter Austria's had in seventy-nine years, he thought. It always is. Where was the *Föhn*, that lecherous Lurleian breeze from the Austrian Alps which reputedly caressed the jeweled hair of Danube's Queen? Gone, gone with all the winds of myth and fantasy. Gone with *Wiener Blut, leichtes Blut*, now a sullen mass of crimson icicles; gone with the *Frühlingsstimmen*, the spring voices, stilled by the throttling winter and the shrilling of boys crying the postwar *Morgenblätter*, such as they were; gone with the *Geschichten aus dem Wiener Wald*, now tales imprisoned in an antique musicbox which was forever broken . . . Ellery shivered, stamped, and blew as the disguised Himmler whined to him about *die guten, alten Zeiten*.

In the gas chambers, Ellery thought unreasonably. Tell it to Hitler, he thought.

*An der schönen, blauen Donau . . .*

Ellery kept his refrigerated feet pumping and blew *pfuis* on the whole postwar European world.

Professor Seligmann came along at a little after 10 o'clock. The mere sight of that huge body, made huger by the black sheeplined greatcoat collared with Persian lamb and topped with a Russian-style *bashlyk*, was thawing; and when he took one of Ellery's disembodied members in his great, dry, warm hands Ellery melted to the inner man. It was like wandering lost over the earth and coming unexpectedly upon the grandfather of your tribe. The place did not matter; where the patriarch was, there was home. Ellery was struck by Seligmann's eyes particularly. In the lava of that massive face they were eternal fumaroles.

He barely noticed the changes in the Karlsplatz and on the Mariahilferstrasse as they rode in the psychoanalyst's ancient Fiat, driven by a scholarly looking chauffeur, into the Inner City through toppling streets toward the Universität district where the old man lived. He was too agreeably occupied in warming himself at his host.

"You find Vienna not as you expected?" asked Professor Seligmann suddenly.

Ellery started; he had been trying to ignore the shattered city. "It's been so many years since I was here last, Herr Professor. Since long before the War—"

"And the Peace," said the old man with a smile. "We must not overlook the Peace, Mr. Queen. Those difficult Russians, *nyet?* Not to mention those difficult English, those difficult French, and—*bitte schön*—those difficult Americans. Still, with our traditional *Schlamperei*, we manage to drag along. After the first War there was a song popular in Vienna which went, '*Es war einmal ein Walzer; es war einmal ein Wien.*' And we survived. Now we are singing it again, when we do not sing '*Stille Nacht, heilige Nacht.*' Everywhere in Vienna people are speaking of *die guten, alten Zeiten*. How do you say this? 'The good old days.' We Viennese swim in nostalgia, which has a high saline content; that is how we remain afloat. Tell me about New York, Herr Queen. I have not visited your great city since 1927."

Ellery, who had flown an ocean and crisscrossed half a continent to talk about something else, found himself giving a Times Square sightseeing busman's description of postwar Manhattan. And as he talked his sense of time, numbed by his hyperborean flight, began to revive and tick away; and he experienced the shock of recognition, as if this—now—were something very old insisting in a flash on being re-experienced. Tomorrow the trial of Edward Cazalis began and here he was, gossiping with a very old man over four thousand miles away by any route. A pulse began to clamor, and Ellery fell silent as the car drew up before a shellpocked apartment building on some broad *Strasse* whose name he had not even bothered to watch for.

Frau Bauer, Professor Seligmann's housekeeper, greeted her aged employer with aspirin, tea, a hot-water bag, and imprecation—and Ellery with a reminiscent frigidity; but the old man brushed her aside with a smiling *"Ruhe!"* and led Ellery by the hand, like a child, into the land of *Gemütlichkeit*.

Here, in Seligmann's study, were the best of the grace and charming intelligence of *Alt Wien*. The décor was twinkly with wit; it had animation, a leisurely joyousness, and it was a little sly in a friendly way. Here the self-conscious new did not intrude; there was nothing of Prussian precision; things had a patina, they were fine and they glowed.

Like the fire. Oh, the fire. Ellery sat in the lap of a motherly chair and he felt life. And when Frau Bauer served a starving man's breakfast, complete to melting, wonderful *Kaffeekuchen* and pots of rich and aromatic coffee, he knew he was dreaming.

"The best coffee in the world," Ellery said to his host, raising his second cup. "One of the few national advertising claims with the merit of exact truth."

"The coffee, like almost everything else Elsa has served you, comes to me from friends in the United States." At Ellery's blush Seligmann chuckled. "Forgive me, Herr Queen, I am an old *Schuft*, as we say, a scoundrel. You have not crossed an ocean to indulge my bad manners." He said evenly, "What is this now about my Edward Cazalis?"

So here it was.

Ellery left the motherly chair to stand before the fire like a man.

He said: "You saw Cazalis in Zürich in June, Professor Seligmann. Have you heard from him since?"

"No."

"Then you don't know what's been going on in New York this summer and fall?"

"Life. And death."

"I beg pardon?"

The old man smiled. "I assume it, Mr. Queen. Has it not always? I do not read newspapers since the war begins. That is for people who like to suffer. I, I do not like to suffer. I have surrendered myself to eternity. For me there is today this room, tomorrow cremation, unless the authorities cannot agree to allow it, in which case they may stuff me and place me in the clock tower of the *Rathaus* and I shall keep reminding them of the time. Why do you ask?"

"Herr Professor, I've just made a discovery."

"And what is that?"

Ellery laughed. "You know all about it."

The old man shook silently. He didn't when I phoned him from New York, thought Ellery, but he's done some catching up since.

"You do, don't you?"

"I have made some inquiries since, yes. Was it so evident? Sit down, Mr. Queen, sit down, we are not enemies. Your city has been terrorized by a paranoid murderer who strangled nine people, and now Edward Cazalis has been arrested for the crimes."

"You don't know the details."

"No."

Ellery sat down and related the story, beginning with the discovery of Archibald Dudley Abernethy's body and ending with the capture of Cazalis in the First Avenue alley. Then he briefly indicated the subsequent conduct of the prisoner.

"Tomorrow, Professor Seligmann, Cazalis's trial begins in New York, and I'm in Vienna—"

"To what purpose?" The old man regarded Ellery through the reek of his meerschaum. "I treated Cazalis as a patient when he came first to Vienna with his wife eighteen years ago, he studied under me subsequently, he left—I believe in 1935—to return to America, and since that time I have seen him once. This summer. What is it you want of me, Herr Queen?"

"Help."

"Mine? But the case is concluded. What more can there be? I do not understand. And if there is more, in which way could I be of assistance?"

"Yes." Ellery fingered his cup. "It must be confusing. Especially since the evidence against Cazalis is so damning. He was captured in the act of attempting a tenth murder. He directed the police to the hiding place of a stock of strangling cords and they were found where he said they would be, in the locked medical files in his office. And he confessed to the previous nine murders in considerable detail." Ellery set his cup down with care. "Professor Seligmann, I know nothing of your science beyond, let's say, some intelligent layman's understanding of the differences among neurotic behavior, neurosis, and psychosis. But in spite of—or perhaps because of—my lack of knowledge in your field I've been experiencing my own brand of tension, arising from a rather curious fact."

"And that is?"

"Cazalis never explained his . . . forgive me for hesitating . . . his motive. If he's psychotic, his motives proceed from false views of reality which can have only clinical interest. But if he's not . . . Herr Professor,

before I'm satisfied, I've got to know what drove Cazalis to those murders."

"And you believe I can tell you, Herr Queen?"

"Yes."

"How so?" The old man puffed.

"You treated him. Moreover, he studied under you. To become a psychiatrist he had himself to be analyzed, a mandatory procedure—"

But Seligmann was shaking his great head. "In the case of a man so
old as Cazalis was when he began to study with me, Mr. Queen, analysis
is not a mandatory procedure. It is a most questionable procedure, Mr.
Queen. Very few have been successfully analyzed at the age of 49, which
is how old he was in 1931. Indeed, the entire project was questionable
because of his age. I attempted it in Cazalis's case only because he interested me, he had a medical background, and I wished to experiment. As
it happened, we were successful. Forgive me for interrupting—"

"At any rate, you analyzed him."

"I analyzed him, yes."

Ellery hitched forward. "What was wrong with him?"

Seligmann murmured: "What is wrong with any of us?"

"That's no answer."

"It is one answer, Mr. Queen. We all exhibit neurotic behavior. All,
without exception."

"Now you're indulging your *Schufterei*, if that's the word." The old
man laughed delightedly. "I ask you again, Herr Professor: What was the
underlying cause of Cazalis's emotional upset?"

Seligmann kept puffing.

"It's that question that's brought me here. Because I know none of the
essential facts, only the inconclusive superficial ones. Cazalis came from
a poverty-laden background. He was one of fourteen children. He abandoned his parents and his brothers and sisters when a wealthy man be-
friended and educated him. And then he abandoned his benefactor.
Everything about his career seems to me to point to an abnormal ambition, a compulsive overdrive to success—including his marriage. While
his professional ethics remained high, his personal history is characterized by calculation and tremendous energy. And then, suddenly, at the
apex of his career, in his prime—a breakdown. Suggestive."

The old man said nothing.

"He'd been treated for a mild case of what they called 'shell shock' in
the first war. Was there a connection? I don't know. Was there, Herr Professor?"

But Seligmann remained silent.

"And what follows this breakdown? He abandons his practice, one of the most lucrative in New York. He allows his wife to take him on a world cruise, apparently recovers . . . but in Vienna, world's capital of psychoanalysis, another breakdown. The first collapse had been ascribed to overwork. But to what was the second collapse, after a leisurely cruise, ascribable? Suggestive! Professor Seligmann, you treated him. What caused Cazalis's breakdowns?"

Seligmann took the pipe from his mouth. "You ask me to disclose information, Mr. Queen, of which I came into possession in my professional capacity."

"A nice point, Herr Professor. But what are the ethics of silence when silence itself is immoral?"

The old man did not seem offended. He set the pipe down. "Herr Queen. It is evident to me that you have come not for information so much as for confirmation of conclusions which you have already reached on the basis of insufficient data. Tell me your conclusions. Perhaps we shall find a way of resolving my dilemma."

"All right!" Ellery jumped up. But then he sat down again, forcing himself to speak calmly. "At the age of 44 Cazalis married a girl of 19 after a busy life devoid of personal relationships with women although in his work all his relationships were with women. During the first four years of their married life Mrs. Cazalis gave birth to two children. Dr. Cazalis not only cared for his wife personally during her pregnancies but performed both deliveries. Neither infant survived the delivery room. A few months after the second fatality in childbirth, Cazalis broke down— and retired from obstetrics and gynecology, never to go back to them.

"It seems to me, Professor Seligmann," said Ellery, "that whatever was wrong with Cazalis reached its climax in that delivery room."

"Why," murmured the old man, "do you say this?"

"Because . . . Professor Seligmann, I can't speak in terms of libido and mortido, Ego and Id. But I have some knowledge of human beings, and the sum of whatever observations I've been able to make of human behavior, and of my own and others' experience of life, impels me to the conclusion.

"I observe the fact: Cazalis turns his back with cold purpose on his childhood. Why? I speculate. His childhood was predominated by a mother who was always either carrying a child or having a child, by a laborer-father who was always begetting them, and by a horde of other children who were always getting in the way of his wishes. I speculate. Did Cazalis hate his mother? Did he hate his brothers and sisters? Did he feel guilt because he hated them?

"And I observe the career he sets for himself, and I say: Is there a significant connection between his hate for maternity and his specialization—as it were—in maternity? Is there a nexus between his hate for the numerous progeny of his parents and his determination to make himself an expert in the science of bringing more children into the world?

"Hate and guilt—and the defenses against them. I've put two and two together. Is this permitted, Herr Professor? Is this valid?"

Seligmann said, "One tends to oversimplify in your sort of mathematics, *mein Herr*. But go on."

"Then I say to myself: Cazalis's tensions lie deep. His guilts are profound. His defenses against the unconscious becoming conscious—if that's a fundamental identification of neurotic behavior—are elaborate.

"Now I observe his marriage. Immediately, it seems to me, new tensions—or extensions of old ones—set in. Even a so-called normal man of 44 would find a first marriage, after a life of overwork and little socializing—would find such a marriage, to a 19-year-old girl, unsettling and conflicting. In this case the young bride was from a thin blooded New England strain. She was emotionally of delicate balance, rather rarefied, on the frigid side, and almost certainly inexperienced. And Cazalis was as he was. I speculate.

"I say: It seems to me Cazalis must at once have found himself involved in serious sexual dissatisfactions, frustrations, and disagreeable conflicts. I say: There must have been recurrent episodes of impotence. Or his wife was unresponsive, unawakened, or actually repelled. He began to feel an erosive inadequacy, perhaps? Yes, and a resentment. It wouldn't be unnatural. He, the highly successful entrepreneur of the biological process, can't master the technique of his own marriage. Also, he loves his wife. She is an intelligent woman, she has a fragile charm, reserve, breeding; even today, at 42, she's handsome; at 19 she must have been extremely attractive. Cazalis loves her as only a man can love who is old enough to be the father of the highly desirable object of his affections. And he's inadequate.

"So I say: A fear is born. Undoubtedly this fear arises from altogether different causes, but it expresses itself in a disguised form: he becomes afraid he will lose his young wife to another man."

Ellery drank some coffee and Seligmann waited. The ormolu clock on the mantelpiece kept a sort of truce between them.

"The fear is nourished," continued Ellery, "by the great difference in their ages, temperaments, backgrounds, interests. By the demands of his practice, his long hours at the hospital assisting other men's wives to bring other men's children into the world, by his enforced professional absences from Mrs. Cazalis—frequently at night.

"The fear spreads, like a cancer. It gets out of control. Cazalis becomes violently suspicious of his wife's relationships with other men, no matter how slight, no matter how innocent—especially of her relationships with younger men.

"And soon the fear grows into an obsession.

"Professor Seligmann." Ellery eyed the old Viennese. "Was Edward Cazalis obsessively jealous of his wife during the first four years of their marriage?"

Seligmann picked up his pipe and rather deliberately set about knocking it out. "Your method, Mr. Queen, is one unknown to science," he said with a smile. "But this is of great interest to me. Continue." He stuck the empty pipe in his mouth.

"Then Mrs. Cazalis becomes pregnant." Ellery frowned. "One would imagine that at this point Cazalis's fears would recede. But no, he's passed the point of reasonableness. Her very pregnancy feeds his jealousy and becomes suspect. Isn't this a confirmation of his suspicions? he asks himself. And he insists—he insists—on taking care of his wife himself. He is undoubtedly excessively devoted, solicitous, and watchful. Gestation unfortunately takes nine months. Nine months in which to watch a fetus grow. Nine months in which to torture himself with a question which at last bursts forth in the full deformity of obsession: Is this my child? Is it?

"Oh, he fights it. He fights an endless battle. But the enemy is discouraging. Kill it in one place and it springs up, viciously lively as ever, in another. Does he ever tell his wife of his suspicions? Accuse her outright of infidelity? Are there scenes, tears, hysterical denials? If so, they only serve to strengthen his suspicions. If not, if he keeps his raging fears bottled up, then it's even worse.

"Mrs. Cazalis comes to term, goes through labor.

"And there she lies.

"In the delivery room.

"Under his hands.

"And the baby dies.

"Professor Seligmann, do you see how far I've traveled?"

The old man merely waggled the pipe in his jaws.

"Mrs. Cazalis becomes pregnant a second time. The process of suspicion, jealousy, self-torment, and uncertainty-certainty repeats itself. Again Cazalis insists on seeing his wife through her pregnancy. Again he insists on performing the delivery.

"And again his baby dies in the delivery room.

"His second child, dead like the first.

"*Under his hands.*

"Under those powerful, delicately nerved, practiced surgeon's hands.

"Professor Seligmann." Ellery loomed over the old man. "You're the only being on the face of the earth in a position to tell me the truth. Isn't it a fact that when Edward Cazalis came to you eighteen years ago for psychiatric treatment he had broken down under a dreadful load of guilt—*the guilt of having murdered his own two children in the act of delivery?*"

After a moment old Seligmann took the empty pipe from his lips. He said carefully: "For a physician to murder his own unborn children under the delusion that they were another's—this would be psychosis, Herr Queen, no? You could not expect him to follow his subsequent brilliant, stable career, most particularly in the field of psychiatry. And my position, what would that have been? Still, you believe this, Herr Queen?"

Ellery laughed angrily. "Would it make my meaning clear if I amended my question to conclude: 'the guilt of *fearing* he had murdered his own two children'?"

The old man looked pleased.

"Because it was the logical development of his neurosis, wasn't it? He had excessive feelings of guilt about his hates and a great need for punishment. He, the eminent obstetrician, had brought thousands of other men's children into the world alive, but under his hands his own children had died. *Did I kill them?* he agonized. *Did my obsessive jealousy and suspicions make my hands fail? Did I want them to be born dead and my hands saw to it that they were? I did want them to be born dead. And they were born dead. Therefore I killed them.* The terrible illogic of neurosis.

"His common sense told him they had been breech births; his neurosis told him he had performed countless other breech births successfully. His common sense told him that his wife, let's say, was not ideally constructed for motherhood; his neurosis told him her babies were fathered by other men. His common sense told him that he had done his efficient best; his neurosis told him that he had not, that he might have done this or that, or not done that or this, or that had he not insisted on performing the deliveries himself but placed his wife in the hands of another obstetrician, his children would have survived. And so on.

"Because he had an overwhelming compulsion to believe it, within a short time Cazalis had convinced himself that he'd murdered both babies. A little of this mental *Schrecklichkeit* and he broke. When his wife took him traveling and he came to Vienna—odd coincidence, wouldn't you say, Professor?—lo, he collapsed again. And went to you. And you, Professor Seligmann, you probed and analyzed and treated and . . . you cured him?"

When the old psychoanalyst spoke, his rumbling voice held a growl. "It is too many years and I know nothing of his emotional problems since. Even at the time there was a menopausal complication. If in the past few years he has been pushing himself too hard—at the present stage of his life . . . Often in middle age people are unable to defend themselves by means of neurotic symptoms and they break down completely into a psychosis. We find, for example, that paranoid schizophrenia is frequently a disease of late middle age. Still, I am surprised and troubled. I do not know. I should have to see him."

"He still has guilt feelings. He must have. It's the only explanation for what he's done, Professor."

"What he has done? You mean, Mr. Queen, murdering nine persons?"

"No."

"He has done something else?"

"Yes."

"In addition to the nine murders?"

"To the exclusion," said Ellery, "of the nine murders."

Seligmann rapped the bowl of his meerschaum on the arm of the chair.

"Come, *mein Herr*. You speak in riddles. Precisely what is it that you do mean?"

"I mean," said Ellery, "that Cazalis is innocent of the charge for which he's going on trial in New York tomorrow morning."

"*Innocent?*"

"I mean, Professor Seligmann, that Cazalis did not kill those nine people. Cazalis is not—and never was—the Cat."

# 13

Seligmann said, "Let us expose Fate, whose other name is Bauer." He bellowed, "Elsa!"

Frau Bauer appeared, pure jinni.

"Elsa—" began the old man.

But Frau Bauer interrupted, stumbling from a secure "Herr Professor" into uncertain English so that Ellery knew her remarks were intended for his ears also. "You have breakfast eaten when it is already lunch. Lunch you have not eaten. Now comes your time to rest." Fists on bony hips, Frau Bauer glared challenge to the non-Viennese world.

"I'm so very sorry, Professor—"

"For what, Mr. Queen? Elsa." The old man spoke gently, in German. "You've listened at the door. You've insulted my guest. Now you wish to rob me of my few remaining hours of consciousness. Must I hypnotize you?"

Frau Bauer whitened. She fled.

"It is my only weapon against her," chuckled the old man. "I threaten to put her under hypnosis and send her into the Soviet zone to serve as the plaything of Moscow. It is not a matter of morals with Elsa; it is sheer horror. She would as soon get into bed with the Antichrist. You were telling me, Mr. Queen, that Cazalis is innocent after all?"

"Yes."

The old man sat back, smiling. "Do you arrive at this conclusion by way of your unique, scientifically unknown method of analysis, or is this based upon fact? Such fact as would, for example, satisfy your courts of law."

"It's based on a fact which would satisfy anyone above the mental age of five, Professor Seligmann," Ellery retorted. "Its very simplicity, I think, has obscured it. Its simplicity and the fact that the murders have been so numerous and have dragged on for so long. Too, it's been the kind of case in which the individuality of the victims has tended to blur and blend as the murders multiplied, until at the end one looked back on a homogeneous pile of carcasses, so many head of cattle passed through the slaughter pen. The same sort of reaction one got looking at the official pictures of the corpses of Belsen, Buchenwald, Oswiecim, and Maidanek. No particularity. Just death."

"But the fact, Mr. Queen." With a flick of impatience, and something else. And suddenly Ellery recalled that Béla Seligmann's only daughter, married to a Polish Jewish doctor, had died at Treblinka. Love particularizes death, Ellery thought. And little else.

"Oh, the fact," he said. "Why, it's a mere matter of beginners' physics, Professor. You attended the Zürich convention earlier this year, you told me. Exactly when this year?"

The white brows met. "The end of May, was it not?"

"The meeting lasted ten days and the concluding session was held on the night of June 3. On the night of June 3 Dr. Edward Cazalis of the United States read a paper entitled *Ochlophobia, Nyctophobia, and Ponophobia* in the convention hall before a large audience. As reported in a *Zürcher* scientific journal, the speaker scheduled to precede Cazalis, a Dane, ran far over his allotted time, to virtually the adjournment hour. Out of courtesy to Dr. Cazalis, however, who had attended all the sessions — according to a footnote in the journal — the American was permitted to deliver his paper. Cazalis began reading around midnight and finished at a few minutes past 2 o'clock in the morning. The convention was then adjourned for the year. The official adjournment time was 2:24 A.M. 4th June."

Ellery shrugged. "The time difference between Zürich and New York being six hours, midnight of June 3 in Zürich, which is when Cazalis began reading his paper to the convention, was 6 P.M. June 3 in New York; 2 A.M. June 4 in Zürich, which is about when Cazalis finished reading his paper there, was 8 P.M. June 3 in New York. Assuming the absurd — that Cazalis whisked himself from the convention hall immediately on adjournment or even as he stepped off the platform at the conclusion of his talk, that he had already checked out of his hotel and had his luggage waiting, that the slight matter of his visa had been taken care of, that there was a plane ready to take off for the United States at the Zürich airport the instant he reached there (for which specific plane Cazalis had a ticket, notwithstanding Dr. Naardvoessler's windiness, the unusual hour, or the impossibility of having foreseen the delay), that this plane flew to New York nonstop, that at Newark Airport or La Guardia Cazalis found a police motorcycle escort waiting to conduct his taxi through traffic at the highest possible speed—assuming all this nonsense, Herr Professor, at which hour could Edward Cazalis have reached midtown Manhattan, would you say? The earliest conceivable hour?"

"I have a poor acquaintance with the progress—if that is the word—of aeronautics."

"Could the entire leap through space—from a platform in Zürich to a street in Manhattan—have been accomplished in three and a half to four hours, Professor Seligmann?"

"Obviously not."

"So I telephoned to you. Whereupon it came out that Edward Cazalis did not go from the convention hall to an airfield that night. Came out not as speculation but as fact. For you told me you had kept Cazalis up talking in your hotel room in Zürich all through that night until 'long past dawn.' Surely that would mean, at the very earliest, 6 A.M.? Let's say 6 A.M., Professor, to please me; it must have been, of course, even later. 6 A.M. in Zürich on the 4th of June would be midnight in New York on June 3. Do you recall my giving you the date of the first Cat murder? The murder of the man named Abernethy?"

"Dates are a nuisance. And there were so many."

"Exactly. There were so many, and it was so long ago. Well, according to our Medical Examiner's report, Abernethy was strangled *around midnight' of June* 3. As I said, a matter of simple physics. Cazalis has demonstrated many talents, but the ability to be in two places thousands of miles apart at the same moment is not one of them."

The old man exclaimed, "But, as you say, this is so basic! And your police, your prosecutors, have not perceived this physical impossibility?"

"There were nine murders and an attempted tenth. The time-stretch was almost exactly five months. Cazalis's old obstetrical files, the strangling cords hidden in his psychiatric case history files, the circumstances of his capture, his detailed and voluntary confession—all these have created an overwhelming presumption of his guilt. The authorities may have slipped through overconfidence, or carelessness, or because they found that in the majority of the murders Cazalis could physically have committed the crimes. Remember, there is no direct evidence linking Cazalis with any of the murders; the people's entire case must rest on that tenth attempt. Here the evidence is direct enough. Cazalis was captured while he was in the act of tightening the noose about the throat of the girl who was wearing Marilyn Soames's borrowed coat. The noose of tussah silk. The Cat's noose. *Ergo*, he's the Cat. Why think of alibis?

"On the other hand, one would expect the defense attorneys to check everything. If they haven't turned up Cazalis's alibi, it's because of the defendant himself; when I left New York, he was being extremely difficult. After attempting to get along without legal help altogether. And then there's no reason why a lawyer, merely because he is a lawyer for the defense, should be immune to the general atmosphere of conviction about his client's guilt.

"I suspect, however, a more insidious reason for the alibi's remaining undiscovered, one that goes to the roots of the psychology which has operated in this case virtually from its outset. There has been a neurotic anxiety of epidemic proportions to catch the Cat, drive a stake through his heart, and forget the whole dreadful mass incubus. It's infected the authorities, too. The Cat was a *Doppelgänger*, his nature so tenuously drawn that when the authorities actually laid their hands on a creature of flesh and blood who fitted the specifications . . ."

"If you instruct me whom to address, Mr. Queen," rumbled old Seligmann, "I shall cable New York of my having detained Cazalis all night until past dawn of the 4th June in Zürich."

"We'll arrange for you to make a formal deposition. That, plus the evidence of Dr. Cazalis's attendance throughout the Zürich convention and of his return passage to the United States, which can't have begun earlier than June 4, will clear him."

"They will be satisfied that, having been unable physically to murder the first one, Cazalis did not murder the others?"

"To argue the contrary would be infantile, Professor Seligmann. The crimes were characterized and accepted as the work of the same individual almost from the beginning. And with abundant reason. The source of the supply of victims' names alone confirms it. The method used in selecting the specific victims from the source of supply confirms it. The identical technique of the strangulations confirms it. And so on. The strongest point of all is the use in all nine murders of the strangling cords of tussah silk—cords of East Indian origin, exotic, unusual, not readily procurable, and obviously from the same source."

"And, of course, in a sequence of acts of violence of a psychotic nature showing common characteristics—"

"Yes. Multiple homicides of this kind are invariably what we call 'lone wolf' operations, acts of a single disturbed person. There won't be any trouble on that score . . . Are you sure you wouldn't like to rest now, Professor Seligmann? Frau Bauer said—"

The old man dismissed Frau Bauer with a scowl as he reached for a tobacco jar. "I begin to glimpse your destination, *mein Herr*. Nevertheless, take me by the hand. You have resolved one difficulty only to be confronted by another.

"Cazalis is not the Cat.

"Then who is?"

*   *   *

"The next question," nodded Ellery.

He was silent for a moment.

"I answered it between heaven and earth, Professor," he said at last with a smile, "in a state of all but suspended animation, so you'll forgive me if I go slowly.

"To arrive at the answer we must examine Cazalis's known acts in the light of what we've built up about his neurosis.

"Just what was it Cazalis *did?* His known activities in the Cat cases begin with the tenth victim. His very choice of 21-year-old Marilyn Soames as the tenth victim must have arisen from his application of the same selective technique employed by the Cat in hunting through Cazalis's old obstetrical case cards—I used the technique myself and arrived at the same victim. Anyone of reasonable intelligence could have done it, then, who had access to both the facts of the preceding nine crimes and the files.

"Having employed the Cat's method in selecting the next victim in the series, what did Cazalis then proceed to do?

"As it happened, Marilyn Soames works at home, she was extremely busy, and she didn't regularly come out into the streets. The Cat's first problem in each case must have been to become familiar with the face and figure of the victim he had marked for destruction. Had the real Cat, then, been working on Marilyn Soames he would have attempted to lure her from her home in order to be able to study her appearance. This was precisely what Cazalis did. By a subterfuge, he lured Marilyn Soames to a crowded public place where he could 'study' her in 'safety.'

"For days and nights Cazalis scouted the girl's neighborhood and reconnoitered the building where she lives. Just as the Cat would have done. Just as the Cat must have done in the previous cases.

"While he was apparently on the prowl, Cazalis exhibited eagerness, cunning, disappointment of an extravagant nature at temporary frustrations. The kind of behavior one would have expected the unbalanced Cat to evince.

"Finally, on that climactic October night, Cazalis waylaid a girl who resembled Marilyn Soames in height and figure and who was accidentally wearing Marilyn Soames's coat, dragged this girl into an alley, and *began* to strangle her with one of the tussah silk cords associated with the Cat's previous homicidal activities.

"And when we captured him Cazalis 'confessed' to being the Cat and reconstructed his 'activities' in the nine previous murders . . . including an account of the murder of Abernethy, committed when Cazalis was in Switzerland!

"Why?

"Why did Cazalis imitate the Cat?

"Why did he confess to the Cat's crimes?"

The old man was listening intently.

"This was patently not the case of a deluded man's identifying himself with the violent acts of another by merely claiming, as many psychotics did in those five months—every sensational crime brings such people forward—to have committed the Cat's crimes of record. No. Cazalis *proved* he was the Cat by thought, plan, and action; by creating a new and typical Cat crime based upon exact knowledge and a clearly painstaking study of the Cat's habits, methods, and technique. This was not even imitation; it was a brilliant interpretation, consisting of omissions as well as of commissions. For example, on the morning when Cazalis actually entered the Soames apartment house, while he was out in the court, Marilyn Soames came downstairs to the vestibule and stood there for several minutes looking over her mail. At this moment Cazalis re-entered the hall. No one was apparently about except Cazalis and his victim; it was early morning, the street beyond was deserted. Nevertheless, at that time Cazalis made no move to attack the girl. Why? Because to have done so would have broken the consistent pattern of the Cat's murders; those had been committed, to the last one, after dark—and this was broad daylight. Such scrupulous attention to detail could not conceivably have come out of an ordinary psychotic identification. Not to mention the self-restraint exhibited.

"No, Cazalis was rational and his deliberate assumption of the Cat's role in all its creative vigor was therefore rationally motivated."

"It is your conclusion, then," asked Seligmann, "that Cazalis had no intention of strangling the girl to death in the alley? That he merely made the pretense?"

"Yes."

"But this would presuppose that he knew he was being followed by the police and that he would be captured in the act."

"Of course he knew, Professor. The very fact that he, a rational man, set out to prove he was the Cat when he was not raises the logical question: Prove it to whom? His proof did not consist merely of a confession, as I've pointed out. It consisted of elaborate activities stretching over a period of many days; of facial expressions as well as of visits to the Soames neighborhood. A deception presupposes that there is someone watching to be deceived. Yes, Cazalis knew he was being followed by the police; he knew that each move he made, each twist of his lips, was being noted and recorded by trained operatives.

"And when he slipped the silk cord around Celeste Phillips's neck—

the girl he mistook for his victim—Cazalis was playing his final scene for his audience. It's significant that the tenth case was the only case in which the intended victim was able to cry out loudly enough to be heard. And while Cazalis tightened the cord sufficiently to leave realistic marks on the girl's neck, it's also significant that he permitted her to get her hands between the noose and her throat, that he did not knock her unconscious as the Cat had done in at least two of his assaults, and that Celeste Phillips was able within a short time of the attack to speak and act normally; what slight and temporary damage she sustained was chiefly the result of her own struggles and her terror. What Cazalis would have done had we not run into the alley to 'stop' him is conjectural; probably he would have permitted the girl to scream long enough without fatal injury to insure interference from some outside source. He could be certain detectives weren't far away in the fog, and it was a congested section of the City.

"He wanted to be caught in the act of a Cat murder-attempt, he planned to be caught in the act of a Cat murder-attempt, and he was successful in being caught in the act of a Cat murder-attempt."

"Whereupon it becomes evident," murmured the old man, "that we approach our destination."

"Yes. For a rational man to assume another's guilt and to be willing to suffer another's punishment, the rational mind can find only one justification: the one is shielding the other. *YES*          *MLP August 7, 2011*

"Cazalis was concealing the Cat's identity.

"Cazalis was protecting the Cat from detection, exposure, and punishment.

"And in doing so Cazalis was punishing himself out of deeply buried feelings of his own guilts as they centered about the Cat and his emotional involvement with the Cat.

"Do you agree, Professor Seligmann?"

But the old man said in a curious way: "I am only an observer along this road you travel, Mr. Queen. I neither agree nor disagree; I listen."

Ellery laughed. "What did I now know about the Cat?

"That the Cat was someone with whom Cazalis was emotionally involved. With whom he was therefore in a close relationship.

"That the Cat was someone whom Cazalis had an overpowering wish to protect and whose criminal guilt is tied in Cazalis's mind to his own neurotic guilts.

"That the Cat was a psychotic with a determinable psychotic reason for seeking out and murdering people who a generation and more before had been brought into the world by Cazalis the obstetrician.

"That, finally, the Cat was someone who has had equal access with

Cazalis to his old obstetrical records, which have been stored in a locked closet in his home."

Seligmann paused in the act of putting the meerschaum back into his mouth.

"Is there such a person, I asked myself? To my certain knowledge?

"There is. To my certain knowledge," said Ellery. "Just one.

"Mrs. Cazalis."

"For Mrs. Cazalis," said Ellery, "is the only living person who fits the specifications I have just drawn.

"Mrs. Cazalis is the only living person with whom Cazalis is emotionally involved in a close relationship; in his closest relationship.

"Mrs. Cazalis is the only living person whom Cazalis would have a compulsion to protect and for whose guilt Cazalis would feel intensely responsible . . . whose criminal guilt would be tied in his mind to his own neurotic guilt feelings.

"Mrs. Cazalis has a determinable—the only determinable—psychotic reason for seeking out and murdering people her husband had brought into the world.

"And that Mrs. Cazalis has had equal access with her husband to his obstetrical records is self-evident."

Seligmann did not change expression. He seemed neither surprised nor impressed. "I am chiefly interested in pursuing your third point. What you have called Mrs. Cazalis's 'determinable psychotic reason' for murdering. How do you demonstrate this?"

"By another extension of that method of mine you've characterized as unknown to science, Herr Professor. I knew that Mrs. Cazalis had lost two children in giving birth. I knew, from something Cazalis told me, that after the second delivery she was no longer able to bear children. I knew that she had thereafter become extremely attached to her sister's only child, Lenore Richardson, to the point where her niece was more her daughter than her sister's. I knew, or I had convinced myself, that Cazalis had proved inadequate to his sexual function as a husband. Certainly during the long period of his breakdowns and subsequent treatment he must have been a source of continual frustration to his wife. And she was only 19 when they married.

"From the age of 19, then," said Ellery, "I saw Mrs. Cazalis as leading an unnatural, tense existence, complicated by strong maternal desires which were thwarted by the deaths of her two infants, her inability to have another child, and what could only have been a highly unsatisfactory and unsettling transference of her thwarted feelings to her niece. She knew that Lenore could never really be hers; Lenore's mother is neurotic, jealous, possessive, infantile, and interfering—a source of unending trouble. Mrs. Cazalis is not an outgoing individual and apparently she never was. Her frustrations, then, grew inward; she contained them . . . for a long time.

"Until, in fact, she was past 40.

"Then she cracked.

"I say, Professor Seligmann, that one day Mrs. Cazalis told herself something that thenceforward became her only reason for living.

"Once she believed that, she was lost. Lost in the distorted world of psychosis.

"Because, Professor, I believe the oddest thing occurred. Mrs. Cazalis did not have to know that her husband thought he had murdered their children at birth; in fact, she undoubtedly did not know it—in her rational life—or their marriage would hardly have survived the knowledge for so many years. *But I think she arrived at approximately the same point in her psychosis.*

"I think she finally told herself: *My husband gave thousands of living babies to other women, but when I was to have my own babies he gave me dead ones. So my husband killed them. He won't let me have my children, so I won't let them have their children. He killed mine; I'll kill theirs.*" And Ellery said, "Would it be possible for me to have more of that wonderful non-Viennese coffee, Professor Seligmann?"

"*Ach.*" Seligmann reached over and tugged at a bellpull. Frau Bauer appeared. "Elsa, are we barbarians? More coffee."

"It's all ready," snapped Frau Bauer in German. And as she returned with two fat, steaming pots and fresh cups and saucers, she said, "I know you, you old *Schuft*. You are in one of your suicidal moods." And she flounced out, banging the door.

"This is my life," said the old man. He was regarding Ellery with bright eyes. "Do you know, Herr Queen, this is extraordinary. I can only sit and admire."

"Yes?" said Ellery, not quite following but grateful for the gift of the jinni.

"For you have arrived, by an uncharted route, at the true destination.

"The trained eye looks upon your Mrs. Cazalis and one says: Here is a quiet, submissive type of woman. She is withdrawn, seclusive, asocial, frigid, slightly suspicious and hypercritical—I speak, of course, of the time when I knew her. Her husband is handsome, successful, and in his work—his obstetrical work—he is constantly in contact with other women, but in their married life her husband and she have disturbing conflicts and tensions. She has managed nevertheless to make an adjustment to life; in—as it were—a limping fashion.

"She has done nothing to warrant special notice. In fact, she has always been overshadowed by her husband and dominated by him.

"Then, in her 40s, something occurs. For years, secretly, she has been jealous of her husband's rapport with younger women, his psychiatric patients—for it is interesting to note that in recent years, as Cazalis told me in Zürich, he has had an almost totally female clientele. She has not required 'proof,' for she has always been of a schizoid tendency; besides, there was probably nothing to 'prove.' No matter. Mrs. Cazalis's schizoid tendency bursts forth in a delusional state.

"A frank paranoid psychosis.

"She develops the delusion that her own babies were killed by her husband. In order to deprive her of them. She may even think that he is the father of some of the children whose successful deliveries he performed. With or without the idea that her husband is their father, she sets out to kill them in retaliation.

"Her psychosis is controlled in her inner life. It is not expressed to the world except in her crimes.

"This is how the psychiatrist might describe the murderer you have delineated.

"As you see, Mr. Queen, the destination is the same."

"Except that mine," said Ellery, his smile slightly bitter, "seems to have been approached poetically. I recall the artist who kept depicting the strangler as a cat and I warm to his remarkable intuition. Doesn't a tigress—that grandmother of cats—go 'mad' with rage when she is robbed of her cubs? Then, Professor, there's the old saying, *A woman hath nine lives like a cat*. Mrs. Cazalis has nine lives to her debit, too. She killed and she killed until . . ."

"Yes?"

"Until one day Cazalis entertained a ghastly visitor."

"The truth."

Ellery nodded. "It could have come about in one of a number of ways. He might have stumbled on the hiding place of her stock of silk cords and recalled their visit to India years before and her purchase—not his—of the cords. Or perhaps it was one or two of the victims' names striking a chord of memory; then it would require merely a few minutes with his old files to open his eyes. Or he may have noticed his wife acting oddly, followed her, and was too late to avert a tragedy but in quite sufficient time to grasp its sickening significance. He would go back in his mind to the recent past and discover that on the night of each murder he could not vouch for her whereabouts. Also, Cazalis suffers from chronic insomnia and he takes sleeping pills regularly; this, he would realize, had given her unlimited opportunities. And for purposes of slipping in and out of the

building at night unobserved by the apartment house employees, there
was always Cazalis's office door, giving access directly to the street. As
for the daytimes, a woman's daytime excursions are rarely examined by
her husband; in our American culture, in all strata, 'shopping' is the
magic word, explaining everything . . . Cazalis may even have seen how,
in the cunning of her paranoia, his wife had skipped over numerous eligi-
bles on the list in order to strike at her niece—the most terrible of her
murders, the murder of the unsatisfying substitute for her dead children—in order that she might maneuver Cazalis into the investigation
and through him keep informed as to everything the police and I knew
and planned.

"In any event, as a psychiatrist Cazalis would immediately grasp the
umbilical symbolism in her choice of cords to strangle—as it were—babies; certainly the infantile significance of her consistent use of blue
cords for male victims and pink cords for females could not have escaped
him. He could trace her psychosis, then, to the traumatic source upon
which her delusion had seized. It could only be the delivery room in
which she had lost her own two children. Under ordinary circumstances
this would have been a merely clinical, if personally agonizing, observation, and Cazalis would either have taken the medical and legal steps
usual in such cases or, if the prospect of revealing the truth to the world
involved too much pain, mortification, and obloquy, he would at the least
have put her where she could do no more harm.

"But the circumstances were not ordinary. There were his own old
feelings of guilt which had expressed themselves through and revolved
about that same delivery room. Perhaps it was the shock of realizing
what lay behind his wife's mental illness that revived the guilt feelings he
had thought were dissolved. However it came about, Cazalis must have
found himself in the clutch of his old neurosis, its tenacity increased a
thousandfold by the shock of the discovery that had brought it alive
again. Soon he was persuaded by his neurosis that it was all his faut; that
had he not 'murdered' their two babies she would not have erupted into
psychosis. The sin, then, was his; he alone was 'responsible,' therefore he
alone must suffer the punishment.

"So he sent his wife south in the care of her sister and brother-in-law,
he took the remaining silk cords from his wife's hiding place and stored
them in a place identifiable with him alone, and he set about proving to
the authorities that he, Edward Cazalis, was the monster the City of New
York had been hunting frantically for five months. His subsequent 'confession' in detail was the easiest part of it by far; he was fully informed
through his affiliation with the case of all the facts known to the police,
and upon a foundation of these facts he was able to build a plausible,

convincing structure. How much of his behavior at this point and since has been playacting and how much actual disturbance I can't, of course, venture to say.

"And that, Professor Seligmann, is my story," said Ellery in a tightened voice, "and if you have any information that controverts it, this is the time to speak out."

He found that he was shivering and he blamed it on the fire, which was low. It was hissing a little, as if to call attention to its plight.

Old Seligmann raised himself and devoted a few minutes to the Promethean chore of bringing warmth back to the room.

Ellery waited.

Suddenly, without turning, the old man grumbled: "Perhaps it would be wisdom, Herr Queen, to send that cable now."

Ellery sighed.

"May I telephone instead? You can't say much in a cable, and if I can talk to my father a great deal of time will have been saved."

"I shall place the call for you." The old man shuffled to his desk. As he took the telephone, he added with a twitch of humor, "My German—at least on the European side, Mr. Queen—will undoubtedly prove less expensive than yours."

They might have been calling one of the more distant planets. They sat in silence sipping their coffee, attuned to a ring which did not come.

The day was running out and the study began to blur and lose its character.

Once Frau Bauer stormed in. Her bristling entrance startled them. But their unnatural silence and the twilight they sat in startled her. She tiptoed about, switching on lamps. Then, like a mouse, she skittered out.

Once Ellery laughed, and the old man raised his head.

"I've just thought of something absurd, Professor Seligmann. In the four months since I first laid eyes on her, I've never called her or thought of her or referred to her as anything but 'Mrs. Cazalis.' "

"And what should you call her," said the old man grumpily, "Ophelia?"

"I never did learn her Christian name. I don't know it at this moment. Just Mrs. Cazalis . . . the great man's shadow. Yet from the night she murdered her niece she was always there. On the edges. A face in the background. Putting in an occasional—but very important—word. Making idiots of us all, including her husband. It makes one wonder, Herr Professor, what the advantages are of so-called sanity."

He laughed again to indicate that this was pleasantry, a sociable introduction to conversation; he was feeling uneasy.

But the old man merely grunted.

After that, they resumed their silences.

Until the telephone rang.

The line was miraculously clear.

"Ellery!" Inspector Queen's shout spurned the terrestrial sea. "You all right? What are you still doing in Vienna? Why haven't I heard from you? Not even a cable."

"Dad, I've got news for you."

"News?"

"The Cat is Mrs. Cazalis."

Ellery grinned. He felt sadistically petty.

It was very satisfactory, his father's reaction. "Mrs. Cazalis. *Mrs.* Cazalis?"

Still, there was something peculiar about the way the Inspector said it.

"I know it's a blow, and I can't explain now, but—"

"Son, I have news for *you*."

"News for me?"

"Mrs. Cazalis is dead. She took poison this morning."

Ellery heard himself saying to Professor Seligmann: "Mrs. Cazalis is dead. She took poison. This morning."

"Ellery, who you talking to?"

"Béla Seligmann. I'm at his home." Ellery took hold of himself. For some reason it was a shock. "Maybe it's just as well. It certainly solves a painful problem for Cazalis—"

"Yes," said his father in a very peculiar tone indeed.

"—because, Dad, Cazalis is innocent. But I'll give you the details when I get home. Meanwhile, you'd better start the ball rolling with the District Attorney. I know we can't keep the trial from getting under way tomorrow morning, but—"

"Ellery."

"What?"

"Cazalis is dead, too. He also took poison this morning."

*Cazalis is dead, too. He also took poison this morning.* Ellery thought he was thinking it, but when he saw the look on Seligmann's face he realized with astonishment that he had repeated these words of his father's aloud, too.

"We have reason to believe it was Cazalis who planned it, told her just where to get the stuff, what to do. She's been in something of a fog for some time. They weren't alone in his cell more than a minute or so when it happened. She brought him the poison and they both swallowed a lethal dose at the same time. It was a quick-acting poison; before the cell door could be unlocked they were writhing, and they died within six minutes. It happened so blasted fast Cazalis's lawyer, who was standing . . ."

His father's voice dribbled off into the blue. Or seemed to. Ellery felt himself straining to catch remote accents. Not really straining to catch anything. Except a misty, hard-cored something—something he had never realized was part of him—and now that he was conscious of it it was dwindling away with the speed of light and he was powerless to hold on to it.

"Herr Queen. Mr. Queen!"

Good old Seligmann. He understands. That's why he sounds so excited.

"Ellery, you still there? Can't you hear me? I can't get a thing out of this goddam—"

A voice said, "I'll be home soon, goodbye," and somebody dropped the phone. Ellery found everything calmly confusing. There was a great deal of noise, and Frau Bauer was in it somewhere and then she wasn't, and a man was sniveling like a fool close by while his face was hit by a blockbuster and burning lava tore down his gullet; and then Ellery opened his eyes to find himself lying on a black leather couch and Professor Seligmann hovering over him like the spirit of all grandfathers with a bottle of cognac in one hand and a handkerchief in the other with which he was gently wiping Ellery's face.

"It is nothing, nothing," the old man was saying in a wonderfully soothing voice. "The long and physically depleting journey, the lack of sleep, the nervous excitements of our talk—the shock of your father's news. Relax, Mr. Queen. Lean back. Do not think. Close your eyes."

Ellery leaned back, and he did not think, and he closed his eyes, but then he opened them and he said, "No."

"There is more? Perhaps you would like to tell me."

He had such a fantastically strong, safe voice, this old man.

"I'm too late again," Ellery heard himself saying in the most ridiculously emotional voice. "I've killed Cazalis the way I killed Howard Van Horn. If I'd checked Cazalis against all nine murders immediately instead of resting on my shiny little laurels Cazalis would be alive today. Alive instead of dead, Professor Seligmann. Do you see? I'm too late again."

The grandfatherly voice said, "Who is being neurotic now, *mein Herr?*" and now it was not gentle, it was juridical. But it was still safe.

"I swore after the Van Horn business I'd never gamble with human lives again. And then I broke the vow. I must have been really bitched up when I did that, Professor. My bitchery must be organic. I broke the vow and here I sit, over the grave of my second victim. What's the man say-

ing? How do I know how many other poor innocents have gone to a de-
center reward because of my exquisite bitchery? I've had a long and honorable career indulging my paranoia. Talk about delusions of grandeur!
I've given pronunciamentos on law to lawyers, on chemistry to chemists,
on ballistics to ballistics experts, on fingerprints to men who've made the
study of fingerprints their lifework. I've issued my imperial decrees on
criminal investigation methods to police officers with thirty years' training, delivered definitive psychiatric analyses for the benefit of qualified
psychiatrists. I've made Napoleon look like a men's room attendant. And
all the while I've been running amok among the innocent like Gabriel on
a bender."

"This in itself," came the voice, "this that you say now is a delusion."

"Proves my point, doesn't it?" And Ellery heard himself laughing in a
really revolting way. "My philosophy has been as flexible and as rational
as the Queen's in *Alice*. You know *Alice*, Herr Professor? Surely you or
somebody's psychoanalyzed it. A great work of humblification, encom-
passing all the wisdom of man since he learned to laugh at himself. In it
you'll find everything, even me. The Queen had only one way of settling
all difficulties, great or small, you'll remember. 'Off with his head!' "

And the fellow was standing. He had actually jumped off the couch as
if Seligmann had given him the hotfoot and there he was, waving his
arms at the famous old man threateningly.

"All right! All right! I'm really through this time. I'll turn my bitchery
into less lethal channels. I'm finished, Herr Professor Seligmann. A glorious career of *Schlamperei* masquerading as exact and omnipotent science has just been packed away forever without benefit of mothballs. Do
I convey meaning? Have I made myself utterly clear?"

He felt himself seized, and held, by the eyes.

"Sit down, *mein Herr*. It is a strain on my back to be forced to look up
at you in this way."

Ellery heard the fellow mutter an apology and the next thing he knew
he was in the chair, staring at the corpses of innumerable cups of coffee.

"I do not know this Van Horn that you mention, Mr. Queen, but it is
apparent that his death has upset you, so deeply that you find yourself unable to make the simple adjustment to the death of Cazalis which is all
that the facts of the case require.

"You are not thinking with the clarity of which you are capable, *mein
Herr*.

"There is no rational justification," the deliberate voice went on, "for
your overemotional reaction to the news of Cazalis's suicide. Nothing
that you could have done would have prevented it. This I say out of a
greater knowledge of such matters than you possess."

Ellery began to assemble a face somewhere before him. It was reassuring and he sat still, dutifully.

"Had you discovered the truth within ten minutes of the moment when you first engaged to investigate the murders, the result for Cazalis would have been, I am afraid, identical. Let us say that you were enabled to demonstrate at once that Mrs. Cazalis was the psychotic murderer of so many innocent persons. She would have been arrested, tried, convicted, and disposed of according to whether your laws admitted of her psychosis or held that she was mentally responsible within the legal definition, which is often absurd. You would have done your work successfully and you would have had no reason to reproach yourself; the truth is the truth and a dangerous person would have been removed from the society which she had so greatly injured.

"I ask you now to consider: Would Cazalis have felt less responsible, would his feelings of guilt have been less pronounced, if his wife had been apprehended and disposed of?

"No. Cazalis's guilt feelings would have been equally active, and in the end he would have taken his own life as he has done. Suicide is one of the extremes of aggressive expression and it is sought out at one of the extremes of self-hate. Do not burden yourself, young man, with a responsibility which has not been yours at any time and which you personally, under any circumstances, could not have controlled. So far as your power to have altered events is concerned, the principal difference between what has happened and what might have happened is that Cazalis died in a prison cell rather than on the excellently carpeted floor of his Park Avenue office."

Professor Seligmann was a whole man now, very clear and close.

"No matter what you say, Professor, or how you say it, the fact remains that I was taken in by Cazalis's deception until it was too late to do more than hold a verbal post-mortem with you here in Vienna. I did fail, Professor Seligmann."

"In that sense—yes, Mr. Queen, you failed." The old man leaned forward suddenly and he took one of Ellery's hands in his own. And at his touch Ellery knew that he had come to the end of a road which he would never again have to traverse. "You have failed before, you will fail again. This is the nature and the role of man.

"The work you have chosen to do is a sublimation, of great social value.

"You must continue.

"I will tell you something else: This is as vital to you as it is to society.

"But while you are doing this important and rewarding work, Mr.

Queen, I ask you to keep in mind always a great and true lesson. A truer lesson than the one you believe this experience has taught you."

"And which lesson is that, Professor Seligmann?" Ellery was very attentive.

"The lesson, *mein Herr*," said the old man, patting Ellery's hand, "that is written in the Book of Mark. *There is one God; and there is none other but he.*"

# A NOTE ON NAMES

If one of the functions of fiction is to hold a mirror up to life, its characters and places must be identified as in life; that is, through names. The names in this story have had to be numerous. For verisimilitude they are common as well as uncommon. In either category, they are inventions; that is to say, they are names deriving from no real person or place known to the Author. Consequently if any real person finds a name in this story identical with or similar to his or her own, or if any place in this story has a nominal counterpart in life, it is wholly through coincidence.

The story has also required the introduction of certain official- and employee-characters of New York City. Where names have been given to characters in this category, if such inventions should prove identical with or similar to the names of real officials and employees of New York City, again the resemblance is coincidental and the Author states in the most positive terms that no real official or employee of New York City has been drawn on in any way. Where names have not been used, only official titles, the same assurance is given. A special point should be made in the case of the characters of the Mayor ("Jack") and the Police Commissioner ("Barney"). Neither the present Mayor and Police Commissioner of the City of New York, nor any past Mayor or Police Commissioner, living or dead, has been drawn on in any way whatsoever.

The list of person- and name-places invented follows. If any occur in the text which do not appear on the list, it is through failure of a weary proofreading eye and the reader should assume its inclusion.

Abernethy, Archibald Dudley
Abernethy, Mrs. Sarah-Ann
Abernethy, Rev.
Bascalone, Mrs. Teresa
Bauer, Frau Elsa, *Austria*
Beal, Arthur Jackson
Castorizo, Dr. Fulvio, *Italy*
Caton, Dr. Lawrence
Cavell, Dr. John Sloughby, *Great Britain*
Cazalis, Dr. Edward

Cazalis, Mrs. Edward
Chorumkowski, Stephen
Cohen, Cary G.
Collins, Barclay M.
Cuttler, Nadine
Devander, Bill
Ellis, Frances
Ferriquancchi, Ignazio
Finkleston, Zalmon
Frankburner, Jerome K.
Frawlins, Constance

Gaeckel, William Waldemar
Goldberg (Detective)
Gonachy, Phil
Hagstrom (Detective)
Heggerwitt, Adelaide
Hesse (Detective)
Immerson, Mrs. Jeanne
Immerson, Philbert
Irons, Darrell
Jackson, Lal Dhyana
Johnson (Detective)
Jones, Evarts
Jurasse, Dr., *France*
Katz, Donald
Katz, Dr. Morvin
Katz, Mrs. Pearl
Kelly's Bar
Kollodny, Gerald Ellis
Larkland, Dr. John F.
"Leggitt, Jimmy"
Legontz, Mrs. Maybelle
MacGayn (Detective)
"Martin, Sue"
Marzupian, Harold
Mayor of New York City ("Jack")
McKell, James Guymer
McKell, Monica
Merigrew, Roger Braham
Metropol Hall
Miller, William
Naardvoessler, Dr., *Denmark*
"Nostrum, Paul"
O'Reilly, Mrs. Maura B.
O'Reilly, Rian
O'Reilly, Mrs. Rian
Park-Lester Apartments
Petrucchi, Father
Petrucchi, Mr. and Mrs. George
Petrucchi, Stella
Phillips, Celeste
Phillips, Simone
Piggott (Detective)

Police Commissioner of New York
    City ("Barney")
Pompo, Frank
Quigley (Detective)
Registrar of Records, Manhattan
    Bureau of Vital Records and
    Statistics of the Department of
    Health
Rhutas, Roselle
Richardson, Mrs. Della
Richardson, Leeper & Company
Richardson, Lenore
Richardson, Zachary
Sacopy, Mrs. Margaret
Sacopy, Sylvan
Schoenzweig, Dr. Walther,
    *Germany*
Selborán, Dr. Andrés, *Spain*
Seligmann, Dr. Béla, *Austria*
Smith, Mrs. Eulalie
Smith, Violette
Soames, Billie
Soames, Mrs. Edna Lafferty
Soames, Eleanor
Soames, Frank Pellman
Soames, Marilyn
Soames, Stanley
Stone, Max
Szebo, Count "Snooky"
Treudlich, Benjamin
Ulberson, Dr. Myron
Velie, Barbara-Ann
Whithacker, Duggin
Whithacker, Howard
Willikins, Beatrice
Willikins, Frederick
Xavinzky, Reva
Young (Detective)
Zilgitt (Detective)

# ABOUT THE AUTHOR

Will the real Ellery Queen please stand up?

The name "Ellery Queen" denotes a host of things. He's a fictional detective. He's a movie and television character. He's a mystery magazine. But the flagship Ellery—the Ellery where it all began—is a pseudonymous author who is not one person at all, but a pair of cousins.

The cousins had a lot in common. Both were born in 1905. They both changed their names: Manford Lepofsky became Manfred B. Lee, and Daniel Nathan became Frederic Dannay. They both wanted to be writers—Dannay longed to be a poet, while Lee claimed a desire to become the next Shakespeare. And in the late 1920s, they both wanted to win a $7500 prize being offered for the best detective novel.

Putting their heads together, the cousins collaborated on a story entitled *The Roman Hat Mystery*. They were both media-savvy—Dannay was a copywriter for an advertising agency, and Lee was a film-company publicist—so with an eye on future marketing potential, the writing duo gave both the hero of the story and the pseudonymous author the same name. If you couldn't remember Ellery Queen the author, you certainly would remember Ellery Queen the detective. The cousins didn't win the money, but the book did get published in 1929. It was the beginning of one of the most important crime-writing dynasties of all time.

Lee and Dannay eventually wrote thirty-three Ellery Queen novels and numerous Queen short stories. From the beginning, the series featured not only the intellectual mystery author Ellery Queen, but also his father, Inspector Richard Queen of the New York Police Department. These tales were in the tradition of classic puzzle stories like the works of Agatha Christie, a strong influence on the cousins.

Over time, the series evolved to fit the trends of the day. The stories got a little more hard-boiled, father and son stopped living together, and their houseboy, Djuna, disappeared altogether. Ellery even got to solve some crimes on his own, as in *Calamity Town* (1942), although his father never completely disappeared from the canon, appearing right up to the final entry in the series, *A Fine and Private Place* (1971). The cousins' collaboration, which in later years was conducted almost exclusively over the telephone, as they lived in different states, lasted until Lee's death in 1971. Dannay died in 1982.

Ellery Queen's popularity was not limited to the written word. Lee and Dannay were determined to get their hero everywhere they could, including Hollywood. The first Queen book to be filmed was *The Spanish Cape Mystery,* released in 1935. A string of features followed, the most famous being those starring Ralph Bellamy in the early '40s. The cousins tried writing directly for films, serving a short stint at Paramount, but nothing came of it. They did manage to break Ellery into radio in 1939, however, starting with scripts they wrote themselves. And when television came along, the characters appeared on the small screen, most notably in a series starring Jim Hutton as Ellery and David Wayne as his policeman father. *Terrific casting is my belief!   (MP, August 9, 2011)*

Probably the most effective attempt by the cousins to turn their creation into a brand name came at the magazine stands, when the Mercury Press launched *Ellery Queen's Mystery Magazine* in 1941. The magazine was touted as the brainchild of author Ellery Queen, but it was Frederic Dannay who was running things, serving as editor in chief from 1941 till his death forty years later. His goal was to raise the mystery genre to a "genuine literary form," and he did his best to publish short stories with mystery aspects from great writers both past and present. The result was the inclusion of more than forty Nobel and Pulitzer prizewinners in the magazine. But Dannay also sought out new writers, and this mixture of big names and up-and-coming authors set a standard for the magazine that continues to this day as one of the great success stories in mystery publishing.

The combination of books, stories, films, radio programs, television shows, and a long-lived magazine did exactly what the cousins set out to do, making the name "Ellery Queen" synonymous with detective fiction in America. The cousins may now be gone, but Ellery Queen lives on! *Yes!*